The Egg Man

Christopher Riebli

The Egg Man
© 2021 by Christopher Riebli

ISBN: 978-1-941066-52-2

Book design: Jo-Anne Rosen

Wordrunner Press
Petaluma, California

for:

ABR and CM-R

Contents

• • • • • • • • • •

PART TWO: HARNESSED

The Egg Man

Prologue

· · · · · · · · ·

We buried my dad, Arnold Bert Miller, a month ago in Santa Rosa. He lived nearly sixty-five years, and oddly enough, it wasn't the drinking or broken hearts that killed him, but a wild boar charging his horse above Skaggs Springs, instead. He would have liked the spot where he was buried—surrounded by tall oaks, with coveys of quail running among the tombstones, deer browsing on the wild oats, and his plot high on a hilltop where he could look out over the town that brought him such joy and such disappointment—both within the same week.

The gathering for the funeral was small—he'd burned some bridges in his time and was the first to admit it. My mother Christina, his former wife, was there, but Irene his oldest daughter wasn't. No surprise since the two of them had feuded almost from the day they pulled little Irene out of her mother's womb. Our younger sister, Nanette, had died years earlier from a blood disorder. John B. Miller, my dad's brother, and John B.'s extended family attended and Tino Morales, who had known my dad since they were teenagers growing up in Sonoma. Also at the funeral were all the fellows in his hunting party that fateful day, and a distinguished-looking couple—the man, a former California state senator named Charles Amos, and the woman, Carlotta Stamm, who I knew to be my dad's former employer at her ranch on Napa Road just southwest of Sonoma.

Was I close to my dad, you might ask? We were as close as the long intervals when he disappeared from my life would allow. At heart, he was a loner who loved most people, loved good bourbon, telling stories, being outdoors, loved animals—work horses, in particular. He was stubborn and he was a doubter—had to first see and feel and taste things for himself. I remember my earliest years with him the best, when all of us still lived together and Ma hadn't divorced him—the times when we fished and hunted together, and I rode with him on his egg routes with Little Ike, his horse, pulling a Studebaker wagon.

But like most people, he kept parts of him closed off from those around him. "You can't ever tell a person too much about yourself," he once told me, "because they'll end up using it against you." There was so much I didn't know about the man, how he spent his time while away, what he thought about different things. I'd only heard stories about him—the drinking, the womanizing, some of it rumors, some of it gossip—little parts here and there that never added up to a complete picture. How could it?

After he died, I drove up to Slim Casper's ranch west of Healdsburg where he last lived to gather up his few belongings. He didn't own much by this time—his horses were long gone, his wagon, his chickens, his pet dog, Jigs—nothing much left to call his own. I'd brought some boxes with me and set about emptying the dresser drawers, scooped up his personal effects, and in the top drawer of a maple desk in the corner of the living room I found a whole sheath of writing he'd done—all in his perfect long-hand. I'd never known my dad to be this kind of writer—sure, there were the postcards he'd sometimes send me and occasionally a long letter when he was down in his cups, mostly saying how sorry he was to make such a mess of his life—but what I found here was different. I started reading it and soon realized that he was telling a story about his life starting out with his teen years in Sonoma but going back earlier, too, before even arriving in this country. I took the sheath of papers to an editorial service in Petaluma, and asked if they could polish up and type out what my dad had written. Two weeks later they contacted me and said they'd completed the job. It was now all typed and bound almost like a book. I sat and read it through in one whole evening and well into early morning. I couldn't put it down. It was about him, and my mother, and me, and just about everyone he'd ever bumped elbows with. I found it a good story—a story about a man nose-to-nose with the hard truths about himself. He was the only one who could tell it—no one else—and the only one who could have written it.

1939: Petaluma, California

PART ONE:
Long Shots

1

Drinking, Women and God

· ·

1890: Sonoma, California

With our skiff hidden behind a tall stand of cattails, and the tide just right, we could bag ten ducks by dawn and deliver them to the Chinaman Ho Tzu by noon for a quarter a bird. A good day's pay around the valley—not the hundreds the cash hunters made filling their boats to the gunnels—but enough for us two hell-raisers. Sometimes as a kicker, Ho slipped us a little wad of opium that Tino and me smoked under Cooper's bridge, a whole different high from the bourbon—making everything seem like it was moving through molasses, and making me want to lie down and dream away the time—something my old man said I did enough of wide awake.

When the ducks weren't flying, we'd track down a buck above Carriger Creek and haul whole and half carcasses to Angie Botelli, the Italian butcher and sausage-maker. We sold quail and doves during season, and when not hunting, we fished the best holes up and down Sonoma Creek. When the steelhead were running we rode our bicycles straight out to Schellville, climbed into our skiff and drifted out past Wingo toward the mouth of the San Pablo Bay, casting into gray waters until our arms were tired and the bottom of our boat filled with squirming fish. Sometimes a wayward sturgeon would wander into the sloughs, and if we hooked one it gave us a helluva fight. Back in town we could trade it for a good bottle of rye—or my preference—bourbon. We sold most everything we shot or caught to the markets and back-alley shops around the plaza, and what we didn't sell we either took home or traded for shotgun shells, fishing tackle, bottles of bourbon, new boots, even a pair of gingham aprons for Ma and my sister, Josephine.

Tino and I were poachers, and we liked to poach best off Percy Sheers. He owned a good stretch of land he'd inherited from his family, part of the original Bear Flaggers, those same folks who ran the Mexicans out and then claimed the land for themselves. Sheers lost different parcels over the years to pay off gambling debts and settle lawsuits brought by his sister, but he still clung to a good chunk of land from the southwest side of the valley all the way south to where the hills collapsed into the San Pablo Bay tidelands. Sheers was a short-tempered, miserable fellow, who wore a Derby hat, chewed on a cigar, and rarely owned anything that wasn't handed to him. He had a following, though, and liked to hold court at the Union Tavern surrounded by his cronies—a collection of dry gulch miners, civil war veterans, locals with nothing better to do than drink and whittle their time away. When he wasn't pissing and moaning about business deals that went belly-up, he saved his harshest words for immigrants, the Chinese, Mexicans, Indians, and right there at the top of the list—his sister, Carlotta Stamm.

Sheers hated everything in general, but saved a special wrath for us poachers in particular. He liked to brag about the time he and two of his ranch hands snuck up on the Edwards boys one morning—caught them completely by surprise, pulled them out of a blind the two brothers had cobbled together, and beat them senseless. Sheers hit one of them—Milton, the oldest, right above the ear with the stock of his shotgun and to this day the boy can't hear anything that side of his head. He would have killed them both if Teddy Abew, one of the ranch hands, hadn't stopped him. Sheers took their shotguns and the ducks they'd bagged that morning and warned the brothers there was stiffer medicine the next time they stepped on his property. Word of the beating spread around town, helped out by Sheers himself who crowed to everyone in earshot what he'd done. "I taught them boys a lesson," he said. "You don't take nothing from Percy Sheers without Percy Sheers getting his cut."

My side-kick in all of this was Tino—Tino Morales— who managed the Union Livery, and gypo'd as a groomer and horse exerciser at the race track on First Street. His mother was half Mexican, half Indian. He claimed he didn't know his father but most folks in town did—it was this same Percy Sheers— something neither Tino nor Sheers would admit to. Tino was wiry, with wavy black hair, barely a hundred thirty pounds. He'd prospected as a jockey until a bad spill launched him over his horse's head, broke his right leg and left him with a permanent limp. His grandfather, old Miguel, one of the last surviving Mission Indians, lived with his daughter, Tino's mother, in a little wooden shack tucked away in the corner of Carlotta Stamm's ranch. Before his accident, Tino played baseball at the local diamond, stealing bases, running down fly balls so fast, the locals, swilling beer in the grandstands, called him "Chief Lightning.' He grew up walking every square foot around the valley, could read animal tracks like most folks read the newspapers and knew every pool along Sonoma Creek from Glen Ellen to the San Pablo Bay.

Besides fishing and hunting, Tino and I did some drinking, too—a habit we'd picked up early on. It wasn't something I took a lot of pride in—it was just something we did. I didn't much like the taste of liquor at first—had even tossed up a couple of stomachfuls, but I liked how it made me feel—lighter and with a different eye towards things—the sharp edges taken off— so I got past the taste in no time. We'd sit on a couple of benches at the livery, share a pail of beer from the Union Tavern and talk until the beer was gone and no money left to buy another. Sometimes Flo would join us—a big-hearted local with lines already bunching around her eyes and mouth. She knew her way around a barroom and knew her way around men. She had a way of coaxing secrets out of you, too, confessing things you never thought you'd confess. If you wanted to know something about someone, or track down a rumor, Flo was the person you went to.

She gave me a turn once—my first—when I was barely fourteen—more of a dare than anything else. I was running at the mouth about women and how I knew so much, and she said I didn't know shit about them and I told her I did—that I knew everything I needed to know—so she called me on it. We went over to the Union Livery, found an empty stall, and I stripped out of my pants right there—I was mostly anxious and scared— hoping she'd call it off—but she didn't. The first time she touched it, I flinched like a snake had crawled inside my underwear. She told me to relax—it wasn't going to hurt—and so I relaxed and the next time she touched it I went off like a powder keg. She started laughing but I didn't see nothing funny about it—to tell you the truth, it embarrassed the hell out of me. "Don't worry," she said, "with some more practice you'll learn to bridle that little guy back."

I quit school early—didn't even make it to eighth grade. All I did was sit in class and imagine what the girls looked like under their dresses—one peek at their bare skin and I'd have me a johnson a cat couldn't scratch. I also figured I'd learned enough— learned the essentials of this life you might say—and didn't see no point of staying in school. For all my self-doubting there was a streak of confidence in me, too. Ma was against my quitting, and my old man told me, "If you think you're gonna do nothing but drink and hunt and chase down tail, you can head right down the road." So I apprenticed with him trying to learn the finer points of carpentry, but the two of us together was like roosters fighting over the same hen. Mostly my mind was somewhere else—thinking about women a lot, and hunting and drinking—something my old man had no tolerance for. I know I disappointed him because he told me often enough—so many times I stopped listening. It wasn't deliberate. I was good with my hands and eager to learn a trade, but inside I was restless and untamed, and my old man saw danger there. I didn't like being barked at, either—nobody does—and he done plenty of that. Work for me was what I did to support my hunting and drinking—it wasn't my whole life like my old man wanted it to be—I just didn't think that way. Sure, I could put in a day's work with the best of them, if I set my mind to it, but always felt I was cut out for something different—not necessarily better, just different—but I didn't know what that was. All I know is that my old man would be explaining something to me—how to plumb a wall or square a corner—and before long my mind would drift off, thinking about Mary Lou Phillip's breasts or how Jeanette Maffia's ass shook through her long skirt—then he'd see that far-away-look in my eyes and lay into me good.

Other times I'd just make up my own idea of a young woman and fly off with that—give her the eyes of the Toscano Hotel maid, the dark hair of the girl washing dishes at the Excelsior—the color of her skin didn't matter. I liked them all. She just needed a warmness about her that invited me in, and she needed to like me—that made everything easier. And I'd give her a lovely complexion, too, without a blemish, hair that blew free in the wind—and a laugh, a great laugh, a laugh that stuck with you—I loved hearing women laugh. But mostly, we could talk to each other. And she had to be in love with me, too, and I'd be in love with her, an unmistakable love and we'd be thinking about each other all the time, especially when we were apart, and we'd make all kinds of vows that there would never be another come between us. And, of course, we'd have beautiful children and live out our days as much in love as the first time we met.

This kind of dreaming just swept me along until right in the middle of it—right when we were naked and about to taste each other's fruits—goddamn, if my old man's voice didn't break in and everything about that little dream went limp. "You got that glazed look in your eye again, son—like you're a dozen miles off," he'd say. It'd frustrate the hell out of him and he'd bite his lip—a bad sign. Biting his lip was never good because you knew all-hell was gonna follow— but you never knew what it was. When I was a little one, it'd be a licking, but as I got older he couldn't lay into me no more, so he'd look around for something to throw—usually one of his hammers.

"What the hell you always thinking about?" he wanted to know.

"Nothing," I said. I didn't think I had to share my little imaginings with a non-believer.

"Nothing?" he asked me. "You stand there for minutes at a time, your eyes glazed-over, your jaw slack, and you're thinking about nothing?"

"Okay, if you really want to know, I was thinking about women—one in particular I saw yesterday," I confessed.

"There's plenty of time to think about them later," he said.

"Well, I was thinking about them now—and you asked, and I think I gave you an honest answer."

"They don't do you no good now," he said. "Besides, you need something that'll attract them first—but more important—something that'll *keep* them," he said.

"Oh, I got that already," and I shot him a little grin like I was King Rooster and knew exactly what they needed.

He looked at me with that exasperated look. I knew it well. "That ain't what I'm talking about," he said. "You need to be a provider—like your brother, John B.—that's what women are looking for. It sure ain't some young buck hanging his pud out to every woman that smiles back. They want someone they can bank on—that won't run off the first sign of trouble—that won't run off when something else comes calling down the road."

"I ain't there yet," I said.

"It'll come up on you faster than you think," he said. "You want to be preparing for it—that's all I'm saying."

"I'll figure it out—don't worry about me," I said.

"I lost my train of thought," he said, and got that exasperated look on his face. "What was I just trying to explain?"

This one stumped me, too. "Building to lay-out?" I said.

"No, that's what I talked about yesterday," he said.

I think the old man got lost in his own thoughts, too, but would never admit to it. What those thoughts were I'd give five dollars to find out—but he kept it all inside, locked up tighter than a bass drum. I wondered if he ever thought about women the way I done or if there was something in this life he really wanted but he couldn't have—and finally gave up trying.

"I want to help you out son," he'd always say. "You know that, don't you?"

"Yes, sir—I know that."

"You know that we all have to work for a living, right? That nothing's handed to us? And if we gotta work, why not make it good work? Honorable work." If he'd told me this once, he'd told me a dozen times—maybe more.

"Yeah, I know that." I think I was just mouthing the words here.

"There's right ways of doing things," he said. "And there's wrong ways—like living this life. There's right ways of living—and wrong ways." He looked at me hard after those last words. I felt another sermon coming on.

"You think I'm living the wrong way, is that it?" I asked him. I don't even know why because I already knew the answer.

"I do." He said it matter-of-factly.

"It's my business, ain't it? Whatever I do? I'm pushing seventeen now," I said.

"Seventeen? Shit, your balls ain't even dropped yet."

"It's still my business."

"When it gets around town—it's all our business," he said.

"When it gets around town?"

"That's right—what people are saying about you," he said.

"What they're saying don't cut no ice with me."

"You're young—you don't know how things work around here."

"I know enough."

"You just think you do—"

Here my old man just shook his head, looked at me and laughed—but it wasn't that laugh at something that's funny—it was that laugh meant to tell me I didn't know shit from Shinola.

"Let me ask you this, son—what good's all this daydreaming do?"

His question stumped me. I didn't know how to answer it. He was right, it didn't do me no good—I mean I couldn't take it to the bank—couldn't order a beer with it—couldn't do much of nothing. But it was what I done—what a lot of folks done—maybe everyone with half a mind done. I wasn't no exception. I was like everyone on this planet, no different. It's like a person playing the coronet and somebody comes along and asks him, "What good does playing that coronet doing you, huh? Is it making the world any better? Can you take it to the bank?" How do you answer that? You can't. If you like playing the coronet, then you keep playing the coronet. If it makes your own world better that's all you got say over—and if it don't kill or hurt no one then you don't need no excuse to be playing it.

My old man and Ma worried too much about what people thought of them. They were newcomers to this country—immigrants—it was stamped on our papers, and felt they had to work extra hard for a good name, to be accepted by those who'd been around here longer. I didn't give it much shrift myself. Folks here longer than my folks weren't no better. They were just here longer, that's all. And the ones that were here the longest—like Tino's grandfather, well, they got treated like shit, like they were cattle. You just had to look at Percy Sheers to see some of them were a whole lot worse. Mostly I found the people who thought bad of me were people I couldn't give a rat's ass about anyway. Let them think and say whatever they wanted.

"I'm not sure—but I tell you what, son," he said. "When I'm explaining something and you ain't listening and you go ahead and run out a foundation—say—and nothing lays out the way you want it to—maybe then you'll wish you'd been listening to me instead of thinking about those 'sweet cheeks' running around town."

He wasn't always wrong—that much I had to admit—and when it came to building, the guy knew his oats. There was no point in arguing with him but arguing was how we talked to each other. Sometimes I'd say something just to get a rise out of the old man—it was meanness, I admit. He had a short fuse, and I knew it, and if he was barking at me, I'd look at him and grin—that's all it took—and that lit his fuse, set him off even more. This was dangerous territory—I knew it—and pretty soon he'd be looking for something to throw at me—a hammer, a shovel—whatever was closest. By then it was time to walk off the job like I'd done a dozen times before. We'd avoid each other back home—if I even went home. More often than not it gave me a good reason to look up Tino and order up a pail and we'd iron out some of the world's stupidities—mostly wondering why people didn't know as much as we did. When it was late enough and I figured he'd gone to bed, I'd ride my bicycle back home. Ma would usually be up if it wasn't too late, like she was this last time.

"Why can't the two of you make peace?" she asked. It wasn't the first time she'd run this question by me.

"I don't know, Ma—we just touch something off inside of us."

"I blame myself," she said—Ma's usual response.

"I know you do and it ain't your fault—it's mine," I said—and it was. I didn't like sugarcoating things—blaming someone else when it was my doing—and Ma was always blaming herself. I hated that habit of hers and told her so many times I lost count.

"He always says, 'Look at John B.—no problem there,'" she'd say. I hated to hear it because it was the truth. John B. was the ideal son and I knew it—anyone with two eyes could see it. She'd get that sad look in her eyes then, and I wished each time I was a different person—someone like my brother John B.—but it wasn't in the cards. You just can't take a horse and make a decent milk cow out of it.

"I know he ain't no problem, but John B. and me ain't the same," I told her maybe the twentieth time.

"That's what I tell him, too," she said. "That you're different from your brother, and it's foolish to think otherwise." Ma wrung her hands,

"Ma," I said, "I hate being compared to him—and it's nothing against John B. because I admire the hell out of him and wish we were more alike, but we ain't." I thought about this since we were young ones. "It's like we got dealt different hands," I said. "His was all Aces and Kings, and mine was twos and threes."

John B. was two years older and lived a life straighter than a hoe handle. No vices to speak of—a real craftsman. He'd picked up carpentry—really anything he put his mind to—like a duck takes to water. He'd already built two small houses on the east side of Sonoma while living at the folks' place in Vineburg, and was earning a name for himself—reliable and hard-working—all the things it seemed I wasn't. I didn't slight him for it. He married Gertie Keebler, the daughter of a well known El Verano dairy rancher, but their marriage wasn't without its bad luck—they lost their first two children at birth—but John B. didn't dwell on it. He saw the one woman in his life, and a year later, married her. I saw women in my life, bought them drinks, ran my hands under their dresses if they let me. He saved his money, too, with an eye toward a thousand acres north of Santa Rosa that he intended to homestead. And me? I blew through mine like there was holes in my pockets—like there was no tomorrows—and had little or nothing to show for it. He had direction—I went where the wind blew. He had purpose—I was scattershot. He was committed—I ran from commitment like it was a house on fire. And responsibility? That meant caring for someone and caring for someone usually meant disappointment— and I hated disappointment—so I said 'to hell with it all,' and chucked it to the wind. For all my dreaming about life-long love and romance, I knew how it clipped your wings, and the only thing I wanted now was to float free like a bird riding a high draft.

"Arnold Bert," Ma said. "I worry about your drinking at such a young age." We were in the kitchen and Ma was peeling potatoes. I hated it when Ma's voice got that serious tone to it because I knew a talking-to was going to follow. She stopped peeling her potatoes and turned toward me.

"It ain't a problem," I said.

"That's what everyone who drinks too much says. You know that? It's what my father used to say to my mother all the time." She wiped her hands on her apron.

"I know when to stop." I did know—when the bottle was empty.

"How do you know, son? You tell me—when you're sick and throwing up? When there's nothing left to drink?" She brushed some loose strands of hair away from her forehead. "I wish you wouldn't even started."

"I'll need a good reason to stop first." I said. "And I ain't found one yet."

"The right woman to come along—someone you love better than yourself," she said. "That's what you need."

"Maybe, but she ain't come along," I said—and she hadn't. There'd been a half dozen of them around town, at least, that I wooed and courted and told lies to and they told me lies back. We'd see each other days later, and there was guilt and hope both on their faces— I know guilt was on mine. I got called names and wished they'd see me in Hell and I felt bad until I didn't feel bad no longer. I didn't set out to treat them that way. It was all good fun at first until I lost interest and started making excuses not to see them again. Most of them, of course, saw right through me. There were some, too, that turned the tables, strung me out thinner than fishing line, dishing me out some of my own medicine. I had it coming—I was the first to admit it.

"I'm praying she does," Ma said.

"You pray, Ma?"

"I do." She reached over and touched my hand. "Little prayers— sometimes just a mumbling to myself—but it's a prayer just the same."

"And you think there's a God that hears you?" I asked her. I'd wondered about this for years but the older I got the less I believed. There was too much wrong in the world for God to be looking over it and if he was, he was doing a piss-poor job. Other times I figured it wasn't in us to know—that we could only guess at it and everyone had a different guess—that's what made up religion.

"Oh, I think there is—don't you?" Here she went again, trying to coax the slightest bit of belief out of me and I wasn't having it.

"I don't know, Ma. I don't think nobody does—they think they do," I said. "Folks pray when they want something—that seems self-ish to me. And even if I did pray, I don't think he'd be listening. I think he's tired of me by now, good and tired, and when someone's good and tired of me I got the decent sense to leave them alone."

2

Waiting on the Tides

· · · · · · · · · · · · · · · · · ·

My old man and I were trapped in something neither of us could crawl out of—like them squirrels you see always running around inside a wheel thinking they're getting somewhere. We'd try, but never got too far. He'd hire me to work alongside him and things went along well enough until they didn't. We'd be working together—everything smooth as country butter—but it didn't take long before I done something that put a burr up his ass—some little thing, too, that's all it was—like pulling a bent nail out with my hammer instead of a crow bar or not checking for plumb every five minutes. Then the barking commenced. "Use the goddamn bar—that's what it's for! You wanna bust the handle on that hammer?" That's all it took. I'd bark back, and before I knew it we were in a pissing contest seeing which one could holler the loudest. A couple minutes of this and I was unbuttoning my tool apron and walking off the job. I guess he thought if I walked off enough times, one of two things would happen: either I wouldn't work with him ever again and find some scrub job I hated, or I'd buck up and be back working with him, grateful he gave me another chance.

It was about this time—early March—that the railroad hired my old man to run a crew building the El Verano Train Depot. I was picking up work around the race track as a groomer and cleaning out stalls, and sometimes I'd sit alongside teamsters and watch them drive teams of work horses. I liked doing that. It paid nothing—I didn't care—I still liked it. John B. had signed on with the depot job, as well, and mostly through Ma's urging, I think, our old man gave me another try and hired me back. I figured, 'what the hell' maybe it turns out different this time. I was glad to be working steady again, showing up and putting a full day in and hoping the bad times between me and my old man were behind us. I liked having money to spend again, and I'd meet up with Tino and Flo and buy a couple of rounds but I was careful to quit early. I missed the horses, though, but they were never far away. If I had some hours free I'd show up at the track and ride with any teamster willing to have me along.

I was trying to turn over a new leaf—you know, not falling into the same old potholes I was always falling into. My old man was the boss, and I didn't argue with him. If he showed me how to do something I did it like he said—if he told me to walk off the edge of the roof, I'd start walking there—and the two of us got along maybe better than ever. We talked civil to one another with hardly an argument and I could tell it pleased Ma to no end. I was walking around town with a couple of dollars in my pocket, feeling like I was on top of the world—my old man finally liked me and my life had straightened out and everything seemed pure gravy. I don't know if this had ever happened before. Still, he'd warned me that first day back: "This time it's different, son—no missing work. Understand?" No second chances." And I agreed—no second chances.

On a Saturday—maybe a month after signing on for the depot job—Tino heard that sturgeon were spotted south of Haystack right where the sloughs broadened out and ran deeper toward the San Pablo Bay. The tides were strong there and that's where they liked to feed. I'd been walking the narrow path for weeks now— no hunting, no fishing, light on the drinking—just work—so the news about the sturgeon sounded good as cold beer in August. The following day we waited until a slack tide before untying our skiff at the Schellville wharf and riding it to where we thought the fish might be biting—but no bites. No sign of them anywhere. We paddled around most of the morning and by noon we finally got our first strikes. Once they started hitting, we baited and cast and within an hour we landed nearly a half-dozen, three-foot long sturgeon. We were so busy thinking what we could trade them for we hadn't noticed the tide turning. We worked the oars trying to head back upstream until our arms went numb. It was slow going, like rowing in mud. Finally we said, "Fuck it," and pointed our skiff to a little spit of land, tied off there and waited. Luckily we'd brought a bottle of bourbon with us and a pocket full of cigars. We passed the bottle back and forth and smoked up all the cigars and we were mellowed to the point where we didn't care what time we got back.

By now, hours had passed, with clouds of mosquitoes hanging around us, and no sign of an incoming tide. When the bourbon was gone, we lay back in the skiff, nursed our headaches until we finally dozed off. Tino was sprawled out in the bow, his feet resting on a pile of sturgeon. The nice edge the bourbon gave us earlier had worn off and now my nerves were jangled, and dark thoughts started seeping in. I was thinking of the promise I'd made to my old man and how I was going to disappoint him again and that bothered me no end. "My old man's going to be pissed if I miss work tomorrow," I said.

Tino grunted. "It ain't lookin' too good right now, is it?"

"It sure ain't." I looked out across the water. Doom seemed written across its surface. "He'll think I done it on purpose."

"What's the worst that can happen? He cans you, right? He's done that before and a week later you're back working with him." Tino dangled his hand over the side of the skiff."

"It's different this time," I said.

"You think so?"

"Yeah, I do. I promised him, and he said he'd hold me to it— no more second chances or third chances or however many he's given me. I miss work this time, he sends me packing."

"If he does, you'll find something else." Tino, at heart, was an optimist.

"I just hate disappointing him all the time," I said and propped myself up on my elbows. "It's different with you, Tino. You ain't got no old man—no one ridin' herd on you all the time—no one wantin' you to be a certain way." This kind of freedom always made me jealous of Tino. He could do whatever he wanted and not disappoint no one. He was his own boss.

"Yeah, I wouldn't know what that's like," he said, "with no one else to worry about."

We both stared at the water with daylight draining out, waiting for the tide to start flowing inland but it didn't move. I closed my eyes and dozed off to the sound of water lapping against the side of the skiff, and in between the lapping I heard the old man's voice bellowing like a bull's and saw myself standing in front of him— my shoulders all slunk down and him giving me that stare that could fry a strip of leather. I wasn't saying anything, just standing there taking my medicine, letting him blow off steam. What could I say? I'd disappointed him again.

"This'd be a good time to smoke some of Ho's tar balls," Tino's voice broke the silence. "Us lounging here like we are—nothing to do—no folks around."

"Normally I ain't that keen on the stuff," I said. "But out here— like this, I'd be inclined to give it another try."

I dozed and dreamed I was sitting in a gazebo by a stream with Helga Reuger, a neighbor from back in Obwalden. She was married to the baker, Peter. In the dream Peter has died, and I've gone to comfort her. She takes my hand and puts it up to her cheek and just as our faces touch, I hear Tino shouting, "The tide's moving! The tide's moving! Let's go!" And that's where the dream ended— the last I saw of Helga.

Tino and me both sat up, grabbed the oars and pushed off into deeper water. We bent into the rowing like our asses were on fire. Over my left shoulder there was daylight leaking up behind Vallejo's hills and everything around us had that eerie but beautiful glow peculiar to dawn. Two hours later we reached the wharf where we tied up our skiff. It seemed like a week ago that we'd first set out. All I could think about was getting to work and facing the old man. My head pounded. We divided up the fish, wrapped them in two burlap sacks and strapped them to our bicycles before pedaling hard back to Sonoma for another hour. I left my fish with Tino at the Union Livery and told him he could sell my share to Ho Tzu. I saved one for my old man as a kind of peace offering, and then rode out to El Verano. I didn't know what was waiting for me out there—but I knew it wouldn't be good.

3

Running My String Out

· ·

By the time I arrived at the job site it was nearly four o'clock in the afternoon. Most of the crew had left, but John B. was still there, measuring and cutting members for the depot framework. I leaned my bicycle against a tree, grabbed the burlap sack with the one sturgeon and walked over to where John B. was working. He was bent over, scribing a line with his pencil. He looked up, surprised to see me. "You just getting to work?" he asked.

I nodded.

"What's in the sack?"

"A sturgeon," I said. Me and Tino went out yesterday and got stuck between tides—that's why I'm so late."

"The old man isn't happy—I'm warning you." John B. gave me that look I'd known for years.

"I figured as much," I said. From the corner of my eye I could see him walking toward us with a copy of the building plans in his hand. My mind fumbled around for the best excuse—something I had some practice with—but it was dulled from too-little sleep and the bourbon and nothing surfaced. I figured I'd just let him get the first shot in and brace myself for whatever followed. I deserved it. He walked up to me and just stood there and didn't say nothing—just pushed his hat back and ran his hand across a stubble of red beard, and looked me over from head to toe—a look meant to ask himself if this really was his son and not someone who happened to wander into his farm one day. His eyes finally settled on mine—a pair of eyes I've already told you what they could do.

"You look like hell," he said. "Been out tomcattin' again?"

I glanced down at my pant legs and boots and they were caked with dried mud. I hadn't seen my face but was sure it didn't look much better. "No, sir—was fishing for sturgeon and got caught between tides," I told him it was the God's honest truth.

"I don't want to hear no bullshit excuses!" He bit at his lower lip. "I thought you was going to buck up—ain't that what you said—ain't that what we agreed on?"

"Yes, sir, I said that." I looked into a face I'd seen too many times by now. "I tried getting back—ask Tino."

He wasn't hearing nothing.

"You got slits for eyes, you know that? And dark circles under 'em." He was giving me a good once-over—from head to foot.

"No, sir, I hadn't looked."

"And you ain't even eighteen years old yet—carrying on like you do." He shook his head until I thought his neck would snap.

"No, sir, I'm not—just a couple more months, though," I said.

"And I can smell the booze on your breath too." He kept shaking his head and looking down at his feet, toeing the dirt with his boot—wondering again, I'm guessing—if this was really his son or someone they gave him by mistake back at the hospital. "You're running your string out, boy—you know that?"

"Yes, sir—I suppose I am."

"Ain't that much left on the spool—damn little," he said.

"Yeah, I guess there ain't."

"No, I don't think you know," he said. "You say you do but nothing sinks in that thick skull of yours—it's like I'm talking to that goddamn wall over there." He pointed to the depot wall nearest us. He ran his hand across the stubble on his chin again, and it made a raspy sound. I could tell he was struggling for the words he wanted to say, words that weren't boding very good for me. His bloodshot eyes stared straight into mine. "I can't depend on you, son, but more than that I'm worried about you—your mother's worried, too. We're afraid you're going to end up like some back alley drunk—either that or shot dead poaching."

I nodded and handed the burlap sack to him. He didn't look down at it. He didn't say nothing.

"It's a sturgeon for you and Ma," I said.

He took the sack without looking inside. For the moment it seemed to calm him. His voice softened. '"We talk a lot about you—me and your mother. She blames herself. She says she never should have left you kids behind in the old country when we come over here."

"I know she does," I said. "And I tell her nothing's her fault—that what I done, I own. And you need to tell her that too. Anyway it's not like I'm some criminal—unless not being like John B. is a crime."

"She worries about you, okay? That's what mothers do with their sons, their kids—they worry about them."

"I'll figure it out—no amount of worrying's going to help," I said. "Can you tell her that?"

My old man started to walk away but then turned around as if he'd just remembered something. "I shoulda had just one son—you know that?"

"And that'd be John B.?" I said, like I didn't know the answer.

"That's right," he said. "That boy works, and you don't ever hear him complaining—he lost two young ones, too, and got a right to complain but not a peep." He looked at me. "And you? You ain't lost nothing but your dignity."

His words pulled me up short. I had to swallow hard to get down what he'd just said. I know it wasn't no surprise—it was the truth— but just to have him come out and say it like that nearly flattened me. It ain't something no son or daughter wants to ever hear out of a parent's mouth—that they weren't wanted. I tried not to let it show—like I done with everything else he said—but this one sunk deep, forced me to turn around and walk away, and suck in my breath a dozen times just to keep from crying.

"Hey, don't walk away from me like that!" he shouted behind me. "I ain't finished."

"Fuck off!" I kept walking away.

"I ain't finished!" he said again.

I stopped and turned around—I could feel warm tears in my eyes now.

"You think there's something better out there than buckling down and listening to me? Well, go out and find it! And stop wasting my time." His voice began trailing off.

"I'll find something!" I shouted back at him. We were just ten yards apart but you could have heard us in the plaza a couple miles off.

"Like poaching from Percy Sheers? You think that's better?" he asked

"Maybe."

"It's all good until you're caught and then your ass is in a real sling." He looked off to where John B. stood. "Percy Sheers would like nothing better than nailing you and Tino. He's a mean son of a bitch, and worse thing—he's got clout in this town."

"He don't scare me."

"That's because you're young and don't know shit." He put both hands on his hips, cocked his head toward me. "I'm trying to reason with you here, son, you know that? Trying to get you to see what's best."

"Yes, sir."

"I'm trying to get you to think about the future like John B. over there has." He nodded to where my brother worked. John B. looked up. He was in earshot now.

"I don't think too much about the future," I said.

"Maybe you should," he said.

"I don't."

"And why not?"

"Because it ain't here yet," I said. "Besides, they're just plans and every time I make one it busts wide open and ends up disappointing me." That's what I'd learned so far in this life—you get some big idea and you finally think—this time my ship's come in—then something comes along and sinks it right in front of you, and you wonder why you even thought of it in the first place. It was all just a waste of time.

"Maybe they're the wrong plans then," he said. "Did you ever think of that?"

"Maybe I just ain't lit on what I was meant to do," I told him. "Or what comes natural to me. Everything I do I see it as work—as taking effort," I said. "Whether I'm swinging a hammer or hauling a buck down off the ridge."

"Maybe so—but there's work and there's *honest* work—and what you're doing ain't honest."

"It's honest—it just ain't *legal* in some books. "

"And what do you do once you're caught?" he asked. "That's what I'd like to know—and when you are, don't come running to me!"

"It ain't happened yet." And it hadn't.

"Because you're lucky—that's why," he said. "That's what the guys in the club say, as well—there's folks that are good and there's folks that are lucky."

"Here you go again with the club and what they think," I said.

"That's not important?" he asked. I could see I touched a nerve.

"Not to me it ain't. What do they know, anyway?" I asked him. "They're like most folks in this town—talking out their asses."

My old man's anger started to boil over now. His face flushed, and I could see him scratching around for something to throw at me. You couldn't say nothing bad about the Swiss Club or its members—that was off-limits—like cursing God. These were his countrymen, folks he'd die and go to hell for. "Let 'em talk," I said. "That's what folks do best around here. You do anything different from the rest and it confuses the hell out of 'em—they don't know what to think. And Percy Sheers? He's the worst of em.'"

Dad shook his head. "Son, you got it all wrong."

"I don't think I do," I said. "Maybe I ain't no journeyman carpenter but I know some things about this life."

"No, you don't understand how that works in a place like this."

"I understand enough," I said. "If you're different or ain't from these parts, you get branded. You get cut out from the herd like the Chinamen do and forced to live in paper houses. And Tino? Tino's folks? Well, you see what they done to them—the ones that are still alive."

"It all gets back to me—and your mother," he said.

"I know you keep saying that, and I'm sorry for Ma, but you know what I think? They can take all that talk and shove it up their asses." A quiet followed. I might have over-stepped my bounds with that last remark.

His jaw dropped. "You think it's some kind of life running off all the time? Not showing up for work?"

"What I do is work," I said. If it took effort, it seemed like work to me.

"Bullshit! Try feeding a family on what you do." He pushed his hat back. "Those days are gone, son. Ask old Miguel, the Indian living up on the corner of the Stamm ranch, he'll tell you. Wasn't anybody who could fish or hunt like him anywhere and look how he ended up— living in a goddamn shack. It's just the way things go."

"Ain't nothing he done was his fault," I said. "His folks got squeezed out—the ones that didn't died from small pox."

"Then go!" he shouted. "And find yourself another place to live, too—'cause I'm cutting you loose!"

"Fine with me," I said, and turned and started to walk away—but he wasn't finished.

"I ain't doing you any favors by taking you back each time," he said. He tucked both thumbs into his tool belt and pinched his lips together. "You figure it out on your own—you got a head on your shoulders—you can do it. But you and me trying to work together? That's done—I reached my limit! Over—you understand? Done!"

And just like that the month of peace between me and the old man ended. I kept walking away and, damn, if he didn't send a hammer flying by my hip pocket! I didn't even look back—just got on my bicycle and rode home and told Ma what had happened— that the old man had canned me for good and wanted me out of the house. She was in the kitchen washing dishes. She stood with her back to me as I talked. From the outside she's a woman who takes disappointment like it's something she's used to, but like me most of what's she's feeling is bottled up inside, churning and boiling. She stopped washing dishes and turned around to face me. "Where are you going to live?" she asked.

"I got a place," I said.

"Where? Where you gonna live?" She wiped her hands on the dish towel.

"At the Union," I said.

"The hotel? How are you going to pay for a room there?"

"No—the stable at the Union."

She shook her head. "The stable?"

"Yeah, I'll stay in a stall until something better comes along." As soon as I said it, I regretted opening my mouth.

"In a stall—like you're some kind of horse?"

"It's not as bad as you think."

Tears started to form in the corners of her eyes.

"Ma, don't cry—like I told dad—I'll figure it out." Now I felt plain lousy to make Ma cry like this.

"You got no money—nothing." She walked over to a drawer in the kitchen hutch and pulled out a small stack of dollar bills. "Here," she said, "take these."

"I don't need them, Ma—you keep them."

"You take them and pay me back when you can." She stuffed the bills into my shirt pocket.

"Okay, that's what I'll do."

I put my arms around her—something I don't remember ever doing in a long time. She was a big, full-figured woman and I could feel little shakes going up and down her back—hear her breathing in bunches. And again I told her not to worry—that I'd figure it out—and that maybe it was all for the best. I apologized for upsetting her. I told her what I needed now was some time and a little bit of luck to come along and I'd right the ship. That's what I promised. We hugged each other again, and I went in and packed the few clothes I owned into a valise. I left out the backporch door, tied the valise to the rack on my bicycle, stuffed a sleeping bag into my knapsack and rode back to town to the Union Livery.

Tino showed me a vacant stall at the far end of the stable. "It ain't hardly used," he said. Tino himself slept in a little room in the loft above. I forked in a thick bed of straw and laid out my bag. The stall wasn't much but it was dry and mostly warm. Tino brought a pail of beer over from the Union Tavern across the street and we drank and talked into the evening over what I could do now that I was sprung from my folks' place. He'd sold the sturgeon and we split the proceeds, nearly two dollars each.

"Pheasants," he said.

"Pheasants? What are you talking about?" I asked him.

"I'm talkin' about them pheasants Percy Sheers' got," he said. "That's what we're goin' after next. He's raised flocks of 'em and turned 'em loose in his hayfields. Ho Tzu said he'd pay top dollar for 'em."

"Oh, I don't know, Tino." My head hurt and every last bit of juice seemed drained from my body. I couldn't think of nothing at the moment. "Tino," I said, "it's been one helluva day. Let's talk about it in the morning."

He agreed. I fell back on the straw, wondering as I always did, what tomorrow would bring—I hoped it'd be different. I was tired of always fighting with the old man and tired of disappointing Ma like I done and tired of being myself, too—and that ain't ever a good thing. It puts ideas in your head—dark ideas about leaving this world before it got any worse. I didn't like thinking that way but I did and I thought of different ways I could do it—a shotgun, string a rope over a tree, maybe row out to the middle of the bay and tie weights to my feet and jump overboard.

I'd lost faith in tomorrows—like they were going to bring some change—but it never seemed to happen. I'd wake up and it took just a few steps before I knew it was the same thing starting all over again. And I already told you about my plans and how they always blew up. It got down to this one thing—I'd lost all faith in myself—my confidence was shot full of holes. I'd gotten so used to playing it off the cuff—taking whatever showed up next and doing what I could—and when I couldn't do that no more, everything inside just crumbled. It was the way life came at me—you'd knock one bad luck bird down and another'd fly up in front of you. They never stopped coming.

Right then I was shy of eighteen years with a few dollars in my pocket, a disappointment to my folks—had just been booted out of the house. I was sleeping in an empty horse stall, with no real prospects—buying drinks for women whose names I forgot the next day—waking up with a hangover that could flatten two guys—and wondering how all of this was going to end. But goddamn it, I was alive—barely, it seemed—and I was my own person and had no one else to blame for it. Right now my head hurt, my body ached—an ant could piss on me I felt so low—but blood was still pumping through my veins and more than anything I hated being a quitter. And maybe—just maybe—tomorrow might be different. We never knew, but there was times when a tomorrow surprised me—and surprised me for the better. I needed one of those now—in the worst way.

4

Teamster

· · · · · · · · · ·

After the old man canned me, I cleaned stalls at the Union and landed grooming jobs at the race track. Folks there said I had a good feel for horses, all kinds—trotters, runners—but big work horses, in particular. I admired the hell out of the Percherons and Clydesdales—massive horses that could pull a house right off its footings—and how they shouldered into their yokes and moved those hay wagons and manure hoppers with ease.

I jumped at every chance to ride along with the teamsters and watch them drive, watched how their hands worked the traces up to the lead horses. I listened to how they talked out loud to them, too—like a foreman talks to his crew—how the drivers clicked their tongues, made certain sounds their horses understood. I listened to them shout commands and watched how the horses' ears slanted back and how the lead horses looked at each other seeming to understand every word. I pestered the drivers with a lot of questions along the way, too. All of it fascinated me. I was a quick learner and pretty soon I was shuttling teams and wagons by myself around the grounds. It was steady work—and damn if I didn't earn a little bit of a reputation around the track. Pretty soon I was hiring out to drive, and when I wasn't driving I was breaking the younger horses to pull and work in tandem, to back up and to jack-knife so a wagon wouldn't block the street. My list of clients grew, and for the first time in a long time I felt good about myself.

JD McCracken heard about me—said I seemed like a natural to him—and offered me a job as a teamster. JD owned a pair of Percherons named Molly and Dolly and a Studebaker wagon and had a contract to haul basalt block from the Schocken Quarry down to the Sonoma Depot twice a day where it was loaded onto flat cars and shipped to San Francisco. He wanted me to ride with him until I learned the ropes and I said that was fine. I liked sitting high up on the wagon's seat and watch Molly and Dolly—his two mares—snort and fart and work together in their easy rhythms, their ears flicking back and forth, their powerful necks sinking into the yokes. I liked to see the country slide by me, too, smell the smells, hear the sound of the harness creaking, the wagon wheels biting into the road. No one was criticizing me when I sat up there—I felt like a king in my own little world.

"When you're coming down off the hill," McCracken looked over at me quickly. We were just leaving the quarry with a load of block.

"You don't want that wagon gettin' away from you—that's when you ride that brake—not hard or you'll burn it up—but just a gradual bite that keeps too much of the weight from goin' forward. You wanna hold them horses back, too—not much 'cause they read the traces good. They got tender mouths and don't like bein' yanked on. After awhile you'll learn the feel. Not right away—but after awhile you'll get a sense of just how the rig should feel." He looked right at me, and his voice got serious. "As big and strong as them horses are—a load of block'll push them right off the road. Then you're in some deep shit, son. Ain't nothin' worse than hurtin' a horse." He looked at me like that was the most important lesson. "Sometimes it hurts me more than hurtin' a man," he said.

I liked JD and we took to each other right away. He was patient and always explained why he did things one way and not the other. Sometimes I compared him to my old man and how they were different but how they were alike, too. They both knew their stuff, and loved what they done. I think with my old man, though, it was just a matter of us being around each other too long, and how we ground into each other's parts—and what we needed was some separation. And I know after working with John B. and seeing the kind of work my brother done, I disappointed my old man even more. He'd told me more than once—and as much as I wanted to please him—I knew I wasn't no natural at carpentry— wasn't something I took to and embraced the way he or John B.

did—certainly not the way I took to driving teams. I wanted to show him I'd amounted to something—that maybe I wasn't no carpenter like John B.—but I could drive a team like no one's business. What I looked forward to more than anything was the day I could drive past him where he was working—with Molly and Dolly in an easy, high-stepping trot—and me sitting high up there like I was some kind of prince—waving to him as the dust curled behind us. I wanted to show him that I'd learned something besides coaxing the last drop out of a bourbon bottle or poaching game to sell in some back alley. I wanted him to be proud he had two sons—not just one.

Two months after signing on with JD McCracken, he made me an offer that about knocked my boots off. "I'm gettin' old, Bert, and thinkin' it's time to hang up the reins." He held up his hands to show how arthritis had bent his fingers and knuckles away from both thumbs. "Don't ever let 'em get like this," he said. His hands, big and gnarled from working all his life, looked like claws now.

"It's in my hips, too," he said. "The only thing worse than climbin' up to the seat is when I have to climb back down." Both his long legs had bowed out. "It's the shits but it's how it turned out," he said. "Wear and tear on all the joints."

"You've lived a good life," I said.

"I watched how you worked them two horses, and you're gentle with him," he said. "That's important 'cause I love 'em like they was my kids and I wouldn't take to no one abusin' 'em. And horses—you know—when you love 'em, they love you back."

"They're fine horses," I said.

"And if you take good care of 'em,' they'll give you ten more good years—maybe more." He paused a moment here. "You're a young feller just startin' out—and I ain't."

"Yeah, I'm a young fellow all right."

"The missus and I were talkin' the other night—talkin' 'bout you and how we think you'd be ripe to take over Molly and Dolly." He paused again. "What do you think?"

I had to catch my breath. "Really, JD? You're not fooling with me?"

"No, I ain't foolin' with you," he said.

"Goddamn, I'd love it!"

"We were thinkin' two hundred fifty dollars for the horses and wagon," JD said.

I didn't know values exactly but it seemed like a fair price. The wagon was a solid one, and like JD said, the horses had ten good years left in them. Besides, I'd worked with Molly and Dolly now and we understood each other.

"Well, then, do we got a deal?" He held out his hand.

"Hell, yes, we do!" And we shook hands on it.

I told him I'd need a place to board Molly and Dolly and he said go talk to the widow Emma Hansen on Grand Avenue about renting her barn and the pasture behind it. I took his advice and rode out to Emma's a day later, and she said she'd already talked to JD. Emma and I agreed on five dollars a month rent. The next day after hauling two loads of block, I filled the empty trailer with hay I bought from Louie Rocca, the hay dealer, and drove the team over to Emma's. I backed the wagon into Emma's barn and unloaded the hay, unhitched the wagon, and turned Molly and Dolly loose in the pasture. They took to it right away. I converted a corner tack room into a little apartment, and eventually moved a cot and chest of drawers in, and hung the one jacket I owned on a harness hook. Emma liked having the company.

She sat on her front porch often, with a glass of bourbon or red wine—waiting for me when I returned from work. It seemed like the twists and turns in my life had straightened out some. I was making payments on my own team and wagon—had moved from sleeping in a horse stall to a converted tack room. With all the recent events, I felt like someone else—like another person had slipped into my skin and pushed the old person out. I didn't know how to account for it. Maybe like the old man said, I was luckier than most. If it was luck, then I'd take it.

A day later I went into G.T. Pauli's General Merchandise to buy household items—things like towels, bars of soap, a new shaving brush, a pot to boil water. I walked up and down the aisles and all kinds of items caught my eye—but what caught my eye the most was a young lady who worked there. She was lovely—a ribbon in her hair, a beaming smile caught between two, round cheeks blushed red—cheeks so round and big they forced her lips into a natural pucker—add a pair of wings and she could have been an angel. At the first sight of her I felt my heart do a little flip inside like it does when you first stumble onto something and it's a total surprise—but a good surprise.

"Can I help you find something?" She stood in front of a display of chewing gum.

"Sure." Our eyes caught each other's.

"What are you looking for?" Her eyes stayed on mine.

"Well, I'm moving into my own place now and need to set up for it," I explained.

"Is it a house or apartment?"

"Hmm—an apartment—it's an apartment. Yeah, that's what it is." Tack room didn't sound very impressive.

"You're sure about that?" She laughed. "And what do you need?"

"Well, just about everything it takes to set up housekeeping," I said.

"Dishes? Cutlery? Is it you alone? Your wife? Other family members?"

"No, I'm not married—it's just me."

"How about we start with some toiletries?"

"Some what?"

"Bathroom items—you know—like towels, soap. Follow me—they're over in the next aisle."

I walked behind and yes, I admit—I was checking out every moving part of her I could—as much as her long skirt allowed. I loved how she walked in such an easy motion—flowing almost—and how her long hair swayed from one shoulder to the other—and like with most young women—I imagined what she looked like under that long skirt.

"What's your name?" I asked when we'd stopped in front of a stack of towels.

"Cameron," she said. "Cameron Landers."

"I'm Bert—Arnold Bert Miller—but folks just call me Bert."

We shook hands. "Nice to meet you, Bert Miller." She fingered through the stack. "They're all cotton—the same color. That doesn't matter, does it?"

"Not at all," I said. "How long have you worked here?"

"About six months now." She looked at me. "Miller," she repeated my last name. "Any relation to Josephine Miller?"

"She's my sister."

"We were in the same grade together," she said. "I don't remember ever seeing you at school."

"No, I left early," I said.

"It wasn't for you?" she asked.

"No, it wasn't," I said. "I had other plans."

I picked out more items—just random now because I was nervous and thinking of her—so I carried each armful to the front counter. By now I'd bought everything I needed—and some I didn't. Whatever Cameron suggested, I bought.

"What do you do when you're not working here?" I asked.

"I'm active in my father's church—he's the pastor. I sing in the choir there and conduct Bible classes." She looked at me—fishing, I think—for some kind of reaction. "Do you belong to a church?"

"No, I don't."

"Are you a believer?"

"I'm not sure what I am," I answered back—it seemed like a safe-enough answer.

"You're certainly welcome to join us at a service sometime—then you can judge for yourself."

"Let me think about it, okay?" I said. Any other time there was no thinking involved—church services and me? God? A perfect way to waste a Sunday—not a chance. I'd tossed all of that away years ago and thought myself a better person for it—well—maybe not better—just truer to myself.

Cameron pressed the keys on the cash register and a bell sounded each time. When she'd totaled all the items, the register's bottom tray slid open. "Two dollars and fifty cents," she said, looking at the numbers displayed at the top of the register. I paid for them and she slid the sack across the counter toward me.

"Thank you for your help," I said.

"It was a pleasure," she said. "I hope you enjoy your new apartment." There was that smile of hers again, flashing my way like a beacon—like a lighthouse beacon. I turned to leave but stopped. "What's the name of your church?"

"Souls' Haven," she said. "It's on Vallejo Street."

"Maybe I'll see you there."

"That would be great—everyone is always welcome."

"Sunday—maybe this Sunday," I said.

"Wonderful!" She looked at me and I looked back at her and I heard the words I'd just said that I thought I'd never say again—that I'd see her in church. But stranger things could happen. I figured I was in the middle of a run of good luck—the horses, the wagon, a place at Emma's—so why not push it a bit further? Why not see what happens between Cameron and me and maybe that run of good luck stretches out further?

5

Pheasants

· · · · · · · · · ·

The depot job was barely finished when the railroad and the land boom that followed went belly-up. Lots from the Craig Ranch that once sold for hundreds—sometimes thousands of dollars by speculators—now sat idle with just stakes in the ground and faded signs that promised "Little pieces of Paradise." Some of the signs had fallen over, and a couple more were blasted full of shotgun holes. All of the signs announced some grand future that didn't look so grand just then. Ma told me the railroad had stiffed my old man, too—folding up while still owing him nearly a hundred dollars. I felt bad for my family—especially bad for my old man. Sure, we didn't see eye-to-eye on a lot of things, but no one worked harder than he did and if you stiffed one of us, you stiffed us all. If he thought he didn't put in an honest day's work, he said you didn't have to pay him. He had some hard bark to him—and I rubbed all his wrong nerves—but he was a decent man and didn't deserve what had happened. Ma told me he wasn't out of work for more than a day or two before Carlotta Stamm hired him to be her ranch foreman. She wanted a hen house built, too, for some prize chicks she'd ordered from a mail order catalog. To help with the construction, she hired my older brother, John B., as well.

My teamster work was steady—before long I had a couple of dollars in my pocket and a new pair of boots. I was paying off my debt to JD and could even afford an occasional steak dinner at the Union. I bought new harness, a chambray shirt and a Stetson hat, and worked enough to take a day off at times to rest the horses, so Tino and could go out and hunt or fish. He was still keen on poaching Sheers' pheasants and wouldn't let up on the idea. He'd mapped it all out, where we could sneak in, where the pheasants were thickest and how we could get out of there fast enough without getting caught.

"Ho Tzu's offerin' us top dollar, too—it's some kind of special bird to the Chinamen," Tino said.

"Sounds too risky to me, I told him. "I mean, those birds are his prizes. And there's only one place they can come from—and, besides—I'm flush now."

"That's why I want to do it," he said. "That and the money. I'm tired of that son of a bitch calling me 'half breed' in front of folks. If I had my way I'd kill him. I mean it—I think about it sometimes—so I'll kill his goddamn pheasants, instead, while I'm bidin' my time."

"But he's your old man—"

"Is not! And don't ever say that again or you ain't my friend! My old man's dead! Sheers is nothin' to me!" Tino drilled his finger into my chest. "Nothing!"

This cut right to Tino's core—the notion that Percy Sheers had fathered him. He wouldn't accept it, never believed it—Sheers never owned up to it, either. It seemed such an insult, such a wrong-doing neither of them could admit to it. And, for me, whose relationship with my own father—strained to the gills like it was—it didn't seem possible that a father and son could hate each other the way they done. But the two of them stayed at it—exchanging threats, cussing up and down at each other—any second waiting for one of them to throw a punch or worse. I never seen bad blood like this. So, I knew better than to stir it up because I saw how it rubbed Tinos' nerves raw, but sometimes it just slipped out— sometimes I wanted him to talk about it, at least—and not keep so much of it boiling inside.

"I don't know, Tino, about these pheasant," I said.

"What don't you know?"

"We've been lucky so far—why push our luck?" I asked him.

"Oh, 'cause you're all respectable now—is that it?"

Tino's remark stung me—it wasn't like before when I had noth-ing to lose. Now I had two horses and a wagon, and a bit of a solid reputation, and I guess when you own things and rely on people's business, it changes up the situation, how you look at things—you got more at stake—more skin in the game. And I remembered, too, what my old man had said about keeping a good name. I always thought that didn't mean shit, but when you rely on regular customers and keeping your reputation—you ain't so quick to write it all off. But I hated Percy Sheers too—not as much as Tino, of course—but I had no love for the man—and against my better judgment—I softened up to Tino's plan.

"We ain't been caught yet, right?" Tino said.

"I know but there's always a first time."

"Not if we're careful." He showed me what he'd drawn out on the back of a livery invoice with the hay fields seeded with oats and the reeds and thickets where the pheasants nested, and the railroad tracks to the east.

"You really want to do this, don't you?" I'd rarely seen Tino draw anything out.

"Been thinking about it a lot." Tino's fingers traced over the map he'd sketched.

"You're crazy, Tino, but I've always known that—it's part of your charm."

"Charm? Sheeeet!" he said, and we both laughed.

But I did like that craziness and daring about Tino. He took chances and wasn't like so many of the stuff-shirts around town. What most folks called foolish, I thought adventurous —that it raised the pulse and made the ordinary exciting. There were too many dull days in this town like it was—too many days of just watching the sun go and then watching it go back down again. And Tino had a mind of his own, too—he went against the grain—and I liked that about him. He didn't follow folks around like sheep in a herd—and most of all, because he was alone, there was no one to disappoint, no one to tell him he was living his life all wrong. He seemed free to me, as free as a bird—free as anyone I knew.

"And you're sure about this?" I asked again.

"More than anything," he said."I'll pick when the time's right, okay?"

"Okay," I said. I've gone this far with you—why turn back now?"

"It'll work—don't you worry." He never lacked for confidence.

6

Advice for the Lovelorn
· ·

Emma and I were sitting on her front porch one evening, sipping a little bourbon—chewin' on our cuds' as folks around here say. I didn't tell her about Tino's plan because she never much cared for the poaching even if it was off someone like Percy Sheers. So I kept it to myself, sitting there on Emma's porch mulling it over, wondering if it was worth the risk or not, until I realized neither Emma or me had talked in awhile. The silence wasn't uncomfortable—it was just a silence—a sign that we'd grown used to each other by now. My feet were propped up on the porch railing while I stared east across Grand Avenue to the open hay fields, watching the last bit of sunlight drain from the sky and feeling the bourbon seep out to the ends of my fingers.

"How come a young fellow like you doesn't have a girl?" Emma's question jarred me out of my thoughts.

I had to think about this one. "I don't know for sure, Emma. With a town that talks like this one does, I'm sure word gets around about me," I said. "It gets around pretty much about any one— good or bad." That seemed a plain truth to me and a good enough reason for being single.

"What do you think they're saying about you?" Emma leaned forward, resting her arms on her lap.

"Depends on who you ask," I said. "If you're listening to someone like Percy Sheers, it ain't full of compliments—I can tell you that. He don't like me 'cause he sees me with Tino, so I'm sure he can fill a person's ear about how we poach and make the rounds and how we spend time with women like Flo—women my old man calls 'floosies'—and how we drink too much and don't ever think about tomorrow—all those things that scare good women away."

"And you think that's what women hear?" she asked.

"I don't know what they hear." I said.

"You don't seem like no hooligan to me." Emma wore glasses and they often slid down her nose.

"Well—having my own team of horses—I guess you could say having my own business—has changed things up some," I said. "I can't just run around no more like I used to." And I couldn't—didn't have the time or the energy mostly.

"You're growing up, Bert," she said.

"Is that what they call it?"

"You got responsibilities now."

"No, maybe I am changing, Emma—things are different—I can feel it," I said. "Even Tino noticed. It snuck up on me."

I wasn't sure I'd left any of my past behind if that's what changing meant. Mostly the past still seemed in arm's reach—calling distance—close enough that I could sneak back to it any time and make myself right at home—just like I'd never left it. I mean, it just didn't disappear because I owned a pair of horses and a wagon now, and had a business to look after, did it? How could it? I think the past hangs around a long time—as long as you want it to—or until all the excuses for wanting to hold onto it run out. For some folks it never leaves. I know, I seen them around town, overheard them at the Union talking about the grand old times and wishing the earlier times would come back and how everything now had gone to hell—but I never bought into it. I still liked parts of my past—like drinking with Tino and Flo, and poaching off Percy Sheers—but I think folks remember just the good parts of the past and forget about all the bad. For me, the past was slipping away and there was nothing I could do to bring it back. I was okay with that. Let it slip away—that was my feeling. Lately I was ready for a new day—something different, something that'd put my mistakes behind me.

"Anyone you got your eye on?" Emma asked.

"It's a long shot and I don't even want to tell you," I said. I had this feeling if you told someone about a hunch—some long-shot wish—that you'd jinxed it from the start so I hesitated to say anything to Emma, but I also knew when I was excited about something, I couldn't keep it to myself. I had to spill it out or it just ate me up inside—besides, Emma had become someone I trusted.

"Now c'mon, Bert, you can't do that to old Emma here. You can't leave a person hanging—tease them with a couple of details and then pull it all back." Emma drank from her glass. "Besides, it's not like I'm going to tell the whole town is it?"

"I guess not." I set my glass down on the little table. "Yeah, there is someone—Cameron Landers." I blurted her name out, hoping Cameron didn't hear me from miles away.

"The girl who works at G.T. Pauli's?" Emma chuckled to herself.

"That's the one—I just met her." I glanced over at Emma. "Why you laughing?"

"She's a plain thing." Emma held an opinion on just about everyone.

"What do you mean "plain thing?""

"I mean the way she dresses. The times I go in there she's always wearing that same long white dress like she don't have a curve to her—not a frill in it. And her hair's always combed straight not a wave or curl—yeah, she'll add a ribbon or two." Emma looked over at me. "Plain—like I said—not good or bad—just plain."

"What does that matter?" I asked. "Besides, I'm tired of being with women with all the rouge and the lipstick and enough toilet water to knock a horse over."

"It don't matter—I'm just talking, that's all." Emma set her glass down on the table. "Time was I didn't care what they looked like and now I care even less." She paused here. "Tell me—what do you find so attractive about her?"

"She's friendly, very helpful."

"But that's her job, Bert—what she gets paid to do."

"I know, but her friendliness seems—what's the word?"

"Genuine?" Emma said.

"Yeah—genuine—that's it!" I said. "It don't seem forced like she's trying to sell you something you don't need." I could see Cameron's face just then in my mind. "And she has a beautiful smile—and green eyes. I had to look at them a couple of times deciding what color they were—but they're green."

"When did this all start?" Emma leaned toward me and I could tell I'd piqued her interest.

"Ain't nothing started yet," I said. "I just met her at Pauli's store. She said she knew my sister Josephine and that they'd gone to school together, and I asked Josephine about her and she said Cameron didn't mingle much with kids that weren't in their church—she's got a brother named Chester, too."

"Her folks are fundamentalists, something like that—Bible toters," Emma said. "The father might even be a minister but I don't know for sure. That's probably why she dresses that way—they're less a temptation is what they figure."

"What's a fundamentalist?"

"They're people who read the Bible a lot, and swear by it—everything in it." Emma shook her head. "There's folks in the Bible that live to be seven, eight hundred years old—and those believers—they swallow it all—hook, line and sinker."

"Six, seven hundred years old, huh?"

"Yes, sir—and don't ever argue with them about it, either—because you can't. Their minds are already made up. There's no talking any kind of sense into them."

"You believe in Jesus, don't you?" I asked her.

"Yes, I'm a Christian but I take it in small doses—not like those folks. They take it real serious."

"How are they different?"

"Lordeee!" Emma leaned back in her chair. "They get excited at their service. I mean *excited!* I ain't been to one but you don't have to—I walked by their church one morning—it's more like a barn painted white—and I could hear them inside. You would have thought a swarm of bees got loose. Those church walls were shaking and the preacher was reading verses and folks were singing and shouting after him. If they said "Jesus" once they said it a thousand times. Hands were clapping—it was one lively affair—a lot livelier than what us Lutherans are used to."

"She invited me to one of their services," I admitted.

"Of course, she did," Emma said. "And what'd you tell her?"

"I told her I'd go maybe this Sunday."

"Well, I don't want to discourage you, Bert, especially if it's a budding romance, but I'd say she's already trying to get her hooks into you."

"I don't know—maybe I'll change my mind between now and Sunday." I pictured Cameron's face again. "You know me, Emma—I ain't too big on all this religious stuff."

"But you won't know unless you go and see for yourself," Emma said.

"I'd just be fooling myself—I ain't no believer," I told her. I knew inside me I was interested in Cameron for all the wrong reasons—it wasn't her church or God or religion or any of that. I was drawn to how she looked, pure and simple—drawn to how she smiled at me—and that was the simple facts. God and religion? I didn't give a lick about them.

"You don't never know, Bert—maybe you'll see the light and get filled with the Lord and turn from your sinful ways." I think I saw Emma wink her eye here.

"Filled with the Lord," I repeated. "Wouldn't that be something? Bert Miller walking around spouting the Bible—folks in half the bars in town'd fall over dead seeing that." We both laughed.

"Stranger things could happen," Emma said.

"She's different from the other girls I know in town," I said, trying to get serious.

"Oh, I'll give you that," Emma was quick to chime in. "Real different."

"Maybe that's what I need," I said. "Someone different—someone to turn my life around."

"Your life don't need no turning around," Emma said. "You might think it does, but it don't. You got a good heart and you don't hurt nobody and that's what matters most."

"Thank you, Emma, for those kind words," I said. "It's true," she said. "You ain't a bad person."

"Well, I hope not!" And at that, Emma poured us one last drink for the evening although I was never sure if it was the last.

"See what it's like being around her first," Emma said. "She may end up doing things that just get on your nerves, and you don't want be around someone like that, do you?"

"I guess not," I said.

"Of course you don't!"

"If it looks like you can stand each other—ask her out for a little date then. Buy her an ice-cream soda." Emma looked at me. "A soda, Bert! Nothing stronger 'cause I'm sure those folks don't take to the bottle—they probably think the devil's corked inside."

"She'll just say no."

"You won't know until you ask her."

"I suppose." No drinking, I thought. I'm sure you couldn't cuss around them, either—and getting inside their dress? The world would probably end first.

"And if she says 'yes,' don't go bringing up 'God' or how you don't believe in any of that biblical stuff—not right off, at least. If you do, she'll send you packing. Just tell her your mind ain't made up yet—that you're considering all the possibilities." Emma smiled to herself.

"What if she brings him up?"

"Then she does, and you'll have to be honest and tell her what you feel—but Bert, you have to be square with her. If you're not, it'll all catch up with you. One look into those 'beautiful green eyes' and there's no telling what you'd say."

"That's what I'm afraid of."

"Would you be ready to convert?" Emma asked. She looked at me with a little grin on her face. "I'm getting the cart before the horse here, but that's what it might get down to—but talk with her first and see what that's like. It may turn out you got nothing in common and that all that appeal of hers was just something you wanted to reach out and grab a handful of—something you made up—something stuck in your mind and no place else."

"I can do that," I said—and I could. I prided myself with being able to talk to anyone, to listen whatever they had to say even if it was just a load of horseshit.

"Sure you can! Don't over-think it, though."

"I'm wasting my time."

"That ain't buliding any confidence." Emma finished the last of her bourbon. "With an attitude like that you might as well be thinking of someone else."

"No, she's the only one."

"Well, then."

"And you don't think I'm wasting my time?"

"Can't answer that—if I could, I'd hang out my shingle and give advice."

"I'm just going to forget about her." It was already getting too complicated.

"That's the simplest thing," Emma said. "She's got you going in circles and you don't even know her yet. Go ahead and forget about her then—if you can. No worries then. No wondering or 'what-if's—but it might be harder than you think."

"There's other girls out there, anyway," I said.

"Sure there are—dozens of them." Emma waved her arms around. "Here they come now! Better go inside and hide!" And we both started laughing.

"Girls whose beliefs line up more with mine—whatever those are," I said.

"You just have to find them."

I laughed. "Girls with no beliefs."

"No beliefs, huh?" Emma shook her head. "Better yet."

"Why do we even have beliefs?" I asked.

"Bert, that's a question folks have been asking longer than I've been around," Emma said. "You find the answer—you let me know, okay?"

Beliefs complicated things. Most folks, maybe *all* folks had them, and I couldn't always understand why because everyone believed something different, and those folks whose beliefs lined up with someone else's, well, they huddled up and formed churches or clubs—whatever they could agree on—and made a list of things they could all believe in and things they could do and couldn't do. Nothing wrong with that, I guess—it's what folks did. But then there'd be another group come along with different beliefs, and more often than not these groups disagreed and worse than that they grew to hate each other and started wars and then the slaughtering began. Over what, I wondered? Beliefs? That's what—something you couldn't put your hand on. Show me a solid belief and I'll give you five dollars. And beliefs about God? Those were the worst—this God was different from their God because he didn't descend from some other God—something with no more grit to it than a horse's fart. I didn't understand none of it.

Religion to me was like trying to learn carpentry from my old man when my mind was somewhere else—just a lot of words that I wasn't ready to listen to just yet—but, at least, with carpentry, if you stuck to it, you could eventually learn a skill. What did you ever learn from religion but more religion?

I remember this religion stuff after Ma and the old man had left for the states, leaving us with Nana, our grandmother, back in Switzerland. Nana dragged us to Mass every Sunday—it was like pulling teeth with us—all mumbo-jumbo to me—the priest in those funny clothes saying things in a language I couldn't understand. And all those sermons about God and the Church and believing in him to save your soul? They went right past me because I couldn't place exactly where the soul was. Sometimes I thought it might be right next to my heart—that's where folks always pointed. Other times when my stomach growled, I thought it might be down there. Still other times I wasn't sure it was anywhere—that maybe I never got one in the first place and that was my problem. I hated the whole church thing and Nana knew it, but she dragged us along just the same and would give my ear a good twist when she saw me not paying attention—like when John B. and I would be making faces or punching each other in the arms.

One time I farted out loud—broke off a big one like a cow does when it starts running—and church-goers around us turned to look at me and John B. and we couldn't stop laughing—we were doubled over, practically howling, fighting to take a breath. Nana clenched her teeth, grabbed our shirt collars, pulled us outside and gave us both a good thrashing. We went back inside vowing to behave ourselves while Nana walked up to the front of the church like nothing had happened. The priest put a wafer in her mouth and she made the sign of the cross, and that was that. Nana's soul was saved—but I still wasn't sure about ours.

"To hell with it! I'll ask her out." I broke the silence.

"Maybe you'll get lucky and she'll ask you out first."

"I ain't holding my breath."

"Maybe this is all a set-up, Bert—like she's got it all planned."

"What do you mean?"

"She'll sense you're a poor lost soul that's strayed from the flock and she'll want to take you in—it's what folks like her do," Emma explained. "They want to save the world. And those green eyes? They're like the shiny lure the fish sees—snap at it and you're hooked!"

"You think so?" It sounded like Emma had it all figured out.

"I don't know, but like I said, there's a lot more to it than 'beautiful green eyes.'"

"I'm a lost soul, Emma."

"Bert, we all are." Emma smiled. "Who knows? She might be just what you need?"

"Emma—no bullshit—give it to me straight. What do you think?"

"You keep asking me, and I can't answer that. It's probably what attracts her to you in the first place."

"Being a long shot?"

"Yeah, it's safe in a way—knowing in the back of your mind it won't work out and that way you won't have to change—you won't have to put yourself out there. You'll tell yourself, 'At least I tried' but the hand was played out before the cards were even dealt."

"Goddamn, this gets complicated."

"It doesn't have to be. Look—there's some steps to this." Emma shifted in her chair. "First of all—and this might be the hardest—be clear-headed about things. I mean, you don't go making a bid on hauling paving stones or grapes or whatever without taking into account distance and time involved, right?"

"Yeah, that's right."

"No different here," Emma said. "Ask her out. See what she says. If she says 'no' then the guessing's taken out of it. If she says 'yes' then next step is how are you going to move forward?" Emma motioned with her finger in the air, ticking off each thing I should do. "It starts with walking into Pauli's store, making small talk that leads up to the real reason you're there in the first place. Then you pop the question—it's not like you're proposing marriage, is it?"

"No, it's not."

"Whatever happens, you're going to feel foolish—it's part of the game," she said. "So, don't over-think it. And, Bert, a couple more things—"

"What's that?"

"A bath. A clean shirt. No drinking."

"Not even before?"

"No, not even before—those church folks smell alcohol a block away."

"All right, that's what I'll do!"

"Good for you, Bert!" And she gave me a light punch on the shoulder.

"Let's drink to it."

Emma poured another splash into my glass and added one to her own. I'd figure out what I wanted to say to Cameron—maybe even write the words down and rehearse the lines so I got them just right before I walked into Pauli's and rattled them off. If it all went to hell, then it all went to hell—it was where I was headed anyway—and it wouldn't be the first time. I'd grown a thicker skin for things going to shit, but it still wasn't thick enough. Something always managed to seep through—no way of avoiding it. The trick was not to let if flatten you, and if it did, you jumped right back up, ready to take your lumps all over again. You'd been around long enough to know more were coming. They sat out there waiting for their chance. My old man taught me some of this—the rest I just learned along the way.

7
A Plan and Church-Going
· ·

With all those thoughts of Cameron Landers and church-go-ing swirling inside my head, and whether I could change or not, and if there really was a God, or if Cameron and I could even match up, I said to hell with it—there's only one way of finding out. I'd been chasing floosies for too long and they'd been chasing me, and I was tired of waking up alongside one, staring at a set of bad teeth or a pillow case dusted in orange by her rouge. I was ready for something different—something pure and good—some-one to turn my life around. So I began rehearsing what I'd say to Cameron Landers—some of the things I thought could soften her up. First of all I'd figure out what I wanted to buy at Pauli's so it wasn't like I'd gone in there cold just to ask her out. I thought about that, and right off I could see I was already being dishonest. There was a whole list of things I needed though: a mirror, a tin of boot oil, some buttons that were missing on one of my shirts that Emma said she'd sew back on, so there was a reason, after all, to go in there. No, I had a reason for going in there—I wasn't being dishonest after all.

I took a piece of paper and wrote out some opening lines: "Good morning, Cameron. Very pleasant to see you," seemed as good an opener as any. I'd make certain, first of all, it was just the two of us in the store, too. I didn't want to ask her in front of other customers—too embarrassing. No, it had to be just me and her. If there was other folks around, I'd scrap the plan and return later.

"Can I help you find something?" she might say, and I'd reply, "Yes, you can. I'd like a small mirror, and some boot oil." Then I'd follow her to wherever these items might be. She might hand the items to me or carry them back to the counter. Without over-thinking, I'd take a deep breath and blurt it out: "There's a band concert this Sunday at Union Hall and would you like to attend it with me?" Then I'd await her answer. If it was' yes,' I'd tell her more details, but if it was no, then I wasn't sure what I'd do. Just accept it—buy the items, wish her a good day, and try not to show any disappointment. Then later maybe go out to Sonoma Creek, find the deepest hole, jump in and drown myself.

A week after Emma and I talked about Cameron on Emma's front porch, I decided the day had come to walk into G.T. Pauli's and pop the question. I put on a clean shirt and parted my hair and even splashed on some rose water. I was ready. I stopped the team in front of Pauli's, stepped down from the wagon and walked up to the front door. When I opened it, the door struck a little bell in the jamb above and the bell tinkled to announce my arrival. I looked up to the front of the store and Cameron was behind the counter, but right alongside her was G.T. Pauli's wife. Cameron saw me and a smile creased her lips—not a big smile but not an unwelcoming one either.

"Good morning," she said. "Back to buy more items?"

"Good morning, Cameron," I said. "Yes, there's a couple more things I need."

"Oh, you remembered my name." She seemed surprised.

"Yes, I did." I couldn't tell her that I repeated it to myself a hundred times already. "Remember, you and my sister Josephine were in the same class at school?"

"Oh, yes, I remember her—she was very smart."

We looked at each other and I had to look away, afraid she might be reading my thoughts. This happened almost every time a woman looked deep into my eyes—it unsettled the hell out of me.

"How can I help you?" she asked.

What a question! How could she help me? And if I needed help, what kind of help did I need? And here I wasn't talking about picking out articles at Pauli's store when I'd gone there for something entirely different. I'd gone there because of how I felt toward this girl, and how the feelings were new and powerful. They were feelings different from what I'd felt toward earlier girls—at least, I thought they were. I didn't know yet how she was different but it was just a sense about her—call it a hunch. Better yet—call it a wish. I had to admit that I was smitten by her looks, and maybe that was all there was to it—that it didn't go any deeper and I was trying to convince myself it did. But something felt different to me inside, and I wanted to follow it and see where it led. But as much as I wanted to talk with her and ask her to the concert, and get it all off my chest, with Mrs. Pauli standing there, the timing wasn't right so I bought the mirror and the boot oil, wished her a pleasant day, and walked out of the store.

Two days later, I decided to try again. I wore another clean shirt, parted the hair, splashed on the rose water and headed into town. This time when I entered Pauli's, Cameron was alone behind the counter. I walked up and down the aisles, rehearsing yet again my lines, before stopping in front of a rack of leather belts, my heart pumping like a blacksmith's bellow. I picked one out and put it around my waist to see how it fit. By this time she was standing right next to me. Her nearness gave me the trembles.

"It looks like it fits," she said. "It's a very handsome belt."

"I think I'll take it," and I handed her the belt and followed Cameron to the front counter.

"Is there anything else?"

"Ahhh—"

"Can't remember what it was?" she asked.

"Yes, there is." I stammered. "You know me, right?"

"Well, not really. You're Bert Miller—that much I know."

"Do you know much about me?"

"I don't know. Should I?" Cameron laughed. "I don't know how to answer that."

"If you did hear stories about me, they're probably not true," I said.

She gave me a puzzled look. "That's an odd thing to say," she said. "What if they were good stories I heard?"

"Well, then they'd be true," I said, and we both laughed and then her laugh settled into a smile—the same one that flashed across my mind a hundred times in the past weeks.

"Would you go to the band concert this Sunday at Union Hall with me?" There, I said it—all in one breath, too. I looked around and the world hadn't ended—the roof hadn't crashed in.

"My—that was sudden," she said. "Certainly something I wasn't expecting."

"I'd been meaning to ask you—and now I did."

"I should ask my folks first."

"And what'll they say?"

"I don't know. My father's the pastor at our church and Sunday morning is reserved for services. Why don't you join us this Sunday?" She looked at me and flashed those green eyes. "I might be able to persuade them if you do."

"What time do the services start?" I asked her.

"Ten in the morning," she said. "The service begins at ten."

"I can meet you there?"

"Of course—I arrive early to warm up with the choir and review which hymns we're going to sing." She paused a second or two. "Do you like to sing?"

"Only to myself and my horses," I said. That much was true. I sang a lot when I was alone—folk tunes and spirituals I'd heard passing by the different churches. My horses seemed to like the singing. I sometimes even thought about buying a guitar and learning to play it, but never did—I ain't much on practicing. I start out all hell-fire with an idea—vowing to myself I'll do whatever it takes to get good—until something else comes along and catches my eye, and days—maybe weeks—pass and I ain't done the practicing—ain't done nothing. I know I started out wanting to whittle wood like old Henry Wohlford and must have started on a dozen pieces—never getting very far on none of them—until a pile of my whittlings just sat by my chair staring at me. One day I scooped all of them up and chucked them into the stove—and that was it for my whittling.

She laughed.

I stole another glance at her, at those green eyes, at that smile, breathed in the air around her, as though I could take it all with me, store it in a little box, until we met again. I wondered what the chances were that the gift of faith would hit me alongside the head, strike me dumb before next Sunday. It might even be a bolt of lightning—a burning bush. It could happen—even to the worst of sinners. Anything could happen. That's what I told myself—it could happen. I paid for the belt and headed toward the door.

"Bert—"

I turned around.

"Your belt," she said. "You forgot your belt."

"I sure did." And I laughed to cover up my embarrassment.

"I'll see you next Sunday then," she said.

"Sunday it is."

At first I didn't want to mention nothing about Cameron to Tino. I knew he'd be hounding me about getting suckered into the Lord and the Bible and all that crap but it was eating at me, and I couldn't be around him without getting it off my chest. He and I had talked enough about God and religion plenty and we both agreed that religion was intended for other folks, but not for us. He told me about the time he'd put up Pastor Hiram's horse and carriage at the livery, and how the pastor had cornered him more than once and asked if he'd received the Lord yet, and Tino told him, 'no', but he was being patient. Pastor Hiram also told Tino about the power of prayer, and if you prayed long and hard enough, he said, those prayers were usually answered. He wanted Tino to get down on his knees right there in the livery and start praying. "I wanted a gold pocket watch," Tino said, "and I prayed for almost a week—every night, and most mornings. Wasn't no pocket watch that ever showed up. But I did find a fifty cent piece on the floorboard of Doc Andrieux's carriage."

I finally told Tino about asking Cameron out, and that I'd promised that I'd go to her father's service.

"Why did you do that?" he wanted to know.

"I like her and want to know her better." That seemed the simplest answer.

"And you're going to a church service with her?"

"Well, I'm meeting her there so we ain't exactly going together—but yeah—I'm going to a service."

"Same thing." Tino shook his head and laughed. "Bert Miller going to a service and gettin' the Lord! Hallelujah!"

"I ain't getting the Lord."

"Not yet, you ain't, but if you don't get the Lord you ain't gonna see inside her bloomers—I'll tell you that."

"That ain't the only thing," I said.

"Oh, yeah? What else is there?"

That one stumped me.

"It's okay, Bert—you don't have to bullshit me—we're friends, remember?" Tino wasn't finished. "Maybe you do get that ticket."

"What ticket you talking about?"

"The ticket on that train to heaven, Bert," he said. "You ain't heard about that train? It glides upwards on them golden tracks."

"You're an asshole, Tino—you know that?"

"Watch your language now Bert—you don't want to be left off that train." And Tino laughed—a big horse laugh because he thought me going to heaven was funny—the more I thought about it, though—the more it seemed funny to me, too.

8

Sunday-Go-A Meetin'

· ·

Sunday morning arrived and I had a bad case of the nerves—so
bad it felt like a cat had crawled inside my stomach. I filled a
wash pail with hot water, soaped up and rinsed most of my body,
concentrating on the arm pits and my privates. I even soaped up
my hair, rinsed it out good and combed it back and parted it. I
clipped the hairs of my beard with a pair of scissors and brushed a
thick lather into the shortened stubble and shaved—nearly losing
a quart of blood. I dressed in clean underclothes and slipped into
the one starched shirt I never wore because it chafed my neck. But
I put it on just the same, buttoned it to the top button and slipped
a string tie around my neck. Moths had already eaten the elbow out
of my dress coat, but figured if I kept my arms close enough to my
body, nobody would notice. I rubbed a coat of boot oil into my
shoes, coaxed a half-assed shine from them, then turned to study
myself in the glass mirror I'd bought at Pauli's. My face was flushed
from the scrubbing and still bleeding in places from the straight
razor, but I thought I looked passable. I put on my hat, grabbed my
bicycle and had taken two, three steps from the barn, prepared to
meet Cameron and the Lord when I saw Emma leaving her garden.

"Lordee!" she said. "You going to church—or a funeral?"

"Both," I said. "Take your pick."

"Is this about that Landers girl?"

"It is." I rocked my bicycle back and forth. "I'm taking your
advice, Emma. Rather than wonder about what the odds are, and
wearing my mind to a frazzle, I thought I'd just wade in and find
out for myself—take all the guessing out of it."

"Good for you, Bert!" She patted me on the shoulder.

"We did a kind of trade—if I go to her church service, she'd see
about going to the band concert with me."

"Sounds fair enough," Emma said. "The service's not going to kill you. And you might even do your soul some good."

"What can I lose?" I was wary of expressions like that.

"Well, good luck to you!" By the tone of her voice, you would have thought she was sending me off to war.

"Thanks." I nodded and rode off toward town, toward Cameron's church. Who knows—maybe even toward salvation? I was trying to keep an open mind about the whole thing.

I arrived at the church and Emma was right—it looked more like a barn than any church I was used to seeing. No steeple or stained-glass windows—just a plain-looking building, white-washed and bright in the morning sun with all its windows opened wide and its front doors peeled back. A sign nailed to the front wall, painted in black letters read: *Souls' Haven—All are welcome.* I checked my pocket watch—ten minutes to ten. A little cluster of folks stood in front of the church and the women waved fans in front of their faces while the men talked amongst themselves. I could hear an organ playing inside and the choir members' voices as they warmed up. I found a sycamore that I could lean my bicycle against and waited behind it until a man came out with a bell in his hand and rang it, and folks filed inside. I waited as long as I could, and just as church doors closed, I slipped in front of them, found an empty space on the last row of pews and sat down. The organist continued playing. I took a deep breath and felt my heart pounding all the way into my throat.

I looked around and tried to pick out folks I knew, but it was mostly the backs of heads and women's hats I saw. The choir stood at the front of the church—twelve of them I counted—a mix of men and women, but mostly women. My eyes settled on Cameron—the only reason I was there in the first place. She stood very erect, holding a hymnal in her hands, and like the rest of the choir, looked out over the small congregation—maybe twenty five, thirty folks. All the choir members smiled. The women adjusted each other's collars or tamed an errant curl. Mrs. Hoskins, whose husband was the pharmacist in town, stood directly in front of them and I figured she was the director. To her right, Florence Riggles, whose family owned a haberdasher shop on the east side of the plaza, sat at the organ. My eyes kept returning to Cameron. Maybe it was my imagination, but she seemed to glow in the morning light. When our eyes finally met, I raised my hand and waved to her. She smiled back.

For their opening hymn, the choir sang "I'll Fly Away" which seemed to capture a deep-seated wish of mine at the moment. I felt out of place, that I'd made a mistake—and everyone there knew it. Then it seemed I was a spy who'd slipped in behind enemy lines and was gathering intelligence to carry back to headquarters, and at some point they'd all turn around and point their fingers at me, and shout, "Non-believer!" but I tried to push aside these feelings and just concentrate on listening to the singing even though the words to the hymn were a little disturbing. The hymn talked about when life is over and like birds we're going to fly from these prison walls and the shackles on our feet being cast aside. And the hymn went on about how we'll all fly away to heaven. I'd always had a hard time understanding any of this—and an even harder time believing it. Our best shot, our *only* shot, it seemed, was how we spent our time here on earth—that's what mattered to me more than crossing through those pearly gates the preachers all raved about. Sure, there was suffering and all that down here, but there were good times, too. And how could you cross into something you didn't even think existed? I know Tino and me had batted around these questions until our heads hurt, never arriving at any conclusion except if there was a heaven, and we managed to reach it, we hoped it had a saloon. Hell, we figured, had closed theirs.

After the choir finished their hymn, they sat down in their respective chairs and a quiet spread throughout the church until Cameron's father stood up and approached the pulpit. He didn't wear no preacher's robes, only a long-sleeved white shirt and tie and dark wool pants. He combed his hair straight back, was tall, wore rimless glasses—a thin man with an athletic built like he might have played basketball or ran long distance on his high school track team. He stepped up to the lectern, surveyed the congregation. "Welcome everyone," he said in a powerful voice. The inside of the church was already warming in the late July sun. The starch in the shirt chafed my neck and I thought how a glass of beer would taste like just then, a big tall glass, cool and frosty—it would have to wait.

Reverend Landers announced several church events: a bake sale to benefit the church's auxiliary, and an upcoming meeting of the church board, Bible classes Tuesday evenings. When he finished with the announcements, he paused, looked upwards toward the rafters before his eyes passed over the congregation once again. He picked up his Bible, opened it and read a parable about the prodigal son. This son had wasted his life and yet his father still took him back. Cameron was attentive, and like most everyone there kept her eyes focused on her father. After he'd read the passage, he set his Bible down. The parable led into the meat and potatoes of what he really wanted to say—that we're all sinners, but if we repent and believe in the Lord he'll always take us back. It was the Lord working within the Holy Trinity—three folks, he said, that showed us the way to heaven. And when we strayed, it was the Holy Ghost that kept our faith alive in the Lord Jesus Christ!

"In this trinity," he said, "God the father heads it, but he sent his son, Jesus Christ, to earth when we started to waver and because of our sinful ways we nailed Jesus Christ to a cross. Our sins nailed him to the cross, but he's coming back, brothers and sisters! He's coming back! I'm here to tell you the good news! And when we need a helping hand, when we need that strength in us to keep our faith alive, there's the third person in God, the Holy Ghost! Say Amen, brothers and sisters! Say Amen!" He looked upward and the whole congregation erupted with "Amen!"

"Shhhh," the reverend put two fingers to his lips. Everyone grew quiet. "Hear that sound? Like someone knocking at the door?" Reverend Landers asked. "Shall we let him in?"

"Let him in! Let him in!" the congregation shouted. "Let the Lord in!"

I strained my ears but try as I might, I couldn't hear nothing resembling a knock on a door. I heard folks shifting in their seats, heard a couple of sneezes from dust rising up from the wooden floor, but nothing like the sound I figured the Lord'd make knocking on a door.

Someone yelled out, "Now I hear it!"

Another person shouted, "I hear it, too!"

Then folks stirred everywhere, asking each other if they heard it, and they nodded their heads 'Yes', they had, and before long everyone was hearing the Lord knocking on a door except me and I wondered if I'd suddenly gone deaf. The fellow standing to my left elbowed me in the ribs, "You hear it, brother?" and I nodded yes, and told him I sure did.

"Don't worry if you don't hear it right now!" Revered Landers assured the congregation. He seemed to be looking straight at me. "But pretty soon you will. Right when you don't expect it—he'll be knocking and it's up to you to open that door."

I took that as a sign of hope.

"We're waitin' for you Lord! We're all here waitin' for you!" Reverend Landers continued. And the congregation answered, "We're here, Lord! We're here!" He waved his arms. "Be patient! C'mon, let me hear you say it! Jesus!" And the congregation answered back, "Jesus!" And once again the whole gathering jumped to life and folks started clapping their hands and swaying back and forth and then the organ pealed, and pretty soon the choir joined in, and the whole place sounded just the way Emma had described it earlier—like a hive of bees got loose. It was hard not to feel the commotion—impossible, really—and and I swayed right along with them, clapped my hands, shouted out to the rafters like I'd been a believer all the time. I couldn't help it. All that energy and swaying and people shouting like they done just rubbed off on me and if I couldn't hear Jesus myself then maybe he could hear me.

Through it all I watched Cameron. She was smiling and clapping her hands and singing with the choir. When our eyes met,

I raised both my arms over my head and she did the same. Then I swayed both arms to the right, and damn, if she didn't follow suit and move her arms to the right! And my arms went to the left and her arms went left. I rolled my head and she rolled her head and I could see her lips move like she was saying something and whatever it was I hoped it was something I wanted to hear. And when the choir sang, I pretended she was singing just to me, instead, and changing the words around to say how glad she was that I was there at this very moment.

Pastor Landers motioned with his arms and a quiet resumed inside the church. He returned to his sermon and was back talking again about the holy trinity but I wished we were still clapping and swaying back and forth because I liked that part of it. It was the sermonizing and Bible quoting that gave me trouble. I tried to imagine three people—like this "Holy Trinity" the reverend described—all crammed into one, and was having a hard time with it. How do you find a suit that fits someone like that? And what if God wanted to go one way and the Holy Ghost another, who won out? And if everyone believed in Jesus, why were there so many versions of him? Why couldn't the Methodists agree with the Presbyterians and what made the Catholics so different? And that didn't even include the Jews—or the Muslims. Nobody could agree on nothing, it seemed. And I'll tell you straight out—the whole affair confused me more than ever, but I was going along with it just the same.

Spirits? I could understand them. Tino said spirits were everywhere. But one Holy Spirit for everyone? That was a stretcher. I'd have to tell Tino about this because even though Tino believed in spirits he just didn't think they liked to hang around inside a church. In fact, he thought churches the last place to find them. Spirits wanted to be free, he said, and were happiest in the trees, the rocks, floating in the air—even the game he killed, the fish he caught. Everything had a spirit. In fact, when he killed something, he felt almost apologetic, like he'd harmed its spirit and as a way to make up for it, the first thing he'd do after the killing was to go up and touch it, close his eyes and mutter something. "What are you saying just then?" I'd ask him. He said he was talking to the spirits, that all things contained a spirit of his ancestors and even though they were dead, this spirit remained alive. "Spirits, huh?" I said. He looked back at me. "That's right, spirits."

At the sermon's end, the choir rose again and sang "Amazing Grace" and when the hymn ended, Pastor Landers led them in prayer, their heads all bowed, and when they finished praying, their heads lifted and a silence followed. I heard a fly buzzing, looked over and saw it beating against the one closed window. Then, as if on cue, everyone stood, and Pastor Landers announced "Go in peace!" and everyone shook hands with those nearest them, greeting each as 'brother' or 'sister.' That same fellow who'd elbowed me earlier, turned and shook my hand and called me 'brother' all over again. I called him 'brother' back. I could see he wanted to talk some more—share his feelings about Jesus—but I was anxious to leave and high-footed it out in front of everyone, found that same sycamore where I'd left my bicycle and stood in its shade and watched folks leave the church.

Cameron was the last to leave the church along with her fellow choir members. I watched how she interacted with different folks, trying to learn as much as I could about her, who the folks were that she moved toward—trying to find out the least little clue— anything I could. A young man approached her—I'd seen him before around town—Daniel, I think his name was Daniel—they shook hands and talked, and it made me even more curious—maybe even a little jealous, and reminded me of how little I knew about her. Here she seemed so at ease, so talkative, different from the shy, quiet girl I took her to be standing behind the counter at Pauli's. She moved from church member to church member, her laughter sometimes breaking above the sound of everyone's talking. I stepped away from the tree, our eyes met and we walked toward each other.

"Well," she said, "it didn't kill you, did it?"

"No, I'm still alive," I told her. She seemed radiant in her yellow Sunday dress. "You look lovely," I said. She blushed.

"The service always invigorates me," she said. "It fills me with an energy that I can only describe as the Lord's."

"It had me going, too," I said, although I wasn't sure I could blame the Lord.

"I know—I watched you. Did it all seem crazy to you?"

"No, it didn't seem crazy," I said. I didn't know what it seemed like other than a bunch of people all clapping and believing the same thing and following their minister like they were trained monkeys.

"You have to give yourself up to it," she said. "It's like a surrendering—but not in a bad way. You put yourself in his hands and you trust in him and he shows you the way forward."

"That's faith, ain't it?" I asked. Folks walked over hot coals with this same faith—I'd read about it somewhere.

"Yes it is."

I figured the worst thing I could do just then was confess to her how little faith I had in most things. I don't know why I felt that way—maybe all the bruises in this life added up to it, all the disappointments, all the hawkers selling snake oil and promising miracle cures done it, but faith to me was an overused word and I steered clear of it. I liked things in front of me—things I could touch and feel—not all this airy crap. Still, I remembered Emma's advice and avoided the subject the best I could.

"Do you have faith?" she asked, not wasting any time popping the question. Her eyes were giving me a good going-over, looking for any cracks—any signs of doubt.

"Let's just say I'm a natural doubter—one of those guys who likes to think things over a lot," I said. "I do it all the time like deciding whether to buy something or not—it's a habit of mine." That seemed a safe enough response. "I like to think these things out for myself," I added. "Figure out what's real and what ain't— what works and what don't."

"But you're not buying anything with the Lord," she said.

"In a way you are. Isn't he trying to sell you on himself?" I asked.

"I think you're missing the point here." This seemed to stir her blood up a bit—something I didn't want to do just then.

"Maybe so," I said. "Let's talk about this later, okay?" Our conversation took a sudden serious turn and I wanted to keep it light. I knew there were issues that sooner or later we would have to face but right then I didn't want to think about them. "How does the concert sound?" I asked, hoping to lighten the mood. That was the problem with Jesus and religion and all that –it was so goddamn serious.

"Like fun—but first I want to say hello to my folks," she said. "And I want you to meet them—formally, I mean." She took my arm and pulled me toward where Pastor Landers and her mother were standing. They were a handsome couple. I could see Cameron's features in her mother—the puckered little smile, the big round cheeks, even the green eyes.

"Mother, father, this is Bert Miller," she said.

I shook both their hands. "Pleased to meet both of you," I said. The preacher gave my hand a hard squeeze. The mother's was much softer. She wore her hair up and under a large hat—the fashion these days.

"Likewise," her mother said.

"Bert Miller!" Her father gave me the once-over—seeing if he could remember my face on a 'Wanted ' poster before shaking my hand. "I didn't know you were a church-goer," he said. I feared he already knew about me—maybe even peeked through the window of the Union or Poppe's Tavern, and seen me there indulging in one of my favorite past-times—and it wasn't reading the Bible .

"It took a little persuading." I glanced toward Cameron.

"Are you going to make it a habit?" He kept his eyes focused on me.

"I don't know, sir, maybe." At this point I was searching only for safe answers—didn't want to stir any feathers up. For a few minutes I could stand being a Christian.

"There's worse things you could do. You realize that, don't you?" he said. This guy had a serious set of eyes to him—like little flames behind each of them.

"Oh, much worse things," I said. And, of course, I'd done them, almost every worst thing I could think of.

A slight smile creased his lips.

"Father, mother, Bert's invited me to a concert this afternoon," she said. "With your permission, I'd like to go with him."

Pastor Landers looked straight into my eyes again with that same look he'd cast over his congregation a half hour earlier—looking straight inside me, trying to see if I had a soul or not. Did he sense I was an imposter? "A concert?" he asked.

"Yes, father. It's at—"

"The Union Hall," I said. "Down at the square."

"Trust me, young man," he said. "I know where the Union Hall is."

There was a hint of disgust in his voice. Oh, no, I thought. I already knew about the liquor, but were they forbidden to listen to concerts, too? What other joys in this life were left?

"Please, father." There was that look in Cameron's eyes—one that might persuade me to walk over coals.

He looked over at his wife and then at me. "Normally we spend Sunday afternoons in quiet contemplation," he said.

Quiet contemplation? What the hell is that I wondered?

"We could make an exception, though, couldn't we, Harold?" Mrs. Landers looked at her husband and then back to Cameron.

"I suppose," he said. "Just this once."

"Oh, thank you, father!" Cameron kissed him on the cheek.

"Bert," Pastor Landers said, "If you don't mind, would you help me close up the church before we leave?"

"Not at all, Pastor."

We left Cameron and her mother and walked inside the church. The pastor started closing windows on one side of the church and I closed all the windows on the opposite side. When the windows were all closed we were standing together in front of the pulpit where he arranged a pile of papers.

"Bert, could I ask you something?" He stood right in front of me. His voice got that serious tone again and I sensed some hard questions heading my way.

"Yes, sir," I said. I was ready for anything—fire away!

"What are your intentions with my daughter?" There went those eyes of his again—burning a hole right through me.

"My intentions?" I said. I had to swallow twice over this word and felt a lie brewing. I must say, the reverend didn't waste no time getting to the meat of the matter. In spite of all that Hell and brimstone he crowed about from the pulpit, he still had some left-over—I could feel it bubbling behind his eyes.

"Yes, intentions," he said. "When a boy meets a girl, or a man meets a woman, there's often something he has in mind—maybe something they both have in mind."

"You mean, like what will happen to them in the future?" I asked. Okay, reverend, I'll go along with you on this one—I'm not just another bobo that fell off the turnip wagon.

"Yes, that's one way to put it—maybe even the simplest way."

"Well, I can't say right now, Pastor Landers," I said. "We only just met a short while ago." What else could I tell him? That I undressed her every night in my dreams? That I wanted to bed her more than anything—more, even than wanting to meet God and going to heaven? That I'd take whatever she gave me and still hope for more?

"But you have some idea, don't you?" The reverend wasn't letting up.

"About our future?" I said. Big question. "No, not really—like I said—we're just getting to know each other—seeing what that's like." The pastor was concerned, as any father would be, and I couldn't blame him. I don't know what he saw when he looked at me—half the time I didn't know either, when I looked in the mirror. But I thought my answers were honest enough. Sure, I whacked around the bush about what my real intentions were with his daughter—what normal guy wouldn't? But right now I was careful about saying the things a father wanted to hear.

"Our daughter is very special to us—"

"I'm sure she is," I said.

"And we've raised her in the Lord's love and we feel she should be with someone raised equally in that same Lord's love," he said. "We don't want to see that spoiled. We want her to be with someone raised in that same love so they can share it and grow it throughout their lives."

"I understand." I knew you couldn't feed a horse oats, then slip him rice hulls and expect the same results.

With the windows closed and the backdoor locked, the pastor and I left through the front doors. He closed and locked them, then stopped to greet church members while I rejoined Cameron and her mother. I smiled at them and wished that earlier fever I'd felt in church could revisit me but the pastor's questions sucked the air out of me. They didn't dance round the issue. They didn't want to hear no bullshit answers. I figured they were the kinds of questions a father would ask any suitor sniffing around his daughter although I didn't consider myself a suitor.

I didn't know what I was. Like most things, I thought that if I didn't have to define myself then there was always possibility and I could be all manner of folks—like those lizards that change color to match their background. If there were different boxes, I'd fit into them. I only knew I was following a smile and a pair of green eyes and a fantasy big and ripe as a summer melon—there was no other way to put it. Crazy—I know. It was pure whim that had me by the balls and here I was headed down another dark mineshaft, thinking, hoping the gift of faith would come along and shine its light just in time. The gift of faith, I thought to myself? Hadn't I chucked that out the window years ago? And now—somehow—it was going to make some miraculous return? Why? To win over some girl? My old man always told me my head was in the clouds—what he didn't know was that it was mostly up my ass. But if there was anyone that tried and tried at even the most futile of causes, it was me. I deserved some kind of medal—a medal for the guy could go back and forth on any issue—back and forth so many times you'd swear he was a pendulum in some goddamn hall clock. That was my life.

"Cameron says you own your own team of horses." Mrs. Landers smiled and tugged at the sleeve of her dress.

"Yes, I do." Finally a question I could answer that didn't raise a hundred doubts. "Molly and Dolly are their names. I bought them from JD McCracken."

"I've always been afraid of horses," Mrs. Landers said. "I don't know exactly why—I don't ever remember any incident that would cause it, but I am."

"Well, Molly and Dolly are like two big dogs," I said.

Cameron interrupted us. "Bert, Father said I could go to the concert with you." There was that glow to Cameron again, that glow I noticed earlier in church.

"Great! That's great!" I looked toward Mrs. Landers. "Thank you. I'll take good care of your daughter."

Pastor Landers rejoined us and I offered to walk the Pastor and his wife to their carriage. Theirs was a surrey pulled by a single horse. I helped Mrs. Landers step up to the carriage seat. The pastor followed. They looked down at us both.

"When does the concert start?" Mrs. Landers asked.

"Two o'clock," I said. "In about an hour, hour and a half. We can walk there from here."

"Well, enjoy yourselves," she said.

I walked to the nose of their horse and nudged it backwards into the middle of the street. The pastor gave the reins a little snap and the surrey jumped forward. Mrs. Landers turned to look back at us as their carriage rolled down the street. I had my bicycle with me and I pushed it along as we walked toward the center of town, three blocks away. Cameron's arm was in mine. We were finally alone.

9

First Date

• • • • • • • • • •

"How about an ice cream soda before the concert?" I asked her. I put it right out there. No point in over-thinking it. By now it was early afternoon, and a soda seemed a good way to 'break the ice' between us. I was new to this 'proper dating.' With me, if I saw someone I liked, usually in a saloon, I shouldered up to her and bought her a drink and it went from there. With enough drinks, the alcohol did the talking—there was hardly no thinking involved. No parents to meet. No formalities. No talking around each other. We'd go straight to the bare bones. This time, though, it was different—this was a good girl, a virtuous girl—and I'd have to be on my best behavior—filtering every word like it was the last drop out of a bottle and miles away until the next one.

"A soda'd be grand," Cameron said.

"I'm curious, Cameron—but do you drink anything harder?" There—I tossed the first really difficult question out to her.

"Harder? Like alcohol?" She paused here. "Never."

"Why not?" I wondered. "They drink in the Bible, don't they?"

"Yes, there is drinking in the Bible, but we believe it only leads to depravity," she said.

"Even in moderation?"

"Yes, even in moderation," she said. "Better to forego it altogether. It weakens our judgment, loosens our morals."

I didn't say nothing further on the subject. My judgment was weakened plenty of times when I pulled the cork out of a bottle so I couldn't argue with her on that one. And my morals loosening? Well, they got loose all right—scattered like dust in the wind. She had me on that one, too.

"Did you ever try a drink?" I asked her.

She looked around her like her father might be listening in. "I did—once," she said.

"And what happened?" I wondered.

"It tasted very bitter—I didn't even want to swallow, but I did," she said. "And it made me sick—right then I knew it was the Lord watching over me." She looked at me. "How can you even drink it?"

"Well," I said. "The first couple of drinks, I had to sneak up on the glass 'cause I found it a little bitter, too, like you said, but after a couple of tries, I got used to it. It just took a little practice—now it just flows down like honey seltzer."

"At least you're honest about it," she said. My remark even forced a little smile from her.

Our future together seemed to be dimming but there were little flickers of light, still—maybe my honesty—my plain speaking—a meteor falling from the sky—would win her over.

"I don't understand why people want to drink in the first place," she said. "Look at his day, for example." And she spun in a circle and threw her arms out like a ballerina. "I can just breathe it all in— the sunlight, the fresh air—my senses open themselves to the Lord's work around me—every little pore open to receive his gifts. I can't do that with alcohol inside me. With alcohol everything's blurred and blocked up and stupid—it seems really stupid to me." She drew in another deep breath.

"Sometimes it's like that with me—all blurred and the like—but, Cameron, I gotta say that other times it allows me to see things I wouldn't see otherwise—feel things, too."

"Like what?" she asked.

"It slows things down just enough where I can get a better look at them," I said. "Otherwise it all goes racing by—like watching countryside from a train window—and I'm wondering what I missed." I thought about this some more. I had to make a good argument for alcohol. "It gives me a different perspective, too—I see things different than I normally do."

"You're not making a very convincing case for it," she said.

"Aren't there times when you wished you hadn't ever started? That you were all clean inside?"

"There's always times I regretted what I done in the past," I said. "I think with alcohol, though, it'd be like leaving an old friend behind if I ever tried to stop."

"Now you're sounding very foolish, Bert Miller—and very old," she said. "You're still a young man but you're talking like an old one who can't leave his vices behind—like the old men I see sitting on front porches passing a bottle back and forth." She stepped in front of me and started walking backwards at my pace, keeping her eyes on mine. "Is there anything that would make you quit?"

"I suppose there is," I said.

"What would it be? I'm curious."

"I guess it'd be something stronger than my desire to drink."

"Like what? A woman?" she asked. "Would that do it?"

"Maybe—if it was the right woman although I don't really know why I'd have to give up drinking at all," I said. "Maybe drinking too much and being mean and all that—but just drinking in moderation? I don't see how that hurts no one."

"You and I see it differently," she said.

"So, does that mean our date's over?"

"No, it doesn't," she said. "I like you—you say what's on your mind."

That made me feel good about myself—that I wasn't losing her just yet.

At Simmon's Fountain we sat at the marble counter and ordered two vanilla ice cream sodas. We saw ourselves in the mirror behind the fountain and we waved to each other. Cameron put my hat on her head and made a funny face in the mirror and giggled. Once our sodas arrived, we decided to sit at a small table near the entrance to the fountain.

"Bert," she said, once we were seated, "Tell me a little about yourself. I mean, I know a few things—that you work as a teamster. And your sister and I were once classmates but I really don't know very much about you."

The question sort of grabbed me by the throat. What to say? What not to say? How much to tell her? And no lying! I had to be honest—straight up. But you could be honest by not saying too much, as well.

"You talk with a little bit of an accent," she said. "Why's that?"

"Because I didn't come to this country until I was ten," I said. "My folks arrived first and after a couple of years, after they got settled some, then they sent for my brother and sister and me."

"From where?"

"From a canton in the mountains of Switzerland—Unterwalden," I said.

"Do you miss it?"

"Less and less." I thought about what I wanted to say next. "You know, I didn't want to leave there at first. I even hid the day my grand folks were taking us to the train."

Cameron laughed. "You must have had a good reason you wanted to stay?"

I did, but I couldn't tell Cameron—not just then. It involved this childhood crush I had on a neighbor there, Helga Reuger. She was years older than me, already married to a baker named Peter, and because of the ovens they kept lit, their house was always warm and inviting, especially on the coldest of days and it often smelled of baking bread. I helped Helga skim cream, hefted sacks of flour from their little store room and we sometimes crafted little creations together, shaping frosting on the cakes she baked to resemble the snow on the mountains surrounding us. She would hug me, draw me close to her big breasts and I wanted to stay there forever and never leave. Sometimes I imagined that Peter was gone, disappeared one day and never returned, and I was old enough and Helga asked me to marry her and we did, and I never had to leave Unterwalden again.

"What about you?" I asked her. "Where are you from?"

"Ohio," she said. "Father always had a pioneering spirit, and he said in his prayers once, God told him to go west, so we packed up when I was just a little girl, rode the train to Sacramento and ended up here. I didn't want to leave my hometown, either." She sipped from her soda, set her straw back in the tall glass. "What did you think of the service today?"

"It was lively," I said.

"When I was looking back at you, you seemed to be enjoying it." She smiled. "That's the spirit of the Lord at work."

"Yeah, you know, I got caught up in it."

"Did you feel the spirit?"

"I felt something."

"Was it Jesus you felt?"

"I don't know, Cameron. To be honest, I don't know."

"That's important—being honest." She sipped from her soda again, and I could tell more questions were forming.

"Were you always a teamster?"

"No, I apprenticed with my dad learning carpentry, but we didn't always see eye-to-eye. So I'd quit, do something else and then he'd hire me back."

"Why would you quit?"

"I guess there were other things I wanted to do instead."

"Like what?"

"Hunting and fishing, mostly, with Tino," I said. "He works at the Union Livery. He knows all the best spots."

"But you can't make a living doing that, right?"

"Not much of one—but we'd sell to markets around town—make a couple of dollars."

"And you could hunt or fish anywhere?"

"Not exactly. Some of the best hunting and fishing was on private lands."

"Then you'd get permission to hunt there?"

"Not exactly," I looked at Cameron. "Tino and I made a name for ourselves as poachers."

"Poachers?" she asked. "What are those?"

"They're folks that hunt or fish on land that isn't theirs—usually without permission."

"Oh." It seemed to take her aback.

"I'm trying not to do it so much now," I said. "With the team and wagon I keep plenty busy. So there's no real reason to stay at the poaching."

"It's wrong, isn't it, to take something that isn't yours?" she asked.

"Well, yeah—I guess it is."

"It's one of the Ten Commandments, Bert," she said. "Thou shalt not steal."

She was right—it was one of the Ten Commandments. I'd almost forgotten about them.

"Anyway, Bert, I don't want to tell you how to live your life."

"You mean I can do whatever I want?"

"Yes, you can."

"And you wouldn't mind?"

"I didn't say that." She looked into my eyes. "Bert, you do whatever comes natural to you. If that means poaching then so be it, but I won't be part of your life. I think that's as direct as I can be. Two people have to fit together, share the same values, the same beliefs."

There was that word again—beliefs. I knew it wouldn't take long before it surfaced.

"If you think stealing from someone else is permissible, then so be it," she said."But I don't."

"Even if that someone is a terrible person?"

"It doesn't matter—it's still stealing."

I never looked at poaching as a sin—especially poaching from Sheers.

"It starts with opening your heart to God's graces," she said. "Letting him in. Not putting up walls."

"Cameron, could we still see each other if I didn't believe in any of that?" I figured it was the 'do or die' question.

"Why would you want to?" she asked. "I'd be going on about the wonderful gifts of having God and Jesus in my life and you'd be over there like the doubting Thomas."

"The who?"

"The doubting Thomas—he was one of the apostles who was always very skeptical about Jesus, but Jesus understood that and was patient with Thomas."

"Would you be patient with me?"

"I don't know, Bert, maybe—to a point."

"And then?"

"Then you'll have to decide for yourself."

We finished our sodas and walked toward Union Hall, just down the block. We'd talked about important issues between us, and though nothing much was resolved, we'd aired some of our differences and I felt a bit lighter for it. I wanted to be honest and open with Cameron and not do what I'd often done in the past with women and that was lie and be evasive and say anything so I could to win them over. It hadn't got me nowhere, I mean, no place I wanted to stay in or no place where I felt good about myself. Mostly it lead to disappointment and I was trying to change that. I always knew it wouldn't be easy.

We arrived at Union Hall and I bought two tickets. Once inside we found a pair of seats toward the back of the hall. It was like a big cavern inside with a large stage at the front of the hall. The band soon marched in—twenty, thirty members all dressed in the same uniforms—lots of brass buttons and flaps sewn on the shoulders of their coats, and all of them wearing the same hats. They looked like soldiers but instead of carrying rifles they held all kinds of shiny brass instruments—flutes, trumpets, coronets, trombones, large Sousaphones. They arranged themselves on the stage—the little flutes and piccolos in front, the bigger horns behind them and in the back, a row of Sousaphones. Once arranged, they began tuning up. Cameron's arm pressed against mine and it felt good. I wasn't sure what lie ahead between us. How could I know? I didn't want to think about things I didn't have much control over. I did that too much already and it never got me no place. For now, she was sitting next to me and I just wanted to enjoy the music and the company of this lovely woman and not worry about nothing else.

Sousa marches filled the concert's bill. The music was lively, stirring, flooding the air with blasts of sound that vibrated against the Union's wall. Some concert-goers even left their seats and marched up and down the aisles, chests puffed out, their arms swinging. The musical notes, much like the clapping and chanting earlier at Pastor Lander's service, moved me, soaked right through my jacket. Of course, I didn't know how much Cameron herself was responsible for that stirring. It was uplifting. I felt good. I glanced over at Cameron and she smiled back, and when she squeezed my hand—oh, what a sensation!

I daydreamed through most of the concert, lost in a mix of thoughts and imaginings, punctuated with the hard reality of what I might be getting myself into with Cameron. She was lovely—maybe the loveliest young woman I'd ever been with, and when I looked at her it felt hypnotic, like she'd put me a spell on me and I'd do whatever she asked. Silly, I know, to feel this way. Was I just setting myself up for the big crash? For the big let-down? At times I was so lost in thoughts of Cameron, I didn't even hear the music—wasn't even aware of time passing—and then, before I knew it, the concert ended—just like that. Applause filled the hall. We stood up along with everyone else. I looked over at her and she was clapping, too, and smiling. "Did you enjoy it?" I asked her.

"Oh, very much," she said.

Good news—tremendous news!

Outside, the air was still warm. I breathed it in. We walked east on United States Avenue toward her home, her arm tucked inside mine. We didn't talk that much—I figured we covered the difficult things already—and when we did talk, it was to comment on the things we saw around us—the afternoon light, a bed of primrose in a front yard. I tried to be funny—make jokes, see her laugh. When we arrived at her door she took my hand and thanked me and planted a quick kiss on my cheek. "I had a good time," she said. "Now I must go inside."

I felt a slight disappointment that she hadn't invited me in—but maybe her folks were still quietly contemplating. "I had a good time, too," I said. "Maybe we could do this again?"

"Yes, I'd like that."

"I'll see you at the store?"

"Yes, at the store. Goodbye now."

And just like that, she disappeared inside, and my first date with Cameron Landers was over—a full day, to be sure. I'd gone to her father's service and not only survived it, but actually enjoyed parts of it. No serious screw-ups—no cuss word slipping out. I met her folks and though I didn't completely pass muster with her father, I'd made a decent showing. I enjoyed the time with Cameron and she seemed to enjoy her time with me. There were still all kinds of lingering questions about where this would lead to, if it would lead anywhere, but for now I brushed them aside and just thought about the positive— how I felt when we were together, the simple pleasure of looking into her eyes. Was there uncertainty? Of course. Was there potential heart ache? Always—I couldn't rule it out. Were there a hundred different things that could doom all of this? Of course there was. They were out there somewhere—lining up, patiently waiting their turn. 'We'll get you yet, Bert Miller' they seemed to be saying. 'We're waiting for that one wrong word, that one wrong action—then we'll pounce. Then folks will see who you really are.' Usually, they never had to wait too long.

10

An Agreement
• • • • • • • • • • • • •

The day after the concert with Cameron, I hauled two loads of blocks down from the quarry. When the last load was transferred to the railroad flat car, I stopped by the Union Livery before returning to Emma's with the team. Tino was inside, pushing a rental carriage back against the livery wall.

"So, Bert, you ready for a little pheasant hunting?" He wore his usual little grin.

"I don't know, Tino."

`"What do you mean you don't know?'"

"I was thinking it over and wondering if it was worth the risk." I had to be careful with my words here.

"It never stopped you before."

"But it's different now." Cameron's warnings were still fresh in my mind.

"Oh, 'cause you got your own team, and a name around town? Is that it?" There was Tino's sarcasm again.

"Partly," I said.

"That Landers girl got anything to do with it?" Tino waited for a reaction. "Flo said she seen you two yesterday walking arm in arm like you was mister and missus."

I didn't say nothing.

"I figured as much." Tino leaned against the carriage's wheel. "That's what they do with all that religious stuff—they start out slow and before long they're pounding it into your head with a mallet until you don't know what day it is—I seen it before."

"She hasn't pounded nothing into my head."

"Give her time—she will. And if you don't buy it, you're out on your ass with the rest of us non-believers."

"Sounds like you got it all figured out."

"Bert, you know how them folks work as well as I do. Hell, we talked about it enough."

"Now, I'm not so sure."

"Why? Do you get a little taste of it already, Bert? Is that it? She give you a little sample?"

"What do you mean?"

"You know—a little taste of her quim?"

"Screw you, Tino!"

"Oh, my—I hit a nerve."

I turned to leave, figuring I'd heard enough.

Tino grabbed my arm. "Hey, Bert—you're pissed. Okay, I'm sorry for what I said. You and me we go back a long ways and I don't want to see that screwed up. If you got something for this girl, then good, but, hell, don't push me out of the picture because of her."

"I ain't pushing you out."

"I hope not 'cause we still got some pheasant hunting to do." Tino chuckled, trying to lighten the mood.

"You're set on that, huh?"

"Yes, sir! Them birds are down there right now fattenin' up for over a year now, just waitin' for us." Tino rubbed his hands together like he was sitting down to a four-course dinner at the El Dorado.

I'd been thinking about the conversation yesterday with Cameron and how she said poaching was the same as stealing and having a hard time trying to square what she said with what I done. Anything I could take from Percy Sheers didn't seem like stealing to me. It had all been handed to him anyway and I figured for all the times he called Tino "half-breed" and me a drunk, it was a way of evening the score. Still, it had me thinking that somewhere down the road if Cameron and me were ever to pair-up, I'd have to change—I didn't know how or if it was even possible. I hadn't promised her nothing yet. And I didn't say I'd mend my ways. Everything right now was just as it had always been.

"I told you I got it all mapped out, right?" Tino walked over to a little desk in the corner of the stable, opened a top drawer and pulled out the drawing he'd shown me days before. "Well, I do," he said. "Sheers seeded them birds in a field right alongside the east side of the railroad tracks so if we stay along the tracks, we got a direct route down there without crossing any one's property. And the track bed's high enough anyone to the west of the tracks can't see us—it's foolproof."

Tino's plan sounded like a good one, and he was right—we hadn't been caught yet. A couple of near-misses but we always managed to slip by. And, of course I remember my old man's warning that we were "running our spool out" and that sooner or later our luck would disappear. We sometimes wondered if our luck did run out, what Sheers would do if he caught us. By himself he was a chicken-shit, but with his men around him, his balls got bigger. He grew a foot taller. Anyway, I was pulled in two opposite directions about all of it—the way I usually am. It felt that whatever I did, I was going to disappoint either Cameron or Tino. It was a hard choice—on one hand, my one, true friend who I'd go to hell and back for—while on the other, a young woman I'd developed a liking to, and wondered what the future might be like with her with some of my bad ways mended up.

"And you got a market for the birds?" I asked him again.

"Ho Tzu said he'd buy 'em all. Them birds are special to the Chinamen."

"I gotta think about it more, Tino."

"What's to think about?"

"Plenty," I said.

"One time, Bert—one time down there. We bag the birds and that's it." Tino made some kind of sign across his heart.

"And you won't bother me no more about hunting pheasant?"

"Not if it goes as planned."

I thought it over again, and figured one more shot. "Okay, I'll do it—but just this once."

"Can we shake hands on that?" Tino asked.

"All right," I said. And we shook hands.

"Wednesday? How about Wednesday then?" Tino asked.

I thought about it. "Let's make it Sunday," I said. "I'll need a day off by then, and the horses can rest."

"Okay, Sunday it is."

11

Conflict
· · · · · · · · ·

I'd no sooner agreed to hunt pheasant with Tino than I remem-bered Sunday was the same day for services at Cameron's church. I wasn't crazy about the services—I mean they weren't throwing a life-line out to my soul or paving the way to heaven or convinc-ing me to change my life—but it was my link to Cameron, maybe my only link. If anything was to happen between us, it had to be through her old man's church. For now, I could go along with it and maybe some revelation along the way would strike, and change my life, and I'd get the Lord. But as much as I wanted Cameron and me to hit it off, and make something happen, I hated to renege on my promise to Tino. With Cameron, I knew it was a long shot, and I knew, also, that part of me was just playing along with her, but with Tino, he was my friend, a good, true friend, and I didn't want to toss him overboard for some whimsy of mine. And what he said about her, though I didn't want to hear it—that she was just setting a trap to lure me into their fold and once I was in, she'd move on to someone else—had a ring of truth about it. She'd call it 'saving my soul' but I wasn't sure I had one to save.

I did want to see her, though, and thought about her a lot, and several times fought back the urge to stop in to visit but then talked myself out of it. That's the way it was with me—with everything—back and forth, back and forth, weighing this against weighing that, and wondering what to do and half the time doing nothing. My dad used to call this back and forth not knowing whether to shit or go blind. I'd even thought of not seeing her again, letting this whole imagining about the two of us together in the palm of the Lord just vanish. A gut feeling told me that's where it was head-ing anyway, so why stretch the whole thing out? Why not just cut my losses now and move on and save the heartache waiting around the corner? But then another voice broke in, and said, "It's too early to tell. So why quit now? And is there anyone else around that attracts you as much?" And the answer was 'no'—there wasn't. So I held onto the dream like I held on to so many before—with just a couple of fingers around it and always trying to slip my grip.

After batting it back and forth, I did finally stop in at Pauli's with the excuse of buying a pound of coffee. Cameron was alone, and that was a relief. She greeted me with that same radiant smile and her warmth that had drawn me to her months back.

"I enjoyed myself last Sunday, Bert," she said.

"I did too."

"I especially liked the men who were marching up and down the aisles while the music played. They were very funny!" She pushed her shoulders forward, swung her arms out and marched between the store counters. We laughed together easily—another thing I liked about her.

"Yeah, I liked them, too."

"I hope I wasn't too serious with you," she said. "I mean, with some of the questions I asked you."

"No, that's how we learn about each other, isn't it?"

"I think so."

"And you weren't offended?"

"No, I mean, they're some of the same questions I ask myself." And they were many of the same questions—no being dishonest there.

"And do you answer them the same way?" she asked.

"Sometimes I do."

An awkward silence followed. That same kind of silence I remembered with the girls from my past that I'd been truly smitten with—their beauty tied my tongue in knots. That same silence that seemed to stretch out for days as I struggled for a clever line to fill the empty space, but those lines rarely came. Eventually the silence ended, and it was only later as I recounted our conversations that I thought of what I could have said back there in those empty spaces.

Women did this to me. They brought all the nerves out to the edge of my skin, sent my pulse racing, left me hanging helpless like a duck from one of Ho Tzu's hooks. There was an art to meeting and interacting with them that I hadn't mastered yet. With some guys it came easy—but not with me. It was like everything else in my life—a learning process full of stumbling and correcting myself, falling down and then picking the bones back up. It was with women like Cameron, women that I was drawn to that I felt most vulnerable, the most insecure, the most nervous. There was no way I'd measure up in their eyes. I'd always come up short. They'd see every fault of mine—and there were plenty—all laid out before them. So what did I do? I kept talking—filling up as much of that empty space that I could—hiding these faults under an avalanche of words and playing the role of someone different than me—someone that knew the right words to say.

I avoided her eyes and looked around at different articles in the store, instead. "I wanted to buy some coffee," I said.

"Of course," she said. "It's in the first bin over in the corner there." I followed right behind her. Near the bins she handed me a metal scoop and a paper sack. Our hands touched and I fought back an impulse to hold her hand in mine. I reached into the bin, scooped out some coffee and poured it into the paper sack. She placed the sack on a scale. "Just under a pound," she said, and I scooped in more beans until it was an even pound. "You want it ground, don't you," she asked.

I nodded my head.

"Are you doing anything Saturday?" I asked her. No sense in over-thinking it—just spit it out.

She shot a surprised look at me. "I've already made plans. I'm sorry." She looked at me. "What about Sunday? Can I entice you to another of my father's service?"

"Cameron, I just made plans with Tino."

"Oh yes, Tino—the fellow you hunt with."

"He's been after me to hunt pheasant."

"Pheasant? Those beautiful birds with the long tail feathers?" she asked. "They're too beautiful to kill, don't you think?"

"Yes, they are beautiful," I said.

"And that doesn't bother you?"

"It does and it doesn't," I said. "I look at everything I shoot as beautiful in its own way but then there's necessity tied to it."

"Necessity?"

"Yeah—like we all gotta eat," I said.

Cameron ground the coffee and poured it back into the bag. She didn't look convinced about what I'd said. We walked to the front counter together. "How about another Sunday—maybe the Sunday after next? I could be at that service," I said.

"Okay, but only if you feel it here," and she touched me on the chest.

"I feel it, Cameron. I really do." What else could I say? I hadn't ruled out any possibilities. A guy could change. It happened all the time. I'd seen it with Lawrence Stone—a hellion in his younger years who turned town drunk by the time he was twenty. There wasn't an alley in town Lawrence hadn't puked and passed out in. And then all of sudden, a miracle! Lawrence dried up—said he'd seen a vision of himself heading to heaven and when he got there Saint Peter was waiting at the front gate and said to him, "Now you know, Lawrence, I can't let you in here." And Lawrence didn't take another drink; became a churchgoer, passing the basket every Sunday, polishing the pews after each service, and died years later, a sober, God-fearing man. If it could happen to Lawrence, it could happen to me.

"Sometime, Cameron, could I walk you home after work?" It seemed a way I could see her without all the church stuff.

"I think we could arrange that," she said. "I usually work until six in the evening."

"Well, if you see me here around that time, I'll walk you home," I said.

"Terrific," she said. "See you then."

I was clinging to a sliver of hope—it was a slim one but I was hanging onto it like my soul—if I even had one—depended on it.

12

Pheasant Hunting

. . . .

Early Sunday morning I bicycled in from Emma's while it was still dark, my shotgun and knap sack strapped to my back. Tino was waiting at the livery and we pedaled east out United States Avenue to Eighth Street, turned south, crossed through Vineburg and just north of the Schellville train depot we stashed our bicycles under a train trestle. We crossed Fremont Road on foot and stayed east of the track bed for a half mile until arriving at the hay fields where Tino said Sheers had seeded the pheasant. Clouds of mosquitoes flew around us. The oat grass was knee-high on both sides of the track. Morning light was just breaking.

Tino made a squawking sound and waited for a response— nothing. He made it again, and this time a bird called back from the east side of the tracks. We both pointed in that direction.

"If it's over there," I whispered. "We ain't on Sheers' land then, right?"

"I can't say for sure, but I think you're right, that's Pimentel's."

If true, we weren't poaching from Sheers but hunting on Pimentel's land instead and I knew the Pimentels because I'd hauled hay for them when I was still working for McCracken. They'd let Tino and me hunt quail and doves there. No stealing now. It was all, or mostly, legal. That would please Cameron, I was sure of it.

We hopped a fence, unstrapped our shotguns and loaded them with #12 shot. We walked along the base of the track bed, keeping a distance between ourselves. We hadn't gone a hundred yards before two big pheasant flew right up in front of us out of a stand of oats. We cut loose, one shot each, and the two birds dropped like sacks of corn meal. We walked up to the birds, and I looked them over because I'd never seen one up-close before. They weighed about the same as a mallard duck, maybe a little less. They had long tail feathers, too—maybe a foot, eighteen inches in length, and beautiful copper-colored chest feathers, and a white collar of feathers around their neck. They had a little crown of feathers on top of their heads, as well, and long, sharp beaks and blood-red hoods around their eyes that looked like the blinders we put on work horses. Cameron was right—they were beautiful birds—too beautiful to eat—and little wonder why the Chinamen valued the pheasant so much. Tino stroked their feathers before I placed them into my knapsack.

We hadn't walked another hundred yards before two more birds flew up in front of us— shoulder-height in a straight diagonal flight upwards. It was an easy lead with our shotguns, and we dropped them both. Tino held one in each hand like he was figuring what they weighed, before putting them in his sack. Here we crouched down and waited, figuring our shots had scared the other birds into keeping their cover.

By now we were a couple hundred yards from the train tracks. It was full morning light. Tino called out again with his squawking but no movement. We walked on before another pheasant flew out in front of us. Tino dropped this one, walked over and picked it up and held it in his hands. Then he put it in his sack with the others. We had five pheasant by now.

"What do you think?" I whispered. "Head back to the tracks?"

Tino nodded.

Two more birds flew up and we downed them both.

"Seven pheasant—let's head out," I said. I was feeling the nerves and wanting to leave.

We reached the tracks and walked north toward our bicycles before we heard a shotgun blast ring out. It kicked up gravel on the track bed about fifty yards behind us. "Some sonofabitch is shootin' at us!" I said. Tino and I started running. Gimp-leg and all, Tino kept up with me.

"It's Sheers! I know it is!" Tino said. "And we ain't even poachin' his land."

"Ain't no time to argue with him!" I said.

Another blast rang out. We peeked up over the track bed and off in the distance we saw a man tromping through the stand of oats. "Looks like Sheers," I said. We ran until we reached Fremont Road. It was a hundred yards more to the trestle where we strapped our shotguns to our backs, jumped on our bicycles and pedaled hard back up Eighth Street, glancing over our shoulders constantly. "Where we headed?" I asked.

"To Ho Tzu's!" Tino shouted.

We rode back into town, crossed over to Vallejo Street and down an alley to Ho Tzu's little market. We knocked on his door. It opened slightly and Ho Tzu peeked out.

""We've got the birds," Tino said. "Let us in!"

We left our bicycles against the alley wall and once Ho Tzu opened the door we stepped inside. It was cool in there, dark at first, until our eyes adjusted. It smelled of raw meat and was lit with two kerosene lamps that cast big shadows across the wall. Assorted fowl—ducks, chickens—hung from hooks. Ho Tzu looked back and forth at both of us with his penetrating eyes. He smiled, but he always smiled like his smile was frozen on his face, and rubbed his hands together. "Very good!" he said.

We took all seven pheasant out of our sacks and lay them side by side on Ho Tzu's table. Ho Tzu picked each one up and inspected it. "How much?" he asked.

"Three and a half dollars," Tino said.

Ho Tzu disappeared into a back room and returned with a wad of bills. He handed them to Tino. "More birds again?" Ho Tzu looked at Tino and Tino looked at me. I shook my head.

"Maybe," Tino said.

"You want smoke?" Ho Tzu asked.

Tino looked at me. "Sure," he said.

Ho Tzu returned with a little ball of black opium stuck in a pipe bowl. He handed the pipe to Tino and struck a match, and when the opium started to burn, Tino inhaled, held it in before blowing out a cloud of sweet-smelling smoke. Then Tino handed me the pipe and I inhaled and the smoke suddenly entering my lungs started me coughing. Ho Tzu laughed. "Too much," he said. When I stopped coughing, I inhaled again. I handed the pipe back to Ho Tzu but he didn't smoke, only handed the pipe to Tino. Tino sucked in more smoke and handed it to me. The pipe made a couple more rounds. Ho Tzo looked at us both with a little smile. "How you feel?" he asked.

"Nothing yet," Tino said.

The three of us stood there. Tino looked at me. "You feel anything?"

"I don't know," I said. But it wasn't long before I did. I could feel something moving toward my head—a numbing sensation not unlike the bourbon, but different, too—like a train fighting its way through a vat of syrup. In a couple of minutes, it reached the rest of my body—down my legs and out to my fingertips, and my first thought was to leave and leave as quick as I could. The walls felt mysterious—like we were in some sort of cave—and they were moving, closing in on us. Then the shadows started swaying—like the congregation did at Cameron's church—and before long they grew into fingers and I didn't know what to think. I was scared just then—I admit it. I wasn't in control and that bothered me. I pulled at Tino's sleeve. "Let's go," I said. "Now!"

Tino turned to me. "Okay, okay."

I had to get outside. The walls were going to crush us, but Tino kept talking—he wouldn't shut up. Then the shadows from Ho Tzu's kerosene lamp started moving across the walls like dancers and when my eyes settled on the lamps' flames, I couldn't stop staring—it was all goddamn hypnotic! Tino noticed the shadows, as well, and started moving his arms and all the walls swayed together and that was enough for me. Let's go!" I said.

"Goddamn—everything's moving!" Tino giggled and walked around the room.

"Tino, I need to get out of here—right now! No bullshit!" I said.

"Okay, let's go," Tino looked at me. "You sure you don't want anymore of this?" And he held up the pipe.

"I'm sure—I need to get out of here—now!"

I headed for the door and Tino followed behind me. He said goodbye to Ho Tzu; at least, I think he did. I was only concentrating on the door and being outside, away from the crushing walls and exotic dancers. I gripped the door knob and opened the door wide—anxious for daylight and fresh air—anything but being inside Ho's store. Daylight flooded in and through the daylight I saw the dark outline of a man. I had to look twice, maybe three times, to make out who it was—even thinking my eyes were tricking me. And then the figure came into focus. Like a bad dream, who should be standing there but the last person on earth I wanted to see just then—Percy Sheers himself—a bull pistol tucked in his belt!

13

Face to Face With the Man

· ·

It took awhile for my eyes to focus, but when they did, they were staring right into his. They were like rat's eyes—dark and meaning no good. He started to talk and I could see his mouth moving behind his moustache but the words weren't making no sense. He stared back at me and then over to Tino, trying to figure us out—like he'd stumbled onto us years later and couldn't remember our names.

Neither of us said nothing. I wasn't even sure I could talk. He just kept staring at me and I kept staring back at him, no one giving an inch. Then he glared over at Tino and Tino glared back, with a little grin splitting his lips. Sheers didn't know what to think. He looked past us into Ho Tzu's little stall and saw the pheasants on the table. He pointed to them. "Those birds are mine," he said.

"What birds?" Tino asked.

"Don't play stupid with me—you know what birds." Sheers said and he kept looking back and forth at me and Tino, his eyes hardly never settling—like drops of water on a hot skillet.

"No, those birds are Ho Tzu's," Tino said. "He just bought 'em."

"Shut up, half-breed!" Sheers pulled his coat back to expose more of his pistol.

Tino looked down at Sheers' belt. "Oh, the man's carryin' a pistol. You see that, Bert?"

I looked at the pistol and didn't say nothing. I just wanted out of there—I was scared. I tried not showing it but I was near crapping in my pants.

"That's right, and it makes me a foot taller," Sheers said.

"You'll always be a little man," Tino said.

Right then, I felt my whole body shaking—I admit it—even more scared than I'd been inside Ho's. The pistol, the opium—it all added up to trouble. I looked over at Tino. "Easy, Tino—just relax, all right?"

"I'm good," Tino said. "No worries."

When I stood in front of Sheers, my nose was about level with the crown of his hat. His eyes kept moving back and forth between me and Tino, nervous, shifting eyes that made me nervous, too. I wished to hell I hadn't smoked the opium but that was done. It made me feel exposed, like I had no clothes on and couldn't lift a muscle to help myself. Sheers' chest puffed out like a little bantam rooster's. His face went in and out of focus. And when he stared back at me I could see he was nervous, but confused, too.

"What are you guys on anyway?" Sheers looked at Tino and then back at me.

"Don't matter what we're on—them birds ain't yours," Tino said. "We shot 'em on the east side of the tracks and that's Pimentel's land."

"I raised them birds—they're mine. Ain't nobody else got pheasant around here." Sheers' face swelled, got large and then it shrunk back up. Everything around him seemed to be moving—the walls, our bicycles, everything. No wonder the Chinamen had to lay down when they smoked this stuff.

"They weren't on your land when we shot 'em," Tino said. "And you shot at us!"

Sheers looked at Tino. "They wouldn't be down there if it wasn't for me."

Ho Tzu stood a few steps inside the doorway. "No trouble. No trouble—please!"

"The birds weren't on your property, okay?" Tino said. "If they're anyone's birds, they're Pimentel's and we can hunt there—so stick it where the sun don't shine."

"Oh, yeah?" Sheers glared at Tino. "My family owns half this valley and you don't own shit! Your kind is still living in mud huts on land that's legally mine."

"Not no more," Tino said. "You're losing it by the day."

"You're full of shit!" Sheers' anger was brimming over and all I wanted was to be some other place—some place far away from here and fast.

"And you're unlucky," Tino said. "You stake land in your poker games and you lose. It ain't no secret—half the town knows."

Sheers looked confused. "You don't know what you're talkin' about."

"I know enough," Tino said. "Now get out of the way—we got no more business with you."

I wanted all the talking to stop and Sheers to leave because I kept looking at that pistol with its pearl handle tucked in his belt and it kept growing larger and larger. I walked over and grabbed my bicycle.

"We ain't done here, yet," Sheers said, moving his hand toward his pistol. "Not by a long shot! You'll see!"

"Oh, I think we are," Tino said. By now we both had our bicycles pointed toward the street. Sheers stepped back, angry, frustrated, barking out more threats. "This ain't over yet!" His voice echoed down the alleyway.

Tino looked at me. "Here, grab my bicycle!" And I grabbed it. Then Tino hiked down his pants, exposing his bare ass to Sheers. "Here you go!" Tino said. "Come and kiss my brown half-breed ass!"

I wondered how Tino found the balls to do this when all I felt was fear just then and a promise to never smoke Ho's opium ever again.

After we were out on the sidewalk and out of the alleyway, I turned toward Tino. "I'm done with this," I said. "It ain't worth gettin' shot at. I don't like the threats. And I'm done smoking this shit—I don't like the way it makes me feel."

"Ain't nothin's changed," Tino smiled. "What's different now? Yeah, we're high on the smoke but everything else is still the same—plus we got a couple more dollars in our pockets."

I didn't say nothing else because it was pointless. I couldn't think straight—I couldn't think at all. If I started to say something I couldn't remember what it was I wanted to say because no sooner would I start with one thought before another one stumbled in, and I'd follow that one before still another one butted through, and I finally figured—to hell with all this thinking. Nothing seemed to bother Tino, though. He carried on like he hadn't smoked nothing—like it was just another day with him.

"You didn't feel scared back there?" I asked.

"I felt something, but it wasn't fear," he said. "I guess it's just seeing Sheers does it to me—gets all my juices riled up."

Whatever I looked at just then became the focus and that focus only lasted until I looked at something new, and that sent off a run of sensations that spiraled inward and though I might be staring at something I really wasn't seeing it at all. My mind was like one of those honey bees flitting from flower to flower. By now I just wanted to sit down some place where it was quiet and put the brakes on to anymore thinking. I wanted to just lie down like the Chinamen do and take in whatever wandered in front of me and let whatever happened, happen. I didn't want to talk to no one, not even Tino. I didn't want to explain nothing, didn't want to make no decisions. I didn't want no one threatening me or showing me a pistol tucked in his belt. And I didn't care whose pheasants they were or if I even saw another pheasant. I didn't care what they did with the pheasants—they could wear them on their heads like a big feather crown or stuff them and put them in store windows. They could stick them up their asses—I didn't care. I wanted to come down from this opium high and come down fast because it gave me the jitters—from now on it was just whiskey.

We walked up to the cemetery above the ball diamond and found a fat oak tree to sit under. We could look over parts of the town from here and see the rooftops of the tallest buildings around the plaza, but mostly what I saw were the crowns of trees that looked like big green toadstools. Tino plucked a blade of grass near his boot and stared at it, turning it around in his fingers.

"That son of a bitch shot at us today," Tino broke the silence.

"Good thing it was shotgun and not a rifle," I said. That finally coaxed a smile out of me.

Tino and me both laughed.

"I don't understand Chinamen," Tino said.

"How's that?"

"I mean, they go into those dens and smoke this shit and just lie around dreaming, I guess."

"I don't understand them, either," I said. "They're different."

"I couldn't do it—I couldn't sit still long enough."

"Yeah, me neither," I said. "I gotta be moving around." But here we were, sitting under a tree.

"It's a pleasant-enough feelin', though, ain't it, once them distractions are gone?" Tino stuck the blade of grass into his mouth.

"Yeah—I guess. It's different from the whiskey," I said. "I can't say exactly how, but it's different, except I don't want be around folks. More stuff going on inside the head—more mental—more things moving around."

"Yeah, sometimes that whiskey makes you do crazy-ass things if you drink too much of it," Tino said. "Sometimes you can't remember nothing about what you'd done the night before. Folks come up to you the next day and say 'man, you had a case of the crazies last night' and all I can do is shake my head and agree with 'em. And I can't tell you how many times I've woken up in places I don't ever remember goin' before." He blew into the blade of grass. "Opium don't make you do that."

"I can't say one way or the other—ain't smoked it enough," I said. "But I'm pretty sure I take to the whiskey better."

We sat for awhile longer, neither of us talking. I remembered it was Sunday and that meant church services for Cameron and her family. I tried to imagine me being in church right now, and what that would be like. Who knows? It might make the singing and shouting even more powerful! Might make me a true believer! I didn't want to think of Cameron, though, in my current state. If she disapproved of liquor, no telling what she thought of opium.

It'd been a long day and my body was tired, drained. I stretched out, the back of my head against the base of the oak, and closed my eyes. All kinds of colors danced in my mind, and pretty soon I heard Cameron's choir singing and saw her father asking Jesus to come down and bless everyone in his church, and I might have even seen Jesus but he wasn't in robes—no, he was wearing a wool suit instead, and he went around Pastor Landers' church shaking everyone's hand and saying he was glad to meet them. He shook everyone's hand except mine. I opened my eyes and Cameron and the church and Jesus were all gone and I was staring up through the branches of that oak. I felt better then knowing I wasn't in church. I heard Tino poking around, picking up rocks and tossing them, and putting blades of grass in his mouth and making bird calls. He was always the fidgety type, a ball of nerves, but when he had to be still, like when he'd heard something—a movement in the brush, ducks settling on the water—that guy could be so still—not twitch a muscle—you'd think he was frozen in ice.

By late afternoon the opium had worn off, the only remnant a slight headache, and I was back trying to put two thoughts together, recounting that whole Percy Sheers thing earlier in the day. Tino was right—nothing had changed other than Sheers making more threats. Both us had gotten used to them by now. And I felt better, too, knowing that we hadn't really poached from him, that we hadn't stolen anything and if Cameron asked what we'd done, I could honestly say we hunted, but we didn't poach, even though it didn't start out that way.

I tried not to think about Cameron, but how do you tell yourself not to think about something? You can't. I knew that for two people to have any chance together, they had to be honest with one another, and I wasn't being honest—not by a long shot. One voice inside me said I could change and be those things a woman like Cameron could respect—church-going, sober, honest, but another voice said, 'Bert, the die's been cast, and you are who you are.' If you change now, it's only to please someone else, and how often does that work? And for how long? So there I was, like a boat caught between two tides. The familiar tide was the one I'd always ridden that carried me to the places I knew well, to friends, to saloons, up to the hills and down the waterways—to the drinking and telling stories and the knee-slapping laugher, and disappointment, too—I couldn't leave that out. And then there was this other tide, the more recent one, trying to pull me toward a strange new land of belief, to a promise of romance and love, and a woman beside me. But it was a land where I had to reform my ways, where I knew I had to change. And could I? And would I? And there I was, like I'd always been—not knowing which way to go—not knowing which tide would carry me with it.

14

The Contract

• • • • • • • • • • • • •

A day later, late afternoon, my brother John B. was waiting for me at the Sonoma Depot. It was my last load of block for the day. He stood on the dock and I picked him out from a hundred yards away. It was rare to see him anyplace but at his work and I braced myself for some bad news. I pulled the rig up alongside him. "Bert, you got the lumber hauling contract for the Stamm job if you want it," he said.

"No shit?" I said—it didn't sound like bad news at all.

"No, you got it," he said. "The floor beams are due here this Friday. We'll send Alfonso down to help you transfer them from the flat car onto your wagon."

"Ma got anything to do with this?" I asked.

John B. just smiled. "You know Ma—always playing the peacemaker."

"She's good at it."

"I got some other news, too."

"Yeah?"

"Dad and Ma moved out to Carlotta Stamm's ranch. They're living in Carlotta's old house. It's been vacant since she had the new one built. Josephine moved with them. And Gertie and me are living at the folks' place in Vineburg until we save enough to move to Santa Rosa."

"That is news," I said. All sorts of changes were happening.

"Dad wasn't getting home until late at night. And there was always something coming up at the ranch—sick cattle and the like—so they moved," he said. "And then Carlotta got this idea about raising chickens."

"That makes sense," I said. "No need to travel for his work—it's right there."

The hauling contract came as a surprise. My old man and I hadn't talked since he canned me, and my visits to Ma and my sister Josephine became fewer and fewer as my work increased. Whenever there was hard feelings, I stayed away, and let the boiling pot simmer.

"The old man still pissed at me?" I asked.

"You know our old man—he doesn't say much—keeps it all tucked inside his vest." John B. looked over my wagon and horses. "Nice rig you got here, Bert." He stroked the noses of Molly and Dolly.

John fished into his shirt pocket and pulled out a sheet of paper and unfolded it. "I guess we got to make it official, Bert. Carlotta agreed to pay you five dollars per load, if that's okay. So if you could sign this." I reached down and grabbed the contract and a pencil John had handed me, and signed it. "There's more loads after Friday's, so don't run off somewhere."

"Hell, John B., where would I go?"

"I know you, Bert—you get a scent and there's no telling where you're off to," he said.

"Don't you worry—I'll be around." I handed the contract back to John B. "Hey—thanks," I said. "I'll see you then."

The lumpers helped me unload the block onto the flat car. When my wagon was empty I swept the bed out, and wrapped up all the ropes. The hauling contract was welcome news, a way of smoothing the road back to my old man's good graces—if that was possible.

I never liked holding onto hard feelings, especially with family. They eat away at you— fester like an untreated sore. I always thought it best to get grievances out in the open—give them air, let them breathe—and then tackle them, but it's damn hard when mostly you want to just duck around them, hope they go away on their own—sometimes they do, but mostly they don't. They stay in the shadows, breed on disappointment and broken hopes—the hopes parents cling to for their children. They want to see them make something of themselves and I know my old man wanted me following in John B.'s footsteps, but I kept disappointing him at every turn. And that grew those hard feelings between us. And what do those hard feelings do? They spread. I seen how all this upset Ma and I think that's what hurt me most. With folks like Percy Sheers, though, I made an exception. I figured he deserved all the hard feelings I could send his way, and if they ate at me, well, they ate at me, and I hoped they ate at him, too—still, if I had my druthers, I didn't want none of these feelings.

I drove the team back to Emma's and unharnessed Molly and Dolly. I brushed them both down, gave each a big scoop of oats and filled their mangers with hay. I was tired from working all day and my head felt emptier than usual. I think it had to do what we'd smoked yesterday. The opium left my head feeling vacant—like a hot wind that had blown through my brain and dried everything out. It wasn't like no hangover, and I couldn't see smoking it as a regular habit.

Emma sat on her front porch with a bottle of bourbon and two glasses set on a table between two chairs. She filled my glass. "Take a load off, Bert," she said

I sat down and we clicked our glasses together and we both sipped the bourbon. "Oh, that's nice." I said, and felt the bourbon's warmth trickle down my throat. I leaned back in my chair and put both feet up on the porch railing.

"I didn't see you at all yesterday," Emma said. "I thought maybe you'd gone to church again with that Landers girl."

"No, no church yesterday—me and Tino went pheasant hunting, instead."

"Pheasant?" she asked. "Where you find those?"

I told her the whole story about shooting pheasants and them not being on Sheers' land and how he shot at us anyway and then how he followed Tino and me to Ho Tzu's and what happened there. I didn't tell her about the opium—there's some things folks don't need to know. The drinking? That's all right—drinking is common. Sure, there's the temperance groups marching up and down the streets, carrying signs saying it's the devil's tool, but you can ignore them—half the town does. Opium though is a different matter—mostly because folks don't understand it. It's foreign and uncommon. Another reason, too—it's connected to the Chinamen—and gives folks one more reason to hate them.

"Don't push your luck with that Sheers fellow," Emma warned. "He's crazier than a shit-house rat."

"I know that," I said. "Tino likes to dig at him, and I go along with it." Just then I remembered what John B. had told me earlier. "I got some other news today, too."

"Wait—don't tell me—you joined Cameron's church?"

I laughed. "Nope, not yet—don't know if that'll ever happen. But John B. came by the depot and said I got the contract to haul lumber for Carlotta Stamm's chicken houses."

"Chicken houses?" Emma leaned back and laughed. "What she going to do with chicken houses?"

"Raise chickens?" I said. It seemed a logical answer.

"But, why?" Emma asked. "So she can make even more money? She can't even spend what she's got."

"She's an independent woman."

"I'll give her that—she must sit home and dream up things to do—ways to spend her money."

`"John B. told me maybe an hour or two ago. He's going to build them with our old man." I took another pull of bourbon. "Oh, and you know what else?"

"You're just full of news today, aren't you?" she said.

"My folks moved over to the Stamm ranch."

"Now why'd they do that?"

"I guess the old man was spending so much time over there, it made sense. Carlotta had the vacant house, and now John B. can live at the folks' place in Vineburg and take care of it and have plenty of room for his own family until he moves."

"You and your dad going to give it another crack, huh?" Emma asked.

"I'm hauling the lumber and I'll try to stay out of his way."

"I can't slight Carlotta, though." Emma leaned forward in her chair. "If I had her looks and that kind of money, I'd burn my own and wouldn't give two shakes what folks thought," she said. "She's done well just to live in the same town as her brother Percy—who's after everything she's got."

"Emma," I said, "You don't need her money."

Carlotta Stamm, like all beautiful, wealthy women—make that *all* women—was a mystery to me. She was talked about a great deal around town, and like much of this talk it was hard to sift through what was true and what wasn't. Rumors in this town grew like spring grass, and one rumor led to two more, so with Carlotta she'd gained this outsized reputation. She rarely came to town, and when she did, she sat in her carriage at the plaza while Ah Yep, her Chinese houseman, ran errands for her. She always wore large-brimmed hats that covered much of her face and most of the time while sitting there, she read books. What kinds of books? I didn't know—probably no one did. An occasional merchant would approach her carriage, sometimes delivering a package personally. They'd talk briefly and then she was left alone. The rare times I saw her, it was only at a distance, and so, like many of the townsfolk, I imagined all kinds of things about her.

Carlotta Stamm's family—the Sheers—dated back to the Bear Flag Revolt, when land that used to belong to General Vallejo and Mexico was grabbed up by newly arrived Americans, most who'd given up panning for gold in the Sierras. The Sheers at one time owned big swaths of land from the ridge tops west of Sonoma all the way down to the San Pablo Bay. Carlotta, still a young woman, had married Gustav Stamm, a wealthy San Francisco politician forty years older than her, who himself owned prime vineyards east of Sonoma. When Gustav died within two years of the marriage, Carlotta became one of the wealthiest persons in the valley. Rumor was that she'd married Gustav to pay off family debts—most of which her brother Percy had piled up gambling and investing in half-ass schemes that always went bust.

Carlotta and her brother hated each other and were entangled in a string of lawsuits contesting different properties, each of which Percy lost. And because she didn't mingle much with townsfolk either, she gained a reputation as being 'uppity,' and too good for the locals. Alfonso, Carlotta's ranch hand, told me the rare socializing she did was with Gustav's acquaintances from the city. They rode the train to Sonoma and Carlotta would send Alfonso in her carriage to meet them at the depot. Ah Yep, the Chinese houseman, would greet Carlotta's guests at the door, offer to take their jackets and coats. Lavish dinners would often follow. When their stay ended, Alfonso drove them back to the depot.

"She's got some kind of touch, though, I'll give her that," Emma continued. "And I've seen how men stare at her whenever she's in town—like she's the prize of all prizes. I don't even think she notices them."

"She probably don't," I said. "I mean what can a guy in this town offer her that she don't already have?"

"Nothing," Emma said. "Not a damn thing. She's no fool—she knows what they're after."

"Two things," I said: "Money and—I don't have to tell you the other."

Emma leaned back in her chair and laughed. "No, you don't."

15

Square. Plumb. Level.

•

Friday morning came, the day the first shipment of lumber was scheduled to arrive at the Sonoma Depot. The carrier was the San Francisco and North Pacific Railroad, the same one that hauled the block back to San Francisco. I decided to do a double-back—haul a load of block down from Schocken Hill, unload the block at the depot and backload with the lumber for Carlotta Stamm's order. It meant a full day but I was up for it. I awoke at sunrise, a little nervous—the way I am before each job. I fed and harnessed the horses, made sure I'd brought all the ropes I'd need to tie the lumber down. Emma, an early-riser herself, yelled from the porch that coffee was ready. I joined her and while I sipped coffee I looked over the list John B. had given me. It was fir floor beams mostly—forty of them, 3" x 4" thickness, sixteen feet in length.

I drove the team up to Schocken Hill where the cobblestones were already stacked and ready to be transferred onto my wagon. The quarry workers loaded the cobbles as they'd done many times before, and as they loaded them, I always kept a close eye on the wagon and its suspension for any signs of wear, any strain that might cause a break. The two horses waited patiently, dozing off, until the load was completed. I tied the load down with ropes and boards at each corner, looked everything over before beginning the slow descent off the hill and down to the depot. Molly and Dolly knew this route well, knew just the slow pace I wanted them to keep so I hardly had to work the reins at all, just a touching of the brake that kept tension between the load going forward and the weight staying back. By the time we arrived at the depot—maybe eleven in the morning—Alfonso had already ridden his horse in and tied it to the hitching post. The train hadn't arrived yet. Alfonso walked over to my wagon.

"You going to build the houses?" he asked.

"No, that's mostly John B.'s job," I said. "I'm hauling the material."

"I like your father. He live at the ranch now. He talk very loud." Alfonso wore a wide-brimmed Mexican *sombrero*.

"Yeah, he talks even louder when you don't do what he tells you." Alfonso gave me a puzzled look— he wasn't sure what I said.

"He likes *la senora*, Carlotta," Alfonso said. "They work together and draw houses."

I sat up on the wagon seat and waited for the train. Every few minutes I'd look down the tracks. Alfonso untied the ropes and laid them on the ground next to the boards. When he finished, he sat on the end of the wagon, rolled a cigarette and smoked it. It wasn't long before I'd heard the train whistle off in the distance—I guessed as it was leaving Vineburg. Twenty minutes later I saw it rolling towards us, smoke billowing out of its stack. It slowed down as it approached the depot and finally rolled to a stop. The agent came out to meet it. Its engine breathed in and out like a big iron horse. I watched the brakeman jump off and uncouple the cars from the locomotive. It rolled forward onto a turntable that had the locomotive facing back toward the way it had come from. I pulled my team alongside the flat car where a lumper had already started to loosen the ropes holding the blocks in.

The transfer of block from my wagon to the flat car went quick. Four of us worked, two in the wagon and two on the flatcar. Alfonso and I tossed blocks to the lumpers and they stacked them against wooden header-boards at both ends of the flat car. When the wagon was empty I moved it to a forward car that held the lumber. Again Alfonso and I stayed in the wagon and straightened each beam so that the lengths would be firm against the sideboards and not shift when the wagon was in motion. When all forty timbers were loaded, I ran a rope across their lengths and cinched it down on the load hooks. Alfonso and I looked over the load. "Okay?" I asked. He nodded. "Look good." He mounted his horse and rode back to Carlotta's ahead of me.

From the depot I drove the team down First Street, past Pauli's where I slowed to look through the window trying to see Cameron, but only saw my reflection instead. I thought of stopping and 'showing off' the team and load but decided against it. We turned on United States Avenue and headed west to Fifth Street, then south on Fifth Street all the way to Napa Road. Here we crossed Cooper's Bridge to the west and just past the bridge entered the road to Carlotta's ranch. It snaked along Sonoma Creek a quarter mile before opening onto the ranch yard. Carlotta's new house, a two story Victorian surrounded by gardens, was to the right. The older house where my folks now lived was opposite the new one. It was a simple single-story adobe, with a broad portico along its front. Wisteria grew around the portico's columns and wound their way up onto the roof. Ma came out to meet me and I stopped the team and stepped down to give her a hug. "So good to see you," she said. "I have lunch for you."

"Later," I said, "after the lumber's unloaded."

Alfonso met me at the top of the yard and pointed back toward the hay barn, to an area between the barn and creek. "They are working there," he said. I followed behind him in the rig as he walked toward the building site. I kept waiting to see my old man, wanting him to see me driving up with my own team and see how he'd react—maybe even think that I'd turned out okay after all—but he was nowhere in sight. I did see John B., a tool belt around his waist, driving wooden stakes into the ground with a sledge hammer. He looked up. "Hey Bert!" he shouted.

"John B.!"

I halted the team, set the brake on the wagon, and stepped down. We shook hands. His face was sun burnt, covered with a red stubble of beard. He wore a floppy-brimmed hat, the same kind our old man wore, and from a distance you couldn't tell them apart. We both looked over the building site, walked around its perimeter. It was already scraped clean and graded, with a pile of pepperwood saplings and poison oak stacked off to one side. Batter boards were driven into the ground at three corners of the building. John was setting the fourth and last corner. I looked around. "Where's the old man?"

"He's somewhere with Carlotta," he said. "They like to meet in a little gazebo down by the creek. It's screened in—no mosquitoes. It's where they discuss the day's work. She wants to know all the details."

"Just like the old man, huh?" I said. "He wants to know it all."

"Yeah, but that's okay," John B. said. "You know—like he says—do it once, do it right."

"Square. Plumb. Level," I said, repeating what our old man had drummed into our heads more times than I could count.

"That's right. Square. Plumb. Level—they all work together," John B. said.

"Like some law isn't it? The Law of John Miller." I laughed after I said it, the same way I laugh at most so-called laws—most things they say that can only be one way and not another. I never quite believed that and was always out to find another way of doing things. It could never be just one way, I thought—too much chaos, too many ways for it to confound you. And laws—like everything—were meant to change. They weren't carved in stone like folks say. There was no one thing that was always true, always right. As soon as you banked on something, it turned on you, would vanish, and left you feeling foolish once again. There were always exceptions, of course, and I was out trying to find those exceptions, and why things didn't always have to be the way folks said they were.

Once the wagon was positioned away from the building site, I loosened the ropes, rolled them back up and stowed them under the driver's seat. Alfonso joined us. John set blocks on the ground—"stickers" he called them—to rest the lumber on so it'd stay flat and wouldn't touch the ground. We off-loaded the lengths into a neat stack. After the wagon was empty, I swept out the sawdust, and when I looked up, I saw my old man and Carlotta in the distance walking toward us.

Carlotta was a slight woman, spry, maybe half the size of my father. She wore pants and boots and a long-sleeved shirt. This morning she'd tied her hair up inside a bandana and held a notebook in her right hand, a handkerchief in her left. Even wearing boots she had a light step, like she was tip-toeing between puddles of water. My dad walked alongside her, the two of them talking in low voices, both of them looking at the ground in front of them, not even noticing John B. or myself until they were just yards away from us. When she looked up, I tipped my hat toward Carlotta. I could see her eyes were red and swollen, filled with tears. She'd been crying and dabbed at her nose with a handkerchief.

"Hello," she said. Her voice trembled as she put on a brave face. Her eyes looked at mine and then looked quickly away, a little embarrassed, I thought. They were brown, penetrating eyes that threw me off balance. This was the first time I actually met her, the first time I ever heard her voice, the first time I was this close to her. "You must be Bert," she said.

"That's me, I'm Bert." I stared at her. "And you're Carlotta."

She smiled back at me—a lovely smile. A strand of her hair had loosened, and she tucked it back underneath her bandana.

"How you doing, son?" my old man asked. He gave me the once-over as he usually does, starting at my boots all the way to the top of my hat. He was the kind of man that wanted to take in everything about you before he decided whether he liked you or not—before he decided what he wanted to say. He didn't much care for surprises, either. He liked it all drawn out in front of him—wanted to know what the possible losses were before he even started. He liked to be in control—liked to have his hands on the reins.

"I'm doing okay," I said.

"Oh, what beautiful horses!" Carlotta said, and handed the notebook to my old man and walked over to the team.

"That's Dolly you got your hand on. The other one's Molly—they're sisters," I said.

"They're wonderful! Such a beautiful color, too—I'd love to have roses this color," she said.

My old man looked at me. "Bert, the teamster." He said it like he couldn't believe it—like I'd finally done something he approved of and it'd surprised him. He walked over and inspected the stack of beams. He counted them out.

"Bert, have you seen the plans your father and I have drawn up?" Carlotta turned and walked back to me. "John, show him the plans."

My old man handed the notebook back to Carlotta and she opened it to several pages of drawings of the chicken houses. I had to turn the drawings to get my bearings, but what I was looking at was a series of neatly drawn chicken houses, each showing a different view. Along one side of the houses were the enclosed yards, and the openings below where the chickens could move outside and inside. On the other side of the houses were the nests, all framed in little houses that extended past the exterior walls. The nests were waist-high, with roofs over them that lifted up in sections so that one could reach in and gather the eggs without even entering the inside of the house.

"What do you think?" Carlotta looked at me.

"You designed this?" I asked her.

"Your father and I worked together on it." She looked up from the drawings. "We make a good team." She paused. "Do you like it?"

"I do—I mean I'm not much of a poultry guy but they look fine to me," I said.

"I'm excited." Her tears were drying and her earlier shakiness disappeared, and as she showed me the drawings she regained her confidence. Now she was energized, more positive, as she walked around the perimeter of where the houses would be built. "I've read everything I could about raising chickens and I'm excited," she said. "And now it's finally happening!"

I looked at Carlotta. "Whatever gave you the idea?"

"You think it's crazy?" she asked.

"I didn't say that."

"Well, I don't know exactly how I got the idea." She paused, thinking of what she wanted to say. "I love fresh eggs for my breakfast—nothing better to start my day off like a couple of eggs and a strong cup of coffee. And there were mornings I'd send Ah Yep out to gather eggs and it would take him an hour to find them. The hens were laying eggs all over the place. He was finding them anywhere they could make a nest. One time I'd gone out for myself and found a nest cradled in the barn wall, and when I picked one up, it exploded right in my hand. Boom! Like a little fire cracker! I jumped back! And the smell? Awful! Just awful! Like sulphur."

"A rotten one," I said.

"Anyway, I thought, what if I could just walk outside, lift up a little lid and gather eggs right there? No need to go inside the chicken house. No need to look all over the place. And that's what gave me the idea."

"She's full of them," my old man said.

"Do I drive you crazy?" Carlotta looked at my father and laughed.

John B. finished driving in the last stakes to the batter boards and walked over to his tool box and pulled out a ball of string. "You gonna work with us today, Bert?"

I looked at over my dad. "Not today, John B. I've already put a full day in and it's time to head for the barn."

"How you like it out at Emma's?" my old man asked.

"I like it okay," I said. "Emma's good company and she's even offered me a room inside her house." That subject came up the other night when Emma and I were sitting on her front porch, and she said, "You know, there's that spare bedroom that ain't being used. You're welcome to it." I'd gotten so used to sleeping in horse stalls and tack rooms that at first I didn't think much of her offer.

"Where do you live?" Carlotta asked.

"At Emma Hansen's," I said.

"Oh, that's very close—maybe a mile or so?"

"About that." I pointed west toward Grand Avenue.

She smiled at me. "Do you have a family like your brother?"

"No, I don't—just me."

John B. attached one end of the string to a nail on the batter board and ran it out to the next board. My old man set a nail and ran the string to the next corner while John B. put a framing square to where the two strings were to check for square. "Once we set the strings," our old man said to Carlotta, "we'll measure diagonals and re-set strings until the two diagonals measure exactly the same. Then we know the lines are square."

Listening to my old man and watching him was like going back in time and working for him again. I don't know why I found working with him so difficult. I mean, I knew all the reasons. I'd told myself why—the demands he made, the comparisons to John B.—how he told me I was pissing everything away—but what he said and how he treated me, I believe, was for my own good. It took me awhile to figure this out. He had my well-being in mind and it scared him, I think, that I might be falling off the deep end, winding up in some place I couldn't pull myself out of, someplace where I had no control. Maybe he'd even been there himself when he was young—I don't know. He never seemed to venture too far inward—at least, he never talked much about it. But what did I know what people thought? You could only guess at it. Sometime down the road, though, I hoped we could work all of this out— down the road when I was older and not so caught up in myself the way young folks are. Down the road when I could listen better and the two of us—no, with John B.—the three of us could all work together and not be at each other's throats.

I walked around the wagon, checked the wheels, the suspension, for any cracks, any signs of wear, before climbing up to the driver's seat. I looked over the building site where the string was now stretched out that made a neat outline of where one chicken house would be. The old man and John B. continued working while Carlotta approached my wagon. "It was nice to have met you, Bert." She smiled. Her eyes had cleared. She reached up to shake my hand.

"Nice to meet you, as well," I said. The skin inside her hand was smooth and cold.

I released the wagon brake and clicked my tongue and the two horses moved forward. John B. and the old man waved and I waved back. Carlotta stood there and watched me leave. She was lovely. And no wonder men desired her. She was different from most women I'd met—independent, educated, curious—and no denying her wealth. I wondered what had made her cry earlier as though lovely, educated women never cried. What was she really like? What went on inside her? How could someone that lovely, that eligible, not find one suitor among the dozens that knocked at her door? When I looked at her I saw a woman with secrets—a woman hiding something. I didn't know what and maybe I was wrong about all of it—that there was nothing secretive about her at all—nothing mysterious. She was simply a young, beautiful woman with the means to do anything she wanted. If it was gathering fresh eggs just steps from her kitchen door, she could hire two men to build a hen house and that wish was granted. I suppose if she wanted a castle built, she'd have one built—the big house she lived in was like a castle. I wondered what it'd be like having that kind of power—the means to do and buy anything you wished?

I drove the team back to Emma's, thinking of Cameron the entire time—when I wasn't thinking of Carlotta. Why have just one woman on your mind, when you could have two? I checked my pocket watch and it read five o'clock—time enough to ride into town on my bicycle and walk Cameron home. I changed into a clean shirt and within minutes was riding back toward Pauli's store. I arrived there before closing time and Cameron was glad to see me.

"Can I walk you home?" I asked.

"Certainly—just a few things to do to close shop and I'll be right with you."

I watched her move around, pull the shades down on the front door windows and flick a CLOSED sign out. She emptied the cash register and stowed the money into a small safe below the front counter. "Now I'm ready," she said.

16

God's Little Place

· · · · · · · · · · · · · · · · · ·

We walked out the front door together, and then she turned and locked it. Daylight was fading, but still enough light to see all around us. Once on United States Avenue she turned toward me. "Do you have any secret places you go to be alone?"

I had to think about it. "No one place," I said. "All the outdoors is a secret place to me."

"I have one," she said. "Do you want to see it? It's not far from here."

"Sure, I'd love to."

The sidewalk to Cameron's house followed along a little creek to our south, and a block ahead we stopped. She took my hand and led me down toward the creek where she parted the branches of a low-growing oak. "Leave your bicycle here," she said. There was no path to follow but the shrubs gave way easily, and in just a few steps more we were at the creek's side. Here it was quiet, and the creek eddied into a little pool of water with large trees hanging over the pool. The last bit of daylight filtered through the trees in long bands. Cameron walked over to a round rock and sat down and motioned for me to join her. We sat there, neither of us talking, just taking in the quiet, the stillness. Finally she turned to me, "This is where I go to feel God," she said. "He's always here waiting for me."

"Always?" I asked.

"Yes, always—can't you feel him now?" She moved closer to me, our legs now touching. I looked at her in the late afternoon light and she was beautiful—glowing almost—and I had to tell her.

"Why, thank you, Bert, for such a lovely compliment." She smiled, and wrapped both her arms around her folded legs. "I feel wonderful here—a feeling I wish I could share with everyone in this world."

I kept looking at her.

"God makes me feel this way, Bert," she said. "I want you to feel the same way, too."

"I feel fine—I really do."

"Do you feel God? Ever?"

"I don't know—maybe."

"That's why I brought you down here—so you could feel God along with me," she said.

Maybe it was God I felt, but I think it was something else. With her so close, I felt an urge to touch her, and so I put my arm around her. She didn't flinch—seemed to welcome it. "Maybe this is too sudden, but I'd like to kiss you, Cameron," I said. "Would you mind?"

"Not at all," she said, and she smiled without saying a word, leaned toward me and offered her mouth. We kissed. It was a sudden kiss, but her lips were very soft and it felt good. Our mouths separated, but then they came together again and they stayed together, our mouths circling each other. My eyes opened quickly while hers were still shut.

"Are you feeling God now?" she asked. Her eyes were open and looking directly into mine.

"I'm feeling something," I said. And I was—a feeling down in my groin, but I was pretty sure it wasn't God.

"Why don't you join me in God's love?" she said. "Walk into the waters and be baptized and be made whole again? Would you do that?"

"I've already been baptized," I said.

"So? Be baptized again," she said. "We can share God's love together. Wouldn't you like that? Wouldn't you like to feel his grace all about you?"

If I could feel like this all the time, I'd be tempted.

"This is all so sudden," I said. My thoughts were everywhere. I know what my body wanted just then, but I knew where my body wanting something led to, as well, and I knew I'd be pushing my luck. Cameron wasn't the type to just lay down with the first guy she felt God with. And I wasn't sure I wanted to go there just yet—as much as I wanted to, as much as this urge was pushing me on. I was in a fix.

"That's how God's love is," she said.

"I need to think about it, Cameron," I said. "I gotta be honest with you."

She smiled. "Of course, you do—but there really isn't any thinking about God's love—it's just there for you."

We stood up from the rock and walked back to where my bicycle was and then continued on to Cameron's house. I walked her up to her front door and was about to kiss her again when the door opened and the reverend stood there. "Well?" he said, looking toward his daughter.

"Not yet, father," she said.

"Come inside, then, daughter." The reverend looked at me. "Good night, Mister Miller," he said. He held the door open for his daughter and she walked inside their house and the door closed behind her, leaving me on the porch alone. I didn't know what to think. What if I'd told her I'd be baptized again—would that have made a difference? Would she have invited me in? I could have told her that easy enough but I didn't. It wasn't what I felt. I felt all other kinds of things then but being baptized wasn't one of them. And I thought about what her father had said and how she answered, 'Not yet' like they were giving me time—enough time to see the light—but I didn't know when that would be. A part of me hoped it wouldn't be long—when we could wade through the waters together.

17

Cameron/Ultimatum

• • • • • • • • • • • • • • • • • •

Sunday morning arrived—the morning I promised to join Cameron at her father's service. I was up early, fed the horses and washed and shaved and made all the preparations necessary for a good showing. I felt a bit like a man preparing to go onstage, to perform and hopefully please his audience. I didn't know what my act was, though, or what I would do. Was it to say the lines that the actress appearing opposite me wanted to hear? And what were those lines? Somewhere, I know, I'd written them down on pieces of paper and practiced them for those future little scenes at Pauli's store. I remembered bits of them, phrases and the like, and had made a decent showing, a passable audition—enough, at least, to manage another date with Cameron.

I arrived at Souls' Haven the same time I'd arrived two weeks earlier. I propped my bicycle against that same sycamore tree and watched the congregation gather, heard the choir rehearsing inside, and wondered to myself what this day would bring. How it would play out. What I hoped would happen. And would the events of today match those same scenes I imagined in my mind? And what were those scenes? The ones where I saw two people move past the uncertainty each of them felt toward each other and arrive at a common ground—feel such harmony, with everything about them ending in a state of bliss with kisses and embraces and joy? What imaginings! It nearly took my breath away!

A man in a dark suit came out and rang a bell he held in his hand, and the remaining congregation filed inside. Again, I was last to enter. I closed the door behind me and found that same empty spot on the pew's end I'd found two weeks earlier. Part of me thought that if I follow the same routine I'd followed with my first visit to Cameron's church, everything would turn out the same. Cameron would be glad to see me. Her folks would approve, and we could spend another Sunday afternoon together, talking and enjoying each other's company and maybe even visiting God's little place again.

Parson Landers appeared at the front of the church, his hair neatly parted down the middle, a fresh carnation in the lapel of his jacket—as the organ's notes pealed out as before and the choir responded with a raucous version of "Soon and very soon, we are going to see the King." That started the congregation moving back and forth, clapping their hands, and filling the entire inside of that little church with sound. Parson Landers walked down the center aisle, clapping his hands to the music. Again, my eyes returned to Cameron. She sang with the same energy as she'd sung before and swayed along with the choir and smiled with that same smile that had so captivated me. I clapped and sang whatever words I could remember. Then my eyes went to each of the choir members, from woman to woman and then to the two men standing at the far right end. The last man was the fellow I'd seen talking with Cameron at the end at that earlier service, a fellow I thought was named Daniel.

The hymn ended and the church quieted. Parson Landers read from the scriptures, this one about the wedding feast in Canaan, and how they ran out of wine and Jesus asked the host to bring him vessels of water, and Jesus passed his hand over the vessels and changed the water to wine, better wine, even, than what had previously been served. The Parson drew a lesson from it which I couldn't remember because by now I wasn't listening to his words. I was thinking of Cameron instead, and what would happen after the service was finished and whether we'd have a date or not and what we'd say to each other. And I was thinking about that Daniel fellow, too, I admit it. He was a good looking guy, and I figured, believed all the things that Cameron believed, and how they probably matched up better than I did, and I wondered why they weren't together in the first place. I went on thinking like that, so caught up in my own thoughts—one little strand tying into the next— that before I knew it the service had ended. Everyone turned and shook hands with one another, and called each other 'brother' or 'sister' and I shook hands back. The choir sang one last song, a lively version of "Amazing Grace" as the church emptied and I retreated to the sycamore. Mrs. Lander saw me and waved and I approached her.

"Bert, good to see you at the service," she said. "Did you enjoy it?"

"Yes, I did." What else could I say? That I daydreamed through most of it?

"Did you say hello to Cameron's father?" she asked.

"Not yet."

"He'll be glad to see you at the service again," she said. I wasn't so sure of that.

The choir members were the last to file out. Cameron and the Daniel fellow came out together. I tried to catch her eye but she was busy talking to church members. I studied how Cameron and Daniel interacted, watched their every move around each other, how she looked at him and how he looked at her. I compared it to how she acted around me. I hated to admit it, but jealousy was stirring, and felt even more insecure—if that was possible. They both made their way to where Mrs. Landers and I were standing.

"Bert," Cameron said, "I'd like you to meet Daniel Biers. Daniel, this is Bert Miller."

We shook hands. I was right, his name was Daniel. He wore a perfectly tailored suit—he could have modeled it in a store-front window. He was handsome, too. I was careful to keep the torn elbow of my jacket tucked close to my body.

"I talked Daniel into joining the choir," Cameron said. "We needed some male voices. I'd already asked Bert to join but he told me he sang only to his horses." Everyone laughed.

"It sounds like the whole church is the choir," I said.

"I've seen you around town," Daniel said. "But I can't place where."

"Bert's a teamster with a pair of very fine horses." Cameron glanced first at Daniel and then over at me and smiled. "Daniel works at Taylor's Haberdasher."

I wasn't sure how things with Cameron and me were going to proceed. All kinds of doubts were entering my mind by now. Was Daniel going to stay around? Or would he leave? Cameron and I had made no plans, only that we'd meet at the service. No mention was made of what we'd do afterwards, if we'd do anything, and it felt awkward bringing any of this up while Daniel was still around.

"If you'll excuse me," Daniel said, "I see someone I need to say hello to." I felt an immediate relief.

This was my chance. I took Cameron by the arm and nudged her away from her mother. "Have you made plans for the afternoon?" I asked in a low voice, practically a whisper.

"I think I can find some time. I'd like it if we could talk," she said.

"So would I," I said although the tone of her voice made it sound serious.

"We could walk around the plaza. Find a bench and sit and talk," I said. "We could buy sodas again, if you'd like."

"Mother, Bert and I are going for a walk shortly."

"That's fine—but don't forget about our later engagement," Mrs. Landers said.

"No, I won't."

"Shall we go now then?" I wondered about her 'later engagement' but didn't ask.

"Sure," she said. "I'll talk with father later."

I pushed my bicycle alongside me as Cameron and I walked down Vallejo Street toward the plaza. "I'm curious, but do you have to ask permission from your folks for everything you do?"

She stopped briefly. "Most things—they're concerned about me. Why do you ask?"

"Just curious."

"You don't have to ask permission?"

"No," I laughed. "I'm pretty much on my own. I give myself permission what to do and what not to do."

"But you set limits, right? We all have to have limits."

"Sometimes I do—mostly I gauge it as I go along."

When we walked past the El Dorado—any of the watering holes around the plaza— I hoped no one would walk out its front doors and offer to buy me a drink. I still didn't know how much of my past history Cameron knew—if she knew anything.

"Daniel seems like a good fellow." I was fishing for the goods about him, and what exactly their relationship was to each other.

"Oh, he is," she said. "He's completely accepted Jesus into his heart."

"That's important to you, isn't it?"

"Yes, it is."

"And what if I don't accept Jesus into my heart? What then?" I asked her.

"Well, then, you don't. And you would've missed an opportunity."

"And how would that affect you?"

"Affect me? It's you that it'd affect, don't you think?"

"No, I mean, how would that affect how you feel about me if I didn't accept Jesus?"

"I guess I'd be disappointed."

"Disappointed enough to not want to see me again?"

"My, Bert, you get right down to the source, don't you?"

"I've been thinking of you a lot—thinking of what the chances were of us being together," I said.

I knew I was venturing into new territory and maybe venturing in too fast, but I had to get it off my chest.

"It's a bit soon to be thinking like that, isn't it?"

"I guess I don't want to waste my time and waste yours if there isn't a chance."

"My question would be: why this reluctance about accepting Jesus into your heart?"

"It has to be done honestly, don't you think?"

"Yes."

"And not for any other reason other than it's what I wanted to do, right? What I felt deep in my heart?"

"That's right. It's something you should be totally open and accepting to."

"And right now I don't feel that way, Cameron. If I said I wanted to accept Jesus, I'd be saying it only to please you—to increase our chances of being together." Her face lost all expression.

We hadn't even arrived at the park yet and all the heavy matter I wanted to talk about had already spilled out. Better to get it out and get it out sooner than later, I thought. I hated the uncertainty. And I hated the act of trying to be somebody I wasn't. I realized, also, that I might have jinxed any future with Cameron because of these questions.

We arrived at an empty park bench and we both sat down.

"Are you happy with your life, Bert, just as it is?" She took my hand and looked straight into my face. "I mean, do you think it could be better?"

"Sure, I think it could be better—it could always be better, couldn't it?" I didn't know how, but it certainly seemed better than a couple of months back when I was casting around for anything to do and on the outs with my old man.

"And what would that take?" she asked.

That question stumped me. "I don't know. I really don't." I tossed the question over in my mind. "I'd like to have someone in my life—someone to share it with."

"What would this person be like?" she asked. "What kind of person have you imagined?"

Should I say it? Should I tell her? Oh, what the hell! "Someone like you, Cameron," I finally said. There—I spilled the beans.

My response embarrassed her. Her face flushed. "I'm flattered— I mean, I don't know what to say, only that we know so little about each other—but it's a good start."

"That's true, but I've been fighting these really strong feelings inside for you."

"Fighting them?"

"Yeah, fighting them because I'm afraid we're too different— that what you believe and what I believe aren't going to stack up."

"And you still think I'm the person you'd want in your life?" She looked me square in the face. "What do you think that would take?"

"One of us changing—and I think that has to be me," I said.

"Well, this is where I think Jesus can help you," she said. "But like I've tried to explain, you have to let him into your heart—you have to invite him."

"Look, Cameron, I'm trying to be totally honest with you here and it's killing me!"

"It kills you to be honest?"

"It does because Jesus ain't coming into my heart—I mean, not for the reasons you'd want him to. I'd only be doing it to try to win your love. And that's not being honest, is it?"

"You make it so complicated, Bert."

"Because it is," I said. "If I could openly, honestly say, 'Okay, Jesus, I'm ready' then it'd be simpler but I can't say that now. I wish I could, but I can't."

"Let's give it some time, okay?" Cameron took my hand. "I appreciate your honesty, Bert. I really do. Maybe sometime in the future you'll have a change of heart. You'll become more receptive. That could happen, don't you think?"

I nodded. "It could," I said. The chances didn't seem good, though.

"What's most important, though, is keeping love in your heart—keeping it open—not closing it off." She smiled.

"Love?" Sometimes that could be a frightening word—with all kinds of meanings.

"Yes, love—for yourself and for your neighbor," she said.

"And you do that? You love everyone?"

"I try."

"I couldn't do that."

"Why couldn't you?"

I thought of Percy Sheers right off. No way I could love that bastard. "I just can't. There's folks in this world—all kinds of folks I ain't even met—evil folks I've heard and read about that I couldn't love no matter what. Why should I?"

"You have to open your heart—"

"I ain't wasting love on folks that don't deserve it."

"You think it's wasted?"

"I do."

"Why don't you try this—the next time when you want to think bad of someone, just catch yourself and say, 'No, that's what I've always done and those negative feelings never change, and I always end up feeling bad.' Unless you don't ever want to change them?" Her face moved closer to mine. "Is that what you want, Bert? To just keep feeling those same bad feelings all the time?"

"I feel what I feel. I give it free rein—and don't know what ever comes up."

"But again and again?" she said. "And the only result is you're feeling bad, feeling that hate, and it drains away at you."

"I guess I've gotten used to it. Besides, I don't feel it all the time."

"Sure you have!" she said. "Most of the world has, and that's why we're in the state we're in."

"Cameron, I can't say you're wrong but I can tell you this: I've got to *feel* something first, feel it way down inside—whatever that feeling is—and if I don't feel it, I ain't gonna blow any smoke and say I do. I'd be wasting my time."

"You don't feel Jesus?"

"It gets back to him again. Is that it?"

"It does. Give yourself some time—Jesus is patient."

"Are you patient?

"What do you mean?"

"Are you patient with me?" I asked. "What if I never come around to this whole God and Jesus thing?"

"Then you don't—it's your decision."

"And what happens between us?"

"Nothing happens. How could it?"

"I think you answered my question."

And what question was that?" she asked.

"If you and I stood any chance—you know—"

"I think *you* answered the question, not me," she said.

I stood up from the bench, grabbed my bicycle. "C'mon Cameron, I'll walk you home."

"I feel like I've disappointed you, Bert, and I'm sorry," she said. "But I don't know what else to say. We come from different places in this matter of belief and I don't see right now how it can be reconciled. Don't you agree?"

"I think you're right." I hated to admit it, but what she believed and what I believed didn't square up. I knew it all along and thought one of us would eventually cave in, but I could see it wouldn't be Cameron. It'd have to be me. Who knows? Maybe Jesus comes to me one day or one night—stranger things could happen. But for now, I wasn't seeing it in the cards. It pissed me off that at a time I most wanted Jesus to come around, tap me on the shoulder and ask, "You want to be friends?" he was nowhere to be found. And as much as I liked Cameron, I wasn't going to say nothing I didn't believe in all the way through—all the way up and down—from my Stetson to the soles of my boots.

We walked east on the avenue but didn't stop at her secret place. We turned, crossed the creek and walked another block to Cameron's house instead. I left my bicycle on the sidewalk and walked her to her door.

"I do like you, Bert. And I'll pray for you," she said.

"Thanks, Cameron. I guess the prayers wouldn't hurt, would they?"

"No, I don't think they'd hurt at all."

I bicycled back to Emma's. Part of me said I'd rushed everything, and ended up shooting myself out of the saddle as a result. But another part said, better to air everything out at the beginning so those differences don't lurk ahead and blow everything to hell. As usual, I didn't know what to think, didn't know which way to go. I was out at sea with no bearings, no compass, just my own instincts to guide me. That's all I had—my instincts. God wasn't going to help—how could he if I didn't believe in him? That I didn't even think he existed? If he did—and I was wrong—maybe he'd make an exception, and I'd end up with Cameron. Stranger things could happen.

18

The Shooting
· · · · · · · · · · · · ·

October, 1891, Sonoma, California

It was a late October morning and the sun was hot. We'd near-finished transferring the block onto the rail flat car and I was ready to find some shade. The lumpers dripped with sweat, and pitch oozed from the gum trees. Everything seemed to bake in a harsh light.

I thought about yesterday's conversation with Cameron and wishing it'd turn out different, but it aired-out some bothersome matters between us, and I felt the better for it. She didn't say what I wanted to hear but that didn't surprise me. I didn't know exactly what I wanted to hear or what I wanted to see happen, and told myself not to worry about it—I was tossing dice on this one. If God came to me, I wouldn't close the door on him—I'd invite him right in and we could hash this whole thing out. I sure wasn't putting any money on it though, but things had happened to me before I never thought would happen—so I tried leaving it all open.

In the middle of all this thinking and wondering, I looked up and saw Alfonso riding toward the depot in a full gallop. He brought his horse to a quick stop just inches from me, and when the dust cleared, the look on his face told me something was wrong.

"Your father shot." He choked out the words. "Oh, *Dios mio!*"

"What? Where?" I sprang off the wagon grabbbing the reins of his horse.

He pointed behind him. "The north gate—he shot there!"

The north gate, two miles from here, was the Petaluma Road entry into Carlotta Stamm's ranch. It was also a short-cut to the Watmaugh district and further on to the markets in Petaluma. Only those with permission from Carlotta were allowed to use it.

"Who shot him?"

"I think Carotta's brother."

"Sheers?"

"*Si*, Sheers," he said.

"Goddamn it!" Too many questions right now. I turned to the lumpers. "Guys, let's get the rest of those blocks off! Now! Move!"

They tossed the remaining blocks onto the bed of the flat car and I threw the tailgate into the back of the wagon. I jumped up onto the driver's seat and slapped the traces hard against the rumps of Molly and Dolly. The wagon lurched forward. Alfonso rode off in front of us. My pair kept a fast trot through town, their hooves clacking loud on the cobblestones down First Street all the way out Vallejo where the cobble surface turned to dirt. Big clouds of dust followed us.

We crossed Sonoma Creek onto Petaluma Road and headed straight west. Several hundred yards ahead, I saw a carriage and a wagon, a couple of saddle horses and a group of folks standing in a circle. The closer I got, I saw a wagon outside the gate loaded down with chicken coops. Inside the gate was my folks' carriage and Ma was sitting in it by herself. I pulled my wagon within twenty yards of the gathering, set the brake, jumped off and ran over to the circle of onlookers. John B. stood there looking down at whatever the other folks were looking at. I shouldered past one of the men and saw a body lying on its back, its face looking straight up to the sky, its mouth wide open like it was trying to say something. One leg was folded over the other. A familiar hat lie a couple of feet away—it was my old man's. I looked again and again, hoping I'd see something different—but I didn't.

It was him lying there. A circle of blood had spread across his chest and another on his right arm. And down near his groin two more dark circles. Dust and dirt were mixed into his hair. His eyes were still open, still clear blue looking straight up at the sky like he'd taken a break from work, found a bit of shade and decided to lie down and rest on this October afternoon. I knelt down beside him, touched him on his shoulder. "Dad? Dad?" I whispered. No answer. I brushed a fly away from his mouth. He didn't move. My father was dead.

I turned around and looked up at John B., "What happened?"

"Ma saw it all," John B. said. "What she told me was Percy Sheers tried to open the gate and cross onto Carlotta's property, and Dad wouldn't let him, and they got to arguing, and Dad picked up a post and went at him and Percy Sheers shot him—four times."

"Just like that? He shot him?" I asked. "Goddamn it!"

"Ma said Dad grabbed a picket when Sheers went to open the gate, and Dad told Sheers 'You're not coming on my property.' Ma yelled for Dad to put the picket down and then he swung it at Sheers. That's when Sheers shot him—once in the arm—Dad kept coming at him and Sheers shot him again, another below his belt and two in the chest, she said. Just before the two shots to his chest killed him, Dad yelled out, 'I been shot'"

"Son of a bitch!" I looked around but there was no sign of Sheers, only his wagon loaded down with chicken coops and his wife sitting on her half of the wagon seat. "Where's Sheers?"

"He rode off on a horse to get Sheriff Sparks," John B. said.

I started toward Sheers' wagon and John B. grabbed me by the arm. "Don't do anything stupid, Bert. We'll get it settled."

"You think so?"

"Somehow, we will," he said.

I felt a dozen different feelings just then—anger, confusion, hate—and spread over all of them was this numbness like I was sleepwalking through this entire scene, imagining that it wasn't real—like it was some kind of opium dream. But I only had to look down at my father lying in the October dust, and the circle of folks with puzzled looks on their faces, and Ma over there still sitting in their carriage, staring straight ahead, dazed, to realize it wasn't no dream. It had really happened.

My first impulse was to walk over to Sheers' wagon, and tell his wife what a no-good coward her husband was, but John B. talked me out of going. I walked over to Ma, instead. She sat there, like I said, just staring straight ahead like she was frozen—a handkerchief up to her nose. By now Josephine had run up from their house after hearing the news and moved in next to Ma, embracing her with both her arms. Ma sobbed. I watched how her body shook.

"I told your father, please—you don't know what he'll do." Ma finally spoke through her subbing and crying. "He picked up a post and I said, 'Johann, no—"

John B. joined us. We stood there, neither of us talking until he finally said, "We're waiting on the Coroner Blaney now. Then we can move Dad."

I glared over at Sheers' wife again. She sat in the driver's seat and standing alongside her was Rennie McDonnell, their hired hand. The wagon was loaded with chicken coops and the chickens looked out through the wooden slats with confused eyes, cocking their heads one way, then the other.

"Sheers' been taking this short cut through his sister's property and Carlotta's been warning him all along he was trespassing," John B. said. "But then by pure chance both Dad and Sheers met up here and that's when the argument started." John B. looked over to where our father lay. "I was working on the chicken houses when I heard the shots. Didn't think anything of it at first, until a few minutes later Sheers' hired hand there run into the yard shouting, 'Your old man's been shot! At the north gate!' and Alfonso and me we took off running. Halfway there, I told Alfonso, 'Go back and get your horse and find Bert."

I was still trying to make sense of it all—everything had happened so fast—but how do you do that? How did any of this make sense? A man works hard every day and does good work, cares for his family and his friends, rare for him to speak an unkind word toward anyone unless they deserved it—minds his own business—is a good citizen as they say around here.

Sure, my old man could fly off the handle at times, and I'd been on the receiving end of his temper more than most, but this was a decent man who didn't deserve to die, a man who loved animals and couldn't bear to see them or anyone else suffer. And then it comes to this. He's shot and killed. How does any of it make sense? There's Sheers' wife twenty yards away, talking with her hired hand, and there's my father lying in the dirt there dead. And just a few feet away, there's Ma in their carriage crying her eyes out. It didn't seem fair. Again, I thought, maybe if I closed my eyes and opened them again all of this would disappear, like a bad dream you wake from and you rub your eyes and at first you're worried but then you're awake and all of it's gone and you don't feel scared like before. But this was real—no closing of the eyes would make it go away.

Sheriff Sparks arrived on horseback along with Sheers. He dismounted and walked over to where my father was lying, pushed the holster carrying his pistol to one side, knelt down on one knee and looked Dad's body over from head to toe. He pulled a notebook out of his shirt pocket, checked the time with his pocket watch and wrote into the notebook.

Sheers joined his wife at their wagon. A few minutes later, Coroner Blaney arrived in his carriage. He was a round, formal-looking man with a sour look as though his lunch had just been interrupted. He carried a clipboard in his hand and clamped to it was a sheath of official-looking papers. He walked over to Ma and tipped his hat to her and said he was sorry about the circumstances, and proceeded to ask her a series of questions. Like the sheriff, he wrote down her responses. Ma answered each one of them, sobbing through her handkerchief as she talked. When she didn't understand the question, John B. translated for her. Then Blaney walked past the onlookers and knelt down alongside the body and pulled my father's jacket back to expose more of the wound. By now the blood had dried all across his upper chest. He picked up dad's right arm and felt the wrist for a pulse, then shook his head, and set the arm back down in the dirt.

The sheriff walked over and the two of them—Blaney and Sheriff Sparks—talked between themselves. "A goddamn shame," I heard one of them say. The coroner looked over the sheriff's notes and took out his pocket watch and wrote down the time. It was 1:20 in the afternoon.

Sheriff Sparks approached John B. and me. "Have you made preparations for the body?" he asked us.

John B. and I looked at each other. "It's been so sudden, sheriff," John B. said.

"We'll take it to Carlotta's," I said. "With the heat like this, we'll put it in her cellar."

"Coroner Blaney wants to impanel a jury, enter the evidence so we can reach a quick conclusion to this matter." Sheriff Sparks removed his hat and wiped his brow on his shirt sleeve. "The two of you will sign off on the body, then?" he asked.

"What does he mean a 'quick conclusion'?" I wanted to know.

"He'll listen to the evidence and then decide if there's any wrongdoing," Sparks said.

"And who's the jury?" I asked.

"Citizens of the town," he said. "Blaney will choose and impanel them."

I looked at John B. and then at the sheriff. "Does our mother know this?"

"I believe Coroner Blaney has informed her, yes," the sheriff said.

The folks' carriage, with Ma in the front seat, was still inside the gate. By now Sheers had moved his wagon out along Petaluma Road. Sheers avoided looking at me. "John B.," I said, "Why don't you turn dad's carriage around and I'll move my wagon closer to the body? We can lift it on the wagon easier then." I still wanted to confront Sheers.

With my wagon positioned, John B. and I went over to the body. I grabbed dad's arms and he grabbed dad's legs. I could feel the body had already started to stiffen. Two more men joined us and together the four of us lifted his body onto the back of my wagon. Little shards of cobblestone and pieces of dry grass stuck to his clothes. I climbed up to the wagon's seat and started the team toward Carlotta's. John B. was ahead of me in the folks' carriage with Ma and Josephine. I turned around and the sheriff and the Coroner Blaney were still talking with Percy Sheers.

Carlotta and Ah Yep, her houseman, met us in the ranch yard. By the looks on their faces they'd heard the news already. Carlotta held a handkerchief to her mouth and looked past me and over the sideboards of the wagon where our father lay. She began to sob loudly. "This is horrible!" she said. "I'm so sorry."

I looked at Carlotta. "We need to put dad's body in your cellar."

She motioned to Ah Yep. "The wine cellar! Open the doors to the cellar!" she said. Ah Yep trotted off toward a little clapboard shack built on top of stone walled foundation. He swung open two doors to the side of the cellar and inside a series of steps disappeared into the darkness.

I pulled the team into the shade and John B. and I stepped down into the cellar to look things over. Cobwebs hung across the cellar opening. We brushed them aside. With each step down to the bottom of the cellar it grew cooler. It was dark inside and Ah Yep brought a kerosene lamp and a broom. The cellar walls were lined with wooden shelves filled with dusty bottles of wine and jars of preserves. In the middle of the cellar was a wooden table. We cleared the table, and Ah Yep swept it clean with the broom, then wiped it down with a damp cloth. We climbed out of the cellar and back into the heat. Carlotta tried to comfort Ma, stroking Ma's back and talking to her in low tones. "Regina, I'm so sorry—so sorry," she said. "Come, let's get out of this heat."

I positioned the wagon in front of the cellar entrance and John B., Ah Yep and myself lifted the body to the edge of the wagon and then slowly brought it out of the wagon and down the cellar steps and carefully lowered it onto the table. By now the body had stiffened even more.

"I don't know what else we can do right now," I said to John B. once the body was placed on the table.

"Make funeral arrangements?" he said.

"We need to talk to Ma and Carlotta first—and see what they say"

"Let's wait on that," I said. "I don't think Ma's in any condition right now to make decisions."

I wanted a drink. More than anything I wanted a drink, a good, stiff one. And I wanted to tell Tino, too, what had happened—I wanted to tell the whole world— wanted to do and say anything to lighten this terrible load inside me.

The three women were now inside the folks' house. I pulled the team back into the shade and remembered that weeks ago I'd stashed a bottle of rye wrapped in a burlap sack under the driver's seat. I slid the bottle out of the sack and motioned for John B. to come over. I handed him the bottle and he drank from it. He handed it back to me and I did the same. "I can't believe it," he kept saying. "I can't believe it. The old man's dead." John B. wiped the tears on the sleeve of his shirt.

I just shook my head.

Inside with Ma, Carlotta and Josephine, I told them that Coroner Blaney was going to impanel a jury to decide on the case.

"But they're all my brother's friends," Carlotta said. "There's no chance of a fair verdict."

"What do we do then?" John B. asked.

"I'll talk to my attorney," Carlotta said.

I unharnessed Molly and Dolly and put them into the two empty stalls at one end of Carlotta's stable. I fed them and after they were settled, I borrowed a saddle horse, tucked the bottle of rye into a saddle bag and rode into town to see Tino. By now it was almost dark. When I arrived at the stable, Tino had already heard the news.

"I'll kill the bastard for you." He took a pull from the bottle. "They won't find out who did it, either."

"You're the first one they'll go after."

"I'll plan it out—you'll see."

"Forget it, Tino."

"You aint gonna just let it go, are you?" he asked.

"I don't know what I'm going to do." And I didn't.

We finished what was left of the bottle and then I rode back to Emma's on the borrowed horse. I was good and drunk by the time I left Tino's, but the evening was a warm and pleasant one and I looked up at the sky and saw the stars swirling around and the dark shapes of trees along the creek and I found a little bit comfort just then in this world—the big, outside world without any humans in it messing it up—a little break from the confusion hammering at me from all sides.

Times like this I seemed small—barely a fleck of dust—and wondered about life and if there was a God—that same God Cameron talked so much about—and if there was, how did he let something like this happen today? I wasn't convinced about him by any stretch; I felt that everything that happened, happened by chance—an explosion in the stars that started it all—and not some spirit looking down on us from his perch in the sky. That all seemed like bullshit to me. What happened down here was a big crap shoot and folks dressed all their ignorance up in religion and ceremony to try to explain it—no different from those earlier tribes slaughtering lambs as an offering for a healthy son or a good harvest. There was no reasoning behind it. No greater lesson. Most of it seemed pointless. We were on our own. I hated to admit it, but we were. All this thinking made me realize yet again the worlds that separated Cameron from me—big worlds—but did it really matter in the end? We were all headed for the same place. Maybe I'd see my father there.

I re-hashed all the day's events, from hauling block down from the quarry, to Alfonso riding to the depot to tell me the news, to driving the team out to where the shooting happened, and seeing my old man lying in the dry adobe, to comforting Ma, and finally hauling the body back to Carlotta's. I wondered what life would be like now without the old man around—I didn't know—but mostly I worried about Ma. Who would fill up that empty space around her now that her husband was gone? And what would it be like for her not having my father around? So many questions. Everything always circled back to that same place, though—that place where I didn't know any of the answers—that place of uncertainty—like going down a mineshaft, dark and feeling for each step, and not knowing where you'd end up or what you'd find or even how you'd get back.

19
Preparing the Body
· · · · · · · · · · · · · · · · · · ·

With the hot spell breathing down on us, we knew we couldn't waste time. Dad's body had stiffened and was already hard to the touch. It had begun swelling, too, and his pants had already started to tighten around his legs and his bare feet had swollen into stumps. An odor about the body was growing, too. Carlotta offered her parlor for the funeral service, and even hand-printed cards we could post at the Swiss National Club and leave at the Index Tribune's newspaper office. The funeral was set for Saturday, two days from when Dad was killed.

Everyone in our family settled on a particular chore. Josephine would contact the undertaker. I bought black bunting at Pauli's to drape on the wagons for the funeral procession. Cameron had already heard news of the shooting and she hugged me and said she'd pray for my dad. I thanked her, told her I'd like to see her again when all this with my father was done—I don't know why I said it unless it was just to be saying something. She smiled at me and nodded her head.

Ma and Josephine agreed they'd undress and clean the body before Cecil Mortensen, the undertaker, arrived for the final preparations. On Friday morning they removed Dad's clothes—some of them they had to cut off because the body had swelled—and wiped his body down. Ah Yep's wife helped, too. She brought stacks of cold, wet cloths she'd soaked in the creek and once Dad's clothes were cut off and his body washed, they draped him in these wet cloths to cool his body until dressing him for the service. Later that morning I joined them in the cellar. A stack of dad's clothes was on one of the shelves. I pulled a cloth back from his chest and there, right above the heart, was a thumb-sized hole where the bullet from Sheer's pistol had entered. Another bullet hole was down near his groin. Dad's eyes were now closed. His body was the color of paraffin wax and just as cold to the touch. Josephine had combed his hair.

"I'd just bought a coat two weeks ago for your father, too," Ma said. "I want you to have it. We can bury him in his other coat." She handed me the coat and with a slight smile said, "I noticed the hole in the elbow of yours." She took my arm. Ma was a practical woman. "Another thing," she said."Your dad's mare's with foal— she could drop any time. You know how he loved that horse."

"Alfonso and I'll keep an eye on her," I said, and put my arm around her. She leaned into me.

"Your dad already wanted to name the foal," she said. "I'll tell you what name later."

Mortensen, the undertaker, arrived in his carriage by late morning. Carlotta had poured him a cup of coffee before beginning his work. After coffee, he climbed down into the cellar carrying his black satchel. He asked for two buckets—one empty, the other filled with water. He asked if he could work alone. An hour and a half later he rose out of the cellar. His satchel in one hand, his coat draped over his left arm. "The buckets are still down there," he said. "Would you mind disposing of their contents?" He walked toward his carriage. "Oh, yes, I left some foundation powder down there, as well—you know—to add some color to the face." We thanked him and he drove off.

Inside Carlotta's house, Ah Yep and Alfonso had removed furniture from the parlor and carried in chairs they placed in rows, and brought in two benches from Carlotta's garden. At the front of the parlor was a table where the casket would set. John B. and our cousin Emil had already started building a casket out of pine slabs and Emil said he'd deliver it later in the afternoon. John B.'s wife contacted Father Whyte at Saint Francis Solano Church to preside at the service.

Ah Yep's wife brought out a dozen flower vases and lined them all on the kitchen counter. She went out and began cutting flowers in Carlotta's garden—mums, roses, day lilies—brought them in and arranged them in the vases. She set out bowls of water and sprinkled them with rose petals until the entire downstairs of Carlotta's house smelled of fragrant flowers. A large coffee urn was brought out, and rows of Carlotta's fine china cups and saucers lined the counter.

Back in the cellar, Ma and Josephine began dressing Dad. The swelling in the face and body was now gone and Josephine had wondered how Mortensen had done it. "He's got a big syringe," I told her. She recoiled at the thought of it. Dad's cheeks and mouth were shrunk in now—his nose as sharp as a blade. He lay there as if asleep. Ma and Josephine slipped a shirt on him, turning his upper body first one way and then the other. With his shirt buttoned, they added the jacket, and then pulled a pressed pair of pants up both legs. He was still bootless. "He's so stiff," Josephine sobbed. "—and cold! I never thought I'd see him like this. It's awful!" Ma hugged Josephine as the two of them looked over the body.

"He didn't deserve it," I said. "The last man on earth that deserved this." Ma and Josephine nodded their heads.

This is the time when you think of all the things you could have said to that person, but didn't—all the times you should have apologized for disappointments, the grief you caused—all the times you wished you'd bucked up and been half the person he expected you to be. It was a time of regret for me that I hadn't done none of this. I always thought there'd be some time in the future—we all do— when we could lay aside our differences and accept each other and finally say those things that'd been just below the surface all this time. I hoped for that moment when I could tell him how much I loved him—I always thought it'd be out there waiting on me to just say the words, but time and death don't work like that—it don't wait on no one.

Despite our differences, I always knew him to be a good man without a dishonest bone in his body. He told you straight-out what he felt—no varnishing his feelings, no blowing smoke up your ass. No circling around what he wanted to say—no bullshit. He was loyal to friends, too, and to those who employed him—loyal to a fault—and it's what killed him—that and his bad temper and hard-headedness. To make it even worse, he got caught up in the cross-fire between Carlotta and her brother. After Carlotta had shared with our old man her long history of disagreements with Percy, we guessed our father felt he had to defend her. Sheers had been using Carlotta's land as a short-cut to haul goods to Donahue Wharf— this same land that Sheers had contested in court— eventually losing his claim as the rightful owner. "I told him, 'Johann, it's Carlotta's property, not yours—don't get involved,'" Ma said, "But he wouldn't listen."

Ever since learning Sheers killed my dad, I wondered what I could do to even the score, if there was anything I could do. Vengeance didn't run in my blood like it ran in Tino's, but there was this thing called family honor that told me I just couldn't walk away from it. I didn't know what to do, but Tino did—he wanted to settle matters with Sheers right out, and if I wouldn't, he would. He'd endured Sheers' taunts of 'half-breed' and 'Indian-nigger' since he was a boy, and now my old man's killing seemed like the perfect excuse for him. "No, Tino," I said. "You can't kill him. They'll hang you in this town if you do."

"They won't know it's me," he said.

"You're the first one they'll suspect." Their hatred for each other was known all around town.

"You'll see," he said. "You know how I hunt, right? How I don't make a sound? How my feet don't even touch the ground? And then—BANG!—whatever I'm hunting drops. It'll be just like that with Sheers. He won't even know he just died."

20

The Funeral

· · · · · · · · · · · ·

Word of my father's killing spread fast through town. Early
Saturday morning, hours before the service was to begin,
Christina Kessel and her two brothers, Jack and Frank, were already at my folks' house. My old man had helped Jack and Frank
build a hay barn years earlier at the Koblentz ranch where the
Kessels worked. Christina cooked there. She'd made a huge pot of
her potato salad and baked several loaves of bread the night before.
Jack and Frank brought strings of sausages and bratwurst they made
there at the ranch. They set out big pots of water to boil the sausages. They brought crocks of sauerkraut, as well, and several bottles
of schnapps they liked to drink in quick gulps. Christina's fiance',
Jimmy Murdoch, was enroute from Petaluma. Oddly, the house
seemed so full of life at this time of death. Everyone moved about,
talking, hugging, laughing and hiding back tears at the same time.

Later in the morning, more guests arrived. Each of them brought
something—cakes, pastries, a large block of cheese and a bowl
that could be heated for fondue, a favorite of the Swiss. Fritz Weiss,
who worked at the Excelsior Brewery, brought a keg of beer. A procession of carriages and wagons and a dozen saddle horses began
filling the ranch yard. Alfonso opened a gate into an adjoining field
to allow more space for the overflow of carriages and wagons. He
and his brothers brought buckets of water out for the horses. It was
another hot day and flies already circled the piles of horse dung.
The bay trees along the creek oozed out their peppery smell while
down in the cellar, Dad's body was ripening. We lifted it into the
casket Emil and John B. had built, and the four of us—John B.,
Emil, Alfonso and I carried it out of the cellar, across the yard and
into Carlotta's parlor. We set the casket on a table and Ah Yep's wife
surrounded the casket with vases of roses and mums and garlands

of wisteria. Josephine colored our father's face with the powder Cecil Mortensen had left. She spilled a bit of the powder on his shirt and then wiped the excess away.

Out in Carlotta's garden the funeral guests gathered. Under a trellis overgrown with wisteria, Ah Yep had set out a punch bowl of water filled with lemon slices, and on each side of the bowl he lined up rows of glasses. There was a coffee urn, as well, and stacks of coffee cups. Many of the guests were members of the Swiss National Club who I knew by name, these same members who'd shared their concern about me to my old man. I didn't like them at the time, didn't like that they were talking about me but I realized this is what they did at their meetings: they talked about one another and especially the ones that were problems. As my old man often told me, the name you earned was important. Other guests were past clients, acquaintances of our folks I'd seen around town. Within his small circle, he was well-liked, well respected among his kind. Tino eventually arrived, too, in a fancy buggy he'd borrowed from the Union. He'd picked up four elderly Swiss Club members in front of their clubhouse on the corner of the plaza.

Ma and Josephine, each dressed in black with dark veils covering their hair, greeted the guests as they arrived. Ma spoke in Swiss-German to several of the guests, a language that best expressed their grief. Carlotta had finally emerged from her seclusion and moved about, a handkerchief never far from her nose. She'd taken Dad's death particularly hard, blaming herself that it had happened. When Father Whyte's carriage pulled into the yard, Alfonso directed the priest to a reserved space near the garden's entrance. He was a round man, and the folds in his neck nearly covered his priest's collar. He talked with Ma and Josephine. He shook my hand and then waded into the small gathering.

My old man and Ma weren't church-goers. They were Catholic by name but rarely entered the church except on Christmas Day or to attend a funeral. I never saw or heard my folks pray. Never heard them recite the rosary. No pictures of Christ or the Blessed Virgin hung on the walls. They saved their faith for times like these—times of grief—and kept their beliefs, like they kept everything else, largely to themselves. It was Ma's choice to have the service at Carlotta's and not at the church, and no one questioned it. They led good lives and to them that seemed enough. I doubt if they'd even met Father Whyte before today but you'd have never known it by the way the priest carried on—like they'd been childhood friends. Father Whyte hugged and shook hands, laughed, and carried on like he was running for mayor.

After Father Whyte made his rounds and entered Carlotta's house, the guests followed and quickly filled the parlor, filing first past the open casket before taking their seats. Fans were provided to the women. The parlor air was already thick, heated with all the folks now inside. I stood at the back of the parlor with John B. ready to help with any need that might arise. Father Whyte walked to the front of the casket and made the sign of the cross over dad's body.

"Welcome, everyone," he began, "to this very sad occasion— but a happy one, too. For John is surely in heaven."

How he knew that I didn't know. He looked around the parlor to the different faces, then turned toward the casket before opening a black book. I heard sobs throughout the room, saw women dabbing their eyes and noses with handkerchiefs. Flies circled and landed on the hats of the women. He read a passage, one he'd probably read dozens of times before at these very occasions, and when he finished reading, he looked up again, paused, took a breath and assured folks there that John was in a better place now. I tried to imagine what that place was like and how my dad could think it better than strapping on his tool apron and building something. Father Whyte went on about how important it was to keep the memory of John Miller alive in our hearts, not to lose hope and that God had a plan for everything, regardless of how senseless things seemed.

I guess I'd heard the words too many times before because they didn't mean much anymore—just hollow sounds coming out of a priest's mouth meant to reassure everyone that life had a purpose. I could understand that folks needed to be reassured, and I saw the need for belief and hopes for an afterlife. What else could the priest say—that this life didn't mean shit? That we scraped and sweated and in the end they slabbed us up, sucked the fluids out of our bodies, powdered our faces and then lowered us into the ground before the worms started eating us? Then what? If you were lucky, you made it to heaven. If you weren't lucky, you didn't.

I heard sounds coming out of Father Whyte's mouth, but they were just sounds—like when my old man would be lecturing me or showing me how to square a corner, and my mind went wandering off somewhere, imagining my latest love at the moment lying on a bed of straw next to me and the whole afternoon in front of us. Then his frustration boiled over. He clenched his tongue between his teeth before laying into me again. But now, I realized, he couldn't do that anymore—that he wouldn't be around to straighten me out when I needed straightening out. No, he was gone—Sheers took care of that. To where? I didn't know, unless it was just the six feet into the ground and nowhere else.

Maybe, though, if there was a heaven—and I was pretty sure there wasn't—but if there was, I hoped he made it there. I tried to imagine what heaven would be like for my old man—a place where all the walls were plumb, all the corners square, the floors level—where his cousin played the concertina and everyone drank schnapps and talked and laughed about one another until they couldn't catch their breaths.

In the middle of all my thinking and wondering, and Father Whyte carrying on—invoking the Lord and describing heaven in such glorious terms—I started to think maybe dying and getting there wasn't so bad after all. Then Alfonso came in and motioned for me to follow him outside. "The horse—it ready," he said. An anxious look spread across his face.

"My father's mare?" I asked him.

"*Si.*"

We trotted toward the stable.

"The horse it walk around and around—making circles." Alfonso drew a circle with his hand.

"Yeah, that's what they do when it's time," I said.

When we entered the stall, the mare was lying on its side, breathing heavy. I took my coat off—my old man's coat Ma had given me—and draped it over the stall door. The mare's fluids had already broken and were draining out its rear into the straw bedding. I pulled the tail up and there was one of the foal's hoofs starting to show—gleaming like porcelain. I reached in to clear the hoof, then pulled the leg until the other hoof appeared. I saw the nose of the foal covered in a bluish film. The mare had birthed before so it made the foaling easier for her, but there could always be problems.

First, the nose of the foal, then its head appeared and then as the mare contracted and heaved, contracted and heaved, the rest of the foal's body slid out whole inside a bluish sack. Alfonso stood at the mare's front, stroking its head, and talking to it in Spanish. "*Eso! Eso! Asi—muy suave.*" I broke the sack away from the foal's nose and heard it take its first breath outside of the mother, a little bubbling, fluttering sound. I peeled the rest of the sack away from the foal's body and lifted one of its long, spindly hind legs. It was a colt, grayish black. Within minutes, it was trying to stand, its rump jutting high in the air, its front legs splayed out as though walking on ice. The mare was now standing over its foal, licking any of the fluids away, nudging it with its nose, helping it to stand. Alfonso looked at me and smiled. "*Es* good," he said.

"Yes, good," I said. The foal looked healthy. No problems that I could see. Finally, it stood, and looked about with large, dazed eyes, and instinctively went to its mother's jugs. "I stay for now," Alfonso said.

"Good. I need to harness the horses," I said.

When Molly and Dolly were hitched to the wagon, I drove it to the entrance of Carlotta's garden. I washed my hands in a bucket of water and dried them against my pants. I put dad's jacket back on—no, I guess it was my jacket now.

The service had concluded—Father Whyte ran out of things to say—and guests were filing out of Carlotta's house. John B.

approached. "Where'd you go?" he asked. I told him about dad's mare. "We're ready to put dad's casket in your wagon, okay?"

"Sure," I said. "Let's get some helpers."

Frank and Jack Kessel, along with John B. and I, carried the casket out to my wagon and slid it inside. Black bunting was draped over the wagon's sideboards and with the few loose strands of bunting, I placed them over the casket. I drove the wagon to the south end of the yard and kept it moving forward as more carriages and wagons formed in a line behind me.

Ma and Josephine rode with John B. and his wife, Gertie, in his carriage. Alfonso drove Carlotta's buggy. By the time the procession moved east on Napa Road, fifteen wagons and carriages were behind me. I drove the team slowly east, little clouds of dust billowing up behind the wagons, until we came to the cross roads of Fifth Street and Napa Road where we turned north toward the cemetery. Fifth Street ended at United States Avenue about a mile north, and fifty yards east was the entrance to the cemetery. The grave-digger met us at the gate and directed us to where the plot was dug. The wagons and carriages wound their way into the cemetery and parked along the lanes separating the plots. While we waited for Father Whyte to arrive, we unloaded the casket and placed it on a set of stands alongside the newly dug grave. The guests formed a circle around the gravesite. Many of them held roses from Carlotta's garden. The women opened their parasols against the harsh October sun.

Father Whyte finally arrived, lowered himself from his carriage and approached the casket. He opened that same black book he'd read from in Carlotta's parlor, looked around at the gathering and then back at the casket before reciting more prayers. He took out a little wand from a silver bucket and shook holy water over the casket. The gravedigger placed two big leather belts around the casket and John B., Tino, Alfonso and me each took an end to the belts, lifted the casket from its stand and slowly lowered it into the ground.

Ma began sobbing loudly seeing the casket resting at the bottom of the grave. Josephine tried to comfort her. Carlotta stared at the casket. Father Whyte continued reading from his book, as different guests dropped their roses on top of the casket. When the prayers ended, and before the guests began to leave, Carlotta invited them back to her house. "Please, feel welcome to come back to my house. We have food, drinks and dessert waiting," she announced.

21

The Funeral Wake

· · · · · · · · · · · · · · · · ·

After the interment, I drove the team back to Carlotta's and stopped
them in front of the stable entrance. Inside I checked on the
mare and foal. Both were doing well. By now the little colt was already walking around on its spindly legs, never straying far from its
mother's side. I heard a carriage pull up outside. It was Tino's. He
joined me and we both looked over the mare and her colt. "He's a
beauty," Tino said, then fished a little flask from his hip pocket. "To
your old man," and he raised the flask before taking a pull. Then he
handed it to me. "It's the shits to have it end like this," he said.

"Sure is," I said and drank from the flask, passing it back and
forth until it was empty. "The old man got a nice colt, though," I
said. "I wish he was here to see it."

"Ain't doing him no good now, though, is it?" Tino said.

"You're right—it ain't." I kicked my boot toe through the straw.
"Guess we better get back to the gathering," I said.

In Carlotta's garden, under a broad trellis, Ah Yep and his wife
had laid out roasted cuts of beef and three chickens on platters,
along with bowls of steamed rice and stir-fried vegetables—brocco-
li, peppers, late summer squash from the garden they kept behind
their quarters. There was a platter of sliced tomatoes and cucumbers, as well. Carlotta had baked two sheet cakes the night before.
All the food was covered with cheese cloth until the guests arrived.
Tables and chairs were spread out in the shade of towering oaks and
once the guests had filled their plates and filled their glasses, they
sat down.

I moved from table to table, welcoming guests, shaking their
hands, receiving condolences. We reminisced about my father
and tried to squeeze a bit of merriment out of an otherwise sad
situation. Frank and Jack sat with their sister, Christina and her

fiancé Jimmy Murdoch. Christina rarely talked. She sat there staring at the flowers in the middle of the table. Christina cooked and kept house on the dairy where her brothers worked. She was a hard worker. We talked about the time we all helped build a hay barn up at the ranch and Jack fell when he was framing the roof and dislocated his hip. "I was lucky," he said in his Swiss dialect. Everyone laughed. A slight smile creased Christina's lips.

"It only bothered his head," Christina finally spoke, and everyone laughed again.

I saw Ma and Josephine at one table and walked over to join them. As soon as I sat down, I told them that Dad's mare had thrown a healthy colt.

"Wonderful! He'd be glad to know that," Ma said. "You know how he loved that horse."

"You told me Dad already had a name for it?" I said.

"He did." She paused. "He wanted to call it Ike, if it was a little colt."

"Why Ike?" Josephine asked.

"Because the song he liked to sing with his cousins most was 'Sweet Betsy from Pike,' you know the line that goes, 'she crossed the wide prairie with her lover, Ike'? Don't ask me why, but he liked that name—it stuck in his head."

"So we'll call him Ike," I said.

"And I'd like you to have little Ike," Ma said to me. "I know your father would, too. He told me no one knew horses like you did. Did you know that?"

I shook my head. "No, I didn't." My old man was stingy with his compliments—especially when it came to me.

"Josephine and I have been talking, and we're thinking about moving back to our place in Vineburg," Ma said. "With Dad gone, I don't feel we belong here anymore—you know—the memories and such—and there's room out there even with John B. and his wife. And it won't be long before John B. and Gertie move to their own place in Santa Rosa."

"I understand."

"You'll help us move?" Ma asked.

"Of course I will."

Isaac Gustafson, a member of the Swiss Club, approached Ma's table to pay his respects. I stood up and shook Isaac's hand and excused myself. I headed toward the drink table and once there, poured myself a stiff bourbon. When I turned around, Carlotta stood in front of me.

"I'd like to talk with you sometime, Bert, about the project your father and John B. were working on." She dabbed at her nose with her handkerchief. Her cheeks were slightly sun burnt, her eyes as dark as ground coffee. "This isn't the time or place, I know, but perhaps sometime in the near future we could discuss it?"

"Sure," I said. "Anytime."

"Bert, I want you to know how very sorry I am for everything that happened. Words fail me, they really do," she said.

"I understand. And I understand, too, how you might blame yourself, but it wasn't your fault."

"I knew my brother to be a scoundrel, but didn't think he could do such a thing," she said. "I'm afraid I filled your father's head with my ill will toward Percy," she said.

"My dad had a temper—we all knew that."

She touched me on my arm. "You do understand—I'm sorry, I truly am." Then she walked away.

I finished my bourbon and poured another. I looked around and saw Emma seated at a nearby table and joined her.

"Carlotta's got quite a place here," Emma said.

"Yes, she does."

"Chinese servants, Mexican ranch hands. It's like a little kingdom here, and she's the princess."

"She's torn up about dad's killing."

"She should be."

"Why do you say that?"

"Filling your father's head with stories about her brother—she should have known."

"She had no way—"

"I guess I'm being a little too harsh on her—always have." Emma looked at my glass. "Anymore of that bourbon?"

"I'll get you a glass."

At the drink table, I poured a fresh glass for Emma, refilled my own, and then rejoined her.

"Ma and Josephine are moving back to Vineburg," I said. "Too many memories for them here."

"I can understand that." Emma looked away, and then back at me. "Bert, what did you think about my offer of you moving into the spare bedroom at my place?"

"The barn's okay."

"I know—you could probably sleep standing up—but I wanted to offer it to you. No ulterior motive, if you know what I mean." She winked and sipped her bourbon. "The room's got a decent bed and there's a carpet under your feet, and if you wanted to slip someone in some night, well—my hearing isn't what it used to be."

I laughed. "If I wanted to do that, I'd stay in the barn."

"Women like a clean, tidy nest," she said.

"Sure. A respectable room might be just fine."

After dessert, the guests began leaving in groups, returning to their carriages and filing out of Carlotta's ranch yard. We stood in a line—Ma, Josephine, John B., Gertie and I, and bid each guest goodbye before they left. It was early dusk by now, the air still warm and loud with crickets chirping. Tino had already left for town with the elder Swiss Club members. I walked Emma out to her carriage. Ah Yep and his wife were clearing the tables, carrying the dirty plates and cups back to the kitchen, and bunching the table cloths up to be laundered. After all the guests had left, I walked with Ma and Josephine back to their house across the yard. We sat on chairs in the front portico.

"It's going to be different now," Ma said.

"You'll manage." I assured her.

"Twenty-five years. We've never been separated—leaving Obwalden, arriving here. All that distance, all that moving, and we were always together your father and I—we were good for one another." She began crying again.

I felt helpless. What could I say that I hadn't already said to comfort her? I'd run out of words. Everything now was in time's hands. If anything could heal the wounds that our father's death had opened, it was time—not prayers. Not lighting votive candles in church, no kneeling before a statue. Of all the uncertainties, I banked on time. Nothing stopped time from moving forward. You had to let it happen, though. You had to let go and trust yourself that you'd get through it. Ma was strong and Josephine was, too. If I clung to any faith, it was this faith that they'd move past it. We'd all get past it somehow. What other choice was there?

I hugged both Ma and Josephine, and before leaving, checked in on little Ike. He was asleep next to his mother. The mare looked up at me with those soft, knowing eyes peculiar to a horse. I drove the team back to Emma's, unharnessed Molly and Dolly and gave them an extra scoop of oats. I hung my new coat on a hook, peeled out of my clothes before collapsing onto my cot. "We buried my father today," I whispered to myself. "We buried my father."

22

Moving Ma and Carlotta's Offer

W ithin days of the funeral, I was back at Carlotta's ranch, helping to move Ma and Josephine back to the family property in Vineburg. John B. had brought his wagon, as well, and the two of us, with help from Alfonso, loaded three beds, an oak table and six chairs, three chest of drawers, a couch and two smaller tables into the two wagons. There were clothes, too, and kitchen implements, our father's tools and other smaller items that Ma and Josephine packed into wooden boxes for the second trip.

Ma was in the bedroom closet, removing Dad's clothes one item at a time. "There's shirts and pants for you two boys," she said. "You're all about the same size, so take what you want."

"I'll pick through them later," I said.

"Me, too," John B. added. "I'll look through them when all the moving's done."

The folks' property was in Vineburg— once part of the Huichica Rancheria—straight east out Napa Road about three miles, and just the other side of the railroad tracks. Dad had built a little house and a barn there on ten acres, right before us kids arrived from Switzerland. He'd added two bedrooms later off the south end when he saw how cramped we were. We liked living out there. I know that Ma and my old man did, and they both felt like their dreams of striking out for a distant place and putting down roots had finally come true.

After we'd unloaded the wagons, we pulled the teams into the shade. John B. and I sat in our wagon seats alongside each other.

"You know, Carlotta offered me the ranch foreman's job," John B. said.

"I didn't know that," I said. "What'd you tell her?"

"I said 'no.' Told her I got my place over at Mark West. I think she was disappointed." We passed a canteen of water between us. "I said, 'What about my brother, Bert?'"

"And what she'd say?"

"She said I'll have to ask him." John B. passed the canteen back to me. "I know you got your hauling business, but I was hoping we could finish those chicken houses together. The sooner I finish them, the sooner I can head out."

"Sure, I can help. I think the old man would have liked us working together, don't you?"

"I think he would."

John B. and I returned to Carlotta's with Ma and Josephine riding along with us in the empty wagons. They'd left brooms and mops at the ranch house, cleaning cloths and a bucket, and once the house was completely empty, the two of them started at the backporch and worked their way to the front entry door, sweeping, mopping, dusting as they moved along. John B. and I went over to the stable. I wanted to show him Ike, the new colt.

"He's a beaut—" John B. said. By now Ike was running about, frisky, ducking in and out of his mother's legs. We walked back to the ranch house.

Carlotta soon joined us. She peeked in through the front door. She wore pants and a shirt and her hair tucked up into a stiff-brimmed hat. "My, my," she said. "I've never seen the place so clean—or so empty." No sooner had she said those last words, than she brought a hand to her mouth. "I'm sorry—that didn't come out right."

"That's okay," Ma said. "You're right. It is pretty empty."

With the wagons finally loaded with all the remaining boxes, we were about to set off for Vineburg. Carlotta approached my wagon. "Bert, can we talk sometime soon?"

"How about in a couple of hours?" I said. "I'll be passing by here then on my way back to Emma's."

"That'll be fine," she said.

As we drove back to Vineburg, I wondered whether Carlotta would offer me the job, and if she did, what would I do? It might mean giving up my hauling work and moving from Emma's after she'd already offered me a room in her house. I thought about it all the way to my folks' place. Once there, we unloaded all the boxes, everything we'd hauled. When the wagons were swept out and the heavy lifting done, I hugged Ma and Josephine and turned the team west toward Emma's with a stop at Carlotta's in between. It was late afternoon. Once across Cooper's Bridge, I turned the wagon onto Carlotta's road, and brought the team to a halt under the big oak. Carlotta walked out to meet me.

"You want something to drink?" she asked. "With alcohol or without?"

"With," I said, "If you don't mind."

"How about some red wine? I just opened a bottle over in the garden," she said. "Join me."

We sat down under the trellis. The sun was slipping behind the hills to the west. We clicked our glasses together. She held hers up. "This one's a burgundy from the colonel's vineyards," she toasted." And we both drank.

"The colonel's?"

"My husband's."

"Oh." I let the wine stay in my mouth briefly then swallowed it slowly. Excellent. I wasn't a big wine drinker but I knew what tasted good. "Very fine," I announced, trying to impress her.

"He took great pride in his vineyards." She set her glass down on the table. "But I didn't ask you here to taste my dead husband's wines, did I?" She paused. "There's other matters now that your father has passed." A silence lingered between us.

"Passed," I thought to myself. First time I'd heard the word describe my father's death. I finished the glass and she re-filled it.

"There's two things, actually that I wanted to discuss," she said. "One of them is the absence now of your father here, and the need to find his replacement. So, I'll get right to the point—are you interested in the foreman's job here?" She set her glass down and peered straight into my eyes. She didn't waste any words. Although John B. had already alerted me to the offer, the actual offering still took me by surprise. And I still hadn't decided what to do.

"Carlotta, could I think about it for a day or two?" I asked.

"Of course you can!" she said. "The job would include the house across the yard there where your folks lived and a fifty dollar a month salary. I have a list of the duties if you'd like to look it over."

"Sure," I said. "I'd liked to see the list." She handed me her copy. I glanced at it quickly before folding it and slipping it into my shirt pocket. "I'd have to give up my hauling business?"

"Unless you have the time and energy for both. It's full-time here," she said. "I'd like you to work with your brother to finish the chicken houses. That will involve hauling more lumber, so you'll still be driving your team. And we'll be finding work for them, don't worry. I know that's important for you." She refilled my wine glass.

"I love my horses."

"And now, I understand, you have a new one?"

"I do. Little Ike." And I motioned toward the stable. I finished my wine and she poured what was left into my glass.

"Well, little Ike can stay here where he was born."

"After he's weaned from his mother, Ma and Josephine will need the mare," I said. I emptied my glass and set it back down on the table. "Time to go," I said.

"Wait, there's a second item," she paused. "I intend to retain a criminal attorney to represent your father because I see this matter heading to court. I'll discuss this in full with the rest of your family, but I wanted to alert you beforehand."

"I don't understand how none of that legal stuff works," I said.

"I have some familiarity with it. The point is my brother can't kill someone and get away with it, don't you agree?

"I do." I stood up.

"Do you feel all right?" She looked into my eyes.

"I feel fine. Why do you ask?"

"Well, you just drank most of that bottle of wine."

"Oh, were you saving it?"

"No," she laughed. "I wasn't saving it." Carlotta turned the empty bottle in her hands. "You hold your drink well."

"Yes, ma'm." I'd had plenty of practice by now.

"And you'll give me your answer soon?" she asked.

"I will—by tomorrow, no later than the day after."

"I hope we can work together." She touched me on the arm, and again looked straight into my eyes. They riveted on mine for a second or two and I had to look away—like they were looking too far inside me and I was afraid of what they'd find. Cameron looked at me with those same kind of eyes, those prying, curious eyes that seemed to bore deep into my bones.

I was back in the wagon's seat, feeling a nice little buzz from the wine. I turned the team around and Carlotta stood there near the garden entrance and waved to me as I left. She was smiling. There in the lingering dusk stood a lovely woman, I thought to myself—maybe the loveliest one in the entire valley and she'd just offered me the foreman's job. I waved back. Molly and Dolly knew they were headed to their barn, and they high-stepped it along Napa Road and right onto Grand Avenue.

Emma was sitting on the front porch when I drove past her. She held up a glass. "Got something for you here!" she shouted. Once inside the barn I unharnessed Molly and Dolly. They followed me to their stalls like two big dogs, and waited for their scoops of oats. I slapped each of them on their rumps and they turned their heads and snorted.

Back on the porch, I sat down next to a glass of bourbon. "Got some news for you," I said, leaning toward Emma.

"What now?" Emma rocked back on her chair. "You always got something to tell me."

"Carlotta offered me the foreman's job."

"And what'd you say?"

"I told her I'd have to think about it."

"You'd live there on her ranch?"

"Yeah, that's part of the job," I said, and reached into my shirt pocket and pulled out the list Carlotta had given me. I unfolded it and started to read the items out loud: "Oversees all daily jobs in running ranch, supervise help, feeding cattle, harvests, maintenance of all equipment. Temperance important." I stopped reading. "Does temperance mean what I think it means?"

"It means you can't drink too much."

"That might be a problem."

"Damn, Bert. I don't want you to go!" Emma said. "I gotten used to you being around and who's going to drink with me then?" Emma sat back in her chair. "Here, temperance is not a problem!"

"I know—I like it here fine."

"But it's a step up for you, right?"

"A step up?" I wondered. "I guess—but I'd have to give up the hauling business pretty much."

"But you'd have your own house." She laughed. "Imagine that: Bert Miller in his own house! You won't know what to do in it."

"Sleep and eat just like I do out in your barn."

"You be careful around her, Bert." Emma's voice got serious.

"What do you mean?"

"I mean, she's a beautiful woman and beautiful women have charms about them—and you've told me enough about how you are around women—"

"She's out of my class, Emma. I mean, look at me—ain't ever read a book. I drink more than's healthy. My best coat used to be my dad's. She's got culture or whatever they call it—I got two horses—three now with little Ike—and a wagon."

"Culture? Now that's a fancy word." Emma laughed.

"Something like that."

"Don't sell yourself too short, Bert," Emma said. "You're a good-looking guy and maybe you ain't read a lot of books, but that don't make you stupid—stupid is what people do. And it doesn't make you any less than somebody who's read a whole library. You don't forget that."

"Okay, Emma, I won't."

I'm just telling you—be careful," she said. "I know a little bit of how women work—you may not think so looking at me, but I turned a few heads in my time—I know what women can do."

23

I Accept Carlotta's Offer

I went to bed thinking about Carlotta's job offer. It caused me a lot of tossing and turning through the night—something I don't usually do—wondering what I'd decide. I weighed the advantages and disadvantages: steady work on a beautiful ranch, a steady salary, a house of my own, less wear and tear on my horses and wagon. All of that sounded pretty good. Then I thought about what I'd have to give up: one thing for certain—I was a restless soul, always moving around—not far, but always moving, not gathering dust, and I liked that most working as a teamster. I liked to see the ground moving under my feet—it always meant I was doing something—and not wasting time. I'd like having my own say in matters, too, so if there were days I didn't feel like working, I didn't have to. I could grab my shotgun or rifle and head out with Tino and no one would be barking at me wondering where I went. And there was life out at Emma's and Emma's company, which I'd grown to like. Still, the offer was a chance at something new, a chance to learn more of the ranch trade and see if it was something that suited me. Carlotta figured into my thinking, too—she had to. She was the boss. I wondered what it'd be like working for a woman like her living just yards away, how we'd get along, what disagreements we'd have. I hated to admit it but like most beautiful women, she fascinated me. I realized it was simple foolishness, something any normal man would feel around an attractive woman, but being around her, looking into those eyes, my thoughts got jangled around. I fantasized about her like I fantasized about all the rest until she had me going in circles. I made love to her in these fantasies—I did everything I could to please her. But I remembered Emma's warnings, too. With all this in mind, the next day I rode my bicycle over to Carlotta's and—maybe like a fool—decided to accept her offer.

She was sitting in her garden when I arrived, reading a book with a tea pot and cup in front of her. Her hair was up, exposing her long, slender neck. I leaned my bicycle against the garden fence and said hello. It startled her. She sat upright in her chair.

"I was so caught up in my reading," she said. "You scared me."

I opened the garden gate and approached her. "Sorry." She'd set her book down on the table. "What are you reading?" I asked her.

"Jane Austen."

"Jane Austen?" I asked. "You learning more about chickens?"

"No." She laughed. "She's an English novelist. You haven't heard of her?" She passed me the book and I looked at the cover and thumbed through its pages. There were a lot of words. "Would you like a cup of tea?" she asked.

No, thanks, ma'm—not a big tea drinker." I looked the book's cover over again and handed it back to her.

"Just wine?" she asked.

"Other things, too."

She poured herself another cup of tea.

"I'd like to write someday," I said.

"You would?" She looked at me surprised. "What would you like to write about?"

"Hunting and fishing, maybe—and what my life's been like so maybe someone a hundred years from now would know what I seen and felt—a hundred years from now folks could pick up what I'd written and know somebody like me lived on this earth. I wished my dad had written something, too, because I don't know much about what went on inside him—and now, I'll never know."

"Just get a pen and some paper and start writing, Bert," she said. "Write what's in your heart."

"You think I could do that?"

"Sure you can," she said. "And read—that helps."

"I ain't much of a reader—started some books but never finished them—they put me to sleep. I don't seem to have the patience, either, and ain't ever been a person in a book that I wouldn't rather meet just standing in front of me." I sat across the table from

Carlotta now and studied the book some more. "What does she write about?"

"Relationships, mostly—between men and women."

"Some spicy stuff, huh? Murders and betrayals—that dime-novel stuff?" I asked.

Carlotta laughed. "Yes, I guess you could say that—but more literary." She paused. "Not all relationships are 'spicy' though, as you put it."

"I guess if that's what drove you to read about 'em, you'd want 'em spicy though. Otherwise—"

"Nothing happens?" She finished my sentence.

"Oh, I don't know," I said. "I ain't no expert on relationships, but I can't see reading about what goes on between a man and a woman unless it spikes my interest."

"You're not interested in learning more about the nature of these relationships?" she asked.

"The nature?"

"Yes—you know—what's underneath them—what makes them work or not work."

"I guess things got their own reasons for working or not working," I said.

"Well, I'm no expert, but I do enjoy reading about them." She fingered the corner of her book. "You're not in a relationship?"

"No, m'am—that's John B.'s line of work," I said. I thought of Cameron and my budding interest in her but that was no relationship yet by any stretch. Relationship was a big word and it happened over time and I was mostly impatient to develop one. I wanted it happening right out of the gate.

She laughed again. "Did you get a chance to look over the list I gave you?"

"I did."

"And what did you decide?"

"I'm going to accept your offer," I said.

"Wonderful!" And she clapped her hands together.

"And if I don't pan out, you'll tell me, right?" I said.

"I will." She reached to take my hand. "And if it's not to your liking, you'll tell me, as well?"

"I will."

"You've already worked with Alfonso," she said. "He's got two other brothers that work here with him. You might have to brush up on your Spanish, though."

"We understand each other enough," I said.

"And I do want those chicken houses finished, so that's a bit of a priority."

"I understand." Right up to arriving at Carlotta's a half hour ago I was still uncertain about taking the job, and thought I'd see how our meeting unfolded first, and then decide. Maybe it was her eyes. Maybe it was how beautiful she looked sipping her tea. Maybe it was a chance at something new—- another step moving forward. Maybe I was a fool—maybe it was all of these—I didn't know. I'd take my chances—roll the dice and see what numbers came up.

"How soon can you start?" she asked.

"Give me a couple of days," I said. "I need to give notice to Schocken up at the quarry that I won't be hauling block for him anymore."

"Will that be a problem?"

"Shouldn't be—there's plenty of gypo teamsters around."

"Do you need furniture?" she asked. "If you do, there's a store-room with a bed, chests of drawers you can have. It was left over from the move over here from the east side." Her expression changed just then—like she'd suddenly remembered something—maybe something painful. I didn't know—I was always trying to read people's faces—seeing how the faces matched up to what they were saying—or weren't saying.

"Sure, I could use some furniture," I said. I didn't want to tell her that the only furniture I owned was a cot and a cheap set of drawers but it was all I ever needed.

"Alfonso can show you where the storeroom is."

I stood up. "I guess that's it for now?"

"I think so. There'll be questions, I'm sure, as we move along, but we can address them when that time comes."

"I think so."

Carlotta followed me out the gate. When she saw my bicycle she walked up to it and ran her hand across its handlebars.

"I love it!" She looked at me. "Where did you buy it?"

"At Breitenbach's."

"Here in town?"

"Yeah, here in town."

"I want one!" She flashed that little-girl delight once again.

"I'm sure they'd love to sell you one."

"Oh, I'm excited!" She moved the bicycle away from the fence. "Are they hard to ride?"

"Not if you've got good balance—"

"Oh, I do—I once took ballet lessons, if you could imagine that!"

"Well, then, you're set."

"Okay, Bert," she said. "I look forward to working with you."

I pushed off on my bicycle and Carlotta watched me closely as I rode away. She smiled like a little girl would smile, like a wish she'd made just came true.

24

Moving Day

• • • • • • • • • • • •

I drove the team up to Schocken's Quarry the morning after telling Carlotta I accepted her offer, and gave the boss there, Hal Wise, notice I wouldn't be hauling block anymore. He asked me why, and I told him, and he said he'd miss seeing me around and wished me luck. I hauled one last load before saying goodbye to the quarry workers, and they all shook my hand. Down at the depot I told the lumpers, as well, and when they found out I'd be working at Carlotta's, Diego, one of the lumpers, winked his eye at me and said, "Maybe you end up owning the ranch?"

I laughed. "Not a chance."

"But you never know, do you?" He smiled and we shook hands.

"No, you don't."

After leaving the depot and shaking everyone's hand, and promising to stop by and see them, I paid a visit to Tino. I felt bad in a way that I hadn't smoked my decision over with him before meeting with Carlotta. I don't know why I didn't—maybe because I knew Tino wouldn't approve—that he never liked Carlotta—was suspicious of her from the get-go. And I knew that Carlotta wanted my decision soon and I went ahead with my gut instincts although my gut instincts told me to be careful with this one. I know that if either Tino or I had to decide something, we'd hash it out over a pail of beer or a bottle of the harder stuff. Each of us could see things the other couldn't. We were like business partners that way—an extra set of eyes for each other.

"Why'd you do that?" he wanted to know.

Right off, his response confirmed what I'd suspected. "Seemed like the right thing to do."

"The right thing to do?" he repeated. "But what about your hauling business? And what about having time for yourself? That's seven days a week out there."

"No, it ain't seven days a week."

"You saw the hours your old man worked, didn't you?"

"Well, yeah."

"I hope she's paying you good."

"Fifty dollars a month, a house to live in, a couple of other benefits," I said.

"Sounds to me like you're giving up your freedom, Bert—your independence." Tino shoveled oats into a wheelbarrow. "You were doing pretty good with your team and wagon. Steady work. Folks liked the work you done. If you got a wild hair up your ass, you could take some days off." He stopped shoveling and looked off. "I don't know—I don't think I would've done it myself."

"But that's you," I said.

"Yeah, I know that's me. But how different are we? We like pretty much the same things. We think the same."

"I don't know how to answer that, Tino. I mean, we're alike in a lot of things, but we're different, too—we just are."

"And Carlotta? She's a weird one, Bert. A beauty, for sure—and you can't tell me that didn't enter into your decision, right? I know you and pretty women, Bert Miller." He stopped shoveling. "But watch out for her."

"Why? Because she's got money?" I asked.

"No, it's more than that," Tino said. "She sits out there in her big house with the Chinaman running around powdering her ass, or whatever he does, and she reads her books. And then *her kind* come up from the city to visit her because she's too good for folks around here." A scowl ran across his face.

"What does it matter what she does? What company she keeps?"

"You'll just be another one of her servants, that's all."

"I'll be working for her. If it's not to my liking, I'll walk," I said. "I got the horses, the wagon, plenty of folks to haul for." I put my foot up on the wheel of a nearby carriage. "What the hell, it's worth a shot."

"Then there's that no-good brother of hers."

"She hates him as much as we do," I said.

"Yeah, but he's still on the scene, even more so now with what he done to your old man."

I'd heard enough— no point in mentioning Carlotta's offer to hire an attorney—none of that. Right then it didn't matter because Tino wasn't interested in hearing anymore of what I had to say. "Okay, Tino—I gotta go." We shook hands. "You got me thinking about it."

"Just don't go into it blind, that's all," he said. "Look out for yourself 'cause no one else will."

I drove the team toward Carlotta's, and now after talking with Tino, thinking I'd made a mistake accepting her job offer. Back and forth, back and forth I went as usual, and even thought of just passing by Carlotta's and not stopping, and telling her later that I changed my mind. But I couldn't bring myself to do it. I couldn't pass by her place. I drove the team into her yard instead, and up to where John B. was working on the chicken houses. By now he'd dug out a hole where each pier post would sit. The floor beams would run across the tops of these pier posts and over these beams the tongue and groove redwood flooring.

John B. looked up from where he was working. I stepped down from the wagon and joined him.

"Carlotta says you signed on here," he said.

"I did. I won't ever replace the old man, but I'll give it a shot."

"Yeah, it's odd not seeing him here," John B. said. "I keep looking up and expecting him to be walking across the yard, and instead, I look up and I don't see any one."

I shook my head. "I think about him a lot," I said. "Replaying what happened and hoping it'd turn out different but it never does. He's lying there in the dirt with four bullet holes in him, staring up at the sky and I'm wondering what his last thoughts were." I saw the scene yet again in my mind. "We're stuck with it, John B. and we gotta make sense out of something that don't make sense."

"How do you do that?" he asked.

"I don't know."

By now Carlotta had joined us. She wore what I'd often seen her wear around the ranch—khaki pants and shirt, a bandana around her neck and her hair tucked up into a stiff-brimmed hat.

"Good morning, Bert!"

"Carlotta." I tipped my hat.

"How are you boys doing?" she asked.

"We're getting through it," John B. said.

"It's a shame, it really is." Carlotta looked at both of us. None of us said anything. Then she looked at me. "Bert, did you tell John B. about my offer to retain an attorney?"

"No, not yet," I said.

"John B., I'll tell you what I told Bert earlier—that I intend to retain an attorney when this matter of your father's death goes to trial. Your mother and I have talked it over and we're not accepting a hastily called jury's decision—not when it's all my brother's cronies."

"You think it'll go to trial?" John B. asked.

"Oh, it will. My brother just can't walk away from killing someone, especially someone like your father."

"We're for it," John B. said. "I know Ma's having a hard time with it, but she's not the vengeful type."

"It's not a matter of vengeance, John B," she said. "It's a matter of justice." Another stretch of silence followed. Carlotta took a paper out of her shirt pocket and walked around the job site. It was a drawing of the brooder house and she rotated it, trying to orient the drawing to what John B. had laid out. I moved closer, guiding her hand. "Okay, now I see it," she said.

"Carlotta, I thought when you had time, we'd look at that furniture you mentioned," I said.

"Of course," she said. "Let's look at it now. It's in a storeroom in the corner of the barn. I'll show you."

We walked to the barn and just inside to the left was an enclosed room. She opened the door, brushed aside some cobwebs, and we entered. It was stacked with furniture: tables, chairs, bed frames, head boards, mirrors. Some of them were covered with canvas tarps, and she pulled the covers back. "You could furnish a whole house here," she said.

"Why don't you use them?" I wondered.

"After we had the house built here and moved from the colonel's property on the east side, it was all his furniture, and honestly, it didn't suit my tastes."

"So you bought new furniture?" I asked her. Of course she could buy new furniture if the old didn't suit her—people with money could do that sort of thing.

"We did." She pushed more of the coverings back to expose several chests of drawers. They were big, bulky pieces built from dark wood—maybe a teak or a walnut—and all of them engraved with fancy scrolls and branches of trees with broad leaves—very different from the simple furniture I was used to.

"You can use whatever you like," Carlotta said. "Alfonso can help you move them."

"I think I'll walk through the house first and see what might fit and what won't. Then I'll decide."

"That sounds like a good idea," Carlotta said.

I closed the storeroom door after us, and we walked over to the house where I'd be living. It was the original ranch house, a single story white-washed adobe with a tile roof and a portico that ran along its front wall. Wisteria wrapped around each of the portico's posts. It was cool inside, even on the hottest days, and it had a fireplace for heat during the winter. Once inside, we walked through the entire house. The floor was a checkerboard of big square fired tiles. As we walked through, Carlotta pointed to where some of the pieces might fit—a couch in the front room with end tables, a bed and chest of drawers with a mirror in one bedroom, where to hang some of the pictures brought over from the colonel's. She delighted in making suggestions. And me? Did I care? I was fine with any of it. After all, I was used to sleeping in barns and empty horse stalls, sometimes on a cot, other times on a bed of straw, hanging my clothes on harness hooks, washing my face in a bucket full of water, so having a place of my own with furniture and a real bed, a kitchen, a pump outside for water—it was like having my biscuits with an extra serving of gravy spread over the top.

"So, what do you think, Bert? Does it suit you?" She pushed her hat back.

"I think it's fine," I said, and looked around once again at the bare walls, the empty rooms. My folks lived here briefly, I thought, and pictured them moving about the rooms—the little touches Ma made to make the place their own—but most of the time they lived here, I'd been booted out of the house and not talking to my old man, so I rarely visited, and for that, the place didn't hold any special memories for me. It's not like I'd look at the kitchen and see my folks sitting at a table there—or see them sitting in the living room—the old man asleep in a stuffed chair. No, the house didn't hold those kinds of memories for me, and that came as a relief.

"I think I'll head out to Emma's and gather my things there," I said.

"Let me know, and I'll alert Alfonso so he can help you move the furniture," Carlotta said.

"Sure thing," I said. I climbed back onto the wagon, said good-bye to Carlotta and drove out Napa Road, heading west to Emma's. Once there, I backed the wagon into Emma's barn, lifted the tail-gate out and swept the wagon clean again. I slid my cot in first with all its bedding, emptied the contents of the chest of drawers into a pair of wooden boxes and lifted the chest onto the wagon. By now Emma appeared.

"So you're really going, huh Bert? Can't talk you out of it?" I could hear the disappointment in her voice.

"I am, Emma—for better or worse." I slid one of the wooden boxes onto the back of the wagon. "Hell, I'm just down the road—it ain't like I moved out of the county."

"I know," she said. "And you better stop by for a glass every now and then, or Emma here will never forgive you."

"I promise—on a stack of Bibles I'll never read."

"Did you forget about that Cameron gal already?" Emma laughed.

"Not entirely. I did stop by her store and bought the bunting I draped around the wagon, but it was an awkward visit with my dad's death and all, and I mostly stared down at the floor, not knowing what to say or what to tell her—like I said—it was mostly awkward."

"You losing interest?"

"Hell, Emma, I don't know. So much has been going on lately I ain't had much time to think about her."

"Just as well. Let things settle out." Emma stepped away from my wagon. "Well, I'll let you get about your business here," Emma said. "Stop by the house before you go."

"Sure will."

There wasn't much left to load—some extra harness I kept, and my box of tools, some spare parts for the wagon, my bicycle—that was it. I looked over the room where I'd been living for over a year now and thought it'd been a good room, and except for what happened to my old man, a pretty good stretch of time in my life: I got my own horses and wagon and carved out a decent living and was able to do pretty much as I pleased. I had a couple of dollars in the bank too, and no one trying to reel me in—no one telling me how to live my life—that was my father's job and now he was gone. I was walking away from an earlier lifestyle and trying on a new one—like a suit I'd outgrown—but didn't know exactly why. Was it opportunity? A chance for something bigger? That's the word I overheard so often before coming to this country—opportunity—spelled out in big letters.

There was pickings here—a chance to make something of your life, a chance to start out small and if the chips fell right, a chance to keep adding on. But that kind of thinking didn't hold me so much. I didn't care for accumulating a lot of things. I didn't really care if I was a success or not. Sure, I wanted things to work out and not have them fall apart—who wants to end up sitting on a pile of rubble after they worked so hard? And I didn't want to work for nothing, neither. But I wasn't aiming to be any Rockefeller—I just wanted my cut, that's all—a small cut from the bigger pie. Some days that cut was just a good bourbon that went down easy and pleasant company—and maybe hidden in the crowd somewhere, looking over someone's shoulder, was a woman whose eyes were set on me.

I walked over to Emma's for a parting drink, still wondering why I was making this move. I knew I couldn't live in a tack room all my life and there were some comforts I felt were overdue. But then I started thinking about Carlotta and wondering how much the draw of a lovely woman's eyes had to do with my decision, a woman so distant from my own world she could have been from another planet. I hoped she wasn't the reason—the only reason— that I was making this next move. I wanted to be clear-headed about it, but honestly, I didn't know. Honestly, when it came to me and a clear head we were sometimes strangers and I could be fooling myself all over again.

25

Settling In
· · · · · · · · · ·

With Alfonso's help, we moved Carlotta's furniture from the storeroom into the ranch house. She directed where she thought the pieces best fit, and Alfonso and I just followed her orders. We placed a couch and a low table in the living room, a table and chairs in the kitchen, a bed with a massive headboard and a chest of drawers in one bedroom, a smaller bed and chest of drawers in the other bedroom. My cot went out to the storeroom, the extra harness and tools to the stable. I looked around at a house that for the first time in my life I could call my own.

"You'll need dishes, silverware, pots and pans, too, won't you?" Carlotta asked.

"I'll buy them at Pauli's," I said. It'd be a chance to see Cameron and take the temperature between us. I'd been busy, true, but there were times I was tempted to stop in and see if anything felt different, but I never did. I thought it best just to let things simmer between us.

"Why don't you look over what's in the store room," Carlotta said. "No point in buying things we already have, is there?" She stood in the doorway, sunlight framed her silhouette. "What about bed linens? Sheets? Towels?

"Yeah, I guess I'll need them." I'd never been much on the domestic stuff—a towel, a straight razor, long underwear, a few pair of stockings—I travelled light.

"You guess?" she asked. "How did you live before?"

"Different than this—simpler," I said.

"Bert, these are just suggestions. You realize that, don't you?"

"I know—I guess I've always lived simple—making do with what I had."

"And now you don't have to—unless that's your choice."

"No, I think I'm ready for a little more comfort."

Carlotta laughed. "You're such a primitivist," she said.

"A what?" Carlotta was hell for throwing words at me I didn't understand. I sometimes wondered why she did it—was it to show my ignorance? Or was it her attempts at trying to enlarge my world?

"Never mind—it's someone who lives simply." She half-turned toward her house and then stopped. "Can you start work tomorrow?"

"I can."

"Alfonso and his brothers handle most of the feeding and daily livestock work," she said. "I was hoping you could work with your brother and speed that project along."

"Sounds good to me," I said.

She started to leave but saw my bicycle leaning against a post in the front of the house. She pointed toward it. "Bert, can I try riding it?"

"Sure, go ahead."

She wheeled it out into the yard and straddled the frame. She tried to sit in the bicycle seat but her feet didn't reach the ground. "What do I do?" She looked confused.

"The bicycle's too big for you but you can still pedal it."

"How do I do that?"

I stood alongside her. "Now sit up on the seat and I'll steady you."

"Like this?" She raised herself up to the seat. The bicycle wobbled from one side to the other. I held her around her waist. "Don't let go!"

"I'm going to push you along—now steady yourself! That's it! Now, I'll give a big shove and you'll be on your own."

"Oh, Bert, I don't know—"

"There's no other way to learn." I was trotting alongside her now. "Get ready! I'm going to let you go!" I could feel the muscles in her back working to keep her balance.

"All right," she said. "I think I'm ready. Let go!"

I gave her a big shove and the bicycle rolled away from me and across the yard with Carlotta still sitting on the seat. "Pedal!

You need to pedal!" I shouted. Her feet caught the pedals and she circled the yard.

"Oooooooweeeee!" She circled the yard. "Now, how do I stop?"

"Don't worry about that now! Just keep pedaling until you feel the balance."

She circled the yard several more times. "Okay, now I want to stop," she said.

"This is the tricky part," I said. "Push back on one of the pedals and that will be the brake. But once the bike stops rolling, you'll need to get a foot down on the ground to catch your fall."

"Do I have to stop?"

"No, you can just keep riding for days and days," I said. "Why stop?"

She laughed. "Okay, I'm ready to stop." The front tire started to wobble. "What do I do again?"

"Push back on the right pedal and that should stop you."

The bicycle came to a near-stop and began to teeter.

"Lean the bicycle over so your foot touches the ground!"

"Like this—"

Carlotta and the bicycle both crashed to the ground. I ran over and helped her up. My hands fit neatly around each of her hips as I lifted her. "Are you okay?"

"I'm fine," she laughed. "Just my pride that's hurt."

"You did fine."

"What about the bicycle?"

"Don't worry about it."

She dusted herself off.

"You need a smaller-framed bicycle."

"They have those?"

"They do. They can make one to fit you."

"Wonderful!"

I pushed the bicycle over to the portico and leaned it against the wall.

"That's my lesson for the day," she said.

"You're a natural," I told her.

I watched her walk away across the yard, open the gate to her garden and disappear among the roses. I sat down on a kitchen chair and found the jobs she'd listed on the piece of paper and looked them over once again. It was mostly a beef and a dairy cattle operation spread over five hundred prime acres, three hundred for grazing and two hundred for growing oat hay that was harvested early to mid summer. Alfonso's brothers milked a small herd of dairy cattle twice a day. Carlotta had teams of horses, as well, a hay wagon, a regular work wagon like the one I owned, and her own carriage pulled by a chestnut-colored mare. There were different farm implements, too: a rake, a mower to cut hay, a two-bottom plow and a disc. Alfonso and his two brothers lived in another, smaller house on the ranch and they did most of the daily work. My job was to supervise, make sure everything was in working order, to help John B. finish the chicken houses, and to meet with Carlotta before any major decisions were to be made on ranch operations.

Later that evening I was lying on the couch, staring at the ceiling, thinking about all the recent changes in my life—that regardless how much you plan for things, events happen you could never foresee— and those plans that once pointed you in a certain direction didn't hold much water anymore. When that happens, you're forced to strike out to some new place—most often a place you haven't been before and it can be strange and scary—like those shadows on Ho's wall. But that seemed the nature of this life—it was full of unknowns, things that could lift you up and just as quickly drag you down. It was hard finding one thing one day that didn't run opposite it the next. You'd look for a solid piece of ground and before you knew it, everything that seemed solid was melting away under your boots and you'd think, 'goddamn, I was fooled again.' In the middle of all this thinking there was a knock on my door. It startled me. I opened it and there stood Carlotta.

"I wanted to show you something your dad built for me." She shifted from one foot to the other. "Do you have a few minutes?"

"Sure," I said.

"It's down by the creek," she said. I followed her. It was the first time I'd seen her without a hat or bandana on her head and her dark hair flowed in long waves down to her shoulders.

We walked through her garden, past the trellised patio and followed a path that led down between stands of oak and bay trees. I heard the creek running below us. The path led us to a little structure build of redwood with a pointed roof, its walls covered with a mesh screen.

"It's a gazebo," she said. "I saw a picture of it in a magazine and showed the picture to your father and asked if he could build it, and he said he could. So, here it is. The mesh keeps the mosquitoes out."

She opened the little door to the gazebo and we both stepped inside. There were two chairs and a small table. A book sat on the table, and alongside the book, Webster's dictionary. She closed the door behind us. From the gazebo you looked down onto an open stretch of creek with oaks towering above it on the opposite bank. "This is my little retreat," she said. "I love to come here and think—or sometimes not to think at all."

"I don't really need a place to think," I said. "It just happens wherever I'm at."

She laughed. "But sometimes don't you want to turn all the thinking off?"

"I guess." I looked up at how my father had framed the roof with all those intricate mitered saw cuts that joined each other right at the top point. "What do you think about?" I asked her.

She laughed again. "All sorts of things—life, love, death—you know, the lighter things in this world."

We both sat down. I glanced over at her as she shifted in her chair and when she looked over at me, I quickly looked off to the creek and then down at the books on the little table.

"Sometimes I come out here *not* to think, too." She turned toward me, brushing a loose strand of hair from her forehead. "Do you ever not want to think? Just have a blank mind? Just have immediate things be your only concern—what you see or touch or smell and nothing else?"

"I guess—I mean, my mind goes blank plenty of times."

She laughed again. "You're funny, Bert."

"Did my dad ever sit out here with you?" I'd often wondered about the two of them together.

"He did."

"And what did you talk about?"

"The work here—plans—the future," she said. Her eyes got that far-away look. "He talked about you and John B. and Josephine. He was a dear man, and I miss him. I really do."

I wondered just then what my father had told her about me. That I was the troublesome son? The one who kept him up at night worrying? He didn't have a lot of good words to say about me—I knew that, but sometimes folks changed their tune when talking to someone else and say things about you they'd never say straight to your face. What I done or what he said about me is what I deserved—and if he said anything different, it'd be a lie.

"Yeah, I'm looking at this little house and admiring his work," I said. "I forget at times just how good he was."

"It's funny, though, with you sitting there, it's like he's back again with me, but only a younger version. You two look so much alike—even more than John B. does—the color of your eyes—that kind of grayish blue. The nose—everything." She touched my hand. I just kept it there with her hand resting on the top of mine. It was quiet enough to hear the creek water below, quiet enough to hear my own heart beat, I thought. In the distance, a cow bawled from across the creek.

"I wanted to ask you something," I said.

"What's that?"

"The day I first met you—when I delivered the lumber." I stumbled for more words. "Do you remember that day?"

"I do."

"And when you and my father showed up, I could see you'd been crying. Why?"

She gathered herself, moved her hand off of mine. "Because Alfonso had told me earlier that he'd seen my brother crossing the property after I told him if he did he'd be trespassing. My brother had just ignored a court injunction issued against him, an injunction I thought would finally put an end to this matter." She paused here and looked out across the creek. "Then your father offered to intercede, and he stiffened up the gate out there and told me if Percy tried it again, he'd stop him at the gate. I thanked him for the offer—it was reassuring but I asked him not to get involved. Your father had a way of calming me down."

These were sides to my father that I rarely saw, but then again there were sides to all folks that we didn't see—we couldn't see. How could we? We only knew a fraction of what someone was really like—the rest of it hidden behind the walls and underbrush of the heart and mind. You could talk to two different people about a third, and discover things about that person you never imagined, sometimes things so different you'd think it had to be another person entirely.

And as I sat and listened to Carlotta, I was seeing a different side to my father—one he kept mostly hidden—a warmer, more thoughtful side he rarely showed to me but I could understand why. I wondered, too, what my father's feelings were toward Carlotta. Could he look at this beautiful woman the way I'm looking at her now and only see her as his boss and not feel anything deeper? Anything romantic? Could he somehow resist the draw toward her that I was feeling myself? And if he did feel something, what happened to those feelings? Did he bury them somewhere? Deny they even existed? This was about emotions I rarely, if ever, saw my father show. The more common ones, yes—anger, frustration, the grief I brought him. But love? Affection? Tenderness? Those seemed strangers to him—not really part of his language. I knew he felt something somewhere—he wasn't an unfeeling man by any stretch. He just didn't show them. He didn't express them—even with Ma. They rarely touched. There were few signs of outward tenderness. What existed between them was something understood, something unspoken. Something they had both accepted about being together. And maybe this quiet acceptance was something stronger, even, than anything they could have said to one another.

"Maybe we should go?" Carlotta suggested. "I'm sure you have things to do."

I opened the door for her and she stepped down onto the path. I followed. We shook hands and parted at her garden gate. I walked across the ranch yard to my new old house, walked inside and looked around to make sure everything was real, that it wouldn't disappear with the blink of an eye. I laid down on a bed without any sheets or blankets and fell asleep.

26

The Work Routine
· · · · · · · · · · · · · · · · · ·

My first full morning at Carlotta's ranch started out with John B. and the chicken houses. We were building two of them. The first one, a brooder house, was where the young chicks would stay their first eighteen weeks before moving them to the second house, the layer house, where they'd mature and begin laying eggs as young pullets and live out the rest of their lives. The plan was to build the brooder house first and once completed, Carlotta could move her chicks in. Then we'd start on the layer house and finish it by the time the chicks had grown into pullets. Carlotta and Dad had designed the layer house to have nesting boxes built out from the exterior walls along the building's east side. These boxes had a roof built over them that lifted in sections, so that one could reach in and gather eggs without having to enter the inside of the house.

John B. wanted to pour concrete around each of the pier posts, so he sent me off with my team and wagon in the early morning to William Green's lumber yard at Sonoma Landing for gravel, sand, and cement. I returned by early afternoon. Alfonso mixed the sand and gravel right out of the end of my wagon and then shoveled the mix into wheelbarrows where we sprinkled in the cement and water until it was a thick, gray slurry. We then poured the mixture around the base of each post. We worked late into the afternoon and poured roughly half the posts. The three of us worked together well. John B. was more forgiving than our father, more patient, too, didn't bark at me when my focus wandered. The old man's name came up more than once, and we'd stop, lean on the end of our shovels, and share a story about him and have a good laugh. For all our differences, I missed the guy.

By mid-week, we had poured concrete around all the pier posts and had spanned the posts with 3x4 floor beams running from one side of the structure to the other, a distance of twenty feet. Now it was time to lay down the tongue and groove redwood flooring across those beams. John B. had placed the flooring order two weeks before the shooting and it was scheduled to arrive at the Sonoma Depot on Thursday morning. I hitched up Molly and Dolly, Alfonso jumped up on the seat next to me and we drove to the depot.

"How you like work?" Alfonso asked.

"Good. *Bueno*," I said.

"And *la senora?* Very pretty, no?" He smiled.

"Yes, she is," I said. We drove east on Napa Road, turned onto Fifth Street and followed United States Avenue to the plaza before turning north toward the depot. The morning was still cool, the air so clear, everything seemed surrounded in big drops of rain water. The harness creaked and the wagon shuddered when it hit a pot hole.

`"To me she seem—how do you say—*triste?*" He lit a small cigar.

"She seems sad to you?"

"*Si*—*m*aybe because her husband die—and now your father. I don't know." Alfonso looked over and offered me a cigar. I took it and thanked him. He struck a match against his thigh. "I do not understand women—sometime the most beautiful the most sad."

"Well, Alfonso, that makes two of us," I said. And we both laughed.

I thought about what Alfonso had just said. Why would a beautiful, wealthy woman not feel sadness? Why wouldn't she feel what every other woman felt? Every other man, for that matter? What made them different? Was it because they were beautiful and wealthy, and most others weren't that we looked at them different, apart from the rest? I know I did—I had to admit it. As much as I knew all of us were heaped together in this mix and we all had about the same feelings, I knew there were those at the top—the upper crust—and the rest of us were somewhere below,

and we looked at those at the top different—not necessarily better, just different—like money and wealth could spare them from
feeling what the rest of us felt. I knew it wasn't like that. The rich
had the same reasons for feeling miserable as the rest of us—and
sometimes it was the money itself that made them miserable.

This was a time a few at the top were making grand fortunes—
the Rockefellers, the Carnegies—and folks wondered how these guys
could ever feel sad having all that money. But it didn't work out
that way. Rich folks could be just as miserable as the poor—sometimes even worse. Still, I looked at Carlotta as different, astounded
that someone as lovely as her could feel sadness when so much in
her world seemed perfect, provided for. She was like a princess in
her own little kingdom. But I knew the world—anyone's world—
isn't perfect. No such world exists. No matter the wealth, we all had
to slog through this life—this imperfect life—but having a couple
of dollars in your pocket made the slog easier. Just a couple of dollars—that's all I ever needed.

"Did you know her husband?" I asked.

"*Si*—*a*n old man—older than my father even. It did not seem
right to me."

"Right?" It seemed an odd word to use.

"The two of them together—more like father and daughter, you
know? He walk around always in good clothes—a fine suit. Not
clothes for work like me and you."

"He was a politician," I said.

"*Si. Un politico. Un jefe.*" Alfonso laughed.

I tried to imagine the two of them together—young Carlotta and
the older Stamm. Alfonso was right—it did seem an odd pairing.
The older Stamm in his coat and starched shirts, probably smoking a fat cigar the way most politicians did. The much younger
Carlotta, escaping in her novels—one moment wandering about
the ranch in her khakis, the next, in a splendid dress—entertaining
her husband's guests from the big city.

"*Muchas fiestas.*"

"What kind of parties?" I wanted to know.

"*Gente* from the city come here," he said. "The men all look like colonel. The women in big dresses. Drink wine, eat all *fin de semana.*"

Here I was trying to piece together this puzzle of a woman. Why, I asked myself? What was the point? What did I need to know about her other than she was my boss, my employer? Why stray any further? Why tease myself into thinking it was anything more? Why even consider such a long-shot?

Every little piece I learned about her, though, seemed to pull me further into a hole that got deeper and deeper. I'd done the same thing with Cameron, now that I thought about it. Cameron was a woman as distant to me as Carlotta was. But with Cameron it wasn't a class difference so much but a difference in beliefs—her Bible, a book of fairy tales to me, and her faith in an all-knowing, merciful God that I'd stopped believing in years ago. If he was so all-knowing, so damn merciful, I thought, why did he allow my father to get killed? Why did he allow all the suffering that I seen, that I'd read about in the newspapers? But it didn't matter for a time with Cameron because I thought romance, if it ever showed its head, would bridge those differences—maybe even change her.

But people don't change so easy. They don't cough up their beliefs on a whim—not for some guy who comes along and tells her how beautiful she looks while they're sitting alongside a creek. I know I hung onto whatever I thought was right. Something seems stamped into us when we're born, and growing up our folks pound their beliefs into our heads and we swallow them whole until we don't swallow them anymore because they don't line up with what we're seeing. Then what do we do? Fight hard to hold on to them? Or toss them overboard and believe in something else? Or, like I done, not believe in anything at all—that seemed the safest.

We arrived at the depot with the train and its flatcar loaded with tongue and groove lumber pulled off to a side rail. I positioned the wagon, and the lumpers loosened the ropes securing the lumber and began handing down the individual lengths to Alfonso and me. As the wagon filled, we could see it would take more than one trip to off-load all the lumber. With the wagon load topped off, we made a separate stack at the depot yard that we could return to later.

"Chickens," Alfonso said. "*Gallinas*. What she want with more chickens?"

"She likes eggs for breakfast," I said.

"*Si*, but cheaper to buy them, no?"

"She doesn't think that way, Alfonso. Maybe she wants to sell the eggs, too."

"*Si, es posible.*"

"She can do whatever she wants, can't she?"

Alfonso nodded his head. "*Si, eso.*" He looked over at me. "My cousin he raise the—how you say *'gallos'*?"

"You mean 'roosters?' For fighting?"

"*Si, eso.* Maybe you go with me sometime and we watch them fight?"

"No thanks, Alfonso. I don't go for that kind of thing."

"No?"

"No, I don't like to see animals made to do that—just seems too cruel," I said. Our conversation about the fighting cocks ended.

Back at the ranch, we unloaded the lumber. John B. looked over the different lengths. "Good stuff," he said as he sighted down some of the pieces. "Nice and straight—hardly any knots, either."

Once the wagon was unloaded, Alfonso and I drove back to town to load the balance. When we passed Pauli's Dry Goods, I slowed to look through the window to see if I could spot Cameron. She was inside, waiting on a customer, so Alfonso and I drove on. We loaded the remaining lumber with the stack head-high, so we tied it down tight so the load wouldn't shift forward. We set out back to the ranch, and unloaded the second load by late afternoon. I unhitched the wagon, and led the horses into their new home in Carlotta's stable where I unharnessed them, and they followed me into their stalls. It was my first day working for Carlotta and a good, full one.

27

Building
· · · · · · · · ·

Once John B. and I had laid the tongue and groove flooring
across the 3" x 4" beams, Alfonso and I hauled three loads of
redwood siding from the train depot back to the ranch. There was
another load of framing lumber, as well, that we'd used to frame
the walls of the layer house. By now the brooder house was starting
to take shape. You could see its length and width and the height
of its walls. Once we added diagonal bracing and the redwood siding—wide 1" x 12" boards—the entire structure stiffened so that
we could start framing the roof.

In our trips back and forth, Alfonso talked freely in his mixture
of Spanish and English, and I learned more and more about life at
Carlotta's ranch and about life in general around Sonoma. He told
me about the ranch boundaries, and how Carlotta had expanded
her holdings to include the western boundary of the ranch that
ran up to the foothills, and it was here where Tino's mother and
grandfather lived. I'd visited there with Tino several times before
we went out hunting doves. Miguel, the grandfather, was very old,
and his eyes had the blue and white circles inside them common to
old folks, but he still worked around the little homestead, tending
to his chickens and a goat, and a garden patch where he grew corn,
beans, and squash. "*La señora* work at the rancho before," Alfonso
said.

"Tino's mother?" I asked.

"*Si,* many years before."

"You're sure?"

"*Si, estoy seguro.* She leave—I think something happen with
Carlotta's brother."

I knew Tino's mother worked at the ranch years before but
left to care for her aging father, at least, that's what Tino told me,

although I never understood why old Miguel didn't move closer to town. When I asked Tino, he said his grandfather was scared of being sick from the white men. He'd seen many of this tribe wiped out years before from small pox.

"And Tino lived here with her?" I asked.

`"No she move away. Tino come later."

"And Tino's father? Where was he?"

Alfonso shook his head. "*Pues, yo no se.*"

"You don't know? Or you won't tell me?"

"No, I don't know—only rumors."

"Rumors?" I asked. "What kinds of rumors?"

"Several different fathers."

"Alfonso, there can only be one father."

"*Pues, yo no se.*"

Alfonso clammed up, lit another cigar and said nothing else until we arrived back at the ranch. When we pulled up to the building site, Carlotta was standing next to John B. with a copy of the building plans in her hand. I pulled the wagon to a halt, stepped down and walked toward her.

"It's really starting to take shape, isn't it, Bert?" she said.

"Yes it is."

She looked back at John B. "How long before I can order the chickens?"

John B. looked at the structure. "Let's see—once the walls are up, we can frame the roof. Then there's the skip sheeting to nail on and then the shingles." He thought a few moments. "I'd say two weeks should do it. Then there's fencing for the pen—yeah, I'd say about two weeks."

"I'm going to order the chicks out of Petaluma, Bert," she said. "I thought we'd ride over together when they're ready to pick up. Is that okay?"

"Sure," I said. "You're the boss."

"It's exciting, isn't it?" she said. There was that smile of hers again, that little girl's delight all across her face. "And you know what else?"

"What else?" I asked.

She looked at me and then at John B. "I went down to Breitenbach's and they fitted me for a bicycle of my own! It'll be a week or two, they said."

"Great!" I said. "You'll be riding everywhere in no time."

"And I don't care if it's not lady-like to ride one. I really don't care," she said. It was this independence, this fiery spirit of Carlotta's, that attracted me so.

Alfonso had positioned the wagon and began loosening the ropes holding the load of siding down. We'd made several stacks of siding and set up saw-horses along the stacks where we could cut the different measurements. Once the work started, John B. would call out a number and I'd measure it on the board and saw to that mark. The siding went up quickly where there were solid walls, but where there were windows we had to cut and fit for the openings, and frame door openings at each end of the building.

Once we'd hauled in the material to frame the gabled roof and ran all the rafters out, we hauled in two loads of skip sheeting, 1" x 4" planks, 16 feet in length that ran along the tops of the rafters and what we nailed the shingles to. The shingles arrived in bundles two days later. With each trip down to the depot with Alfonso, I learned more about the ranch, about Carlotta and the colonel. I always had questions for Alfonso, and I didn't know exactly why, except I was driven to learn everything I could about Carlotta—it was becoming an obsession of mine. Who were her guests? How long did they stay? What did they do during their visits? Alfonso would look at me and ask, "Why you have so many questions?"

"Because I'm curious," I said. In manyways it was my undoing.

"Why you curious?" He fished a cigar out of his pocket and lit it.

I couldn't tell him the real reason why, how I thought about her, and the more I learned the more I believed these thoughts might put her in reach. No, that was a secret I kept to myself, not even telling Tino—Tino most of all—because I know how he'd laugh at me. "The farm hand and the princess," I could hear him say. "You're a goddamn dreamer, you know that?"

Once Alfonso's brothers, Raul and Jose, had finished the morning milking and done all the feeding, they helped us nail skip sheeting down, then hefted the bundles of shingles onto the roof. It was a slow and tedious job, but with all of us working, we finished it in two days. Now the building was near weather-tight and once the fence posts set for the outside yard, we could string chicken wire between the posts. At least twice a day Carlotta came out to check our progress. She often brought a pitcher of lemonade and a tray of glasses. We'd sit in the shade of an oak tree, and look over our work while Carlotta talked about the chicks she was buying, the type of feed they'd be eating. When she wasn't reading her novels, she was reading up on how to raise egg-layers.

I sat under the oak, listening to her talk and looking over our work on the chicken house and thinking my life hit another one of those calm stretches. They never lasted very long before another storm blew in, but for now I'd sit with it. Sure, I thought about the shooting and the sour taste it left with me, but I didn't want anything stirred up with Percy Sheers the way Tino wanted. It just seemed more trouble. I wanted those feelings to go away. I wished that the shooting didn't happen—but it did, and now I had to learn to live with it. I couldn't see any other way.

28

At the Mill

· · · · · · · · · ·

O nce the brooder house was finished, Carlotta gave me an order
for feed troughs, watering stations and a chick mash starter
mix to be picked up at Golden Eagle Milling in Petaluma. The
feed was in one hundred pound burlap sacks. It'd be heavy pulling
for Molly and Dolly. I set out early in the morning when it was
coolest, and three miles later, just past the Watmaugh District, I
stopped at the Chancellor Ranch to water the horses. They nosed
at the water but didn't drink much. From Chancellor's, the road
narrowed into Stage Gulch and followed the creek until it rose to
the top of a hill that overlooked the Petaluma Valley.

I lingered here just a bit, and let the horses take a blow. I liked
to look out at the hills that resembled rolling ocean waves, watch
the vultures circling above us, take in the smells—the tar weed in
August, the oat stubble, the adobe dust, and listen to the sound of
red-tailed hawks screeching from the gum trees. This is what I enjoyed most about being a teamster—letting the world around me
soak through my skin.

Just below the hill, the road split: straight ahead was Adobe Road
and Vallejo's old adobe, but if you turned to the west, Stage Gulch
Road continued, curving around even more hills that looked like ocean
swells until it dropped down into the little town of Lakeville. Here you
could smell the brackish air seeping up between the hills long before
the river basin opened in front of you. Here stretching out in front of
you was tidal land, flat as a tabletop, so flat that from the little town,
you didn't even see the water, only tule weeds growing along the river
banks. South a half mile was Donohue's Wharf and to the north six
miles was the wharf district of central Petaluma where I was bound.

I followed Lakeville Road north, a good, long level stretch, and
here Molly and Dolly broke into their rhythmic trot; the sounds

of their hooves making a clatter like a drummer tapping a snare drum, the leather creaking, the metal jangle of harness trees and rolling bass of the wagon wheels all working together to sound like a little marching band to my ears.

This was the music I loved to dream by, where my mind took flight, and I'd be off to any number of places with any number of women. Helga, the wife of Peter, the baker, from our little village in Obwalden had crept onto my makeshift stage lately. Once my father and Ma left our village for America, I spent many cold mornings in Peter and Helga's bakery. With the ovens lit, it was always warm inside, and Helga would give me chores: churning butter, sifting flour, pouring batter into cake pans. We loved to frost cakes together.

I loved the smell of baking bread, loved her smile, and the feel of her touch when our hands met. I sometimes wished that it had been Helga's family I was born into, rather than my own. When word finally came that our folks were sending for us and we had to leave Obwalden, I didn't want to go. I felt safe here. No reason to leave. The morning our grandfather was to take John B., Josephine and me to the train depot, I hid in the hay loft at Helga and Peter's, hoping grandpa would leave without me. Up and down the street I could hear his voice calling out, hear it echoing through our village. "Bert! Arnold Bert! Where are you?" John B. found me, and I boarded the wagon never to see Helga again.

At Washington Street, I turned the team toward the center of town. The Golden Eagle Milling Company was just before the creek, on the south side of Washington Street. It was a massive brick building, with its wharf area just to the west, its loading dock for wagons just off Washington. By now it was ten o'clock in the morning. Several wagons were ahead of me, most of them four-teamed and six-teamed, because of the weight of the feed. I braked my wagon and walked into the shipping office with my order. It was a tiny office, not much bigger than the desk and two chairs that occupied it with a row of sliding windows that looked out onto the dock area. The clerk reviewed my order. "You got a few wagons ahead of you," he said. "So sit tight."

I walked back onto the dock and at the far end I saw a wagon with stacks of feed sacks nearly four feet high, a good load for four horses, but when I looked at what was hitched to the wagon, I saw only one, and it was under-sized, its ribs showing, its withers high, its back already swayed. I walked up to a big-bellied man in overalls standing near the wagon. The stub of a cigar was stuck in the corner of his mouth, the brim of his hat eaten away.

"You ain't expecting your horse to pull that, are you?" I asked him.

He turned and looked at me like I'd insulted him. "It's my horse, ain't it?"

"Yeah, it's your horse, but the load's too heavy for it."

"You don't know—you're just a young feller." He looked me over and then spit off to the side.

"Maybe so, but I know when a load's too heavy for what's pulling it," I said.

"You take care of your horses—I take care of mine." He gave me a disgusted look, chewed a bit more on his cigar before spitting out another dark wad that landed near my boot.

He lowered the tail-gate back in place, climbed down off the dock and onto the seat of his wagon. Once there he loosened the reins and slapped them against the rump of the horse. It leaned into its collar. The wagon inched forward, but it was clearly a strain for the horse. Its hind legs stiffened again, its rump lowered, the rear hooves slipped as the horse pushed into its collar. The wagon jerked ahead. He slapped the reins again, and shouted, "Move! Let's go! C'mon!" Again the horse strained into its collar and again the wagon inched forward. He pulled a leather strap from underneath the seat and whipped the horse's rump. By now I stood at the back of his wagon. Several other teamsters had joined me.

"Stop it, goddamn it! The load's too heavy!" I yelled, and jumped from the dock and ran up alongside the wagon. "You got too much weight for that horse."

"Fuck off!" he shouted back to me. "You mind your business—I mind mine."

"At least back your wagon up and lighten the load."

"I ain't backin' up," he said. "Been waitin' here all mornin' already."

"But the load's too heavy!" I repeated.

"I get another horse," he said, and pulled his wagon out to the top of the yard and stopped it there. He stepped down from his wagon and began loosening the harness. I felt better that he was replacing the horse. It was still too heavy a load for a single pull, but with a bigger, stronger horse and no hills to climb it was do-able. I backed my wagon into the vacant stall at the loading dock, removed the tail-gate and waited for the dock workers to bring out my order. I talked with the other teamsters there on the dock, and occasionally would look out to the guy with the overloaded wagon. By now he'd freed the horse from its harness, led it to the back of his wagon and tethered it with ten feet of rope. The mash mix had been hand-trucked out and I was loading the sacks over the wagon's axles.

Then I heard someone on the dock shout out, "What the hell's he doing?"

When I looked up, I saw the fat man dousing his horse with a can of some kind of fluid, sprinkling it all over its back and neck and on top of its flanks, emptying the entire can. The horse just stood there. Then I watched him strike a match and goddamn, if he didn't set the horse on fire! I couldn't believe it!

It was kerosene he'd poured on it and it burned right through the horse's hide like dry tinder. In seconds the entire horse was covered in flames, pulling back on its rope until I thought it would break, and squealing out like a stuck pig—its mouth wide open, its long teeth showing—its eyes as big as saucers.

It was awful to watch. I looked around for something—any-thing—and saw a pile of empty burlap sacks, grabbed a fistful and ran over to the horse but by now the flames were so hot, it hurt to get near it. Its back legs had collapsed and the horse tottered then fell over on its side, parts of it smoldering away. I beat out most of the flames but it was too late. The horse was dead, its hide burned through until you could see its blackened ribs. An awful smell of singed hair and burnt horse flesh hung in the air.

I grabbed the horse's owner by his shoulder and spun him around. "What the hell's wrong with you, man?"

"The horse no good!" He snarled back.

I clenched a fist, swung and hit him on the side of his head—I felt bones in my hand crack. He fell against his wagon. One of the teamsters from the dock grabbed onto me from behind. "That's enough," he said.

The fat man in overalls stayed leaning against his wagon, holding the side of his head. "I call the police on you!"

"Go ahead!" I said.

By now the mill boss was at the scene. He looked over the burnt carcass of the horse and shook his head. "George," he said. "I've told you about overloading your wagon now, haven't I?"

"But it's your guys that overloaded the wagon," I said.

The mill boss flashed a look of guilt toward me. I held my right hand, rubbing its bruised bones.

The fat teamster stroked the side of his head and didn't speak.

"Why do you even let your guys load up a wagon like that?" I asked the mill boss. "They got eyes—they can see."

"It won't happen again," the mill boss promised.

I walked back to the loading dock and the workers there slid the metal feeding troughs and the water stations in behind the sacks of feed. I checked the order against what was in the wagon. Everything was there. I tied the troughs down. The water stations were in boxes. I climbed onto the driver's seat, released the wagon brake.

A few onlookers still gathered around the horse's carcass, one of them kicking at the dead horse's hoofs. A policeman came and the folks standing around the carcass pointed at me but the policeman never approached. I clicked my tongue and Molly and Dolly leaned into their collars, and the wagon rolled forward. We drove east out Washington Street then south on Adobe Road. It was a flatter route than the Lakeville/Stage Gulch Road. The whole ride back, I kept seeing that skinny horse going up in flames, its eyes close to bulging out, its mouth open wide like it was yawning, showing those long teeth, and how it pulled back at its rope until I thought the rope would snap, and the fat man in overalls just standing there, an empty kerosene can in his hand, watching his horse thrash about like nothing had happened—like it was just a natural thing for a horse to do. It made me sick thinking about it, wondering how people could do such cruel things, but I knew they did. I'd just seen them do it. And worse yet, they did it to each other. None of it made any sense to me.

29

Setting Up the Operation

· ·

John B. and I sealed up a store room for the feed, plugging every little hole we could find to keep the rats out. We set traps, too, because those critters were persistent and always found a way in. We moved the feeding troughs into the brooder house and set up a watering station at each end. The watering stations were big glass jars that screwed into crock lids shaped like a circular trough. Little holes in the crockery allowed water to seep out into the trough. When the chicks drank and the water level lowered, water would seep down until the water reached a certain level and stopped.

Carlotta was concerned about how to keep the chicks warm and suggested we install a wood burning stove inside the brooder house, but it seemed too risky for John B. All that loose straw and wood shavings invited fire, so John B. went to a sheet metal fabricator in Sonoma, a fellow named McKendrick, and this fellow shaped pieces of sheet metal into broad hoods that resembled near-flattened cones. These hoods could be hung from the collar beams on chains or rope to adjust their height. The chicks could huddle under them for warmth.

Once the brooder house was finished, Alfonso and his brothers cleared out more brush and poison oak and scraped the next building site clean with shovels and hoes. The layer house would be built just north of the brooder house, separated by twenty feet. Unlike the brooder house, this one would have an enclosed yard where the chickens could wander, as well as nesting boxes built out from the east wall of the house. On the west side, we would place a framework of metal rods set at one inch centers into openings in the wall. This would allow the chicken to poke its head between the rods and feed from the trough just below the opening. John B. also thought of replacing the tongue and groove flooring over where the chickens fed with stiff wire that would allow their droppings to fall through to the ground and not build up inside the house.

Once the site was cleared, we set up batter boards at each corner and ran our string lines out, moving our strings until the diagonals measured equal and the building outline was square. I hauled in a load of flat rock, and Alfonso and his brothers dug out where each of the pier posts would be and set the rock into the depressions, tamping down the ground surrounding the post until it was good and firm. Another load of floor framing lumber was due at the depot and once again Alfonso and I set out with the team.

"You miss your father?" he asked as I turned the wagon toward town. He lit another of his little cigars and offered me one.

"I do."

"He get a bad deal."

"The worst," I said.

"But he make this building with the *gallinas*—with *la senora*," Alfonso said. "It will be his altar—his shrine."

"His shrine?"

"*Si,* where you can go and think of him."

"I hadn't thought of it that way," I said.

"*Si,* a shrine for both of them—*una iglesia*," and Alfonso laughed

"Yeah, they drew it out together."

"They spend much time down by the *rio*. When I look for him, I find him there in *la casita*—those two *juntos*." Alfonso placed his two index fingers together.

"Well, they had to discuss the details of the houses."

"*Si.* I think she like him and he like the *senora.*"

I nodded my head. Of course they liked each other or respected each other—that might be a better word. I did wonder if there was anything romantic between them—I always wondered about that kind of thing—but it seemed to me a pure business-type of arrangement—you do this, and I pay you for it.

Truth was I rarely thought of my father as being romantic at all—or spiritual. He was a practical guy and he allowed himself few emotions—least of all, romantic ones. The one he did allow—anger—ended up getting him killed. Sure, I could see a certain gleam in his eye when he was in the company of women, particularly attractive women, and when he was with Carlotta, his manner changed—his rough edges smoothed out, his voice softened—but I didn't give it a second thought; some harmless flirtation if it even came to that, and I don't think my old man did, either. I figured as we got older we grew out of those fascinations and ended up with whatever feelings were left us—mostly how to survive with all our aches and pains. But romantic feelings? They didn't travel with us. They got sloughed off. The sap inside dried up.

But like everything else, it wasn't always true—nothing was. I'd heard about guys in their eighties falling in hopeless love with women half their age, howling at the moon trying to win their love—promising them houses, wealth, anything—but it was all in their heads, all some crazy way to recapture their youth—but that was romance. On the outside, it made no sense—you could slice it a hundred different ways for a hundred different people.

The flat car with the floor timbers and tongue and groove flooring was waiting at the depot when we arrived. After checking in with the station master, I positioned the wagon alongside the flatcar and the lumpers once again loosened all the ropes to the load. The fir and redwood came down from the north coast on ship, into San Francisco harbor where the lumber was transferred onto river scows and delivered to the rail head at Sonoma Landing and from there transferred onto flat cars and railed into Sonoma. By land it would have taken days to transport this lumber.

We loaded the floor timbers first, twenty foot lengths that stuck out the end of my wagon another six feet, and headed back to Carlotta's ranch. The whole way back my mind was dancing from one woman to another—from Carlotta in her khaki ranch outfit, to Helga with pastry flour dusting her nose, and then to Cameron singing in the choir, breathing in Jesus with each breath and breathing him back out again. It was like I couldn't make up my mind which one to think of—so I thought of them all. What harm could it do? Sometimes, too, I'd see my old man and Carlotta in the little kiosk, looking over the building plans and imagine him with that same hunger I felt moving through him, and wondering what he thought—wondering what he'd do. What was he feeling, sitting so close to her? What was she feeling? Questions—I had a million of them.

We rolled into the ranch yard and John B. directed us where to drop the lumber. I drove the team up past the hay barn and came down alongside the creek where we'd cut a road earlier through the brush to the top of the building site. Alfonso's brothers had laid out a tape measure along the ground and placed flat stones in half the pier post locations. Once the wagon was positioned, we loosened all the ropes and unloaded the floor beams.

By now it was midday and time for lunch. Alfonso and his brothers brought tortillas wrapped in towels and refried beans in a metal pot, and sat down in the shade of a nearby oak. Ah Yep came out to the site and motioned to John B. and myself to follow him. "You eat in garden," he said.

We washed our hands in a bucket of water and sat down at a table under the trellis. Ah Yep's wife brought out two plates with sandwiches, slices of cheese, tomato and cucumber, and a pitcher of water with lemon slices. I looked over at John B. "You eat lunch like this every day?"

"No, this must be a special occasion," he said.

Carlotta soon joined us, said hello, and sat opposite me. "We can pick the chicks up anytime now," she said. "They're at the hatchery, ready to go." She sliced her sandwich into little wedges and separated each wedge on her plate.

"How about tomorrow?" I asked. "John B.'s got the floor framing lumber now and Alfonso and his brothers to help him set posts. What do you think, John B.?"

"Sure, I've got the help I need," John B. said.

"I'd like to go with you, if you don't mind." She placed a wedge of sandwich into her mouth.

"Not at all," I said. "I look forward to the company."

"John B, the brooder house is ready, right?" Carlotta asked.

"It is. We've got a half foot of shavings on the floor and those metal umbrellas hung which should keep the chicks warm enough at night," he said.

"Wonderful!" She ate another of the sandwich wedges and while she ate, she looked past me. After she swallowed, she paused. "I wish your father was here to see this."

John B. and I both nodded our heads.

"I think he'd be very pleased," she said.

John B. looked over at her. "I know he would."

We finished lunch and both John B. and I thanked Carlotta, and returned to the job site. Alfonso's brothers were back digging out where the flat stones would be placed. They worked with us each day until three o'clock before leaving to gather in the dairy cattle and begin the afternoon milking. They worked into the early evening, washing down the milking barn afterwards, straining the milk that was then poured into thirteen gallon cans and picked up each morning by a team and driver that hauled the milk back to the creamery in town.

This was the daily rhythm of work around Carlotta's ranch. I worked on the brooder house and layer house with John B. overseeing the job, and by day's end returned to my own place. This time it wasn't an empty stall or converted tack room but a house, an honest-to-goodness house, with a bed and furniture and a kitchen—everything but a wife and family, I thought. I hadn't seen Tino in awhile, either, and I hoped he didn't think I'd forgotten about him because I hadn't. I know he was against my taking this job, and he told me so—one of the things I appreciated about him—about my old man, as well. You never had to guess what was on their minds. They didn't try to hide it—they told you straight out where they stood, and maybe you didn't agree with them, but at least they told you. Overall, this was a good time in my life despite my father's death, and maybe because of it, John B. and I worked together with hardly a hitch—maybe because we were trying to make up for his absence, trying to fill in for him and that space his death had left us, and build something he'd be proud of.

I had feelings for Carlotta, too—I had to admit it. They were deep inside me, growing each time I saw her, even though I knew they'd only complicate things—but how do you tell a feeling to stop? It was push and pull, push and pull, all the time with her, as it was with most women. I hadn't forgotten about Cameron, either, although that one seemed a long shot, too—still I thought of her and wanted to see her again and thought maybe there was still some outside chance that we'd be together.

I always remembered, too, what Emma had told me about chasing women I could never catch—that it was all part of my plan. I didn't much agree with her, but looking at it from a different angle, it seemed to pan out that way. The more I wanted a woman, the further away from me she moved. Sometimes I even wished the nut inside me was cut or dried up, and I didn't have to chase women anymore—the way they gelded a stallion. It'd make things a lot simpler but the more I thought about it, the more I asked myself—do I really want things that simple? I didn't think so. Not yet, at least.

30

To the Hatchery With Carlotta

I was up early the next morning, earlier than usual. I hadn't slept that well, my head full of thoughts about Carlotta, thinking about the trip over to Petaluma, what it would be like being alone with her, what we'd find to talk about and wondering if there was some way I could inch further into her life. I walked out to the stable and fed Molly and Dolly and Little Ike. Once weaned from his mother, the little colt had taken to my pair of mares like they were his mother, following them around, never straying more than twenty, thirty feet from them, nuzzling up to them every chance he could. When I had to harness Molly and Dolly and take them from the ranch, Little Ike grew upset, threw a temper tantrum, pacing back and forth in his corral, whinnying, throwing his head back and carrying on. Once he grew more, I'd start tying him to the back of the wagon for the shorter trips so he got the feel of a halter, of being out on the road with the different noises and distractions he wouldn't hear around the ranch.

With the horses fed and harnessed, I pulled the team into the yard just outside Carlotta's garden gate and waited. She left her house, carrying a woven bag in one hand, a coat draped over her other arm—her hat cocked to one side. She beamed a wide smile. "Good morning, Bert!"

I tipped my hat. "Good morning to you!"

She handed me her bag. "It's got sandwiches and some pieces of fruit—some canteens with water." She looked up at me. "Do you think we should bring blankets to cover the chicks in case they get cold?"

I shook my head. "It'll be plenty warm today and they'll be right behind the wagon seat here and out of any breeze."

I stowed the bag under the seat and she climbed up and sat down next to me.

"I'm excited." And she touched my arm.

"You're always excited," I said. "I like that about you."

"Am I?" She looked at me. "Do you think I'm childish? You do, don't you?"

"In a good way, though," I said. "You don't ever want to hear someone say, 'Now you're acting like an old person' do you?"

"No, I guess not," she said. "It's just that there's so much heart-ache in this world that any chance to feel a little joy—well, I jump at it."

The west end of Napa Road tee'd onto Grand Avenue, and from here I could see Emma Hansen's barn off in the distance and the grove of oaks that surrounded her house. I pointed the team south on Grand, turned into the Watmaugh District and passed the lit-tle school house there. Past Watmaugh, we turned onto Stage Gulch Road and continued until we reached the Chancellor Ranch. Here we stepped down from the wagon and watered the horses— like I'd always done— in a trough just yards from the road. I glanced at my pocket watch: seven thirty. The night cold was still trapped in the steep gulch with patches of fog hanging in the trees like big balls of cotton. Carlotta put her coat on. We wound our way through the gulch to the top of La Franchi's hill that looked out across the Petaluma Valley. A layer of fog hung over the creek to the west. We paused here.

"Beautiful—absolutely beautiful," Carlotta said as she leaned into me. "We are so fortunate!"

"Let's stay on Adobe Road," I said, "so we don't have to ride into that fog."

By now Carlotta had taken a scarf out of her coat pocket and wrapped it around her neck.

"The chicks we're picking up," she said. "They're half Leghorns and half Rhode Island Reds. Sixty total. They're both pretty hardy birds and good layers." She tightened her scarf. "They should reach egg-laying stage by spring. In winter, you know, they practically stop laying."

"What gave you the idea to raise chickens?" I asked her this once before but thought it a good way to keep us talking. I was nervous around her.

She laughed. "We kept them when I was a little girl and they became like pets to me, following me around, always clucking like they were trying to tell me something. I even gave some of them names—Millie, Gwen, Betty, Mildred—after aunts of mine. I would talk back to them and they would cock their heads like they were trying to understand what I said. They seemed like the perfect animal, too—they'd pick at bugs and scratch around the yard, you fed them, and then at the end of the day they walked back to their roosts for the night. You closed the door behind them and opened it for them the following morning. They weren't particular about what they ate, either, and they gave you eggs in return. It seemed like a very fair deal, don't you think?"

"Yes, it does—very fair," I said.

"My brother was mean to them, though." Carlotta put her boot up on the footboard and rested her chin on her hand. "He'd throw rocks and chase them, and he once grabbed one—he was with his friends at the time and trying to show off—and wrung its neck and tossed it to the ground. For no good reason—just to show off to his friends. I ran out shouting and started hitting him. He and his friends just laughed."

"Sounds like the two of you never got along—that it goes back a ways."

"We never did. I tried to like him, tried being a good sister to him, but it never worked."

"And it carries on right to today."

Yes, it does, unfortunately. Now we do our fighting in court. I've faced him so many times, I've lost count." She paused here. "And looks like we're going to face him again," she said.

"What do you mean?"

"Your mother and I have been talking, and she's upset about the sham acquittal of my brother by the locals, most of them my brother's cronies. So we've talked and I think I told you already I've retained an attorney?"

I nodded my head.

"Well, this attorney is demanding your father's case go to trial. He's already filed an appeal, and if it does, he's demanding a change of venue."

"What's a venue?"

"Where the trial is held," she said. "He wants it held in Santa Rosa—any place but Sonoma, and he's trying to get it scheduled for sometime later this year."

"And you think that could happen?"

"He's awfully good. So, we'll see."

"More stuff to think about."

"Yes, more stuff."

This was a long stretch of Adobe Road ahead of us, mostly straight and mostly flat, where the horses settled into that easy trotting rhythm of theirs—what I liked to call their 'marching band' rhythm. I pointed out all the different sounds to Carlotta—the leather creaking, the snare drum tapping of their hooves striking the road's surface, the metal jangle of the harness tree, the bass sound of the rolling wagon wheels. She listened, not saying anything, her head tilted to one side. Then her hands began moving as if conducting a band. "You're right! It is like a marching band!" she said. And always that little girl glee about her when she laughed. By now, she'd loosened the string on her hat and it hung down behind her head, allowing her hair to flow free in the breeze, strands of it sometimes wrapping about her mouth and forming circles on her cheeks.

"I was just thinking of your father," she said, half to herself, half to me. Her voice broke into my thoughts. "You think of him, don't you?"

"All the time," I said.

"I was thinking that I'd infected him with my own hatred toward my brother—and it's why your father did what he did."

"He had a temper—something, I'm sure, he didn't show much around you," I said, "but he had one and it made him do things he don't normally do."

"He was usually so pleasant—"

"But you never crossed him."

"And you did?"

I laughed. "All the time—I mean, we're father and son after all—and isn't that what fathers and sons do—they disagree, they argue, they get in a shit-toss with one another? I'd piss him off and the next thing I knew he was throwing something at me."

"A shit-toss," she repeated. "Such colorful language." She laughed. "What did you ever do to cause such a reaction in him?"

"I'd miss work—tell him I was tired of listening to him—that's all it took," I said. Here again I didn't want to tell her too much. Didn't want to admit to all the things my old man faulted me for. The drinking, the womanizing—a dozen other things I couldn't even remember now. No, she didn't need to know none of that. "He said I was a dreamer—that my head was always in the clouds—or someplace else I'd rather not say."

"Nothing wrong with being a dreamer—"

"No, there ain't—he just didn't want me doing it on his time or when he was trying to explain something to me."

"Oh," she said. "I guess there is a time and place for everything."

At the old adobe, we turned down Casa Grande Road and followed it west until it reached Lakeville Road. From here we stayed on Lakeville north all the way into town, past the train depot, the United Ice Company, the feed mills, and over a little spur of the Petaluma Creek until we reached Main Street. Poehleman's Hatchery was just a hundred yards further north up Main. We pulled the team into the hatchery yard, and Carlotta and I walked into the hatchery office. She held the order for sixty chicks in her hand. The secretary looked over the order and directed us to a door leading to the interior of the hatchery. Once we opened the door, we heard the sound of hundreds—maybe thousands— of chicks cheeping. Carlotta looked at me and smiled. "Isn't this wonderful?"

I agreed. It was a pleasant sound, all that young life sounding out in such a small area. A hatchery worker took Carlotta's order and pointed to a small dock area just outside. "Think you can pull your wagon to it?" he asked me.

"Sure thing," I told him.

I walked out onto the dock and down a set of steps. Once up in the wagon seat, I had the horses make a wide turn in the yard that brought the back of the wagon and the horses square to the docking area, then reined them gently backwards in an arrow-straight line. By now the hatchery worker hand-trucked out a stack of wooden boxes with openings on each of their sides covered with a mesh wire. He watched as I brought the back of the wagon to the edge of the dock, shook his head. "I can see you've done this before, young feller," he said.

"Cut my teeth on it a few years back," I said, and climbed down. I removed the tailgate to the wagon and he trucked in the boxes onto the floor of the wagon. I took each box off the stack and placed it right behind the driver's seat. When all six boxes were in the wagon, Carlotta opened the top of each box to check on the chicks inside. When the tops were opened, the chicks looked up and scrambled to the corners of the box. Carlotta counted the chicks. "Look at them, Bert! Aren't they precious? They're like little balls of yellow fur."

I smiled.

She counted each chick in each box, then looked at the hatchery employee. "They're all here." She signed a receipt and handed it back to the worker. I tied a rope around the boxes furthest to the back so they wouldn't move across the wagon's floor. Back in the driver's seat, we pulled out of the hatchery yard and started back to Sonoma.

"The chicks are so cute," Carlotta said. "It's a shame they have to grow up—it's a shame anything has to grow up." There was a common ground between us after all—we were both dreamers.

We drove south on Lakeville Road and turned east once again onto Casa Grande. At the top of Casa Grande, by the old adobe, Carlotta suggested we stop and eat the lunch she'd brought. I pulled the team off the road right by the creek, and we walked down to the water, found a couple of big rocks to sit on. She opened the bag she brought and handed me a cheese sandwich.

"It's been a wonderful day, Bert. Thank you so much!" She touched me on my arm. "Those little things go right into the brooder house, right?"

"That's where they go—until they start laying eggs in the spring." I found a couple of pebbles and tossed them into the water and watched the ripples spread out across the creek's surface. "I'll bet this is good trout fishing here," I said. "Tino could look at a place and know right off if it was good fishing or not."

"You two are good friends, aren't you?" She wrapped both arms around her legs and hugged her legs close to her body.

"We are—maybe my best friend." I tossed another rock into the water. "Your brother's sure got it in for him, though." I looked over at Carlotta. "He's chased us every chance he could and never caught us. The more he tries, the more he hates us—especially Tino. I've never seen two guys that hate each other the way those two do."

"I don't know." Carlotta looked out across the creek. "Years ago, Tino's mother worked at the ranch when my brother lived there. She did house cleaning and cooking for the ranch hands. This was before I bought the ranch from the family estate. And then she left suddenly, moved off to the foothills where her father, Miguel, lived, and where they're living still. My brother never gave a reason why. And sometime later Tino was born."

"You don't think—"

"That my brother's Tino's father?"

"It's the biggest secret in town that really isn't a secret." Carlotta covered her mouth. "I just wished he'd come out and admit it—but that's not my brother's style. It's hard for him to admit anything that doesn't put a feather in his cap."

"Tino denies it, too," I said. "How could you hate someone that way knowing he's your father?"

"It's like a Greek tragedy."

"A Greek tragedy?"

"Years ago, a Greek dramatist wrote a play about a person who unknowingly kills his father and he doesn't find out until a blind prophet tells him," she said.

"And then what happens?"

"It doesn't end well—like most tragedies," she said.

"There's so much I don't know about," I had to admit. Just then my world and Carlotta's world were drifting apart.

"It's all right, Bert," she said. "We grew up differently. It doesn't make you any less a person."

"I don't know. When you talk about these things—Greek tragedies and English novels and all those other books you read, I realize how ignorant I am—how little I really know." It was the truth—I had to face it—all those times of sitting in a classroom, my mind wandering off, staring out through the windows, and the teacher's voice sounding somewhere in the distance but nothing the teacher saying sinking in. I thought I knew it all—everything there was to know about this life—and I wasn't even ten years old.

"I'm sorry if I make you feel that way," she said. "It's not my intention. You know that, don't you?"

"But it's the truth—I am ignorant," I said.

"You could read about these things if you wanted—couldn't you? I'll gladly loan you any book I own." She turned to look at me. "Besides, you've spent your life doing other things. Could Jane Austen drive a team of horses the way you can? I don't think so."

"Yeah, doing other things," I repeated out loud—like poaching, drinking, chasing women, disappointing my old man. I'd wasted a good part of my life, I thought to myself. But that was behind me now—now I was trying to change.

"What's important is in here," and she leaned into me and put her hand on my heart. "That's what matters—not how many books you read."

Her touch made me flinch. Despite all my so-called conquests of women—the luring, the big talk, the bedding—at heart, they scared the bejesus out of me. "Maybe we should go?" I said. "And not leave those little peepers in their box too long?"

"Let's finish eating first." She reached into her sack and came out with a pair of apples.

After we ate the apples, she stuffed the cloth napkins back into her bag and brushed the crumbs off her lap. She reached for my hand as she stood up. I took it and felt its coolness. I tossed one last rock into the creek while she walked ahead to the wagon. "Do you want to check on them?" she asked. I leaned over the wagon's sideboards and opened the tops of the boxes nearest me. The little chicks looked up at me with eyes like little circles of polished flint. "They're fine," I said.

I hated to see our trip together end, and wished we could keep traveling for days and days, talking and laughing and learning more about each other. We talked about all kinds of things along the way—family, friends, books I hadn't read—life in general and how it comes at you. I asked her questions, some of them bordering on the personal, about her earlier marriage, and what life was like living alone. She always worded her answers careful, tossing out just enough information to make me hungry for more. I wanted to find out everything I could about this woman even though I knew how foolish, even impossible that was. Like a fool, I wanted to solve the mystery of her, but mostly I wanted to know how she felt about me, if there was even a chance between us. A chance? I asked myself. For what? Romance? Something deeper? More permanent? My head was in the stars thinking like this—but it didn't matter.

When we weren't talking, and I wasn't thinking these crazy thoughts about her, we looked around us at the world passing by—the outside world—the one that didn't always break your heart the way people done. It was early November and the hills were brown like a lion's hide. Clusters of oaks grew to the ridge tops, and dust from the wagon wheels curled up behind us. Once the road dropped into the gulch, the pepperwoods' smell rose like a trapped perfume. Neither of us talked much.

We finally arrived at Carlotta's and I drove the team up to the brooder house. John B. and Alfonso were setting pier posts for the layer house and bracing the posts off to hold their plumb. John B. looked up, "Everything go all right?"

"Fine!" Carlotta said. "We've got them right here." She turned behind her and pointed to the wooden boxes.

"The brooder house is ready," John B. said. "Alfonso spread out more shavings this morning and filled the feeders and the water stations."

Once the tailgate was removed, I slid each box to the edge of the wagon where Alfonso and John B. lifted them and carried each one inside the brooder house. When all the boxes were inside, we closed the door behind us, opened the top of each box and tilted the boxes onto their sides. The little chicks fell over each other as they scampered out onto the brooder house floor. They looked about them, at their new surroundings, while wandering further from their boxes. I looked over at Carlotta and she was smiling a big broad smile.

"This will be your home, little ones, for the next few months. I hope you like it," she said.

"They should do fine," I added.

"Tomorrow," John B. said. "More gravel and sand and bags of cement so we can set the pier posts. These little guys'll grow fast and we'll be moving them before you know it."

"Carlotta doesn't want them to grow up," I looked toward her. She tried to conceal her embarrassment.

"I don't," she admitted. "I mean—look at them! Why would you want them to?"

John B. and I looked at each and then at Alfonso who shrugged his shoulders.

"The problem is," John B. said, "they can't lay eggs when they look like this."

All of us laughed. "No, they can't," Carlotta agreed.

31

Ranch Work and
an Evening Bicycle Ride

· ·

The day after delivering Carlotta's chicks, Alfonso and I drove out to Green's Supply at Sonoma Landing to haul back sand and bags of cement. The landing was at the mouth of the San Pablo Bay, and here the river scows unloaded their cargo. Some of it was transferred onto railcars, but other material, like sand and cement was loaded onto wagons. It was about six hours round trip from Carlotta's to the landing and back. Because of the added weight, I hitched Molly and Dolly to Carlotta's ranch wagon that had a harness tree set up for four horses. Behind my pair I added two of Carlotta's horses. We set off early for the landing. The route was flat and followed Sonoma Creek down through the tidelands.

"How was *el tiempo* with *la senora?*" he asked. We were now south of Schellville, where winds off the bay whipped up the brackish air.

"Good. It went well," I said.

"You like her, no?"

I laughed and shook my head.

"You no like her?"

"Of course, I like her," I said. Alfonso's questions almost always had a deeper motive to them—always trying, it seemed, to wrangle some sort of confession out of me.

"You learn about her?"

"I did—I asked her some questions. And she asked me some questions."

"What you think?"

"What do you mean?"

"A chance for you?" Here Alfonso laughed.

"I don't think so." No point in telling Alfonso what I really thought, or, at least, what I hoped for. I was superstitious that way. My gut feeling, the one I trusted most, told me there was no chance—only blind good luck that anything would develop between us. A one-in-a-million shot. But gut feelings hadn't stopped me before—at the very least I could still think about her.

"*Por que no?*"

"We're different," I said. "You know that."

"No, I don't know that," he said and lit another one of his little cigars. "You're a man and she's a woman. How different can you be?"

A silence followed between us until we both thought about what he'd just said. Then I heard a little grunt. "How different?" he repeated. Alfonso looked at me and I looked back at him and we laughed. How different could a man and a woman be?

"How different?" I repeated once again. "A man and a woman, Alfonso? Tell me!" And we laughed again until my eyes watered. Maybe it was all the difference in the world.

We continued down through the tidelands. At first the two horses behind Molly and Dolly made my pair nervous. Molly and Dolly were used to working alone and kept turning their necks to check on the two behind them, but once underway, they adjusted and settled into their regular rhythms. Patchworks of levees were built across the upper tidelands to keep the salt water out and behind these levees were broad, flat fields where oat hay was grown. The raised bed for the train track followed the road here to the terminal at Sonoma Landing where the river scows unloaded bags of cement and all kinds of other cargo bound for the valley. Some of it was transferred onto rail cars like the lumber I'd hauled from the Sonoma Depot, but sand and cement went to William Green's Supply Yard right there at the landing.

Once we arrived, I drove the team into Green's yard and positioned the wagon near a shoulder-high pile of sand. Inside the yard office I paid for the materials and shortly after, yard workers hand-trucked several bags of cement out to the rear of the wagon and lifted them onto the wagon's floor. Alfonso carried the bags to the front of the wagon. Once the cement was loaded, the yard workers began shoveling sand onto the rear of the wagon. I kept a close eye on the wagon's axles and when I felt enough sand was shoveled on, I signaled the workers to stop. I placed the tailgate back into place, climbed up onto the driver's seat and we were off for the return trip. I checked my pocket watch: eleven o'clock. From the feel, it was a heavy load to be sure, and I was glad we'd added the two horses. The wagon's wheels dug into the road surface and we wound our way back to the ranch.

"Every year *la senora* give big *fiesta* for Christmas," Alfonso said. "*La gente* come from San Francisco—*muchos politicos.* Maybe she invite you?"

"Maybe," I said.

"*Si,* every year," he said. "It start with the colonel and his friends—much eating and drinking the whole time."

I wondered just then if she would invite me. And what her friends from the city were like. What would I wear if I was invited? What would I talk about? What would it be like in the company of folks I wasn't used to keeping? Folks better off than me, folks with culture and education? And I wondered, too, how would I feel if she didn't invite me? It was still weeks off, and already I was setting myself up for disappointment. I tried not thinking about it but these thoughts kept finding their way in.

We pulled into Carlotta's just before three in the afternoon. I drove the team up around the hay barn and down along a little road that followed the creek and ended where we built the chicken houses. I unhitched the horses there and led all four back to their stable. Alfonso's brothers had already begun the afternoon milking and would unload the sand the next day.

Back at the building site, John B. and I were running string lines out where the pier post holes would be dug, marking each spot with a short wooden stake. When I looked up, I saw Carlotta on her new bicycle, pedaling it like she owned it for years. "Hey, Bert! John B.!" she called. Her hat was blown back on her shoulders, the hat's string around her neck.

"Look at you!" I shouted.

She stopped just short of where we were working. "I got it this morning—rode it all the way out here from Breitenbach's!"

John B. and I walked to her and looked the bicycle over. "It's just your size," I said. "We'll have to race and see which bicycle is faster."

Carlotta laughed. "Let's go for a ride later!"

"Sure thing," I said.

We marked off the remaining pier post locations, but all the while I kept thinking about where we'd ride to when I'd finished work. I remembered Carriger Creek. Most of the ride out there, maybe two miles, was smooth, packed road, and we could stash our bicycles and walk up into the creek. It was cool and shaded there, with dark pools and water skippers that glided across the creek's surface.

When work was done, I washed up and went over to Carlotta's and knocked on her backporch door. "You ready?" I asked when she appeared.

"I am." She wore light cotton pants and a light top. A bandana covered her hair. "Where we going?"

"I thought we'd head up to Carriger Creek," I said. "It's not too far."

"Like a maiden voyage, right?" she said.

We pedaled out of her yard and turned west onto Napa Road. We rode alongside each other, and the faster I pedaled, the faster she pedaled, keeping up with me. "Oh, you wanna race?" I shouted. A broad smile spread across her face as she stood up in the pedals for more speed. The wind whipped past my ears. I looked over at her, and she looked at me before looking back to the road in front of her. "I love it!" she shouted. "Why didn't I do this years before?"

"I don't know. Why didn't you?" I shouted back.

"Maybe it wasn't lady-like? I don't know."

We arrived at Carriger Creek, but she wanted to keep riding, so we stayed on Grand Avenue and rode all the way north on Grand to the El Verano train depot. We stopped at the depot and sat on a bench just outside the depot office. "I used to work with my dad here," I said.

"I remember," she said. "I hired him after he left this job."

"Yeah, after that whole Craig Ranch thing went belly-up," I said. "That seems like a long time ago, don't it?" I said. "Like another century, a whole different lifetime." I remembered the different dust-ups I'd had with my old man here—all the times I showed up late to work—when I showed up at all—and watching his face flush red—like a boiled crawdad's—when I fished around for some half-ass excuse. I hated myself when I remembered those things, and wished he was here so I could apologize—so I could make it up to him somehow.

"It does," Carlotta said.

"We fought a lot then," I said. "We just couldn't seem to get along. I tried to but I guess I didn't try hard enough. And he was a pretty demanding guy. I walked off the job so many times I lost count. He was always giving me one more chance, until finally he didn't. "You're running your string out, son," he said—he told me that more than once—before he sent me packing."

"But that's typical of fathers and sons, isn't it?" she asked. "The father's always trying to do what he thinks is best for the son, right? Isn't that what parents do?" She'd turned toward me and the late afternoon light struck her face in such a way I resisted just leaning over and kissing her.

"But if the son don't agree, then there's trouble," I said. "He'd try to convince me, but I was as stubborn and head-strong as he was. All we ended up doing was butting heads."

Carlotta nodded and looked south down the railroad tracks.

"That's mostly what it was like between us," I said. "Not all the time, but a good part of it. Ma says it was all those years of being apart at such a young age and never getting to know one another again once we were together, but look at John B., I told her. He was separated just as long as me and the two of them never had any trouble."

"You're different, you and your brother," Carlotta said.

"I wanted to be more like John B. but I never could—so I gave up trying," I said. "I was stuck with who I am—."

"There's nothing wrong with who you are, Bert."

"You don't think so?" I wanted to hear a compliment from her just then.

"No, I don't. You're perfectly fine," she said. "You have a good heart. I told you that at the creek the other day. You care about things." She touched me on my thigh. "We can't be like other people. I mean, we can't just turn a switch and be someone else. It doesn't work that way. We all have to live out our lives the way life comes to us. We have to make choices, too"

"Make choices," I repeated.

"A big part of it is making the right choices. Don't you think? We choose how we're going to act, what we're going to do. It's called free will," she said.

What Carlotta said made sense to me. It was months now since my father had been killed, and it seemed every day I thought about him more and more, still trying to come to terms with him not being around but still having trouble accepting it. Every day I'd turn a corner and wonder where he was. And every time that happened, I remembered he was gone and that whole scene at the north gate would play out again behind my eyes. Every day I felt that if I'd been a better son to him, and hadn't disappointed him so many times and had lived up to that person he wanted me to be, he'd still be alive. I know that didn't make no sense. Nothing I'd done would have kept him from meeting up with Percy Sheers and everything that happened after, but I was trying to understand the sadness I was feeling—a sadness so big I was afraid it would swallow me up at times. The more I thought about it, the more I could see this sadness was big, too big to understand all at once, and what I tried to do was break off little pieces of it, one day at a time, and swallow up these pieces until the sadness was gone or nearly gone although I knew how long that would take—I'd always be feeling something.

"You're quiet for such long stretches," she said. "You're a thinker, aren't you, Bert?"

"I'm sorry—yeah, I guess I am."

"No, I understand. We both have a lot on our minds."

"My dad would always ask what I was thinking of, especially when he was trying to explain something to me."

"And what would you tell him?"

"I'd make up something different because I didn't want him to know," I said. "It was like my secret, and if I told someone, it wouldn't be a secret anymore. Besides, there was never one thing I was thinking of. My mind wandered everywhere—mostly though, I was wondering where I was heading, and where I was going to end up, and what that would be like."

"Are you happy with where you are now?"

"Right now? Right at this very minute?" I caught her off guard.

"Yes, okay—at this very minute."

"I'm very happy," I said. "I couldn't think of any place I'd rather be—and it's kinda scary."

"Scary?"

"Yeah—I got so used to things blowing up that when I hit a good stretch, I'm afraid it ain't ever gonna last—that some big disappointment is waiting around the corner."

"Just enjoy the good stretch—that'd be my advice," she said.

"You'd think it'd be easy, wouldn't you? Just enjoy one day at a time—and I do—but I know the good times never last—it's just one those facts about this life I don't argue with."

"Maybe you just need a bit of practice—like me trying to learn to ride that bicycle." She touched me on my hand again and looked up at the late afternoon sky. "Maybe we should start heading back?"

We mounted our bicycles and followed Riverside Road along the creek until we came to Petaluma Avenue. If we turned here, we could ride up to the north gate and cross the fields back to the ranch yard. But it was the gate where Dad was shot—and ever since the shooting, I'd avoided it.

"What do you think?" Carlotta asked. "Go through the north gate?"

"I don't know. What do you think?"

"We don't have to. We can go around," she said.

"Let's try it," I said, curious how I'd feel seeing it again.

We rode up to the north gate. Some loose pickets were stacked along the fence, those same pickets that he'd grabbed when facing-off with Sheers. Nothing here, though, suggested any earlier violence. It was just a wire gate, with extra pickets wired to a gate post. His blood by now had dried into the soil, and Sheers' wagon tracks were gone, and all the boot prints of the onlookers had long since disappeared. We opened the gate and pushed our bicycles through and wired the gate shut behind us. We both stopped and looked over the site again for several seconds. Earlier scenes moved across my mind, but like the footprints and wagon tracks and my father's blood—I knew if I let it, the bad memories of this place might disappear, too—or at least lose their hold on me. I just had to let them go—simple enough but not easy to do. We mounted our bicycles again and rode them across Carlotta's field and into the ranch yard.

"I enjoyed our ride, Bert. We'll have to do more," she said. "But longer ones, don't you think?"

"Much longer," I said. "There's so many other places to explore."

She smiled at me. I bid her a good evening and she bid me one back. We shook hands and I walked home, wishing she was walking home with me, right through that front door and into my heart where I'd built a little room for her—a little room for both of us. I leaned the bicycle against a porch post. I opened the front door and it was dark inside, so I struck a match and lit a kerosene lamp and held it in front of me as I walked into the bedroom. I stripped out of my clothes and fell onto the bed—a real bed this time, with a big head board all carved with grape vines and clusters of hanging grapes. It was the colonel's bed but now it was mine—at least, for now it was. But like most beds from before, I was sleeping in it alone.

32

Before the Rains

• • • • • • • • • • • • • • • •

By mid-November the first rains fell. Days earlier, Alfonso, his two brothers, Raul and Jose, and I had taken the wagon and team and gone down along the creek, chopping and sawing up lengths of dead oak for firewood. We filled the wagon, and unloaded portions of it at Carlotta's, my house and the brothers' bunk house. We finished as much other outside work as we could before the winter rains would set in: repairing fences, bringing hay into the barns, spreading dry cow manure in the fields, cleaning out the horse stalls. By now both the brooder house and the layer house were finished, and John B. found other work in town, so I didn't see him near as often. He did stop by to invite me out to the folks' place for Thanksgiving dinner and to say if all went well, he was moving to his property north of Santa Rosa in the spring. He'd saved enough money and was itching to move.

The chickens became my responsibility. I liked caring for them right from the start, but there was another reason, too, I took on the work—it was a chance to see Carlotta when she wasn't hidden away in her big house, reading novels or baking her fancy cakes— doing whatever else she did there to pass her time. She checked on the chickens each day, usually by eight in the morning, and so it was my chance to see her. They grew fast and soon were young pullets, "And no longer cute," as Carlotta said. But they were healthy and thriving and by spring I had no doubt they'd be good layers. At times, too, I'd stop and admire the work that we'd done building these houses, the tight miters we cut, how the windows slid easily in their tracks, the doors closed tightly in their jambs. I admired also how our old man had designed the houses, how everything seemed to fit together. The old man was never far from my mind nor was the idea of Percy Sheers still walking around like he'd done nothing wrong at all. Tino reminded me of it whenever we were together.

Carlotta and I managed a few more bicycle rides before the rains came. We'd ridden to Glen Ellen one afternoon, stopping at the Mervyn Hotel there for a glass of wine on a terrace just above the creek. She told me about her plans for an upcoming Christmas party at her house and how it was an annual event. She invited several of the colonel's friends from the city, and they'd gather for dinners and exchanging gifts, sometimes staying two to three days before returning home. "They love the country," she said, "but never felt it was for them and always looked forward to returning to the city."

"Are they stuff-shirts?" I asked her.

"Well, that's not a terribly complimentary term, Bert." Her lips twisted.

"I was just asking," I said.

"They're different—that's all," she said. "They're city folks and used to certain refinements."

"Different from me?" I asked.

"Yes—different from you," she said. "They were raised differently—wealth, position, certain entitlements, I guess you'd say." She turned toward me. "This is to take nothing away from you, Bert, but they're from a different part of society."

"The upper crust, huh?"

"Yes, you could say that."

"Are they different just because they have money?" I asked her.

She'd started to drink from her glass, then set it down and stared across the creek. "Money's a big part of it—yes, but not the only part—."

"But it's what gets them through the door, right?"

"The door?"

"Yeah, the door into the room where they all gather," I said.

"I'm not sure I like your tone of voice, Bert. They're good folks—and yes, you'd say privileged, but good people nevertheless." She finished her glass of wine. "Let's talk about something else, okay? I don't like the direction this conversation's headed."

"Sure," I said. And so Carlotta talked about the autumn light through the trees, and the coming rains, and her plans for Thanksgiving, while my mind hummed away with other questions—was the difference between us too wide to ever bridge? Would I ever own up to how I felt about her? Or, did I even have to? Couldn't she see right through me? Women had that power.

Another time we rode out to the Buena Vista Winery tucked away in the eastern corner of the valley. Enroute, she pointed out vineyards that the colonel used to own, and the estate they lived in until he died. I know it wasn't her intention, but as I listened to her and looked at these properties, I felt pretty small. What did I have that could even compare? Nothing, really—a wagon and three horses? Hardly nothing. And once again, any hope of ever winning her heart seemed to shrivel up and blow away. I don't know why I hung onto this imagining like I done. Well—yes I do. I was hungry and alone and following my heart—that's what I told myself, at least—but the heart can lead to some dangerous places—places that are hard to find your way out of. And if one woman wasn't enough—in the middle of all this imagining, there was Cameron, too—another one of my long shots.

"Is it important that someone has wealth, owns a lot of things?" I asked her again. I kept returning to this thing about money because it seemed the biggest of the many obstacles between us. We were sitting under a large oak at the Buena Vista at the time, sharing a bottle of wine.

"Important for what?" she asked. "To be with that person?"

"Yeah, to be with that person."

She didn't answer—just stared off.

"Yes or no? Is it important?" I repeated the question.

"I think it depends on the individual," she said. "What's important to me is the quality of a person's character and not their wealth."

Her answer came as a relief to me but also as a kind of dodge—a way of stepping around the question. Money had to figure in—it always did. And the quality of a person's character? Wouldn't that depend on who you asked?

"Why these questions, Bert?"

"Curious mostly," I told her.

"No other reasons?"

"Well, yes, there is—I'm—"

I knew the words I wanted to say, but I couldn't say them.

"What's on your mind? Don't be shy—tell me," she said.

"I'm really growing to like you," I admitted.

"Well, I'm growing to like you, too, Bert."

"And it doesn't matter if I'm not like your rich friends from the city?" I asked, still trying to dig deeper.

She laughed. "Oh, heavens, no! I think what I like most about you is that you're *not* like them," she said.

"Really?"

"Yes, really, Bert," she said. "We're talking friendship here, right? A bond between two people? And how they understand each other?"

I nodded yes but I was thinking of something deeper than friendship. Let's get right down to it—I wanted her. I wanted to give my feelings free rein and fall in love with her and in return, I wanted her to fall in love with me—that seemed like the end-game here. Anything less and I'd be fooling myself. Friendship? If it led to love—then fine. If it didn't, I'd just be disappointed all over again. I wanted to take the great leap and not waste my time with anything in between. There was no patience for anything less. I wanted to get right to the quick of it. To me there were no in-between stages: your heart fastened on someone and you rode it until you fell in love.

And then what? What happened after falling in love? You made love. And after making love? Then what? It grew—if you were lucky the love grew and kept growing. And what made it grow? Was it just luck? No, you had to find that right person. And who was the right person? And how would you know this? That's where they had me by the short hairs—territory I hadn't crossed into yet, but like most things with me, I trusted my gut and my heart—that's what I went on.

"Bert, I'm a free-spirited woman," she said. "Do you know what that means?"

"No, I don't—not exactly."

"It means that, in ways, I don't follow the rules," she said. "I do what I feel is best for me, and I don't give a hoot about convention—or what other people might think of me and sometimes that disappoints them—or shocks them—maybe even both."

"Sounds like I'm a free-spirited man then."

Carlotta laughed. She finished her glass of wine and I finished mine. I refilled my glass and motioned toward hers. "No, I've had enough. We're on bicycles, remember?"

What Carlotta had said about being a "free-spirited woman" didn't really sink in with me at first. It made her more daring in my eyes—more desirable—but it gave her power and a voice that scared me, too. Despite her wealth, I looked at her as I looked at most women—someone to win over, someone to conquer with charm, persuasion, persistence—someone to have my way with. I didn't know how I'd do it—or even if I could—but I hung onto the stubborn belief that I'd find a way. It became the thing I most wanted in this world. But our worlds were different—it always came down to that. What gave me this confidence, I wondered, that I might win her over? I don't know where it came from—unless it was just being ignorant—trying to hold on to those little slivers of hope. Where all of this led, I didn't know—I didn't think that far ahead. I hardly ever did, but I'd figure it out as I went along—that's what I told myself.

"Shall we go?" she asked.

We left the winery on a late fall afternoon. Once again we rode past the colonel's vineyards and his estate, but this time neither of us said anything. She rode beside me into the setting sun and every few moments I'd steal a glance toward her, drinking in her beauty, at the wind whipping at her hair and the last golden rays of the sun on her face and hands. I'd have to remind myself—is this really Carlotta Stamm riding beside me? Carlotta, the mystery woman? The one I used to pine for from a distance? The one sitting in her carriage at the plaza? I was falling for her by the day and wondered if she knew it. If she had any clue? How could she not? How could she not notice how I looked at her? How I acted around her? How my eyes could never stray from her for very long? But if she knew, she was good at hiding it. She didn't want to disappoint me—I know. Whatever happened, I believed I'd manage. It wasn't going to kill me. That's what I told myself again and again. I don't know where I got my confidence—how it'd spring up in the middle of all my doubting—but it showed up, and it never failed to surprise me when it did.

33

Thanksgiving and
a Grammar Lesson

• • • • • • • • • • • • • • • • • • •

Tino and I managed to slip away the morning before Thanksgiving and rode to Schellville on our bicycles to hunt ducks. I'd
promised Ma I'd bring back a couple of mallards for the Thanksgiving dinner. It was good seeing Tino again, too, and hearing all the
scuttlebutt around town. The news was pretty much the same—just
the faces changed. Since starting work for Carlotta, I wasn't making
the rounds with Tino like we'd done before—wasn't up on all the local
heart break and who was sleeping with who—who was feuding—all
the stuff that folks talked about. Since Dad's death I didn't have much
stomach for that. No, it was mostly ranch work, staying in during the
evenings, going to bed early and getting up while it was still dark. I
missed not talking and drinking with Tino—Flo, too—but I figured
there'd always be time for that. But time was moving fast.

Tino was ready when I arrived at the Union Livery. It was still
dark, and he'd lit a kerosene lamp that made long shadows on
the stable walls. He had a knapsack packed, and his shotgun was
strapped to his back. "Just like old times again, huh?" he said.

"Yeah, old times," I said. "It feels good." And it did—like we
were younger again and not giving two shakes about our futures
and not caring whether a beautiful woman loved me or not. All this
thinking about Carlotta had me sideways.

We rode south out of town and decided we'd follow the creek
down through the tidelands and when we spotted any ducks, stash
the bicycles and see if we could work our way to within shooting
range. A mile south of Schellville, we spotted what looked like a
promising pond, left our bicycles in the tule grass and worked our
way quiet-like, to the edge of the pond. We found a spot we'd

hunted from before, a blind we'd made out of tall reeds, and sat there and waited.

"You moved in with that Carlotta yet?" Tino whispered.

"No, not yet," I said and laughed it off.

"Gettin' any closer?"

"No, keeping my distance." Which was only partly true—any distance I kept was closely measured.

"Flo said she seen you and her riding bicycles the other day."

"Is there anything that woman doesn't see?"

"She's the eyes and ears of this town, Bert—you know that." Tino looked over at me. "You ain't gonna sneak nothing past her, that's for sure."

Tino fished two cigars out of his shirt pocket and handed one to me. He lit mine first. "Keeps these goddamn mosquitoes away," he said and puffed on his cigar. "I read where Coroner Blaney put a jury together and declared Sheers innocent—it was in the paper."

"Yeah, I read it, too," I said. "Pretty white-washed account but what do you expect? All favoring Sheers and crowing about what an upstanding citizen he is and how my old man caused it all. Pure bullshit! Carlotta's got an attorney, though, and she and Ma are appealing the decision, claiming Dad was denied due-process. We're hoping for a trial."

We sat in the blind and waited.

"I'm still gunnin' for him, Bert," he said. "Just waitin' for my chance."

"Like I told you before, Tino—forget about it. You do anything, they'll string you up faster than a cat running with its ass on fire."

We heard ducks squawking in the distance and saw a wedge of them flying straight toward us. We both crouched lower, held our breath, waited for them to get within range. "Let 'em get close to us, okay? We got no boat," I whispered. When they were just twenty yards off, we stood up and fired. Two dropped right off, and we downed two more as they veered away.

"How we gonna get 'em now?" I asked, since we usually had our skiff with us.

"I brought a rope," Tino said. He took off his boots and socks and then his pants, and waded out into the pond with a length of rope. With the water nearly to his hips, he twirled it over his head like he was roping a calf and the broad loop dropped over the furthest duck. He pulled the rope toward him and brought the duck with it. When the duck was close enough, he grabbed it and tossed it back to me. He twirled the rope again and after a couple of tries landed the loop over the next duck, pulled it toward him like he'd done with the first and then threw it into the blind.

"Good work, Tino," I said as he brought the last duck in.

"Goddamn water's cold!" He walked out of the pond and I could see his knees were shaking. His legs looked spindly and white as candle wax.

"I brought something for that," I said, and pulled a flask of whiskey out of my knapsack.

"There is a God!" Tino said.

"You earned it. Drink up!"

Tino took a long pull and passed what was left to me. A couple more gulps each and the whiskey was gone and I wished I'd brought more. We stuffed the ducks into our knapsacks, walked back to our bicycles and headed north to town.

"Let's drop the birds off, first," I said, so at Four Corners we turned onto Napa Road and pedaled to the folks' place in Vineburg. When we arrived there, I turned toward Tino. "C'mon in and say hello," I said.

Tino and I walked inside. I was holding two ducks. Ma and Josephine were in the kitchen, cutting up slices of bread for stuffing. "I brought dinner," I announced.

My voice surprised them. When Ma turned around, I could see she looked different—older, thinner, too. She'd always been a big woman with big coarse hands, who could outwork most men, but now when I saw her she looked frail and tired with little pouches under each eye. The rosy color to her cheeks was gone, too. Dad's death had been hard on all of us, but particular hard for her. It was written across her face, the way she walked—how she stared off so much of the time. I walked over and put my arms around her. We held each other for several seconds until she stepped back. "Tino," Ma said, "Long time since I've seen you."

Tino tipped his hat. "Wait a minute, I've got something else." He left the house and returned holding his two ducks. "I can't eat them."

"Sell them to Ho Tzu," I said.

"No, why don't you keep them all?"

"That's very generous," Ma said. "You're welcome to join us tomorrow."

"Thank you, Mrs. Miller," he said, "but I've got two carriage rentals tomorrow."

We laid the four ducks on the kitchen counter, and Josephine set to plucking their feathers. Ma brought a pail in for the ducks' innards.

"Ma, I'll see you tomorrow," I said.

"Early afternoon—but come anytime. John B. and Gertie'll be here," Ma said. "They're both in Lakeville now visiting Gertie's brother, but they'll be over tomorrow," Ma said. "Gertie's going to bake pies."

I rode back to Carlotta's and checked on the young chickens first thing. They all looked healthy and were growing fast. When I left the brooder house, I walked back home and turned to see Carlotta sitting by herself on her patio. She wore a coat with its collar pulled up around her neck.

"Hello!" I called out.

She raised her hand and waved, and I walked over to the garden fence. I'd been around her enough times to read her moods. She looked sad now, her face drained of any color.

"Are you okay?" I asked.

She nodded her head.

"What happened?"

"I was planning a little Thanksgiving dinner for the senator and a couple of his friends and they cancelled," she said. "I just got the message yesterday."

"There's always Christmas," I said.

"You're right, there's always Christmas," she said. "Silly of me to react this way, but I was so looking forward to their company." She took a handkerchief out of the jacket pocket and dabbed at her nose. "Where did you go so early this morning? I don't mean to be spying on you."

"Tino and I went duck hunting. We each got two. Ma and Josephine are going to stuff and roast them for dinner tomorrow."

"Bert, the hunter!" she said.

"Would you like to join us?"

"Oh, I don't think so, but thank you anyway."

"Roast stuffed duck with all the trimmings. John B.'s wife is baking pies."

"That's very kind. Thank you."

"I'm sure there's room for one more. Ma would be glad to see you."

Carlotta looked at me and thought about my offer. "You know—on second thought, I think I'll accept your invitation—no point sitting here feeling sorry for myself."

"No point at all," I said.

"We can ride out in my carriage," she said. "I'll make something from the garden. I think there's still some squash out there for a casserole. Yes, that's what I'll do." She looked at me. "See, Bert, I feel better already. And, I've got some news for your family, too, but I'll wait until you're all together."

Thanksgiving Day couldn't come fast enough for me. I was up early, fed the horses, tended to the chickens. I walked down to the milking barn where Raul and Jose were halfway through the morning milking. Alfonso had taken the wagon out and was filling the mangers with hay for all the dry stock and heifers. He'd return and fill the wagon with hay for the milk cows. I wished them all a happy Thanksgiving.

By noon I'd hitched Carlotta's horse to her carriage and drove it into the yard. I went inside and washed up and changed into my good clothes and put on my old man's coat. I always thought of it as the old man's, like it was his parting gift to me just like I thought Little Ike was his—the horse and coat were mine just to take care of.

I knocked at Carlotta's backporch door, and she came out of the kitchen holding a wicker basket, and inside the basket was her casserole wrapped in towels to keep it warm. She wore a full-length dress, with long sleeves and a band of lace sewn in at each wrist— the first time I'd seen her dressed-up since starting work at the ranch. She looked like a fairy tale princess, her hair worn up, showing her long, elegant neck. She handed me the basket. "I'll bring some bottles of wine, too," she said and disappeared inside. I set the basket in the rear of the carriage. She soon joined me and placed another basket in the carriage. I helped her up to the carriage seat.

"You look different, "I said.

"How so?"

"All dressed up the way you are."

"Is it okay?"

"It's perfect."

"Well, you look different, too, Bert, so I guess we're even."

We drove out to Napa Road and headed west to Vineburg, four miles away. It was a crisp, cold day. For now the rains had let up, and the countryside was damp and quiet. The vineyard leaves—the ones still clinging to the vines—were bright yellow, the trees bare. It was the first time I'd driven Carlotta's carriage with Carlotta's horse. It responded differently than Molly and Dolly—a bit more headstrong, lighter on its feet. The carriage was a comfortable one with big springs that absorbed much of the road shock.

"Did you tell your mother you invited me?" she asked.

"No, I didn't. I thought it'd be a surprise."

"That's not good manners, Bert."

"She don't mind," I said.

"She *doesn't* mind," Carlotta said.

"That's what I said, 'she don't mind.'"

"The correct way to say it, is 'she doesn't mind' and not 'she don't mind,'" Carlotta said. "It's a habit of mine—corrrecting other people's grammar."

"I don't speak very good, do I?"

"It's 'speak well,' Bert."

"Does it matter?" I asked her.

"I don't know—in some ways it does, it some way it doesn't," she said. "But good grammar says something about a person."

"What does it say?" I wondered.

"That they have some level of education, some level of refinement. And it makes for clearer understanding, too," she said, "particularly when you're writing." She thought a few moments. "A diamond stays a lump of coal until it's polished."

"You can correct me then when I'm speaking bad—"

"Speaking *poorly*," and she laughed. "When you're speaking *poorly*."

"Either way, you can correct me," I said.

"And you won't mind?"

"No, I won't mind," I said. "I don't want to sound ignorant all my life."

"Reading helps, too," Carlotta said. "And listening to how other people speak."

"Okay, I'll try speaking more correctly—did I say it right?" Carlotta laughed. "Yes, you did."

"At any rate, Ma will be glad to see you." I looked around at the vineyards on each side of us and remembered how it felt seeing Ma in the kitchen yesterday. "I'm worried about her," I said.

"Why so?" She hesitated. "I mean, I can understand how she must feel—I lost a husband, too."

"She *doesn't* look good—like this whole thing has aged her twenty years. Did I say that right?"

"Yes, you did."

When we arrived at the folks' place, I stopped the carriage at the front steps. Ma soon appeared on the front porch. "Carlotta! What a surprise! I didn't know you were coming."

"I hope it's all right, Regina." Carlotta took Ma's hand.

"Of course it's all right," Ma said.

I carried the baskets inside and said hello to everyone. Gertie and Josephine were working in the kitchen. I handed them the basket with the casserole. Three pies lined the kitchen window sill where they were cooling. John B., they said, was in the barn repairing a broken harness. The smell of roasting duck filled the entire house. I opened one of the bottles of wine Carlotta had brought and poured out several glasses. Written across the front of the bottle was: *Burgundy/Verano vineyard.* Carlotta and Ma sat on a couch in the living room. I brought them each a glass of wine.

"I hope you enjoy it." I winked at Carlotta. "It's from our private stock."

"Someone get John B.," Ma said. "It's time for dinner."

I grabbed two glasses of wine and walked out to the barn where John B. had just finished splicing a new piece of leather into the harness. "Damn, John B. is there anything you don't do?" I handed him a glass of wine. "Happy Thanksgiving, brother."

"Same to you," he said. We raised our glasses and drank.

"Ma says you bagged two ducks yesterday."

"Yeah, Tino and me—south of Millerick's. Tino gave me both of his."

"Not as much time for hunting now with the work out at Carlotta's, is there?" he asked. John B. finished his glass of wine. "How's that going anyway?"

"Good," I said. "The chicks seem happy—growing like weeds. I got my own place now, and that's different. And Carlotta's teaching me how to speak proper, too."

"Speak proper?"

"Yeah, she says I use a lot of poor grammar," I said.

"Well, you weren't ever much on schooling."

"No, I wasn't, but I don't want to sound like I'm some dumb bastard, either," I said. "She even left a grammar book outside my door. I've taken to studying it—practicing my writing, too."

"Damn, Bert—all this because of her?"

"I guess."

"What do you write about?" he asked.

"I bought one of those journals down at Ruffner's and I try to write in it every day—things I done around the ranch, what I see, how I'm feeling—stuff like that. To tell you the truth, John B., I enjoy doing it. I lose track of what I do every day, and looking back in the journal it's like I can remember it."

"Maybe you'll write one of those books like Carlotta likes," he said. "With good grammar, too."

We walked back to the house, and by now everyone was seated, ready for dinner. Two platters of roasted duck sat in the middle of the table, surrounded by Carlotta's casserole, a bowl of mashed potatoes, several pitchers of gravy and a loaf of bread with a slab of butter next to it. An empty chair was next to Carlotta, and before I sat down, I walked around and filled everyone's glass with wine.

"Here's a toast to Dad," John B. said. We all raised our glasses.

"To Dad!" all our voices joined in.

"And next Thanksgiving, I hope to invite you all to our place in Santa Rosa!" John B. announced.

"Here! Here!" I said.

The platters were passed around and each of us filled our plates. Ma and Josephine had stuffed the ducks with cubes of bread, grapes, celery and onions. The oils from the ducks' skin moistened the stuffing. The talking stopped when we ate.

"John B., will you miss Sonoma?" Carlotta asked.

"I won't have time to miss it," he said. "There's plenty of work to do over there."

"Well, the little chickens sure like the brooder house you and Bert built." Carlotta sliced a piece of duck breast and brought it to her mouth.

"It turned out fine," John B. said.

I ate an extra serving of everything. I didn't eat like this very often because I wasn't much of a cook—didn't have the patience for it. I ate a lot of dried beef and bread instead—and eggs, lots of eggs—fried, hard-boiled, poached—it didn't matter.

"Save room for the pie, Bert!" Gertie said.

"Don't you worry—I got a hollow leg!" I said.

Everyone laughed.

After pie and coffee, Ma and Carlotta sat together in the living room. Carlotta held Ma's hand. "I do have some news to share with you," Carlotta said. "My brother and I have finally reached a settlement on the ranch. He's agreed to accept eight thousand dollars to relinquish all claims to the property. This bickering has been going on too long, and I don't have to tell all of you the costs."

"That's good news," Ma said.

Carlotta turned toward Ma on the couch. "I realize it won't bring your John back, but it will avoid any future confrontations." She paused. "He won't try to cross the ranch again."

"I worried about that happening again with Bert," Ma said. "I thought about it a lot."

"No, that shouldn't be a problem. I only wished I'd acted earlier," Carlotta paused. "There's other news, too, that I want to share with you. John's case is going to trial. My attorney has filed an appeal to the earlier verdict by the locals, and the appeal has been granted by the courts."

"That whole thing was a farce," John B. said.

"My brother has a lot of clout in this town," Carlotta said. "My entire family does, I have to admit."

"But there's so much bad feeling toward my husband," Ma said. "John B. read to me what they wrote in the newspaper."

"Because everyone knows my brother—which is why we need a trial outside of Sonoma."

"I don't know, Carlotta," Ma said. "Do you think it's a good idea?"

"Well, I do," Carlotta said. "I'll file the papers."

We finished our coffee and talked about what might happen if it goes to court. "It won't bring John back," Carlotta said, "but it's a way of showing our love toward a very decent man."

The afternoon light was fading fast. "Carlotta," I said. "I think it's time to leave. I'll get the carriage."

Ma, Josephine, John B. and Gertie followed us out to the front porch. They'd put together a plate of leftovers: slices of duck breast with a big scoop of dressing, and a piece of pumpkin pie. I helped Carlotta into her carriage and walked around to the other side and climbed up to the driver's seat next to her. We waved good-bye to everyone and set out back to Carlotta's ranch. "Did you have a good time?" I asked Carlotta once we were out on the road.

"I did, thank you," she said. "And thank you for including me."

I rubbed my stomach. "I think I ate too much."

Carlotta laughed. "Well, there was plenty to eat—and you can certainly put it away."

We drove west. Carlotta chuckled to herself. "What's so funny?" I asked.

"You don't mind me correcting your language?"

"No, I don't."

"I mean, so much of what you say is colorful—very colorful—and I don't want to discourage that."

"But it ain't correct, is it?"

"No, *it's* not correct—not *ain't* correct."

"I won't ever get it right, will I?"

"Sure you will—with some practice and me reminding you," and Carlotta laughed again.

"I'm working on it." I didn't mention the journal because I was afraid she'd ask me to read from it sometime, and there were plenty of days I was writing about her, and how I felt, and I knew it'd be embarrassing if she ever heard what I wrote.

She sat close to me on the carriage seat and with her body next to mine it felt good. We both commented on the late afternoon sunlight and how it slanted across the sky and seemed to outline every tree, every little dip and swell on the eastern side of the valley behind us. It was a carriage ride I wished could have lasted for hours more but soon—too soon—we were turning onto the road that led to her ranch. I stopped the carriage at the garden gate and she grabbed her baskets from behind the seat.

"Thank you again, Bert." She offered her gloved hand and I took it. "Don't forget your leftovers."

"No, thank you and thanks for the grammar lesson," I said.

"I hope it wasn't *no* bother," she said.

"That don't sound right."

"Because it's not— I purposely misspoke— and it wasn't *any* bother."

"Well, I purposely misspoke, too, so we're even."

I drove the carriage back to the barn, and unharnessed her horse and led it back to its stall. Molly and Dolly watched me as I led Carlotta's horse by them. "Don't worry, you two," I said to them. "You ain't being replaced—no, let me say that right—you're *not* being replaced." I gave all the horses a scoop of oats. Little Ike nuzzled up to my hand as I dropped the oats in his manger. "Grammar's important," I told them.

34
Preparing for More Holidays
· ·

The rains fell again a day after Thanksgiving—a good, long rain that lasted nearly two days. It swelled the creek alongside Carlotta's ranch, and the little trickle of water I'd heard all summer during the quiet times of working on the chicken houses was now a loud, moving, mud-colored flow. And then as suddenly as the rains started, they stopped. A slight wind blew the remaining clouds away and left a sky as clear and blue as a polished gem stone.

Alfonso always liked the rains. He'd come from a part of Mexico where rains were scarce and when they did fall, it was always, he believed, because he remembered to pray. His mother, he said, often walked out into the middle of a downpour, her arms outstretched, her eyes looking toward the heavens, thanking God. "*Gracias, Dios! Gracias!*"

"Did you pray last week?" I asked him.

"*Como?*"

"I said, did you pray last week and that's why the rains came?"

He laughed. "No, *senor* Bert. I forget to pray."

Carlotta was excited because already she was starting to plan the Christmas festivities. She'd sent Alfonso to cut a Christmas tree in the hills above Glen Ellen where friends of the colonel owned property. Alfonso returned with an eight foot tall tree that towered above him as he removed it from the ranch wagon. I built a stand for it and we set it up out on the patio for Carlotta's approval. She loved it, and already she and Ah Yep's wife had taken out boxes of ornaments to decorate it. We moved the furniture back against the walls in her parlor and brought the tree in and stood it up in front of the parlor windows.

"Splendid!" she said. "I'm so excited! And, so far, all my guests have answered their invitations. It's going to be a full house."

Carlotta was like a little child in manyways. When things went well, she was spirited, happy, a constant smile on her face, talking all the time—everything seemed to fascinate her. She was filled with energy—her feet never seemed to touch the ground. But when things didn't go good, I should say 'when they didn't go *well*,' when something happened to change her mood—and it was a rare time she told me what that was—a sadness spread across her face. Her eyes lost their sparkle and she'd hold-up in her house, sometimes for days before I'd see her again. I hated those times, wanting, somehow, to help her but knowing there was nothing I could do. So I went about my work, always looking toward her house, hoping for any sign of her, hoping to see her out in the garden or over at the layers' house—but nothing. I'd ask Ah Yep, her houseman, about her and he'd offer that wry smile of his and say, "She inside."

But now with Christmas quick approaching, and all the planning that involved, Carlotta was that little child again, making lists of things to do, sending Alfonso, and sometimes me, on different errands into town. One of those errands involved buying red and green streamers she wanted to string from the ceiling. I went to Schocken's New Store to buy the bunting but they were all out, so it meant I'd have to go to Pauli's where Cameron worked. I'd been avoiding her for weeks now, not knowing what to do, what to tell her. Every day that passed, I'd come up with more excuses that seemed to draw out our meeting up even longer. I still wanted to see her—realizing that Carlotta was a long shot—and that maybe there was still a chance with Cameron—that maybe she'd lighten up on me not accepting Jesus and not following the ten commandments closely like she done, and maybe, just maybe, we'd be a couple after all. I thought about this a lot—too much, maybe, but my hopes with either of these women rested on somebody changing and all fingers pointed at me.

I pulled my wagon in front of Pauli's, sucked in my breath and walked through the store's front door. Cameron was with a customer and didn't notice me. I walked up a different aisle to the front counter and Mrs. Pauli was standing behind it. "Can I help you, young man?" she asked.

"I'm looking for streamers. Holiday streamers," I said in a low voice. I didn't want it to carry.

"Streamers?" Mrs. Pauli looked at me. "You mean bunting?"

"Yes, that's what I mean."

"Follow me."

When I turned around, Cameron was looking right at me. It was a puzzled look. Or a surprised look—one of those two. I wasn't sure. In the next aisle, Mrs. Pauli had taken down several boxes of colored bunting all tightly wound into coils.

"There's red and green," she said, "the favorite holiday colors."

I didn't hear a word she said, but I took the coils of bunting out of their boxes and walked them to the front counter. When I turned around, Cameron was standing behind me.

"Hello, Bert," she said. "I thought the earth might have swallowed you up or something."

She looked as she always looked, with that simple glow of hers. Those wonderful green eyes the color of jade—the milky complexion, that wonderful puckered smile. I did what I usually did in these situations—I fumbled around for an excuse, trying to avoid those jade-colored eyes as best I could because I always felt they saw right through me. "I've been busy with the new job," I told her.

"New job?" she asked.

"Yeah, I'm working full-time now out at the Stamm ranch. I took over there after my dad's death," I said.

"That's when I saw you last when you came in to buy the bunting for the funeral wagon." She paused and looked into my eyes. "That was such a tragic event. I prayed for you and your family."

"And here I am buying more bunting," I said, "but this time for a happier event."

"You're not hiring out as a teamster anymore?"

"No, but I still have my horses and I use them around the ranch, but, no, I'm not hiring out anymore," I said. "Going to be doing something different."

"Do you miss not being on the road?" she asked.

"I do. I like being out there, but work around the ranch has been good, too," I said. "I even have my own house now—more room than I know what to do with."

She lowered her voice and glanced behind her. "I miss not seeing you at the services."

I looked back at Mrs. Pauli behind the counter. "Cameron, could we step outside a moment?"

She looked over at Mrs. Pauli—there were no other customers in the store. "Yes, for just a moment," Cameron said.

I opened the door and followed her out onto the sidewalk. "Would you like to go on another date with me again?" I asked. "I've been thinking of you a lot."

She looked at me and didn't answer, then looked away. "I can't," she said.

"You can't?"

"No, I can't," she said.

"Why not? You don't like me anymore?"

"No, that's not it," she said.

"What is it then?"

"My father doesn't want me seeing you again," she said.

"He doesn't?"

"He said he heard some stories about you—they were not very flattering."

"And that's all it took—some stories?" I asked, and looked at her, but this time she looked away. "What about you? How you feel about me?"

"I don't go against my father's wishes," she said.

"Ever? You always do what he says?"

"I do."

"Why?" I asked. "Even if it's something you want to do?"

"He knows what's best for me," she said.

"I don't buy that—don't we know ourselves, what's best—well, maybe not best, but what's in our heart?"

"We're different—you and me," she said. "More than I realized."

We stood there and looked at each other and then I stared off like I often done—hoping I'd find the answer to all of this written in a tree across the street—a sign in a window—but nothing was written there—nothing. "I'm sorry—I do really like you, Bert—but we are different—you're set in your ways and I'm set in mine—and I don't think that's ever going to change—you said as much, didn't you?"

"I said a lot of things—I know." And I did. But now it was all coming out in the open from where it'd been hiding—what I'd been ducking from these past months and what she'd been avoiding, too. "It's that whole God-thing, isn't it?" I asked. I looked at her again. "We can't seem to get around it, can we?"

"No, we can't," she said.

"I was fooling myself that we could—that we'd look past these differences—"

"They're too big—too important—to look past, Bert."

"Yeah, you're right—they are." I took her hand. God was important to her—he wasn't to me. "Better to know now, isn't—than dragging the whole thing out?"

"I think so," she said.

I felt bad—lousy, even, to have it end like this. I thought it'd be different—that I could buck the odds—but I knew from the start it was a long shot. Folks have their belief in God—their beliefs in anything— and it's hard changing them. You can argue it back and forth and offer all your proofs until you're blue in the face, but it doesn't do a lick of good. "Oh, well," I said, "I still need the bunting."

"We can still be friends, right?" she said. "And if you change or whatever—"

"I'll let you know," I said.

"And you're always welcome to join us for services—you know that, too."

"Sure, I know that."

"Maybe during Christmas?" she said. "That's a special time for us."

"Sure, maybe then," I said, but it was me just talking, saying words she'd like to hear but knowing nothing more was going to happen between us—I was pretty sure of that. She'd just hammered the last nail into the coffin.

We went back inside, and I paid for the bunting, said goodbye to Cameron, and left the store. And that was that—another hope of mine crashing to earth. Was I surprised? No, not really. I had no intention of going to her father's services—no more I figured than the Lord'd be knocking on my door anytime soon. I didn't see it happening. The world would end first. Still, I didn't want to toss all of it away—something inside made me reluctant to do that, something inside still hung onto a little shred of hope. Maybe I would go to her father's services— I didn't know. I'd have to think about it—see how things went first. That's how it was with me—saying one thing one minute, then backtracking and saying something different, the next—always trying to figure out a situation, a certain predicament I found myself in and how I could best land on my feet. I spent too much time doing this—worrying and thinking 'til it had me going in circles.

The whole ride back to the ranch I thought about Cameron and all the hesitation I felt around her. What was that about, I wondered? It got back to beliefs—hers and mine. Why was it so hard to believe what she believed? I couldn't answer why, except it was. We were different. We'd been raised different. I didn't see God the way she did—most of the time I didn't see him at all. She saw him everywhere except when there was bad happening, and then she'd make some excuse for him, saying it was some kind of "divine plan" nonsense. I wasn't buying it. I did try looking for him, though— especially when all my luck had run out—but he must have been hiding in the shadows or somewhere far off where he couldn't hear my voice. He was unreliable, too, because when I most needed this guy, he wasn't anywhere around. He'd become like a friend that was no longer a friend, because I was no longer useful to him. He only wanted to be around when I had something to offer him—so what was the point of keeping him? I didn't see any point in it at all.

I delivered the bunting to Carlotta and like everything else these days, she was happy. "Alfonso's set up a ladder in the parlor," she said. "Would you mind hanging the bunting for me?"

What could I say? No, I have to think about belief more? Or, I may have a toothache sometime in the next few years and have to prepare for it? Of course I said 'yes' and followed her inside. Once in the parlor she handed me a coil of bunting and a can full of tacks and a little hammer—almost like a toy hammer. She instructed me exactly how she wanted the bunting hung with it starting from each corner of the room and all four points joining together at the center—and, oh, yes, I had to turn the bunting to give it a spiral effect.

I wished I could share her joy about the holidays, but I couldn't—not yet, at least. I was glad the holidays made other people happy and it was certainly welcome to see Carlotta's change of mood. Ma and Josephine, too, especially liked them, and I didn't want to dampen their joy—especially now when joy in their lives was so hard to come by. I did everything I could to make them special for Ma and Josephine and Carlotta, too—maybe that was my holiday spirit. It actually made feel pretty good. It broke down some of the walls I'd built around me, helped me think of other folks and not spend so much time thinking about myself, and wondering where I was going to land in this crazy world. Where was I going to land, I wondered? I thought about this so much, but as I thought about it more, I realized I'd landed already—every moment in my life was a landing of sorts. I had to keep reminding myself—this was it—right here where my feet touched down—right at this very moment and all the moments like them. No more wondering—no more mystery. I'd landed.

35

The Christmas Party
· · · · · · · · · · · · · · · · · · · ·

Carlotta's holiday guests started arriving two days before Christmas. Alfonso met them at the train depot in Carlotta's carriage which she'd trimmed with holly and sprigs of mistletoe and some of the bunting I'd bought at Pauli's. The first day two couples arrived, both men with big round waists that looked like they put barrel hoops inside their pants. The women wore long dresses and hats that from a distance looked like a duck had squatted on each of their heads. They all talked a great deal as they moved from the carriage to Carlotta's house, fluttering their arms about, stopping to breathe in the country air, and marveling at the quiet all around them after the noise and bustle of the city. Alfonso made two trips to the house carrying their luggage.

The following day another couple arrived. The man was trim with a large moustache, and like the others before him, wore a suit and vest and doffed a derby hat. The woman was slim, as well, dressed in the fashion of the day—frilly sleeves and a puffed-out bodice—her hair bobbed and wearing a hat not quite as laughable as the two before her. They stepped down on opposite sides of the carriage, Alfonso taking the woman's hand. She looked around her as though she'd been here before and was trying to remember when. Neither of them spoke to each other. The man straightened the lapels on his suit and surveyed his surroundings. Carlotta came out to meet them. She and the woman embraced, but it was a stiff, formal embrace, just their shoulders touching each other. Carlotta held her hand out to the man, and he took it, and she bowed slightly. I heard her say the word, "Senator." They proceeded to the house followed by Alfonso carrying their baggage. Ah Yep greeted the party at the front door, bowing as he always did.

The weather was cold and damp, typical for December, and the house guests remained mostly indoors. Few of them even stepped outside, including Carlotta. I worked around the ranch and tended to the young pullets, shoveled out the dirty shavings and shoveled in the new. The pullets scrambled about whenever I went inside, but one or two of the more curious would approach me, cock their heads and stare with their dark eyes. I'd put mash in the palm of my hand and these same curious birds would come up to me, stare at my hand and then peck at the mash.

I'd ridden into town mid-afternoon to say hello to Tino and share a couple of rounds, thirsty for a little of my own company. With Carlotta tending to her guests, it was a good time to slip away unnoticed. Carlotta didn't invite me to join her guests, and for that I was put-out a bit and didn't want to stay around. I wasn't drinking as much at the ranch—maybe a glass of wine or two when invited over by Carlotta—but not my normal drinking habits. Generally, I liked company around when I drank. I told myself I was a social drinker.

When I arrived at the livery, Tino was sitting behind a desk in his little office with a stack of invoices in front of him. He was glad to see me and I was glad to see him.

"You married yet?" he asked.

"Not yet," I said. "Just getting the papers in order though—any day now it'll be high cotton." We both laughed. He pulled open a drawer in his desk and brought out a half-filled bottle of bourbon. He reached to a shelf behind him and grabbed a pair of glasses.

"Accounts payable," he said, and poured me a drink.

"Good—then pay me up."

He filled his glass and we raised them and toasted. "Merry Christmas and all that other horse shit that's going around," he said.

"Merry Christmas to you, Tino." I drank and felt the warmth in my mouth and as it trickled down my throat.

"How's life at the rancho?" Tino asked.

"Carlotta's got her guests from the city visiting now—all the big-wigs."

"So she don't want you around?"

"No, that's not it," I said. I bristled a bit at his comment. "Let them hob-nob or whatever they do—it doesn't interest me." That wasn't entirely true. I wanted to be included.

"The big shots from the city—the big deal-makers." Tino laughed.

"Yeah, they get out of the carriage and breathe in the air and start pissing their pants about how good it smells," I said. "I take a whiff of this same air and all I can smell are the milk cows knee-deep in their own shit."

"Ah, yes, the captains of industry," Tino said.

"You've been reading too many newspapers."

"You read the local one lately?" he asked. "What a crock of shit they've been writing about Sheers and your old man—like Sheers is some kind of hero—wouldn't harm a fly and had to protect himself against your father's vicious attacks. It's right there in the paper."

"I read it, too," I said "But you don't need any newspaper to know how half the town feels."

"Half?" Tino laughed. "It's more than half."

"We're aiming for a trial. Carlotta's got her attorney involved."

"Good luck on that one," he said. "I still think there's a better way of handling it."

"What? Shooting the son of a bitch?"

"I'm plannin' it out," Tino said. "Plannin' about how I can make it look more like an accident."

"My advice is to just let it go."

"I know—that's what you keep sayin'."

It'd been over a year since the shooting, and Tino still hadn't let go of it—still thinking how he was going to even the score with Sheers.

"You got plans for Christmas?" I asked Tino.

"Working here—carriage rentals, maybe drive a couple of drunks home—the usual."

"You're welcome to join us out at Ma's," I said. "I thought the holidays might cheer her up but it isn't turning out that way. If anything, she's feeling worse and I worry about her."

"That's a big load to carry when your husband's gone like that."

We drained the remaining bottle and Tino filled me in on the gossip around town. Flo, his usual source, had taken up with Marvin McKinnon, a jealous type who didn't like her spending time with Tino—didn't like her spending time with any one— so gossip was thin. "How long's that going to last?" I asked Tino.

"Who knows around here?" Tino said. "It's still early and the shine ain't worn off yet."

I looked out through the livery doors and could see it was fast getting dark. I said goodbye and rode home, my head swimming in a pool of good bourbon. The night air bit at my face. The sky was filled with stars and once or twice I'd stop and look up at them and think of my father and what I'd say to him if I could see him now. Would I tell him he was right all along about me? That he could see where I was headed before I could? Would I tell him I could have been a better son? You always think of these things after it's too late to say them. When I reached home, I stood my bicycle against a porch post, sat down in a chair in the portico and stared out at the night. My mind kept wandering, thinking about the upcoming holiday and Carlotta's guests and whether I'd be invited over or not. Then I'd think of my father. I slipped into the chair, took a couple of deep breaths and listened to the quiet around me. I was half-hidden by wisteria vines, and as I sat there I heard a man and a woman approach, then stop maybe twenty yards off in the ranch yard.

"I want to go home—now!" I heard the woman say.

"Be reasonable," the man said. "We just got here—and, besides, there isn't another train until tomorrow."

"Then I want a hotel room for the night" she said. "I'm not staying here and watching the two of you carry on."

"Mildred, you're imagining all this," the man said.

"No, I'm not! I've got two eyes—I can see. I know your little histories together. I can see it in the glances you pass back and forth—I'm not blind. I wasn't born yesterday, either." A silence followed then I heard the woman say, "Don't touch me!"

"Oh, for crissakes," the man said. "Let's go back inside and enjoy the company, okay?"

"Company? They're your friends, not mine! I don't like anyone here, so how can I enjoy it?"

"Try, will you? For the next two days, okay?"

"That's all I do is try—this was all a big mistake," the woman said. "I knew it from the start."

"Let's go back in and make like nothing happened."

"That's all we do, you know that?" she said. "Make like nothing's happened when everything's happening and it's all falling down around us."

"Now you're exaggerating."

"I am not! Every bit of it is true!"

"Please, let's go back inside," the man pleaded.

I heard them walk away, and as they did, I looked from behind the wisteria vines to see it was the man Carlotta had addressed as 'senator' and the woman was his wife. I could make out their outlines against the lamplight through Carlotta's parlor windows—they were the only two skinny guests. Several times they stopped and he'd take her arm and she'd jerk it away. They were across the yard now, and I couldn't hear their conversation. He finally persuaded her to rejoin the rest of the guests. When they entered through the front door, the noise of the gathering inside spilled outside—the bursts of laughter, the tinkling of glasses, and when they closed the door behind them it grew quiet again outside.

The following morning, Christmas Eve, I woke up with a headache, built a fire in the kitchen stove, heated a pot of water and made coffee. After drinking two strong cups, I slipped on my boots and walked over to the brooder house to check on the pullets. Inside, I poured more mash into their troughs and refilled the water crocks with a bucket of water kept just outside the door. The young chickens scampered toward the troughs, sometimes trying to climb over one another, and pecked away at the mash. We'd lost one pullet a few days back. It wasn't healthy from the start, its eyes always half-closed—a white film growing over them—and when I'd gone into the brooder house the next day, there it was lying on its side, dead. It upset Carlotta, but I told her she had to expect it, that if just one or two died, we'd be lucky.

I'd closed the door behind me, latched it and when I turned around Carlotta was walking toward me. "Merry Christmas, Bert."

"Same to you." I was at the bottom of the steps now. "How's the party going?"

"Fine, everyone's in good spirits."

"No problems?" I asked, fishing around for more information on the senator and his wife.

"No, not really," she said. Her tone of voice didn't fool me.

"Who's the tall, thin guy that arrived with his wife after your earlier guests?" I asked her.

"Oh, you mean Senator Amos and his wife, Mildred?" She paused here. "Why do you ask?"

I didn't know whether to tell her what I'd overheard the night before or not. "Just curious," I said.

"Mildred does not like the country," Carlotta said. "She's a born and bred city girl."

"And what about the senator?"

"The senator is a politician—he likes everyone and everything." She laughed. "He's a dear man, though, with a very good heart."

"The chickens are doing fine," I said. "No deaths."

"Oh, good!" She seemed to welcome the change of subject. "Ah Yep picked up a turkey yesterday. He's going to prepare it this morning."

"Prepare? You mean, kill and pluck it?"

"I gave him specific orders that he do it far away from the house and out of my sight. I can't bear to see those kinds of things."

It was one of the many aspects about Carlotta that puzzled me. She didn't want to see a turkey killed or anything killed for that matter, but she gladly ate it. She hated the sight of blood, and the thought of any animal suffering, but she raised beef cattle on her ranch. And one time she nearly fainted when I dragged a cross-cut saw across the top of my hand—blood spurted out and John B. caught her as she fainted.

"Do your guests ever wander outside?" I asked. "Or do they stay in all day and night?"

"They're talkers," she said. "Give them a glass of brandy and a good cigar and they're a happy bunch of Republicans, who could talk about President Harrison and Governor Markham until I have to leave the room. Politics just doesn't interest me."

"And yet all your guests are politicians."

"They're friends of the colonel, and I felt I just couldn't abandon them after the colonel's death."

"So you endure them?"

"Well, I don't think 'endure' is the right word." Her eyes fastened on mine. "Aren't you being a bit sarcastic?"

"Sorry, I don't much care for politicians," I said.

"Oh, that's right—they're stuff-shirts—aren't they?" she said. "I was going to introduce you to them but in that case, maybe I shouldn't."

I looked over Carlotta's shoulder and Senator Amos was approaching. He stopped alongside Carlotta and the two of them looked at each other, smiling. He breathed in deeply. "Ah, the country air! Nothing like it." He looked at me. "And who is this young man?"

"This is Bert Miller," Carlotta said. "He's the foreman here. Bert, this is State Senator Amos."

The senator reached out and we shook hands.

"Bert, his brother and his father built these chicken houses."

"A fine job," the senator said. "I was inspecting them yesterday. You might have something here, young man, something you might want to expand on."

"Expand?"

"Yes—become more commercial," he said.

"I hadn't look at it that way," I said.

"It could be a money-maker, especially with the market for fresh eggs the way it is."

Carlotta looked at me and then at the senator. "Is Mildred feeling better?"

"She was still in bed when I left her—maybe it's the country air that doesn't agree with her," he said.

"The poor soul." Carlotta reached out and touched his arm.

The senator hadn't taken her to a hotel after all.

"Hopefully it's just a passing thing," Carlotta said.

"She doesn't travel well, either—the least little change sets her off."

"But as a senator, aren't you travelling around a great deal?" I asked.

"I am," he shot back. "She often chooses not to accompany me and I'm fine with that arrangement—we both are."

"Bert, if you'll excuse us, I wanted to show Senator Amos the little gazebo your dad built."

The pair disappeared down the path and I walked over to the stable and fed the horses. Stupid me, I was trying to make sense of this whole gathering, trying to fit more puzzle pieces together that would add up to Carlotta but there were too many pieces. I knew it. I was jealous of the senator just then—I admit it because it was Carlotta that concerned the senator's wife, and the reason his wife wanted to leave. And I remembered, too, how disappointed Carlotta felt at Thanksgiving when a certain guest had postponed his visit, and my gut told me that guest was the senator. Right then I didn't feel too good about my prospects—in fact, I felt about as low as I'd ever felt. The real world was catching up with me and the pretty picture I sometimes imagined between Carlotta and me now seemed as far away as those stars I was watching last night. That's what happens when you give the imagination just a little free rein— it runs off and it's hard pulling it back. I let the little things we done together—the times we rode bicycles or when she laid her hand on mine or how she looked with the setting sun on her face—fool me into thinking there was more there than there really was.

No, I'd been fooling myself, and could see things weren't lining up the way I wanted them to, and wasn't much I could do about it. And here I was, stuck right in the middle, wishing I was back being a teamster again, drinking with my friends, and making the rounds—not putting my heart out there only to have it hung on a line and dried out. I'd taken this job on a certain long-shot—I knew it—and now I was seeing just how long a shot it was. Already I was thinking of ways I could walk away from all of it.

I was working with Little Ike in my spare time. He was halter-broke now and I'd just say the word "Stop" and he'd halt in his tracks. He liked to nuzzle up to me and nibble on my ear, too. He was like a dog—a big dog with long stilt legs. I'd talk to him and he'd look back at me like he understood everything I said. "Women, little Ike, will break your heart if you let them." He'd look at me and nuzzled some more. "Pretty soon, though, you'll be gelded and won't have to worry about females," I said. "I'm sparing you some grief later—trust me. You're not going to like it at first, but later, you'll see—you're gonna thank me."

I went back home, emptied my nap sack and slipped it onto my back. I rode my bicycle into town and stopped at Pauli's to buy Christmas gifts for Ma, Josephine, John B. and Gertie. I decided I'd buy a gift for Carlotta, too. Cameron was working there, wearing green and red ribbons in her hair, and I was glad to see her. Partly I figured that since chances with Carlotta were looking slimmer with the senator around, I wouldn't give up entirely on Cameron—you know, try to keep that one alive. Sure, there was all that religious mumbo-jumbo and quoting the Bible—and it didn't take any genius to see I wasn't one of her old man's favorites—but when I looked down at my page of prospects, the page was blank—not a name on it.

"Hello, Bert! Merry Christmas!" she said.

"A merry one to you, as well, Cameron."

"Buying gifts?"

"I am—maybe you could help me out?"

"Of course," she said. "Who are they for?"

I told her and she led me down one aisle with mostly household items: table cloths, napkins, towels, aprons. I picked out three aprons, one each for Ma, Josephine and Gertie. One aisle over were women's accessories, and what caught my eye were pocket watches but they weren't watches at all— but little women's compacts, and when you opened them up, there was a mirror inside. I picked out three of those and three little round boxes of rouge powder with puffs inside each. I didn't like seeing powder on women's faces mostly because it reminded me of all the floosies I'd ended up with after a night of drinking—I didn't like how the powder found its way into creases on a woman's face and made her look like a mannequin in a store window. It was one of the things I liked about both Carlotta and Cameron—they didn't use powder—but it was in style and so was bright red lipstick. I bought the powder and the lipstick anyway. I looked around for something I thought Carlotta might like, and decided I'd look at books instead at J. Ruffner's.

"Would you like those wrapped?" Cameron asked.

"I would, but could I come back a bit later and pick them up?" I asked. "There's one other gift I need to get."

"They'll be ready when you return."

"Maybe we could talk sometime?" I asked her. There I was still clinging some little bit of hope—when everything's gone—shot to hell—there's always hope, isn't there?

"Sure, but not now." She looked back at the counter where Mrs. Pauli stood.

I walked just a couple of doors down to Ruffner's and went inside. The shop walls were lined with books from floor to ceiling. "Can I help you?" Mr. Ruffner asked. He had a pipe stuck in the corner of his mouth and he smelled like pipe tobacco—his whole shop did.

"I'm looking for a novel—something popular," I said.

"Literary? Pulp fiction? Modern?" Ruffner asked.

"She reads novels by Jane Austen."

"Follow me." And I followed Ruffner down an aisle of books.

He walked with a stoop—bent over at the waist—maybe from reading too much.

"This is one that's been very popular and we only have two copies left." He pulled the copy from the shelf and ran his sleeve across its cover before handing it to me. The title read "The Picture of Dorian Grey."

"It's quite well written—a bit controversial, but a fine work nevertheless—the author's English."

"I'll take it. And could you wrap it, please?"

"Of course," he said.

I paid for the book and thought I'd go over to Wegner's Pharmacy. I bought little bottles of perfume for each of the women there, and then returned to Pauli's. By now several customers were in the store and Cameron was occupied. She motioned toward the counter. "Your items are there," she said.

"We'll talk later?" I said.

She nodded yes.

I wanted to talk to her but I didn't know what I'd say. My little fantasy with Carlotta looked like it'd run its course, finally crashing to earth—and grasping for straws—I thought of giving Cameron and God one more shot even though nothing had changed between us. Maybe it'd change, though—maybe I'd start praying—maybe a meteor would hit me—maybe she'd accept me just the way I was— but then I remembered about her old man, too—the Reverend Landers raising both arms toward the rafters and asking Jesus to come down like Jesus was some kind of trained pigeon—and the reverend's eyes—like there were little fires built behind each one and him asking what my intentions were toward his daughter— and any hope between us just petered out.

I took my gifts, waved goodbye to Cameron and left the store. I rode back to Carlotta's, feeling a bit sorry for myself and wishing the holidays would soon be over—all they did was remind me of the joy I wasn't feeling. I rode into the ranch yard and glanced over toward the main house. Carlotta's male guests were bundled in jackets now and sat out in the patio in the cool sunlight. They smoked their cigars and clouds of blue smoke hung over them. Senator Amos sat at one end of the table, and when he saw me he got up and walked over to the garden fence.

"Bert, hello there!" he called from behind the fence.

I said hello back and turned away, not wanting to talk. Before I knew it, he opened the garden gate and was walking toward me.

"I was sorry to hear about your father," he said. "Carlotta told me the details."

"Just his bad luck, you know?" I said.

"I told her and I'll tell you—that I'll do what I can to see that justice is done. I have contacts in the courts." The senator twisted the ends of his moustache.

"I appreciate that because the jury's already decided here that it was self-defense."

"I know, but that can be appealed," he said. "I'll see what I can do—enjoy the holidays." He turned and rejoined the other guests in the patio.

It was hard to hate the senator after our conversation. I didn't hate him though—I envied him. He had what I wanted—all the right qualities to win over Carlotta—qualities I listed again and again, the kinds of qualities I always came up short on. Of course, I was jumping to all kinds of conclusions here, but I figured the worst. If I figured the worst, my reasoning went, I'd never be disappointed. I was looking for exits, too. My thinking had already shifted. I'd rat-holed money away each month, I had a good pair of horses and a wagon, and plenty of work out there, and if I couldn't bear it anymore having the senator around and him and Carlotta carrying on, I'd be gone. No sense staying around, letting my heart take a beating—because I knew that's what would happen. No, I'd be gone—like dust blowing down the road—I'd be gone. I didn't know exactly where, but that didn't matter—I'd find a place.

36

Dealing With It

• • • • • • • • • • • • • • •

Ispent Christmas day with family out in Vineburg. We tried making it a happy affair but the dark cloud of dad's death still hung over everything. Ma sat in her chair and forced a smile until her smiled disappeared. I sat next to her and held her hand. Then she'd take to staring blankly at the Christmas tree that Josephine and Gertie had decorated. I hated seeing her like this—we all did—and wished there was something—anything—we could do to change it, but we couldn't bring dad back. Each of us comforted her as best we could.

We ate turkey dinner with all the trimmings and had pumpkin pie and coffee for dessert. After dinner, we gathered in the living room to open presents. Josephine and Gertie liked the compacts I'd bought for them at Pauli's, and right after opening their little boxes, the two were patting their cheeks with powder and giggling in front of the tiny mirrors. Each of them had dabbed a bit of perfume on their wrists, and dabbed a bit on Ma's wrist, as well. Ma smelled it and wrinkled her nose. John B. gave me a pair of gloves, "riding gloves," he called them. The leather was thin, made for riding and not for work, he said. Ma gave me a new work shirt, said she was tired of seeing me wearing ones with frayed collars. I bought John B. a new level from Green's Supply. I'd dropped his several times working on the chicken houses and the bubble was off kilter.

By mid-afternoon I was ready to go home. I hugged Ma, my sister and Gertie goodbye and shook John B.'s hand and thanked him for the gloves. I rode my bicycle back to Carlotta's, leaned it against the porch post and went out to check on the horses. All three nickered when they saw me, fluttering their big horse lips. I gave each a scoop of oats. Halfway back to my house I glanced over, and there was Carlotta and the senator walking back from the path down to the gazebo.

"Hello, Bert!" Carlotta called out. "Don't go away! I have something for you."

"Well, I have something for you, too," I said.

"Wait just a minute," she said, "I'll go inside and get it."

"That's quite a little gazebo your dad built," the senator said. "All those different cuts on the rafters and each one fitting perfectly into one point—a nice piece of carpentry."

` "He was good at what he did." I stepped back from the senator. "If you'll excuse me, I'll get Carlotta's gift."

"Of course," he said.

When I returned, Carlotta was again with the senator. She handed me a little gift-wrapped box. I handed her my gift.

"I'll open it later," I said. "I don't want to keep you from all your guests."

"Oh, they're gone," she said. "They left on the train this morning—everyone, of course, except the senator." The two of them smiled at each other.

"It's so rare to get a chance to stay in the countryside, and I thought I'd take advantage of it," he said. "There's nothing I like better."

Sure, I thought—that, and getting rid of your wife.

"Why don't we go inside and open the gifts there?" Carlotta suggested.

I followed them into the parlor. Carlotta and the senator sat together on a small couch. Carlotta motioned to Ah Yep and he returned shortly with a bottle of brandy and three glasses.

"Open yours first, Bert," she said.

I undid the wrapping and opened the little box. It was a compass with its own leather pouch, a beautiful silver compass with a bronze needle painted red at its very tip.

"In case you ever get lost out on the road," she said. "You'll always know where North is."

I thanked her. Carlotta then opened her present, handing the loose wrapping to the senator. She read its cover. "Oscar Wilde!" I love it! Thank you so much! He's a very daring writer, you know."

I didn't know—only what Ruffner told me. I nodded my head though as if I did, and rotated the compass watching its needle move between the bold letters. The senator filled each of the glasses. We toasted a 'Merry Christmas' and drank.

"What do you like most about the country?" I asked him.

He and Carlotta looked at each other and smiled. I was fishing for more information.

"The quiet," he said. "And this time, I'm thinking of taking in the waters out at Aqua Caliente. A little bit of rheumatism is creeping into my bones and the warm mineral water is just the ticket for it." He looked over at Carlotta. "Maybe we could all go out there together sometime?"

"Sure. I'd like to try them," I said.

"What about tomorrow?" the senator asked. "Have you made plans?" He looked right at me.

"Just some work here in the early morning but afterwards I'm free," I said.

"And you, Carlotta?" the senator smiled again at her.

"I think that can be arranged," she said.

"I'll have the carriage ready," I said. "What time?"

"Late morning?" Carlotta suggested. "We leave here at, say, ten thirty?"

"Capital!" The senator clapped his hands together.

The following morning, I harnessed Carlotta's bay horse to her carriage still decorated with holly and mistletoe. Carlotta and the senator met me promptly at ten thirty, each carrying a little bag with them. It was a chilly morning and steam came from our mouths whenever we talked. Carlotta and the senator sat in the rear seat of the buggy.

We drove east out Napa Road to Grand Avenue, then north to Boyes Springs until we arrived at the Aqua Caliente bath house. It was built of stone with a wide, welcoming entry door, and folks walked through its lobby in long bath robes. We paid our entrance, went to our respective changing rooms and slipped into our bathing costumes. I was anxious to see what so much of Carlotta's ranch outfit kept hidden. The rest of her body was left to my imagination.

I went out into the pool area first, dipped my toes into the larger pool. It was bath-water warm. I walked down its steps into chest-high water and flailed my arms about. The warm water felt good. The senator followed. He was skinny with a little paunch of a stomach and his skin was white as milk. I waited for Carlotta to appear.

"This is the life!" the senator said. "Don't you think?"

"Feels pretty good!" I said. And it did. My joints welcomed the warm water around them, like millions of tiny fingers. My little aches and pains dissolved away.

Carlotta finally appeared. Her bathing costume wasn't as revealing as I'd hoped, but it did expose her slender arms and shoulders and the round cup-shapes of her breasts. There were little red marks on her shoulders where the straps dug into her skin and her bathing cap made her neck seem even longer, as slender as a swan's. She plunged right into the water. "Heavenly! Just heavenly!" she said.

Carlotta and the senator soon joined me. I watched how the water dripped off her body and how she tugged at the lower part of her costume. Her legs, the little bit I could see, were shapely and firm. The usual desire rose inside me. She was even more appealing than I'd ever thought and already I regretted going to the spa. It only made me want her more. The more I learned about her, the more I wanted her, and the more that seemed impossible. Somehow I'd have to deal with it, right? Either that, or head down the road. And if she hadn't invited me? I would have felt just as bad, felt excluded. Either way, I was at the losing end of this one. Impossible—that's the word that kept coming up.

When we'd had enough of the waters, and the skin on our bodies was as wrinkled and shrunken like dried prunes, we eased out of the pool and back to the changing areas. Within a half hour we were back in the carriage. Both Carlotta and the senator were bundled into their winter coats with scarves around their necks, the senator's right arm firmly around Carlotta. An hour later, we arrived at her garden gate. Carlotta's cheeks were still blushed pink from the mineral baths, her eyes bright. They thanked me for driving and I thanked them for including me. Then they both disappeared into Carlotta's house. I drove the carriage back to the stable, unharnessed Carlotta's horse and led it back to its stall. I said hello to Molly, Dolly and Little Ike and gave them their oats. I took out the compass and watched its needle move as I walked toward my house, first in one direction, and then in another. The needle moved with me. How odd, it seemed, for her to give me such a present! For all the confidence I'd felt about finally landing in a comfortable place, maybe even the promise of romance, I wasn't feeling that way at all right now. Instead, I was feeling passed-over, foolish, feeling adrift once again like that boat I kept seeing in my dreams.

37

After He Left
• • • • • • • • • • • • •

Senator Amos soon returned to the city, and for days afterwards Carlotta moped around the property, sad that he was gone. I'd learned to read her moods the way other people read a book. Even from across the yard, I seemed to pick up on them—I don't know how, but I did. I could feel it in the air between us. Maybe it was the way she carried herself, her head low, lost in thought—the eyes empty and looking far away—that usual energy that surrounded her now drained off. She'd avoided me for several days after until one morning we found ourselves together in the brooder house. I tried consoling her without being too prying, a delicate balance. "He can always return here, right? It's not like he's gone forever," I said while pouring mash into the pullets' trough.

"Am I that transparent?" she asked.

"You are—like me, you don't hide your moods very well." I was about to say 'hide your moods very good' but was remembering Carlotta's grammar lessons, trying to become more "refined."

"It's a bit of a challenge with the senator."

"How so?"

"If you must know, it's his wife. She's a terribly jealous sort," she said.

"Well, Carlotta, in fairness to her, she is his wife."

"Oh, I know, and don't think that doesn't trouble me—it troubles Senator Amos, as well."

"Why do they stay together then?"

"His career, mostly—how it'd look with him being divorced. He's invested so much into it."

"So, in the meantime, everyone's miserable."

"Silly, isn't it?" Carlotta leaned against the brooder house wall. "I have broached an ultimatum with him—several times."

"And what does he say?"

"He wants more time to think about it—to see how it plays out," she said. "'Be patient', he says. Just be patient.'"

"How do you feel about that?"

"Well, I'm anxious a great deal of the time—always wondering what's going to happen," she said. "And I confess, my patience can run thin at times."

"I can't offer you any advice," I said. "It's really up to what he decides, isn't it?"

"I know—and I don't like being in that position. I've always had the say in what I do."

"Then you decide," I told her.

"Oh, I've tried," she said. "Just when I think I've built up the courage to ask 'me or her,' I look into his eyes and can't bring myself to do it—I'm afraid of never seeing him again."

"Sometime down the road it's going to come to that, though, don't you think?" I said. "When he's going to have to decide—or you?"

"I suppose it will," Carlotta admitted.

"I heard the two of them argue," I finally told her. "I wasn't going to say anything, but in light of what's happened, I think I can."

"When did you hear them?"

"Christmas Eve," I said. I'd just ridden back from town and was sitting in a chair out on the porch. They didn't know I was there. His wife wanted to leave, return to the city that night, and he told her to be reasonable, but she insisted and said she'd take a hotel room instead until the train arrived."

"Did she give a reason?"

"She did."

"And what was the reason?"

"She said that he was carrying on with a woman at your party, exchanging glances, being flirtatious."

"And did she mention that woman's name?"

"She didn't, but it's plain who she was talking about."

"The senator and I tried to be discreet, but apparently not discreet enough," she said. "It's awfully hard to hide these kinds of feelings, isn't it?" Tears were forming in Carlotta's eyes. She took out her handkerchief and dabbed at them.

I agreed with her, even though I'd done a pretty good of hiding those feelings myself. So good, that even Carlotta didn't know about them—at least, I fooled myself that she didn't. The sky had broken open—a good time to change the conversation—and for now the rain clouds were gone. It was brisk, clear—a perfect day for a bicycle ride and so I suggested one.

"That sounds perfect—just the thing to shake me out of this dreary mood," she said. "Where would you like to ride to?"

I thought about it. "How about some place we could ride to, stash our bicycles and climb up to some view point?"

"Do you know of any?"

"I do—there's a trail above the cemetery."

Within a half hour we were on our bicycles riding toward town and eventually up Schocken's Hill where it overlooked the plaza. Once the grade became too steep, we left our bicycles in a thicket of manzanita and hiked the remainder of the way to a lookout point above the cemetery. From there we could see the entire town laid out before us, the smoke curling out of the chimneys, teams of horses driving up and down Broadway—sometimes a steam whistle sounded from the brewing company.

"It's like a miniature town," Carlotta said.

"With miniature people."

We both sat on the same large rock. She moved closer to me. "I should fall in love with someone else—someone like you, Bert—and not someone who's already married. It'd be so much simpler."

"Maybe it would be," I said. Falling in love was simple enough—I'd done it enough times. Often it was just a glance, a first-look, and that's all it took before everything started moving, started shifting inside. My mind just took-off, imagining all kinds of outcomes. The challenge, it seemed, was staying in love—keeping those early fires burning hot—something much harder to pull off. I admit, I didn't know how to do it, didn't know what it required. In truth, I never got that far before the fire began smoldering out.

"But the whole process is so irrational," she said. "It doesn't follow any reason."

"Did you love the colonel?" I asked her.

"That was one time it was rational—I married him for my family's sake," she said. "It was all very reasonable—made perfect sense." She paused here. "Did I love him? Yes, but not in a passionate way—it was more dutiful, if you know what I mean. He was a dear man and would do anything for me."

"But you didn't love him the way you love the senator?" I figured this was chance to dig deeper—to learn more about their involvement. I don't know why I needed to know more—I already knew enough—and she picked the senator, not me.

"No, I didn't," she said. "It was different with the senator—very passionate, perhaps because it was forbidden—like Madame Bovary."

"Madam who?"

"Madame Bovary—she's a character in a French novel by Flaubert. She's married but has an illicit affair. It arouses her passions in an otherwise passionless marriage."

"How did all of this start with the senator?" I asked.

"When the senator first confessed his feelings toward me, the colonel had just died," she said, "And I told the senator it was not an appropriate time to be discussing this. He apologized. I felt bad that I may have discouraged him entirely, and in our following social gatherings I dropped little hints that I was still interested—but that certain things would have to change."

"Like his being married?"

"Yes, like his being married," she said. "I'm hopeful at times that he'll end his marriage—I know that's a terribly selfish thing to say—but neither of them are happy so why prolong it? Other times though, I'm not so sure."

"Do you think he'll ever end it?"

"If what he tells me is true, he will." Carlotta put her hand in mine. "Bert, you're such a dear to let me share this with you. I know it must sound very melodramatic to you—two people's personal affairs."

"Actually, it's three," I corrected her.

"Yes, that's right—there are three people involved," she said.

In truth—it was four people. But I saw any chance with Carlotta quickly disappearing so why make it any more complicated than it already was? Clearly her heart had settled on the senator and I wasn't going to change that. My imagination could take things only so far before reality stepped in, and said, "Bert Miller, enough of this fooling yourself." I'd get over it—with enough time I got over most things.

"What's been happening with the attorney you retained?" I asked her. I thought a change of subject might be in order, another subject just as depressing.

"He filed an appeal, so we're waiting to hear how the courts decide. There could be a trial as early as February or March," she said.

"I hope so because I don't like what I read in the papers about the whole incident," I said. "How your brother was the upstanding citizen only defending himself and my dad the hot-tempered guy who started it all."

"Bert, it will always be that way around here—I hate to say," she said. "My brother has clout with the locals—they eat up everything he says. And your dad? He'll always be the immigrant—the foreigner—the one trying to take away what my brother thinks is rightfully his."

"Yeah, I've learned that living around here," I said.

"Anyway, your mother and I have an appointment with the attorney just after New Year's, and we should have a better idea then how the case proceeds." Carlotta stood up and stretched her arms out. "I'm ready to go."

We hiked back to our bicycles and coasted down the remaining grade. Her hair flew behind her and she smiled like she was that young girl again—like she was the only one my heart desired. Some days I didn't care how impossible the situation. It didn't matter. Some days the senator never existed, they never set eyes on each other, and my foolish heart could run away with itself. Some days the compass inside Carlotta's heart always pointed to me. She was the one my heart hungered for even knowing by the day how hopeless that hunger had become. At times, it didn't matter though. I could indulge myself in those brief moments until sleep overtook them, or more often the big, heavy boot of reality stomped them down— then it was back to where I'd always been—footloose, ignorant, on my own—wondering what the next day would bring— some days looking forward to it, other days not. I never knew— like I said, it was all one big crapshoot.

38

The Trial
· · · · · · · · · ·

Most town folk felt that Coroner Blaney's jury finding Percy Sheers innocent of killing my father was trial enough. Blaney had slapped together a gallery of the town's finest—all friendly to Sheers—just a day after the shooting, and their verdict of "Not Guilty" satisfied most folks. But Carlotta's attorney's appeal for a trial by jury had been granted and the trial was scheduled for February in the Santa Rosa Superior Court.

When the local newspaper wrote of this upcoming trial, it went on how Percy Sheers was now being persecuted by a "vindictive sister" and "the aggrieved widow of John Miller." These newspaper accounts described Sheers as a model citizen, protecting himself and his wife against my hot-tempered father. They even described an incident where hunters crossed into Sheers' property, tore down his fence and scared his cattle off, even pointed a double-barreled shotgun at him, and Sheers' response was a gentle "Please don't trespass on my property," and let them go without any further action. It certainly wasn't the Sheers that Tino and I knew—the guy that tracked us down with a vengeance—even shooting at us. But he was from a long-standing family, and I realized by the day how much water that carried around here.

The arraignment was set for early February, and, as expected, Sheers pled 'not guilty.' Two weeks after the arraignment, the trial of the People vs. Percy Sheers began in the Superior Court of California in Santa Rosa. Judge Dougherty presided. We rode the Donahue train to Santa Rosa, took a taxi to the downtown courthouse, and shortly before ten o'clock found our seats in the gallery. Ma and Carlotta sat with the district attorney at a table to the right of the judge's bench. A roll call of the selected jurors was taken and found that the twelfth juror, Andrew France, was missing. Judge Dougherty postponed the hearing until three in the afternoon. France, it turned out, had suffered a brain hemorrhage at his home near Grant's Station, so an alternate juror was selected, and the entire trial was postponed until the following morning at ten o'clock.

Once again, we took a taxi to the Santa Rosa depot and returned home, set to ride again to Santa Rosa the following day. Ma looked tired through all of it and we worried about her. I couldn't tell if it was the grief all of this brought up inside her, or if there was a more serious ailment. She wasn't well—I could see that—but she brushed it all off and refused to see a doctor.

We arrived back at the courthouse the next day, Thursday, and the entire twelve man jury was now assembled. At ten o'clock sharp, the court was brought into session and the opening remarks made. The District Attorney, James Satler, then called Ma to the witness stand. She placed her hand on the Bible and swore to tell the truth.

After a series of questions by J.P. Rodgers, Sheers' attorney, she pointed her finger at Sheers. "He shot my husband. He had no right." There were objections from the defense. Ma looked confused. "That's what he did," she said. "You ask me and I tell you." After the defense rested, Satler then questioned Ma about our dad's character. "A good man," she said. "A hard-working man." Carlotta was called next and she recounted the long, bitter legal history with her brother of contesting title to certain properties, and the right-of-way dispute ending in my father's death. "You're a wealthy woman by most standards," Rodgers said.

"Objection, your honor!" Satler followed. Mrs. Stamm's wealth is immaterial to this case."

Sheers' attorney, then called their witnesses for the defense . The first person called was Ah Yep, Carlotta's Chinese houseman. He'd arrived just minutes after the shooting. "But you didn't witness the actual shooting?" the district attorney asked him.

"No, just see Mister John on ground," Ah Yep said. "Not moving."

The next witness called was Rennie McDonnell, Sheers' hired hand. He had a shock of red hair and wiped at his nose constantly.

"Mister Sheers went to undo the wire on the gate and John Miller said, "I wouldn't do that," and Mister Sheers went ahead and undid the wire and John Miller went at him with a fence post. That's when Mister Sheers shot him. The first two shots didn't slow Miller down but the last two to the chest did. Then Miller yelled, 'I been shot!' When McDonnell finished testifying, he gave his nose a final swipe and stepped down from the bench.

Sheers' wife was the next witness and she pretty much repeated what McDonnell said. She had a small, nearly shrunken face, half hidden by a mass of dark curls, all sandwiched under a woolen hat. Finally, Sheers himself was called and sworn in, and he started his testimony with an apology to Ma and my family. "I wouldn't have shot him if I didn't feel my life and my wife's life was threatened." He went on about how he'd always been a man who hated violence, but it didn't square up with my experience, but none of that mattered here. I wasn't on trial and Tino wasn't either.

After all the witnesses testified, the court went into a recess while the jurors filed into a separate room to decide their verdict. It wasn't ten minutes later that the jury foreman came out from the room and handed a slip of paper to the judge. "Has the jury reached a verdict?" Judge Dougherty asked.

"We have, your honor," the foreman said.

"And what is that verdict?" the judge asked, looking down on everyone from his high bench.

"Not guilty, your honor," the foreman said.

All of Sheers' supporters in the courtroom—and and there were many—clapped their hands and let out a cheer. The judge banged his gavel and shouted out, "Order in the court!" I looked at Ma and she just stared down at the table in front of her. Carlotta had put her arm around Ma's shoulder to comfort her.

"Time to head home," John B. said. We filed out of the courtroom and onto the sidewalk where John B. waved down a taxi that took us back to the train depot. Just behind us was Sheers' group headed for that same train. At the depot we waited inside while Sheers and his attorney, Rodgers, and the rest of his followers, stayed out on the train platform passing bottles and flasks between them. When the train arrived, we took seats in a different car from Sheers although through the entire trip back we could hear their laughing and shouting. None of us talked. It was like a funeral train in one coach—a wedding train in the other.

Word of the Sheers' verdict reached Sonoma, and when the train pulled into the Sonoma Depot that evening, a throng had gathered, dozens of all the town's dignitaries, council members, business owners—all the important people. The women held bouquets of flowers. Bon fires burned and cannons boomed, and the Sonoma Valley Brass Band—the same band that Cameron and I had listened to months earlier—played loudly as Sheers and his following stepped off the train. There were endless hand-shakes and congratulations as Sheers moved through the crowd like he was some kind of returning war hero.

At the other end of the platform, though, it was a very different scene. Carlotta and my family stood there like refugees, our heads low, dejected, waiting for Tino to bring us back to the Union Livery. We were quiet and even a bit stunned at the reception Sheers had received. All through these events, I kept my eye on Ma, fearful that her condition was worsening and there was nothing I could do about it. I watched her face reflected by the bonfire light and saw tears in her eyes as she looked on at a town celebrating the man who'd killed her husband. I pitied her—felt the deepest pity I'd ever felt for anyone. It was yet another wound she had to suffer, and I wondered what it would take for her to heal. Would there be enough time? Could time even last that long? I didn't know.

Tino soon arrived and drove his carriage to the end of the platform. He helped Ma and Carlotta into his carriage, and glared over at the gathering honoring Sheers. I could feel the rage simmering just below his skin. "It don't seem right," he said. "It just don't seem right."

39

After the Trial

· · · · · · · · · · · · ·

With the coming of spring, Carlotta's chickens were soon nearing their laying time. They had grown from tiny chicks to pullets to now nearly full-sized hens with thick layers of colorful feathers. Already pecking orders had been established, and certain hens went out of their way to chase off others. I'd watch their behavior and marvel at how much they were like humans—picking on one another, trying to banish certain chickens from the group.

Ma's health hadn't improved. She stayed indoors much of the time now and rarely went outside, content to sit in her chair and knit when she had the energy, but mostly she sat there absorbed in her own thoughts, staring out the window as if waiting for her husband to climb the front porch steps. She did help Gertie in the kitchen when she could and managed a share of the housecleaning, but our father's death had left such an empty hole in her life that we felt helpless—like there was nothing we could do to lighten her suffering.

Carlotta had offered to take her in, but Ma would hear nothing of it. "I'll die here in Vineburg," she said. The rest of us went about our lives. John B. and Gertie had set up a tent at their property at Mark West Springs. I'd hauled several loads of redwood lumber out of the Russian River basin for John B., and we slapped together a little shack with a wooden floor that kept them dry when it rained. We'd set posts, as well, for a corral for his horses and cows, and pretty soon he'd started on the main house. Before long you could see a little homestead popping up before your very eyes. It couldn't happen soon enough because by now Gertie was pregnant again. "And she's not going to live in a shack," Ma said.

I worked over at John B.'s for two or three days at a time until we had the main house framed, but work at Carlotta's couldn't keep me away too long. Eggs were now starting to appear in the nests, and of course, that excited Carlotta. She'd forced a hen off its eggs once, and the hen clucked angrily at her before joining the others in the flock. "Pretty soon, we'll have to find a market for these eggs," she said. "That is if they keep laying."

"Oh, they'll keep laying all right—don't you worry," I said, and scooped more chicken feed into their troughs. "I'll ask around at some of the markets. Ho Tzu might be interested, as well."

We'd all settled back into our routines as best we could after the trial ended. The jury's verdict didn't surprise me, but the town's reaction did. It was hurtful, especially for Ma, and it only worsened her condition. Nothing excited her anymore. She didn't want to venture out but was content just sitting in her chair, looking out the window, dozing off, then waking to drink a cup of coffee and then dozing off again. Each of us tried to reason with her, tried to convince her that life still went on and we all had to be a part of it. She looked back at us with that hollow stare—that same stare I probably flashed to my old man dozens of times—and she'd nod her head that she was listening, that she agreed but she didn't convince any of us.

Carlotta's spirits were generally high—a sign that she and the senator were still managing some kind of relationship in spite of the senator's wife. He'd visited just once since the Christmas gathering, but he and Carlotta exchanged regular letters. She sometimes read me a line or two from them, and commented on how like a poet the senator put words together. I listened, but my heart sank each time she mentioned his name, each time she read a passage from his letters. My chances with Carlotta—a long shot from the very start—grew even longer as the days went on. That fantasy of the two of us together had all but faded away, and I figured with enough time, it'd be gone entirely and I might have my peace of mind back. I'd let my imagination run off with me—something I'd made a habit of— and though the thoughts and scenes in my mind were sweet and sensual, it made the reality even more bitter and harder to swallow. Sooner or later I'd give up the ghost—that's what I told myself, at least—I'd give up the ghost.

I saw her one morning and the excitement surrounding her told me the senator would be visiting. I was right. He'd arrive on the Saturday train and leave the following day. I decided it was a good time to visit John B. over at Mark West for the weekend and avoid the two of them. I was jealous—I admit it. I hated the feeling, but it had me in its grip. I had no control over it—it just came up inside me like a reflex, like a muscle twitching—like a sudden storm you're caught in.

When I told her I'd be gone for two days, she appeared disappointed. "You don't like the senator, do you?" she asked as I was cinching down a saddle on one of her horses named Sammy, readying for the trip to John B.'s. I'd decided not to take the wagon—and Ike was still too young to ride. I filled the saddle bags with an extra change of underwear, strips of dried, salted beef and a handful of winter apples I picked from Carlotta's orchard.

"I don't really have an opinion about him one way or the other," I said.

"You don't?" She tried to catch my eye. "It doesn't bother you that he's a married man carrying on with someone other than his wife?"

"I'd say it's his business, and not mine," I said, and closed the buckles on my saddlebags. "Maybe it's the sneaking around that might bother me but I've done the same thing."

"You have?"

"Yes, ma'm—been out the back door a couple of times," I said.

"And what happened?" Curiosity flashed across her face.

"One time we got caught—he walked right in with the two of us in the sack," I said. "There was some terrible shouting and accusations, and for a minute I thought someone might get shot but no one did."

"And what did she do?"

"She called it off," I said. "Said it was taking too much of a toll on her—all the lies and excuses." I checked the saddle's cinches. "I learned one thing from it, though."

"What was that?"

"When you tell the truth, there's less to remember," I said.

"Well, I'd feel much better if the senator would just tell his wife that their marriage is over because I don't like all this maneuvering behind her back, either."

"But he won't?"

"Not yet, at least. One more election cycle, he says, and then he'll end it."

"So it's all for appearances?"

"It is—and I try to accept that."

I re-tightened the cinch on the saddle and swung up onto the back of the horse. I looked down at Carlotta. "I hope your time together this weekend is a pleasant one."

"I hope so, too." She looked up at me. "Which way you riding?"

"I'll head up to Glen Ellen and out through Bennett Valley—that takes me into the east side of Santa Rosa. There's a way of cutting over the hills from there and dropping down to where John B.'s property is. He's described the route but it sounds like a lot of bushwacking so I may just go through Santa Rosa and head north from there. I ain't been in the big town since the trial and I always like seeing the ground move under me." I tipped my hat toward her and turned the horse toward Napa Road.

"Be careful!" she said. "When will you be back?"

"Monday—I should be back by Monday."

"Give my best to John B. and Gertie."

Sammy, one of Carlotta's saddle horses, was a good one—big, strong, sure-footed. We rode north up through the valley and stopped at the Rustic Inn in Glen Ellen for a glass of beer. I didn't dally long and was soon climbing up the ridge in Bennett Valley that dropped into Santa Rosa. Chinese coolie labor had piled lines of stone into fences here, and I just followed the fence line to the ridge before it dropped down on the Santa Rosa side. An hour and a half later, we were in town and I stopped at the Union Hotel there for another glass. Eight miles more and I was at John B.'s. He'd bought a beautiful piece of property there—1200 acres with a creek running right through it and an artesian well that bubbled water right out of the hillside. There were flat areas for his house, and further up the little valley a place for a barn and corrals. There were plenty of hills, too, covered with oak and madrone where the deer ran wild.

John B. had hauled in a load of roofing shingles from the Russian River valley the day before I arrived, and his plan was for the two of us to frame the roof, and once that was done, he'd shingle it himself. It was a modest house he'd laid out, about eight hundred square feet with a front porch and a backporch he planned to add on. He had already made plans about forming a water company, as well, because parcels of land around him were selling, and these parcels didn't have the water that John B.'s had. Gertie helped where she could—she'd set up a little kitchen with a wood-burning stove in the shack we built. A bed was squeezed in there, as well. She was showing her pregnancy by now. Ma had wanted her to return to Vineburg when the birthing was near.

"How's Ma doing?" John B. asked.

"Not very good—she just sits in her chair most of the day," I said. "Like she done at Christmas."

We dragged roof rafters from their pile and set them on saw horses. John B. had taken out his framing square and calculated the angle cut he had to make at the ridge top for the butting rafters to marry. This was the more technical side of carpentry that I found scared me a bit, but to John B. it was just another challenge. We cut end rafters for each end of the house and braced them in place before adding the ridge beam that the top end of each rafter butted to. Once the ridge beam was in place, we cut our rafters that butted to this beam. By the end of the day, the skeleton of the roof had taken shape. Next, we'd run out the skip sheeting that we nailed across the rafters, just as we'd done with the brooder and layer house at Carlotta's. Roofing shingles would then be nailed to the skip sheeting.

We worked until daylight drained off. John B. had shot a little buck two days before and Gertie had cut it up and dried big slabs of deer into jerky, and with the other cuts we ate chops and what was left went into a big stewing pot. They put fresh meat into water-tight pots and set the pots into the cold creek water to keep the meat from spoiling. I walked back to where I'd left the saddle and saddle bags and pulled out a bottle of whiskey I'd taken along for the ride. I passed it to John B. and he offered it to Gertie who just wrinkled up her nose, and said, "No way!"

"Well, that's good, Gertie," I said, "because that's more for John B. and me to drink."

The following morning we were up early. Gertie had built a fire in the stove and made coffee and we sat in a circle of tree stumps and talked about the day's work. "I'd like to finish framing the roof," John B. said, "and then start running that skip sheeting out. If you can give me today that'd sure help."

"I can—and I'll try for more time next month," I said.

"I appreciate it. You got plenty going on over at Carlotta's, I know."

"Those chickens of hers have started laying now," I said. "We've already moved them into the layer house."

"I want some here, too—but with coons and foxes and everything else, I'll have to build some solid pens and houses to keep those critters out."

"Well, you know how to do that," I laughed.

We finished framing the roof and ran skip sheeting out all day. By late afternoon we climbed off the roof, stood back and admired our work. "It's starting to look like a house now, ain't it, John B.?"

"It sure is," he said.

We ate stew and biscuits and finished off the bourbon. We smoked a cigar and drank our last cup of coffee for the day. I was tired. I took my bed roll out of the little shack and unrolled it where I'd slept the night before. Owls hooted in the night and the sky was filled with stars overhead. I closed my eyes and fell asleep.

When morning came, Gertie had already started a fire in the wood stove and was boiling water for coffee. We ate biscuits and venison chops and finished off two pots of coffee for breakfast.

Gertie made a little sack lunch for me with biscuits and deer jerky and a little pot of stew. I thanked her and put the sack into my saddle bags, mounted up. John B. had drawn a little map that took me through the little valley here and over the ridge and into Rincon Valley, and from there I could ride to Bennett Valley or head down through Sonoma Valley following the same route the train took. "It'll save you a couple of hours," he said. "This way you don't have to go back through Santa Rosa."

John B.'s map was easy enough to follow and before long I'd dropped into Rincon Valley, and in a couple more miles was at the upper end of Sonoma Valley heading toward Kenwood. From Kenwood, I followed Warm Springs Road along the creek that took me into Glen Ellen, where I stopped again at the Rustic Inn for a glass of beer. The beer went down so easy I had another glass. By now it was mid-afternoon. Right at dusk, I rode Sammy right into the stable, took his saddle off and brushed the sweat out of his hair. I fed all the horses and made my way back home. It was a full day.

40

A Night Visitor

· · · · · · · · · · · · · · · ·

I'd risen early the next morning, made my coffee and ate one of the left-over biscuits Gertie had made the day before. I walked over to the layer house and checked the nests for eggs. Several of the chickens were already laying. I filled their troughs with mash and topped off their water, and went out to find Alfonso to see if anything needed attention around the ranch. He was feeding the dry stock from the ranch wagon when I found him. "Everything okay around here?" I asked him.

"*Si*, everything good." He pointed toward Carlotta's house. "The man there, he take your place while you gone."

I laughed. "No, it's his place now."

"You think so?"

"I do."

"You give up?"

"Alfonso, I was never in the race."

"The race? What you mean?"

"She likes him and not me," I said—about as simple a way as I could put it.

It felt hopeless—like a person caught in some kind of trap, but the more he moved to try to free himself, the tighter the trap clamped down. At one point I'd even thought about quitting the job here, moving away, and starting all over with some kind of clean slate—move to some place far away where I didn't have to see her everyday, where I could let the memory of her burn away and not have to disguise my feelings and hide the jealousy eating me up inside.

There was plenty of work around the ranch and that distracted me—for awhile. It was calving season and I was spending more time on Sammy, herding calves and their mothers into separate fields, sorting out the bull calves from the little heifers, letting the bull calves suckle and then selling them off for veal. It'd been three days since I returned from John B.'s and I fell back into the work routine, but still, I thought of her, looked constantly toward her house, but no sign of Carlotta. Ah Yep had come out of the milking barn to skim for cream, and I asked him about Carlotta. "She inside," he said. "No talk much. Maybe sad."

I'd start to walk toward her house a dozen different times, then reconsider, stop, turn around and walk away. I didn't know what I'd say to her—what was there left to say? Maybe she was ill, I thought, and needed my attention, but if it was anything serious, Ah Yep or his wife would have told me. No, this was the Carlotta I always knew, the Carlotta who locked herself away when the storm winds blew, who days later would appear among the roses with her cup of tea, who when she saw me would ask how the chickens were doing like nothing had happened, like she'd slept-in late that morning. All kinds of thoughts filled my head but in the end they were just thoughts—wasted thoughts at that. This was Carlotta—as unpredictable as she was independent—so I did the only thing I could and stayed away. In time she'd reappear and the old rhythms would start again.

I'd put in a full day's work, mostly herding cattle from one field to another before turning in for the night. I fell right asleep, but sometime later the sound of the front door opening awoke me. I heard footsteps and called out, "Who's there?"

"It's me." It was Carlotta's voice.

I sat upright in my bed. "What's wrong? Is anything wrong?"

She sat on the edge of the bed. I could see her dark outline next to me.

"I'm sad," she said. "Very sad."

"What happened?"

"It's the senator," she confessed.

"Did something happen to him? He didn't die, did he?"

"No. He sent me a letter—it arrived today." Her voice broke as she spoke.

"And?"

"He's going back with his wife," she said. "He doesn't want us to see each other again." And she began sobbing.

I reached out for her and felt her body trembling.

"I feel so sad, I don't know what to do," she said. A silenced followed. "But I've always been able to talk to you, to tell you things about me I've never told anyone else."

"That's right—you've done that," I said.

"Can I lie down next to you?" she asked.

"Of course," I said, and moved toward the middle of the bed to make room for her. She lay down next to me and I put my arm across her back.

"I'm sorry to trouble you with my concerns." Her mouth was just inches from my face. I could feel her warm breath when she talked. "This was all predictable, wasn't it?"

"You followed your heart," I said. "Not everyone does that."

"I was foolish," she said and moved her face close to mine and her lips were now against my cheek. I turned slightly and our lips met. We kissed. She moved even closer and we both turned toward each other. My right arm stroked her back. "Can I get under the covers?" she asked.

I pulled the blankets from under her and moved her next to me and then covered us both with the blankets. We kissed and then she pulled her face away from mine. "This isn't right," she said. I could feel her body move away from mine. "But right now I don't care."

"Don't go—please—just stay for awhile," I said. "Talk to me—tell me everything."

She relaxed and moved back beside me.

"Do you think I'm like one of those—what do you call them—floosies?"

"No, I don't think that at all."

"What do you think, Bert?" she asked. "You've always been like a puzzle to me."

"A puzzle?"

"Yes, a puzzle," she said. "You live over here in your house across the yard and no one ever comes to see you—and I think what a lonely person you must be. But I know you have friends and family—"

"I do."

"And I wonder what you think of—what goes on in that head of yours?"

What a question! Is this the time I crack open my heart like an egg and tell her everything I've felt about her since the day I saw her walking with my father back from the gazebo? Do I tell her all about my secret longings for her ever since? The jealousy I felt when I found out about the senator, and now the relief—even the little bit of joy—now that the senator was no longer on the scene? "I've always felt something for you, Carlotta—you must know that by now," I said.

"I know—I could sometimes see it in your eyes," she said. "Women have an extra sense about those things. It's flattering in a way—and I was pulled one way and then another. It was difficult for me."

"I'm not a very good actor—am I?"

"But I didn't want to lead you on—and I still don't." She stopped talking. I could hear her breathing close to my ear. "So, you're wondering, what am I doing here, then?"

"I guess I'm someone to be with when you don't want to be alone," I said. "Someone you can talk to, right?"

"Yes, that's it."

"And later today? And tomorrow? What then?" I asked her. "How will you feel then?"

"I don't know—that's the future," she said, "and I really don't want to think about the future—but I don't want to feel shame either for being here."

"There's no shame." I said. "You do what I do—we both follow our feelings and never quite know where we'll end up—where they'll lead us. I know that can be dangerous." The whole time we're talking the urge is growing within—I can feel it like a strong pulse all the way down into my groin—I want her more than I've ever wanted a woman—she must feel it. She must feel me. I moved her face close to mine and kissed her again on her mouth.

She moved away from me. "I want to be held right now—that's what I want—nothing more for right now," she whispered. "Just hold me."

"Sure—I can do that," I said, disappointed to hear this because what I wanted more than anything was to undress her, excite her like she's never been excited—then slip inside her. That's all I knew how to do in these situations. I kept my arm across her back and pressed her tightly to me—my mind crazy with desire—my entire body. We held each other and our mouths met again and her breathing quickened. Soon she was pressing her body against mine and I pressed back, pulling her night skirt above her hips and moving my hand between her legs. She didn't say "stop," she didn't push me away—she just continued breathing heavy, seeming to welcome it.

Any second I waited for her to bolt up—say this was a mistake—but she didn't. Instead she moved over on top of me and with her hand guided me inside her. There were short little thrusts at first until I felt it move deeper inside—she let out a sharp sigh until we found a rhythm between us.

How do you describe it? I won't even try. We stayed like this— in rhythm— until I could no longer hold it and then I released. Ahhhh! That feeling! Those few seconds that all the world builds up to, all the world wants to last longer. And then it's over.

Her breathing slowed, then deepened—we continued holding each other. I tried closing my eyes but I was afraid once I did, she'd disappear. Sometime later she fell asleep. I covered her with more of the blankets and lay there wondering at times what this meant, if it meant anything. I ran my hand across her back again to make sure she was still there beside me. Eventually the entire day caught up with me and I fell asleep.

When I woke later to reach for her, she was gone. I lie there and wondered if everything that happened earlier had been some kind of dream—that I'd only imagined her coming to my bedside and then lying down next to me. But no—I could smell her fragrance on the pillow case, saw a long strand of her hair, remembered her touch, the smell of her on my hands, and the feel of her lips on mine, and knew I hadn't imagined any of it. What I'd imagined and hoped for all this time, what had occupied my mind more than anything else these past months had finally come true. Now what do I do? Or, more important, what does she do?

41

The Aftermath
· · · · · · · · · · · · ·

Carlotta stayed out of sight the entire next day—it was maddening. Now I wanted to see her more than ever, felt a hunger I've never experienced before—felt like a crazed man. I wanted to hold her once again, and bare more of my heart, make what had happened last night spill into all the days and nights that followed, but she was nowhere to be found. I thought of pounding on her door, but decided against it. What was she thinking, I wondered? Regret? The shame she mentioned the night before? What would happen now? How would things change between us—would they change at all? I didn't know and I wanted answers. I wanted to know exactly where I stood in her eyes, hated being in this kind of limbo but I knew something about Carlotta and her free spirit, and there would be no easy answers to these questions. I fed the chickens and gathered eggs and put the eggs in metal baskets, constantly looking toward her house, hoping Carlotta would come out and join me, but no—I didn't see her anywhere. Ah Yep came out for eggs and I asked him about Carlotta, and it was his usual reply, "She inside."

The more I thought about her—and I thought about her the entire day—I regretted her visit the previous night. All it did was fill my head with even more expectations—hopes of how things would be between us, but it was a head already crowded with imaginings—and along with these hopes came the uncertainty—the second-guessing of what things would be like between us now. I know she came to me in a moment of weakness—had the senator not contacted her and told her he would stay with his wife—things would be as they always were between us.

Before last night I was the hired hand, a guy she rode bicycles with and wished was more like the senator—probably no more than a whim with her—somebody at a safe distance—but had that changed now? I hoped it did, but she was a 'free spirit' after all, and I knew how that frightened me—that she was beholden to no man. Now I'd gotten a slight taste of her—but it wasn't enough. I wanted more—like opening that bottle of bourbon and not satisfied until all of it was gone. I paced back and forth, unable to concentrate on anything. My heart beat fast, sometimes so fast I thought it would explode. A dozen times more I thought of knocking on her door, of even just walking right into her house and demanding to see her. I was in a state—crazed, half-delirious.

In the afternoon—still beside myself—I decided I had to get away and rode into town to have a drink with Tino to try and settle me down. I bought a bottle of bourbon on the way and found Tino cleaning stalls. He looked at me and could tell right-off something was wrong. "What the hell happened to you?" he asked.

"I look that bad?"

"Yeah, you do—like you been run over and left to die."

I told him about the night before and how Carlotta'd been avoiding me all day.

"Now you gone and done it," he said. "I warned you about her—she's trouble."

"I don't know what to think."

"She's sleeping with a married man—he calls it off and she's all broken-hearted and crawls into the sack with you," he said. "What's to think about?"

"It ain't exactly like that."

"The hell it ain't—how's it different?" he asked. "You tell me." Tino polished off his glass of bourbon. "Oh, is what you're saying is that she was really in love with you and it took the senator breaking things off for her to realize that? Is that what you're thinking?" Tino looked at me. "You ain't that stupid, are you?"

"I don't know—maybe I am."

"Bert, I've been telling you this all along—she's out of your class," he said. "It don't make you any less—it just makes you different from her—too different for anything to happen."

I didn't say anything—truth sometimes had a bitter taste to it.

"You're not liking what I say, but it's true," he said. Tino poured himself another glass. "She's used to them big shots from the city—them senators and attorneys and them folk—not someone like you—some broke-dick teamster that stares at his horses' asses all day."

"But you don't know everything about her," I said.

"I don't need to," he said. "And you do?"

"I know enough—"

"You don't know shit," he said.

"I know we spent some special times together—times when I thought we'd connected—"

"Oh, you connected all right—"

"I don't mean it that way—I mean there were other ways, too."

"Don't matter how you mean it," Tino said. "You're one and done."

"You don't know that—"

"Maybe I don't—she might give you another try."

Here was Tino again saying things I didn't want to hear.

"And all the time she's thinking of someone else," he said. "How special can that be?"

"You don't know what she's thinking," I said.

"And you don't either—so that makes us even."

Tino was throwing a big dose of reality right into my face, and wished now I hadn't gone to see him. I filled my glass with more bourbon. It was going down easy—too easy—the way it does when I'm either real happy or real troubled, when I'm looking for answers that keep hiding from me.

"Fact is, Tino, I don't know shit about what's going on with her—not until we talk."

"What do you think she's going to tell you, Bert—that you were the one all along?"

"I don't know what she's going to tell me."

"I hate to spoil your dream, old man."

"Ah, fuck it! Let's just drink and forget it ever happened," I said.

We finished the bottle I brought and it was all I could do to stand up and go outside and piss. The world was wobbling all around me and I couldn't walk two steps in a straight line. Tino disappeared and came back with a brand new bottle and I couldn't say no. He opened it and poured two fresh glasses and we toasted all the broken-hearted people in this world—all the millions of them wandering around just like me. "You're not alone there, Bert," Tino said. "It's crowded with folks like you."

Halfway through the bottle, my vision started playing tricks on me—I'd look at something—a harness hanging on a hook—and instead of one harness there'd be two or three, all going around in circles. I had trouble talking, too—like someone tied my tongue into a bowman's knot. My thinking was shot full of holes, too—I could hardly get two words out that made any sense. Tino finally told me I needed to go home. "You're too fucked up to ride your bicycle," he said. "And I ain't loanin' you one of my carriages. Stay here and sleep some of it off."

"I want to go home—I need to talk to her," I said. I could spit that much out.

"You're in no shape to talk to no one."

"I don't give a shit—I gotta talk to her!"

Tino laughed. "Okay, old man—have it your way," he said. "I'll saddle up old Milo and you can ride him home and talk to Carlotta all you want—talk to her until all her cows come home."

"Okay—I will—I'll do just that." I poured me a final glass of bourbon—I sure-as-hell didn't need it—but I poured it anyway. Next thing I knew I was on the back of Milo the horse and Tino slapped him on the rump and we took off in a trot up United States Avenue. I just hung onto the horn of the saddle so I wouldn't fall off—gave old Milo a free rein—and goddamn if that horse didn't know its way to Carlotta's because in no time it had stopped at her garden gate, where I slid off him—landing flat on my back when I hit the ground and staring at more stars than I could count.

The rest of what happened was a blur. The last thing I remember is lifting myself off the ground and walking toward Carlotta's front door. After that everything went black and when I finally came-to, I was in Carlotta's parlor—flat on my back again—with a terrible pain on the top of my head. Everything was out of focus at first until I saw Ah Yep standing over me with a rolling pin in his hand. I got up on one elbow and when my eyes finally focused, standing behind Ah Yep was Carlotta and Ah Yep's wife.

"What happened?" I wondered.

"You broke into my house, Bert," Carlotta said. "We couldn't reason with you and Ah Yep had to hit you in the head."

"You drink too much," Ah Yep said.

"I wanted to talk to you," I said to Carlotta. "But you've been avoiding me all day."

"I wasn't avoiding you—well, maybe I was," she said. "I had nothing to say to you."

"What do you mean nothing?"

"Just that—nothing."

"I wanted to talk to you but you avoided me."

"So you just walk into my house drunk? Is that it?" she said. Her face was out of focus but I could tell by the tone of her voice she was pissed. "What's so important to talk about that it couldn't wait until morning?" she wanted to know.

"I needed to talk to you—tell you how I feel."

"How you feel?" she said. "In this state? How would you even know? You can hardly talk without slurring your words—"

"I needed to tell you—I—I—I love you!" I blurted it out. "Screw it—it's what I felt." I tried looking at Carlotta but she was still out of focus.

"You love me?" she repeated. I may have even heard her laugh slightly. "Oh, dear—you're mistaken, Bert—confused—you've had too much to drink." She'd moved closer to me.

"Yeah, I drank too much—but it's how I feel about you," I said. "It took the drinking to tell you."

"There's other ways—other times—of expressing how you feel, you know?" Carlotta looked at Ah Yep. "And this is not the time."

"I had to get if off my chest."

"I'm sorry, Bert—now you've done that—"

"And you don't feel the same, do you?"

A silence followed. "No, I don't." She stared at me. "No reason to tell you any different. I'm sorry about what happened the other night—I regret ever going over there."

"You regret it?"

"I do—very much. I was vulnerable—it was a moment of weakness for me," she said. "A lapse in judgement."

"You can't do that," I said. "You can't do that and then say you're sorry and act like nothing's happened."

"And why not—don't you do it all the time with your local ladies?" she said. "Now the shoe's on the other foot, isn't it?"

"You can't do that!"

"I can do whatever I want, Bert. Don't you remember what I told you—I'm a free spirit?" She looked down at me. "And what I want right now is for you to go back home."

"I want to talk."

"You're in no condition to make any sense—"

"I want to talk."

"Tomorrow, maybe—when you're sober." She turned and walked away. I heard her footsteps going up the stairs.

"I help you," Ah Yep said. He stood behind me and put his arms around my chest and lifted. Once my heels were under me I was able to stand up and walk to the door and down the front steps and across the yard to my house. Ah Yep walked alongside me the entire distance, opening my front door and helping me to the bedroom where I collapsed onto the bed. That was the last thing I remember about the night—Ah Yep saying "You home now," and then I collapsed onto the bed—my mouth dry from the whiskey and my head aching bad—before passing out.

42

Decisions
· · · · · · · · · ·

The morning sun was a harsh one, so I did the only thing I could do—I rolled over in bed and wished for the all the world I was somebody different—some lucky bastard who'd never laid eyes on Carlotta. Some guy so far way from here he couldn't find his way back and wouldn't recognize her if he did—one of those guys. But I wasn't—I was here, instead, with my own sorry-self, wondering why I kept following that trickster heart of mine. Sooner or later I'll stop chasing it—that's what I keep telling my-self every time I'm left sifting through the ruins that following it leaves behind. I'm thick-skulled, I admit it, and I go where common sense tells me not to—I just wish my heart was as thick as my skull. Maybe it wouldn't hurt like it's hurting now.

Last night came back in snatches—falling off the horse, looking up and seeing Ah Yep holding a rolling pin, my head feeling like it'd been split in half, Carlotta looking down at me like I was something that had just washed ashore. I kept hoping none of it had happened, but there was a lump on the top of my head that told me different. I hoped it was all a bad dream— except it wasn't any dream. I remembered the two of us talking, the words tumbling out of me. It didn't matter the timing was all wrong. Nothing mattered, except I had to tell her something, something I kept mostly hidden until the whiskey built my courage up to puke out the words. Then it put the bit in my teeth and there was no stopping until all three words came out—you know the ones I'd been storing up—'I love you.' Foolish words.

I finally climbed out of bed. I still had my boots and all my clothes on, and stoked a little fire in the stove to heat water for cof-fee. I looked out the window and Milo, the horse from the livery, was still tied to Carlotta's hitching post. While the fire built up, I went out and led Milo to the stable, took his saddle off and tossed him a couple of forkfuls of hay. I walked over and stroked the noses of Molly and Dolly and Little Ike and fed them, as well. What would people think if I told them my three best friends in this whole goddamn world were my horses—that they were the only things I could talk to? The only ones that made any sense?

The fire was roaring and the water boiling by the time I returned to the kitchen. I poured hot water over the coffee grounds and sat down at the kitchen table wondering what I was going to do now. Would I still have a job here? And even if I did, would I want to stay after all that happened last night? I didn't know. What I did know was that I got myself into another jam—made another wrong turn—and now I had to live with what I'd done. I'd figure things out—it'd take some time, but I'd figure them out. Maybe not right now—but eventually I would.

Sooner or later I'd have to talk with Carlotta when my head cleared and see what the future looked like going forward. I wasn't tied down to any one thing. If she sent me packing, well, she sent me packing—I deserved it. I still had my horses and wagon and folks wanting my services—and Emma Hansen would take me back in a shake so it wasn't the end of the world.

One thing for certain, though—my little fantasy with Carlotta had run its short course. I suspected it all along even without the drinking bout the night before and the scene in Carlotta's parlor. I misread the signals, the way people blinded by love often do. Still, with her little visit to me the other night, and the senator no longer on the scene, and our bicycle rides and her hand on top of mine— and all that—I started to think I had a chance—that I was some- one special in her eyes. For a few days there I was walking on air, thinking I was somebody—top of the heap—and not just a down- on-his-luck jackpot teamster who liked his bourbon. But that little imagining didn't last too long—no, it sure didn't. It crashed to earth like a meteor—like so many of my big hopes. Now I was back to where I started and had to figure out my next move. It seemed that's where I was most of the time—at the starting gate and wondering how I'd finish the race, if I'd even finish it all.

After coffee, I walked over to the corral and plunked my head into the watering trough—that sent a shock down my body but it cleared out some of the fog. I saddled up Milo and rode back to the Union Livery. I didn't want to see Tino because I knew another earful was waiting for me, but maybe he could help me piece together what happened last night. I don't know why it needed piecing together though—I seen enough of the pieces already. When I arrived at the livery, Tino came out of his little office looking a little rough himself—big bags under his eyes and his hair in tangles. "Did you make it home all right?" he asked.

"I did—unfortunately," I said. "Wish to hell I hadn't."

"You just point old Milo in the direction you want to go, and he takes you there," Tino said.

"Well—I wish he'd forgotten his directions just this once," I said.

"That bad, huh?" He was giving me the once-over. "You don't look too good," he said.

"You oughta be on this side," I said.

I didn't know how much to tell Tino about what happened at Carlotta's—whether to tell him anything at all. He'd been warning me about Carlotta all along and I chafed at his warnings—wrote them off as someone jealous of my good luck. The simple fact was we looked at her different. I wasn't going to change his mind and he wasn't going to change mine, but in the end it turns out he was more right about her than I was. He said our worlds were different, that I was chasing my own tail, and he was dead-on.

"You were pretty shit-faced last night," Tino said. "As wasted as I've ever seen you—in fact, I'm amazed you even made it home."

"I wish I hadn't," I said. "You can blame your goddamn horse for that."

"Why? What happened?" He had a little shit-eating grin on his face.

I opened my big mouth and now I had to tell him. "I had a little encounter with Carlotta last night."

"A little encounter, huh? How'd that happen?" he wondered. "Didn't you just go straight home?"

"Not exactly," I said, and hesitated here to tell him anymore.

"She came over to your house?"

"No—I went over to hers—like a goddamn idiot." I took off my hat and felt the lump on my head. "She said I barged right in out of control and Ah Yep, her Chinaman, cracked me on the head with a rolling pin."

"No shit?" Tino laughed.

"Yeah, no shit—and then I spilled my guts out to her."

"Whiskey'll do that," Tino said, and leaned against the office wall. "What'd you tell her?"

"I don't remember everything—"

"What do you remember?"

"I told her I loved her—"

"Bert! Bert! You're supposed to wait til last before you tell 'em that—don't you know? I ain't no big romancer but it seems you gotta build up to it," he said. "You tell 'em out front and all the surprise is gone. Keep 'em guessing." Tino looked at me—I could tell he was eating it all up. "Then what'd she say?"

"That I was mistaken—confused," I said.

"She got that right—now what?"

"I don't know—I guess we'll have to talk and figure out where I stand—or fall," I said. "It ain't like it's the end of the world."

"I told you all along, didn't I—that it was a bad idea signing on with her?"

"You did, Tino."

"And I was right, wasn't I?"

"Yeah, Tino, you were right—okay?" I looked around and spotted my bicycle. "Anyway, I'm returning Milo and riding my bicycle back."

"You want a little 'hair of the dog' for the road?"

"No thanks," I said. "I'm going to dry out for awhile."

"Why don't you look up Cameron?" he said. "She'll save you—get a good serving of the Lord to wash that whiskey taste out of your mouth."

I laughed. "Yeah, Cameron—she's all I need right now." I got on my bicycle and rode back to Carlotta's—with the usual hundred thoughts coming at me—entering my head and just as quick passing on through. None of them stopped for very long—but the one that kept circling around and returning was the one I already knew—the one that kept telling me, "Bert Miller, you're a fool!"

I wasn't inside the house but for a few minutes when I heard a knock on the door. I opened it and there stood Carlotta. She had the questioning eyes and a look of concern, too. "How are you feeling, Bert?" she asked.

"A little rough, but doing okay—better," I said.

"I wanted to talk to you about the other night—to clear the air between us about what you said." Her voice had that serious tone to it.

"I was pretty drunk."

"You were, I realize that," she said. Her eyes were as intense as I'd ever seen them. "You said some startling things—do you remember any of it?"

"Some of it—"

"You said you were in love with me. Do you remember saying that?" she asked.

I nodded my head.

"That's unworkable, Bert."

"Unworkable?"

"Yes, meaning it's not going to work out." She paused here. "I mean—look at us. I'm years older than you—we're just so different—everything about us." She paused again. "I'm sorry if I gave you the wrong impression. I know I visited you the other night and it was a vulnerable moment for me, and I'm sorry if I gave you the wrong idea." She looked into my eyes. "But it meant nothing beyond the moment."

"Nothing? Nothing at all?" I asked. This was a hard pill to swallow.

"That's right—nothing—it was of the moment."

"But we kissed and—"

"I know—there were some tender moments, yes—"

"And they didn't mean anything to you?"

"No they didn't—not now, at least," she said. "It's what happened in that particular moment and nothing else." She looked at me with pitiful eyes. "And now those moments are gone—I'm sorry."

"Nothing else—just that moment?" I asked her again. I had to make sure I heard her right.

"Yes—just that moment."

"So what happens now?" I asked her.

"Nothing else happens," she said. "It started and it ended there."

"Like nothing at all happened?" I repeated her words—not the words I wanted to hear.

"That's right—like nothing at all happened," she said. "We just go on with our lives." She looked away and then back at me. "I'd like you to stay on and continue working here, but I can understand if you want to leave. It's your choice."

I couldn't believe it—what seemed like magic to me was something she'd already forgotten about—like a passing thought—like a page she turned in a novel she was reading—and nothing more. "I don't know what I'm going to do," I told her. The truest thing I'd said in days—months, maybe.

"You can think it over—when you've decided, let me know," she said. I could tell she wanted to end this conversation. She kept turning her head toward her house.

I nodded again—no words were coming to me.

"I'm sorry, Bert, if I disappointed you. It was a weak moment for me and I was careless. I'm sorry." She turned and walked back to her house.

A weak moment? What was a joy to me and thrilling and all those feelings that night was just a weak moment for her—goddamn! Like eating too much chocolate—or staying in bed too long—those kinds of weak moments? This hope for romance that filled my head for weeks, months—I'd lost count by now—just turned out to be yet another heart-breaker—like all the ones before it. Why did I even bother, when all that I imagined never lined up with reality? I always knew that. I kept holding out hope someday it would—but no luck. Well, now I knew. No more wondering—no more speculating on what life would be like with Carlotta—that game was up. No more dreaming. I'd feel bad for awhile. It was like a death, in a way—like how I felt when my dad was killed. I'd be angry and feeling helpless—then struggle like hell convincing myself it never happened until I realized it did— and then I'd feel even worse. Eventually, though, I wouldn't feel as bad, but the feelings never quite went away. They lingered inside— hidden somewhere—until some little connection—a word I heard, something I smelled or touched—the least little thing—would stir them all up again. I was learning that life was like that—you could never shed all the bad feelings—they followed you around—hounded you sometimes—and the best you could do was gird yourself when they came back around again, find a place where they could be on their own—out of the way—so you could live your life mostly without disturbing them, without letting them bury you in the process.

43

Options
· · · · · · · ·

I continued on at Carlotta's for another week—I'll tell you straight out, it wasn't easy. I thought about her all the time, tried all sorts of ways to rid her from my mind, but how do you do that? How do you turn the thoughts off? I sure-as-hell didn't know. The more I tried not thinking about her, the more she was right there, front and center, crowding out the rest of my thoughts. I avoided seeing her—went out of my way to skirt her house—anywhere I thought she might be. There was nothing much left to tell her, except it didn't stop me at times from rehearsing a whole new set of lines that might win her good graces again, but the lines had been tried before in a bourbon haze and now they were shot full of holes.

No, I had nothing to say to her that hadn't been said already. In fact, I'd already said too much. And, as it turned out, she had even less to say to me. We were different—she said as much. I was just her hired hand, someone to replace my father, someone to help finish her chicken houses so she didn't have to walk all over creation to find fresh eggs for breakfast—that was it and nothing more. As much as I wanted it to be something else—as much as I wanted to be someone special in her eyes—that wasn't in the cards— another hard pill to swallow.

I was thinking of where I'd go next, and had some choices: Emma Hansen would always take me back—she'd told me that every time I saw her. And, since John B. and Gertie made the move to Mark West, there was room out at the folks' place in Vineburg. Ma would welcome the company and I could help out around the farm with chores. And with Ma's declining health, it was a chance to spend time with her while I could. I thought about packing up and moving over to John B.'s, as well, and helping him finish building his house. I liked it over there with the hills all around and water like

I'd never tasted before—and deer that ran through the oaks like mice. It was just up the road from Santa Rosa, too, if I wanted a taste of the city life where I could wet my whistle and when the time came, maybe even dip my wick.

I'd soured on Sonoma. Seeing the kind of reception Percy Sheers received after his acquittal just turned my insides. I felt like the whole town was against us, and I didn't know why. We were honest, working folks—at least my folks were, without any airs. The move to Mark West would put some miles between me and Carlotta, too, and maybe help me get past her a bit quicker. I knew as long as I stayed on at her ranch, that dark cloud called Carlotta would hang over me.

And, in the middle of all this, who shows up but Senator Amos? He arrives one Friday morning in Carlotta's carriage with a pair of suitcases. I watched his arrival from the kitchen window and it was a sure sign—as if I needed another—that it was time for me to pack up and head down the road. Carlotta met him out at the carriage and they embraced, and if there was anything left of my shredded heart by now, well—it was pretty much gone—just some little bloody fragments—if that. I speculated on what brought the senator back but what was the point? He'd finally decided to leave his wife was my best guess, at least for now. I watched the two of them and jealousy flowed through me like a big swallow of bad-tasting bourbon—it was a terrible feeling. One minute you want to kill yourself and end the whole goddamn parade—the next minute you want to run out there and shoot both of them—the senator first—and then make her beg to take you back and she does just to save herself from being killed—no other reason. Jealousy made for some terrible thoughts!

I decided to move out to Vineburg first—let the dust around my life settle there. I was thinking again, too, of drying up, staying away from the bottle, and calming my devils down. I knew that'd be hard to do around Emma Hansen. After a day's work, I could see two glasses and a bottle waiting on her front porch just calling out my name. That kind of willpower to resist wasn't in me yet, not by a long shot. But with Ma, there'd be no bourbon waiting. She'd made that clear long ago, warning me where I was headed if I didn't put a cork in the bottle. She reminded me again when I rode out to see her and told her I was leaving Carlotta's and wanted to move in if just for a short stay.

"Why you leaving?" she asked. "I thought you liked working there."

"I figured it was time," I said.

"Just like that—you figured it was time?" she asked. "How long you been there?"

"Since right after the shooting," I said. We fixed all our dates now by when the shooting occurred.

"What? A year, and some months?"

"Yeah, about that."

"Did something happen between you two?" Her eyes dug into mine, expecting a straight answer but a straight answer wasn't coming out.

"Yeah— but I don't much care to talk about it right now."

"Why not?"

"Because it concerns me and her and no one else—and you got enough on your mind already."

"Okay—fair enough. Keep it to yourself," she said. "But I don't want no drinking done in my house, is that understood?"

"Yes, ma'm. No drinking."

"And sometime when you feel more like talking," she said, "you can tell me what happened over at Carlotta's."

"Sure, some other time but not right now."

"You can take John B.'s and Gertie's room," she said. "It's all swept and clean. That girl's neat as a pin."

I hugged her and told her I'd return that afternoon with my belongings and I thanked her for taking me in. I promised her no drinking and that I wouldn't be the pain-in-the-ass like I was before. Then I rode back to Carlotta's and tracked down Alfonso in the hay barn to tell him I was leaving.

"*Por que?*" he wanted to know.

I motioned back to Carlotta's house.

"Oh, *si, el politico.* How you say 'big shot'?" I laughed and we shook hands. "There are others," he said. "*Muchas chicas.*"

"Yeah, they're everywhere." We smiled at each other. "You're a good man, Alfonso. I liked working with you and your brothers."

"Maybe you come back?"

"I don't know—I never know."

I walked back to the stable and harnessed Molly and Dolly to their wagon. I drove it into the middle of the yard and then backed the team up to the front door of where I'd been living. I dropped the tailgate on the wagon and lifted the chest of drawers in first, then the cot, the bicycle, followed by everything else—maybe a half dozen boxes. In half an hour I'd emptied the house of all my belongings. It still looked completely furnished inside, as if I'd never left, with all the colonel's furnishings still in place. Back at the stable I put a lead rope on Little Ike and led him to the back of the wagon and tied him off. Then I wrote a note to Carlotta and tacked it to the front door. "I'm leaving here. I think we're all paid up. Thanks. Bert." I climbed up to the driver's seat and looked over at Carlotta's one last time, but there was no sign of her or the senator. Just as well, I thought. There was nothing else to say, and besides, I'd had a belly-full of awkward scenes by now.

I'd get over her—I told myself a hundred times or more. It'd take some time but it'd happen. I drove the team out to Napa Road and pointed it east to Vineburg. I'd left just like I'd arrived—with a wagon, three horses and everything I owned stacked behind me. I thought I'd be at Carlotta's longer, but I thought a lot of things that in the end never worked out. As unlikely a pairing as we were, I still thought something might happen between us—that she saw something in me and I saw something in her. All the ingredients were there—at least, I thought they were. I'd fallen in love with her, but it turned out I'd just fallen, and now it was time to pick myself up again and see what tomorrow might bring. It didn't feel good—it never did. I can say that straight-out.

I was back on the road, listening to the sound of the horses' hooves—the drum tapping I called them—and the jingle of the harness and the creaking of the oiled leather and watching the countryside roll past me. I'd missed this—I'd missed the road. I could let my mind wander out here, and I was learning that for every disappointment, something else was waiting to take its place—maybe it was just another disappointment and nothing ever changed—but I liked to think it'd be different—that somewhere out ahead of me was a surprise—a good surprise—one that didn't rip my heart out every time. I was all paid-up for now with that account and was looking forward to something new. I didn't know what it was—who did? That's partly what kept me going—the not-knowing.

44

Starting Over

• • • • • • • • • • • • •

Once I got settled in at Ma's, I made the rounds telling former clients that I was hanging my shingle back out, ready for hire. Haying season was fast approaching and there'd be plenty of work in the fields, and later in the summer, grapes, and there was always the cobblestone hauling down from Schocken Hill. Fact is, there was work everywhere, and I had to turn a lot of it down. Jack and Frank Kessel had looked me up, too, about building a brooder house out at the Koblentz ranch where they worked. They'd seen the one that John B. and I built at Carlotta's and thought it was just the ticket. They'd pay me by the hour. Christina, their sister, besides cooking and cleaning at the ranch, was earning a steady income making crocks of her potato salad that the local markets sold. And for these salads, she used eggs, lots of eggs.

I made a list of the lumber they'd need for the brooder house, and another list for the layer house, and told them if they were serious enough about building it, I'd go ahead and order the material through Green's Supply. The three of them ponied up the cash for the brooder house—nearly sixty dollars—and I made the order. Two weeks later I drove Molly and Dolly down to the Sonoma Landing to pick up the first load of structural lumber and haul it back to the Koblentz ranch. Jack directed me to where he wanted the lumber unloaded and I positioned the wagon, untied the ropes, and we set to unloading. Christina came out midday with sandwiches and a pail of lemonade and filled glasses for Jack, Frank and me. Christina was engaged to a fellow named Jimmy Murdoch who worked along the wharves on Petaluma Creek. Jimmy and Christina were saving up for their big day and hoped to buy a little house on the west side of town there.

Christina struck me as a serious woman, hard working, sober, not given to a lot words. She had sharp features—high cheekbones, a nose like a knife blade, and her skin was always flushed red from working over steaming pots of boiling water. She was older than her brothers, a devout Catholic who prayed the rosary each night before bed. They'd all emigrated together from Switzerland, from a little town named Sarnen in Canton Obwalden, not far from where my relatives lived. Christina was pleasant enough, and when I coaxed a smile from her, that serious side to her slipped away. She had an eye for numbers, too, for keeping everything in order, and after we'd unloaded and sorted the lumber, Christina asked to see the receipt. I gave it to her and she set about counting all the lengths of lumber to make sure we weren't being shorted. I watched her pencil out each line, and when she was finished, she walked over to where we were working and said, "It's all there. I checked it."

Jack, Frank and I began preparing the building site. We worked with pick and shovel most of the afternoon. Christina would sometimes watch us from the front porch. When we finished for the day, Jack wandered off and returned with a bottle of schnapps. I was still nipping at the bottle since leaving Carlotta's—not nearly as much because it was a hard habit to break—but goddamn it—I liked the taste! I kept my promise to Ma, though, and didn't drink around her. I'd try a couple of days doing without, but my hands would start shaking and all I could think about was finding something to end the shakes.

I tried all different kinds of methods, but just going dry didn't work for me. After a couple of days, I'd be climbing the walls, wanting a drink so bad, it's all I could think about. I'd set to working, trying to get my mind off of it, and for awhile I'd be doing okay and then the craving came back stronger than ever. I never thought drink could do this to a person, that you drank until you've had your fill and then you didn't drink anymore, but the longer I drank and the older I got, there seemed no end to it.

So what I done when these cravings hit, I'd take a drink, just a small one, so I didn't think about it all the time, and that'd calm me down. I'd visit Tino and ask him to leave just a shot or two in a bottle and I'd take that bottle home with me and keep it there. It was like a safety rope to me. I'd try to stay away from it as long as I could, but I always knew it was there, staring back at me. Sometimes I'd write the number of days down that I hadn't touched the bottle—two seemed to be my limit.

I even went to see Ho Tzu, bought a ball of opium from him, thinking I could smoke my cravings for liquor away. I rode out to Cooper's Bridge, stashed my bicycle in a little stand of pepperwoods, and climbed down the bank and found the spot me and Tino liked right under the bridge. I wadded a little ball into a brass pipe Ho Tzu gave me. The opium was sticky, like tar. I lit up, sucked the smoke in. And sucked it in again and waited.

It was beautiful, this spot—the light through the trees, the water slipping over the rocks, the coolness, the quiet. I'd brought a couple of girls down here at different times—one of them was a maid from the Toscano Hotel—a pretty Italian who struggled with her English. She was looking to get married and I told her in a mix of Italian, German and English that marriage wasn't high on my list. That was all she cared to hear and didn't want to see me again.

This spot under the bridge was like my little haven—maybe even like the creek Cameron retreated to where she went to talk to God. I could feel the opium working its way through my body.

Pretty soon a numbness started spreading out to my fingers and toes and it felt like I'd dipped into those warm waters again out Aqua Caliente. The sounds around me got bigger, louder—the water in the creek, the magpies, the cows bawling—everything magnified, bigger. I took my boots off and plunked my feet into the cold creek water, and goddamn, if that didn't start me shaking again! I took them right out and laid down and watched the sun play between the oak leaves. It was like seeing gold coins floating above me. I tried not thinking about anything, but the thoughts came anyway. I wanted to lie there and let everything soak through my skin and not have a thought in my head because once I started thinking, I knew that'd be the end—that I'd be drawn back into the world I was trying to forget for an afternoon. But try as I might, those thoughts came knocking at the door. They wanted in. I ignored them as best I could, but they were stubborn, persistent bastards, and pretty soon I was thinking about that bottle wrapped in burlap under my wagon seat and hoping no one would take it.

Then Cameron flashed across my mind—then the whole bedroom scene with Carlotta, and the whole time I'm thinking about this, I see a thief sneaking up on my bottle, too. He was sniffing around my wagon like a hound that picked up a scent, and when he spotted me, he made a run for it. He was fast and I couldn't catch him, but he didn't find the bottle and that's all I cared about. I took the bottle out of its burlap and turned it in my hands like it was a precious vase. I wrapped it up again and put it back under the seat without taking a drink from it. That was good, I thought. I didn't drink from it. I lie there for some time—I don't know how long. The numbness eventually left me and that was good.

I wasn't cut out for this opium stuff even if it stopped the cravings. I liked being high, but I liked being able to do things when I was high, as well, and you couldn't do much with a strong hit of opium in you, but just lie there half-dreaming, half-awake.

I remembered peeking into one of them opium dens behind Vallejo Street and seeing the Chinamen sprawled out this same way, and it all seemed pretty mysterious to me. It was trading one vice for another, and for now I didn't like the trade. I wanted to get back to the real world even if it meant shouldering up to the bottle. I'd figure it out—learn how to live with it. Where I got this faith in myself, I sure don't know—maybe I inherited it— learned it from my old man or Ma—but I had it. Things could all go to shit—and they usually did—but I had this faith I'd get through it even if they did.

Alcohol and women seemed to have the same effect. They both jostled my brain, threw me out of any routine—like crew members who tired of the captain and tossed him overboard. It wasn't hard drawing a line connecting my cravings for bourbon with the cravings I felt for Carlotta, either. They could have been brother and sister. Both had their beginnings inside me, somewhere inside my head, and way down in my groin, too—a place that sometimes seemed entirely separate from the rest of my body. They both wanted control, too—they wanted to call the shots.

More than once I'd wished I'd never started down that road, but I did, and it seemed there was no going back, and now it was time to pay the piper. Times like these I heard my old man's voice warning me, but I was young and I knew all the answers and laughed off his warnings. I wished he was here right now. I wouldn't mind him shouting at me—throwing a hammer my direction, pounding some sense into this thick skull of mine. I'd welcome it, in fact—anything to have him back. Maybe I was the type that needed threats and punishment, the heavy hand coming down because nothing else seemed to work. Looking back, it seemed I spent most my life trying to save one half of myself from the other half.

Moderation and me weren't on talking terms—it was like we met and couldn't agree on a common ground. Moderation was a word that escaped my vocabulary—like God and heaven and salvation. Most folks around me didn't have an issue with the bottle. They could take it or leave it, and when they took it, it was small doses—manageable, saved for those special occasions.

Tino was the exception, and I knew that as long as we hung out together there was no cure for this fever. We were both given to finishing the bottle—anything less seemed criminal and we didn't need any special occasion, either—they were all special to us. But Tino was my friend and I just couldn't turn my back on him—I couldn't. Alcohol bonded us. Right or wrong, it mixed our blood together and made us like brothers, and I'd go down in flames first before turning my back on him.

In the middle of all this, I starting thinking about Cameron again, and how she might save me. But the more I thought about her, the more I realized that I'd been down that road before and how would it be any different now? Was God going to rip the bottle from my hands? Command me not to drink? I didn't think so. And would the love of a woman do it? I hadn't felt that kind of love strong enough yet, but that didn't stop me from thinking about Cameron. If I thought about Cameron, it took my mind off Carlotta—so what was the difference then? I was just trading one for the other. So, back and forth I went—back and forth— like a goddamn tennis ball. Should I go see Cameron and try another service at her father's church and maybe convince the Lord that this time I was serious? But if he knew everything like folks said he did, he'd see right through me, wouldn't he? Wouldn't he know right off I was bullshitting him to save my soul? To win the girl over? That if I didn't make some changes I was heading down that slippery road to Hell? So, I did what I thought I'd never do again—I went to see her.

It's been several months, maybe longer, since last seeing her. She was standing behind the counter at Pauli's, looking as pure and wholesome as the last time I saw her—those same green eyes, that long blonde hair—not a whiff of sin about her. She still had that same smile—like she'd borrowed it from an angel—sandwiched between two generous cheeks. She was like that maiden you saw in an advertisement for hand soap—anything to wash you clean, and I got this half-assed notion that I'd follow her anywhere if it meant no more drinking—maybe even follow her to heaven. She seemed glad to see me—a good sign. "Hello, Bert! What a surprise! Where have you been hiding?"

"Hello, Cameron." I gave her a good once-over. She still looked pure. "I've been around."

"I haven't seen you since last Christmas when you came in to buy those streamers," she said.

"Over a year," I said. "Time goes by fast, doesn't it?"

"How are you doing now?" Her voice went lower, the tone more serious—like I'd gotten over a life-threatening disease and she wanted to know how I was recovering .

"You mean, since my dad's been gone?" I asked her.

"Yes, how are you doing with that?" she said. "It must be hard."

"I still think of him—it makes me sad," I said. "But mostly I'm getting along."

"That's understandable," she said. "I don't know what I'd do if father wasn't around." She twisted her hands inside one another. "How's the new house coming along—except by now it isn't so new, is it?

"No, it's not—except I don't live there anymore," I said. "It's a long story."

"A change for the better?"

"I think so. I'm back to driving again, and I like that," I said. "And I'm living at my folks' place. Ma's health ain't good and with John B. and Gertie gone, I figured I could move in and help out."

"You always had a good heart about you, Bert." She paused. "So, what brings you in?"

I'd wondered what to say if this question came up—and I knew it would. Should I go right to the salvation reason—that I'm trying to save my soul while there's still a chance? And save my body too? Or should I be more direct and tell her I wanted to quit the bottle and with someone like her around, it might make that easier? Or, should I be just as honest and tell her I was hoping to rekindle an earlier affection and seeing if I still had a shot at it?

"I hit a little rough water," I said, "and wondered if you'd like to go on a date—or just spend some together? Maybe go to your little place by the creek?"

"Rough water?" She had a puzzled look.

"Yeah, with dad not being around—some bad choices I made." I could feel the nerves building. "I thought it'd be good to have someone to talk to."

"That's kind of you to think of me," she said.

She hesitated here, hardly ever a good sign.

"I should tell you, though, that there's been some changes in my life, too."

She held out her hand and showed me an engagement ring, a tiny, glittering diamond that stared back at me. If a diamond could laugh, this one was having a good chuckle. My heart sank—I mean, it fell like a lead sinker. Rough water? Hell, this was an out and out storm!

"Who's the lucky guy?" I looked at her and then at the ring—as if I didn't already know.

"Daniel," she said. "Daniel Brescup—you met him at our service. Do you remember him?"

"I do—a very handsome fellow," I said. "Well dressed, too." Here I was trying to say anything to keep from falling apart. "I could tell by the way he looked at you, Cameron, that he felt something for you."

"You could? Even then?" she said.

"I could. I've got a decent eye for those kinds of things." I didn't, really. I was duped all the time and just imagined the worst. "Have you set a date?" I was sinking fast, trying to swim to the surface but the currents kept pulling me down.

"Late summer—maybe early autumn," she said. "It's our favorite time of year." She looked at me and I could see pity in her eyes—that same pity I'd seen in Carlotta's when she told me I was just a flash in the pan. "You're still always welcome at our services, Bert. You know that, right?"

"I do."

"And I'd like to remain your friend, too," she said. "Maybe the three of us could do something fun together?"

"Sure, Cameron—I could always use another friend," I said. "I'm running short of them in this town."

"The three of us," I thought to myself. Just how I wanted to spend my time—watching the two of them carry on while holding my dick in my hand. I couldn't think of anymore to say. So I stood there for a few more moments, twisted in my boots—fought off another wave of self-pity before telling her I had to get back to work.

"Take care of yourself, Bert," she said. "And don't forget about our service and don't forget about Jesus—he takes us in right at these moments."

I thanked her, wished her and Daniel luck, turned and walked out the door—what else could I do? It was worth a shot—seeing if there was anything still there, and now I knew. Another attempt gone bust, Bert Miller.

Someone said disappointments came in bunches, and I'd have to agree—a bunch of them was just dropped on me. I guess it all got balanced out though—that disappointments didn't hit me any harder than they hit the next guy. We all took our lumps. What was a disappointment to me was good fortune for Daniel, just like my disappointment with Carlotta was good news for the senator. Some won—some lost—that's just the way it was. I thought with enough losing, though, I'd get it all out of my system—the tables would turn, and things would start leaning my way—but it doesn't always work out like that. There's no guarantees in this life. I'd had a whole string of setbacks lately, and they were testing me—taking me sometimes to my limit—and finding out that my only friends, the only things I could count on, were my horses and a good bottle of bourbon.

45

Getting By

· · · · · · · · · ·

The brooder house out at the Koblentz ranch was going up fast. Jack and his brother, Frank, were good workers, good carpenters, too, and I barely kept up with them hauling lumber. Christina noted our progress and would write our hours worked, any expenses into her little ledger—she kept track of every penny—every board I hauled in, practically every nail we used. Between hauling for the Kessels and other jobs, I'd gone back to running block off Schocken Hill, and lumping grapes to the wineries around town when harvest rolled around. I was spending time with Little Ike, too, in the evenings, breaking him for harness. Little Ike wasn't so little anymore, though. He stood almost as high as Molly and Dolly at the withers, but without their bulk and muscle. His coat was coal black that turned to gray in the winter, with a blaze of white down his nose—as handsome a horse as you'd find. My old man would have been proud of him, real proud. He'd been gelded and for a few days wasn't happy about it, but he was a good-natured horse and took it in stride.

Little Ike liked Ma and Ma liked him, and he brought her a little bit of joy every day—and for that I was grateful. He'd follow her out to the garden and then back to the house, stopping at the backporch steps, waiting for a handout. He liked apples and carrots, especially, but he wasn't particular. I'd seen him eat cooked potatoes, anything green, and he liked sweets, too—cake, candies, sticks of peppermint. Ma spoiled him terribly, and I'm sure if the door was big enough, she'd invite him into the house—maybe give him his own room. "He's got an appetite like your father's," she said.

Ike was getting to the age, though when he needed to earn his keep, and in the evenings I was breaking him for harness. He'd be an ideal single puller. With his long legs he could send a light carriage flying down the road.

After a couple of trial runs around the folks' place, I hitched him to the folks' carriage, and took him out on Napa Road to see how he'd do. He was nervous—frisky, too—and I had to work the traces hard to keep him from running back to the farm. He'd seen Molly and Dolly pull, and now he thought he could be just like them. A couple of weeks later he was responding to the bit, and he stayed right where I wanted him to stay, whether it was a slow walk or a fast trot. Eventually I decided he was ready for a longer drive, and we set out for town. The sights, the noises, the smells were all new to him, and his ears worked back and forth, listening to my commands. The other horses, the new sounds around him, spooked him a bit but he adjusted.

I stopped at the Union Livery to say hello to Tino. I'd avoided him the last couple of months so I could ease back on the drinking—and that whole scene with Carlotta had me talking to myself more than usual, and I didn't like Tino reminding me of it. I was glad to see him, though, and he seemed glad to see me. He looked over Little Ike, ran a hand across his back. "Damn, Bert, look what he's grown into," he said.

"Yeah, he's something, isn't he?"

"How old is he now?" Tino asked.

"Born the same day of Dad's funeral," I said. "Two years and counting."

"That long, huh?" Tino went quiet for a few seconds. "You think he likes beer?"

"I don't know."

"I got a pail right here—too stale to drink," Tino said. "Let's see."

Tino brought the pail over to Little Ike, and the horse dropped his nose inside it, sniffed at the beer and then slurped it up like he hadn't drunk in days.

"Well, that answers that question," Tino said. We both laughed. Tino looked at me. "I can't believe it's been over two years."

"Yeah, it goes by, doesn't it?" I said.

"I still think about your dad."

"I think of him all the time, too," I said. "It's true—you don't miss folks 'til they're gone and then it's too late."

"I'll tell you who else I'm thinkin' of, too—and that's Percy Sheers."

"Shit, Tino—that's all in the past."

"Maybe for you—but not for me," he said and motioned me to follow him into his office. He walked behind his desk and I heard a bottom drawer slide open. He took out a bundle wrapped in cotton cloth and laid it down on top of the desk.

"What you got there?" I asked him.

"Open it up and see."

I picked it up. I recognized the weight and unwrapped the cloth—it was a pistol with pearl handles.

"It's a Remington, Model 1888—a service revolver, single shot action," Tino said. "I bought it off old Tom Lancaster. He was drinkin' away the money he had and owed the Union here for boardin', so we made a deal—traded him straight across."

I picked the pistol up and held in my hand and aimed it away from Tino. "Got good balance," I said.

"Shoots a 44 caliber shell—good up to about 150 feet."

"I thought you were mostly a rifle and shotgun guy, Tino."

"I'm branchin' out." And he laughed.

"You weren't thinking of Sheers when you bought this, were you?" Sheers was never far from Tino's thoughts. We both knew it.

"Maybe I was—maybe I wasn't."

"I keep telling you to let it go, Tino. It's done—over. My dad's six feet under and that's where he's going to stay. Killing Sheers ain't bringing him back."

"We all got scores to settle, Bert," he said. "Some folks just back away from 'em, think they'll settle themselves, but I ain't that type."

"Okay, so you kill him," I said. "Then what? You think you're going to get away with it? You think the town's going to give you a parade? You seen how they treated him after my dad's trial, didn't you? Cannons going off and the band playing. You won't get any farther than the nearest tree, 'cause that's where they'll hang you."

"They gotta catch me first," he said.

"How long you think that'll take?"

"I don't know—"

"Well, I do—not very long. You can't run fast enough." I looked at Tino and he looked away from me and picked up the pistol. "Why do you hate this guy so much?" I asked him.

"You don't know by now?" he said. "You see how he treats me, Bert—how he treats us. He runs us off his property, takes shots at us, but there's other shit goin' on, too—shit you don't even know about. What he says to me over at the Union when I'm runnin' pails of beer. 'Hey half breed!' and all his friends laughin', and slappin' the top the bar, eggin' him on. I don't forget any of it."

"I wish you could—more than anything I wish you could," I said.

"Like I said before, Bert—I'm bidin' my time. Pickin' the place—waitin' for those ducks to land."

"I'm your friend, Tino, and I know Sheers is an abusive son of a bitch—he killed my father, after all. And I'll tell you there's times when I lie awake at night planning to get even with him—how I could do it and not spend the rest of my life in the slammer, but in the end I can't see anyway," I said. "I try to, but can't see it."

"Well, I can see a way and I won't forget—I can't," Tino said.

"I hope you change your mind," I said. "I like having you around."

I climbed back onto dad's carriage and Little Ike and I headed south on Broadway before turning east back to the folks' place. I thought of everything I could do to change Tino's mind, but he was a stubborn fellow—even more stubborn than my old man. When he got something in his mind, it was hard for him to let go of it—you might just as well try pulling one of his molars out. I was beside myself thinking of ways to get Tino to change his mind, when I thought of Tino's mother, and wondered if there was something she could do or say that might change Tino's mind. I'd see her around town, with her skinny horse, pulling a wagon loaded with folks' discards but had never talked to her. I decided I'd go and visit her and see if she could talk some sense into her son. It was worth a try.

46

Maria and Miguel

· · · · · · · · · · · · · · · · · ·

Tino didn't talk much about his mother or his grandfather. I
don't know why. He wasn't ashamed of them, and the few
times he mentioned Miguel, it's what the old man taught him about
hunting and fishing, and how he hoped his grandfather would outlive the white man. Miguel had already survived small pox and the
herding of his tribe into the mission. In earlier years, Maria and
Miguel lived on the Sheers' ranch before the ranch was sold off,
partly to pay off Percy Sheers gambling debts and the half-dozen
half-ass get-rich schemes of his that all went belly-up. Maria did
domestic work, cleaned the Sheers' house and did the family's laundry. Once Carlotta inherited her share of the ranch, which Percy
disputed from the beginning, she moved Miguel and Maria to one
of the ranch's far corners, to just where the valley floor climbed
into the oaks and pepperwoods. A creek flowed nearby most of the
year, and there was enough flat land where Miguel and Maria grew
corn, tomatoes, squash, kept chickens and a small herd of goats.
Someone had built a little wooden shack there, maybe an early
homesteader after the Mexicans left, and Miguel and Maria added
a wooden floor to it and salvaged a door and a pair of windows. It
had a wood-burning stove, too.

They had one horse between them, a tired, sway-backed mare
that Maria drove to town maybe once a month. Maria was a good
scavenger and filled her wagon with discards, broken furniture,
shovels with handles missing, stale bread for her chickens, things
folks had thrown away or saved for her that she could find useful.
She hauled it all back to their little place and stacked it in piles,
and Miguel would pick through it, fix what he could fix, and throw
into another pile what he couldn't. She was a grateful woman, often
thanking folks for what they left her. At the mill, they gave her

half sacks of feed the rats had eaten through, but she said her goats and chickens didn't mind. She'd stop and visit Tino at the Union Livery, and he'd load as much hay on her wagon as there was room, and then she'd return home. No one saw her until a month later when she returned again and made her rounds.

I didn't tell Tino about my intended visit to his mother's, and I wasn't even sure why I was going except that maybe if I told Maria about Tino's plans to kill Sheers, she could talk some sense into him. Mothers could often do that with their sons when no one else could. And, there was the long-shot, too, that Maria might open up about Sheers being Tino's father—finally admit it—but I wasn't sure that would change Tino's plans—it might even make him hate Sheers more than ever. I'd seen bad blood before and it sometimes ran deepest between family members.

I rode out to the west end of Napa Road, turned north on Grand, and at Carriger Creek I followed a rough stretch of road that led up into the hills to Miguel and Maria's, a stretch so rough I had to get off my bicycle and walk it that last half mile. I wondered how their wagon made this trip each month without falling apart. The road wound up through a little grove of oaks and then right after the oaks, it flattened out and ended right where their yard began. An old, gray-muzzled dog walked out to meet me, barked once and sniffed at my boots. Right after the dog barked, Maria appeared from behind their little shack. She wore men's pants, several sizes too big and gathered at the waist with a length of rope, and a moth-eaten sweater over a blue work shirt. Her hair was long and straight with strands of gray running through it. She looked at me and didn't say anything.

"Maria," I said. "It's me, Bert Miller."

She walked closer. "Oh, yes—now I see. My eyes, you know? But I remember you," she said with a heavy-accented English. "Why you come here?"

"I wanted to talk with you," I said.

"Okay—you talk."

"About Tino."

"He's in trouble?"

"No—not yet," I said.

"Sit down," she motioned me toward a chair with its back missing. "I make you coffee."

"Thank you," I said, and sat down on one of the chairs. Two more chairs just like it surrounded a fire pit lined with blackened rock. I watched Maria disappear inside their little house. I could hear her speaking Spanish. A short while later, old Miguel walked out toward me and took a chair next to mine. We shook hands. "*Buenos dias,*" he said. He wore a hat and long, gray hair spread out from under its brim.

"*Buenos dias,*" I said.

He looked at me with those old man eyes—dark, the color of chocolate with circles inside the colored part of each eye— eyes that seemed older than the hills around us. His hands were gnarled and he leaned forward on a wooden cane.

"*Como estas?*" he asked.

"Good," I said. "*Bueno.*"

Maria soon joined us. "The water will boil." She looked at Miguel. "My father doesn't speak English," she said. "Only Spanish and what he remembers from his own language."

I nodded. "We seem to understand each other."

"And Tino?" Maria asked. "How is Tino? A problem with Tino?"

"Not yet," I said. "But I worry about him."

"Why you worry?"

"Because he bought a gun."

"He has been with guns all his life."

"But this time it's different—he wants to shoot a man," I said.

Maria looked at me. "And who is this man?"

"Percy Sheers," I said. Her expression changed—the muscles in her face seemed to collapse.

"The man who killed your father?" she asked.

"Yes, that man."

"And what can I do?"

"Talk to him. Tell him not to do it."

"He's a grown man now. No listen to his mother."

"Maria," I paused here. "I need to ask you something—something very personal."

She looked at me, and I sensed fear in her eyes like she knew the words that were going to follow.

"Tino says you told him his father is dead," I said, "but I don't think that's true."

"What do you know? He's dead, I tell you!" she shouted. "You know nothing!"

"I know that you worked for the Sheers family years ago and that something happened there with you and Percy Sheers—something his family kept hidden."

"Nothing happened—nothing there," she said.

"Maria, you're not on trial here. You've done nothing wrong but what you say might keep Tino from killing someone."

"How?"

"You tell him—yourself."

"No! No! It's not true! His father is dead!" She stood up and ran off behind their little house. Miguel looked up at me. His expression hadn't changed from the time he sat down to now as he watched his daughter run off. I got up from my chair and walked around the corner of the house. Maria stood crying in the middle of a patch of dried corn stalks. "Go! Please, go! Now! Tino's father is dead!" she said without looking at me.

"You must tell him," I told her.

"Why you need to know?"

"Maybe it'll stop Tino from killing Sheers."

"If he knew he'd want to kill him even more," she said. "Better he never knows."

But Tino knew—I was sure of it. He denied that Sheers was his father just as his mother did, but inside—deep inside—Tino knew. He wasn't stupid—he just couldn't admit it. It was complicated—too complicated for me to understand—but when someone fathers you and then abandons you—what's left? Nothing of the father.

You can track him down and beg him to take you back—try in your own way to make amends—or you could do what Tino did and Tino's mother—deny he ever existed—deny any kind of kinship. It's what both Tino and Sheers settled on.

"Can you talk with him?" I asked her. "At the very least, talk to him."

"And tell him what?" she said. "What he already knows—that his father wanted nothing to do with him? That his father's family sent us away to live in the hills to be forgotten? He knows that already," she said. This time she looked right at me. "Why do I need to remind him?"

I couldn't answer her except she might be the only one Tino would listen to—that was my hope.

"Maria," I said. "I'm sorry for coming up here—it was a mistake." She fingered the end of the rope around her waist like it was a pair of rosary beads. "Tino doesn't need to be reminded of his past, but he needs someone to talk some sense into him, and I thought you might be that person."

"He has his own mind," she said. "I don't change it." She walked toward the entrance of her house. "I can tell him nothing."

"He might listen to you."

"I think you go now." She turned away from me and disappeared inside the little shack.

There was nothing left for me to do here, nothing left to say. When I walked past Miguel, I said "*Adios,*'" and he bowed his head slightly.

I walked my bicycle down the rocky path along the creek, and when I'd reached Grand Avenue my head was filled with what to do about Tino's situation. My one hope was that Tino would do nothing—in time forget about his hatred toward Sheers—but I knew for myself how strong feelings lingered, particularly feelings of hatred and loss and being abandoned. They burned into your heart and mind the way a branding iron burns into the hide of a steer and it's hard to outlive them. The best I could do was try to change his mind, talk to him about the consequences of killing another man, especially when this man was prominent. It was different when someone like Sheers killed a man. The law and most folks was on his side, but when you were someone like Tino—with a half Indian, half Mexican mother, and she was the town scavenger living on a hard-scrabble piece of land—folks and the law looked at you different. You weren't the same. It was this thing all over again about 'taking sides' that always cropped up in my thinking. It's what we did—it's what we thought would make sense of everything when there was no sense to be found.

I passed Carlotta's ranch again on the route home, and it always set off a tumble of memories even these months later. I thought of taking alternate routes to avoid her ranch but it would add miles to where I was going. And even if I went another way, I'd be thinking why I went this way and not the shorter one and then all those thoughts came at me again—thoughts I couldn't control no matter how I tried. I hadn't gotten over her yet—that much was clear—even though I tried convincing myself I had. Sometimes she was everywhere I looked. I couldn't see an egg without thinking of her—or a chicken—even a book—even certain sunsets were burned into my mind. And there were times I pulled the compass out of my jacket pocket and looked down at its dial, and it was her face staring back at me and not those big, bold letters.

This, in a way, was maybe the same thing happening with Tino and Percy Sheers—that try as he might, Tino couldn't shake thinking about him—that Tino saw Percy Sheers everywhere, too— and saw things that reminded him of Sheers the same way I saw things that reminded me of Carlotta. I wanted to stop thinking about her more than anything and wished there was a pill or liquor strong enough to do the trick, and I think Tino would have wished he didn't think about Sheers either—but I couldn't say for sure. You think it'd be a big load off his mind, just like not thinking of Carlotta would be a big load off of mine, but I couldn't crawl inside Tino's mind to know what he was thinking. I had to rely on what he told me instead—and he didn't tell me much—but what he did tell me spelled out trouble for my friend.

47

More Bad News
· · · · · · · · · · · · · · ·

The Kessel brothers were making good progress on the brooder house—pretty much building it the same way my old man and Carlotta had drawn it out. I helped them when I could, offered any advice when they asked, but they'd done most of the work themselves. They'd ordered shingles and another load of lumber for the layer house and I drove the team down to Sonoma Landing, loaded it up and headed back to the Koblentz ranch. When I pulled into the ranch yard midday, something felt different—I couldn't put my finger on it exactly—but different somehow. Usually the two brothers were out working on the chicken houses, waving at me, and Christina would be out hanging laundry or beating a rug with the back of her broom, but today no one was in the yard. It was quiet. The only movement, their dogs running alongside my wagon, waiting for it to stop so they could piss on its wheels. Finally the front door opened, and Jack walked out of the house, and looking at him I could tell something had happened. I'd grown another sense about bad news.

He walked up to my wagon. "Jimmy Murdoch was killed yesterday," he said. "A whole unit of lumber fell on him down at the wharf, and by the time they picked the load apart, he was dead."

"That's terrible," I said. "Where's Christina?"

"She's in Petaluma with Frank," he said. "I had to stay behind and finish the milking. I guess they gotta sign papers and make arrangements."

"Like we done with my dad."

"It's a shame. They was planning on marrying and everything," Jack said.

I shook my head.

"He was a good boy—a hard worker and he'd do anything for my sister."

"I just met him that once at dad's funeral," I said. "He doesn't talk much—real quiet."

"No, he won't fill your ear with a lot of chatter, that's for sure."

"But Christina doesn't talk much, either," I said. "So that was a good pairing."

"Well, Bert, that depends if she knows you or not," Jack said. "Around here she talks all the time and it's mostly to give orders. And when she's not talking, she's thinking—and when she's not thinking she's adding numbers up and writing them down in her book."

"Sides to people you never see, I guess."

"Yeah, all different sides," Jack said.

"If I can be of help, you'll let me know, won't you?" I looked Jack in the eye. "I know a little something about this funeral business."

"Yeah, I guess you do," Jack said.

I backed the wagon to where Jack wanted the lumber unloaded and untied the ropes. We worked without a word between us until all the lumber was stacked on the ground and the wagon was empty. I swept out the sawdust.

"How about a drink?" Jack asked.

"Sure—I think we're owed one."

We walked over to the front porch and while I sat down, Jack went inside the house and came back with two glasses and a bottle of schnapps. He filled each glass and we raised them. "To Jimmy," Jack said. We emptied our glasses and Jack refilled them.

"It's a goddamn crazy life, ain't it, Jack?"

"It sure is—you just never know what's going to happen."

"And if somebody told you they did, you know they'd be lying," I said.

"Sure as shit they would."

"You think Christina will be all right?"

"She's a tough, strong woman," Jack said. "And she's got her faith. She was never much of a socializer—none of us are—so Frank and me were a little surprised when she started talking about Jimmy. She'd met him one time when we went to Petaluma to buy supplies. He was in the same store we were and they struck up talking about the best way to cook up an old chicken. I didn't see nothing happening between them, and then one day Jimmy shows up here, his hair parted and skin scrubbed— shining like a pearl in a goat's ass—and I figured something was up." Jack finished his glass of schnapps. "I was glad for her, Bert—real glad. She was stuck on this ranch, working day to night and not seeing nobody but me and Frank—that ain't no life for a young woman."

"Yeah, that's no life," I said.

"Another glass?"

"Sure—one for Christina this time." We both toasted his sister.

I said goodbye to Jack and headed back to Vineburg for the day. Molly and Dolly settled into their easy rhythm and I nearly nodded off in the driver's seat. The schnapps lightened everything on an otherwise dark day, and it was a welcoming feeling—one I'd grown familiar with. It seemed to slow everything down, and in an odd way, put things in a better focus. I don't know if that's the right word or not, but it made me see things different than when I was cold sober—made me see different sides, different angles. It broke me out of the sober routine when I just saw things one way.

All this thinking led me back to Christina and Jimmy and what Jack had told me earlier, and I remembered the two of them at my dad's funeral and how neither of them talked or interacted much with folks around them. At first I thought Jimmy might be a bit feeble-minded and hid his feebleness by not talking, but then I remembered it was still early in their being together—a time when two people can't see much past themselves. The rest of the world could be up in flames and they'd be putting another log in the fireplace. It was a time, too, when feelings were strong and so much understood between them, that maybe they didn't have to talk every little thing over like most people done—not everything had to be all spelled out. I envied that kind of arrangement because I'd never been in one—not for very long, at least. I had to spell things out and when everything was going

good, it was easy enough—the words just flowed out when they had
to—but when things took a bad turn—when feelings changed or
someone got hurt and the finger pointed at me—then I didn't want
to talk about it—didn't want to hear about it neither. I wanted it
to either mend or just go away without having to hash over all the
problems—I guess that's why relationships befuddled me, why I
slept alone most nights. I didn't want to go through all the work
of keeping one healthy, but more than that, I hated someone telling me what to do even when it was for my own good. I figured I
knew best what was good for me and what wasn't—but there were
enough times when I knew that wasn't always true.

I was passing Carlotta's ranch now and, as usual, wondering about
her, wondering how she and the senator were doing—wondering
when I'd ever reach that point when I could see her again without
feeling hurt and jealous and all those other troublesome feelings
that nagged me at times. I wished I'd talked to her before I left and
cleared the air between us, and told her how I felt without a belly
full of bourbon in me, but I didn't. Just leaving a note tacked to
the door seemed cowardly, but I was in the grips of something that
had me by the balls. She'd picked someone else and not me, and it'd
be a long time getting over it. I didn't like losing, and I didn't like
being passed over. Who does? It doesn't matter how many times it
happens, either—you just never got used to it. Again and again, I
wondered when was I going to build up that thick hide so when
the hurt and jealousy tried to get at me, it slid off like water on a
duck's back. It wasn't going to happen, I thought—not any time
soon, at least. I'd have to find a way—some way—not so much
around it, but taking the direct route *through* it. I wasn't ready yet.

48

Jimmy's Funeral and Christina
• •

The funeral service for Jimmy Murdoch was set for 11 o'clock at Sorensen's Funeral Home in Petaluma. I borrowed a two-seater carriage and a pair of dependable mares from the Union Livery and was at the Koblentz ranch by just after daybreak. The four of us, Christina, Jack, Frank and I, drove to Petaluma early that Thursday morning. Ma was down with a cold and a fever and couldn't make the trip. Christina was dressed all in black with a black lace covering on her head—the only other time I'd seen her wear a dress outside of her work clothes. She smiled slightly at me as I helped her into the carriage. Jack and Frank followed and took the back seat. The brothers were freshly bathed, their hair neatly parted, before they donned their hats. Their moustaches were combed to points on each sides of their mouths.

The first part of the ride to Petaluma was a quiet one, the silence broken at times by Frank pointing out where he'd shot a buck a year earlier in Stage Gulch or where Jack had nearly been gored to death by Koblentz's bull near the Chancellor ranch. Christina sat looking straight ahead, listening but rarely talking. She thumbed through a pair of rosary beads in her hand. Her lips muttered the Hail Marys, the Our Fathers. I felt like I had to say something to her—something to break up the quiet—but I didn't know quite what to say, so I leaned toward her. "I'm sorry I didn't get to know Jimmy better," I said. "He seemed like a good boy."

"He was—he treated me well." She stared straight ahead when she spoke.

"It's too bad the things that happen to people," I said.

"We never know what God's will is—that's why I pray," she said. "For the strength when these things happen."

"Was Jimmy Catholic?"

"Oh, yes," she said. "He went to the grammar school until sixth grade, until his father died. He fell away from the Church, but I made him promise to go to Mass each Sunday, and he did."

We crossed Petaluma Creek a half hour before the service began. Christina wanted to stop by Saint Vincent's church and light a votive candle in remembrance of Jimmy. The church was just a few blocks from the funeral home. The four of us entered the church. It was nearly empty save for a person or two sitting in pews near the front altar. Christina walked to the front of the church, while Jack, Frank and I sat in the last pew. To the left of Christina were rows of votive candles in red glass, some of them already burning. She struck a match and lit one more and placed it in a row with the others, knelt at the communion rail and bowed her head for several minutes. Then she got up and rejoined us, and we drove to Sorensen's.

We arrived at the funeral home and Jimmy's mother was already there, seated by herself in the tiny funeral parlor, her son's open casket at the front of the room. Candles were burning at each of the casket. When she saw us, she stood up and she and Christina held each other, both of them sobbing. Unlike Jimmy, who was a big, brawny sort who'd lumped cargo most his working life, his mother was short, slight, with tiny, gloved hands.

I walked up to the casket and looked down at Jimmy, dressed in a suit, looking shrunken, half the size as when I saw him at my father's service. His face was drawn in and powdered, his lips still with a little pucker to them, his curly hair trained down onto his forehead. No mistaking his mother's nose and mouth, either.

When I looked at him, I couldn't help thinking of Dad in his pine box, and his gray hair parted down the middle, and how quick people were taken from us—too quick. You never expect it, either. You figure we're all going to live out long lives, and if we're lucky, maybe just die in our sleep at a ripe old age, but you can't bet on that—you can't bet on anything in this life. Something always comes along and throws a wrench into the works—someone shoots you over a right-of-way dispute, or a whole stack of lumber falls on you, and that's that—so much for the long life and dying in your sleep. Your number was called up.

Behind me I heard voices, and when I turned, I saw the priest arrive, talking with a man I assumed was Sorensen, the funeral parlor owner. Later the priest introduced himself as Father McIntyre. I sat down with Christina and her brothers, with Jimmy's mother sitting in front of us while Father McIntyre walked up to Jimmy's casket, made the sign of the cross over it. He turned, welcomed us to the service and said a few things about Jimmy's life that Jimmy's mother must have told him earlier because I figured he didn't know Jimmy.

He began reading from his black book. It was mostly what the other priest read at my old man's service—all about Jimmy being in a better place now, and how God was welcoming him to heaven, and, as usual, it set me wondering how the priest knew any of this. I didn't know where Jimmy was now other than lying in a box fifteen feet away. And Jimmy's spirit? Jimmy's soul? All those things about Jimmy that you couldn't touch but were asked to believe in? I didn't know about them either, and didn't think I ever would—they were all a big mystery and I left it at that. Whatever happens, happens. It wasn't anything I had control over. If Jimmy had a spirit and a soul, Christina was his best bet in keeping them alive down here on earth.

After the service, we followed Sorensen's funeral wagon carrying Jimmy's casket up to the cemetery on Magnolia Avenue. There were more prayers there, and more Holy Water, and a couple of red roses thrown on top of Jimmy's casket before it was lowered into the ground. Both brothers had their arms around Christina, trying in their own feeble way to comfort her, but there wasn't much you could say when you're dropping somebody into the ground for the last time, especially when that somebody was still a young man and you were engaged to marry him. It was sad—no getting around it. Maybe Jimmy was in heaven— I didn't know—but I'm guessing Christina would have traded heaven—traded anything—to have Jimmy back.

We invited Jimmy's mother to join us at the Petaluma Hotel for coffee and pastries before we returned to Sonoma. She welcomed the invitation. We sat at a round table in the hotel's dining room. The waiter filled our coffee cups and returned with a tray of Danish pastries. We each chose one from the tray and he placed them on small plates in front of us.

"It's hard when it's your only child," Jimmy's mother finally spoke. She sat just to my right. "There's no one left after he's gone."

"Just his memories," I said. "And you must have plenty good ones, right?"

"Oh, I do," she said. "He was a blessing—he really was—and such a devoted son." She looked toward Christina. "And he thought the world of you."

Christina nodded her head. She'd barely said ten words the entire time. After coffee and pastries, we dropped Jimmy's mother off at her flat on Lakeville Street near the silk mill. She invited us in for more coffee but it was already mid-afternoon, and we thanked her and said no.

We drove south on Lakeville, turned east on Casa Grande and followed Adobe Road as it skirted the hills off to our left. An hour and a half later we arrived at the Koblentz ranch. Jack insisted that we drink a glass of schnapps before I left, and I told him I didn't think that'd be a problem. All of us sat on the front porch with our glasses filled—all of us except Christina. "I don't drink," she said.

"Never?" I asked.

"No, hardly ever," she said.

I discussed the next load of lumber for the layer house with the two brothers. Christina listened. After we agreed on what materials we'd need, I got up to leave.

"One more," Jack said, "for the road."

"Well, okay." I sat down and Jack poured me another glass. Christina watched the glass fill and something told me my choice to have another didn't agree with her, but right then, I didn't care. It's what I wanted and I didn't owe her anything. The schnapps warmed me up. I said goodbye to everyone and drove the rented carriage back to the Union Livery. It was twilight by now. Tino sat in his office, his feet on top of the little desk, a bottle of bourbon and a glass nearby. "Bert, pull up a chair and help me with this bottle."

"Sure—why not?" I said. I wasn't having much luck cutting back on the drinking. I had no will-power—none at all, it seemed—and everyone I spent any time with drank, so it made any vow of leaving it alone hard to keep. "Sure," I said to Tino. "Pour me a glass."

The deeper we got into the bottle, and the more I thought about death and funerals, the more I wanted to tell Tino what Tino didn't want to hear—that Percy Sheers was his father—something he needed to come to terms with it. But I didn't know how to break it to him. I kept waiting for an answer as I drained off each glass. Tino pulled open the desk drawer and brought out the pistol he'd bought from old man Lancaster and laid it on the desk. "You seen this, right?" he asked me.

"Yeah, you showed it to me already." I looked at the pistol and then I looked at Tino. "I don't like your reason for buying it, though," I said.

"What reason?"

"That you're gunnin' for Sheers."

"That ain't the only reason."

"It's what you told me the last time," I said.

The whiskey was working, flowing through my body the way it does, lightening my head until it felt like a balloon bobbing on my shoulders. I fumbled for words but figured this was as good a time as any to get them out. I set my glass of whiskey down on Tino's desk. "You know how you've always told me your old man was dead?" I said.

Tino looked at me for several seconds and didn't say a word. "Yeah?"

"Well— he ain't."

"Is too—and don't tell me any different!"

"No—he ain't—he's alive as me and you, and you know it—he's living right here in this town."

"I'd say you were full of shit," he said. "How would you know, anyway?"

I told Tino what Alfonso had told me when we were hauling lumber that day and how he'd heard something had happened between Tino's mother and Percy Sheers, but he didn't know what, only that Tino's mother was soon gone from the ranch and moved out to where she is now with her father. I told him what Ah Yep had said, as well. Both accounts seemed to support each other. Tino just stared down at his glass of bourbon, his mouth open.

"I don't believe it," he said. "It's all bullshit."

"I went to see your mother, too," I told him.

"You what?"

"I went to see your mother."

"Why'd you do that?"

"Because you got that pistol and all you were talking about was getting even with Sheers. And I didn't want any more people getting killed—I seen enough already."

"And what'd my mother tell you? Huh? What'd she say? Did she come right out and admit it?"

"No, she didn't."

"Then you don't know, right? It's just a hunch, but you don't really know."

"It adds up."

"Fuck you, it don't! Sheers ain't my old man!"

"Then who is?"

"I don't know, but whoever it is, he's dead—gone! Not part of my life no more."

Tino was upset and I'd caused it. I wanted him to see that the man he was gunning for was his own father—but maybe Sheers being his father didn't matter. Fathers could hate sons, and sons fathers. I know I sometimes hated my own. It's another one of those feelings—like jealousy— that gets you in its grip and won't let go.

"But what if he wasn't dead?" I asked him. "Let's just say Sheers is your father, then what?"

"I'd still kill him—even more of a reason—it don't change nothing," he said.

"I don't know, Tino. I don't have the clearest of heads right now, but drunk or sober, you're headed down the wrong road." I fumbled for the right words. "If anyone had a reason for killing the bastard, it's me. He shot my old man four times; the juries sided with him, and the town celebrated. You saw it. Ma saw it— saw Sheers gloating the way he did. Right then is when I could have done it, too," I said. "Right then I never hated anyone like I hated Sheers at the moment, and if you'd handed me that pistol right there, I would have gone up and plugged Sheers right in front of everyone—the band, the big wigs—I didn't give a shit. And it wouldn't have taken four shots, either."

"But you didn't," Tino said.

"No, and I'm better off for it," I said. "You think we'd be sitting here talking, drinking like this if I had? You can bet your last fuckin' dollar we wouldn't." I turned the glass in my hand. "Tino, there's things we all wanna do in that first heat that we think'll settle it but it never does. That's why you gotta let things cool. Think things over."

"I don't know." Tino put his elbows on the desktop and held his head between both hands. He seemed close to crying. "It's got me in its grip," Tino said. "Go figure—the person you hate most turns out to be your old man."

"I know about being in the grips of something," I said. "Carlotta's had me there—still does. And, I'd say that bottle's got me in one, too. Awful at times, but sweet, too—you don't know what in hell to do."

Tino stared at me and back at the empty bottle. I didn't know what else to say. I'd drunk enough—too much, in fact—and now I just wanted to go home, lie down and go to sleep. Let everything settle out. I wanted folks to stop hating—stop killing each other, too—but that was a tall order. There'd been enough death for the day without talking about more killing. I wanted Tino to put that pistol back in that desk drawer and never take it out again. I wanted him to forget about any long-held grudges with Sheers, as well, and in a dream of all dreams, I wanted to see the two of them embrace like a father and son that loved each other, and not two that hated like they done. I know this was asking for a lot, maybe too much.

"At least, think about what I said, Tino. Okay?" I rolled my bicycle out the front door of the Union.

"Okay, I'll think about it," he said. "Ain't making any promises, though."

49

Delivery Day and More Building

· ·

With all three of us working together—Jack, Frank and me—we finished the brooder house and were halfway through the layer house in just under two months. We worked well together—each of us knew his job and there was rarely a cross word between us. Both Jack and Frank had swung a hammer before, so they weren't new to it, and what they didn't understand about building, my explaining helped. They took to it right-off. Christina prepared lunch for us every day and we ate in the kitchen and on the nicer days, out on the front porch where we could look across the valley floor. She shuttled hot dishes from the stove to the table, heaped our plates with her popular potato salad, strings of bratwurst, piles of sauerkraut, but generally didn't say much. But she listened to every word, and she kept a ledger on all expenses, right down to the penny. She collected all receipts, wrote our hours down each day we worked, and if the price on a grade or type of lumber varied from an earlier delivery, she wanted to know why. If my explanation didn't satisfy her, she wrote out her complaint in English, which she'd learned through primer books left by the Koblentz children, and asked me to deliver her note personally to Mister Green at Sonoma Landing.

I'd accompanied Christina one day to town with my wagon filled with crocks of her potato salad to be delivered to her different accounts. Her brothers' wagon was being repaired and so I offered mine. I still felt sorry for her after Jimmy Murdoch's death. I also felt an odd kind of relief that this was a woman I wasn't pulled toward. After Carlotta and the beating my heart took there, and the disappointment with Cameron, I was leery of women and how I ended up feeling after each encounter. I didn't feel that threat with Christina. She wasn't constantly on my mind. I wasn't babbling her name to myself or wondering when I'd see her again or feeling heartsick like a goddamn puppy pulled from its mother. No, I didn't feel any of that.

She wasn't a homely woman by any stretch—she was mostly plain-looking, shared her brothers' blade-sharp noses and high cheekbones, and those blue eyes of hers could be warm one second then cold and piercing as a December frost the next. But she didn't excite me the way Carlotta or Cameron did—she often seemed distant and removed—and for that I was grateful. I was good and tired of being led around by my heart and then left behind. There were times, though, when she didn't look so plain—I guess there's times like that with most of us—times when I'd catch her looking at me a certain way, the sun light on her just-so, or the colors in her blouse matching the colors in her eyes, and I could see what attracted a guy like Jimmy Murdoch toward her.

The two of us seemed like opposites, though, and that was fine with me. She did everything by the book, and it all had to add up and balance out, and there was no peace until it did. She wanted to see every receipt, and every stick of lumber. Every nail we used had to be accounted for. But I didn't live that way. I didn't live by any book, and ledgers were as foreign to me as algebra. I stuffed cash in my pocket after being paid, hid a dollar or two away for a rainy day, and spent the rest just as fast as I made it—spent it like the bills themselves were on fire. But Christina, she banked whatever she saved. I bought rounds of drinks, the best harness for my horses, a comfortable pair of boots—bought whatever Ma wanted. Where I spent it and how I spent it, half the time I couldn't tell you, but I did and had no regrets. I wasn't much for things gathering dust—especially my money. But with Christina, it was a rare time she spent anything on herself.

And she had her faith, too—not that wall-rattling commotion I'd witnessed at Cameron's church, but the more solemn Catholic stuff with everything in Latin, and Christ on the cross, and folks genuflecting and the priest raising his golden chalice toward the heavens, and every time he raised it a goddamn bell would ring and people beat their chests. But she loved the Church and every-thing about it—loved all the ceremony, the fancy vestments the priests wore, prayed to the different saints, fasted during Lent, lit votive candles, returned from Ash Wednesday with a blaze of charcoal across her forehead, and thought Easter the finest day of the year because Christ walked out of the tomb where they'd buried him. If her faith offered her comfort and gave her life meaning down here on earth, who was I to slight it? If religion offered me half of what it offered Christina, I'd be kneeling right beside her and pounding my chest every time those bells rang, too. But it didn't.

She lived by a strict set of rules, more rules even than the Ten Commandments—too many rules, in my opinion. All the things I most enjoyed, it seemed, were forbidden to her—swearing, im-pure thoughts, an occasional lie—you name it and she was against it. She had no tolerance for alcohol, either, and drunkenness was right up there with coveting your neighbor's wife or worshipping more than one God. I'd noticed the disapproving way she looked at me when I drank a glass of Schnapps, and if I let out with a profanity—something I did on a regular basis—she'd turn her head away like it was foul-smelling air aimed straight toward her. She had to go to Sunday Mass, too, and would never miss it. It could be raining fire from the heavens, or floods washing across the countryside—it didn't matter—come Sunday morning, she'd be in her brothers' wagon heading straight toward Saint Francis Solano, her purse full of nickels and dimes to put in the collec-tion basket or to light votive candles for Jimmy Murdoch.

On this particular day, her hair was tied back and the cold made her cheeks red, but her cheeks were almost always red, even on the warmest days, from working over pots of boiling water. She wore a simple long skirt with a blouse and vest, and sticking out of one of the vest pockets was her ledger book. She hardly went any-where without it. We carefully loaded ten five- gallon crocks of her potato salad into the back of my wagon. She wrapped each one in a flannel cloth so they wouldn't crack into one another. Each one had a lid that sealed the contents from any dust or dirt kicked up by the road, and each crock had a number written on its side.

"How long it take you to make this much salad?" I asked her.

"Two days—sometimes three—working all day and into the night," she said.

"And you do all of this working on just one stove?"

"That's right—one stove," she said.

"You know, once those chicken houses are built and the hens start laying, you can be selling eggs right along with your potato salad. Did you ever think of that?" I asked her.

"I did—I thought of hard-boiling eggs, too," she said. "You can charge even more for those."

"Then you'd be working twenty-four hours a day—that something you want to do?"

"No, I'd hire some help if it comes to that," she said. Once up in the wagon seat, she turned around to re-count the crocks. "All there—ten crocks."

On the ride into town, she pulled the tiny ledger book out of her vest and showed me the different accounts. In very neat handwriting she'd entered the name of each client, the exact amounts of potato salad she'd delivered, the dates it was delivered, amounts paid or owing on the accounts and sometimes a comment written in a blank margin off to the side "Simmons difficult today" she'd written to the right of the Simmons' account.

Clearly, she was an organized woman, and as the day wore on, I could see she was a good business woman, as well—no question about it. Not shrewd or calculating, not trying to take advantage of anyone, but direct and plain-spoken—cash on the barrel, an even exchange. If the Excelsior Market, for example, hadn't paid her for their previous delivery, she gently but firmly reminded the manager there, a Mister Frank Burmis, of its overdue status. She rarely argued with a client, and if there was a disagreement over price or amount of salad delivered, she immediately brought out her ledger as proof, opened it to the proper page and showed it to the concerned party. Clients that were persistent headaches to her—failure to pay, complaints about product—she listened to politely—once—before dropping them from her list.

We'd spent all morning delivering the crocks of salad, and loading the empty crocks back into my wagon. She had accounts all around the area—Poppes Store, Schocken's, the Toscano Hotel, the El Dorado, a dozen different restaurants and stores from Sonoma to El Verano—all the way out to Glen Ellen. She knew everyone's first name, their families, the amounts they typically ordered, how often they paid. After each delivery, she wrote the amounts into her ledger and recounted the cash received which she slipped into a purse that fit into a large pocket sewn onto her long skirt.

"You don't worry about being robbed?" I asked her.

"No, I don't," she said. "I keep sacks separately when I'm out delivering—just in case."

"And how often do you make these deliveries?" I asked her.

"The deliveries? Twice a week, depending on the time of year," she said. "Then two to three days of making the salad, washing out the crocks, and Jack and Frank loading them onto the wagon for me."

"Plus all your work here around the ranch?" I was adding up the hours in my head—a full week's work by any account.

"That's right."

"You work a lot," I said. "Don't you ever rest?"

"I take Sundays off and go to Mass in the morning. I never miss Sunday Mass." She said this in a matter-of-fact tone like asking her if she thought the sun rose every morning. "I try to get Jack and Frank to go with me. Sometimes they do depending on work around the ranch." She looked at me. "Do you go to Mass?"

"I don't."

"I suppose that's your business, but why not? Why don't you go?" she asked.

"I used to, when I was younger, but not no more. It doesn't do anything for me—nothing," I said. "Just a bunch of words in a language I don't understand."

"Oh."

"I'm not a good Catholic," I said. "I don't make any bones about it. Me and the Church had a falling-out."

"A falling out?"

"Yeah—I stopped believing in it and it stopped believing in me."

"Are you at peace with yourself?" she asked. "That's important."

"Yeah, mostly," I said.

I didn't know what to make of her question. Peace, I thought to myself? What the hell was peace, anyway, but those times between all the roiling up inside? And those times never lasted very long—not for me they didn't. Something would always crop up—it seemed in my nature—and there I went battling it, but there was times when I felt everything settle out all right, when I could take a deep breath and all the nerves were calm and I wasn't worrying about anything—mostly when I was outside, driving my team, when I was hauling just a paying load behind me in the wagon and not the weight of the world. "Weight of the world," I thought to myself. You can't find horses big enough to pull that load.

"And you lead a good enough life to go to heaven?" she asked.

"I can't answer that—I don't think you can, either— because I don't know about heaven or what it takes to get there—everybody thinks they know, but they don't," I said. "Anyway, I'm more concerned about what's down here—how I live my life right now. Mostly I try not to hurt anyone."

"You don't know if you'll get to heaven or you don't know if it exists?" she asked.

"Both," I said.

We didn't talk much after that. Maybe she was writing me off as another non-believer—another guy without a soul. I didn't know, and for the time being, I didn't care. I said what I felt about God and religion—they had no sway over me—and if what I said riled a few feathers, well, then that's what it done. Talking about either was sure grounds for an argument, so I kept my mouth shut after that conversation, carried the crocks into the different businesses for her and carried the empty ones out while she took care of all the transactions. By late afternoon, we'd made the last of the deliveries and headed back to the Koblentz ranch, the empty crocks jangling around behind us in the wagon. Once at the ranch, I unloaded the crocks and lined them up on the front porch.

"If you had more stoves, wouldn't that cut your time making salad?" I asked her.

"It'd mean less time boiling potatoes," she said. "I wouldn't have to wait on each pot to boil. I could boil several at once." She looked off across the ranch yard. "Why do you ask?"

"I don't know—why don't you buy more stoves?" I suggested.

"And where would I put them?"

"Build out. Frame a roof and line the area with stoves," I said. "You got plenty of firewood around here already."

"I'll think about it," she said.

She thanked me for my help that day and offered to pay me and I said, no, it was just one friend helping another. I said goodbye to Frank and Jack, and drove the team back to the folks' place in Vineburg. Little Ike was glad to see me and glad to see Molly and Dolly. He pranced around the yard and threw his head back and kicked up his hind legs and followed us right into the barn and nudged at my hip pocket for his oats while I slipped the harness off my two mares. I hung the harness on its hooks and fed the horses. It was nearly dark by now. Ma had made a pot of stew earlier, and I dug into it and finished two bowls before heading off to bed.

50
Routine, Calm
and a Ranch for Sale
· · · · · · · · · · · · · · · · · · · ·

While Jack and Frank were nailing down the last squares of shingles to the brooder house, Christina and I drove to Petaluma and picked up a hundred Leghorn chicks she'd ordered weeks before and three sacks of chick mash. It was a late fall morning and Christina wore a woolen jacket with a scarf wrapped around her neck. She'd brought a basket containing lunch, as well, and set it just behind the driver's seat. Earlier memories with Carlotta and this same drive to Petaluma shouldered their way into my memory and I was tempted to talk about them with Christina but didn't. I don't know exactly why except I didn't feel like picking through the bones of a left-over memory—was getting tired of it, to tell you the truth, always lugging around its weight, and besides, I didn't think it was something Christina much wanted to hear about. Actually the memory of Carlotta was slipping further and further away, off to some back corner where it belonged, and not standing right in front of me, waving its arms, always tugging at my sleeve, reminding me again and again what losing felt like.

So Christina and I rode over together, sometimes the jangling of the harness and the clopping of the horses' hooves, the wagon wheels turning, the only sound stirring between us. She wasn't a big talker—I was finding that out, but she was a thinker—you could tell right off. She didn't talk much about Jimmy Murdoch anymore, either, and I didn't talk about Carlotta. That seemed a fair enough trade—all it done was stir up old embers and start them breathing again.

"When we're in Petaluma," I asked her, "do you want to visit Jimmy's mother?"

As was her habit, she stared straight ahead for some seconds before answering. "I don't think so," she said.

It seemed odd she didn't want to visit her, but I didn't ask why. Folks have their own reasons for doing and not doing things. Some time passed and we'd just climbed out of Stage Gulch and into a bit of warming sunshine. A layer of fog hung over the Petaluma valley below us like a thick cotton blanket.

"I think she's trying to heal, and my visiting her may just open up those wounds again," Christina said, maybe ten, fifteen minutes after I first mentioned Jimmy's mother. "It takes time to heal." She shifted toward me. "Have you healed yet?"

"Healed? From what?" Her question caught me off-guard.

"Your father's death," she asked. "What other deaths were there?" she asked.

"His was the only one," I said, though I thought of what happened between Carlotta and me as a death—maybe not four bullets to the body or a unit of lumber crushing the life out of you, but a death just the same. Something that once was alive in me that wasn't alive any longer.

"I think of him all the time, so I don't know if that's healing or not," I said. "And there's times I want to ask him something— when your brothers and I are working on the brooder house, for example, and our saw cuts aren't coming out right and I'm wondering why—then I remember he's not around."

"You don't pray, do you?" she asked.

"No, I don't," I said. "It's always asking for something—something I probably don't deserve."

"My praying is a way I still talk to Jimmy."

"And what do you talk about?" I wondered.

"That maybe we'll see each other in heaven if it's God's will," she said.

"What do you think heaven's like?" I asked her. I wanted to know since most believers were striving to get there—that for a lot of folks, they thought life here on earth wasn't that important, didn't mean that much, and it was heaven they were all shooting for— that was the grand reward. I couldn't see it myself. There was just this one life we had, and I could see that a lot of people got dealt bad hands and wanted something more, wanted another life where they could start over and not suffer so much. I know, at times, I wanted more, wished for more, but it seemed like all this wishing was just me trying to piss up a rope.

"It's a place of spiritual warmth—"

"Spiritual? Meaning no bodies?" I asked.

"That's right. We leave our bodies behind at death," she said.

"Do we feel anything then, if we don't have our bodies?" I asked. I couldn't imagine feeling anything if we didn't have our bodies. My whole life was wrapped up in feelings—feelings and thoughts coming at me all the time. I couldn't imagine anything else.

"We feel God's love and God's grace." She turned in her seat and looked at me. "Bert Miller, I sense you're a skeptic about all this—and I won't try to change your mind."

"That's good," I said, "because I don't need no converting—not yet, at least. What you say might be true, but has anyone ever come back and told us what heaven was like? Or hell? That's the guy I'd listen to—the guy who seen it and came back to tell us about it."

"You never know," she said. "There might come a time when you do believe."

"Yeah, maybe when I'm dying and grasping for a hand-hold and I figure, 'what the hell, maybe there is a heaven.' What have I got to lose? Can I believe then?"

"If you're sincere, God'll know."

"And if I'm not?"

"He'll know that, too." She raised her arm like she was swatting away a house fly. "Enough of this talk about God for now—let's talk business."

And we did all the way into Petaluma. She had her ledger book out and her pencil and had calculated when these chicks would go into production, approximate egg count, cost of feed, the number of new clients she'd need for all of it to balance out.

"You're a woman who counts her eggs before they hatch," I said.

"No, not quite—I count them before they're laid." We both laughed.

At the hatchery, while Christina went inside and paid for the chicks, I unwrapped the burlap from around a bottle of bourbon stashed under the driver's seat, looked around me before taking a long pull. I felt its warmth trickle down my throat and into my stomach. "Spiritual warmth," I said to myself. I let it settle and I felt good. Then the hatchery worker hand-trucked out a stack of wooden boxes with holes cut in the sides and tops, and the little chicks cheeping inside, and we loaded them into the back of the wagon. From the hatchery, we headed to Golden Eagle Milling, the same place I'd witnessed the guy burning his horse to death, and Christina bought three one-hundred pound sacks of chick mash.

Once Christina was in the wagon, she turned toward me with that suspicious look in her eye that told me she knew I was nipping at the bottle. Guilt sometimes made me imagine things. "Is that everything?" I asked.

"That's it," she said. "I'd like to make a little detour on the way back, if you don't mind."

"Not at all."

"It's a place my brothers and me have been talking about."

"Talking about?"

"About maybe buying," she said.

We drove out Lakeville Road almost four miles from the center of town and followed Freitas Road, turned south on Ely, almost to Brown's Lane. Just before Brown's Lane she asked me to pull into a yard in front of a white house with a big porch, a hay barn, and a smaller house built just north of the hay barn. It was cross-fenced with maybe twenty, thirty acres of flat land around the buildings before two big hills swelled up behind. The place was vacant.

"Jack and Frank told me about this place," she said. "It might be for sale soon. The owner's dying—a guy named Fred Markleson—and his family doesn't want to keep it."

"And your brothers are thinking of buying it?" I asked.

"We all are," she said. "Let's have a look around. We can eat lunch here, too."

I drove the team to the top of the yard, and braked the wagon. We walked up the front steps to the house and looked through the windows. It was still furnished inside.

"I feel odd doing this," I said. "Like we're looking at something before it's right to look it over."

"We're just looking, Bert—that's all," she said. "Not wishing or waiting for anyone to die—none of that."

So we looked around. The house had a stucco exterior with a dormer window built out on the front hip of the roof. There was a living room with a big picture window that looked over the farmyard, and because it was built on the side of a hill, you could look over the farmyard across to the Petaluma Creek and the ridge of hills further west. The smaller house wasn't nearly as solid, and maybe intended for the help or to live in while the bigger house was under construction. There was a good-sized hay barn across from the big house and a smaller milking barn with a concrete floor to the north. The two hills behind were shaped like a woman's breasts with a gradual slope to them that could be farmed for oat hay.

"It's a fine place," I said.

We walked all around the yard, went inside the hay barn, and poked around in the smaller house. We walked back to the wagon and Christina took out the basket with our lunch. We sat on two chairs on the front porch like we owned the place, and she unwrapped a cut-up chicken and handed me one of its legs. She'd brought along a bowl of potato salad, as well, and two plates, with forks and napkins.

"This is as good a place as any, don't you think?" Christina asked.

"You'd have to build layer houses," I said.

She nodded her head. "I know just the guy who can do that," and she smiled

"And you'll need some milk cows, too," I said. "You're starting from scratch here."

"How else is there to start?" she asked. She worked the meat off a chicken wing and put it in her mouth. "We talked it all out, the three of us, and figured no sense in paying rent, making improvements on land that isn't ours."

My eyes moved from the hay barn to the milking barn, and the smaller house just above. I turned around and looked again through the living room window and past the living room was the dining area and through another door, the kitchen. Yes it was an ideal set-up. "There's so much to do to get it up and running," I said.

"Work doesn't scare me," she said. "It doesn't scare my brothers, either."

"I've learned that much about you," I said.

We finished our lunch and headed down to Lakeville where we'd catch Stage Gulch Road back to Sonoma. We talked back and forth about the farm we'd just looked at and when it'd be for sale and what price we thought it'd bring. In a stretch of silence, though, damn, if I didn't start thinking of Carlotta again and imagining her and not Christina showing me this vacant farm, and how much more excited I would have been if it was Carlotta. That's what my mind did—it went after the things it couldn't have—and the more it couldn't have it, the more it wanted it. And the things it could have? The things right in the palm of your hand? It took them for granted and didn't want them nearly as bad.

Thoughts of Carlotta came just when I thought I'd finally rid myself of any memory of her, but here they were arriving like some uninvited guest, showing up at the oddest of times. What was it now—some two years and counting since I left her ranch, my head hung low, looking for a cliff I could jump off of? Two years and counting it took me to finally realize Carlotta and I were from different worlds, and no amount of book reading or money in the bank or fine manners on my part was going to change that.

It was bred into our blood what we were destined for. Bred into our blood what class we fell into. For awhile there I thought I could buck it and win her over—I guess that part of being American rubbed off on me—that we could be and do whatever we put our minds to, but that wasn't always the case. There was always something working against you. But I was young and ignorant and full of that juice, and, hell, it was in front of me—at one point laying right beside me— warm as a pair of mittens, and I was fool not to give it a shot.

We hauled the chicks back to the Koblentz ranch and let them loose in the brooder house. They scattered about like buckshot, cran- ing their heads around at the new surroundings until they found the mash and dipped their little beaks into the trough. The chicks delighted Christina and it was good to see her smiling. She could be such a serious woman at times, with a thick hide pulled over her emotions and her feelings kept in a ledger of their own, so for me, it was a relief to see her lighter side, to see a smile break through on that face of hers. She still mentioned Jimmy Murdoch but less and less, and like the rest of us dealing with death, she put a brave foot forward each day and lived life without him. What else could we do?

A day after delivering the chicks, I hauled the last of the ma- terial for the layer house to the Koblentz ranch and we finished its construction by early spring, just in time to move the pul- lets out of the brooder house. Christina wanted more chicks and we made another run to Petaluma and brought back a hundred more Leghorns. I'd built a lean-to off the back of the ranch house and moved in two more stoves, and every week hauled in hundred pound sacks of potatoes. Christina hired a young Portuguese girl, Filomena, from the Sousa ranch down the road to come in help her boil potatoes and peel them afterwards. Filomena ended up work- ing so much with Christina that Christina gave Filomena her own little bedroom off the backporch.

Christina had her own method for making potato salad, a method she'd learned from her own mother back in Obwalden: she preferred the large russet potatoes and she liked to peel them just after removing them from the boiling water. She sliced them rather than cutting them into cubes. She then made a mixture of olive oil, red wine vinegar, salt, a pinch of sugar and a little water and stirred it all into the potatoes, adding sliced hard-boiled eggs, celery, onion after it cooled; she then added a slight amount of mayonnaise, for what she called a "creamy dry mixture" and then fresh parsley, stirring it all together once again before letting everything thoroughly cool.

"I keep my recipe a secret," she said.

Her business was growing, and there was no question the woman could work. She was tireless. From before sun-up to well into the evening, she cooked, cleaned, kept pots of boiling potatoes on three stoves but rarely missed Mass on Sunday and often prepared a full Sunday dinner, as well. She invited Ma, Josephine and me to these dinners, and Ma enjoyed the company. Ma loved talking in her dialect with Christina's brothers, and it was the rare time she ventured out of the house.

Ma's health wasn't good. She carried too much weight, for one, and it was straining her heart. Her breathing came hard, sometimes in big gulps like someone surfacing after diving into the water, and she often had to sit down after taking just a few steps. She refused to see a doctor. And now, nearly three years later, she still hadn't gotten over Dad's death. I could read the sadness in her eyes, and how her head jerked to attention if Dad was ever mentioned. I drove her out to the cemetery once a week, and she'd bring fresh flowers to put at the head of his wooden grave marker. An empty plot was right alongside Dad's.

"That's mine," she told me. "That's when we'll finally be together again."

I was picking up seasonal work around town: hauling oat hay through the summer months from the Schellville tidelands. I'd hauled several loads to the Koblentz ranch with the loose hay stacked fifteen feet above me on the wagon. Christina would walk onto the front porch and gawk at the load. In the fall it was grapes to the wineries up and down the valley. I hauled lumber, as well, for a couple of local carpenters, and there was always the block up on Schocken Hill if I had free day and felt like putting in more hours, Jack and Frank had jobs for me, too—they were cutting and selling firewood and I was hauling it into Sonoma for the local fuel company. If I was in town, I'd stop in and visit with Tino when I could, and sometimes land hauling jobs for clients of his at the Union Livery. We hadn't hunted or fished in months, it seemed, and I felt bad about that, like I was turning my back on a good friend. I promised him I'd come in some afternoon with a good bottle and we'd sit down and drink what we could, but that time never seemed to happen. All in all I was staying busy, pocketing sometimes ten to fifteen dollars a day, and not finding much time to spend it. I helped Ma around the place with expenses, all the while rat-holing money away like I'd never done before and thinking of ways to spend it.

I still sipped at the bourbon and offered myself a stern lecture anytime I sipped too much. I'd even drawn up a truce of sorts: rather than always beat myself up every time I popped the cork out, I allowed myself a good swallow or two just to keep it all in balance, as a kind of reward for working like I done, and not poaching, and not whoring, either. For the first time in a long time, I stayed mostly level-headed, careful not to drink around Ma unless it was some special occasion. It was good practice for me to go without, even if it was just for a half day or so. I don't know why, other than to prove to myself I could do it. I hated having to lean on things to get by, but that's the road I cut out for myself.

When I worked at the Koblentz ranch I never kept track of my hours because sometimes I didn't know if it was work or just spending time out there. I wasn't big on numbers, either, or about keeping tight records. I'd start to and then days, sometimes weeks, would slip by where I hadn't written anything down. But come pay day, Christina always had a count of my time worked. She'd ask me, "Let's see your hours," and I'd make up some total, and she'd say, "Now, Bert Miller, you know you've worked more hours than that."

"I suppose," I told her.

"No supposing about it—you did," and she'd show me the count, the day and date and the number of hours I worked. "Fair's fair." Sometimes she'd often toss in an extra ten dollars.

"How you'd get so good at numbers?" I asked her.

"My father," she said. He kept a count of everything and I guess it rubbed off on me even though I didn't much like it."

"You didn't like it?" I wondered.

"Something was always missing in his count," she said. "He always suspected someone was trying to short him. Then he'd blame me or one of my brothers. And I'd ask him, 'what's the point of trying to keep such a close count if it's never right? Then he'd look at me with that certain look—it was a scary look—and then he'd explode. I hated his constant suspicion that someone was trying to cheat him."

I was unloading firewood in a lean-to I'd built near the stoves. Chrstina was stirring the boiling potatoes. "What are you going to do with all your money?" I asked her.

"I got my heart set on that place I showed you near Brown's Lane," she said. "I like it here fine, my brothers do, too, but we talk about that place a lot. And working like we do here for someone else? Well, it doesn't make sense." She moved to the next pot of boiling potatoes. "I don't know if Jack's told you, but he's met a woman named Esther."

"Jack met a woman?" I asked. I'd pegged both brothers as life-long bachelors.

"She's a friend of some cousin, and Jack's been talking about her, something he doesn't normally do," she said. "She's a city girl, though—don't know what she'll think of the farming life."

"It's that serious? They're talking about getting married?"

"You know Jack.—he's a man of few words," she said. "And it's not like he goes out of his way to meet people."

"You think it might change how Jack looks at the Brown's Lane place?" I asked.

"I don't know. We haven't talked about that yet."

"What if you don't get it?"

"Then we'll find another," she said, "where I can grow potatoes and cabbage, too. I'm thinking about making sauerkraut to sell right alongside the potato salad and for that I'll need room for a cabbage patch."

"Don't you get tired of working so much?" I asked her.

"It keeps me going." She looked off past me. "Jimmy and I'd made plans for a family and that's what I thought about when I was working—that all the work would add up to something of our own." She went back to stirring the potatoes. "What are you working for, Bert?" she asked.

"I don't know," I said. "At times I think I do—other times I'm not so sure."

"But if you could wish for anything and have that wish come true, what would it be? More horses and wagons? Maybe you'd like to own your own tavern? I could see you standing behind a bar. Or maybe you'd just like to cash it all in and spend your days out fishing and hunting with that friend of yours, Tino?"

"You know about Tino?" It surprised me when she mentioned his name.

"I know about Tino—at least, what my brothers tell me."

"And what do they tell you?"

"They say he's a fellow who's pulled himself up by his bootstraps—that he's done okay and is a good man. He had a tough upbringing—not knowing his father and all that."

"He's that," I said. "I don't have a better friend around here."

"I know him and Percy Sheers got a long-standing feud between them," she said.

"You knew that?"

"I don't think it's any secret around here," she said. Christina stopped stirring one pot and then moved to the next. "This is a small town but folks got big mouths. And big mouths never stop talking, especially when it's about someone else. And when it's bad luck that's fallen on someone else, they like to talk even more." She paused here. "But then there's secrets,too—they just get whispered behind people's backs."

"You think Tino's had bad luck?"

"I can't say one way or the other," she said. "It started out bad. But I know there's plenty of secrets passed around about him."

"What kind of secrets?" I wanted to know.

"I suppose the biggest is who Tino's father is."

"And what do folks say?"

"I think it's as plain as the nose on your face—his father's Percy Sheers."

She said it like she'd known it all the time, and here I was walking around thinking I was the only one who knew, the only one who suspected who Tino's father was—that I alone held the secret to solving Tino's father's identity—like I held the key that unlocked the room. Fooled again! If there's a God or many gods, they're all looking down on me right now and having a good laugh because Bert Miller thought he knew what no one else did. This Bert Miller who thought he was special, thought he was the keeper of the mystery, and it turned out it wasn't any mystery at all, that he was the last one in the room to know—this one caught me by surprise. "When did you hear this?" I asked her.

"Hear it? I don't remember exactly," she said, "but I'm a person who can put faces together—who sees the resemblance in families better than others. Folk always said that about me. So when I saw Percy Sheers and I saw Tino, right away I noticed the resemblance between the two—sure, Tino's got his mother's coloring but he's got Sheers' traits, too—the eyes, the nose, the short build. No question about it."

"You think Tino's known this all along?" I was asking just to confirm what I already knew.

"I can't answer that," she said. "But there must be a reason why they hate each other so much, don't you think?"

"Because they're father and son?"

"No, it's not just that. Fathers and sons, like everyone else, need a reason to hate." Christina stepped in front of me and grabbed two pieces of firewood. She opened the firebox door to the first stove, stoked its embers and then added the two pieces. "I don't know what it is, to tell you the truth," she said, "but folks don't like getting left behind—it scars them. They don't like being dropped off and forgotten. They don't like being disowned and they don't know who to blame, whether it's the person who left him behind or the person who got left behind himself thinking it's his fault. I'm guessing that's what happened to Tino."

"He doesn't know who to blame?" I asked.

"Again, I can't answer that," she said. "It's just my own ideas—that's all."

I stacked the remaining firewood from the wheelbarrow and watched Christina work around the stoves. Filomena walked in from the kitchen and Christina handed her a wooden spoon. "Stir all those pots there." Christina pointed to the three pots on the last stove.

"You know," she said, "we're all orphans in a sense. Or, we're going to end up like one. My folks didn't leave me—I left them and except for Jack and Frank, I'm alone in this world. That might have been the reason I latched on to Jimmy the way I did. I didn't want to be an orphan."

51

Sunday Dinner and Engagements

· ·

I saw Jack Kessel in Breitenbach's early one morning having a section of harness repaired, and I asked him how Christina was doing. "Working, as always," he said. My hauling business was steady, going from hay through the summer, to grapes in the fall, so I hadn't been out to their ranch in six, maybe seven weeks. I thought of Christina now and then, but not in the same way I used to think of Carlotta, and I know I keep repeating myself here, but it come as a relief. I felt like I'd wrestled control of my life again—yeah, there was the drinking I had to answer to—but, at least, I didn't have any woman constantly on my mind, wondering what she was doing, and if she was still with the senator, and muttering to myself what a fool I'd been and the all the things I could have done different. That kind of thinking takes its toll on a mind—it wears you down. I'd run through a whole list of mistakes I'd made every time until those affairs of the heart beat on me harder than any of my drinking.

"She's got several pots on the fire," he told me. "Those chicks you bought in Petaluma last fall are laying, so she's selling eggs, too. Come winter they shut down but she's figured out a way to keep eggs so they don't spoil. She'll have another flock laying in spring, as well." Jack twisted at his moustache.

"I'm not surprised," I said.

"And she's making sauerkraut from her cabbages," he added.

"When does that woman sleep?"

Jack just laughed.

"I was sitting at the Excelsior the other day having a drink after work," I said, "and what's staring back at me but a jar of hard-boiled eggs? I asked the bartender where they came from and he points west and says, 'From that German girl who lives on the Koblentz place.' I just shook my head."

"Why don't you, Josephine and your mother join us for dinner this Sunday?" Jack asked. "We'd all be glad to see you. I got someone I'd like you to meet, too. I know Christina would like having you there." Jack looked at me and winked his eye.

"How's she doing since Jimmy's not around?" I asked.

"She don't talk about it much," Jack said. "None of us do—I think that's why she works like she does."

I thanked Jack for the invitation. "It's hard to get Ma out of the house but I think for you and your family she'll make an exception."

That evening I told Ma and Josephine about the dinner invitation for Sunday but Ma didn't seem that interested. "Ma, you need to get out and mix some," I told her. "You just sit in your chair and think too much, and that's not good—you haven't died yet."

"I wish I could," she said.

"And then what would Little Ike do without you?" I asked her. "I'll tell you what he'd do—he'd mope around the place worse than you."

Mention of Little Ike brought a smile to her face.

"I'm thinking we can hitch him to Dad's carriage for the ride out to the Kessel place. What do you think?"

"He's old enough for that?" she asked.

"He's going on three years—plenty old, and I've been working with him in my spare time."

"Three years?" she said. It's been that long?"

"It has," I said. "Time goes by whether you want it to or not."

Time was galloping by. When you most want it to pass fast, it slows to a crawl, every day seeming like it's a year in itself, and then when you want it all to slow down—take some moments to breathe it all in and enjoy it—then it races by, faster than a trotter on the homestretch. Tino and I hadn't fished or hunted in months. I'd stop at the Union Livery and we'd raise a glass or two, but those days of making the rounds like we were young Rockefellers and bedding any woman who'd stayed awake long enough to listen to our palavering—well, they were gone. I didn't much care, though. Sure, I wanted time to slow itself down and let me get my bearings, but other times I wanted to put the quirt to it—make it speed up and lift me over a rough patch so I could stumble on ahead and see what the next day brought.

On Sunday at noon, I harnessed Little Ike to the folks' carriage and brought it up to the backporch steps. Josephine's boy friend, William McGrath, was with Josephine and Ma, and though I knew it wasn't good manners to bring an uninvited guest to dinner, I knew Christina and her brothers wouldn't mind.

"Look at Little Ike, how handsome he is!" Ma said from the backporch steps. "Your father would be so proud!" She walked over and stroked Little Ike's neck.

It felt good to see Ma smile, to be glad about something. She'd become like a fixture in the house and it scared us, especially Josephine who spent much of each day with her. The two of them had baked a pair of apple pies and we set them inside a wooden box at the rear of the carriage. Once everyone was seated, I looked over and Molly and Dolly were both staring at us, their big necks draped over the top corral board, wondering why they were left behind, and the young guy got to leave.

We drove out onto Napa Road, past the Vineburg General Store, and over the railroad tracks, heading west toward the Koblentz ranch. It was a clear late September day, crisp but not cold. The oak and grape leaves were yellowing. Little Ike was feeling his oats, keeping a fast trot but I was sensing he wanted to go even faster. I held some tension on the traces, not enough to bite on his mouth, but just enough to let him know who was in control. His ears flashed forward and to the sides, mindful of the sights and sounds all around him. Ma sat in the front seat, marveling at Little Ike. "I remember him when he had those long stick legs," she said. "I thought he'd never grow into them. And now look at him!"

We arrived at the Koblentz ranch just after noon. I pulled the carriage up to the front steps of the house. Jack was sitting in his rocking chair next to a woman I hadn't seen before, and I figured it was the person he wanted me to meet. They were both drinking glasses of white wine. He waved to us. The woman smiled.

She was plain-looking—even homely, you might say—with a mat of tight curls around her face and big full cheeks like a chipmunk's with its mouth stuffed with seeds. One look at her and you could tell she wasn't any country girl—the soft hands, all the make-up. Frank soon appeared from the inside of the hay barn. Christina was nowhere in sight. William and I helped Ma down from the carriage and we each took one of Ma's arms as she made her way up to the front porch. Ma sat down on a chair next to the woman, and Jack introduced her as Esther Ross to the rest of us. Ma and Jack both started talking in their dialect, and I could tell Esther didn't understand a word, but looked away, smiling to no one in particular. William returned to the carriage and carried the pies inside the house. He looked at Josephine and the two of them gushed at each other. I was glad Josephine had met a guy she'd struck something up with. She'd been house-bound for months caring for Ma, and it was a rare time she stepped out. And I was glad Jack had met someone, too. He and his brother Frank never struck me as ladies' men—but here he was with Esther Ross right by his side.

I drove the carriage over to the stable and took the bridle off Little Ike. I separated him from the carriage but left him in his harness and led him into a vacant stall. I gave him a big scoop of oats. He'd done well on the drive over, like he was already an old hand at it, and I told him so. I could talk with Little Ike and the way his ears moved, and they way his eyes looked at me, I knew he was listening. I joined the others on the front porch where I could smell chickens roasting from inside the house.

Christina finally appeared. She wore a bandana to keep the hair out of her face which, as usual, was flushed red from working over the stove. She and Ma embraced. She went back inside and brought out more glasses for Ma and me, William and Josephine. We all toasted to good health, good crops and long lives. "Prost," Ma said.

Christina disappeared inside the house and several minutes later came out. "Dinner's ready," she announced.

We walked into the dining room to a fully-set table, complete with linen table cloth, silverware, soup bowls and linen napkins. Christina had done a lot of preparation. We all found chairs, and in an open space in the middle of the table, Christina set down a platter of roasted chicken. On each side of the platter sat a bowl of mashed potatoes and a bowl of string beans, another with a loaf of bread and two small plates with cubes of butter. The room soon filled with a warm, delicious aroma of Christina's cooking. I poured wine into the glasses around me and we made another toast. "To Christina," I said, "for all her work in making this meal." We raised our glasses. Christina smiled, and as usual, appeared embarrassed by the attention.

We passed the dishes around and everyone filled their plates. Just as we started to eat, Jack tapped his wine glass with a spoon. "I have an announcement to make," he said. The room grew quiet. He paused, and I could see him assembling the words he wanted to say. "Esther and I are going to get married!" A hush followed the announcement, and then a round of applause.

"When did you decide this?" Christina asked. I couldn't tell if she was happy about the announcement or troubled.

"About an hour ago," Jack said. We all laughed. "No, really, we talked it over and decided last week."

"Have you set a date?" Josephine wanted to know.

Jack and Esther looked at each other. "Sometime in spring?" he said, and looked over at Esther again. "Isn't that what we decided?" And Esther nodded her head.

"There's still lots of decisions we have to make," Esther said. "Where we'll live and what Jack will do."

I looked at Christina to see her reaction. Jack, as far as I'd known, was part of the deal in buying the Brown's Lane place and now it was sounding like that wasn't the case.

"Where would you like to live?" Christina asked her.

"I'm kind of a city girl myself," Esther said. "I'd like to live in Petaluma, right in town—or maybe Santa Rosa."

I looked at Jack. "And what would you do?"

"Oh, I'll find work someplace," he said. "You know me."

"You don't want to keep farming?" I asked him.

Again he looked at Esther. "I don't know just yet—maybe."

This all came as news to me, and it seemed, news to Christina, as well. I had a hard time imagining Jack living in town and not farming—not doing ranch work and not being outside. As far as I knew that's all Jack had ever done—never seemed to talk about anything else—but women can make you change your mind, make you do things you never thought you'd do, and I guess Esther was one of those women.

"And I have a close friend who's interested in meeting Frank," Esther announced. "I told her all about Frank and she's just tickled to meet him."

This was even more news—Jack and Frank both with women? What were the odds of that? These were two guys I could see milking cows into their eighties—milking cows until they were both slabbed up and slid into the ground—wearing out a path between the barn and the house all their lives, changing their underwear maybe twice a week, depending on whether Christina did their laundry or not.

But again, what did I know about what attracts a man to a woman, and a woman to a man? It's the oddest sort of thing, and nothing you can predict. Two people can seem like opposites and end up living together with hardly a voice raised, everything smooth as whipped cream, and then there's couples that seem meant for each other right out of the chute, but they end up fighting like cats and dogs, arguing over the least little thing, slamming doors behind them, the woman emptying a cupboard of dishes against the wall and the man shaking his head, wondering how he ever married a woman like this.

"Did I let the cat out of the bag, Frank?" Esther asked him. "I mean, you two haven't even met yet but she's a nice girl, and I told her about you and she thinks the two of you'll do just fine."

Frank fidgeted in his chair, staring down at the plate in front of him.

"This sounds like an engagement party," I said. "Anybody else getting married?" I looked over at Josephine and William, and Josephine's face flushed red. "You, too?"

They both smiled. "Yes, us, too."

"What do you think of that, Ma?" I asked her.

"She told me earlier," Ma said. "And I said I think it's time. She needs a life of her own."

"What about you and Christina?" Jack asked. "Let's just go around the table and see who else is getting married." Everyone laughed again. It was my turn to be embarrassed. I glanced over at Christina and she looked away like she'd heard something behind her.

"No, no engagement here," I said.

Christina stared at her plate of food, avoiding my eyes. I couldn't tell if I hurt her feelings or if I'd disappointed her. I just spoke the truth. There was nothing in the oven between us. We were getting along fine with both of us keeping our distance, keeping everything like a business arrangement and that suited me fine. After Carlotta, I was gun-shy when it came to women—built a wall around me meant to keep out any attractions of the heart, thinking I was better off being the captain of my own ship and not welcoming anyone else aboard. My past affairs always sent me through the ringer, and it was months, sometimes years, before I could piece myself together again. And with Christina, I figured she was still mending after Jimmy's death and wanted no part of another man which seemed good with me. We didn't talk much about our feelings, and when we did, it was feelings we had toward others and nothing between us. I didn't know how she felt about me beyond being friends, and I didn't know, really, how I felt about her, other than wanting to keep my distance, wanting to keep it business-like. As I said, we didn't talk about those things. We talked about chickens, the cost of potatoes, new accounts, instead—things could put your hands around, add a number to.

When dinner was over, Josephine helped Christina clear the plates for dessert. Christina had made a pot of coffee and Josephine brought out the two apple pies she and Ma had made.

"Oh, what beautiful pies!" Esther said. "And the crusts—how did you get them so perfect?"

"Practice," Ma said. "Spending time in the kitchen."

"Are you ready for that, Esther?" Jack asked her.

"Being in the kitchen?" she asked. "I suppose I can learn even if I have invested some time into my professional career," she said. "Two years at the Burbank Secretarial School in Santa Rosa—graduated with top honors."

The more Esther talked about herself, the less likely a match she seemed for Jack but what can you do but wish them luck? I wasn't a match-maker by any stretch, and I learned people either worked out their differences—or they didn't. I heard it from plenty folks that marriage was a tough road, and I wasn't so sure I wanted to travel down it.

By now Josephine had cut into the pie and put a generous wedge on each dessert plate before passing them around the table. Christina filled each coffee cup. "There's cream in the little pitchers," she said. "And sugar in the bowls."

"Everything has just been marvelous," Esther squeezed Jack's hand.

When dessert was over, Jack, Frank, William and I walked out on the front porch and lit up cigars. Jack brought out his bottle of schnapps. The women stayed inside and cleared the table, and once the table was cleared they stepped outside onto the porch, into a cloud of cigar smoke. They brushed the smoke away from their noses, coughed, and went back inside.

Out on the porch, Jack filled our glasses with schnapps.

"So you're going to tie the knot?" I asked him.

"Looks like it," he said.

We all lifted our glasses in a toast. "What do you think married life's going to be like?" I asked.

"I don't know—different, I guess," he said.

"You haven't thought about it?" I asked him.

"What's to think about?" Jack drained his glass of schnapps. "You're either in the water or you're standing on the shore—ain't no halfway. I'll learn as I go—like everything else I do."

"And you're ready for it?" I asked.

"Well, I'll have time to prepare."

"How do you prepare for marriage?" I wondered.

"You just practice saying, "Yes, honey. Anything you say, honey," he said and all of us laughed.

"And, Frank, you're thinking about walking down the aisle with someone you haven't even met?" I looked at him with a bit of disbelief. "Is that right?"

"I don't know yet," Frank said. "It's mostly Esther talking— but I'm thinking about it." He tucked his hands into his pants pockets. "But you know how a man can get—wanting company and all that and thinking about the future."

"It's your turn next, Bert." Jack looked at me.

"Why's everyone in such a rush to get married?" I asked. "I don't understand it." All of this news about marriage and engagements surprised the hell out of me. Again, looking at Jack and Frank, and knowing them like I done, I would have bet the ranch I was looking at two life-long bachelors—two guys that'd rather look at cows' asses all day than settle down with a woman.

"It's what folks do," Jack said. "You want to live alone the rest of your life?"

"I thought about it," I said. "There could be worse things to do."

"And carry around that choad all the time?" Jack laughed.

"There's ways to lighten that load," I said.

Frank spit into his hand. "There sure is!" We had another good laugh over that one.

Esther came out and put her hand on Jack's shoulder. "Sounds like you boys are having a good time out here," she said. "I hate to break it up, but I'd like to go home now." Esther had moved back to Sonoma after completing secretarial school and lived with her folks on the east side of town. Her father owned a barber shop on First Street just across from the plaza's eastside.

"Could we have just one more round first?" Jack asked her.

She gave him a look I imagined he'd be seeing often in his married life. "Well, okay, but getting up for work comes early for me," and she walked back inside.

"You got to be firm with them," Jack said, turning around to make sure she was out of earshot. "Otherwise they walk all over you."

All this news of marriage and engagements made me wonder about the status of the Brown's Lane place, and if that had changed. Esther seemed to be leaning toward town life, and I didn't know much more about Frank's fiancé than Frank himself. What would all these engagements mean about the Brown's Lane place, the one Christina seemed to have had her heart set on?

Esther appeared on the porch again, her hands on her hips, and this time in no mood for more excuses—she wanted to go home. Josephine had come out earlier, as well, to say that Ma was fidgeting and acting restless and wanting to leave, so I walked out to the barn and harnessed up Little Ike. Jack walked out with me, as well, and harnessed up his horse to take Esther home.

"Where'd you get that horse?" Frank asked when I pulled the carriage up to the front of the house.

"You ain't ever seen Ike before?" I said. "This was the colt dad's mare threw the day of his funeral."

"I'll be go-to-hell." Frank walked down the steps and up to Little Ike and patted him on his rump. "That's a fine looking animal," he said.

Josephine and William helped Ma down the steps and up into the carriage. Jack drove his buggy alongside ours, and he helped Esther climb aboard. Christina stood between the two carriages and thanked everyone for coming out for dinner. She touched me on the arm. "You take care, Bert Miller," she said. "And don't go getting engaged."

"Don't you worry about that," I said. And we drove back to Vineburg. There was a bite in the air by now, and Josephine and Ma spread a thick comforter across their laps for the ride home. William sat in the driver's seat next to me. I looked over at him. "So you're going to marry my sister, huh?"

"Yes, I am." He looked back at me. "Anything I need to know about her?"

"It's too late, now, William," I said. "You shoulda asked me months back."

"Bert!" Josephine poked me from the back seat.

"She's perfect," I said. "You couldn't have made a better choice."

52

Another Year, Death and Marriages
· ·

The following spring, Ma's health took a turn for the worst. She said there were times when her heart felt like it'd stopped beating, and she'd collapse on the nearest chair. Josephine found her on the living room floor one time, and after that incident I brought her to the hospital. They told us what we already knew, that she had a serious heart condition but there wasn't much they could do to treat it. I brought her back home and three mornings later Josephine went to wake her and found her dead. "She was cold to the touch," Josephine said. "Now she's with Dad."

According to her earlier wishes, she wanted no funeral service—only to be buried next to Dad—so that's what we done. And just like that, both my parents were gone without a chance of saying good-bye to either one. In the following days, I kept telling myself—like I told myself when Dad died—that Ma was no longer around, that I wouldn't be seeing her anymore out in the garden with Little Ike trailing after her, or sitting in her stuffed chair reading the newspaper.

It was sad thoughts. The Vineburg place seemed empty now, quiet—like everyone moved away sudden-like. Ma's death hit Josephine the hardest because the two of them were always together—almost like two sisters. But I knew after Dad's death that a big part of Ma had broken off and gone with him. I could see it in her blank stares and the way she looked off into the distance hoping the man walking toward her was the man she missed the most.

John B. and Gertie drove over for the burial with their new son, Friedolin. We laid Ma to rest right next to Dad, according to her wishes. After the burial we gathered out at the Vineburg place. The men drank bourbon, the women white wine. Josephine baked a cake. Christina brought cold chicken, her potato salad and sauerkraut, and we slapped together some tables and benches in the backyard and talked about Dad and Ma, and all the twists and turns their lives had taken, from the time they left Obwalden for the states, to working on dairies in Brisbane, the move to Napa and eventually to here in Sonoma where they both died. We laughed and we cried, too. I couldn't help it. They'd worked so hard trying to stake out a new life in this country and by all measures had done well. Our dad got cheated out of his life, and, in a way, Ma got cheated out of hers, too, by not having him around, but there wasn't anything we could do about that. Call it God's will if you're a believer. I called it fate, the luck of the draw—something none of us had any say over. When your time was up, it was up—there was no bargaining involved.

John B., Gertie and Friedolin spent the night. John B. and I stayed up past the others, sipping on bourbon out on the front porch and talking about our lives.

"Whatever happened between you and Carlotta?" he wanted to know.

"My heart went where it shouldn't have," I said. "It wrote a check the real world wasn't ready to cash."

"She's a beautiful woman, and I can't blame you."

"Yeah, beautiful women make you do foolish things, all right," I said. "And I done them all—but what's life if you don't stick your neck out every once in awhile?"

"You stuck it out more than most," he said.

"I thought I had a shot—the things she told me, the things that happened. I thought it was all lining up—but I was wrong," I said. I finished my glass of bourbon and felt like talking more. "She was out of my class and it took me taking some lumps before it sunk in."

"They'll be others," he said. I poured him another glass. "What about Christina? I see the way she looks at you."

"We're both avoiding that," I said. "She's thinking there's probably no one after Jimmy Murdoch and I'm thinking there's no one—period."

I finished my bourbon and wanted to change the subject. I'd been hashing over thoughts about Christina and what I'd do, and all of it put a load on my mind. I liked things the way they were between Christina and me and didn't see any reason to change them—didn't see any reason to make it more complicated.

"How you liking it over there in Santa Rosa?" I asked him.

"More work than you can shake a stick at," he said, "but I like it fine. We finished the house just in time for little Friedolin to come along—couldn't have done it without you."

"It was nothing. I enjoyed the ride over, and think that's a fine area you settled in," I said. "Real fine and I'll give you more time when I can."

He swirled the remaining bourbon in his glass. "Got so many things I want to do I don't know when I'll find the time."

"Like what?"

"I already put in an orchard but the goddamn deer ate my saplings to the ground, so I gotta replant in the spring. There's fencing to put up, too," he said. "I want to raise some sheep over there, too, and right now, cutting and selling firewood has brought in some cash. And then there's the water issue. I'm thinking about forming a water company for users around me."

"You're an ambitious guy," I said.

"Why don't you come over and we'll hunt some deer?" he said. "You can take some venison home with you."

"I might just do that," I said. "Okay if I invite Tino along?"

"Sure."

"What about the folks' place here?" John B. asked. "I hate talking business so soon, but it's something we should probably hash out, don't you think?"

"If Josephine and William are going to tie the knot, don't you think they should live here? We can figure out the legal stuff later if it comes to that."

"That's what Gertie and I said, too." John B. finished his bourbon. "I think it's what Ma and Dad would have liked, don't you?"

"I do."

By now everyone was asleep in the house with just John B. and me awake. The crickets were sounding and there was a screech owl that flew out of an oak along the creek.

"When was the last time you saw Ma?" I asked John B.

"At the hospital, but before that it was last Christmas."

"You always think there's time to talk to them, tell them thanks for busting their nut, and telling them things you always wanted to tell them about like how much you loved them but could never find the words to say it—couldn't find that courage. Then they're gone—just like that," I said. "I know I felt that way about Dad because we always argued and I thought he was wrong and he thought I was wrong and things just never seemed to change. I figured in time we'd get it squared away—that we'd both come around, but before we could, time run out on us."

John B. yawned. "Time for me to turn in," he said. "I don't normally stay up this late." He looked over at me. "But what you say is true, Bert—every word of it. We think there's time but we don't ever know."

"No, we don't," I said.

We both stood up and shook hands and John B. went inside. I was alone now and thinking of Ma and remembering again how it was after Dad died and all the adjusting I had to go through, all the times I had to remind myself that he was no longer around and should I get even with Percy Sheers and finally deciding to let that go, let life take its course.

I figured it'd be the same with Ma, the big empty spaces she left behind, and I wondered what would fill them in. I didn't know. I could always talk to her, something I couldn't do with my father—not without fearing the big hand coming down. Ma and I, we just seemed to understand each other more. And now she wouldn't be around to talk to. It would be different. I sat there on her front porch—the night all around me, things so quiet and dark and lonesome. I felt a real sadness well up inside—so real and big it seemed I could reach out and touch it. The sadness came in waves and I couldn't stop it—just one wave after another—and before I knew it, tears were spilling out of my eyes and running down my cheeks.

53

Visiting John B.
• • • • • • • • • • • • • •

Two days after Ma's service, a letter of condolence arrived from
Carlotta. Inside the card, she'd written, *"So sorry to hear of your
mother's death. We miss seeing you around the ranch here. Best wishes,
Carlotta.* I stared at the front of the card—it was embossed with a
colorful bunch of roses in a glass vase—and I opened it to read what
she'd written several times—maybe hoping for some clue to want
me back. The "we" she'd referred to was, no doubt, the senator, and
now two years later, I still felt a stupid longing for her, and pangs
of jealousy, and I wondered if they'd ever go away or if it was something that would stay with me the rest of my life.

I remember it took awhile before finally realizing that whatever
fantasy I'd clung to about Carlotta was gone, buried—as dead now
as my mother and father. In an odd sort of way, this realization
was freeing. Everyone says we should always have hope, but hope
to me was a weight around my neck, a buttermilk biscuit just out
of reach, and for months and longer, I clung to some far-off chance
that something might still happen between me and Carlotta. For
several years I lived my life for that hope, keeping every opportunity open, not chasing other women, avoiding any kind of closeness—saving myself for her, for that hope. It was a foolish thing to
do—hoping like that—and I finally come around to seeing it.

William, Josephine's beau, spent more time around the Vineburg
place now, and the two of them were planning their springtime
wedding together. Josephine had moved into Ma's bedroom and
changed some of the furniture to fit her tastes, and I was starting
to feel like I was another piece of that discarded furniture, and
that maybe it was time to move on to other quarters even though
Josephine had reassured me that I was welcome to stay at the place
long as I wanted. Hauling had slacked off, and I decided it was a

good time to visit John B. and help him with his place up at Mark West, so in between February rain storms, I harnessed up Molly and Dolly, loaded my tools and whatever else I thought I'd need, tarped them all under a sheet of canvas, tethered Little Ike to the rear of the wagon and set off for John B.'s.

We drove north up through the valley, and by Kenwood the clouds covered the mountains on both sides before the rains cut loose again and drenched us good. I wore an oil-cloth coat and that kept the upper part of me mostly dry inside, but my boots filled with water, my feet got cold and that bothered the hell out of me. We just kept going, though. The horses didn't mind the rain. Every few minutes they'd shake their big bodies and the rain drops flew off like confetti. By the time we pulled into Santa Rosa, I was good and ready for a drink. We stopped at the nearest tavern where I braked the wagon and walked inside, my toes squishing around in the insides of my boots. I hung my oil-cloth on a hook near the door, walked to the bar and ordered a shot of whiskey with a beer-back. As the bartender set the glasses in front of me, he asked what I was doing out on a day like this.

"Going to visit my brother," I told him. "It's what folks do with no sense. I thought I could do it between storms—wrong again."

"You didn't want to take the train?" he asked.

"No, couldn't," I said. "Needed to bring tools and horses with me."

I banged the whiskey down and felt its warmth all the way into my stomach, and then followed it with a wash of beer. I ordered another shot.

"Where's your brother live?" he asked.

"Up in the Mark West Springs area—he bought twelve hundred acres up there," I said.

"Beautiful country, but lots of hills." The bartender grabbed a glass and began polishing it with a towel. "Dry during the summer, too."

"He's starting from scratch—just bare land, but he's got a house up already." I sat there and finished my beer. A big cloud burst cut loose and pounded the roof so hard we could hardly hear ourselves talk. It felt like the roof would cave in. We both looked up and shook our heads. I walked to the tavern door and looked out. My horses' heads were hung low the way they do in bad weather. Water was pouring off the rooftops and collecting in big pools on the streets.

"I'll have another round," I called out to the barkeep. "I ain't going out there now."

I walked back to my barstool, sat down, downed the whiskey and let it mellow in my throat. I followed it with another beer and by now I had a good glaze on, a nice tingling throughout—the way I liked it, but still in control of my faculties—no stumbling, no fighting to get words out—just a little buffer between me and the outside world. When I looked out the tavern door, it'd stopped raining, and I figured now was my chance. I paid my tab and thanked the barkeep, put my oil-cloth back on and walked out to the wagon. I apologized to the horses for taking them out in weather like this. They looked at me with those sad, curious horse eyes that I hoped forgave me.

I pulled into John B.'s place nearly two hours later. The rain had stopped by the time I left Santa Rosa, and save for my feet, I'd stayed reasonably dry. He came out to meet me along with his little terrier dog who went from wagon wheel to wagon wheel, sniffing furious before lifting his leg on each wheel. John B. and I hadn't seen each other since Ma's burial. A growth of beard had spread across his face, and when I looked at him it was like looking at our dad, the resemblance was that strong—the high cheekbones, the sharp nose, the eyes the color of robin's eggs. I marveled at how much work John B. had done since last visiting here, over a year ago. The house was nearly finished, and he'd built several small outbuildings for his work shop and a lean-to for his flock of sheep, and had laid out an area where he planned to build the hay barn. He'd cross-fenced most of the level land around these buildings, as well, before the land rose into the steep surrounding oak-covered hills.

"Damn, John B., you've been busy!" I said.

"What else is there to do?" he said and ran his hand across this mouth.

We walked to the back of my wagon and he looked over Little Ike. "You know, I can't look at this horse without thinking of Dad," he said. "It's like he took up Dad's spirit."

"Yeah, he's a good boy. Dad would have been so proud," I said. "I can ride him. He'll pull. Does whatever I ask him to—and Molly and Dolly there—they treat him like he's their own."

Gertie came out of the house holding their son Friedolin. He was already a year old with a shock of red hair on top of his head. She was pregnant with another child. We hugged each other. "You going to stay for awhile?" she asked.

"Yeah, for awhile," I said. "I was feeling like a fifth wheel on a wagon over at the folks' place. William and Josephine are making it their own."

"Well, Bert, that was couples do," Gertie said. "They make nests—you'll find out someday."

I untied Little Ike and walked him over to a hitching post and retied him before returning to the wagon and removing its tailgate. I climbed up on the back of the wagon and loosened the rope and pulled it through the canvas' grommets and then folded the canvas back to expose what was under it. Everything looked mostly dry.

"Let's get those horses out of their harness," John B. said, "and let that harness dry. There's an empty corral and a lean-to they can hunker under if it starts to rain again." He looked over the back of the wagon. "You can put those things on the front porch for now."

"I brought just about everything I own," I said. "I'm set to haul lumber up from Guerneville, too, when we need it."

"Let's see what the weather does first," John B. looked up at the sky.

After we unharnessed the horses and led them to a corral and emptied the wagon, Gertie called us in for coffee. She had a fire going and the house felt warm as an oven.

"If you don't mind, I need to remove my boots and stockings," I said. "My feet been wet all day."

"Set 'em by the stove to dry," Gertie said. "I'll get you a pair of John B.'s socks."

We sat at the kitchen table and Gertie poured each of us a mug of hot coffee. I looked around the interior of the house. Nothing fancy about it, just plain, good design and building. The kitchen area spilled into the living room, and on each wall was a window that opened out to the woods. "You built yourselves a fine place here," I said.

"It took awhile, but we got it done," John B. said. "And we appreciated your help, too, Bert."

Gertie sat down with us. "So, any news from Sonoma?" she asked.

"Nothing much since Ma's service," I said. "I've had hauling jobs and stay as busy as I want. And now I need to find another place to settle into."

"I'm sure Josephine wouldn't mind you staying on," Gertie said. "I mean, it's as much yours as it hers."

"I know that, and she's told me so, but with the two of them starting out like they are, I'd feel better just giving them their space."

"What about returning to the Stamm ranch?" Gertie asked. "Carlotta thought the world of you and John B."

"No, I don't think that's going to happen." I looked at John B. and he looked back at me. I didn't know how much he'd shared with Gertie. Hard to believe he hadn't told her, but knowing Gertie like I did, I figured she was fishing here to see how I felt about Carlotta.

"Do you see Christine at all?" Gertie asked. "It was a shame about her fellow, but she's a good woman, Bert, and they're hard to find." Gertie looked at me to see what my reaction might be.

"Not sure I'm looking now," I said. "I helped her brothers build the brooder and layer house and saw her pretty regular. And once the hens started laying, she was selling eggs along with her potato salad. I even loaned her my wagon when theirs was down."

"Don't you think she'd make a good partner?" Gertie asked.

"Listen to you!" John B. said. "Playing the match-maker."

"I'm only asking," she said.

"She's a by-the-book person and I'm not," I said. "She figures everything down to the penny while I don't. And she keeps a ledger and writes down every little expense inside it. I don't work that way. Sure, I jot some things down, but mostly it's what happened on that day."

"So what if she does?" Gertie asked. "It just shows she's a good business woman. Would you rather be with someone who just spends it all without knowing where the money went?"

"Bert likes the dangerous woman," John B. said. "The long-shot ones, the ones he's never sure he can get—otherwise he loses interest."

"You don't know that, John B." Gertie said.

"It's just what I've seen with my brother," John B. said. "And what he's told me. Isn't that right, Bert?"

"I don't know, John B.," I said.

But I remember Emma Hansen telling me the same thing a couple of years back—that I chased after the ones I couldn't catch because I knew I couldn't catch them in the first place. It seemed like a terrible waste of time and something that only ended up tying me into more knots, but Emma said it didn't matter—it's what I done.

Those long-shot ones drove me crazy with desire—I didn't have to look any further than Carlotta to know that was true. And then there was Cameron right behind her. The ones that showed any interest in me—the Hoaglen girl at Poppes Store or Crawford's daughter who worked at Breitenbach's—even the chamber maid at the Toscano, who'd once asked me to a Sunday concert—I didn't gave a shake about. The pickings were too easy with them. I needed someone who could really test me, take me to the limits of desire—and that's just where I ended up—out on the limits, always looking in, and never satisfied.

"Now why would Bert, or anyone, chase a girl he knew he couldn't win over?" Gertie asked. "Doesn't it just seem like a waste of time?" She paused. "It does to me, at least."

"He doesn't know, though, until he tries," John B. said.

"And, if a woman was honest, she'd tell him outright he's wasting his time, wouldn't she?" Gertie sipped from her coffee cup. Friedolin had crawled up on her lap and she loosened the top buttons on her blouse, exposed a nipple and he began to nurse.

"How many guys—and women, too—been told to 'shove off' and eventually wins over the guy or the woman that sent him away?" John B. asked. "That's happened to half the people I know. If they didn't persist, nothing would have happened."

"Listen to us," Gertie said. "The two of us offering advice to Bert like we know all about it—we don't. It was simple with us, wasn't it, John B.?"

"Yes, it was," he said.

"The first time we looked at each other, both of us knew," Gertie said. "We didn't have to jump through all kinds of hoops like those tigers in the circus either. And we didn't have to think the other was out of reach to add to the desire, either—no, the desire was already there."

"I'm glad for the two of you," I said. "I've always been jealous of your relationship and how uncomplicated it seemed—"

"Oh, don't think it's doesn't have complications," Gertie said. "There's plenty of those."

"What I mean is both of you seem in-step with one another, something that's avoided me. I don't know why, either," I said. "Is it because I'm waiting for the perfect person to come along?"

"She doesn't have to be perfect," Gertie said. "Just perfect for you."

"Or, is it the other reason I fall back on?" I said.

"And what's that?" Gertie asked.

"That I don't deserve it—that everything about me spells trouble—my drinking, my not taking nothing serious—this independent streak of mine that tells me I'm better off alone than making someone else's life miserable trying to live with me."

"You beat yourself up too much," John B. said. "And you over-think everything."

"You're a good person," Gertie said.

I nodded my head. It was something I was never certain of—my goodness, my self-worth. I'd convince myself, that, yes, I'm a decent person that cares about others and is worthy of being loved, and then the next second I'm not sure—that self confidence gone and so is any reason someone could find to love me in return. Like I've said all along, this was me—back and forth, back and forth. First on one side of the fence—king of the hill—and then on the other where I'm wallowing down in the hogs' mud. Everything always in turmoil. Was it any different with other folks, I wondered? Did they go through life just like me but only they figured it out faster? I didn't know.

"Well, I still think Christina would make a fine partner for you," Gertie said. "By-the-book or not." She looked at me. "Why not ask her to a concert in the park? Would that kill you? Or, are you afraid she might say 'yes'?"

"I'll think about it," I said.

"Gertie," John B. looked at his wife. "Bert'll figure it out." And then to change the subject, he looked at me. "How long you plan on staying?"

"I thought until we get that barn framed," I said. "I can haul the lumber in from Guerneville once you place the order."

"I placed it already," he said.

"Well, once this rain stops, I'll head down there with the team and wagon."

"It might be a few days."

"Anything else we can do?"

"Cut and haul firewood into town," he said. "That's what's paying some of the bills now."

I stood up from the table and went over to check on my boots by the wood-burning stove. They were nearly dry by now. I slipped them back on and John and I went outside to feed the horses. All three of mine met me at the corral fence and shoved aside each other trying to nuzzle into my jacket. Their coats were caked with mud after rolling on the ground. It had stopped raining but the clouds seemed just a couple of feet above my head, muffling the sound all around us like we were in a closed room, but somewhere in the middle of this quiet, I could hear wind in the trees above, and off in the distance, Mark West Creek swelling up with the new rains.

I liked it here. I liked being in new places, being outside, and breaking up routines I found myself in for too long. I knew it was routine, the work routine, that got us to produce and get things done, but still, I liked a break from it, to wander around and take in new sights and sounds. I liked my time with John B. and his family, too. I've told you all along that I envied him, and I do. He was the model for me on how to do things, and sometimes I could follow him and other times I couldn't. But even though we were brothers, growing up pretty much the same, something made us different, and I had to keep reminding myself of that. No better, I thought deep down—just different.

54

Cutting Firewood

· · · · · · · · · · · · · · · · ·

The following morning, John B., Gertie and I were back at the
kitchen table, drinking coffee and deciding what the day's work
would be. A light rain pattered down on the roof. John B. walked
over to the kitchen window and looked out. "Probably going to piss
down like this all day," he said. "We can still cut firewood, if you're
up for it."

"Sure," I said. "I don't feel like staying in all day. We can hitch
up my rig if you want."

"Those big horses of yours sure-footed?" he asked. "Might get a
little slippery up there."

"They should do all right—I mean, there's some kind of road
they can follow isn't there?"

"There is," he said. "We'll keep 'em on it and haul the wood
back to the wagon."

Gertie fixed us a breakfast of eggs, venison and fried potatoes. I
drank two more cups of coffee and felt like I wanted to go back to
bed I was that full, but once outside and moving around, breakfast
wore off and the juices started flowing and I was ready for work. I
harnessed up Molly and Dolly, and John B. loaded a two-man saw,
some smaller saws and a pair of axes into the back of the wagon.
Little Ike stayed behind in his corral, pacing back and forth, and
wondering why he couldn't come along. "He's sure taken to you,"
John B. said.

"You know, John B., I ain't that big on all this spiritual stuff," I
said, "but I think some of the old man's spirit made its way over to
Little Ike that day of Dad's funeral—just walked over from Carlotta's
parlor and right into the stall where Little Ike was being born."

We were on a path now that John B. had cut earlier in between
the stands of oaks and we followed it up a little draw that opened

into a flat area the size of a baseball diamond. The two horses picked their way upward around the jutting rocks.

"I've been loading the wood here," John B. pointed to piles of bark and branches. "Any further up it gets too steep for a wagon. Sometimes I'll take my horse and have him skid a good-sized tree down here for cutting up. I don't cut anything that's alive, just the downed stuff. It's already seasoned and makes for good burning."

"Who do you sell to?" I asked him.

"Mostly to hotels and taverns, wherever they can keep a wood-burning stove going," he said.

I braked the wagon and stepped down. John B. had removed its tailgate and was up in the wagon handing the tools back to me. "You'll have to excuse Gertie," he said. "She thinks everyone in this world needs to pair up, and until they do, they're just plain miserable."

"I can understand that," I said. "Most of us don't like being alone."

"But it either happens or it doesn't," he said. "It's all that rushing it that I don't understand."

"No, I don't think you can rush it," I said. "It takes its own time and both folks gotta be ready for it."

He took one saw and looked at its teeth closely, then brought a file out of his hip pocket and filed in one direction with each tooth. "You ain't going to force it," he said. "But I know plenty folks that just get married because they think they have to, or because they don't want to be alone—wrong reasons if you ask me."

"Social pressure," I said. "Seeing people around them hitching up and they don't want to be left out."

"I don't know if I'd be married if I hadn't met Gertie like I did." He looked over at me. "Gertie and I sometimes ask each other that question."

"Someone else would have come along," I said. "She's a hive filled with honey and you can't keep the bees away from her."

John B. laughed. "I'm going to tell her you said that. And me? Am I a hive, too, that women can't resist?"

"Hell, yes! We both are! Just two big fuckin' hives!" We laughed. "I'm fighting women off all the time—it's why I came up here—to get away from them."

We both laughed again and then picked up the saws and axes and climbed up through stands of oaks to an area where John B. had been working. An older oak had toppled and it had a big trunk that John B. didn't want to tackle unless he could use the two-man saw. The two of us set to work on it, pulling and pushing that two-man, and before long I was peeling off my shirt and working up a good sweat.

"You ever thought of going back to work at Carlotta's?" John B. wiped the sweat from his forehead. "I mean after all your commotion with her blows over?"

"No, I'm done there," I said. "If the dog's bitin' you, you don't keep stickin' out your hand, do you?"

"I guess not—but maybe if you keep sticking it out, the dog gets used to it and stops biting you."

"I don't see it that way, John B."

I took a handkerchief out of my back pocket and wiped my forehead. "She gave me a little taste one night—and that was all. And being human, it was just natural to want more, but she wasn't having it—about drove me out of my mind." I looked over at John B. "Anyway, I told you all this out at the folks' place that night, didn't I?"

"Yeah, you told me some."

"I told you all I knew," I said. "She was laying right beside me and blubbering over the senator and how sad she was that he'd gone back to his wife, and I was rubbing her back and telling her things ain't that bad and pretty soon her mouth was next to mine and we started kissing and getting all excited and it led up to what those things usually lead up to."

"Just a one-timer, then, huh?" John B. asked.

"Yeah, later her conscience kicked in, something like that, and she said what we done was wrong—or in a moment of weakness— and I told her wasn't anything wrong about two people enjoying each other."

"But it wasn't wrong with the senator?" John B. asked.

"I guess not," I said. "But what I knew all along was there were winners and losers in this kind of thing—we all took our turns. I had mine and hoped it would last longer than it did, but it didn't. You feel lousy for awhile—it's the dues you pay—but if you let it alone and don't keep teasing it, time smooths out the rough patches."

"Bert Miller and Carlotta Stamm," John B. said to himself. "Who'd have thought?"

"Yeah, for one night I was in the catbird seat," I said, "but I was fooling myself—I must have known it. But we go along with it just the same. It was all too easy to be real, but when you're in the middle of it, who's going to ask questions? Who's going to wonder why it's happening or how long it's going to last? Not me—didn't see any point in asking those kinds of questions—just let whatever happens, happen."

"Look at all I'm missing being married," John B. said.

"You're not missing anything!" I grabbed my end of the saw. "So, to answer your question—no, I'm not going back to Carlotta's."

We sawed away at the big trunk and rolled the oak rounds down to the wagon. The rain had let up and the moss on the trunks of the trees turned bright green. John B. and I each took sledge hammers and splitting mauls and split the rounds into smaller pieces.

"Do you ever see her?" John B. asked.

"Who? Carlotta? No, I go out of way to avoid her," I said. "I have to pass her place all the time, and I try not to think of her, but the memory just has to wear off in its own time—and, god-damn, it takes its own time."

"That's why you need to meet someone else," he said. "And I don't want to start sounding like Gertie here, but some of what she says is true. You meet someone else and pretty soon you're not thinking of who you're trying to forget."

"I don't know," I said. "I've been with a couple of women since then—mostly one-nighters—and all I end up doing is comparing them to Carlotta."

"Because they don't mean anything to you, that's why, Bert. If you met someone who did, any memory of Carlotta'd be gone in a horse's fart."

"I guess."

"Yeah, I ain't no expert in it, but I think it would." He started to raise his sledge hammer and then stopped. "You want to go through the rest of your life just carrying around her memory, huh? Is that what you want?"

"No, it isn't."

"It don't do you a lick of good, does it?"

"No, it doesn't—not a lick."

"It ain't making her break it off with the senator because you're thinking of her, right?" he asked. "She doesn't even know what you're thinking—and probably couldn't give a shit if she did. So, you're just wasting your thinking—burning up thoughts you could be using for something else."

"I know all this," I said. "But it's that stuff deep inside I can't seem to control—they just come up. I don't want them to—but they just come up."

"What did Dad say? 'He don't know whether to shit or go blind'? Isn't that what he said when you're stuck between two places?"

"Yeah, that's what he said all right."

"I don't know what to tell you, Bert. I got lucky when it came to women."

"And I didn't."

"Well, you don't know that yet," he said. "You got years left—still plenty of time to fall on your face again—time enough for at least a dozen more heartbreaks."

"Thanks for the encouragement," I said.

"Don't mention it."

By noon, we had a wagon full of split firewood and our stomachs were growling. We tossed the saws, axes and sledges into the back of the wagon, and I put the tailgate back in place. We both climbed up to the driver's seat, I loosened the traces, clicked my tongue, and the horses made a U-turn in the opening and we headed back to the farmyard. Gertie had made a stew and baked several loaves of bread, and after I washed up, we sat at the table and I dug into the stew like I hadn't eaten in days.

"You boys have a good morning?" she asked.

"Pretty good," I said. "John B. here straightened me out on a few things."

"Oh?" Gertie said.

"Yeah, about what I was doing wrong," I said. "Now I know."

"John B.'s helpful that way, isn't he?" she said.

"He is," I said. "Now I'll know I'm doing wrong when I'm doing it and not have to wonder."

"You're an odd one, Bert Miller," she said.

"Yes, I am."

"You got enough left in you to head to the Occidental Hotel this afternoon with the firewood?" John B. mopped the remaining stew out of his bowl with a slice of bread.

"Yeah, I think so."

The rain had let up, but we both brought our oil-cloths with us and stashed them under the driver's seat. I turned the team onto Mark West and we headed down the road that would take us into Santa Rosa, eight miles away. It was flat all the way into town and the two horses made good time.

"I wonder if old JD wishes he had these two horses back?" John B. asked.

"He was all stoved-up with arthritis," I said, "And as much as he liked to drive, it was hurting him too much. I know he misses them—hell, he treated them like they were his kids."

John B. looked around. "Rain's given everything a good soaking—but we needed it."

We drove past bare orchards and bare vineyards, everything soaked and gray, until we arrived at the outskirts of town, staying on Mendocino Road to within a block of the courthouse. The Occidental Hotel sat at the corner of the block and there was an alley behind it where all the deliveries were made. "I ain't been up here since Dad's trial," I said.

John B. directed me where to stop. The alley was bound on both sides by brick buildings three stories high. John B. knocked on a metal door and soon a man with a white cook's hat appeared. "John B.," he said. "I didn't know with the weather if you'd come or not."

"We're here. I brought my brother along, too, Arnold Bert, but we just call him Bert. Bert, this is Mario." We shook hands. "He helped me cut the wood."

"What you think of his place up there?" Mario asked me.

"It's a fine place," I said.

"I tell my wife I want a place like that, and she say, 'just keep cooking.'" And Mario let out a loud laugh. "Besides I don't know all the work you need to do —the building, the cattle—too much to know."

"It is a lot of work, but that never scared my brother," I said.

Mario went back inside the kitchen and we began unloading the firewood, stacking it neatly against the back wall of the hotel. A little roof overhead kept the firewood dry. We loaded-in over a cord and a half of firewood and when we were finished, Mario invited us in for a drink at the hotel's bar and we both accepted. The bar room was like a big cavern paneled in dark wood, with ten foot high ceilings covered in a pressed metal, and except for a couple of patrons at the far end of the bar, it was nearly empty. A mirror ran the length of the bar and lined in front of the mirror on a series of shelves was liquor I'd never heard or seen before. "Bruno," Mario said to the bartender, "Give them anything they want."

I looked at Bruno. "How about a good bourbon?"

"You got it." He took down a bottle of Jack Daniels from a shelf behind him. "I think you'll like this one."

I sipped it, let it wallow in my mouth to get its flavor. It was mellow, strong but not hard, like drinking liquid hickory. I swallowed. "Very good," I said and turned to John B. "You should try it." And he did, and we both agreed that if there was a heaven, they'd be serving this bourbon.

Bruno refilled my glass and I thanked him. There's times when liquor—particularly a good bourbon like this one—goes down better than other times, and you wish there was a lake of it you could jump into and never have to leave until it was all gone— this was one of those times. If it weren't for John B. and Gertie, I would have stayed at that Occidental Hotel bar until that bottle was dry, just letting the bourbon work its magic on me, but I knew Gertie drew a strict line when it came to alcohol. It'd killed her father and so I stepped lightly around it. It didn't stop me though from banging down a couple more shots until John B, said we'd better head back before it gets too dark.

I got up from the barstool and it took a few seconds to find my legs. I propped myself up and waited for my equilibrium to kick in. I had a nice glow on and when I turned my head, the barroom spun like a carousel you'd see in a park. John B., who'd had only one drink, maybe two, looked at me. "You all right?" he asked.

"Fine—never better," and I laughed.

We thanked Bruno and I left him a tip and he told us to come back anytime. Out in the alley, the horses nickered when they saw us. They weren't crazy about being left in that damp, dark alleyway, I could tell. They shifted their weight from hoof to hoof and rocked forward and back. I went up and talked to them and told them I was sorry, but now we were headed back to John B.'s where they had a dry place for the night and plenty of hay.

"You always talk to them like that?" John B. asked.

"I do, especially when I've had a couple of belts under me," I said.

"Can you drive?"

"Now what kind of question is that?" I asked him. "The only way I can't is if they slabbed me up and stuck me in a pinebox."

The first hour driving, my bearings were all tossed around, and John B. had to keep directing me. "You sure you're all right?" he'd ask.

It was all new surroundings to me. Some of it I remembered from the drive in, but much of it, I didn't. The longer I drove, the more the cool night air cleared my head, and that earlier glow from the bourbon wore off. The last two miles, maybe three, we drove in the dark. The hills to our east loomed like big shadows with rain clouds running along their ridges. Overhead the clouds had broken up into big pieces, exposing stretches of clear sky sprinkled with stars, and there was a nearly full moon trying to poke its way out, as well.

We climbed up Mark West for the last mile and brought the horses into John B.'s. I let him off at the house and continued up to the stalls with the team, unharnessed them and led them into the corral where Little Ike was glad to see us. I fed them and walked back to the house exhausted. It'd been a full day, this first one with my brother, since Ma's funeral, and though the bourbon now left me with a bit of a headache, I didn't much care. I looked up at the sky above and breathed in the cool, clean air a couple of times, and listened to the creek water below sliding over the rocks before I went inside.

55

Factory Girl
• • • • • • • • • • •

1895: Santa Rosa, California

John B. and Gertie made it clear I was welcome to stay with them as long as I wanted. I didn't know how long that would be, maybe a few days, maybe a few weeks, maybe even longer. When I felt like leaving, I'd leave. As long as I could help them out and not feel I was a burden, I'd stay. There was nothing in Sonoma calling me back. I'd honored all my hauling contracts and left town with a clean slate. I told Christina and her brothers I'd be leaving for awhile and she looked at me and then looked away quickly as was her habit, and nodded her head. Putting some distance between Carlotta and me seemed a good idea, as well. She still hid in a corner of my memory, walking out from the shadows now and then, smiling that smile, and reminding me she wasn't completely gone.

Things with Christina were uncertain at best. We both kept our cards close to the vest—I know I did—and neither of us leaked out any signs that our interest was other than being friends. Like I said, there wasn't that strong draw with her like I'd felt with Carlotta and Cameron. I wasn't mumbling her name or wondering what she was doing every minute of the day or imagining some glorious future together. Some days I didn't even think of her that much. I'd convinced myself I could take her or leave her, and if someone else came along to claim her—well, someone else came along. And if someone came along to claim me, then that's what they done. She could have me. I know I didn't want to get hung out on a line the way I'd been with Carlotta. I'd done that and it hurt like hell, and I wasn't into fooling myself again.

John B. and I each hitched up our wagons for a trip down the Russian River valley to Joshua Murphy's sawmill in Guerneville, where we picked up lumber for the brooder and layer houses John B. wanted to build. They mirrored the ones we'd built at Carlotta's and the ones I'd helped Jack and Frank build at the Koblentz ranch. We hauled the lumber back and stacked it on stickers near the building site. In between our trip to Guerneville, we'd cleared an area for his orchard, using Molly and Dolly to pull out stumps, and brought in fifty bare-root apple trees to plant. We dug holes for each bare-root and back-filled with a mixture of good topsoil and a mixture of horse and cow manure. We worked from sunup to sundown nearly every day, and Gertie kept us well-fed. She'd set up my own bed in the back bedroom meant for little Friedolin when he was old enough to have his own room. On a rare day off, John B. and I grabbed our shotguns and hunted for quail, or we'd take his fishing poles and cast into a couple of good holes he knew along the creek. Sometimes after lunch, I'd just take a long nap, hear the creek talking to me through the firs and oaks, and rest up for the next bout of work.

The weather broke long enough for us to set the foundations for both the brooder and layer houses. We followed the drawings Dad had made, kept pretty much his same measurements, and using all available daylight and working every day, we had the floors to both houses laid and the walls stood up in two weeks. We returned to Murphy's in Guerneville for the roofing members and the shingles, and in two more weeks, the roofs were framed and the shingles nailed in place. "Now all we need is the chickens," John B. said. "There's a hatchery down by the railroad depot, not far from a section of town you'll want to stay away from. It's okay during the day but it turns different at night."

"Why's that?" I asked.

"Hard-timers, folks down on their luck, loose women—take your pick," he said. "They come out at night."

Of course, what John B. said stoked my curiosity, so on our next day off, I cleaned up, put a saddle on Little Ike, and decided to see what the seamier side of Santa Rosa could offer me. I left Mark West early afternoon and rode straight into Santa Rosa on the Healdsburg Road, and stopped at the first bar I saw on the north end, a little place called Bailey's and ordered a double shot of bourbon and a glass of beer—my usual. Both went down like pinching the pit out of a soft peach, and I thought of another round, but there was still so much to see, so many temptations ahead, I decided against it, got back on Little Ike and rode further into town. It was a Saturday afternoon, lots of folks out after the rains, with wagons and carriages and saddle horses tied up along both sides of the streets, and mounds of horse manure piled behind them. Little Ike and I toured the town like two sailors on liberty, taking in all the sights and sounds and smells of what I considered the big town. It was a welcome break from working up at Mark West.

I rode up to the front of the Occidental Hotel, tied Little Ike to its hitching post and went inside to say hello to Mario and taste some of that fine bourbon from weeks before. This time the bar was filled with folks—all kinds—but mostly well-heeled types wearing suits and smoking cigars—the talking and laughing so loud you couldn't hear yourself think. Cigar smoke hung in the air like rain clouds. I found an empty stool at the end of the bar and Bruno eventually made his way toward me. "Bruno! Remember me?" I asked.

He looked me over but I could tell he didn't remember.

"Bert—Bert Miller," I said. "John B.'s brother—we delivered the firewood a few weeks back."

"Oh, yeah! Now I remember." He looked me over. "Bourbon, right? You liked the Jack."

"You got it!"

"I forget faces but never what someone drinks," he said, turned and grabbed a rock glass from the counter behind him and set it in front of me. Then he turned again and grabbed the bottle of bourbon and filled my glass. "Where's your brother?" he asked.

"Home with the wife and boy—resting like I should be doing," I said. "But something was pulling me toward town and I think it's sitting right in front of me now," and I pointed at the glass of bourbon. "John B.'s wife doesn't like having it around and since

I'm staying there I honor her wishes." I brought the glass up to my mouth and polished it off.

"Well, drink up and enjoy your day off." Bruno started to walk off.

"Bruno, could you refill it before you leave?"

He smiled, grabbed the bottle and topped off my glass. He poured me another beer, as well. "There you go," he said. "All set."

I thanked him. This time I sipped the bourbon slower and turned and looked around the bar. The tables and bar were all filled—folks talking back and forth, some of them nearly shouting at each other. There were spittoons by my feet, and big chandeliers hung from the ceiling. I looked in the mirror at the folks' faces seated down the bar and then looked at myself, and when I did, I wondered what folks saw when they looked at me. Was it just another young guy drinking by himself on a Saturday night? What did this young guy want, anyway? What was he waiting for? And what did he hope would happen? I wondered, too, if folks saw me the same way I saw myself—but half the time I never knew what that was. And how would I know if they did? It depended on the day—depended on my mood and how things were going. It depended on all kinds of things—there was nothing set about me. Everything was in motion—everything always changing. Too much thinking, Bert Miller!

The bourbon was already making its way through my body and up to my head. Goddamn, I knew too much of it could kill you, but I liked this feeling better than most and wished I could stay right at this moment when the alcohol kicks in and numbs but doesn't deaden, doesn't lay you out on the floor—not yet, at least. It closed off some of my senses, but opened up others. What the hell am I talking about, you wonder? My hearing, for example, would sharpen but my eyes didn't see. Or I'd take in smells and not be hearing anything. And as long I didn't drink too much—which sometimes happened—my eyes stayed good and focused. I could read all the fine print, too, until it ran together into dark lines. I didn't like getting falling-down drunk, either. I'd liked keeping some of my wits about me. And I liked being in control, too, and knowing when to stop.

I could have stayed at the Occidental and kept drinking but I felt restless and eager to see more of what the big town could offer. I paid my tab and thanked Bruno and left the bar. Little Ike nickered when he saw me. The sights and sounds around him were as new to him as they were to me, and they made Little Ike a bit jittery. I loosened his reins from the hitching post and climbed up in the saddle, took a couple of deep breaths and thought of riding back to Mark West and calling it a day. I had my drunk on and felt tired but relaxed—that would have been the smart thing to do. But sometimes I'm not a smart person. I rode over to the train depot and crossed the tracks and came upon a row of bars and restaurants and narrow hotels with wooden sidewalks in front of them. I told myself I was looking for the hatchery that John B. had mentioned, but I was really looking for something else—I was looking for a woman.

Folks shuffled in and out of the bars. These were the workers and the loafers, some dressed in coveralls, others in tatters, a couple of them passed out, their heads on the wooden sidewalk and the rest of their bodies sprawled out on the street. I dismounted and led Little Ike behind me. Further down the block, two ladies leaned against a wall in front of the Rose Bud Hotel. They both smiled at me. "Where you going, *guapo?*" one of them asked. She wore red lip stick and her eyes were outlined in black. She had brown skin—a Mexican, an Indian—maybe both. "You wanna go upstairs?" she asked. "But you leave your horse tied up." And she laughed. I did, too.

"You mean I can't bring him upstairs with me?" I said. "He'd love to watch."

"It cost extra," she said.

"How much extra?"

She looked Little Ike over and held up two fingers. "Two dollars," she said.

"Too much!" I said. "He'll have to stay down here but he hates being alone."

I thought about giving her a whirl but decided I wanted to look around further, drink in more of the big town, and so Little Ike and I kept walking down the street.

"Where you going?" one of the ladies asked.

"Down the street," I said.

"There's nothing to see down there." She walked toward me and touched my arm. "Everything you want to see right here." She pulled the top of her dress away and showed me the cleavage in her breasts. I smiled back at her.

Little Ike and I walked another block until we came to another bar, The Golden Bobbin. It was long and narrow, just wide enough to fit a table and chairs and the bar itself. Sawdust was sprinkled across the floor and everything about it was bare—no big mirror like the Occidental's but a smaller one, streaked and yellowing, and no fancy chandeliers or grand assortment of liquors, either. The place was spare—stripped down to just the essentials. The bartender, a big, barrel-chested man, stood behind the bar polishing glasses with a towel. Two men sat at the end of the bar closest to the street, while at the other end sat a young woman by herself. I walked in and took a stool a couple of places down from the woman and ordered my usual. The barkeep set a glass in front of me and poured the bourbon and then followed it with a glass of beer. I raised the glass of bourbon, looked over at the woman, and said, "Cheers!" She forced a smile. Her glass was nearly empty.

"Can I buy you a drink?" I asked her.

She thought about it for awhile and finally said, "Sure, why not?" She turned toward me. "But don't get too friendly, okay? My boyfriend's coming any time and he doesn't like me talking to other men."

"I'll be careful," I said.

I motioned the bartender over. "Could you pour that young lady there another drink?"

He nodded his head, turned and poured a splash of gin into a glass and followed it with a big blast of tonic water. He set the drink in front of her. I looked over at the woman, raised my glass and she raised hers and I said, "Cheers!" We both drank.

I leaned toward her. "Can I ask what your name is?"

"Della Bellamonte—Della, for short."

"I'm Bert— Bert Miller." She nodded her head. "What do you do, Della, for a living?"

"I work at the woolen mill. I'm a seamstress," she said. "I was there when it shut down and they hired me back when it reopened. I sew flannel shirts—at least, I used to."

"And your boyfriend?" I asked. "What does he do?"

"He's the shift boss." She brought the glass to her mouth and sipped slowly. "You ask a lot of questions," she said.

"I'm sorry if they bother you. If I see somebody near me, my inkling is to talk to them—I don't mean any harm."

"Like I said, if he comes in here, you make like we don't know each other, okay?" She kept looking past me toward the street—her eyes never settling—nervous the whole time. I felt bad I'd even started talking to her.

"Well, we don't know each other," I said. "So we wouldn't be lying."

"I mean, like we haven't talked or anything, okay?"

"Sure," I said. Della's hair was black as coal and braided into two long tails with bangs cut straight across her forehead. Just below her bangs was a pair of thick, dark eyebrows. Her eyes were as dark as her hair and her hands were the hands of a working woman—not dainty hands by any stretch—not like Esther Ross' hands.

"It's none of my business but you act like you're afraid of this guy," I said.

"He's got a temper."

"And he's your boss?"

"That's right."

"And your boyfriend?"

"Well, I think he'd like to be—but not sure I want to go there." She drank again. "He's been friendly to me and I don't want to upset him—it'd mean my job." She looked past me again. "He said he'd meet me here but he's late and I don't much care for that."

"You have family?" I asked her.

"No, not here—they're in the city," she said. "I wanted to live in the country and so I came up here. I rent a little apartment

a couple of blocks away, but to tell you the truth, it doesn't seem
much different here than the city. I work inside all day and these
mills are all the same." She turned toward me. "And you, Bert
Miller? What do you do?"

"I'm a teamster, mostly," and I told her about staying with my
brother north of town, and building the brooder house and layer
house and cutting firewood—that I'd been living in Sonoma and
hiring out as a teamster, and wanted a little change and ended up at
Mark West working with my brother. I didn't tell her much else—
no need to. I didn't tell her that part of the reason for staying at
Mark West was to shake off a woman—she didn't have to hear that.

"You're not married?" she asked

"No, I'm not," I said.

` She laughed. "Every man I meet isn't married—until I find
out they are."

"Well, I'm really not married," I said. "And that's the truth."
I would have married Carlotta if she'd asked me—at least, that's
what I told myself—but she didn't ask me, and here I was talking
to a pretty girl in a bar west of the tracks who was waiting for some
guy she seemed afraid of.

"Why's that?" she asked. "You're a good-looking guy. You got a
trade. I'd think women'd be following you everywhere."

"They don't."

"Maybe you just haven't noticed." She finished her drink.

"You want another?"

"No, I think I've waited here long enough—time for me to go."

"Where are you off to?"

"Home—back to my apartment," she said.

"Can I walk you there?" I asked. "Me and Ike?"

"Who's Ike?"

"My horse—he's tied up outside." I pointed out the door. "He
was born the same day we buried my father."

"Then he must be special?"

"Yeah, it is."

"How did your father die?" she asked.

"He was shot four times," I said. "But it might have been his temper that really killed him—he had a bad one—and he was hard-headed."

Della stood up, straightened her long skirt, and slipped a pair of gloves onto her hands. "You have an honest face—so, sure, you can walk me back to my place." She looked into my eyes. "But that's all, understand? Don't go thinking it's something else."

"Sure—that's all."

"I hate being stood up," she said, "but he'll have some excuse when I see him on Monday." She forced a smile and then wrapped her shawl more tightly around her shoulders. I paid the tab and the two of us left The Golden Bobbin together. We walked over to Little Ike and she pat his neck. "If I lived in the country—the real country—I'd have a dozen horses," she said. "And chickens and sheep and a big garden."

I untied Ike and we walked west past another block of shops and dimly lit bars until we were in a neighborhood of row houses with big, bare trees overhead lining each street. Another block further west was more row houses facing a park. The night was cold and clear, and as we walked, she tucked her arm inside mine. It surprised me. At the park we stopped. I looked at her in the moonlight. "I don't know anything about this guy—"

"His name is Russell—"

"I don't know anything about Russell, but in the little time I've been around you, you don't deserve being stood up," I said. "I don't think anyone does."

"Thanks—that's a nice thing to say."

"I'm serious—you don't." I looked at her. "What's his hold on you?"

"He's my boss—I told you that already—"

"Yeah, you did, but you have a life outside of your work, don't you? And choices."

"He's given me promotions at the mill—promotions I haven't asked for," she said. "And it's made for hard feelings with the other ladies I work with."

"He's playing favorites?"

"Yeah, that's what he's doing—workers I used to be friends with now won't even talk to me—I hate it."

"And yet, there you were waiting for him at the bar," I said.

"I know—stupid, isn't it? The kind of crap we put ourselves through?" She laid her head on my shoulder and tightened her embrace. "Truth is, Bert, I'm afraid of him. You know what you said about your dad's temper? Well, he's got one, too. I've seen it, and other women at the mill have warned me about him, and now I wish I'd just turned down the promotions and not feel like I owe him something."

"You don't owe him anything," I said.

"At first, I thought they were just jealous of me."

She looked so sad that my first impulse was to embrace and comfort her, so I moved closer and put my arms around her—I think anyone with a half a heart would have done the same. It just seemed a natural thing to do. She relaxed into my embrace and for several seconds neither of us moved. We just stood there holding each other and it felt good—like we were keeping each other from falling over. Then we separated slightly, our faces close to each other.

"There's other jobs, other places to work, aren't there?" I asked her.

"There are."

"So, what keeps you from leaving?"

"He's persuasive—a sweet talker," she said. "He seems to know when I've reached my limit and then he changes up, softens his language—throws out another little treat to me like I'm his pet dog."

"And you fall for it?"

"I do—every time I talk about leaving, he talks me out of it." She looked at me. "I'm such a fool." Her face moved closer to mine. "It feels good being able to tell someone this—otherwise it just stays inside me—always building up until I feel I could explode."

"Well, I usually don't offer a lot of advice but I'd tell you to dump this guy and dump this job, and find another place to work." Here I was giving advice—me, of all people—the one guy who could have used advice the most. "And I wouldn't tell him when you do, either," I said. "Just give your notice and walk out the door."

"I don't know why I don't," she said. "I think part of it is I don't trust myself—that I'm weak."

"You came up here all alone, didn't you? And you found a job and you're supporting yourself, right?"

She nodded her head.

"That says something about you."

"You're sweet, Bert. Very sweet." Again she moved her face in front of mine, but this time kissed me softly on the lips. Our mouths stayed together until they moved apart gentle-like. "I'm getting cold," she whispered. "Let's go to my place—it's just across the street."

"What about Ike?" I asked.

"There's a carriage house behind my place—just down the alley," she said. "There's usually an empty stall or two there."

Ike and I followed her as we crossed the street from the park and walked down an alley that separated one row house from another. She opened the door of the carriage house, and at first it was pitch black inside, but then my eyes adjusted, and with the little bit of moonlight that leaked in, I could make out the horse stalls. I led Ike into the empty one and took his saddle off, found a pile of hay and tossed in two big forkfuls. Ike took to the hay right off. I patted him on the rump and closed the stall door. "You be good," I said to him. Della and I walked back up the alley, and at her apartment door she took a key out of her coat pocket and unlocked the door. Just inside, she struck a match and lit a gas lamp. A little puff of black smoke tumbled from the lamp's glass before the inside of the room was illuminated. It was a small with a bed in one corner and a chest of drawers, and facing the bed was a tiny counter with a sink and cupboard. Against another wall, standing by itself, stood a wood-burning stove and next to the stove a pile of firewood.

"You want me to make a fire?" I asked.

"No," she said. "Let's just get under the covers."

The suddenness of all this caught me by surprise. Della removed her skirt and unbuttoned her blouse, but kept her long underwear on. I slipped out of my pants and shirt and kept my underwear on, too. She pulled the blankets back and I crawled across the bed. Its sheets were icy. She followed me into bed and pulled the blankets across both of us. "Brrrr, it's cold," she giggled. Our bodies were next to each other.

`"You feel good," I said. "A little cold, but very good."

"You'll have to warm me up," and she giggled again.

We held each other like we were clinging to buoys in a rough sea, neither of us talking, afraid that one word and the woman I was holding would vanish—that everything that had led to this moment would disappear. I slipped my hand inside her top shirt and stroked her bare back. Her skin felt smooth as the satin on a wedding dress. "My hands aren't too cold, are they?" I whispered.

"No, they're fine," she said. "You could rub a little harder, if you'd like."

We kissed and held each other and when I opened my eyes hers were open, too, and we both smiled. Lamplight tumbled across the ceiling. "You don't think I'm cheap do you?" she asked. "I mean, this is so sudden."

"I think it's what both of us were looking for," I said. "Some comfort, some warmth—someone to talk to—like we were both reading each other's minds—waiting to meet each other."

"Isn't it odd that of all the places you walked into tonight, that you picked the place I was in?" she asked. "There must be something to that."

"Yeah, it is pretty strange," I whispered.

"I was lonely living in the city," she said. "And it's followed me up here. I can't seem to shake it." She began sobbing. "I'm afraid I'm one of those people that always feels alone, and I don't want to be—I really don't."

"Of course you don't," I said. "Who wants to feel alone all the time?" And yet, when I said this, I remembered that being alone often felt the safest for me—no one to please but myself—no one else to worry about. No one to wonder if I'd hurt their feelings by something I said, something I'd done. And yet, in the end, I didn't want to be alone either—I had to admit it. I wondered where the trade-off was—if that place even existed.

"You understand, don't you?" she said and ran her fingers through my hair.

"Maybe better than most," I said.

She got up on her elbows and slipped her top shirt off and then slid down beside me again. I rubbed her bare shoulders and then my hands found her breasts. I gently massaged them, cupped my hands around them. They were warm and firm, the size of small melons. Her breathing grew louder. "You're okay with this?" I asked.

"I am."

We kissed and rubbed and touched each other all over. When her hand came down to my groin and touched it, I was afraid I'd shoot right there. I moved her hand away and caught my breath. "Not yet," I said, and placed my hand inside her thighs and gently worked my fingers into her quim.

Her breathing grew heavy and rapid now, her whole body trembling as she lifted herself on top of me and in a series of gentle movements I was inside her.

How do you describe this feeling? You can't. There are no words for it—and what all of it leads up to before those few seconds of coming? Of releasing? It's why men toil the way they do or go to war or wander down some forbidden alley. It's why they open themselves in ways they never thought possible, or lie, or do things they never thought of doing. And women? Were they any different? I didn't know. I couldn't crawl inside their minds, but right then it didn't matter what I knew.

She raised her upper body as if she was straddling a log and then lowered herself again, moving forward so that her breasts were just above my mouth. I kissed them and suckled like a new-born. We found our rhythm—up and down in gentle strokes, both of us sighing and breathing deep, and any second I could explode but then backed off, waiting on the feeling, then rising again almost to a climax before backing off again. "Go ahead," she said. "Go ahead. I'm ready!" And this time I released. "Ahhh!" we breathed out together.

"Oh, my God!" I whispered. "I'd nearly forgot what this was like."

She stayed on top of me, both of us breathing hard, before she rolled off and lie down right beside me. I kissed the top of her head.

"That was—"

"Wonderful?" she asked.

"Every bit of wonderful," I said.

We lay there together for the longest time. I can't tell you the thoughts that crossed my mind and how I wanted them to just go away and be in this moment—but they were all rattling at the door. Then it went quiet and the thoughts trailed off, and before I knew it, there was no movement from either of us. I felt the gentle rise and fall of her breathing and how it deepened. "Della?" I whispered, but she was already asleep.

Sometime around dawn when early light slanted through the top of the window curtain, I woke. I turned toward Della and she was still fast asleep. I studied her face and noticed the tiny freckles almost like pin points scattered across her nose and cheeks. I kissed her on the mouth and she smiled without opening her eyes. I stared at the ceiling and recounted the night before, the wandering about town that led me to The Golden Bobbin and offering to buy Della a drink and her warning me about a jealous boss of hers and all the other events that led to this very moment, events just hours ago I could never have imagined. I got up, slipped my pants and shirt back on and went outside to the privy. While outside I checked on Little Ike. He nickered when he saw me. I tossed him another forkful of hay. When I returned to Della's room, she was awake. "I was afraid you left," she said.

"No, I wouldn't do that" I said. I opened the door to the wood stove and wadded up a newspaper and placed sticks of kindling across the paper and lit it. When the fire was strong enough, I added bigger pieces and then closed the stove door. "I'll boil some water for coffee, okay?"

"Sure," she said, "but Bert I don't think you should stay much longer. I'm afraid that—"

"Russell might show up?"

"Yes—he knows where I live and I don't want you caught up in something that doesn't concern you."

I walked over to her bed and sat down beside her. I stroked her cheek. "Della, you don't have to live like this—afraid of what some man might do to you. It's not right," I told her. "You're a good person—lovely to look at and I hate seeing you so fearful."

"It's my own fault for letting it get this way," she said. "I should have known that every favor comes with a price."

"Then leave—go someplace else—"

"I could do that."

"Yes, you can—but Della—"

"Yes?"

"I want to see you again."

"I want to see you, too," she said. There was a silence between us as we looked into each other's eyes. "I'll deal with Russell—I promise."

"I hope you do—for your own sake," I said. "I hate to see you this way. You're young and beautiful and don't need to be looking over your shoulder all the time."

"You're sweet, Bert, to say those things."

I put her coffee pot on the stove and within minutes the water began percolating. I took two cups from the cupboard, and when the coffee was made, I filled each cup. She was sitting up in bed now, and I handed her the cup. "Thank you," she said and she sipped her coffee.

"It was a good night last night," I said. "A really good night—everything about it."

"Yes it was."

"Can I come back again?" I asked her.

"Of course you can. Maybe next weekend—when I'm not working?"

"I'll be here—I promise," I said.

We finished our coffee and kissed and held each other. "You should go now," she said.

I got up and walked away, holding her hand until it was out of reach.

"Say hello to Ike for me."

"I will."

When I reached the door, I turned and went back to her and we kissed again, a long parting kiss. I walked to the carriage house and saddled up Ike and rode north, my head clouded over with thoughts of Della. I didn't remember anything about the ride, didn't remember anything I saw along the way—it was like being in a trance—the eyes seeing, the nose smelling, the ears hearing—but not noticing any of it—none of it connecting—only thoughts of her and the picture of her face, her smile in the lamplight—all of those things running across my mind.

56

Back at John B.'s
• • • • • • • • • • • • • • •

Like I said, I don't remember much about the eight mile ride back to John B.'s—if I was even sitting in the saddle or floating a dozen feet above it. I was in a daze, thinking about Della and all that had happened the night before. At times I wondered if I was dreaming, making it all up, but I only had to press my chin down inside my jacket and smell her lilac fragrance on my body. I was smitten by her—no question about it, and already I was thinking of the coming weekend and how long a wait that would be. Could I stand it? What if I couldn't wait? But I remembered she was a working girl, putting in her long hours at the woolen factory—and she did say "next weekend."

When I rode into John B.'s yard, he was up in one of the lean-to's, tossing hay to his herd of sheep. He looked up at me. "You're alive!" and he laughed.

"I am alive," I said. "Alive as I've been in months."

"Oh, boy! What was her name?" he asked. "Or, did she even tell you?"

"John B., give me some credit, won't you?" I dismounted from Ike. "If you really want to know, her name is Della Bellamonte."

"Della," he repeated. "And how did the two of you meet?"

I told him about going to the Occidental Hotel first and warming up with a couple shots of bourbon, but the big-wig clientele wasn't to my liking and so Ike and I wandered around the town and finally crossed the tracks. "I remember you telling me to avoid going there after dark, and that was all the temptation I needed," I said.

John B. laughed. "Me and my big mouth."

"No, it's okay or I would have never met her."

"You're sounding awful serious already," John B. said.

"I like her and I think she likes me." I thought was a safe enough thing to say. "There's a couple of things that need working out first."

"Working out?"

"Yeah, she's got a boss hound-doggin' her," I said. "Giving her promotions where she works when she's not asking for them, and causing problems with her fellow workers—and all that comes with a condition—"

"You don't have to tell me what that condition is," John B. said. "But she's going along with it, isn't she?"

"She is—but she's trying to shake him, though."

John B. looked at me. "Be careful, Bert, you don't get caught in a crossfire with her."

"I know."

"You don't know anything about her, right?"

"Just what she told me," I said. "She left the city to work in the country."

"Why'd she leave the city?"

"I didn't ask—and she didn't tell me."

"But that could all be just a line of shit, couldn't it?" John B. always took the hard line when it came to my matters of the heart.

"It could, but I think she was on the straight with me."

"And what makes you think that?"

"I don't know, John B.—just a feeling I had about her that everything she said was on the level—you know you can usually tell when someone's being straight with you or not."

"I ain't telling you how to run your life, Bert, but think about this," he said. "You met her in a bar—not sitting next to you in church—and she was there waiting for another man, right? And I'll tell you something else, Bert—I've met some good liars in my lifetime."

I nodded my head. "Yeah, I have too."

"A man who's her boss that she wants to shake but can't—and then he stands her up, right? It doesn't seem the two add up."

"Yeah, that's what happened all right." I had to admit it.

"I don't know, Bert."

"I don't either, but I'm going to find out one way or the other," I said.

"Be careful—that's all I can say. I don't want to see you run up a pole over some factory girl." John B. finished feeding his sheep and stuck the pitchfork into a mound of loose hay. "You mind if I tell Gertie about this?" he asked. "It's the kind of thing she loves to hear about."

"Sure, tell her," I said. "I'd be interested in what she has to say."

"I've got a few more bare-roots to put in the ground if you want to give me a hand."

"Sure," I said. "Let me get this saddle off of Little Ike and feed him."

"How about some coffee and eggs after?"

"Sounds good." I said, and it did. I hadn't eaten since yesterday. "I'll meet you down at the house when I'm done."

John B. was already seated at the kitchen table with a mug of coffee in front of him. Gertie poured me a cup. "Sounds like you had yourself a little adventure in Santa Rosa last night," Gertie smiled.

"Damn, John B., you don't waste any time do you?"

"Bert, we live dull lives up here, don't we, Gertie?"

She smiled again. "Just work, eat and sleep—that's all."

"So we rely on folks like you to tell us what life is like in the big town," he said. "To tell us all about the things we're missing—the life we can only dream about. You're like a messenger to us."

"You're doing fine here," I said. "You ain't missing anything— I'd trade places with you in a second."

"What's this woman's name?" Gertie asked.

"Della," I said.

"Why don't you bring up here sometime?" Gertie asked. "Give her a taste of the country life."

"I just might—she told me she liked the country—the real country outside of the factory—and, if she could, she'd have a dozen horses and chickens."

"Does she know how much work they are?" Gertie broke several eggs into a bowl and beat them with a fork.

"Gertie, to be honest, I don't know what she knows," I said.

"There's plenty of time to find out, isn't there?" Gertie poured the eggs into a skillet.

"I hope so," I said.

We ate a breakfast of scrambled eggs, toast and coffee and just before heading up to the orchard to finish planting the bare-roots, Gertie touched my arm. "I want something good to turn out for you, Bert—I really do. I know you've been looking for a long time—maybe this is the one."

"I don't know," I said, which seemed the answer to most of my questions.

I joined John B. up at the orchard. The remaining bare roots were tied together with a length of twine. "I'll need to put a fence around these trees—something—or the deer'll eat them right down to the ground like they done before." He loosened the twine holding the bare roots together.

"Maybe put a wire cage around each bare root while they're still small," I said, "but I agree, eventually you're going to need a fence, a tall one because those deer can jump."

"I was thinking of a picket-style one," John B. said. " Set posts or maybe just string two lengths of wire together between trees, top and bottom, then twist the wire so a long picket fits in the opening the twisted wire leaves." He looked at me. "What'd you think?"

"Yeah, let's try it," I said.

"I'll buy the pickets at Murphy's—the wire I can get in town."

We dug holes all morning, stopping for lunch and continued working after lunch until most of the bare roots were in the ground. Throughout the day I kept thinking of Della—thoughts of her poured into my head, seeming to find every vacant space in my mind and filling it—and I wondered what it would be like when we saw each other again. Would she still be as warm? Would she even remember me? What if I was just another man she'd taken home in a whole string of men? What if she'd just made up that entire

Russell thing? As good and positive as I felt about her, sometimes a stubborn doubt would creep in—that all of it was too good to be true—that it didn't happen as easy as this with me and there were always complications, mountains to climb and things I couldn't see. So I warned myself about getting my hopes up. Yes, there was now a new woman on my mind, someone to replace Carlotta and Cameron and even Christina the few times I thought of her, but would Della be any different? Was I just repeating it all over again? Setting myself up for another big downfall?

John B. and I surveyed our work. It was fine-looking young orchard. "A couple of years and these trees'll be producing," I said.

"If the deer don't get them first," he said.

By late afternoon, we finished working with the bare roots. John B. brought his three cows together to milk while I fed the rest of his cattle. After the feeding, I went over to check on Little Ike and gave him a scoop of oats and filled his manger with loose hay. By now it was dark, and I was dog-tired. We ate dinner together and no one mentioned Della. Little Friedolin was already asleep. I thanked Gertie for dinner and turned in early. As I undressed, again I smelled Della's lilac fragrance on my skin and in my underclothes. No, it wasn't a dream—I didn't imagine it. It had all really happened.

57
Back to Town
. . . .

Somehow, someway, the following Saturday arrived—it had taken its sweet time. Each day seemed twice as long, the sun never moving in the sky, and the nights even longer. All the clocks slowed, sometimes their hands moving backwards. But Saturday finally did arrive and I put a morning's work in with John B. cutting firewood just to burn off some nerves. He'd look over at me, shake his head and laugh. "You got it bad, Bert," he said.

"It's that obvious, huh?"

"Like it's written all over you."

"I can't help it, John B."

"It's okay, Bert—you could come down with worse things," he said. "Gertie and I been noticing you all week—laughing to ourselves. She says you're like a whore in church."

I laughed. "Yeah, I'm in a state, all right."

"It's okay, though."

"Were you like this when you first met Gertie?" I wondered.

"Yeah—different circumstances, of course," he said, "but, yeah, I could feel something inside me shifting—something wanting to take control."

"I'm gun-shy, though, about all of this romance, John B.," I said. "And a bit of a doubter about much of it."

"Why's that?"

"Because it kicks my ass almost every time—it does."

"But that's the past," he said. "Maybe it'll be different this time."

"Yeah, maybe—I hope so," I said. "I'm tired of coming out on the short end of the stick, and I don't know if it'll be any different now."

"I can't tell you either way. It might just be the same old story, but you never know," he said. "You take your chances—love's a roulette wheel, Bert. You can't win if you don't play."

We filled most of the wagon with firewood by noon and drove back to the farmyard. I took the harness off of Molly and Dolly and went inside the house, heated a kettle of water and washed up. I changed into clean underwear and stockings, slipped into a clean shirt and pants, and studied myself in the mirror. "I can't do any better than this," I said to myself. "Take it or leave it."

"Can we expect you for dinner?" Gertie asked, a glint in her eye. "Or should we plan for a guest, as well?"

I smiled. "Gertie, it's all a crapshoot—John B. called it a roulette wheel—take your pick."

"Can't win if you don't play," John B. repeated.

Gertie served lunch, but I was so knotted-up inside I could barely eat. She looked at me in disbelief. "Bert Miller not eating—now that's one for the books," she said. I pushed myself away from the table and thanked Gertie and John B. and headed out to saddle up Little Ike.

John B. stood on his front porch when I rode by. "Be careful. It's still west of the tracks—outlaw territory, outlaw women—all bound to get you!"

"Yeah, outlaw women—just what I need," I laughed and pointed Ike out to Mark West and we rode down to where it met Healdsburg Road, good and churned up from the recent rains. It was another cool, late February day with big clouds hanging in the sky, but traces of blue overhead, too, toward the west. Santa Rosa was south nearly seven miles from here, plenty of time to wonder what the rest of the day would bring—maybe too much time. I'd packed along a small flask of bourbon as a bracer, just in case.

Traffic on the Healdsburg Road was mostly wagons and carriages, plenty of folks on foot and several more like me on horseback. In places, the road was a bog and the loaded wagons' wheels sunk into it up to their axles, and I heard the drivers swearing at their horses, and one or two of them taking out their whips and lashing the horses' backs—something I just hated to see, and spoke my mind to those drivers. "Get off your horse, young feller, and come over and tell me that to my face," one burly driver said.

"Can't," I said. "I got a date with the captain's daughter." He just looked at me.

I rode straight through town, and on the other side of the courthouse I dismounted, tied Ike to the hitching post in front of the Occidental Hotel and went inside for a quick bracer—just one and its friend, I told myself—that's all I'd needed. Bruno was tending bar and this time he remembered me. I finished the bourbon and chased it with a glass of beer, paid my tab, and was out the door. I mounted Ike and we wound our way through Santa Rosa's streets, past the railroad depot and into Della's neighborhood on the west side of town. I found the park right out and across the street from the park, the house where Della rented an apartment on its basement floor. By now my heart was in my mouth, pounding hard like a bird's heart. I pulled in some deep breaths, dismounted from Ike and walked back to the rear of the house to Della's room. I knocked. No answer. I knocked again, this time a bit louder—still no answer. I looked around for a note, any kind of message she might have left me, but there was nothing.

This left me confused, wondering what to do. I walked to the front of the house, climbed its stairs and knocked. A gray-haired woman, Della's landlady I assumed, answered. "I was looking for Della," I said. "She doesn't seem to be home."

"You got a lot of nerve, mister, coming back like this," she said. A scowl covered her face.

"What are you talking about?" Her remark caught me completely off-guard.

"You know what I mean," she said. "You're lucky I didn't call the constable—that's what I shoulda done."

"What are you talking about? Calling the constable?" I was clueless.

"After what you done to that girl." She looked straight into my eyes with disgust.

"Do you mean Della?" I asked.

"Yeah, I mean her—she had one eye nearly closed and bruises on the side of her face."

"What happened? Tell me!" I grabbed her arm. "Ma'm, I swear, I don't know what you're talking about!"

"Don't you touch me—you hear!" She started to close the door and I stuck my boot between the door and the jamb.

"No—wait!" I pleaded. "You're confusing me with someone else."

"I heard the shouting and the arguing down below," she said. "You'd have to been deaf not to—"

"What happened? Goddamn it, tell me!" I looked at her—straight into her eyes. "You're confusing me with someone else."

"There was yelling and fighting—"

"Who was yelling and fighting? Who?"

"I'm trying to tell you if you'd just give me a chance!" she said. She looked at me again like she finally believed me. "The girl knocked at my door—this one right here." And she pointed at her front door. "She was crying—and like I said, one of her eyes was nearly closed—"

"When did all this happen?"

"Last weekend—on Sunday back," she said.

"And where is she now?" I was panicking. "That's the morning I left her," I said, half to myself. "Where is she now?"

"Gone," the woman said. "She gave me notice she was leaving the next day, packed her suitcase, and was gone."

"Did she say where?"

"She asked about the train schedule, that's all I know." The woman shook her head. "You men," she said. "It's terrible sometimes how you treat women."

"I need to find her," I said.

"Good luck with that—she could be anywhere."

"If, by chance, she returns—"

"I doubt if she'll do that—"

"But if she does, tell her Bert was here," I said. "And have her leave an address where I can find her—please!"

"Then you're not the one who beat her?"

"Of course, not!" I looked at the woman. "Bert's my name—Bert Miller, and my brother John B. Miller lives off Mark West Road. Can you remember that?"

"I think I can," she said. "My memory's going—I may have to go inside and write it down."

"Please! I'm worried about her," I said.

"I can see that,' she said. "I'm worried about her, too, and hope you find her."

I didn't know what to do. I walked back and untied Little Ike and stroked his nose and felt like crying—felt like someone had stuck a pin in the big balloon of hope I held for Della. I led Ike out to the street, looked west and then looked east—she could be anywhere. I thought about just heading back to John B.'s and giving up on all of it. Instead, I decided to ride over to the woolen mill and hope for any clues there. The mill was shut down when I arrived, but through the office window I saw a woman working at a desk. I knocked on the door. She came to the door and shouted through it, "We're closed."

"I need to find out something," I shouted through the door. I heard the door unlock. "I'm looking for an employee of yours," I said.

"No one's working now. Can't you come back on Monday?" she asked.

"No, it can't wait," I said. "Her name is Della Bellamonte."

"There's lots of employees here," she said.

"But can't you check your books, your time sheets?"

She looked at me and I guess he saw the desperation on my face. "I'll see." She returned to her desk and brought out a clip- board with several sheets attached to it. "These are the employees' daily logs. What was her name again?"

"Della Bellamonte."

She looked down the page and repeated her name out loud. "No record for her on Friday's log, yesterday," she said, and looked at another page. "No record for her on Thursday's, either." She turned to another page. "Nothing on Wednesday, either." She flipped to a previous next page. "Nothing on Tuesday, either—are you sure she even works here?" she asked.

"That's what she told me," I said. "She said she was a shift boss— please, keep looking."

"Nothing on Monday—oh, wait—'Terminated,' it says." She turned the sheet toward me so I could read it myself, then set the clipboard on the counter between us. "Sorry—that's all I can tell you," she said.

My heart sank even lower—if that was possible. "No word about where she went?" I asked.

"No, no word," she said. "Besides, even if I knew, that's confidential information."

I thanked her, left the office, mounted Little Ike and rode through town a lost man—I don't know how else to describe it. I went from near the mountaintop to the lowest part of the valley in a matter of minutes—in the time it took Della's landlady to tell me she was gone and didn't know where. I rode up and down each block, my eyes keened on every woman I saw, but none of them was Della. I didn't know what to do, what to think. I was feeling bad, feeling low, and feeling like this, I leaned on an old friend, pulled the flask out of my saddlebag, unscrewed its top and drained it right there on a street corner in downtown Santa Rosa.

It only made me want more. I rode north out Mendocino Road and stopped at a tavern, tied off Little Ike, and went inside, imagining I saw Della Bellamonte sitting at the far end of the bar waiting for me, wondering where I'd been. It wasn't her—it wasn't any one. I found an empty stool, sat down and ordered a straight bourbon with a beer backer, downed the bourbon in one swallow and pointed to the glass for the bartender to fill it again.

"Take 'er easy there, son," the bartender said. "We ain't gonna run out."

I nodded my head, and drank the beer.

"Troubles?" he asked

"Yeah, troubles," I said.

"Women or money?" he asked. "There's only two to choose from."

"It's a woman," I said.

"I can usually tell." He reached down, grabbed a glass and began polishing it with a towel. "Did she leave you or did you leave her?"

"Well—I guess she left me although it isn't that simple."

"It never is."

I told him my story—-shortened it for his sake—and to his credit, he listened. "The s.o.b. beat her up, huh?" And he shook his head.

"That's what her landlady told me."

"They oughta cut the bastard's balls off—that might cure him." He finished polishing the glass and put it back on a shelf behind him. "You don't think she strung you along, huh?"

"Who—the woman or the landlady?" I asked him.

"Either one, now that I think about it," he said. "Maybe even both—like they're in cahoots together."

"I hadn't thought of that."

"Folks'll do all sorts of things—you just never know," he said.

"I don't think it's that—I mean, I've been snookered before—but no, I think she was on the straight."

"You never know, though." He poured me another beer. "Anyway she can track you down?"

"I left a message with the landlady—whether Della gets it or not's another story." I looked at the bartender. "Tell you what, keep, I want to drink enough to get back to my bed tonight—and nothing less."

"And you know how much that is?" he asked.

"I got a pretty good idea—been doing this for awhile."

The bartender laughed. "One thing for certain—"

"What's that?"

"You ain't gonna find her in the bottom of your glass," he said.

"I figure one more good belt should do it," I said. "That should numb everything enough." So he poured me one last round. I drained it, got off the barstool, and it took a few seconds to find my legs, but when I did, I thanked the bartender again, and asked what his name was and he said, "Earl" and I told him I'd be back again because I liked talking with him. "Sure enough," he said.

Out on the street, Little Ike looked at me and I looked back at him, and saw two Little Ikes instead of one and wondered when I bought another horse. "Goddamn, Ike," I said, "You got a twin!" It took me a couple of tries, but I managed to climb up on the saddle and pointed Little Ike north, tied the two reins together and just let him go. He knew his way back to John B.'s already—just a sense that horse had that always amazed me.

At one point, I fell right out of the saddle—dozed off or something—and landed hard on my shoulder. The soft mud broke my fall, shook me out of my daze, and nearly forgot why I started drinking in the first place. It was minutes before I got my bearings. I was sitting square on my ass—I knew that—and it was night time, with the dark shape of the hills to my right and the night quiet and still like it is after a good rain has fallen. My coat and pants were covered in mud and Little Ike looked down at me, and I knew what he was thinking—he was thinking what my old man would be thinking—I knew it. I was awake the rest of the ride, the cool night air blowing through me head and mellowing my drunk. By the time I reached John B.'s I was near sober—close to it, anyway—unsaddled Little Ike, fed him and Molly and Dolly and zig-zagged my way back to the house.

On the front porch, I stripped out my pants and shirt and walked in as quiet as I could so as not to wake anyone. I found a towel and wiped off the mud from my hands and ran the towel across my face before climbing into bed. All the day's heartache, disappointment, climbed right in with me and I kept thinking I was a man jinxed when it came to women—that even when I met the right one—at least, the one I thought was right—someone comes along and screws it all up. It never failed—whether it was Cameron's fire-breathing God, Carlotta's cigar-smoking senator, or now some short-fused factory boss with a bad temper.

58

Hope and Reality

· · · · · · · · · · · · · · · · ·

The following morning, Gertie saw my pants and jacket out on the front porch covered with mud. When I stumbled out of bed, my mouth was dry as cotton, and as I passed her in the kitchen, she looked at me and asked. "Did Ike throw you yesterday?"

"Pardon?"

"I said—did Ike toss you?"

"Oh, now I get it—no, he didn't toss me," I admitted. "I fell off him somewhere down on the Healdsburg Road."

"You fell off him?" she repeated.

"That's right, I fell off him," I said. "Passed out in the saddle and the next thing I knew I was sitting in six inches of mud."

She looked at me. "I take it things didn't go too well for you in town?"

"No," I said. "They went about as bad as you could imagine."

"She didn't want to see you? You had a fight? I'm dying to hear!" She sat down at the table. By now John B. had come in from his morning chores, and poured himself a cup of coffee. He looked over at Gertie. "What happened to old lover-boy last night?" he asked with a big grin across his face.

"He fell off Ike—for starters," Gertie said.

"I seen your pants and jacket out on the porch and figured something happened," John B. said.

I sat down on a chair next to Gertie and related most of what happened the day before, and how I'd gone to Della's and then talked with her landlady, who thought I was the one that roughed Della up, before convincing her I wasn't the one. I told them about going to the woolen factory and finding out Della had been terminated, and how all this news made me sick to my stomach, and how I kept riding around downtown Santa Rosa, looking at every woman and hoping it would be Della.

"So you stopped somewhere and hoped that enough drinking would make it all go away? Is that what happened?" Gertie asked.

"Yeah, that's what happened all right," I said. "I finally stopped at a little bar on my way out of town. The bartender there was named Earl and I told Earl what had happened."

"It didn't make it go away, did it?" Her eyes riveted on mine.

"Gertie, please, I don't need any sermonizing right now."

"So—she's gone—end of story?" John B. asked.

"I don't know, John B.," I said. "I told her landlady about you, and if she sees Della again to pass along your address—so maybe one day she knocks on that door there. But that seems like another long shot, doesn't it?"

"Maybe—maybe not," Gertie said.

"I almost wish I hadn't met her," I said. "You get all your hopes up and then they come crashing down—it's a story I keep writing for myself—always with the same ending, too."

Gertie poured me a cup of coffee. I stared at the steam rising off the top of the cup and wondered what I'd do now. Should I head back to Sonoma and pick up the pieces there? Or should I stay here and work with John B. and maybe—maybe, Della looks me up? Stranger things could happen—a comet could fall where I was walking or lightning strike me square in the forehead.

"I don't know if you feel like going back into town so soon," John B. said, "but there's another load of firewood to be delivered and a hundred chicks to pick up at Longman's Hatchery. What'd you say?

"Sure, I'll go with you," I said. "You want to take my horses?"

"Yeah, they're easy pullers," he said.

We ate breakfast, and afterwards I harnessed Molly and Dolly and set them on each side of the wagon's tree for the final buckling-in. Gertie had packed us a lunch and we stowed the basket under the driver's seat. Molly and Dolly were anxious to go. They'd been in their corral for several days now without any work, and once out on the road and for the first mile I had to keep a tight rein on them.

"I'm snake-bit, John B.," I said.

"That's 'cause you try more than most—if you didn't try, you wouldn't be snake-bit—you wouldn't be nothing."

"I guess," I said, "but just being nothing doesn't sound half-bad now."

"No guessing about it," he said. "Imagine something different than what happened to you last week—you walk past the bar and look in and there's the girl—I forgot her name—"

"Della—"

"There's Della, and instead of going in and sitting down next to her and buying her a drink and everything that followed—you just keep walking past that bar and the two of you never meet," he said. "What's the trade-off?"

"The trade-off?"

"Yeah, what is it?"

"No disappointment?" I said.

"That's right—no disappointment—but none of that summer butter, either." He chuckled a bit to himself. "So, you get what I mean?"

He held out both hands. "In this one, no disappointment—no taking any chances—probably the way most people live their lives. And in this hand?" He held up the other. "Disappointment, or at least, a good shot at it because you don't know the outcome, do you? And you never will until you try."

"No, I don't—never do," I said. "I go in with high hopes—I guess because I'm just stupid—"

"No, you're not stupid—you're just more of a dreamer than most—the guy that aims for the long-shot," he said.

"I guess I got something fixed in my mind how love and relationships should be—some ideal picture—"

"And, so far, it hasn't turned out that way, has it?" he asked.

"Sure hasn't." I looked at John B. "What am I doing wrong?"

"I can't answer that, Bert. You're one of those folks that's gotta try out all kinds of different things—take chances—"

"And fall flat on his face—"

"Maybe—until you don't."

"You think that'll ever happen—a time when I don't?"

"I can't answer that—don't have any crystal ball I can look into," John B. said.

We made good time into Santa Rosa. The horses kicked up their share of mud and by the time we reached the alleyway behind the Grand Hotel and stepped down from the wagon, its whole undercarriage was covered with six inches of road muck. The horses had mud stockings up to their knees. John B. knocked at the back door and a Chinaman answered dressed in a linen kitchen coat and linen pants. "Firewood," John B. said and the Chinaman nodded.

"Same as with the Occidental," John B. pointed toward a lean-to shelter built against the back of the hotel. I backed the wagon as close to the lean-to as I could, and started unloading the firewood, stacking it neatly like it was a crossword puzzle, making every piece fit. John B. returned from inside and we finished unloading. "The manager invited us in for a drink," John B. said. "What do you think?"

"I think it's just what I need," I said. "A little hair from the dog that bit me last night."

John B. laughed.

I tied the horses off, re-set the wagon brake, and we walked through the hotel kitchen and out into the bar area. It was another barroom like the Occidental's with high ceilings and ornate lamps, leather-covered chairs around oak tables, with dark polished wood everywhere, a long mirror and in front of the mirror and on each of its sides, rows and rows of liquor bottles.

I ordered my usual—a good bourbon and a beer it could talk to. John B. just ordered a draft. "Here's to finding love," he said, and we both raised our glasses. The bourbon went down as it usually did—warm, bracing—like it'd found the home it'd been looking for—and leaving me with what I always felt as an after-glow.

"One more?" the bartender asked.

"Not for me," John B. said.

The barkeep looked at me. I pointed to the shot glass. He filled it, and I raised it like I'd seen the priests years ago raise their golden chalices, and drank—no bells though, this time, no striking the chest. We left the bar and walked through the kitchen and out the rear door to where the wagon and horses waited. "Now to the hatchery," John B. said.

We crossed the tracks near the railroad depot, and a block west on Seventh Street stood the hatchery, a brick building with the words Longman's Hatchery painted in black across the bricks. I pulled into the loading area while John B. stepped down off the wagon and went inside to the office. Waiting there at the hatchery loading dock, I remembered driving to Petaluma with Carlotta a couple of years back—maybe longer now with the years and months all running together—and picking up her first batch of chicks and how excited she was when I lifted the top off the box and she looked in. She giggled like a little girl and it thrilled me as much as it thrilled her. That was two years ago and counting, and now it seemed that little about myself had changed—that I kept walking around the same block and never crossing the street. Here I was again longing for lost love and nothing to show for it but a head full of memories I was trying to drown out every chance I could—memories that seemed at times like a curse, like something I couldn't shake—that followed me around wherever I went—hounding me always about how things could have been, but never were.

John B. came out from the office and walked up to my wagon. "You all right?" he asked.

"Yeah, I'm okay."

"Just checking," he said. "You looked a little distant—just wanted to make sure."

"Distant? Hell, I'm always that—but I'm okay."

"They're bringing the chicks out shortly," he said.

We loaded the boxes of chicks into the back of the wagon and made one more stop at Santa Rosa Feed and Milling for chick mash before setting off for Mark West. It was early afternoon, and John said he was hungry and reached around and brought out the lunch basket. He handed me an egg salad sandwich. "We'll be eating even more of these in a few months," he laughed, and motioned back to the boxes of chicks.

"You've got lots of critters up there that'll want to snatch those birds," I said. "Coons. Foxes. Bobcats."

"Sometimes even a mountain lion'll wander down," he said. "Rare, but I've seen the ass-end of them as they ran away."

"Lots of wire fence," I said. "Maybe even run it across the top of the pens."

We finished our sandwiches and John B. handed me an apple. Neither of us talked for a stretch. The two horses had settled into their usual rhythms and I could feel them wanting to pick the pace up, sensing they were heading back to the barn.

"Let me ask you something, Bert." John B. said.

"Sure, ask me anything—I might just tell you the truth." We both laughed.

"Say Della was at her room when you went back to see her," he said, "and there wasn't any problem with her boss, and the two of you just hit it off fine—and every time after that it was all good between the two of you—then what happens?"

"I'd see how it went," I said.

"But say all of it's good. What's the next step?" he asked. "Would you marry her?"

"If it was all good, and she turned out to be the woman I hoped she was, well—yeah, I'd marry her."

"You're not against it?"

"No, I'm not—don't think I've ever been entirely against it." I looked over at John B. "Why you ask?"

"Gertie thinks it's a game you play with women—she doesn't exactly say that—"

"A game? I don't think I play any games, John B.," I said. "Yeah, I used to—I admit it— but I've gotten more serious now—you might even say I've grown up." I pulled the reins back to keep Molly and Dolly in check. They were feeling their oats. From the back of the wagon, I heard the little chicks cheep-cheeping through the holes in their boxes. The more I thought about what Gertie had said, the more I was forced to agree with her. "But, yeah, when I think about it, there's some women I played games with—women I weren't serious about. But there was women who turned around and done the same to me. I think we both understood the rules."

"Women have that extra sense about them," he said. "They know when you're not on the straight."

"But the ones I was serious about?" I said. "If I meet a woman and if there's something mutual between us, I go where it leads me—the past couple of women, though—they led me straight off a cliff." I looked over at John B. "Does that sound like I'm playing a game?"

"No, it doesn't," he said.

"But I gotta say, though, that marriage is a bit of a crapshoot, isn't it?" I said. "You marry the wrong woman and life can be hell. I know—I seen enough folks suffering through bad ones."

"Yeah, it's a crapshoot all right—but your odds increase if you work at it don't they?" he asked. "Nothing comes natural in marriage—it might seem that way at first—all that excitement running through you on honeymoon night, but it doesn't stay that way. It's all give-and-take—the more you take, the more you gotta give."

"I gotta say that I mostly think about myself, John B. I learned that early on—right after Dad and Ma left us behind back home and came to the states," I told him. "I looked around and couldn't find anyone to lean on, so I reckoned I'd lean on myself—it was all on me." I thought about what I'd just said. "Does that make me selfish?"

"I don't think so," he said. "It makes you a survivor."

We'd passed the town limits by now and were in open country north of Santa Rosa—flat fields that ran all the way up to Healdsburg—prune and walnut orchards, hopyards with hops growing along strings, and straight rows of grapevines mixed in with stands of big oaks, wild oats sprouting up everywhere, and here and there a solitary farmhouse with a barn behind it and a tank house. A little breeze lifted the horses' tails.

"You ever imagine what being married is like?" John B. asked.

"All different kinds of scenes play out in my mind," I said. "My biggest fear is that it'll put a collar around my neck with a short rein and I'd be fighting against it all the time."'

"It's not just you anymore—you can't just do anything you want," John B. said.

"That's my problem, John B. I want it all—the freedom to go and do whatever I want and not have to explain why I did it or why I didn't and still have a woman at home that loves me—that'll forgive me for whatever I did or didn't do."

"I don't know—there might be a woman around like that," John B. said, "but you're gonna have to look real hard. Sure, they'll give you some rein at first, but then they'll start tight pulling it back in—I guess, in a way, you can't blame them."

"Marriage," I said to myself. "There's no law that says you gotta be married, is there?"

"No, there isn't. But most of us want something like a home and kids and not have to be scratching around all the time on our own—that gets damn old," he said. "Maybe you haven't grown into it yet, Bert, that's all. Maybe you will—maybe you won't."

We reached Mark West Road and started heading up the hill toward John B.'s. Our conversation gave me all sorts of things to think about. There was Della, of course, and I thought how little I really knew about her—that I could have been any number of guys that wandered into The Golden Bobbin that night and started gnawing on her ear, but it just happened to be me—like I'd drawn the lucky number—or, was it the unlucky number? And marriage? John B. gave my plenty to think about there, as well. He'd torn up the ideal picture I'd held about it—made me think about the work it took and the compromise and thinking about someone else instead of me all the time and whether I was really ready for it or not. And, I'll tell you straight out—I wasn't sure about any of it.

What I'd also realized was how much I'd learned from John B., what a good teacher and good example he'd been to me—ever

since we were little ones. He had the patience our old man lacked—
didn't fly off the handle when you did something that crossed him—
didn't judge you right-off, either. He let you do whatever you did,
make the mistakes you always made, and then ask you why you
done it. What did you learn that you didn't learn the first time?
The more I thought about it, the more I realized I was trying to
model my life after John B.'s. Foolish, I know, but he was the kind
of person I wanted to be like. I know in the past I envied him, even
resented him at times. I hated myself for not mastering carpentry
the way he' done or how he and Gertie had met and married with
no string of heart-aches following them around—but that wasn't
true, either. They'd lost two children at birth—and had weathered
the loss. My heartaches were different from theirs.

I pulled the team into John B.'s and drove them up to the brooder house where we carried the boxes inside. We'd added a small
feed room to the brooder house and lined it with extra redwood to
keep the mice and rats out—you never could keep all them entirely
out, though. They gnawed and gnawed until they found a way in.
John B. carried the sacks to the feed room, opened one and filled a
bucket with mash, then once back inside the brooder house, filled
the troughs with mash. We opened the tops of the boxes and tilted
them until the little chicks spilled out onto the floor. They stayed
together in a tight cluster before one or two broke from the rest,
found the trough and started eating. By now Gertie and little Friedolin had joined us. "They're precious!" she said. She set Friedolin
down and he grabbed for one of the chicks and it scurried away.

John B. looked at me and smiled. "From now on, Bert, we're
calling you the Egg Man."

"Fine," I said. "Call me anything but late-for-breakfast."

Gertie laughed a good one after that.

59

Gathering No Moss
• • • • • • • • • • • • • • • • • •

I stayed on with John B. and Gertie for the rest of that spring and by late June was feeling the urge to move on. The chicks grew into pullets and within a few weeks, maybe two months, they'd start laying eggs—just a couple at first, but then with enough sunlight and enough age in their bones, their nests would start to fill— enough eggs that John B. could haul buckets of them into town along with his firewood, and earn a few extra dollars to keep operations afloat out at Mark West. John B. had more projects in mind, too: he wanted to start a water company for the neighbors around them and he'd read about a steam-powered plant that could produce electricity, and was sending off for any information he could find. That was my brother—never short on ideas.

And me? I was feeling my usual restlessness, eager to move on but not knowing exactly where. I was thinking less and less about Della and writing it all off to experience—those once-in-a-thousand occurrences you think are written in the sky and mean something special—but in the end they don't. They're written in the skies, all right—but like the clouds up there, they just drift off and don't leave anything behind. What else could I do but let them drift off, too? Still, I'd gone into town several times since and rode the streets up and down like a man looking for his other half, peering into bars and taverns hoping I'd see her sitting there alone, drinking her gin and seltzer—but nothing—not a trace of that woman. Once in awhile I'd spot one that fit her—the long dark hair and the olive skin—and my heart'd jump into my throat, beat like a hammer there until I got closer and saw it wasn't her. Then it'd fall back down to my boots and I'd do what I always done—stop in and see Bruno or Earl and order up my two closest friends. Earl would ask, "Did you find her yet?" and I'd tell him no, no luck, until, after a few more visits, Earl stopped asking. My guess was he could read the news written across my face.

I felt I'd done my part with John B. and he told me that enough times. We'd built the brooder house and the layer house, built enclosed pens, put up hundreds of feet of fencing, planted a good-sized orchard, and finished two smaller outbuildings. The news came, too, that Josephine and William had announced their wedding date for the middle of July, and that made me think of returning to Sonoma and picking up where I left off—starting up my hauling business again and maybe try to set down roots somewhere. Josephine would welcome me back and Emma Hansen told me I had a standing invitation to stay at her place, so, for the time being, at least, that seemed the direction to take. I missed my friend, Tino, as well, and wondered how he was doing, if he was still gunning for the guy that most of us knew was his father.

On an early morning in July after one of Gertie's big breakfasts, I harnessed up Molly and Dolly to their wagon, put Little Ike on a lead rope behind and climbed up into the driver's seat. Gertie held little Friedolin and smiled and waved from the front porch while I reached down and shook John B.'s hand. "We'll see you at the wedding," he said.

"Yes, you will." I clicked my tongue and the wagon lurched forward.

"Which way you going back?" John B. asked. "Over the ridge and into Rincon Valley?"

"No, I'll go down Healdsburg Road into Santa Rosa and take Sonoma Public Road down the valley and into town," I said. "It's an easier pull for my two."

Just inside the town limits, I stopped in to say goodbye to Earl and have a bracer or two for the road. "I like your spirit, Bert," he told me. "You get knocked down and you get right up." I thanked him for the kind words.

"What else can a person do?" I asked.

"Just stay down on the ground, I guess," he said.

"No, that's not my style," I said. "Besides, I got a pretty good chin." I downed the bourbon, let its warmth settle in before following it with the beer. "You see a woman with long black braids whose name is Della, you let me know, okay?"

Earl laughed. "You sure about that?"

"No, I'm not sure about any of it," I said. "But sometimes it's just nice to think about."

"Thinking about it is the easy part," Earl said. "It's the rest of it that's hard."

I thanked him and we shook hands and I was back on the road. At the Methodist College, we turned east and within a mile, maybe a mile and a half, we were on Sonoma Public Road, making good time with a mostly empty wagon, passing through Los Guilicos, then Melita, where they hauled the basalt blocks down from Annadel to the railhead, on to Kenwood and into Aqua Caliente where I'd gone with Carlotta and the senator for the mineral baths, then Boyes Springs, and finally into Sonoma proper. I stopped at the Union Livery and snuck up on Tino and grabbed him by the shoulders. He jumped two feet off the ground. "Goddamn, Bert, you scared the shit outta me!" We both laughed.

"So, you're back in town, huh?" he asked

"I am—for better or for worse."

"What's the plan?" he wanted to know.

"I'll look up my old accounts," I said. "And get to hauling again—block off of Schocken. Grapes pretty soon, maybe some late hay—whatever I can scare up." I looked over at Tino. "And you?"

"Working here as always—sometimes a little action at the track, some rentals." He walked into his office, pulled open a drawer at his desk. "How about a little snort?" he asked.

"I never turn a friend down," I said.

We drank two more rounds before I climbed back on the wagon and set out for Vineburg and the folks' place. We called it "the folks' place," the twenty-five acres they crossed an ocean and most of a continent to call their own, and we hoped it would stay in the family for generations to come. Josephine had been living there, and I figured would stay on after the wedding. None of us had really discussed details about the property since Ma's death. John B. was settled in Mark West, and Josephine here in Sonoma. And me? I didn't know where I'd squat down, but until I did, Vineburg was as good a place as any.

Josephine waved at me from the front yard, and after I stepped down from the wagon we hugged each other. I congratulated her on setting the wedding date, which was now less than two weeks off and told her William was a good choice and asked her if there was anything I could do to help in preparations. "Oh, there is," she said. "I've always wanted an arbor in the backyard to train those sprawling roses Mama planted. And," she added, "I thought it'd be an ideal site where William and I could exchange our vows. What'd you think?"

"You're not getting married at Saint Francis'?" I asked.

"We both thought about it—Dad and Mama liked this place so much—Ma, especially with her roses and the garden—and we decided it'd be a nice tribute to both of them to be married here, right on this spot." Josephine pointed to the ground. "And I went to the rectory and asked Father if he was willing to preside out here, and he said yes. He remembered me from Dad's funeral," she said. "I told him we'd make it worth his while."

"Make it worth his while," I repeated, and then laughed. "No one works for free, even the priests."

I told her it was a great idea—a fitting tribute—and set right off to build her an arbor, brought in a partial load of redwood and within three days had put up a fine one—one even our old man would be proud of. I'd modeled it after the one in Carlotta's garden. It thrilled Josephine. I didn't stop there, though. I built a little platform—almost like a tiny stage—under the arbor with a set of steps on each end and slapped together four long benches for the wedding guests. Across two pairs of saw horses, I laid out eight-foot long planks for tables. I spruced up the rest of the yard, as well—knocked down a stand of dry grass and brought in a half dozen shrubs from Ross' Nursery. Josephine was near tears when she saw my work. "How I wish Dad and Mama could be here to see this," she said.

The horses were glad to be back, as well. They liked a routine, a regular place to eat and bed down, and they showed it. Little Ike pranced around the field like he was leading a marching band while Molly and Dolly just watched the youngster, taking it all in.

I was back to hauling block within a couple of days. The foreman at the quarry, Hal Wise, was glad to see me, as were his quarry workers. "Long time we no see you," Lorenzo said. "We think you marry *la princesa*."

"The princess?" I asked.

"*Si*, you know, the woman with all the *dinero*," he said, and rubbed his thumb and index finger together.

"Oh, you mean Carlotta?"

"*Si, ella.*"

"No, never married her," I said. "At one time I thought I wanted to—"

"You change your mind?" Lorenzo asked.

"She changed it for me."

I thought about visiting Christina, as well, but my days were filled up with hauling basalt block and helping Josephine and William, and I figured I'd see her at the wedding anyway which was now just days off. I told myself all sorts of things about Christina; that if I was really drawn to her—which I didn't think I was—I would have been out to see her already in two shakes of a lamb's tail.

That episode in Santa Rosa with Della left me with another bruised heart and I wasn't that anxious to step right back into courting although I never knew what to call whatever was between Christina and me. It wasn't courting—it was more like helping her and her brothers out, which I liked doing. It seemed safe, no commitment. I was free to roam around, take off for a few months like I done at John B.'s, drink when I felt like it, take a roll in the sack—no one telling me what to do. I didn't know what was in our futures—hers or mine—if there was anything more than what we already done together. And to be honest, I didn't spend a lot of time thinking about it. I thought she'd always be around if things changed between us. Anyway, when it came to women, I figured I was jinxed and best just to keep my distance. It seemed I was meant to be a loner—that was my fate, and the sooner I accepted it, the better off I'd be. All this longing, this desire, drove me crazier than a pet coon.

60

The Wedding
· · · · · · · · · · · · ·

Josephine and William's big day finally arrived. John B., Gertie and little Friedolin had driven down the afternoon before and John B. and I stayed up late, drinking bourbon, toasting the would-be bride and groom, and telling wild tales about Josephine to an unsuspecting William, who took it all in good jest. I woke up the following morning with cotton-mouth, and Gertie already had a pot of hot water ready for me to wash up in. I'd bought a large ham the day before at Angie Botelli's, and he asked why I wasn't selling game to him anymore. "I been busy doing other things," I told him.

After leaving Angie's, I picked up the wedding cake at Lillian Waldmeir's and a keg of beer from Excelsior Brewery while Jack Kessel had stopped by and dropped off a crock of his sister's potato salad, two long strings of bratwurst and another smaller crock of sauerkraut. Josephine fashioned a fine salad from her garden— plenty of fresh tomatoes, peppers and cucumbers, and set the bowl aside in the pantry. Along with the baked ham were fresh string beans and sweet potatoes, loaves of bread, sweetmeats and freshly-churned butter. By late morning, Josephine and Gertie had all the food prepared, the plates, silverware and napkins laid out on the crude tables I'd built. Once all the preparations were finished, Josephine and Gertie disappeared into the bedroom to dress. William, as was the custom, finally arrived without seeing Josephine, his bride, until the very start of the ceremony.

I changed into my best pants and parted my hair and twisted the ends of my moustache. I'd cleared an area in the yard, as well, for the carriages to park, and after I brought down more hay from the loft, I went inside, slipped into a starched shirt and tied a string tie around my neck. Gertie saw me and said, "Hello, handsome," and I thanked her for the compliment. I went to the beverage table and poured myself a glass of beer.

The first guests to arrive were—of all people—Carlotta and the senator. I hadn't seen Carlotta in over two years and that stranglehold she'd once held on my heart now seemed, thankfully, gone. I could face her and not shy away, and not feel that hurt and anger that dogged me for so long. I met them at their carriage. Carlotta and I exchanged a long look before I helped her from the carriage. "Bert," as she gave me her hand, "It's so good to see you after all this time!"

"You, too, Carlotta," I said. She was a lovely woman and no wonder I chased after her like a hound dog following a rabbit's scent. The years had added a few more lines around her eyes and her skin had grown paler, but she was still a looker. I shook the senator's hand. In his other hand he held a bottle of wine and tucked under his arm was a wrapped present. He looked at me. "I still remember those baths out at Aqua Caliente," he said. "They were wonderful!"

"Please," I said to both of them, "Make yourselves at home. John B.'s around here somewhere." I looked around and saw him setting up two large sun umbrellas.

I led their horse and carriage to the shade of a walnut tree and had set out buckets of water earlier for the other horses that would be arriving. William's folks and his sister, Annabel, were the next to arrive. John B. and I greeted them together, and they joined Carlotta and the senator and sat under the umbrellas. Gertie offered them drinks.

The next to arrive was Tino— but he wasn't alone. He'd borrowed the Union's three-seater, and riding with him in the front seat was Christina, and behind them in the second seat, Jack and Esther, and behind them was Frank and a woman I'd never seen before—the woman who, I figured, was the friend of Esther's I'd heard about at that dinner months earlier. Jack and Esther had married shortly after I first met her—a no-frills civil ceremony with a Justice of the Peace in the Petaluma courthouse, and a train ride to a Russian River resort for their honeymoon before returning to the ranch. I'd wondered about that arrangement from the start, and how it would settle out since Esther seemed so set on living in town, but that was their concern and not mine.

Tino brought their carriage to a halt. This funny feeling overcame me seeing Tino and Christina together—it came from deep within and spread quickly like a fast-moving storm—that same feeling that struck me when I saw the senator and Carlotta together years before, and even earlier when I'd seen Cameron and Daniel talking after the church service. It was jealousy—pure and simple. I hated to admit it, but that's what it was. There's no mistaking that feeling. I put on an actor's face, smiled as warm as I could force a smile and welcomed all of them to the wedding. "Frank," I said, "who's this charming woman you're with?" I was really laying it on here. "I don't believe I've met her."

"Bert, this is Eleanor. Eleanor, this is Bert," he said. I took her hand and shook it lightly.

"You're Esther's friend?" I asked her.

"That's right—Esther and I have known each other for years," she said. All the women wore hats, some with feathers and others with netting that crossed their foreheads. Eleanor was plainlooking, plump, very much like Esther, with a face that seemed frozen into a constant smile. Once they'd all stepped down from the carriage, I grabbed Tino's elbow and pulled him aside.

"Tino," I said, "You didn't tell me you were bringing the Kessels when I last saw you."

"No, I didn't," he said, "But do I have to tell you everything?"

"No, I guess you don't," I said. It seemed he would have mentioned something like that when we were together at the Union just days earlier. But I remembered, too, all I kept hidden from him about Carlotta. Still it felt funny seeing the two of them together. Maybe it was just me making a mountain out of a mole hill. Maybe it was nothing at all, but Tino not mentioning anything about Christina bothered me just the same. I watched him as he joined the two brothers and their ladies and how quickly he was at Christina's side. I studied the two closely, watched how they were interacting, how they looked at each other. I studied their every movement. Did he have his arm around her? Did she have her arm around him? Were their faces ever close together? What had happened between them while I was away? I was looking for clues, trying my hardest, it seemed, to find the things most hurtful to me. Why did I do this, I wondered? What was in my history to cause this kind of fascination? I didn't know—didn't have any idea. It seemed to run counter to everything, didn't it? That I would take an unusual interest in a woman only when I saw her with another guy—a woman, whom had I shown enough interest in, could possibly be with me?

I tried my best to shake this dark feeling, to just enjoy my sister's wedding on this beautiful July day in the company of friends and family, but first I had to down a good-sized shot of bourbon. Then with a glass of beer in hand, I migrated from group to group, talking the small-talk, a compliment here, a compliment there, a smile plastered across my face like a clown's face you'd see on a circus poster. All the time, though, in the back of my mind, the questions lined up like railcars. What if Tino and Christina were a couple? What did it matter anyway? Had I taken her for granted? Missed my chance? Didn't I want the best for everyone? Or was that just some feel-good bullshit I told myself? Maybe she'd finally shaken the memory of Jimmy Murdoch and was ripe for some other guy to come along, and there I was forty miles away—hammering down roof shingles, and for one brief week thinking I was the luckiest guy in the world because I'd gone home with a factory girl from the west side of the tracks.

It could have been me with Christina—I had my chances riding with her on her deliveries. I could tell sometimes the way she looked at me—all it would have taken was a few kind words, a couple of compliments, maybe touching her hand, showing her my interest. But I didn't feel it, and the words didn't come out, and I didn't touch her—no, none of that. I didn't feel anything deeper than a friendship and I guessed that was where it'd stay. Was

Christina waiting for me to make the move all this time? I didn't know and didn't much think about it. Was Gertie right when she said I was afraid of commitment? Was that the real reason I spent those months at John B.'s, ducking commitment, avoiding Christina? Too many questions—I needed another drink.

The priest was the last to arrive—Father Whyte, the same one who officiated at our dad's funeral. He drove up in a cabriolet carriage, brought it to a halt and I went out to meet him. The white starched collar around his neck was already wet with sweat, and his face flushed red. Once he stepped down, I led his horse to another walnut tree, tied it off and brought it a bucket of water. I watched him as he made the rounds, shaking each person's hand. He had the air of a politician. Gertie poured him a glass of wine.

The ceremony was about to start. Father Whyte stepped up on the little stage I'd built just days before. I'd woven rose branches through the slats on the arbor and, as if on cue, clusters of pink roses sprang into bloom. We were all seated on benches when William walked up to the arbor and joined Father Whyte while the two of them stared toward the backporch. Shortly afterwards, Josephine appeared in a long white satin dress with lace around each wrist, a white veil across her face. She held a tiny bouquet of white carnations. William's father accompanied her. She never looked more beautiful, and I had to keep reminding myself that this was my sister, the same person I'd teased mercilessly growing up, telling her she was homely and funny looking and would never find someone on this earth foolish enough to marry her. Well—wrong again.

After the usual, "Dearly beloved, we are gathered here—" the rest of the ceremony was short and to the point. Father Whyte read some prayers from the book he carried. William and Josephine promised to be faithful to one another through sickness and health and all those other promises brides and grooms make. Then they exchanged their vows and kissed, and when they did, I was watching Christina to see her reaction. She smiled, her lips making a thin straight line across her face, while her eyes focused ahead at the newlyweds. When Josephine and William were finally pronounced man and wife, and they kissed, everyone clapped and the men let out a *Hooray!* and threw their hats in the air. The couple then turned and walked down the makeshift aisle while the guests stood and clapped. A short line formed and Josephine hugged each guest. John B. and I quickly moved the benches over to the tables while Gertie started carrying the food out of the kitchen and onto the serving table.

With the benches in place, I stood behind the beverage table and filled glasses with champagne and when all the guests had their glasses, I toasted the newlyweds. "To William and Josephine, may they enjoy a long life together! You'd make Dad and Ma proud!"

"Here! Here!" the guests responded together.

After the toast, the guests formed a line and served themselves, buffet-style, from a table set up at the foot of the back- porch steps. Once they filled their plates, they returned to the tables, and for several minutes you could only hear the sounds of people eating, knives and forks sliding against each other, the tinkling of glasses, an occasional laugh or compliment. Gertie hovered over the tables, asking constantly if there was something else she could bring a guest. I stood behind the beverage table, pouring wine, beer, whis-key shots, soda water—whatever they wanted to drink. My glance kept returning to Christina and Tino, though, and whenever she looked my way, I'd turn and look off in an opposite direction. I filled my whiskey glass again and again, and before long that old, familiar numbness came back to me.

I'd gone out behind the barn to relieve myself and stayed out there for several minutes, leaning against the barn wall, soaking in the Vineburg countryside—everything still and outlined in sum-mer light like a landscape painting. I let my mind wander across it. All three horses had surrounded me by now and I was patting each one, and they'd nose each other out of the way for more atten-tion. They weren't much different than humans, I thought. We all want attention, to be recognized, not left out, and, in the end, to be loved. And that desire creates different feelings—and not all of them pleasant—I know because I was in the middle of a whole bunch of them right then. And all of this happening, too, on a day that should be joyous and happy—my sister's wedding—and instead, there I was standing behind a barn, my pud hanging out, feeling a big dose of pity for myself, and about to come apart with envy because a woman I had all the chances in the world to be with was with another guy—my best friend.

I don't know how long I was out there before I heard a woman's voice, "Oh, there you are." It was Christina's. She opened the gate and joined me behind the barn. "I saw you disappear," she said. "You were drinking a lot and I was a little worried about you."

"Nothing to worry about," I said. "Besides, it's a happy occasion, isn't it?" I stood up straight, but my legs felt unsteady.

"Sure it is—but no reason to drink so much, don't you think?"

"I guess not," I said. I looked over at her and noticed her normally straight hair was done in ringlets now. "All those people—they make me nervous. And when I'm nervous, I like to drink to quiet everything down." I looked south down to where my old man and I had strung a fence years ago. "So, you and Tino together now?" I figured I'd get right to the point.

"Why do you ask?"

"Curious, that's all," I said.

"That's all?" she said. "That seems like a funny question to ask."

"Yeah, I guess I'd like to know," I said. "I saw Tino the other day and he never mentioned you and him coming to the wedding together, and then you show up today—it just seemed a little odd to me." I shifted from one foot to the other. "Like he was trying to hide something from me."

"I can't speak for Tino but—"

"So, are you guys together or what?"

"He loaned us a carriage when ours was being repaired," she said, "and he was friendly enough and invited me to a band concert—that's all—and I accepted."

"That's all?"

"Bert, I feel like this is some kind of trial—all the questions. It's very awkward for me." She looked around and I sensed she wanted to leave. "I don't ask about your personal life, do I?"

"No, you don't."

"Does everything I do have to meet your approval?" she asked.

"No, it—"

"You went off for months—not a word from you—and now you come back asking all these questions like I done something wrong, like I done something behind your back. I don't get it," she said. "You have no hold on me, okay?"

"I thought we could pick up where we left off," I said.

"And where was that exactly?"

"Helping each other—me with your route—"

"We can still do that, can't we?" she asked. "If you must know, I don't feel anything romantic toward Tino. I know he'd like me to—he's told me as much—but in all honesty, I don't. It could happen—I've always liked him—admired him, even, for making something of himself despite his upbringing."

"He's my best friend," I said.

"I know that and I don't want to be caught between you two." Christina looked back behind her shoulder. "I should get back—"

"Or Tino will worry?" I said it with a sneer.

"You're making me feel uncomfortable," she said. "I did come with him, Bert, and it's bad manners to ignore the people you came with." She looked at me. "You should join the party, as well. These are all your family and friends—there's no need to be nervous."

She turned and walked back to the gate, opened it, and rejoined the wedding guests. I followed behind her. Tino watched us both appear from behind the barn. He approached Christina and he led her back to their places at the table. I worked my way over to the beverages, poured myself a whiskey but added some water. When I looked up, Carlotta stood in front of me.

"So, Bert, what have you been up to all this time?" she asked. A wry smile creased her lips.

"The usual—my hauling jobs, keeping busy. I spent a couple of months over at John B.'s—built a couple more brooder houses and layer houses and somewhere in there had my heart broken—again." As soon as that slipped out, I regretted saying it. She didn't need to know about my broken heart. "And the chickens?" I asked her. "How are your chickens doing?

"They're doing fine," she said. "I'm sorry to hear about the broken heart—"

"That's okay—I shoulda seen it coming, but I didn't."

"Am I the culprit?" she asked.

I smiled. "At one time you were. You'd think with a little practice, it'd get easier, but it doesn't."

"No, it doesn't," she said.

"You and the senator, you're doing okay?" I asked.

"The two of us are fine," she said. "It's his wife that's the problem."

"Still? After how long now? Months? Years?"

"Please, don't remind me," she said. "But the two of us? We're fine, and that's all I care about really—that's all I have control over." A silence followed and I was about to excuse myself for another drink. "Every time I ride my bicycle I think of you," she said. "Those were special times."

But not special enough, I thought to myself. I poured her two glasses of wine and she returned to where the senator was holding court with several of the guests. By now everyone had eaten and Gertie had cleared some plates from the food table, and brought out the wedding cake—a two-tiered affair with yellow and pink roses fashioned from the frosting. "It's a Lillian special," Gertie announced. A large urn of coffee had brewed and was placed on one end of the table opposite a stack of small plates for the cake.

William and Josephine stood behind the cake, while Josephine sliced into its top layer with a knife, took a small piece and pushed it across William's mouth. Everyone laughed and cheered. I passed out plates with cake to the guests, and Gertie followed with the coffee pot, filling the guests' cups. Father Whyte finished his dessert and quickly walked out to his cabriolet and drove off. By now it was late afternoon, and guests began leaving. Tino, Christina and her brothers and their ladies soon followed. Then William's folks left until it was just Josephine and William, John B., Gertie, little Friedolin and me. We cleared all the tables and shook out the tablecloths. Gertie started heating water to wash the dishes.

I poured John B. and myself a fresh whiskey, and we sat in the backyard, watching the western sky turn the color of a new penny as the sun slipped behind the Sonoma hills.

"It's just you that's left now," John B. said.

"Yeah, it's just me."

"I noticed Tino was with Christina and her brothers," John B. said. "Anything going on there?"

"Between Christina and Tino?" I sipped at my whiskey. "I think Tino's making a play for her."

"How's that make you feel?"

"Weird—it makes me feel weird. What else can I say?" I looked over at the arbor I'd built. "We talked a little about it today—"

"You and Tino?"

"No, me and Christina," I said. "She didn't like all my questions and told me she was free to do what she wants."

"I think she likes you—"

"You do?"

"Yeah, I do," he said. "I can usually tell—not all the time—but a good part of it."

"And what makes you think that?"

"The way she looks at you when you're not looking—but I could be wrong," he said.

"Della hasn't shown up yet at your place?" I asked.

"Della? Oh, the Santa Rosa girl?" John B. laughed. "That's my brother, Bert—lover of the long shot!" He shook his head. "No, Bert, she hasn't stopped by—sorry."

"The long shot," I said out loud. "You're right about that one."

61

Changes in Circumstances

· ·

I brooded over what to do about Christina, but like everything else in my life, I was of two minds—either confess my interest in her or just keep my mouth shut, slip away to someplace else and let things take their course between her and Tino or whomever else came on the scene. Meanwhile, I had my work and that kept my mind mostly off of what to do—but not entirely. I thought of Christina throughout the day and into the night and weighed our past history and how the appearance of another guy—Tino—had changed everything. Without Tino on the scene, I reasoned, there wouldn't be this growing interest in her, would there? Things would go along as before. But you couldn't take any of that to the bank. To think she'd wait around for me and no one else to finally decide seemed unlikely. She was a woman, in her prime, with appeal, and to think she'd go unnoticed by other men was foolish. I was like Little Ike—when Molly or Dolly got all the attention, he nosed in and wanted his share. Otherwise, he seemed mostly indifferent to the other two. And, of course, in the middle of all this, I hadn't completely forgotten about Della, either.

Finally, just tiring of batting the whole thing back and forth, I rode my bicycle up to the Koblentz ranch to see what I could settle. I hadn't thought of proposing to her—that seemed too extreme, too impulsive. I hadn't thought of what I'd do or how anything would get settled other than to try to rekindle some time together—you know—take some small steps, at first. That was about it—no real plan. Just get a read on the situation and follow my instincts.

I knocked on the front door and shortly Christina appeared with the usual bandana around her head, her face flushed from working over boiling pots of water. "This is a surprise," she said. "Come in."

"You're working—I hope I'm not disturbing you—"

"Not at all—come in—have a seat," and she motioned me toward a chair. "Coffee?"

"Sure, I'll have a cup."

"I have a fresh pot—I drink too much of it as it is," she confessed. She disappeared into the kitchen and returned carrying a small tray with two cups of coffee and a little pitcher of cream. "I forgot—do you take cream?"

"Just black's fine," I said.

"So, what brings you here?" she asked.

A tough question—right off the bat. I fumbled around for some safe words to say. "I wanted to see how you were doing up here. How your business is going—"

"That's all good," she said, "but it looks like some changes ahead."

"Changes?" I said and immediately thought Tino had proposed to her.

"A number of them—Esther—Jack's wife—is pregnant as you may have noticed at Josephine's wedding—"

"I did notice."

"Well, she doesn't want to live on the ranch once the child's born—she's made that pretty clear to Jack." She sipped at her coffee, stared out the living room window. "And that makes it a bit complicated for the rest of us here."

"Frank doesn't want to stay on?" I asked.

"Oh, he does, but he says he can only work with Jack—he's always struggled with English, and with Jack, language isn't a problem," she said. "Besides, the two of them have always been together—ever since they were boys."

"That does complicate things, doesn't it?" I said.

"It does—we've talked about some options—but Esther's mind's made up and Jack does whatever she says." A silence followed. "One other thing," Christina said.

"What's that?"

"You remember that ranch we looked at after picking up the chicks in Petaluma?" she asked.

"The one at the end of Ely Road—at the corner of Brown's Lane—the vacant one?"

"Yes, that one," she said. "Well, the owner died and it was sold in a probate sale but the new owner couldn't make a go of it so it's back on the market again."

"And?"

"I liked the place a lot," she said. "You did, too, didn't you?"

"I did—you and Frank thinking of making an offer?" I asked her.

"Frank's out—he won't do anything unless Jack's involved," she said and paused and looked at me. "That just leaves you. You've put some money away, haven't you? And you do have a partial interest in your folks' place that might help as collateral." She ran a finger around the rim of her coffee cup. "What about you and I making an offer on it?"

"Damn, Christina, this is all kinda sudden, isn't it?"

"It is, but the place won't be on the market long—I know that."

"What are they asking for it?"

"Forty-five hundred dollars."

"I don't have that kind of money," I said. "Nowhere close to it."

"We can get a mortgage," she said. "I've got nearly two thousand in savings—enough for a good down payment."

"I don't have that much," I said.

"How much you have?"

"Don't know exactly—maybe a thousand."

"And no debts, right?" she asked.

"No, got a clean bill there."

"Why don't I talk with my banker friend, Aaron Wendall?" she said. "He's always been straight with me. He's in Petaluma, too, at the Bankers Trust, there." She set her coffee cup down. "I guess I should have asked you first—are you even interested in this deal?"

"I am—it's going to mean some changes, though," I said. "For both of us. You've got your clients over here and I've got mine—you thought about that?"

"I have—I'll find new ones," she said. "You can, too." She stood up and walked over to the window and looked out across the farmyard. "I'll make an appointment with Aaron and we'll both go over together. How does that sound?"

"Good," I said. "I don't want to get my hopes up if we can't make a deal, so the sooner the better."

"I'll let you know," she said.

I rode back to Vineburg, my head swimming with Christina's business proposal. Like her, I didn't have a place to land. William and Josephine had tied the knot and they lived at the folks' place, but I'd felt a bit like an intruder ever since, even though Josephine told me again and again it was my place as much as hers. There was Emma Hansen's, too, and she'd take me back in an instant, but I'd already lived there, and as much as I liked Emma, I was looking to strike out to someplace new—maybe even a place I could call my own. This whole notion of finally putting down roots grew bigger in my head. I thought about the ranch deal with Christina and all sorts of possible complications reared themselves. What if we're approved of a mortgage and we move in to the Brown's Lane ranch? What then? Is it a purely a business arrangement? Separate bedrooms? What if it turns out we don't get along? Then what? I'm stuck living with someone I don't want to live with, or she's stuck living with me—both bad outcomes. There was always that smaller house on the property if it all went to hell between her and me. What if I have trouble finding work in Petaluma? Or she does? Then what? I worried myself sick thinking about all these possibilities, but I remembered I'd been taking chances all my life—the poaching, buying JD's horses, the whole Carlotta thing—and it hadn't stopped me yet. I was ready for the next change, the next step into the dark cavern of my life.

Another thing, too—she'd asked me and not Tino. What did that mean? That I'd bumped Tino out of the driver's seat? That I was her favorite now and not him? He'd rat-holed money away, too—maybe as much or more than I had, and he'd always worked—was reliable, and I always felt he'd be a good business partner. Why didn't she ask him, I wondered? Those were questions I'd save for another day. Right now, nothing had changed. Maybe in time, things would, but right now things were as they'd always been. No sense bargaining for a wagon, I reasoned, if you don't already have a horse.

62

Buying the Ranch

· · · · · · · · · · · · · · · ·

Christina sent word that she'd made an appointment with Aaron Wendall for Thursday at eleven in the morning at Bankers Trust in Petaluma. She asked me to dress in my best and to bring a list of my all my assets. It was a short list—four hundred dollars in savings—not the thousand I thought I had— three good horses and a Studebaker wagon, carpenter's tools, two saddles, an extra set of harness, my bicycle, and enough spare wagon parts to build another wagon—that was it. I harnessed Little Ike to the folks' carriage, and was at the Koblentz ranch by just after daybreak. Christina was bundled up warm and brought a lunch basket. "Did you bring your papers?" she asked.

"The few I have," I said.

We set off together down Grand Avenue and onto Stage Gulch, past the Chancellor Ranch and into the chilly shade of the gulch. Little Ike kept up a comfortable trot—so smooth you could have set a glass of water on the floorboards and not spilled a drop. We paused at the top of the hill that looked out over the Petaluma Valley, where a blanket of fog still hung over the creek. I let Little Ike take a blow here before continuing down Stage Gulch road to Lakeville. At Lakeville, we turned north toward Petaluma. "Let's go by that ranch again," I suggested, "before we head into town. We've got a couple of minutes to see if it's still the place we think it is."

Christina nodded her head and smiled.

We turned at Brown's Lane and onto Ely and drove into the farmyard. Nothing had changed since our last visit. Tall weeds followed the fence lines and the barn was still half-filled with hay. Red geraniums grew in front of the house, and behind the house were two hills, brown with summer grass, that rose up like a pair of woman's breasts.

"Do you still like the place?" I asked her.

"Yes," she said. "What about you? You still like it?"

"I do."

We rode into Petaluma and stopped the carriage in front of Bankers Trust. I helped Christina step down and the two of us entered the bank, each of us holding our respective papers. Aaron Wendall spotted Christina and met us just a few steps inside the bank's main doors. "So good to see you, Christina," he said. He looked at me. "And this must be Arnold Bert?"

"That's me—but just Bert's fine," I said.

We followed him to his desk and we both sat down opposite him. He opened a folder. "I did some research on the property," he said. "As you probably already knew, it was originally sold in probate but the buyer has since defaulted on his loan, and now the property has been repossessed by the lending agency."

He looked first at Christina and then at me. "Is this your understanding?" he asked.

"It is," Christina said.

"We sent an agent out to the property for an appraisal," he said, "and I have a copy here."

He handed it to Christina and she looked it over before handing it to me. "There are no liens against the property; there's farm implements included in the appraisal, as well—no livestock, though." He looked first at Christina and then at me. "So, how would you like to proceed?" he asked.

"We want to make an offer,'" Christina said. "We're willing to put two thousand dollars down if your bank can finance the balance."

"And do you have collateral?" Aaron asked. "Other properties? A business with records of income? Other savings? Equipment of value?"

"We both have businesses," she said. "My records are all kept in this ledger, here," and she set her ledger book down on Aaron's desk.

"And, you Bert?" He looked at me.

"I don't have any business records, sir—it's been mostly cash-and carry with me," I said. "I do have some savings and a one third interest in the family property in Vineburg, three good horses and a Studebaker wagon, and some other things I own—all listed here." And I slid the paper across his desk. "I got my good name as a teamster, too."

"And are the two of you married?" he asked.

Christina and I looked at each other. "No, we're not—we're both single." I paused here. "But we've discussed the idea."

She turned sharply and looked at me, her mouth partially open.

"Then for now you'd be listed on title as a single man and an unmarried woman?" Aaron asked.

"For now, yes," Christina said. "Let me ask you—does it make a difference If we're married or not?"

"You can co-mingle your assets if you're married," he said. "Banks tend to look more favorably on that kind of arrangement."

"And, if we don't marry?" Christina asked.

"It doesn't preclude you from making an offer," he said. "You'll hold title differently, that's all."

"Preclude?" I repeated the word.

"It doesn't prevent you from making an offer," he said. "Title would be held differently, should your offer be accepted." He looked at us over the top of his glasses. "We can still submit your offer, and, if accepted, we can work out how to hold tenancy. How does that sound?"

"That sounds okay with me," I said.

"And you, Christina?" he asked.

"That's fine. We can iron out the details—or we can't. Either way we'll let you know, won't we, Bert?"

"Yes, sir," I said. "We'll let you know."

"Very good," Aaron said. "We'll be in contact soon and hope-fully, all of this works out. We do value your business here at the bank—"

"And if the deal goes through," I said, "we'll be doing a lot more business here, I promise."

"Excellent!" Aaron stood up, shook Christina's hand and then mine before escorting us to the bank's door.

Once outside, we climbed onto the carriage and I backed Little Ike onto Main Street, turned at D Street and headed back to Sonoma. "Well, what do you think?" I asked Christina.

"About what?" she asked. "You said a number of things in there."

"You think there's a chance for this to happen?" I asked. We crossed over the D Street bridge and turned south just past the railroad tracks. "Is there a chance for the deal to go through?" I repeated.

"Oh, that." She tightened the scarf around her neck. "I hope it's the right decision."

We drove south on Lakeville and a bit further passed the silk mill, its windows opened and the machinery inside whirring its metallic sound—almost like the sound the wind makes moving through the leaves on a tree. Neither of us talked until a mile or so further I suggested eating lunch down at the ranch we wanted to buy together.

"Sure," she said. "I think I'd like that."

At the Brown's Lane place, we turned into the farmyard and stopped the carriage in front of the hay barn. I helped Christina step down and then grabbed the lunch basket from under the driver's seat. "Where would you like to eat?" I asked her.

"How about up on the front porch?" she suggested.

The house was built just where the hills behind started to rise, so from its front porch you could look over the hay barn's roof to the creek and tidelands beyond. We climbed up its steps and at the topmost one, I set the basket down. "How's this?" I asked her. And we both sat down.

"This is fine." She opened the lid of the basket, took out the sandwiches, unwrapped them and handed me one. I bit into it and surveyed the surroundings, already imagining the place to be ours. I looked over at her. "Christina, I can usually tell when something's on a person's mind—they don't say much," I said. "So, what's on yours? Are you thinking about this whole deal?

Maybe having second thoughts?"

"I am thinking about it, Bert," she said. "But I'm thinking mostly of what you said when we were in the bank—"

"About us discussing marriage?"

"We never did discuss it, right? You just said that sitting there at Aaron's desk?" she asked.

"You're right, we didn't discuss it—I said it mostly to sweeten the deal."

"That's the only reason—just to sweeten the deal? Nothing else?" she asked.

I tried swallowing the last bite of my sandwich but it stuck in my throat. I reached for the canteen of water inside the basket. I was waiting for the words to form—something to come out of my mouth, but the words were bottled up inside.

"Are you going to answer me?" Her eyes were searching for mine.

"Yes—I am," I told her.

I had to gather myself here and figure out what to say. I'd thought of proposing to Christina—in time—but had to admit Tino's appearance had forced my hand, and if Tino wasn't on the scene, I'd mostly hoped things could go along as before. But Tino was on the scene, and life didn't stop in its tracks just because you wanted it to. If not me or Tino, someone else would come along and catch Christina's eye and she'd catch theirs—it's the way those kinds of things went. You can't tighten the reins on it and bring it to a halt no more than you can change the direction a river flows. And with the recent circumstances—Jack's wife not wanting the ranch life, and then the Brown's Lane place coming back on the market, and both Christina and me looking for a piece of ground to stand on— well, now seemed as good a time as any to take the big leap and propose marriage.

"You don't want to get married, do you?" she sensed my hesitation. "At least, not married to me."

"No, that's not true," I said. "You'd be a good partner."

"I know I'm not the prettiest girl around—my mother told me so years ago—"

"Your mother told you that?"

"She did. She said, 'Christina, you're not a beauty so you'll have to be a worker to win someone's heart.'"

"That sounds like an awful thing to say to a daughter."

"Awful or not, she said it."

"Christina, please—that's not it at all. You look fine—as pretty as any girl out there."

"Well, what is it then?" she asked.

"Gertie told me I'm afraid of commitment," I said. "And she's right—it scares the hell out of me."

"Why is that?" she wanted to know.

"I guess it comes down to doing what I want and not having to think about someone else," I said. "Not having that responsibility—and not having it all blow up, either, if things go bad."

"So, you want to stay that way for the rest of your life—doing whatever you want? Not having to think of another? Just thinking of yourself?" she asked. "That seems kind of a lonely life to me."

"I make so many mistakes—so many screw-ups—"

"We all do."

"I'm afraid of taking someone down with me," I said. "With me alone, I can handle it but with someone else—I don't know."

"That's the chances we take, isn't it?" she asked. "I see life—everything, for that matter—as a trade-off. It's rarely a clean deal—for everything we take, we give up something. I don't know if it's ever been any different." She looked around her. "It's nice here, isn't it?"

"It is—real nice," I said.

She glanced behind her. "And this house—I don't want to get my hopes up, but if I lived here, this would be the finest house I ever lived in—big windows like this one has and how it perches on this hill looking out at everything below it."

"Christina, you're sitting next someone who's spent half his life, it seems, living in barns and empty horse stalls." I laughed. "Compared to them, this place is a palace."

"What do you say?" She stared over at me. "Give it a shot?"

"I'm not giving up drinking, okay?"

"You just don't have to drink as much. How about that?" she asked. "Can you agree on that much?"

"All right, I'll try," I said. I knew this would be a tough one to promise.

"And there's no beating on me, either," she said. "The first time, and we split the sheets."

"Right, no beatings—but no church, either," I said.

"Maybe in time you'll change your mind about that."

"Right now, I'm not—no church."

"For the wedding—I want a church wedding," she said. "At Saint Francis'. Mama made me promise her that before she died. It had to be a church wedding, she said."

"All right, for the wedding—but that's the only time I step inside one," I said.

"Then it's a 'yes'?'"

I waited here for just a couple of seconds, watching the anxiousness build across her face. "Yeah, let's give it a shot," I said.

"Do we shake on it?" she asked.

"Sure—we shake on it." And I held my hand out.

"I think we should do more than that, don't you?" she said, and she leaned toward me, put her hand around my neck and pulled my head toward hers. Then we kissed. Her lips were soft, a bit cold like the rest of her face in the autumn air, but still pleasant. We kissed again, both of us a little embarrassed—the way it is with 'first times'.

"Things don't have to change much, do they?" I asked.

"Well, some will." She looked at me. "Don't be so afraid, Bert—we'll just have to sort them out as they come along."

And just like that, I proposed marriage—or she proposed it to me— to a woman I hadn't taken to bed or even kissed yet until that moment. Just like that I took the big leap. Where would I land, I wondered? And what kind of partner would I make? Big questions. I know there were times I could hardly stand myself—times I could be down-right difficult and how would she take to them? Would she send me packing? Would we argue all the time? But I'd been wondering about this all my life—all my adult life, at least, about what kind of partner I'd make. Some days I thought a good one, other days I wasn't so sure. I did feel it was time to turn the page, though, to move on to the next chapter, and see how the story unfolds. Up until now, I'd been reading the same lines again and again, like I often do just before falling asleep. We were both ready for something new without really knowing what that 'something new' was. But who does? Who has the crystal ball they can look into? It's all a leap of faith—a crap shoot—a near-blind leap—take your pick—with nothing to go on except what we see and believe in the other, and what we see and hope in ourselves.

I was ready—I think Christina was, too. After all, she'd already been engaged—one up on me. And all this proposing before knowing we even had the ranch that we'd built part of our dreams on. What if we got the ranch and the rest of it—maybe the most important part—didn't work out? Well, then it didn't work out and the world wouldn't end—it'd just seem that way for awhile. There were other places, too, to be sure. We'd find one, if we had to. Right then, I was sure of it.

We drove back to Sonoma, Christina nestled in close to me, neither of us saying much. She'd let out a little chuckle now and then, and I asked what's so funny and she'd tell me about something I'd said or done earlier that had tickled her. "You can be really funny at times, Bert," she said, "and I don't even think you realize it—that's part of your charm, I guess."

"I never thought of myself as charming—more inward-leaning than charming," I told her.

"But you are! And you're a thinker—maybe too much at times, but better than not thinking, at all," she said. "And—you have a wonderful smile—toothy, I'd call it."

"Toothy? Why, 'cause I have big teeth?"

"Yeah, but it's the smile—big and broad—toothy—like I said," she repeated the word.

When the two of us weren't talking, I took in the early fall countryside—the leaves on the oaks and the buckeyes already shading to yellow, the strong smell of pepperwoods trapped in the gulch, a pair of turkey vultures circling overhead, the jingle-jangle of the harness. My mind was busy, too. It was a big decision we'd made—maybe the biggest one of my life so far—and I was trying to bring all of it into focus, but it was damn hard. If we got the ranch, we'd have to figure out how to keep it—what we'd do for income. I'd never had a debt like this before—the money I owed JD when I bought his horses, but nothing like the balance on this mortgage. Christina was a born worker, though, and I knew she'd pull her weight, and I was a good worker myself—I know a good day's work didn't scare me the way it scared others. We'd have to buy some milk cows and I'd be building more brooder and layer houses, and we'd have to drum up business for Christina's routes and maybe my own where I could sell eggs and cream. I had Molly and Dolly, too, for the hauling work if everything else went to hell.

"What are you thinking about?" Christina asked me as we drove along.

"Things," I said.

"You don't regret what you told me earlier, do you?" She leaned over and looked into my eyes.

"No, I don't regret it—just thinking of all the things we need to do."

"They'll get done," she said. "In time they'll get done. They don't all have to be done all at once—don't worry."

We arrived at the Koblentz ranch by late afternoon. "You want to come in for coffee?" she asked. "Esther's been staying in town with her folks during the pregnancy."

"Sure," I said. "You going to tell your brothers the news?"

"I suppose we should, don't you?"

"Sooner or later they'll know—might as well be now."

Christina stoked up the fire in the stove, filled the percolator with water, and added coffee in the percolator's basket. We both sat at the kitchen table and looked at each other, waiting for the coffee to perk. She put her hand on top of mine. The clock on the living room mantel ticked loudly. "I always thought you were so handsome, Bert," she said. "It seems a bit like a dream what happened today."

I smiled at her and heard footsteps on the stairs. Jack looked through the glass on the entry door. He paused outside and removed his boots before entering the house. He walked in and looked at both of us. "Well, what'd you find out?' he asked.

"The bank's going to review our application," Christina said.

"How long does that take?" he asked.

"I don't know exactly," Christina said, "Maybe a couple of weeks."

The coffee finished perking and Christina got up and went into the kitchen. She came back with four coffee cups. "Frank's coming in, isn't he?" she looked at Jack.

"Should be right behind me," Jack said. "He was separating the last of the milk when I left."

We heard Frank's footsteps on the porch. Shortly, the front door opened and Frank walked in in his stocking feet. He looked at each of us around the table. "Well," he said. "Did you get the place?"

"We don't know yet," Christina paused, then looked at me. "We got some other news, though."

"Yeah? What's that?" Jack asked.

Christina looked at me and put her hand back on top of mine. "Bert and I are getting married," she said.

"I'll be go-to-hell," Jack said, and looked at me and then his sister and then back at me. "You finally popped the big one, huh?"

I nodded my head. "I did."

"What took you so long?" he asked. "She's been waiting all this time—"

"Jack! I have not!" Christina said.

The two brothers laughed. I shrugged my shoulders. "I don't know—I wanted to make sure she was the right one," I said.

Frank sat opposite me and laughed. "Everyone's getting hitched," he said. "It's going around like the flu."

Christina poured coffee into each of the cups. She'd brought out the cream in its little pitcher and a bowl of sugar with its own spoon.

"You set a date?" Jack asked.

"No," Christina said. "It just happened—but it's going to be in the church—Bert promised." And she looked at me again. "You promised."

"I did."

"Either way—church or not—they got you hand-cuffed." Jack laughed.

We finished our coffee. By now it was dark, time to head back to Vineburg. I got up from the table, said goodbye to Jack and Frank and headed for the door. Christina followed after me. At the carriage, we embraced and kissed again. "I gotta say, this all feels a little different, doesn't it?" I said. "Almost like I'm sleep-walking."

"Yes, it does," she said. "It'll take a little adjusting—like everything else."

She tightened her embrace and we held each other for several seconds, kissed again before I climbed up to the driver's seat. "You take care, Bert," she said.

"I will."

Then I drove back to Vineburg, passed Carlotta's, but this time not feeling the hurt or rejection I once felt, but feeling something very different, instead—feeling light and a bit carefree but mixed in with some heaviness, too, wondering if I'd made the right decision or not—wondering if I hadn't jumped the gun—wondering how much of my freedom I'd have to give up. I was wondering all kinds of things—but I'd made my decision and was going to stick to it. Sure, things would be different—but like I said again and again, nothing stands still. You think it does—like being in a boat you feel isn't moving but it's drifting all the time—the currents grabbing at it. You don't feel it moving under you, but it is. It's moving, taking you to places whether you like it or not.

PART TWO:
Harnessed

63

A Split

· · · · · · ·

I kept the news about our engagement mostly to myself though I did tell Josephine and William. We were all living under the same roof and she was my sister—so how could I not tell her? She congratulated me and gave me a hug and asked if we'd set a date, and where we'd live, and all those things folks ask when they see somebody's life about to change. I told them about the Brown's Lane place and how we'd looked at it a year or two earlier, and how Christina thought that she and her brothers might live there, but then Jack married Esther and Frank wasn't sure what he'd do, and the place finally sold.

"We pretty much figured that was a dead deal," I said. "And then we heard the buyer couldn't make payments and the bank repossessed the property."

"Did you ever think of marrying her before this ranch deal even came along?" Josephine asked.

"To be honest—I'd thought of it but didn't want to," I said. "But I looked at my situation and she looked at hers and it just sort of came together—like all the numbers added up or you found the missing key—something like that."

"We're happy for you, Bert," Josephine said. "We really are. I see the way you mope around here at times and think to myself—Bert needs someone."

"That's what you thought, huh?"

"Yeah, that's what I thought all right," she said. "We all need someone."

"I sometimes thought it showed weakness—needing someone."

"I don't think it does at all—it's just a basic human need," she said.

With the prospect of buying a ranch, I stepped up my hauling jobs trying to salt away as much money as I could. I contracted to haul several loads of late-harvest grapes out to the Buena Vista Winery and was back at the Schocken Hill quarry, hauling block down to the rail station. In between, I'd hauled lumber up from Sonoma Landing, volunteer hay from the tidelands, and even several loads of furniture when the Preston brothers moved into their new store. All in all, I was staying busy, working long hours and hardly drinking— I thought about it all the time, though.

One late afternoon after a final haul down from the quarry, I was enroute back to Vineburg when I saw Tino walking south on Broadway. I stopped alongside him. "Can I give you a ride?" I asked.

He glanced up at me and right-off I could see something wasn't right. He didn't smile the way he usually did, and the look he gave me was the look you'd give a stranger who just asked you for a quarter, not someone you considered your best friend. "Been avoiding me, huh?" Tino said.

His question caught me off guard. I looked down at him. "Why would I be doing that?"

"You know why? Don't go playing stupid on me now."

"Tino, I don't know."

"I seen Jack Kessel the other day at the harness shop. He told me you and Christina are engaged." Tino looked off. "You know how to stab a guy in the back, don't you—you're real good at that."

"I haven't stabbed anybody in the back," I said.

"You seen the two of us together at your sister's wedding and you couldn't stand it, could you?" Both thumbs were tucked into the tops of his pants.

"That isn't what happened."

"You disappear for a few months," Tino said, "and then come back and see the two of us together and you couldn't stand it so you decided just to step in and fuck things up between us. Bert, the big ladies' man," and he snarled the words at me. "You wouldn't have paid a cent's worth of attention toward her if you hadn't seen us together, would you?"

"That ain't true," I said, although it was true—at least, partly true. I'd returned to Sonoma from John B.'s with Della on my mind, but after a couple of weeks I had to give up that ghost and move on. She'd disappeared, vanished, and that was that. And it wasn't like I'd never thought of Christina this whole time—I did—but then seeing her with Tino put her in a different light. It's hard to explain, and I could see why Tino felt the way he did—that I'd just muscled my way in and scotched his chances—but something inside me had shifted, like a curtain had been pulled back and I finally saw all these things in Christina I hadn't recognized before. It took Tino coming along to see them.

"It sure looks that way to me," he said. "You couldn't stand seeing the two of us together."

I just shook my head. "I'm sorry you feel this way—"

"Sorry don't cut it," he said. "You'll just fuck her like the others and then toss her aside."

"The others? Who are you talking about?" I asked. "The floosies I met in bars? You had your share of them, too, Tino, and don't say you didn't."

"You were the guy that was never going to settle down, remember?" he said. "No quim was sweet enough for that to ever happen—you told me that once."

"I would have settled down with Carlotta," I said.

"Carlotta!" he laughed. "Wish in one hand and shit in the other, and tell me which one fills up first."

"Goddamn, Tino, you're pissed—really pissed—"

"That's right, I am! I feel like you stabbed me in the back," he said. "Friends don't do that to one another—"

"Tino, I drank with you down at the Union just after I come back from John B.'s and you didn't mention a word about Christina—not a word—"

"I didn't know exactly how I felt about her then," he said. "And whether you still had an interest in her or not—and, besides, I don't have to tell you everything, do I?"

"No, you don't, but if you'd told me straight me out, I wouldn't have—"

"Horned in like you done?" I could see he was getting good and agitated. "You would have stepped aside for old Tino here, is that right? Given me my shot? Mighty considerate of you, Bert."

"It's more complicated than it seems," I said.

"Don't seem that complicated at all."

"To you it doesn't—but it is," I said. I looked down at Tino. "I'm sorry—"

"You already said that."

"Then there's nothing else I can say right now—I'd like to explain everything to you but this doesn't seem the time."

"No, it don't." He turned and walked away. I watched him for several steps before clicking my tongue and the horses moved forward. "I still want to be your friend," I called out as I passed him. He stared straight ahead, didn't say anything and just kept walking.

In the remaining miles back to Vineburg, my head swam with all kinds of thoughts, many of them swirling around colliding into each other. Had I intentionally set out to hurt Tino? I didn't think so. I never thought I could do that to a friend. Had Christina told me that Tino was her interest, I would have backed off and let the two of them work it out, but she didn't tell me that, and it left the door open, and I walked through the door. She was the one who decided the course, not me, but I couldn't convince Tino of that. I couldn't tell him that he wasn't her favorite and that it was me. That would have been even more hurtful. I couldn't tell him anything at this point and just had to let the dust settle between us.

I arrived back at the folks' place and drove Molly and Dolly alongside the barn, and slipped them out of their harness and led them into their stalls. Little Ike craned his neck over his stall door, not wanting to be left out. We weren't any different than horses, in that respect. We didn't want to be left out. We didn't want to be passed over. The horses had taught me this lesson, and now I was learning it again with Tino. I hadn't thought of him when all of this started happening—I was mostly thinking of myself like I so often done. But we have to make choices and some of them are damn difficult. I hoped, in time, I could explain all this to Tino, and he'd understand. But right now, I couldn't. It wasn't in the cards. I'd just have to hope that in time all this would blow over.

64

Engaged

· · · · · · · ·

Bankers Trust sent a letter to Christina two weeks after our visit, notifying her that our offer on the Brown's Lane ranch had been accepted and that the property was now in a thirty day escrow while our finances were checked, and our backgrounds reviewed to ensure we had no outstanding debts, foreclosures or bankruptcies. There was no paper on me—my citizenship papers, yes—but I'd never borrowed money from a bank, and it was only in the last couple of years after going into the hauling business that I even had a bank account—an account I never much used. It was the same for Christina although her bank balance was larger than mine, and may have been the difference in us qualifying for the ranch. We both stayed at our jobs, working as much as we could and salting away every dollar. It was a good ranch, all right, but we'd need start-up funds for cattle and chickens and other expenses we'd encounter.

I helped Christina whenever I could: I hauled sacks of potatoes out to the Koblentz place and sometimes delivered crocks of potato salad and fresh eggs to her clients on the east side of Sonoma, closer to where I lived. We'd gone back to the Brown's Lane place twice—Christina managed to secure a key for the house from Aaron Wendall—and we walked through its empty rooms, imagining a certain piece of furniture here, a table there, which room would be our bedroom and laugh an embarrassed laugh when we talked about the kids' room. She'd look at me with that intense stare of hers, that "truth finder" stare I called it—a probing one that made sure everything I said was what I meant.

Outside, I walked all through the hay barn and the milking barn, and paced-off where a brooder house and a layer house could be built. The sale included farming implements that were left behind, too: a hay rake, a seed drill, a disc, and a two bottom plow, some extra harness that time had dried the leather on. In the milking barn, there were buckets and a milk hopper and a feed room where sacks of feed were stored. When I opened its door, mice scurried in every direction. John B. earlier had offered me one of his terrier pups, "good ratters" he called them, and now I thought that was just what we needed. "Christina!" I called out. "Let's walk up to the top of the hill."

She'd been in the smaller house—built for the hired help—and appeared at its door. "It's a mess in here," she said.

"Never mind, let's climb to the top of one of the hills," I said. She joined me, and we walked up alongside the house and into its backyard where a fence separated the yard from the field above. We opened the gate and crossed into the field and climbed up to the top of the north hill. "It's got a pitch to it," I said, "but I think we can still grow oat hay on these hills."

"I don't know, Bert," she said. "They look pretty steep to me."

"Then we'll grow kale for the chickens on them or cabbages— we'll grow something," I said.

At the top of the hill, we both caught our breath and looked out over the Petaluma Creek and the tidelands below us. The creek wound like a loose piece of ribbon through flat tule land with levees mounded along both sides of the water, and behind these levees, hay fields spreading out, and little wooden shacks with docks that jutted into the creek. A light wind blew up from the bay carrying the brackish scent of the tidelands up to where we stood. "It's really very lovely, isn't it?" Christina said. "I never dreamed anything like this when I was a little girl."

"How could you?" I asked. "Like me, didn't you think you'd always be in the mountains? Always be where you grew up?"

"I guess—but I thought of other places, too," she said. "And father scared me when I was young—he was very strict—and when I heard that Jack and Frank were immigrating to the states, I begged them to take me along, too. Mother reluctantly agreed."

I thought of Obwalden and Peter the baker, especially Peter's wife, Helga, and how—unlike Christina—I didn't want to leave for the states. I wanted to stay with Helga in their warm kitchen and help her bake breads and cakes and fancy strudels. But all that was a distant memory now—over twenty years ago—and Dad and Ma were gone with Josephine and William now caring for the piece of their dream they left us in Vineburg. And I was engaged—not even married yet—with all my life savings bundled into a down payment.

I hadn't mentioned my earlier encounter with Tino to Christina —I don't know exactly why—but it was weighing on my mind and I waited for the right time to bring it up—which seemed now, this moment— with the two of us standing on top of that hill and looking down on the roof of a house we hoped we'd soon be living in, and looking further out to the hay barn and the pastures and further still into the distant future. "I didn't tell you about the run-in I had with Tino," I said.

"Run-in?" she repeated.

"Yeah, I saw him walking down Broadway and stopped to say hello, and right off he came at me about us being engaged," I said. "Your brother, Jack, told him a couple days earlier."

"I wanted to tell Tino myself," she said, "but Jack beat me to it—and I felt bad."

"Tino accused me of stabbing him in the back." I looked over at Christina and a gust of wind blew her hair back from her face. "He was pissed—good and pissed."

"I don't think I played him along," she said. "I never promised anything. I told him I enjoyed his company and maybe—maybe in time—something could have developed. I didn't know and that's what I told him—and then you returned from your brother's and things took off the way they did—"

"I was trying to explain this to him but he wasn't hearing any of it. I apologized several times—what else could I do?"

"Nothing, really—it was my choice," she said.

"And I couldn't tell him that—not without hurting him even more," I said. "There's winners and losers, I guess—we all take our turns."

"I'm hopeful for Tino," Christina said. "He's got a good heart—I've always said that about him. Someone else will come along."

"I hope so," I said. "Because I feel bad about it—"

"But not about us, right?" she looked at me. "You don't regret what's happened between us?"

"No, not at all—I don't feel bad about us—only that Tino feels the way he does," I said.

"Give it time—that's what it needs."

We stayed on top of the hill for several more minutes before walking back down to the farmyard. We climbed the stairs to the front porch, locked the entry door and took a final look around. "It's a fine place," she said.

I nodded and she took my hand and we climbed back down the stairs to the carriage below. We were soon driving south on Lakeville Road, past the Keebler dairy to Altenbach's, where we turned and climbed up Stage Gulch Road. Here, the road turned and dipped through the gulch before spilling out in Sonoma Valley and the Watmaugh District. We turned north on Grand Avenue and soon arrived at the Koblentz ranch. I helped Christina down from the carriage and we embraced. "We made the right decision, didn't we?" she asked.

"Yes, we did—it'll all work out," I said. We kissed and said goodbye and I drove back to Vineburg.

65

The Ranch and Marriage
· ·

Several events happened in the next few months: Christina had gone to see Father Whyte about setting a wedding date, but then just days later, the church caught fire and burnt down. All kinds of donations poured in to rebuild the church and in short time, the debris was cleared and a new church rose up in the footprint of the old one. We were slated to be the first couple married in the new church. Next, our loan was approved. We went to Petaluma and signed all the papers, and just like that, Christina and I were the owners of a hundred acre ranch just north of Lakeville. About this same time, Jack and Esther bought a little house on East Washington Street in Petaluma, and we emptied out the Koblentz ranch house—furniture, stoves, cooking pots, dishes—everything they owned, and hauled it over the hill to both places—to Jack's on Washington Street and ours in Lakeville. Christina and I rented the little house to Frank as partial payment for his labor. He was happy with the arrangement and took to cleaning out the house right-off before moving in.

Christina and I bought a pair of Holstein milk cows from old man Koblentz, and Gertie's brother, Joe Keebler, gave us a registered Holstein along with her heifer calf. Bloss Keebler, her other brother, gave us two fine Holsteins, as well. John B. came down for a day or two at a time with his three sons, Eddie, Joseph and Friedolin, and we built a brooder house to start our egg business. Once the brooder house was finished, we built a layer house. On his last trip, John B. brought along two young lambs. All this and Christina and I weren't even married yet. The marriage came six months later.

We were the first couple to be married in the new Saint Francis Solano church. We exchanged our vows, Christina in a simple white wedding dress and me wearing my Dad's coat. John B. was my 'best man.' We held the reception at the Swiss Club on the northwest corner of the plaza where Dad had been both a member and officer for years. All the immediate and extended family were invited, and it was a good turnout. I'd left an invitation at the Union Livery for Tino—we hadn't talked since our little brush-up on Broadway—but he never responded. I shook everyone's hand and embraced all the women and everyone wished us good luck. We ate and drank, and Lorraine Helger played her accordion. There was a stack of gifts, too, that we decided to open later.

For our honeymoon, Christina and I reserved a room at the Mervyn Hotel in Glen Ellen. We drove there with Little Ike pulling the folks' carriage, stabled him at the hotel's livery and entered the hotel to check in. I wasn't used to this kind of elegance, and Christina wasn't, either. We followed a bell-hop upstairs to our room. He opened the door for us and set our two small pieces of luggage down. He waited. "I think we tip him," Christina said. I handed him twenty five cents and he left. Our room looked out over the Sonoma Creek, and when you opened the window, you could hear the creek running, spilling over the rocks in the stream. Light through the trees seemed to be shifting all the time like looking into one of those kaleidoscopes where you turn its shaft and the glass spills into different shapes and colors. I smiled at Christina and she smiled back a nervous smile. Through our long engagement, we hadn't slept together yet. I wanted to—more than anything else—and the times we laid down next to each other and embraced and kissed, with the sap rising up my tree, I near-pleaded with her, but she held fast.

So, that time finally came. It was late evening, and I'd drunk and ate my fill earlier, and there was nothing more I wanted to do now than to take my new bride to bed. I approached her and we embraced. "I've been waiting for this moment a long time," I told her. She forced a smile, but I could tell she was nervous about the whole thing. I fumbled with the buttons on her dress and she politely brushed my hands aside, and unbuttoned them herself. She was in her slip now, and in the gaslight of the room, her arms and shoulders were as pale as ivory. I looked into her face and ran my hands through her hair. By now it had lost its curls, and the ringlets that had coiled down just hours ago were gone. I unbuttoned my shirt and slipped out of my underclothes and led her to the side of the bed.

"How are you doing?" I asked her.

"Nervous—I'm nervous, Bert."

"So am I," I said. "But we'll be fine."

"You think so?"

"Yes, I do—and we have time," I said, "lots of time," and she slipped the straps off her shoulders and her underclothes dropped to the floor. I pulled her down to the bed where we both embraced and kissed. Her skin felt smooth, soft. We both finally stripped out of our remaining clothes and continued to kiss and fondle each other, our breathing becoming charged and rapid. Finally, I moved over on top of her and her legs separated and with some gentle thrusts—it took some doing—I was inside her. She let out a deep sigh.

"Are you okay?" I asked her again.

She nodded her head. "Yes, I think so—but it does hurt some—so go easy."

I tried to be as gentle as I could, taking my time so she was relaxed, not so nervous, but once inside her, though, I couldn't much tell if she was enjoying it or not. Her expression never changed. "Is it okay?" I asked.

She nodded. It took some doing, but we found our rhythm after several attempts. I could feel the tenseness in her body still. "Just relax, Christina," I said. "It's all fine. Just let yourself go."

She'd nod, a little smile appearing. "This is difficult for me," she said. "I'm so nervous."

I whispered in her ear, told her how good it would all be—that there was nothing to worry about—that it was like this for most newlyweds.

"You think so?"

"I do," I said. "It's a whole different way of getting to know each other."

My whispering seemed to finally relax her. We moved with each other and that felt good. She smiled and seemed to enjoy it more, but seemed embarrassed by all of it, as well. Then I came—a loud ahhhhhhh. She looked up at me. I hovered over her, enjoying the moment. Afterwards, I rolled off of her and we both stared up at the ceiling, neither of us talking, just looking at the shadows the gas light made, listening to the sounds of the creek and the clop-clop of a horse crossing over the bridge below.

"How was that for you?" I finally asked her.

She didn't answer at once. "It'll get better, won't it?"

"Sure it will—we're just getting to know each other that way."

"You think so?"

"Yes, I do."

"I hope that's true," she said. A silence followed. "I didn't disappoint you, did I?"

"No, of course not—like I said we have time."

We both lie there in our hotel bed and it was dark now, and I was thinking about what we'd just said—that the sex between us would get better. I hoped so. She'd learn to relax through it all, learn to trust me—and just enjoy it—then things would smooth out between us.

"Well, Christina, we're married—who'd have thought it?" I said. I wanted us to talk mostly so I could gauge her mood, gauge what she was feeling. Our first go hadn't been all I thought it would be and I could feel her disappointment. "It's funny how things turn out, isn't it?" I said.

"It is," she agreed. She continued staring up at the ceiling, hardly moving her head.

"Did you ever have an inkling that this would happen between us?" I asked.

"No," she said. "It was the last thing on my mind."

"The last thing—really?"

"Well, almost.

"So, what happened?" I wondered.

"It took me some time to realize Jimmy was gone and he wasn't coming back," she said. "And then I watched how you worked with my brothers, and how helpful you were to me—but when you left I thought, 'Well, that's that,' but then I started to miss you and kept asking myself what that was all about. I didn't think I'd ever feel that way again toward another man."

"But I came back."

"Yes, you did, and that made all the difference."

I rolled toward her and put my arm across her breasts.

"All the difference in the world," she said.

Neither of us talked much after that. I lay awake for some time. Christina's breathing grew heavier. "Are you awake?" I whispered to her. No answer.

We both awoke early the next morning, looked at each other while still in bed, and we kissed. Her face was pale and bare, every little detail exposed in the morning light. We dressed. She combed her hair and the ringlets—done by Tikey Rawlins the previous morning before the wedding ceremony—were now completely limp and her hair was straight again. We embraced each other and walked downstairs for coffee. We sat in an empty dining room until finally a waiter appeared from the kitchen. He was still slipping into his white linen jacket as he approached our table. "Did the two of you not sleep well?" he asked.

"We slept fine," I said. "We're farm people—early risers, that's all."

He brought us coffee and we both ordered eggs and toast for breakfast. I looked across our table at Christina. "Well, what did you think?"

"I'm not used to all the service—being waited on and folks carrying my luggage," she said.

I moved my head closer to her and in a whisper, asked, "No, I mean about last night."

She smiled, a bit embarrassed. "Oh, that—it might take some getting used to," she said, and dabbed at her mouth with her napkin.

"But did you enjoy it?" I asked her.

She didn't answer right away. I think my question embarrassed her. "Well, like you said, we've got lots of time," she said.

"Yes, we do."

After breakfast, we stepped out onto the terrace that overlooked the creek. We stood there with my arm around her waist and her arm around mine, listening to the sound of the water. "It's very lovely here," she said.

"It sure is," and I tightened my arms around her.

We checked out of our room and walked over to the hotel livery where Little Ike had been stabled for the night. He was glad to see us, and like us, not used to such special treatment. I harnessed him myself and tipped the stable hand. I helped Christina up to the carriage seat and we headed south from Glen Ellen, all the way down Grand Avenue and Watmaugh and on through Stage Gulch to Lakeville, to our new home. Frank was there to greet us when we arrived.

"How do you like it here, Frank?" I asked him.

"Good," he said. "Very good."

I helped Christina down from the carriage and we climbed the stairs together, but as she opened the door, I took her up in my arms and carried her across the threshold. "It's an old custom, Mrs. Miller," I said. And she smiled. I walked back down to the carriage, and carried up our wedding presents and stacked them on the living room floor.

66

Finding Our Legs

· · · · · · · · · · · · · · · · · ·

Joe Keebler, Gertie's brother, lived right up Lakeville Road. He had a beautiful dairy ranch there—maybe the finest in the south county, with a herd of registered Holsteins, and offered us his help in any way he could. "What are you folks setting out to do?" he asked. He knew about Christina's business over in Sonoma and he suggested she contact Emilio Paroni, who operated one of Petaluma's finest delicatessens. Joe looked at me. "And you?'"

"I've got a little starter herd," I said. "And I'll be raising chickens."

"You're going to need more than a half dozen cows," he said.

"Well, John B. and I plan on building a brooder house and a layer house, so we'll start up with the chickens pretty soon."

"You bought any yet?" he wanted to know.

"Not yet," I said. "Got to catch up on the finances first—money seems to disappear when you're starting out."

"Yes, it does," Joe said. "And it'll keep disappearing—that's what farming's about. Thing is—and I'm no poultry man—but it's damp down here near the creek like we are—and chickens don't take to that dampness."

A week after we finished the brooder house, a delivery wagon pulled into our yard. It was from Sales Hatchery. The driver stepped down from his seat and asked, "You Bert Miller?"

"Yes, I am."

"I got a hundred single-comb Leghorn chicks for you," he said.

"I didn't order any chicks," I said. "Not yet, at least. You sure you got the right address?"

He looked at the delivery receipt. "It says Mister and Mrs. Arnold Bert Miller, Rural Route 3. That's you, isn't it?"

"That's me, all right." I looked down at the receipt. "Who ordered them?"

He read further down. "Mrs. Carlotta Stamm," he said. I took the receipt from him. A little note was attached, too it, as well. It read: *a late wedding present for you and Christina. Love, Carlotta.* She even included a hundred pounds of chick mash."

We carried the boxes over to the brooder house, and like I'd done at Carlotta's and John B.'s, the folks', and a couple other places since then, I opened the top of the box and tilted it over, and the little chicks spilled out onto the brooder house floor. After the last box was emptied, I called Christina over from the house, and told her I wanted to show her something. I opened the door to the brooder house and she looked in at all the chicks and smiled. "That's wonderful!" she said. "Who ordered them?" I told her Carlotta had.

"Your old boss," she said. "She's still thinking of you."

"Yeah, my old boss," I said, and poured chick mash into their troughs and filled the water feeders then closed the door behind us.

We were busy the next days. I'd gone into Petaluma, following the leads Joe Keebler had given Christina and me about finding new clients. I went from restaurant to hotel to tavern to market, drumming up our business. "Fresh eggs and cream delivered right to your door twice a week," I told them. "We've even got potato salad and sauerkraut, "I told them.

"How soon?" they wanted to know.

"Springtime for everything," I said. "Right now I can deliver the cream and potato salad. Springtime for the eggs. We're brooding chicks as we speak."

The reception was encouraging. Emilio Paroni, the delicatessen owner, had tasted Christina's potato salad on an earlier visit to Sonoma and praised it. He'd buy whatever she could make, he told her. And the bar and restaurant owners liked the idea of deliveries right to their establishments.

Back at the ranch, Frank and I set aside two plots of land for kale, potatoes and cabbage, and I brought Molly and Dolly in with the disc and it scratched at that adobe soil. It was hard and dry and pebbly—good for making bricks and growing oat hay, but for kale and cabbage and whatever other vegetables we'd grow, the soil needed something more—manure, mostly. Joe Keebler helped us out there. I took my wagon up to his dairy and loaded it with dried cow manure every day. Once the manure was worked in, Frank and I set out kale and cabbage seedlings for two days.

Christina loved her new house. I'd set up her stoves in the backporch with chimneys that poked through the porch roof and kept smoke out of the house. She'd scrubbed all the floors and hung pictures on the walls—the woman seemed happiest when she was working. We painted the kitchen a pale yellow and she talked about a living room carpet, and when money allowed, a dining room set with matching dishes and silverware. By evening, after all the chores were finished, Frank would join us at the dinner table and the two of them would say grace, and we'd talk about the day's work and what still needed to be done—there was always something left to do. In short order, tired from working all day, we'd eat and then we'd go to bed. Sometimes Christina and I would make love, but often, after a short embrace, we'd both fall asleep.

I thought married life would be different than this—plenty of love-making—but when you worked all day until you could hardly stand up, and then you ate and went to bed, there wasn't much energy left over to do anything else. Sometimes we'd wait until morning and I'd reach for Christina, but she was already up and dressed. And with morning came that drive to start working all over again like you done the day before and the day before that one. The work never seemed to end—that was our lot.

I don't know what I'd bargained for with the married life. My old man had told me again and again what to expect—that if you was banking on sex all the time, you'd better bank on other things, too, but I was of that young age when what he said went in one ear and just as quick, went out the other. He warned me ahead of time about this, that it was a lifetime of working together, learning to live with each other's imperfections—there was no time-off—and it involved compromise and you didn't always get your way. "Find yourself a good companion," he said. "It

don't matter what she looks like 'cause the looks wear off anyway."
I never believed him, until his warnings started to sink in. In no
time, I was missing the carefree life of my younger days—heading
out with Tino and my shotgun or fishing pole, running from Percy
Sheers, drinking whiskey, nibbling at the ear of any woman willing
to listen to me. The more I thought about those times, the more
I wanted them back—but those times were gone—like yesterday's
tides—and I wondered if it was just because they were gone that I
wanted them back so bad. I didn't know.

All through our courtship, it was the hungry hope of sex and in-
timacy that drove me to our wedding day. Once we were married, I
reckoned, we'd have sex every night, and sometimes in the morning
or mid-day if we could fit it in, but now just after a few weeks, the
shine was wearing off that apple. All that stuff about sex and making love was mostly stuck in my imagination, it seemed—probably
where it stayed for most folks. Now it was routine and facing the
sometimes hard-tacks of living together and compromising, and
when things didn't go your way, not tearing at each other's throats.
I was in it for the long-haul, I told myself. I kept saying that again
and again to drown out all the doubts. No running away, Bert
Miller. I had a good partner, a faithful woman, a hard worker—
and, yes, I sometimes thought about the other end of the road, but
she made me tow the line—something I needed— because I think
she understood me better than I understood myself. She knew my
weaknesses—where my wanderings sometimes took me, just like
she knew my strengths, too.

That said, it was a challenge much earlier in our marriage than
I thought, and I figured there'd be plenty more of them, so I had
to work out a plan if we were going the distance. She wanted an
accounting of my day—pretty much everything I done—especially
if I'd gone into town. She wanted to know where I'd stopped, who
I'd talked to. Did I have a drink? How many drinks? How much
did I spend? My life got to be another page in her ledger book. At
first I volunteered the information right-off, but I knew if I'd told
her everything I done—like the day I'd seen Madeline Brewster

at the Tivoli—she'd want to know how that happened, what we talked about, was she still married—like I said, a full accounting. I didn't want to lie. I wanted to be honest with her—everything straight up. I didn't want to hide anything or deny stuff, either, but I wanted a part of my life that was my own, too, that no one could just wander into and pick through what they wanted. I needed to put a fence up, guard my innermost secrets. I wanted something that was just my own and no one else's. The only choice, then, was either tell her everything—which I was reluctant to do—or to just cherry-pick certain things. I adopted the latter. I'd already had a taste of Christina's firmness. She didn't cave in easily, and I didn't want to butt heads all the time, either. I wasn't cheating on her—hadn't even thought of it—regardless of who I talked to. With all the work on the ranch, I needed another woman like my ass needed another cheek.

Within a couple of months, we'd established a routine around the place. Frank was a good worker—we already knew that from his time at the Koblentz ranch. He had the little house just north of ours and other than joining us for dinner on occasion, kept pretty much to himself. We never heard anything further about him getting married. Christina had brought in some furniture for him and hung pictures on the walls. Frank still went into town on Sundays to visit Vivian, but he was back at the ranch by himself by late afternoon. Christina made him a big pot of stew each week and took it over to his house. Sometimes he joined us for dinner, but Frank was a loner—a guy given to work but spending a lot of the time by himself. Like I said, he hardly ever talked about Vivian, and when we'd ask him questions, his answers were always short—maybe one or two words—that's all. "He never talks," Vivian had told Esther. "And when he does, I can hardly understand a word he says."

When Frank socialized, it was mostly just with his brother Jack. Frank was likeable enough but had no friends. I'd look across the table at Frank, sometimes often wondering what went on inside his head—what made him the way he was and what excited him or brought him joy—if anything. His insides were locked tighter than the safe at Bankers Trust. I thought of the times when I wanted to turn my back on everyone—and how I could have ended up the same way—all locked inside myself—even more than I already was. But as long as Frank did the milking and separating out the cream, feeding most of the cattle and was content doing it, what Frank thought or what he did or didn't do, wasn't my concern. I liked having him around. We worked on his English together—I'd point to certain objects and repeat the word in English—"shovel" for example, and he'd say the approximate word back, sometimes several times until he got the pronunciation right. "How are you going to talk to Vivian if you don't know the language?" I asked him. Frank would look back at me and smile and say, "I don't know. Maybe I go back to Switzerland?"

In the fall, after a first rain and the soil had softened, we hitched Molly and Dolly up to a plow and worked the fields above the house. Then we disced the soil, breaking the adobe up even more and followed with the seed drill and planted oats. With the first rains, the oats sprouted and the hills were soon covered with a green carpet of oat seedlings so bright it hurt your eyes. We set out cabbage and kale seedlings and planted nearly two acres of potatoes. The pullets were growing now, too, and Frank and I moved them to the layer house we'd built with John B. and his sons. By early spring, a lone egg appeared, then two, three, and soon their nests were filing up. I'd outfitted another wagon, too, with sideboards that folded down on hinges, so I could access the eggs and cream and Christina's potato salad, and whatever else I was hauling, without having to climb up into the wagon each time. I drew a rough street map of Petaluma's downtown with the creek running through it, and the different businesses on both the east side and west side of the creek. I'd gathered a whole list of clients around town, as well, and with Christina's help, we figured out delivery routes and delivery schedules.

Time just shot by. By early summer, with the days growing longer, I was hitching Little Ike up to the delivery wagon three mornings a week before daylight and loading it with buckets of eggs, tins of whole cream, crocks of potato salad. We'd set out for town just as the sun broke behind us, and I'd have my list of deliveries and what each client ordered on a clipboard next to me on the driver's seat. It took some time working the kinks out—I'd miss a delivery and have to double-back, or I'd be short on an order and have to return the next day. Christina stayed at home, working over her stoves and helping Frank out in the garden until I returned, usually by mid-afternoon.

One afternoon after finishing deliveries, I was back at the ranch slipping the harness off of Little Ike. Christina walked into the barn and came up close. "There's something happening to me," she said and ran her hand across her stomach.

"Nothing bad, is it?" I asked her.

"No, but I skipped my bleeding," she said. "I think I'm pregnant."

The news caught me off-guard. We looked at each and smiled, and I hugged her. "Damn," I said, "I guess that's what happens."

I asked her to not work so hard, to take rests, and get off her feet, but Christina continued on as she'd always done. Further into her pregnancy, she tired more easily, and often I'd find her resting on our bed. I'd come in, sit by her side, stroke her swollen stomach, and ask how she was doing. "Okay, I guess," she said, rarely complaining, and when she did, her complaints were usually directed at me. I tried to be a good husband—to think and care for her—but it meant putting her concerns ahead of mine, and that was often a struggle for me. Why, you ask? Because it was the old habit—another hard one to break—of thinking of myself first. I had to admit it.

I stayed mostly true to what I'd promised her. Yes, I still drank—it was hard not to. Every other stop on my routes, someone was offering me a draft or a shot of whiskey "to get the day off right" and I'd bang one down, shoot the breeze for a few minutes before heading to the next stop. I had to turn a good number of them down, or I'd be flat on my back with a wagon still loaded down with eggs and Christina's potato salad. After awhile, Little Ike was learning the route almost as good as me. He knew the places to stop, where he got his hand-outs, and when the deliveries were close together, I didn't even have to get up in the driver's seat. I'd walk alongside the wagon, click my tongue, and Little Ike would move forward and when I said "whoa!" he'd stop. Sometimes my mind wandered, and I'd walk past a stopped wagon before realizing what I'd done. Ike would turn his head and look at me, and I'd look back at him and say, "You're right, old man, I missed it."

He made all sorts of friends along the way, too. Harvey Milstead, the bar keep at the Central Club, would bring Ike out a little pail of beer, and if there were patrons inside the bar, they'd all crowd the doorway and watch Ike slurp it up right there on Main Street, all of them laughing like hell. The cleaning girl, Margarite, at the Yosemite Hotel loved Ike, too, and she'd often sneak a carrot or two out of the kitchen and meet us on the street. Margarite was pretty, with long braided hair and dark eyes—she reminded me a lot of Della. She had one stiff leg and it caused her to rock from side to side when she walked. I'd once overheard a patron there say she was "simple" and that riled my blood some. She wasn't simple—not by any stretch—but people said things about other people they didn't even know—hurtful things—just to be saying something—mostly because the people they talked about were different from the rest.

At the end of each route, Ike and I would stop and gather up whatever items we needed back at the ranch before heading home. One day we'd picked up a baby crib, a chest of drawers painted white with pictures of rabbits on each drawer, and a high chair. Christina always met us at the bottom of the steps when we pulled into the yard. I'd hand her the cash box with receipts and she'd take them into the house and enter all the numbers in her ledger, while I led Ike over to the barn and slipped his harness off.

There was always work to do: I'd rinse out the cream tins and fill them with the cream Frank had separated. Then I'd take the skim milk and pour it into a big hopper and shake in bunches of kale leaves and mash it all together with a wooden plunger. I'd dip a bucket into the hopper and pour the slush into the chickens' troughs and they loved it. In the remaining daylight, I gathered eggs in buckets and carried them back to the feed room where the coons couldn't get at them. Christina would come out and sort the eggs according to their size, and with a piece of emery cloth, scratch off the scuffs on their shells. When my work was finished for the day, I entered the house through the backporch door, took my boots off by slipping each heel into a boot jack, washed up, and joined Christina in the kitchen. Frank usually followed me in shortly after. They said grace and I muttered along with them, we ate dinner—Christina was a fine cook—we talked a little business, what the day had brought, and then retire to the living room where I read the *Courier* until falling asleep in my favorite chair. Christina would tap me on the shoulder, I'd wake up and wander into the bedroom, wind the alarm clock and fall into bed. Seven hours later we'd get up and start the whole work day over again.

67

Irene and Staying True

· ·

With the pregnancy, Christina was finding it harder and harder to sleep. She'd pace at night, and the following day be irritable, short-tempered, plagued with cramps. I was as anxious as her for it to end—and it did one February morning—the twenty-fifth, to be exact—two weeks earlier than her due date. I'd loaded the wagon the previous evening, and was about to leave for the day's deliveries, when she met me in the barn and told me her water had broke. I helped her up to the wagon's seat, ran back to the house and tore a blanket off the bed and was back down beside her in minutes. I kept Little Ike at a fast trot all the way to the General Hospital on Sixth Street. Christina moaned and held her big stomach the whole way, and I kept pleading with her, "Hold on, Christina! Hold on! We're almost there!" At the hospital, the nurse on duty took her right in while I sat outside in the waiting room and hoped and prayed—I think what I muttered to myself was a prayer—that everything would turn out all right.

An hour later—although it seemed more like weeks—the doctor came out and said, "Congratulation, you're the father of a new baby girl."

I was so glad and so relieved, I nearly pissed my pants. "And the baby and wife are doing okay?" I asked.

"They're doing fine," he said.

Christina and our new daughter—we named her Irene—remained in the hospital for several more days. After Christina and Irene were released from the hospital, they stayed in town with friends until Christina regained her strength. Christina went to Mass first thing every morning, taking the baby with her, praying, lighting votive candles, and thanking God for her baby daughter. I stayed on the ranch, working, doing the daily chores with Frank, before driving into town with a loaded wagon to first check on Irene and Christina and then afterwards make my deliveries.

After two weeks, Christina and Irene arrived back home, but once they did, the little girl required almost constant attention. She was weak and she cried and when she stopped crying she just looked up at the ceiling with those watery eyes. Christina took her in her arms and gently patted Irene's back and for a time that seemed to calm her, but it never lasted. Soon another crying bout would start, and I couldn't stand listening to it and I'd head outside and finish whatever work I'd started. "That's right," Christina would say, "You go off and let me deal with her," and I'd look at Christina and say, "What do you want me to do, for crissakes?"

Christina had prepared the baby's room back home weeks before. It was furnished with a crib, and Gertie and Christina's cousins had given her a baby shower a couple of months earlier with all kinds of gifts: a little wooden table with two chairs, a playpen, baby blankets, baby clothes, cups, dishes, little spoons, rattles, stacks of cotton diapers, packages of pins, even little pairs of shoes in soft white leather.

"You're disappointed it's not a boy, aren't you?" Christina asked me one morning.

"No, not at all," I said. "I just wanted the two of you to be healthy."

"You're sure?"

"Of course, I am," I said.

And so I became a father. There wasn't much for me to do in those early weeks and months—Christina did most of the work—nursing, changing diapers, waking up often two or three times during the night when little Irene began crying. I'd hold her in my arms and rock her back and forth and she'd look back at me with those startled eyes and I wished for all the world she could grow to love and accept me. Sometimes her tiny fingers toyed with the ends of my moustache. She'd grow restless with me, though, would start to cry and want her mother. I'd hand her back, feeling a bit helpless. "I don't think she likes me," I said.

"That's all in your head, Bert," she said.

"I don't think it is."

"Give her time, for lord's sake."

"I'm giving her time," I said.

"Then give her more."

I bought a box of cigars and passed them out to my clients along the different routes. "It's a girl," I announced and they said congratulations and patted me on the back and told me how my life was going to be different from now on with a little one around the house.

"That calls for a drink!" the different bartenders said, and I couldn't turn them down. "Just one," I said, but after a dozen stops, my head got light, my legs unsteady, and I found a shade tree, pulled off, crawled into the back of the wagon and lay down. I thought of what folks had told me earlier about my life being different now with little Irene, and I wondered how different. I had already had a taste of the sleepless nights with her crying and Christina's short temper.

A day or two later, I saw Mickey Palocchi, manager at the Excelsior, and he asked me, "Was that your wagon I saw under that sycamore out East Washington Street?" I nodded my head, a bit embarrassed. "Sleeping on the job, huh?" He looked at me and smiled.

"Mickey," I said, "the little one keeps me up at night—keeps both of us up."

"Get used to it," Mickey said.

Pretty soon it got around town that Bert Miller slept on the job and that it was his horse doing all the work. I had to thank Mickey for that one.

I'd come home some days after I'd stopped for an earlier nip, and Christina could smell the alcohol on my breath ten feet away. She didn't say anything—she didn't have to—the look she gave me said it all. "I'm not breaking any agreement between us, all right?" I said. "You told me I could drink but not get falling-down-in-the-street drunk, not be an embarrassment, and I'm not. And I'm not beating on you, either—I'd never do that."

"Why do you have to drink at all?" she'd ask. "You're a father now—"

"And fathers don't drink? That's bullshit," I said. "You falling in with that temperance bunch now?"

"Never mind—you can't leave it alone, can you? Admit it!"

"If I had to, I could."

"I don't think you can," she said.

Times were tense between us. Little Irene's crying and waking up in the middle of the night made both of us irritable and we'd look for ways to take it out on each other—sometimes little, stupid ways—a harsh comment when it wasn't needed—stuff like that. My drinking was always a sore spot with her, and now she went at me harder than ever.

"You wanna bet on it?" I said. No sooner had the words slipped out that I regretted opening my mouth.

"Sure," she said. "For everyday you don't drink, I won't harp on you. How about we start with a week? And if you stretch it out even longer, I'll up the bet."

"A week?" I said. "And you won't harp on me anymore?"

"That's right, seven days—nothing—no beer, no whiskey." She looked at me and held her hand out. "You want to shake on that?"

I thought about it. Seven days didn't seem that long. It'd test my resolve, too—see if there was any willpower left inside. And it might even win me back Christina's good graces because those graces were slipping away between us—I could feel it and I think she could too. Her warmness—the little bit she could muster at times, wasn't there like before, and those beautiful eyes of hers—the color of robin's eggs—well, they weren't warm like before. In fact, they'd turned hard as a north wind. It was gradual, this coldness, but I felt it happening. "All right," I said, and we shook hands. "Seven days—no hootch."

"Today's Monday," she said. "One week from today and no drinking, I won't harp on you, okay?"

"Until I drink again?" I asked.

"We'll have to see about that," she said. "Is it a deal or not?"

"All right," I said. "I'll give it a shot.

The first day, Tuesday, went all right. I felt calm enough, even a little cocky. I'd walk into taverns and restaurants on my route and they'd have a glass of beer waiting for me on the bar, or an empty shot glass with my name on it, and I'd push the glass back to them, and say, "I can't drink it—made a bet with my wife." And they'd ask for how long, and I'd tell them seven days. They'd shake their heads like I had some terminal disease, then wish me luck.

The second day, it got a little stiffer. I was proud, confident, even, that I gotten through the first, thinking that might be the hardest, but it wasn't the case at all because on the second day, my thirst, my craving came calling—not so much a shout but a loud tone of voice to let me know it was in the room. I'd see that glass of beer waiting for me on the bar, and I'd look away and tell the keep the bet I'd made and that I had to honor it, and he'd pull it back and say, "Let me get you a sarsasparilla instead." I'd drink the sarasparilla, pretending it was a fine bourbon, but you can't sneak sunrise past a good rooster. I wasn't fooling anyone except myself. I felt a little twitching on this day, as well—a little trembling in the hands—and wasn't counting on that happening so soon, but it did. That voice inside—calling my name—well, it got a little louder.

I arrived home, handed the cash box to Christina and she'd look me right in the eye, come up close, first to smell my breath, before planting a sympathetic kiss on my cheek. "How are you doing with this, Bert?" she asked.

"So far, so good," I told her but that was only partially true. It was just the second day, and the twitching started up again late in the morning, especially when I went to write something down, and the numbers or letters started to wander away from me. Along with the twitching came the nerves. So every time the urge hit, I'd drink a glass of water and take some deep breaths and think of what it'd be like with Christina not harping on me like she done. I drank so much water, it felt like all my innards was washing away. I'd piss sometimes for five minutes, too. Was I feeling any better? Was my mind any clearer? That's what Christina said would happen once I got the alcohol out of my system but truth was I felt worse. I had headaches like a splitting maul was finding its way through my skull, and I already told you about the trembling. I regretted the bet I made—thought more than once about saying, 'Fuck it,' I'm taking a drink—but I held true and didn't.

The third and fourth days were bad—pure outright torture. I'd avoid even walking through the bar or restaurant on some of my stops, just making deliveries through the back door and sometimes not even going inside but handing the eggs or cream to the receiving clerk while staying out in the alley. "You okay, Bert?" they'd ask. "You got something contagious? Is that it?"

"Just a case of bottle fever," I told them.

The fifth day was a day of staying at the ranch, no deliveries—catching up on all the work. I thought that might be easier without all the temptations the town's establishments offered, but it was just as bad there because I'd stashed a bottle or two of whiskey in the barn and I knew exactly where they were. If I got anywhere near them, they seemed to be calling out to me, "Bert! Is that you, Bert? How come you don't stop by anymore for a little taste?" No soft voice this time—it was almost shouting at me.

Frank saw the state I was in and he asked if there was anything he could do to help, and I said, "Maybe get a gun, Frank, take me behind the barn and shoot me."

He was unsure of what I said, and I repeated it, and he looked back at me with those same colored eyes as his sister's, not knowing how to react. Then we'd both grab hoes and head to the cabbage patch, and scrape away the milk weed and curly dock trying to crowd the kale and cabbage out. The work, the feel of the hoe in my hands, took my mind off what was in the barn—but not for long. And, if work with the hoe didn't do it, Frank and I would head out to the fields with scythes and cut grass. Frank was a master at it. I watched him as he brought the scythe back and swept it low through the tall grass, leaving the remaining stubble at an even height. When I brought the scythe down, the stubble was tall where the scythe first struck the grass but short where I finished the stroke. Frank looked at me and laughed.

"Frank, your sister says I drink too much." I wiped the sweat off my face and looked over at Frank. "What do you think?"

"Well, do you?" he asked. "And how much is too much?"

"Good question," I said. "If it doesn't interfere with a day's work it should be perfectly fine—that's my opinion. Don't you think?"

"But not hers?"

I shook my head. "Frank, you ever had any habits you tried to shake?"

He leaned on his scythe and thought awhile. "I can't think of none."

"Really? No bad habits ever?"

"Well," and he got a little embarrassed here. "I used to stroke the chicken's neck."

"That's not a bad habit—that's just keeping you ready," I said. "Warming you up," and I laughed, but Frank just leaned on his scythe and looked at me with a sober expression. Maybe he understood me, maybe he didn't. With Frank I never knew. "How about drinking?" I asked him. "Ever struggle with that one?

"I got so sick once from drinking too much," he said. "Neighbors saw me bent over, puking, and they told my father and he shows up, leans over to look at me and says, 'If you feel something like a ball of hair in your throat, just swallow hard because it's your asshole coming up.'"

"And you haven't touched it since?" I asked him.

"I didn't say that—I just don't drink as much."

"Smart man," I said. "Smarter than me."

We cut more grass and the sweat poured out of me. We'd taken a glass jug of water with us wrapped in burlap and we passed it back and forth. He saw how my hands trembled, but didn't say anything. The wind had whipped up and moved through the tall grass, and I stopped a minute to watch it—wishing I was the wind or the moving grass—and not the person I was this moment, shaking from something I needed but shouldn't have. From where Frank and I stood, we could look down on the roofs of the house and barns, and for a few seconds, I set aside feeling sorry for myself and thought how lucky I was despite all the shakes and tremblings. I felt a gush of pride run through me that Christina and I were able to buy this place and that we now had a baby daughter and dreams about the future.

"What ever happened with you and Esther's friend?" I asked.

"Why you want to know?" Frank looked over at me from the corner of his eye.

"Just curious, that's all," I said.

"I don't understand women," he said. "And what I don't understand, I don't like to talk about." He took a file out of the back pocket of his overalls and ran it across the scythe's blade.

"But if you ask questions maybe it's less you don't understand." That seemed a reasonable thing to say.

"What would I ask questions about?" he asked.

"I don't know—maybe why the two of you aren't together."

"I don't need to know why—it's just something else to think about," he said. "And it wouldn't change nothing if I knew."

"Fair enough," I said. It seemed clear that Frank didn't want to discuss it any further, but it only made me more curious just the same. "Maybe someone else will come along," I said. "Look at your brother— Esther's made him a city boy. Did you ever think that would happen?"

"I like it right where I'm at," he said. "No city for me."

"Frank, I'm glad you do."

Frank and I slung our scythes over our shoulders and walked back home for lunch. We both washed up in the backporch sink. From inside the kitchen, I could smell schnitzel, one of my favorites. Baby Irene was in her playpen, on her hands and knees, still not walking. I leaned over the side of the playpen and picked her up and held her in front of me. She looked at me the way she always looked at me—uncertain, it seemed—of who I was, and I wondered how long it would take before I stopped being a stranger to her. Christina had told me to be patient. I sat down as Christina placed a platter of schnitzel surrounded with fried potatoes on the table. She looked at me. "How you doing, Bert?" her eyes searching all across my face.

"Day five and holding true," I held up my right hand and it was twitching.

"Good for you! You'll make it, I'm sure," she said.

I wasn't so sure.

We ate lunch, and I thought how a glass of red wine would taste so good with the schnitzel. But I thought how everything would be better with a drink and without one, I always felt something missing—like when you lose a tooth and your tongue keeps returning to that new space and it just won't leave it alone. If I was cutting grass, I thought of a tall glass of beer; if I was separating milk, it reminded me of a shot of whiskey. Putting the harness on my big horses or the harness on Ike, I thought how good a drink would taste, and how bourbon was same color as the leather harness. And always, always, I thought of that bottle of whiskey over in the barn, waiting so patient for me like a true friend. Every time I got near, it called out, "Hey, Bert Miller! How come you don't ever stop and talk to me anymore? What'd I ever do to you but bring you good times? And make the bad times not so bad? Huh? I want to know why."

Christina saw the changes I was going through, and I hoped she'd just feel sorry for me and call the whole wager off—but she didn't. She'd put her hand on top of mine at the dinner table and look at me, and I couldn't look back at her very long because I hated pity—more than anything I didn't want anyone feeling sorry for me. I'd rather die first.

On the sixth day, I was in piss-poor shape. My whole body shook and my legs felt unsteady. I had just one more day to go, too, but that one day by now seemed like years off and I felt my willpower crumbling away. I got through the route okay although my clients said I had no color to my face, and they were worried about me. I told them, "No problem, in two days I'll be good as new." When we finished the route, Little Ike and I headed south on Lakeville Road back to the ranch, and I would have made it fine except when we passed the East Side Tavern, I saw Bib Romalli standing outside, smoking a cigarette. He motioned me over. I pulled

Ike in front of the tavern and stepped down to shake Bib's hand. He looked at me and said, "You look like you need a drink."

"Truth is, Bib, I do."

"Let me buy you one then," he said.

"Can't—I made a bet with the wife."

"How about a cigarette then?" he said.

Sure, I'll take one of those." Except when I smoked a cigarette, it didn't feel the same without a whiskey to keep it company. "Goddamn it, Bib, I'm in bad shape."

"How about just one drink?" Bib said. "And if she says anything, just make the bet again—but for not as long."

"She'll be disappointed," I said.

"Then just get up in that wagon seat and head home—"

"I want a drink so bad—"

"I'm going back inside—you go home!" he said.

I walked toward my wagon and had one hand up on the seat before I heard voices, little tempting voices, and I turned around, walked back to the tavern and went inside. The little voices kept it up. I took an empty stool next to Bib, and John, the barkeep, asked what I was drinking, and I thought about it a few seconds. "Bourbon," I said. "Give me a shot of bourbon, goddamn it!"

He poured me one and I took it all in one swallow, and—oh, sweet Jesus! It was like what those snake oil salesmen promised how you'd feel—like wading into a warm pool where the warmth surrounds your joints like sheets of velvet, and everything for a time stops aching—like everything inside you moves like melted butter. So I did what any normal man would do—I ordered another. It tasted better than the first one. I was up to my neck in that warm water and the world felt just fine then. Bib looked at me. "You don't tell your wife it was all my fault, okay?"

"I won't say anything, Bib."

I don't remember how many I drank—I lost count. But each one went down smoother and easier than the one before it, and all the time I remember just talking away—holding court right there at the Eastside—banging my fist on the bar for another drink, and folks laughing at my stories about how it was being a new father and a wife crankier than hell—I was in my element. I remember Mario, one of the owners, saying, "Bert, go home," and I remember leaning on someone's shoulder walking out the tavern door and someone helping me into the wagon and the next thing I'm flat on my back and the wagon's rolling ahead with all the shakes and bumps in the road vibrating me to sleep. It felt like I was still in that pool of warm water, never wanting to leave it, letting it bask all over me. But it didn't last long.

Pretty soon someone's shaking me awake. I look up and I'm staring right into Christina's face, and when it comes into clearer focus, it's the kind of face no husband wants to see—no other way to describe it. If disappointment had a face, it'd been Christina's at that very moment. I got up on my elbows and looked around and, damn, if I wasn't back at the ranch. "How I'd get here?" I asked her.

"That fool horse of yours took you home," she said. "It's pretty bad when a horse has more sense than its owner."

"Really? Ike took me home? By himself?"

"You're a fool, Arnold Bert Miller, but you already knew that, didn't you?"

"I had just one day to go, too," I said.

"You couldn't stick it out, huh?" she asked. "Not for me so much but for Irene."

"Irene? It doesn't matter what I do—drunk or sober—that little girl doesn't like me."

"Now that's just the alcohol talking there," she said.

I rubbed my eyes, tried to clear my head. "It's not just the alcohol talking—she doesn't take to me."

"Maybe if you spent as much time with her as you did with your damn horses and your friends in the bars, she might treat you differently."

"I try with her."

"You don't try hard enough," she said. "No sense in arguing with a guy that's been drinking." She stood up, lowered herself down to the barn floor and walked back to the house. I lay there on my back looking up toward the barn rafters, feeling as bad as I've ever felt. Bad because my body was sick and bad because I'd disappointed Christina again. I could disappoint myself—I did that all the time—but disappointing other folks, especially your wife—well, that one crawls inside you and festers.

I pulled myself over to the edge of the wagon, dropped down onto the barn floor and walked up to Little Ike and thanked him. "I think you got some of my old man in you," I told him. "How you look out for me, and I want you to know I appreciate it." I dropped his harness and loosened his halter and he walked into his stall. I closed the stall door behind him and thought to myself, it's a shame when you got more in common with a horse than you do with your own daughter. How the hell did that happen, I wondered?

I tossed hay to all three horses, walked outside and stared up at the sky. It was clear and dark and dotted with stars. I didn't want to go right back to the house just yet—didn't want to face that cool anger of Christina's, so I unloaded the wagon, rinsed out the cream tins. When I finished, I looked up at the house and it was dark inside. I took my boots off in the backporch and walked quietly to the bedroom, stripped out of my clothes, and lay down on my side of the bed. No hand reached out to me and at first, I didn't reach out for her, but then I gently laid my arm across her back and whispered, "I'm sorry." But there was no response. I'd have to win back her trust—have to do something for the long haul—but right then I didn't know what it was. One thing, though, I had to change my ways and somehow figure out how to do it. I'd tried enough times and knew it wouldn't be easy—nothing in this life was when you had to give up the things you liked.

68

Pulling Back the Reins
and a New Addition

· · · · · · · · · · · · · · · · · ·

There's nothing like a guilty conscience to force you to reform your ways—or at least, force you to think about changing them. I learned that when I was a young boy caught pocketing a chocolate at Frau Himmel's store back in Obwalden. She gave me a good talking-to, then she told my folks, and my old man's answer was a good rapping across my knuckles with his meter stick. I never took another chocolate from the Frau. I wish it was that simple now—that I learned my lesson about drinking and how it upset Christina—and I wouldn't drink anymore, but I wasn't betting the ranch on that happening. I was in the throes of something, and couldn't deny it away, but that didn't stop me from adding a dash of reasoning to it. After all, I hadn't killed anyone—hadn't committed any crime. I fell off the wagon, so to speak, and lost a wager—big deal. It happened to folks all the time. The world didn't end. I realized, though, it was more than just losing a wager. I only had to look at Christina's face the following days, feel her coldness toward me and her disappointment, to know I'd damaged the trust between us.

A few days later, when we'd said maybe ten words between us this whole time, she looked at me and asked, "Why don't you go see Father O'Malley?"

"About what?" I wondered.

"About your drinking," she said.

"What's he going to do?"

"Maybe the two of you could pray together?"

"Pray together?" I laughed at that one. "I told you years ago I don't pray. Praying is only asking for something—begging— and I don't beg." I was picturing the two of us—me and Father

O'Malley—kneeling somewhere, looking up at the ceiling and praying—it was like we were talking to ourselves.

"Maybe you should start then," she said.

"Go see Father O'Malley about my drinking?" I repeated her words and laughed. "He pours it down himself. What are we going to pray for? Two glasses instead of one?"

"You have no spiritual life, Bert Miller—that's your problem," she said.

"You mean because I don't go to church?"

"Yes, that's part of it."

"No, I think with you, it's *all* of it," I said. "If you're not at church every Sunday, standing and kneeling and listening to a priest saying words that none of you understand—well, then you have no spiritual life. I don't buy it—and you got your God all dressed up in those white robes looking down at us—telling us what we can and can't do, taking credit for all that's good in the world, and passing the buck on what isn't." I thought of conversations I'd had with Tino about this very subject, and how he saw spirit in everything around us—the trees, the animals—even the rocks, and he never once set foot inside a church.

Christina looked at me with part shock, part disbelief—an equal amount of pity, and hell—let's toss in a bit of disgust, too.

"I've never changed from the person you knew when we first met," I said. "You're just getting to know me better, getting to know all my flaws and the things inside me—just like I'm getting to know all yours. What we got to do is figure out a way to live with them so we're not going to war all the time. Besides, I told you right-off, I wasn't perfect—"

"You don't have to be perfect," she said. "Just don't drink"

"I can't make you that promise—you see what happened when I did."

"I hate seeing you drunk—"

"When you seen me drunk?"

"Plenty of times—with your cousins, at funerals, weddings —plenty of times. You don't even remember, do you?"

"I'm just enjoying myself," I said. "No harm in that."

"You talk loud—you say stupid things to make people laugh, and then when you're sobering up, you're on edge and you got that look on your face—a look that sometimes scares me."

"I told you I'd never hit you, never threaten you, never do anything like that and I'm holding true—-isn't that right? Huh, isn't that right?" I looked at her. "I'm not like some others."

"I know you're not," she said.

"I went six days without, and look what happened—that kind of schedule doesn't work with me," I said. "I need a little taste almost every day so that whole idea of drinking doesn't get so big in my head that it's all I think about. Every day without and that thirst just grows and that idea inside my head grows along with it—I don't know how else to describe it."

"Sounds like something you got no control over," she said.

"It's like a stud bull—you feed it, but you don't jump over the rails trying to make it your friend. He'll stomp you right into the ground if you do. No, you each live your lives on opposite sides of the fence. You make some kind of peace." I looked at Christina. "I think that's what we need to do, don't you think? Make some kind of peace?"

She nodded her head.

"I'll pull the reins back on the drinking," I said, "but I'm not giving it up entirely. We can wager how many days I can go without, but the day comes when I'm walking back to it."

Little Irene began stirring in her crib and Christina left to tend to her. She returned, her blouse lifted up and Irene's head hidden under it, nursing. I stroked the little girl's feet. "I wish she wouldn't flinch from me the way she does," I said. "And I know you keep saying, 'give her time' but I'm being patient—I want you to know I'm being patient with her."

"That's all you can do with children," she said, "Is be patient with them."

"Christina, I want you to know that I'm sorry for the grief I cause you—I don't do it on purpose."

"I know you don't."

"And I'll try not to drink as much—it might take some doing, but I'll try—that's all I can do."

I held true for the next several months, turning down drinks at most of my stops on the routes, and when I did drink, I limited it to one strong one so it wouldn't stay on my mind. Things began healing, too, between Christina and me. We still had our differences—they weren't going entirely away—but we could talk to one another civil again and with all the work around the ranch to do, it wasn't like we had time to dig up old grievances. Frank was milking twelve cows now, and John B. brought down a couple of his Angora goats—a ram and a ewe—and in no time we had a small herd of goats that kept the grass down. Frank even milked the does after we found a market for their milk in town. During late spring and into the fall, our leghorns produced plenty of eggs.

With the egg surplus, we took small barrels that opened on either end and laid rice hulls in the bottom and placed eggs in layers separated by more rice hulls and then stowed the barrels away in the coolest corners of the barn we could find. Then when winter came, and egg production slowed, we'd take out those barrels, turn them upside down, and picked out the oldest eggs first for our customers.

Irene was walking now, growing like a weed, learning her first words, but she still looked at me with those uncertain eyes, like she was seeing me for the first time and trying to figure out who I was. I talked to her and coo-coo'd her and held her and did all the things I thought fathers done with their daughters to show their love, but Irene was a hard nut to crack. She'd cry and carry on when I was around, and Christina would have to hold her to quiet her back down. It hurt me because I didn't know what I'd done to cause her to feel this way.

Still, I tried to follow Christina's advice and just be patient with the little girl and not take so much of it personal. By now, too, my sister Josephine had a young one of her own, and I'd tell her about Irene, and Josephine would offer me advice, as well—things to do and things not to do. Gertie and John B. had lost two children at birth but since then had four that had grown up healthy, and I was happy for them. John B. told me pretty much the same thing Christina had said—be patient and love them without conditions.

All of us just kept working at the ranch—Frank doing the milking and outside work, Christina gathering and polishing eggs, making her potato salad, and shredding cabbage for her sauerkraut, cooking and keeping house while I'd load up the wagon three times a week with eggs, cream, potato salad and make the rounds in town. Our list of clients grew. Christina would line up all the buckets of eggs in the order they'd be delivered, label each bucket, and ask for the cash box as soon as I arrived back home. She'd add up the receipts, asked if I'd spent any money on drinks, and write down that amount in a separate margin. Our entire lives seemed contained in that ledger book—columns of how and when I took money in, and more columns of where and when I spent it. In the middle of all this, Christina told me she'd missed a period, and thought she might be pregnant again, and when she started turning irritable and complaining of cramps, we knew for certain. She kept up her regular schedule of work, even though I'd asked her to do less, and I suggested hiring another hand to deal with the chickens, but she insisted she could handle the work load.

During the summers, John B. came down to Lakeville to help harvest hay. He'd stay for two to three days with his two youngest sons, and leave his oldest, Friedolin, to help Gertie back at the Mark West place. After working all day, the two of us drank on the front porch and watched the sun set behind the western hills. He talked about losing his two children, and how grateful he was to have his healthy ones. He brought me a little terrier pup, too, and we named it Jigs. He said its mother was from a line of good ratters, and I told him I remembered the terrier he owned from years earlier and how it scratched at the feed room door waiting that split second for it to open, before bolting in and chasing down a rat, clamping hard onto its neck, shaking it until the neck broke. We talked and we drank the night before John B. was to drive back to

Santa Rosa. While I played with Jigs, Christina came out holding her stomach. "I think it's time," she said.

I ran out to the barn, led Ike to the front of the carriage and harnessed him up, drove the carriage to the foot of the steps and Christina and Irene climbed in with John B. in the back seat with his boys, holding Jigs, the terrier. I kept Ike at a fast pace all the way to town and right up to the front of the hospital. Christina moaned. "Hang on, Christina, we're almost there," I said.

A nurse met us at the door and lowered Christina into a wheel chair and whisked her off to the maternity ward. Irene, John B., his boys and I sat in the waiting room, and when Irene started to fidget and cry, I handed her Jigs and that quieted her. "Just a few minutes more, Irene," I said. "Then you can see mommy."

Sometime around midnight, the doctor came out and announced I was the father of a healthy baby boy. John B. shook my hand and said, "Congratulations, old man!" I nearly cried from the news. By now, Irene was asleep across the seats of two chairs we'd slid together in the waiting room. Jigs was asleep right next to her. I had a son—it took awhile to sink in. I had a son! I kept repeating it to myself.

69

Irv, Irene and Time Passing

· ·

We named our boy Irv—Irving Earnest Miller in full. I was proud of him from the start, proud of Christina, too, for bringing him into this world, and I couldn't wait for him to grow up, too, because I thought of all the things we could do together, things I could teach him that I couldn't teach a daughter—how to hunt and fish, how to build things and drive horses, run a ranch, but mostly I wanted him to be a good person, to be thoughtful of others. I didn't want him to be any trouble, not be difficult the way I was growing up, testing my old man all the time and pushing against boundaries; but I wanted him to have a mind of his own, as well—but maybe you couldn't have all these things together in one person—I didn't know. He'd grow up the way he chose and I'd try to be an example and rein him back in if I saw him leaving the road, but beyond that, there wasn't much I could do. I remembered how I grew up—how I hated rules and folks telling me to do things a certain way and not the way I wanted.

I passed out cigars to my clients like I done when little Irene was born. Everyone congratulated me and set drinks on the bar and I couldn't refuse them. After several stops, I felt a good buzz, and decided that was enough drinking for the day. Everything had been mostly peaceful between Christina and me—no arriving home with a big heat on for a long time—and I wanted to keep it that way—especially now with two children in the house. I never liked the arguing, the jawing back-and-forth—it upset me as much as it upset Christina, and I figured since I was usually the cause of it, I could try and change my habits some. So, that's what I set about doing.

The ranch was going along okay. We sold everything we produced—prices weren't great but we weren't starving, either. Every day, one day after another, when I wasn't making deliveries, I got up, dressed, worked a spell, then ate breakfast and set out working until lunch time. After lunch, I napped and forty- five minutes later was back at it until the day ended, went to bed and started another day of work all over again. In between, there was family gatherings, weddings, funerals, baptisms—all the things that happen in people's lives.

One by one those days rolled into weeks and the weeks into months, the months into years. You tear a page off the calendar until it runs out of pages and then you tack a new calendar on the wall and start tearing pages off that one. It never stops. Earlier there'd been an earthquake in San Francisco and a good part of the city burned down. It'd struck Santa Rosa, too, and the courthouse where the trial was held and that John B. and me admired so much, was now a big pile of rubble, its dome squatting on the ruins like a big stone mother hen.

By now, little Irene started first grade at Bliss School up near the old adobe, and Irv was already walking and mumbling his first words. I'd rigged up a little box with holes punched through it for his legs and set it alongside me, and tied the box down so it wouldn't wander off the seat. On some of the shorter days, I took him with me, carried him into the different stops to show him off. He'd walk right along the top of the bars like he was onstage. "He's got his mother's eyes," Jess Dye would say. August Grossmuller said he was the finest young boy he'd ever seen. I'd hear compliments like that and felt so proud and when I walked out of those places, it felt like I was walking on a blanket of air.

About this time, the first automobiles started showing up around town. They were noisy things and they scared the horses, but folks said they were the future. There were early trucks, too, and I'd see them lined up at the creameries and feed mills along with the horses and wagons. Every year it was more trucks and more automobiles. "They're going to leave you and your horses behind, Irv," Christina would say.

"You can't talk to any automobile, though," I told her. "They don't listen—and they have no feelings, either."

"No, they don't," she said. "But they don't need them."

"They're temperamental, too—and they smell to high heavens," I said.

"Worse than horse manure?" she asked.

"Worse than horse manure—a lot worse," I said.

Christina was feeling her independence more and more—a lot of women were these days—and without asking me, she bought a horse and carriage of her own. She drove it into the yard one day and I looked it over, and asked her, "Whose is this?" I asked her.

"It's mine," she said. "I just bought it."

The horse had good bones and the carriage was light on wear.

"How much you pay for it?" I asked.

"A fair price—and with my own money," she said. Christina was a stickler about money—almost from the very start—even before we were married. I already told you about how she collected the cash box at the end of each day and counted it all out, and if it didn't match what we'd loaded into the wagon the day before, she'd want an accounting—if I'd spent it on drinks, spent money on any-thing—she wanted to know. You couldn't slip anything past her if you tried. She'd write it all down, every little thing. When the pile of money got big enough back home, she'd ask me to take her to the bank.

Now with her own horse and carriage, she didn't have to rely on me so much. She'd take Irene and Irv to school in her own rig. Molly and Dolly scared her with their size, and she didn't much care for Ike. "I know this is going to sound silly, but he breaks wind whenever I'm around him," she said.

I had to laugh about that one and so did most of the guys on my routes when I told them.

I didn't mind, though—it was one more horse, and they all seemed to get along. Besides, it was less I had to use Ike. He was still in good shape but he was getting long in the tooth—pushing twenty years by now.

A chill still remained between Irene and me—things just never seemed to thaw between us. Christina thought it was all those times

I stared into Irene's face smelling of bourbon and stale cigars, but I said there was plenty of times I didn't smell of either and she still treated me the same way. I tried talking with her and telling her I wanted to be her friend and for her to trust me, but I don't know how much of that talking sank in with her. She had a mind of her own, and it didn't seem like it was going to change it any time soon.

With Irv, I vowed it'd be different. My feeling was that fathers and sons could talk more easily with each other than daughters and fathers, but plenty of men I knew with daughters said that wasn't true. You had to listen to them, they said, boy or girl. Irv started talking before he could walk, and within a couple of years the little guy could keep up a steady stream of conversation. He was always asking questions and wondering why things were the way they were, and some of those questions I had a devil of a time answering.

We were riding into town one morning and he looked at me and asked, "Is Ike going to die someday?"

"He is," I said. "Everything has to die."

"And Jigs here—he's going to die, too."

"All of us—Jigs and Ike and Molly and Dolly—everything, everyone," I said.

"Why is that?"

"Because we all wear out," I said. "Everything, every person, starts out young and strong—-usually—if we're lucky—and then we grow old and eventually we die. Ike there, he's losing a step or two as he gets older—so am I."

"So you and Ma are going to die someday, too?"

"That's right—we're going to die, but not for a long time yet."

"I don't want you to die—I don't want Ma dying either," he said.

"Well, we don't have much choice in the matter—I wish we did, but we don't." I looked over at him. "Let's not talk about dying now, okay?"

We'd drive along with Jigs between us, and little Irv always looking around him, his eyes wide with curiosity, asking questions and just chattering away. Sometimes he'd say something, and I'd look at him in disbelief that a guy so little could think up something like that. He looked forward to starting school, too. He'd watched his sister do her lessons, and she gave him a pencil and taught him to print his own name, and pretty soon he was scrawling all the letters of the alphabet across sheets of paper and writing out his full name and all our names, too.

When I came in from chores one evening, Christina had tacked several sheets of his work up on the kitchen wall. "Look what I taught Irv," Irene would say and I'd never hesitate to thank her.

One morning, Irv and I were driving into town to start the day's route when we passed an automobile stalled alongside Lakeville Road. I brought Ike to a halt. "Need some help?" I asked its driver.

"I guess it ran out of fuel," the man said. The automobile's front lid was open and he leaned over into the motor department. "It just stopped on me."

Irv climbed down from the wagon and began looking over every inch of that automobile. It fascinated him. When I looked up, Irv was sitting in the driver's seat, cranking the steering wheel back and forth. "Irv!" I shouted. "Get down from there!"

"That's all right," the man said. "It doesn't look like it's going anywhere."

"I could give you a tow if you wanted," I said.

"Thanks, anyway. My mechanic's not far from here," the man said.

"Sorry I can't help you then," I said. Irv climbed back in the wagon and we drove on into town.

"Will we ever have an automobile like that?" Irv asked.

"I don't know—I suppose. But right now horses are fine."

"An automobile won't die, though, will it?"

"No, it won't die the way a horse does, but I'm guessing it'll wear out just the same as dying," I said.

"Why did they make automobiles when we already had horses?" he asked.

"Because the world's speeding up," I told him. "Everything's going faster."

"Why is it speeding up?"

"That's a good question, son. I guess because folks want things faster, and want to get from one place to the next quicker—like I said, everything is moving faster and folks don't want to get left behind."

"But there's trains for that—"

"Yeah, but trains aren't enough," I said. "Like what we're riding in now with Ike there pulling us—people want the same thing but they want to go faster and with a horse you can only go so fast—and for folks now, that's not enough. Things are going mechanical."

"Mechanical?"

"Yeah, man-made—-steel and rubber and engines," I said. "Folks are saying in ten years we won't even need horses anymore to do the work."

"So, there wouldn't be anymore Ikes?" he asked.

"That's what they're saying."

"I don't think I'd like that," Irv said. "I always want some Ikes around."

"Me, too," I said.

Irv followed me into the different stops along the route. Sometimes I'd hand him a tin of cream to carry in or a small bucket of eggs. I loved showing him off, and folks gave him suckers and penny candy but he wouldn't eat them all at once; he'd pocket them, and even share some of it with his sister when we were back at the ranch. The boy had such a good heart to him, and I figured it must have come from his mother's side.

I'd had a couple of drinking bouts—once when little Irv was with me—and I got carried away, forgot about my limits and passed out in the back of the wagon; when I came-to we were back at the ranch. When Christina found me still sprawled out in the back of the wagon, she was hopping mad. I couldn't blame her. "I don't want you taking Irv with you anymore," she said.

"Nothing happened," I said. "Okay, I got a little drunk—"

"A little?"

"Yeah, a little drunk, but Ike knows the way home," I tried to explain.

"I don't want him going with you—"

"He likes riding along on the routes—"

"I don't care—I don't want him seeing you drinking."

"C'mon, Christina, be reasonable."

"I am being reasonable," she said. "He's not going with you."

The following morning, Irv climbed up on the wagon next to Jigs. "I can't take you with me today, son," I said.

He looked at me with a confused expression. "Why not?"

"Your mother says so, that's why."

"Because you went to sleep in back of the wagon?"

"Yeah, because I went to sleep."

"And I drove us home, didn't I?"

"You sure did—would have never made it home without you driving Ike," I said.

I drove out from the ranch yard, turned around, and Irv was watching us leave and he wore such a sad face, I wanted to jump off the wagon, grab him up and take him with us—but I didn't. "Irv, go back to the house," I said.

He turned and walked back up the steps, and Ike, Jigs, and I continued onto Lakeville Road, heading north into town. Already I was missing the boy, seeing his sad face in my mind as we drove along and wishing I didn't own the habits I did—or that Christina could be more reasonable. I guessed she was right though—no son wants to watch his father get tanked-up and carried off—but I always had an excuse for what I done. It never stopped me from apologizing and regretting whatever it was, but in the back of my mind there was always some reason. I knew if Ike was there, I was safe, that there was always a way home, regardless of my state. I remembered my conversation with Irv about automobiles and how they'd someday replace horses and I laughed out loud. "What kind of automobile out there could I fall into and take me home the way Ike does?" I asked myself. There wasn't any and never would be.

70

The Calm and the Storms

· ·

Our marriage, I figured, was like most marriages—periods of calm, and in between the calm, dark clouds that gathered before cutting loose. It was that way with Christina and me—like a cycle was set between us that neither of us could change. I figured there'd always be something about me she didn't like or wanted to improve—and there were things about her that chafed me, too. I never liked people telling me what was good for me and what wasn't. I could quit drinking entirely and she'd find something else that needed changing—why I wouldn't go to church with her, for example, or why I swore or kept the company I did. Like I said, there was always something. It got to the point that I completely gave up trying to improve myself—it was futile. I could be perfect, but in Christina's eyes, she'd find another flaw.

It must have been in one of those rare calm periods that our third child was conceived—Annetta—we called her Nanette for short. Like Irene, she came early, though, by nearly five weeks, but the doctor wasn't sure she'd survive. Christina stayed in town with friends nearly this whole time, going to Mass first thing in the morning, praying, lighting votive candles before driving to the hospital—just like she done when Irene was born—awaiting any word on little Nanette's condition. Irene and Irv stayed with me. By now they were both at Bliss School—and I dressed and fed them before dropping them off at school and then driving into town with a loaded wagon to check on Nanette and Christina. Afterwards, I'd make my deliveries and return in time to pick them up from classes.

Nanette survived those early weeks, but the doctors hesitated to say what her future health would be like. "She has some kind of blood disorder," one doctor told us, "so we really can't determine what her prognosis will be."

Christina took the news hard—I did, too—but we were both grateful the little girl had survived. Nanette stayed in the hospital for another two weeks before we could take her home, and once home, she required almost constant attention. She was weak and she cried, and when she stopped crying, she just looked up at the ceiling with those watery eyes. Christina took her in her arms and gently patted Nanette's back and for a time that seemed to calm her, but it never lasted. It was the whole pattern starting all over again like it'd done when Irene was born. Another crying bout would start and I couldn't stand listening to it and I'd head outside just to get away from it. "That's right," Christina would say, "You go off and let me deal with her," and I'd look at Christina and say what I'd said to her a dozen times before, "What do you want me to do, for crissakes?"

I'd suggested when Nanette grew a bit older of putting her in a sanitarium where she could receive the care she required, but Christina wouldn't hear about it. "We're not putting any child of mine in one of those places," she said.

Nanette's health and the attention she needed forced routines to change around the ranch. Christina spent less time preparing her potato salad, and I had to tell our customers for the time being, at least, we couldn't provide the amount of product they were used to receiving. Irv pitched in and fed the chickens, going out in the garden and breaking off kale leaves and hauling them back to a hopper and pouring in skim milk and mashing the whole mix up. He gathered eggs, too, and he'd sand off the dirt and scale them to size, and place them in wooden cartons. Joe Keebler, Gertie's father, brought us a couple of hogs earlier in the year, and Irv wheeled them out curdled milk and the stale bread I'd bring back from town. I taught him how to drive the big horses, and he took right to it. I'd watch him harness Molly and Dolly and saw how they towered over him—how he'd have to bring a step ladder out to reach the top buckles—his head barely meeting where their ribs were. I felt so good having a son like this.

Irene did her part, too. Her mother taught her to cook and keep house—she wasn't always eager to do the work, though, and she still looked at me with that hard glare. "Everyone here does their part," I'd tell her. "You're not any different."

"Why's mom never home?" she asked.

"Your sister's very sick and she needs your mother's care," I told her.

"I want to stay with mom in town," Irene said.

"Right now, you can't," I told her.

I got Irene and Irv off to school on the days their mother spent consulting with doctors on how to best care for Nanette. It was a strain on all of us, and I'd sometimes find that bottle in the barn, pull off its cork and take a big swallow—that's all—one big swallow, and I'd put the cork back in the bottle. Sweet Jesus, though, it felt good! That little bite at first, and then as it trickled down my throat, it was like warm honey the rest of the way.

In early summer, John B. came down with his three boys—like he'd done in past years—to help with harvesting hay, and in the evening after working all day, we'd sit on the front porch and drink whiskey and talk. He knew of little Nanette's condition right after she was born. Word about these kinds of things traveled fast between family.

"We lost the two right at birth or just after," he said. "They lived long enough for us to name them. I don't know if that makes it any easier than losing them later in life—it's all pretty painful."

"I wasn't ready for this," I said. "Christina wasn't either—but she's done better with it than me. I want to be pissed-off at something, somebody, but I don't know who or what. I guess if I believed more in God, I could be pissed-off at him."

"It don't do any good to be pissed-off," he said. "Just bear with it—it's all you can do."

"I thought this whole thing with Nanette might bring me and Christina closer together," I lowered my voice, "but it isn't working out that way." I took my feet off the porch railing and looked toward John B.

"Christina started tearing into me one day about the drinking," I said. "I thought I'd been doing pretty good up til then—keeping it all manageable—-then she started to say Nanette's condition might have been tied to it and that set us off arguing. I know by this time it was her nerves talking—mine were shot, too. And I said if the drinking had anything to do with it, wouldn't the doctors have said something? If it had something to do with it, then what about Irene and Irv? They're both healthy. And she said, no, the doctors don't tell us everything."

John B. looked at me. "I'm sorry to hear this, Bert. I hope it all gets worked out."

"I don't know what's going to happen," I said. "If I didn't have little Irv, I don't know what I'd do. That boy's been a blessing."

"Children are," John B. said.

We cut the oat hay out in the fields with Molly and Dolly pulling a mower, and once the oat grass dried out, Irv and I hitched the two horses up to a rake and built big stacks of loose hay into shocks and from the shocks we loaded it into the wagon with pitch forks and hauled it inside the barn. Irv was a good worker. "I don't ever want to go to school again," he said. "I want to do this kind of work instead."

"Your mother's gonna have something to say about that," I told him.

I kept a little skiff over at the wharf just a half mile from the ranch and once the hay was in, Irv and I and Jigs took our fishing poles and a basket with our tackle and bait, and paddled out into the creek, mindful of the tides. You didn't want to get caught having to paddle against them. "When I was just a little older than you," I told him, "my buddy Tino and me would set out and fish for bass and sometimes float almost to the bay for sturgeon. We'd sell some of what we caught to a Chinaman named Ho Tzu."

"Where's Tino now?" he asked.

"He's over in Sonoma—runs a livery there," I said. "We'd hunt together, too—ducks, deer, whatever was in season—no one could hunt or fish like that guy—he was part Indian and it was in his blood."

"How come I never met him?"

"Well, Irv, it's a bit of a long story," I said. "We had a disagreement."

"You're not friends anymore?" he asked.

"I hope we are—I really don't know."

"What happened between you two?"

"We both liked your mother—you're too young to know about those things yet," I said. "And that caused the split—he blamed me for butting-in on him."

"Is that what you done?"

"Yeah, that's what I done—didn't meant to—but I'm hoping we can patch it up someday," I said. "Maybe we"ll drive over to Sonoma, drop in on him and say hello. Would you like that?"

"I would," Irv said. "And maybe you can be friends again."

"I hope so."

Irv cast his line out and within a few minutes he had a bite. Jigs saw the play in the line tighten and leaned out over the skiff, barking, his stub tail working back and forth. When Irv reeled the fish in, Jigs lunged at it and I caught him or he'd gone right into the creek. "That's a crazy dog," Irv said.

"He's attracted to anything that moves," I said. "I guess it's bred into them."

Irv landed the little bass and Jigs was all over it, smelling it, barking. I finally put the fish in the creel. We were between tides and the boat just floated hardly moving upstream or downstream.

"Is Nanette going to be all right?" Irv asked.

"I hope so—she started off pretty sick but the doctors and your mother are doing all they can do."

"I don't ever want to be sick like that," Irv said.

"No, I don't want you that way either—that would break my heart all up."

71

Tino in Trouble

· · · · · · · · · · · · · · ·

I was delivering the usual three baskets of eggs to the Egg City Cafe on Main Street, when Fred Lazzini, the cook and owner there, told me about a shootout in Sonoma the day before. "Right near the plaza," he said. "Some stable-hand and a big shot from town shooting at each other like it was the wild west."

I immediately thought of Tino. "Names?" I asked him. "Did you get any names?"

"Barney Perkins, a salesman for Pioneer Hatchery, told me—he didn't mention any names—sorry," Fred said. "One's in the county jail in Santa Rosa—the other's in the Sonoma jail—I guess to keep them apart. Keep them locals away from the stable hand, too."

By mid-morning the news was all around town, and from each stop along my route, I learned more and more about what happened. Of course, when news like this spreads, you never know who to believe or what to believe. The stable-hand was in the county jail in Santa Rosa—I heard that enough times. He'd been treated for a gunshot wound to his shoulder—nothing serious—and the "big shot" as Fred Lazzini called him, I later learned was none other than Percy Sheers. He'd been shot, too, but was expected to recover. The rumors grew like they often do in towns like ours: they were fighting over gambling debts, fighting over a woman, a stolen horse—no one knew for certain—but that didn't keep people from making up their own reasons.

I stopped at the constable's office in Petaluma to see what was fact and what wasn't, and Sheriff Reese told me one suspect, the stable hand, was in custody at the county jail, and the other principal had been released after receiving medical treatment. I finished my route for the day and returned home. I told Christina the news. "Is Tino okay?" she asked.

"I don't know—I've heard all kinds of accounts but he's in the county jail and I need to see him. I'm going to Santa Rosa tomorrow," I said.

"It's that feud he's been having with Sheers, isn't it? It just never seems to end," and Christina shook her head.

"Sounds like it," I said. "I'd been telling him for years to forget about it and he just couldn't let it go—and it's his own father, too."

"You don't know that for sure," she said.

"You put two and two together and it all adds up," I said. Then I told Christina about my visit to Tino's mother and her reaction when I told her that Tino had bought a gun and how she denied any connection with Sheers. "Right-off, I knew she wasn't leveling with me," I told her. "I think Tino knew, too, all the time but made out like he didn't—I know for awhile he fooled me."

The following day was my shorter route—up and down Western Avenue and stops along Kentucky and Keller. I raced through them, hardly stopping to talk to my clients at all, just thinking of Tino the whole time and what I'd say to him. I'd emptied the wagon before noon and by three o'clock I was parked in front of the County Courthouse in Santa Rosa. It was a new courthouse now, rebuilt after the big earthquake, and not where the Sheers' trial took place, where John B. and me had run our hands along the polished marble and the dark wainscoting. I stepped down from the wagon, and looked at Jigs. "You stay!" He looked back at me, retreated to his little bed on the driver's seat and laid down. I found the jail section inside and told the deputy I was there to see Tino.

"You his attorney?" he asked.

"Do I look like I'm his attorney?" I said.

"No, you don't, but it's not visiting hours now," the deputy said.

"I drove up from Petaluma and I'm a friend of his and I need to see him."

The deputy gave me a long look-over. "Well, I guess I can make an exception—but keep the visit short, okay?" he said. "I don't want my boss coming in and seeing you there inside—that gets my ass in a sling, if you know what I mean."

"Yes, sir," I said.

I followed the deputy through two doors that led into a hallway with three cells on each side, and at the end of the hallway, sitting on a cot in the last cell, was Tino. His shoulder was wrapped in thick bandages. He looked up at me and then looked away quick—like he'd heard something from the other side of his cell.

"Hello, Tino," I said. His black hair was much longer than the last time I saw him and it was matted together in places.

"What do you want?" he grunted, without looking at me.

"I heard about what happened."

"What'd you hear?" He finally looked up at me.

"That there'd been a shooting—with you and Sheers."

"It didn't go too good, though," he said.

"Why's that?"

"Because both of us are alive—that's why."

"I'm glad for it."

"Why you here?" he asked.

"Because I heard what happened—and was worried about you." I looked through the bars at Tino. "I know how you felt about what I done years back but that's water under the bridge, isn't it?"

"I don't know—I guess it is."

"It is for me—right now I come to see you and make sure you're okay."

"I'm okay—don't know what's going to happen—but I'm okay," he said. "The bullet sliced through my shoulder but didn't hit no bone."

"You're lucky—"

"Yeah, I'm the luckiest guy alive, ain't I?"

"What have they told you?" I asked.

"They ain't said much—wanted to know if I had an attorney and I told him no—don't know no attorney."

I stood there and neither of us talked for some time. It was quiet. The other cells were empty. "I'm sorry about what happened between us—with Christina and all—"

"She went with who she wanted to—and it wasn't me," he said. "That was awhile ago and I try not to think about it. Like you said—water under the bridge."

"Just like you and Sheers," I said. "That was awhile ago, too, but you didn't forget about that."

"You come up here to lecture me again?"

"No, I didn't. I come up here to see if I can help in anyway."

"I don't know nothing about all this legal stuff—what the charges are—what they're gonna do—nothing."

"So, Tino, what happened?"

"I was drinking—we both were," he said. "He come in the livery spoiling for a fight—I'm minding my own business, not stirring up nothing—just in my own cups, that's all—and he walks in bold as brass. He says, 'You're that half-breed from that bitch up on the hill and you got my blood in you, don't you?' and I told him I wasn't spoiling for a fight—wasn't spoiling for nothing, and told him I didn't know whose blood I got in me—I just wanted to be left alone, but he kept pressing and then he pulls out that bull pistol of his—that same one he killed your old man with—and he's pointing it at me except he's so drunk his hand ain't steady—his eyes wandering all over—and that pistol's moving up and down. I figured he couldn't hit the side of a barn with it if he tried."

Tino ran his hand through his hair with his one good arm. "This whole time I'm sitting behind my desk, keeping my eyes trained on his, but slowly opening the drawer where my pistol was so he wouldn't notice. Next thing, my hand's on the pistol grip and I bring it up fast, and he touches off a round that grazes my shoulder and I fire back—just missing his heart. If I hadn't been drunk, I would have killed him for sure and Percy Sheers'd be six feet under."

"Goddamn, Tino—I wish you hadn't a done it."

"Sitting here like I am—I wish I hadn't done it neither—but what else could I do?" he said. "You tell me—he's got a pistol in his hand trying to aim at me, and I'm sitting at my desk thinking I'm dead meat, so I done what anyone else would a done—I tried killing the bastard."

"Sounds like self-defense to me, but I'm not any lawyer," I said.

"I guess I'm going to need one."

"Maybe Carlotta can help you," I said. "She knows lots of attorneys—but I haven't seen her since Josephine's wedding."

"She's still around," Tino said. "Her and that senator pretty much together all the time now. They come in the livery once and rented a three-seater from me. Now she bought a touring car so she won't be needing the horses no more."

I nodded. "That's what she wanted—-she wanted him all along."

"And that's what she got," he said.

"You warned me about her."

Tino nodded his head. "And you? And Christina?" Tino started to open up—I wasn't feeling that coldness from him I was feeling right when first seeing him.

"We bought a hundred acre ranch in Lakeville, just south of Petaluma," I said.

"Yeah, I heard you done that—and you was the big egg man."

"We got three kids now. Irene's twelve—she don't much like me— Irv's nearly eight and Nanette—she's four but she's not doing so good—was born too early and there were complications—things the doctors don't even know how to treat."

"And you're making a go of it?" Tino asked.

"I got routes in town delivering eggs and cream and Christina's potato salad, but it's a little tight right now. Christina spends a lot of time with Nanette—she's even talking about getting a place in town," I said. "I can understand why, but it turns everything upside down at the ranch. Frank and I are juggling chores just to keep things afloat. Irv helps out, too."

"So, you're holding on?"

"Yeah, that's as good a way to put it as any—I sure don't want to lose the ranch, though," I said.

"So, how about you and Christina—how the two of you doing?"

"Good days and bad days—like everything else, I guess," I said. "We argue a lot—we got our differences. I won't bullshit you about that." I leaned my head against the bars of Tino's cell. "She doesn't like me drinking—"

"They never do."

"I told her from the start I was going to drink—that I'd be civil about it—but it didn't matter," I said. "I haven't cheated on her and I've never hit her—haven't landed me in any trouble—only what I make with myself."

"Flo still asks about you. 'Where's that handsome Bert Miller,' and I tell her you're a married man now and you ain't got time to visit us." Tino lowered his head into both hands, staring down at the floor. He didn't say anything—just kept looking down at the floor. "I shoulda turned the gun on myself," he said. "I shot the wrong man."

"Don't talk like that, Tino."

"Why? It's true—would have saved me a lot of grief."

"I guess all of us think about it at times," I said. "I know I do when things go upside down, but I just learned to wait it out and most times always things change—they don't have to change a lot—just a little."

"You still got that horse that was born the day of your dad's service?"

"Little Ike," I said. "He's' right outside the courthouse now—twenty-five years old but you'd never know it."

"Twenty-five years old? Jesus H. Christ where'd the time go?" Tino wondered.

"Yes, sir—twenty-five and still doing all right," I said. "I don't run him like I used to, but he's steady and reliable as a good watch." I paused here. "As to where the time went, I can't say—it just goes."

Neither of us said anything for some seconds.

"You hunted or fished much?" Tino asked.

"Not like me and you used to," I said. "I took Irv out on the creek and we fished awhile back and I told him all about you and how you knew the best holes along Sonoma Creek all the way out to the bay. I told him about us hunting ducks, too, and running from Percy Sheers and how we bagged deer—he's been wanting to meet you."

"I don't want him seeing me like this," Tino said.

"After you heal up, I'll bring him by and you can meet him."

"I don't want him seeing me in here—don't want no one seeing me like this."

"I'll talk to Carlotta and see what she can do," I said.

I heard the door open at the end of the cell block. The deputy walked toward us. "I gotta run you out now," the deputy said. "Visiting time's over."

Tino stood up from his cot, approached me and poked his arm between the bars to shake hands. "It was good to see you, Bert. I'm sorry about all that shit happening between us."

"Good to see you, too, Tino," I said. "I brought it on myself—and I'm sorry for it—but we'll figure something out."

"We always do," and a little smile formed at the corner of his mouth.

I walked out of the jail block and thanked the deputy there at the front desk. Jigs jumped up from his little bed when he saw me, licking my face the whole time it took me to climb to the driver's seat. We drove back south to Petaluma and down Lakeville Road, pulling into the barn just before dark. Christina was home with Nanette, Irene and Irv. She asked how the visit went with Tino. "He was a little stand-offish at first," I said, "but then he warmed up. He's going to need an attorney and I thought of Carlotta—asking her who she might recommend."

"Why'd you think if her?" she asked.

"She's been in and out of court enough with her brother," I said. "She must know a half dozen good attorneys."

"You're not fishing there, are you, Bert?" she asked me.

"Fishing?"

"Yeah, just looking for an excuse to see her?"

"Christina, c'mon—that's long done—forgotten. That horse died years ago."

"I'm only asking," she said. "I guess because I lost my trust in things lately—mostly the trust between me and you."

"You lost your trust in me—is that what you're saying? And why's that—'cause I ain't given up drinking?"

"No, I've seen you around other women—it's all sorts of things."

"Other women? What other women?"

"You got that charm about you—you can turn it on and you can turn it off. I know—you flashed it at me when were courting—but it's been gone between us a long time," she said. "I can feel it gone and I think you can, too."

"Isn't that what happens with married folk?" I asked her. "You see each other day after day and there's nothing new anymore between them. You think everyday has to be like we were courting? All kisses and romance? Is that it?" I looked at her. "Who's the dreamer here, anyway?"

"It doesn't have to be that way," she said. "I think we both gave up trying."

"Maybe it doesn't—but bottom line is—I been faithful to you—there haven't been any others."

"I'm frayed," she said. "Like an old piece of cloth all worn out at the edges—worrying all the time about Nanette and what's going to happen with her."

"You're doing everything you can," I told her. "Anything more and it's out of your hands."

It was hard to hear Christina say these things. Sure, I'd thought about other women—what man hasn't? I'd see one walking down the street or sitting at a counter when I made my deliveries and I'd wonder about them and sometimes say hello and talk them up—all innocent stuff. I liked women—what else can I say? I hadn't figured them out and never thought I would—but I still liked them—was still drawn to them. I'd gone round and round on the carousel with a couple of them more than once—they got off somewhere without me knowing it, but I stayed on—kept going around in circles the whole time, wondering where they went and figuring if I stayed on long enough, they'd come back around again.

Mostly I was wrong. A couple of them had left me for dead and there was some I left the same way—pretty much an even score there. But I wasn't propositioning them now or anything—was teaching myself to look the other way—and it didn't seem any reason to concern Christina. And I wasn't so sure about that "charm" that Christina had mentioned, either. Age had dried it up in me—withered away like an old prune. It hadn't always worked in the past anyway—like a lot of things about me.

"Look, Christina, there's no other reason for seeing Carlotta than to try to help Tino out—believe me."

Christina didn't say anything.

"Who else is gonna help?" I asked her. "Sheers turned the whole town against him."

"I don't know," she said.

"No one—that's who. It's a shame all this had to happen. I thought with enough time it'd all blow over between those two, but it didn't," I said. "And from what Tino told me, it was Sheers that started it all up again."

"Tino won't go to prison, will he?"

"I don't know," I said. "The scary thing about Sheers is he's got pull—at least in Sonoma, he does. I already told you how the town greeted him, didn't I, after he was acquitted from killing my dad? Like he was some kind of hero—the band playing, fireworks—all that horseshit."

"But this is different, isn't it?" she asked.

"I hope it is—for Tino's sake—I hope it is."

I didn't know what would happen—I never did—but I'd do whatever I could to help my friend Tino. I'd disappointed him years earlier—went behind his back and stole his woman away just so he couldn't have her—and now I wanted to make amends for that.

72

Carlotta
· · · · · · · ·

On the Saturday after visiting Tino in the county jail, I drove over the hill to Sonoma to look up Carlotta. It'd been over ten years since I'd seen her—about the same time since I'd last seen Tino. I sent her a card thanking her for the hundred Leghorns she gave us for a wedding present, and thought about her over the years—there's some things you just can't erase from your memory no matter how hard you try. I wondered what it would be like seeing her again after all this time. And I wondered, too, if it would have been different if Carlotta had chosen me over the senator. Would we still argue the way I done with Christina? Would there still be that excitement I felt whenever I'd see her? Or, would it be more of the same thing—disappointing them by being the person you were and no one else? I don't know why I wasted my time with such thoughts, but I did—even comparing her to Christina in different ways. It wasn't fair to do that, but I did it anyway.

Sure, there was more romance, more excitement with Carlotta than with Christina, and I didn't quite know how to account for it other than Carlotta being out of reach—a long shot—and for that reason she found a waiting home in my imagination. With Christina, she seemed available—maybe even an easy mark with nothing much left to imagine. There was no fighting, no big challenge to win her over—the pickings were all there. I guess you could say I took her for granted. It was like hunting or fishing, in a way— the ones that brought you satisfaction were the ones hardest to track or hardest to land, but the ones you wanted the most—the ones you tracked until your boots wore through, well, they were the ones you couldn't have, and they got away.

This wasn't meant to think less of Christina in anyway. She had her many good qualities—more than I deserved from any woman.

I'd just thought of the differences between the two of them—Carlotta coming from a wealthy family, while Christina, an immigrant girl, worked her way up from nothing to what she had now. Christina had her one love—Jimmy Murdoch—and then he got killed and I turned out to be the guy next in line. And Carlotta was with her love now—finally—but not before giving me a turn that spun my head for years. Where was all my charm back then when I needed it? What I had wasn't enough. All this thinking, though—all this comparing the two women—was just a waste of time. I might as well have compared Christina to Queen Victoria, or for that matter—Carlotta to Queen Victoria—they were about the same distance away.

I arrived at Carlotta's ranch, pulled Ike up to a hitching post by the garden fence and walked up to the front door and knocked. Ah Yep answered, surprised to see me. His chin whiskers were long and gray now. "Is Carlotta in?" I asked him.

He nodded his head. Just beyond Ah Yep stood the senator and he approached me.

"You look familiar," the senator said.

"I used to work here," I said. "And we went to the hot springs in Agua Caliente once—"

"Of course! Of course! My memory's not as good as it used to be," he said. "And your name was—"

"Miller. Bert MIller."

We shook hands and from a back room, I heard Carlotta's voice, "Charles, who is it?"

"It's Bert Miller,'" he said.

Then Carlotta appeared, dressed in a long skirt, her hair, now nearly all gray, fixed in a bun on top of her head, exposing that beautiful neck of hers. "This is a surprise!" she said. "You still look the same."

"So do you, Carlotta."

"What brings you over to these parts?" she asked. "You still live in Petaluma, right?"

"I do," I said. "Got a family now—three kids."

"Wonderful," she said.

"And Christina? How is she?"

"She's fine—busy as always."

"But I didn't come over here to tell you about my family," I said. "You heard about Tino—"

"That's all anyone's ever talked about around town," she said. "It's why I avoid going there even more, now. My brother has a way of making the headlines."

"Tino's gonna need an attorney, and I thought of you." I noticed she had more lines in her face but she still held on to her beauty.

"Well, I did contact Morris Graves," she said. "He's a criminal attorney—first rate—when I heard of the incident. He told me it could all get dismissed if both parties would agree."

"Tino and your brother agreeing?" I said. "How likely is that?"

"Percy might want to think about this since I hear he's the one that provoked the incident—he was the one who walked into the Union Livery and drew his pistol," she said. "I read the police report."

"And if they don't agree?"

"There'd be a trial in all likelihood," the senator said.

"He'll need an attorney then and I don't know what Tino's finances are like. I'm guessing they aren't much," I said.

"There's always the public defender option, as well," the senator said. "But I like Tino, and the worst-kept secret in town is that Carlotta's brother fathered him."

"And they end up trying to kill each other," I said. "Father and son—pretty damn strange isn't it?"

"Like a Greek tragedy," she said.

"Don't know anything about Greek tragedies," I said. "I figured sooner or later something would happen between them—I hoped it wouldn't—that it'd just blow over, but that never happened."

"Not with my brother—he's got his pride to worry about," she said.

"And when Tino gets something in his mind—he doesn't let go of it."

"A bad combination." Carlotta looked at the senator and then back at me.

"Can you reason with Tino?" the senator asked.

"He's hard-headed," I said, "but I'll try."

A bit of awkward silence followed.

"Can you stay for lunch?" Carlotta asked.

"No, thank you," I said. "I left work behind and it's waiting for me back at the ranch." I turned toward the door.

"We'll be in touch," she said.

"Good."

She offered me her hand and I took it and held it briefly. Then I shook the senator's hand and walked toward the door. "I'll escort you out," she said. "It's very proper you know."

Jigs leaned over the side of the carriage when we approached. "And who's this little fellow?" she asked.

"That's my partner, Jigs—best ratter in the south county."

She petted Jigs on his head and then she turned toward me. "I often think of you—especially as I'm gathering eggs. I think of your father, too. Everything—such a difficult time but special times in there, as well."

"Do you still ride your bicycle?" I asked her.

"No, I don't. It's in the storeroom gathering dust where I keep the colonel's furniture," she said. "I bought one for the senator hoping we could ride together—like you and I did—but we hadn't gone a half mile before he got such a sneezing attack and was gasping for air—I was afraid he'd die right there—so we walked the bicycles back here and haven't touched them since. I bought a touring car instead."

"I think of you, too," I said. "And things are good with you and the senator?"

"He lives here now for all practical purposes," she said. "We live in sin together."

I laughed. Somehow sin didn't seem to have the hold on Carlotta that it did on others—like Christina. "And his wife?"

"She won't divorce him."

"He does have some health issues—I seem to pick men who do—but I see that he gets good care. My mother moved in with us, too, and spent her final months with us before she died. It was starting to feel like a sick ward around here."

"Well, you're a caring person," I said.

"Her dying wish was that my brother and I would patch things up between us," she said. "I told her I was open to it—that I hated these bad feelings as much as she did." Tears started to form in her eyes. "I do think of those earlier times, though when I was much freer—when I could wander about at will and read my books and paint—you didn't know it but I started painting using watercolors."

"Carlotta the artist—it fits," I said. "And about those earlier times? We all yearn for them, Carlotta. We want them back but forget about all the pain and disappointment mixed in."

"That's true," she said. "If only there was some way you could remember just the good memories."

"Some people do—they filter out all the bad like it never existed." I wanted to go just then, say a final goodbye, and leave it at that, but I felt there was more to say—more things to get off my chest. "I still remember that night you came to me."

She turned to me quickly. "Please, Bert, don't—"

"No, I want to talk about it—because it's never left my mind—even after all these years."

"I'm sorry—"

"I never really understood it for the longest time—but it finally sunk in," I said.

"I was vulnerable and beside myself—and a bit careless. I pulled you in with me—you knew my circumstances."

"I did and thought I'd be strong enough for whatever happened or didn't happen between us," I said. "Turns out I wasn't—turns out I was a lot weaker than I ever thought."

"We're all so fragile, Bert. We don't realize how fragile—"

"I thought I could tough it all out," I said.

"But we can't—not really."

I looked across the yard to the house where my folks lived briefly and where I lived an even shorter amount of time. "You have another foreman now?"

"Yes, Ben Pender's his name," she said. "He's been with us several years now, but Alfonso always asks about you—his brother asks about you, too."

"Good guys, all of them." No sooner did I say that than I saw Alfonso cross the yard. I shouted, "Hello!"

"*Senor* Bert, *como estas?*" he called back. He approached us, tipped his hat to Carlotta.

"Good," I said. "*Bien. Bien.*"

"You come back to work here?" he asked.

I looked over at Carlotta. "No, Alfonso, those days are over," I said.

"*Lastima*—too bad. My brother and me we still talk about you and John B. and your *padre.*" He walked up to Ike and stroked Ike's forehead. "And this is the little one?"

"*Si*, that's the little one."

"Not so little now," Alfonso said. "All grown up."

"All grown up and long in the tooth—but still very smart." I said.

"Long in the tooth?" he asked.

"Yes—he's getting old—like the rest of us."

"*Si?*"

I nodded my head and looked toward Carlotta. "It was good to see you again."

She moved close to me and kissed my cheek. I smiled back at her and then climbed up to the driver's seat and loosened the reins.

"Goodbye, Little Ike," she said.

"You remember when he was born?"

"Of course I do," she said. "You've taken good care of him."

"He's taken good care of me," I said.

"Goodbye, Bert."

"Goodbye, Carlotta."

I swung the carriage around and we headed out to Napa Road with Jigs leaning out over the carriage's side, barking to clear the way in front of us. I glanced behind me and Carlotta still stood there by the garden gate watching us leave. Was it that foolish side within me—that side with the loudest voice, wanting her to run after us and beg us to stay? To take my hand and lead me back to that night years ago that had never left my memory? And I'd say, yes, take me there. Take me back to that night when I was most alive, when the stars sizzled and I was drunker than I'd ever been without even drinking a drop. And, yes—it was that side of me that wanted all of this—that very foolish side.

73

Christina Goes to Mass

· ·

Christina was a faithful Catholic—more faithful than anyone I knew. It was a rare time she missed Mass on Sunday, and when she did, she'd attend Mass during the week, light votive candles, and recite an extra rosary as her penance. She didn't eat meat on Fridays, prayed the rosary, fasted during Lent, giving up her favorite vice—Swiss Chocolate, and there was a string of saints she prayed to whenever a particular need came up—Saint Jude when in despair, Saint Anthony if she lost something, Saint Christopher whenever she traveled—like I said, a whole string of them. She made me promise all our children would receive the sacraments, too: baptism, Holy Communion, the works. And no one followed the Ten Commandments closer. If a soul had a place reserved for her in Heaven, it was my wife, Christina. She wanted me to join her there, too, and begged me to accompany her to Mass, to pull the reins back on my drinking, to confess my sins regular-like—to be a pillar of the church, a Knights of Columbus faithful—but it wasn't in the cards.

On Sunday mornings early, she'd send Irv out to harness up her horse, Daisy Rose, a sweet-natured, but generally lazy creature who'd rather sleep than eat—and she ate all the time. This one Sunday morning, though, after Frank had left the gate open into a pasture of sweet clover the day before, Daisy Rose wandered in and ate until she foundered—her hooves so tender she could barely walk. When Irv saw her condition, he ran back to the house and told his mother and Christina looked at me and said, "That only leaves Ike, doesn't it?"

I said it did.

"But you know that horse doesn't like me, right?"

"Ike doesn't play favorites," I said. "There isn't a mean bone in that horse's body."

"I beg to differ."

"It's all in your imagination," I said.

"It isn't either."

"Well, we can stand here and argue all day about Ike's short-comings, or I can hitch him to your carriage," I said. "Your choice—or you can miss Mass just this once."

She gave me a disgusted look—one that seemed to say, "I won't be seeing you in heaven," and I went into the barn and led Ike out to the front of her carriage. "You know, it wouldn't kill you to go to Mass with us," she said.

"You remember the deal we made, right? No church."

She shot another hard glance at me—her second of the morning—and went inside to set out dresses for the girls and make them breakfast.

"Now once you reach Washington Street," I told Irv, "Ike's gonna have a mind of his own. He's used to stopping all along the way on the egg route and doesn't like just passing by our regular stops—he takes it all kinda personal—if you know what I mean. Folks come out and give him things and he's come to expect it," I explained. "Best thing is don't fight it. Ike moves to his own clock."

"So, you just give him free rein?" Irv asked.

"That's the simplest thing to do. Ike's got a stubborn streak in him, and if it means he misses a hand-out along the way, he can get a little cross-eyed about it."

"I'll tell Ma," Irv said.

"Oh, you won't have to tell her anything—she'll have a front-row seat." I looked over at Irv. "You better go in and get ready for church."

I brought hay down from the loft and wheeled a big load of it out to the milk cows. On my return trip, all four of my family was now in the carriage, Christina sitting next to Irv in the driver's seat and the two girls in the back seat. Irv held the reins in his hands. I looked at them from a distance and wished I could take a photograph—the girls and their mother all dressed up, with their hats on, and Irv in his wool suit, his hair slicked down and parted, still wearing his work boots, and Ike looking proud as ever—like he was leading the July 4th parade downtown. That picture's still burned into my mind.

"Remember what I told you, Irv!" I said.

He nodded his head, clicked his tongue and Ike leaned into his harness and they were gone down Ely Road.

I returned to the milking barn where Frank had lined up buckets of milk to separate out the cream. He'd milked the last of the cows and was washing down the floor. I told him about the trouble between Tino and Percy Sheers and how they shot each other and one was in the Sonoma jail and the other was in the county one. Frank just shook his head.

After I'd separated out the cream, I washed out the buckets. Frank was nearby.

"Frank," I said, "Christina never talks much about life back in the old country. Why's that?"

"I don't know."

"What was it like for your family?"

"Like everyone else, we struggled to get by."

"What were your folks like?"

"Our father was strict—he drank, too," Frank said. "He was hardest on Christina—it's why she couldn't wait to leave. Our mother wasn't the gentlest person, either."

"Probably why Christina never liked my drinking."

"No, it's something she doesn't much talk about."

What Frank said about Christina's father and her attitude toward my drinking now made more sense. We all have our histories—and none of them are perfect. I know mine wasn't. They carry all kinds of wounds, all kinds of slights with them. We think everything will pass and it's all behind us, that those wounds'll heal over and won't affect us anymore—that everything will be like nothing happened to us—but it's not always like that. It's not always a clean slate. Our histories and the hurt inside them never completely die regardless of how much we want them to—regardless of how much distance we put between them and ourselves. The wounds are always there, scabbed-over, maybe, but they're always there—something about them always manages to survive. Something always pops its head up, some little incident— some habit you can't shake—that peels the scab away and opens the wound back up, reminding us it's never completely gone.

As I got older and thought about it more, about how to deal with these wounds if you can't forget them, I figured the best thing was to give them their own room, their own space, let them move about where they wanted to and not stir them up. I didn't like denying them, either. Denying seemed the worst thing to do. It was like passing somebody on the street who'd wronged you, and then not confront him, acting like nothing happened. You had to say something, didn't you? If you didn't, was that like denying anything had happened. I guess you could just walk on by, too, and not say a word. Enough times and maybe you'd just forget the wrongdoing and let everything be.

"Why would Tino do that?" Frank asked.

His question confused me. He shifted back to what we'd talked about earlier that morning, before the family went off to Mass. Frank had a habit of doing that—you could be talking about one thing and right in the middle of it he'd bring something up we'd talked about a week earlier. I don't know why he did it—things just came to Frank that way. Maybe he didn't want to talk about what we'd been discussing, and the best way to do that was to change the subject.

"It's a long history between those two—Tino's been running from him all his life—we both were when we were poaching— and I think Tino just got tired of running from him," I said.

Frank looked at me. "I think they been running from each other."

Frank didn't say a helluva lot. He was a man of few words, but the words he did say—well, most of the time they carried some water with them.

"I went to see Carlotta, too," I said. "I figure I can tell you. I can't mention her name around Christina without Christina getting all upset and thinking I'm carrying on with her."

"I can see why," Frank said. "She's beautiful." He looked at me and asked, "Why did you visit her after all this time?"

And I told him about Tino needing an attorney and how Carlotta had a list of them because of all the legal problems with her brother.

"That was the only reason?" he asked.

"Now you're sounding just like your sister."

"Only asking—"

"Frank, I pretty much gave up on that one—there wasn't any choice in the matter. Anyway, I got a family now and that sort of thing's in the past now."

It was during this time, as well, that the chickens started dying off. Irv would come back from gathering eggs in the morning carrying one or two dead chickens with him. John B., like Joe Keebler before him, had warned me about the dampness that hunkered down around the bottom of the ranch where I'd built a layer house. "Chickens like fresh air," he said, "And they don't like wet air that settles on them and doesn't move. One of them catches something and pretty soon the whole flock's down."

"What do you suggest I do?" I'd asked him.

"Here, I'd be thinking of building some colony houses," he said.

"Colony houses?"

"Yeah, they're just little sheds where they can roost and lay eggs, and you build skids underneath them and attach an eye bolt to the front of the skids," he said. "That way you hitch a horse to them and pull them around to wherever the air moves best."

"And the chickens will know to go back to them at night?"

"Yeah, you feed them around each colony house and they take to that one house," he said. "Chickens are smarter than most people give him credit for."

So, John B. and I had drawn up a sketch of how to build the houses, and I'd driven off to Cavanaugh Lumber to buy material. I'd set up a little workshop in an open area of the hay barn and worked a couple hours each day building them. By the end of the first week, I'd finished one house. This is what I was working on the

Sunday the family took Ike to town. I worked on one all morning after finishing chores, not even stopping for lunch. By mid afternoon I looked up and there was Ike and the family rolling back into the farmyard. I laid down my cross-cut saw and walked over to the carriage.

"How'd it go?" I asked.

No one said anything at first—they just looked at one another, waiting for someone to speak. Irv glanced over at his mother but she looked away, not saying anything. I'd been around Christina long enough to read her moods. She was upset.

"You were right about Ike," Irv finally spoke up. "He done just what you said he would."

"Stupid horse," Christina said.

"What happened?" I asked.

Christina shook her head.

"Well, we were doing fine all the way into town and past the depot, and then we turned onto Washington and right past the ice house, Ike stopped in front of the Yosemite Hotel—just up and stopped," Irv said. "I clicked my tongue and slapped the reins lightly on his rump but he wouldn't move."

"Why do you even keep a horse like that?" Christina asked.

"Ike just stops there, bends his neck toward the front of the Yosemite, and pretty soon a girl comes out the front door holding a fistful of carrots. The girl walks with a limp—-

"Her name's Margarite," I said. "Ike's got a real soft spot for her."

"Well, she feeds the carrots to Ike and then we start moving again," Irv said. "But not for long—until we come to the Chop Suey house and he stops again."

"The horse is doing this on purpose," Christina said. "I know—just to make me mad and late for Mass. It's like you trained him to do this, Arnold Bert."

"No, Christina," I said. "He learned it all by himself."

"A Chinaman comes out with a bunch of China greens, and Ike snorts and takes the greens in a couple of bites, and then we're off again," Irv said.

"That's Charlie, the Chinaman," I said. "Charlie taught me how to say "I have eggs" in Chinese, and now when I deliver eggs, I practice my Chinese with the women working in the kitchen. "Jeetoc," I said, and they all start laughing. One day I asked Charlie what it was I was really saying, and he said, "Just that—'I have eggs'." I didn't entirely believe him.

Christina's arms were folded in front of her. Nanette looked at me. "Then Ma got down from the carriage to lead Ike and he looked at her but he wouldn't move—a couple of seconds later he farted," Nanette said. Both girls laughed.

"Go ahead—laugh it up—the two of you—all of you," Christina said. "Wait'll you want to go somewhere and it happens to you."

"After Ike ate the China greens we drove all the way to the creek and just past the creek, Ike stopped again," Irv said.

"At the Electric Waffle Inn," I said.

"That's right—that place—but no one came out and Ike got tired of waiting before moving on," Irv said.

"They're busy there on Sunday mornings," I said. "Usually somebody comes out with a couple of waffles. Ike likes them with maple syrup."

"I'll tell you one thing that horse is good for," Christina said.

"And what's that?" I wondered.

"GLUE!" she snarled.

"Now that's a terrible thing to say about Ike," I said.

"Why is it a terrible thing to say?" Christina asked. "Because it's the truth?"

"Ma was upset," Irv said.

"You own a horse—and the horse decides where it goes and not you—who ever heard of such a thing?" Christina said. "In front of the Continental Hotel, people came out on the sidewalk and were laughing at me trying to get that fool horse of yours to move! I tell you, Arnold Bert Miller, if I'd had a gun I would have shot him! Right there, in front of God and everyone!"

I laughed—so did Irv and the girls.

"It's not one bit funny," she said.

"Then Ike let his thing drop down," Irv said.

"That's when I got out and walked the rest of the way," Christina said

I laughed even more—I couldn't stop—even my two daughters in the back seat were holding their stomachs, they were laughing so hard.

"Disgusting—that's what it is! That's not a horse," and she pointed to Ike. "That's a jackass—and it's got a jackass for an owner, too!"

By now Irv and me were doubled over—neither of us could stop laughing.

"Ma, what's wrong with Dad?" Nanette asked. They weren't used to seeing me laugh like this.

"You've got a fool for a father—that's what's wrong," Christina said.

"Did you get to Mass on time?" I asked.

"No, I came in at the Offertory."

"So does that count for a full Mass—or do you have to go back?"

"I don't like your sarcasm, Bert Miller—not one bit."

By now Christina had stepped down from the carriage and stared me right in the face. "You should be more serious when it comes to matters of your soul," she said.

```"I'm doomed—I already gave up. Why even try?"

"Fine thing for your children to hear," she said.

"Sorry, kids. It only means there's more room in heaven for you," I said.

Christina walked back to the house and the two girls trailed after her while Irv unharnessed Ike and led him back to his stall.

"I warned you about him, didn't I, Irv?"

"You did, dad, and he done just like you said he would."

"He never disappoints, son—different from a lot of folks," I said.
```

74

Cross-Roads

• •

I built eight colony houses the way John B. and I had drawn them out, hitched-up Molly and pulled them to where they caught the best breezes blowing up from the river—but it wasn't enough to save our flock. One by one, and then by the dozens, they were dropping off—their eyes shuddered at first with a white film before they'd fall over on their sides, linger there maybe a half hour, hour, their feet kicking out before dying. It was hard for me to watch—hard for all of us. You raise them from little chicks and see them grow into pullets and then into layers and they become a part of you. They learn your different sounds, hear you approaching yards away and run out to meet you—their legs scampering fast, their little wings beating hard and for a couple of yards they're in the air—almost flying. You feed them and they follow you around, pecking at your heels, and for a good part of the year give you eggs in return, eggs that you sell around town that keep the whole ranch running. And what do they ask for in return? That you keep them fed and keep them healthy.

With the flock dying like it was, I was forced to buy eggs wholesale from the dealers in town to keep all my accounts, and, of course, that meant a slimmer profit margin. Nanette had now reached an age when she didn't require as much care—she was still sickly—but Christina was back preparing her potato salad, and that helped pay some of the freight. Irene did her part, too, cleaning house, washing dishes, helping to care for her younger sister. But the distance between Irene and me had never closed, and that always ate at my insides. Like so many things in this life though, I learned to buck up and live with it. I didn't like it, but there were things in this life you didn't like—it was just a fact. And Irv—well, there was a special place in my heart for that boy. He worked with me every chance he could get—loved driving the two big horses more than anything and would sometimes miss class so he could mow hay or spread manure out in the fields. His mother would bark at him for missing school, and I'd tell him, "It's okay—there's some classes you can miss. The world ain't gonna end if you do."

"Don't keep that boy from his schooling," she'd warn me. "He's not going to be staring at a horse's rear-end all his life—he's meant for better things."

I didn't know what was better though than doing what you loved.

I'd look at Irv sometimes and see myself when I was his age and imagine that was me right there walking around. It was like having a chance to see your life all over again when you were younger—listening to what you said and seeing what you done, knowing the things you liked and the things you didn't. You could see the mistakes you made, too—the way you took to work, the way, especially, how you loved driving those big horses. "You got a leg-up on me, son," I told him one day.

"What'd you mean?" he asked.

"I didn't start driving until I was sixteen—and how old are you?"

"Ten," he said.

"See—you got six years on me."

"Ma says horses ain't gonna be around much longer."

"Now why'd she'd say that?"

"She says cars and trucks are gonna replace them—-that folks like you are gonna be left behind."

"I'd like to think that horses will always be around," I said.

"So if Molly and Dolly and Ike die, we'll get more horses?" he asked.

"I sure think so."

Christina thought about these things more than I did. She was what folks called a realist and I wasn't—I was what folks called a dreamer. I could see Molly and Dolly and Ike, too, coming near the end of their years, just as plain as Christina did, but I didn't want to think about that ever happening. It meant something painful, and it meant changes, too, and I'd finally found a routine that suited me. I loved my family. Sure—I was at odds with most of them—but I just swallowed our differences, woke up each morning, put one foot in front of the other and pushed forward. I loved the ranch life, shuttling eggs around town and stopping off for a few stiff ones, swapping stories, and I didn't want any of it changing. But I could feel the little quakes under my feet telling me things were changing—it's a fool who thinks they won't. Christina talked more and more about moving to a house in town where Nanette would be closer to doctors, where she wouldn't have to make the eight-mile carriage ride from ranch to town all the time. She said it wore her and Nanette out, and with the flock dying off and Irv spending more time with me than in classes, she thought the move to town made the most sense.

"I ain't giving up the ranch," I told her.

"That's fine," she said, "because you're not moving to town with us."

"I wasn't planning on it anyway—suits me good here."

"Fine. You stay here but we're going—all of us."

The news floored me. "What are you talking about?" I asked her.

"What'd your father used to say to you?" she asked. "Bert, you're running your string out." Isn't that what he used to say?"

"Something like that—"

"Well, I think that's what we done here," she said. "You're not happy with me and I'm not happy with you. I thought by now we'd iron out our differences, but I haven't seen it happening,"

"You can't just pack up and leave," I said.

"I can and I will—I already found a little house at the top of Keller Street. Irv can go to Washington Grammar School, Irene to the high school and Nanette's close to her doctors." She crossed her arms across her chest like it was the final word.

"Why don't we take some time to think it over?" I asked.

"I thought it over—every time you come home with booze on your breath or poke fun at me for going to Mass—or mention other women."

"You been sitting on this awhile, haven't you?"

"Awhile—thinking, hoping it would change—I don't see it happening, though. Do you?"

"And we can't talk it out?"

"What's to talk about that hasn't been hammered over a dozen times already?" she said. "Besides, the separation might do us some good—clear the air a bit."

"I don't like it," I said.

"Well, I don't like a lot of things, either, but what I hate even more is what's come between us—married folk don't have to live this way—"

"Goddamn, Christina, is it that bad?" I stepped back and tried to gather my thoughts. "I told you right-out I wasn't perfect—that I liked to drink but I wouldn't beat on you like other guys done with their wives and I ain't raised my fist once—hell, I hardly raised my voice. And that whole thing about you going to Mass? I ain't ever stood in the way of you going, have I?"

Christina looked down at her shoes.

"I just didn't want to go myself," I said. "Didn't see any point in it sitting there listening to some priest lecture me. What do they know anyway?"

"More than you know, Arnold Bert Miller!"

A bad sign when she called me by my entire name.

"Can they drive a team of horses? No, they can't—tell when a cow's down with milk fever? I don't think so."

"They're concerned with your spiritual life," she said.

"Spiritual life? What a laugh! Spiritual life doesn't put any food on the table—"

"Man does not live by bread alone," Christina said.

"I'm sure you read that somewhere."

"I did—in the Bible."

"Well, let's take that Bible to the bank and see what we can borrow against it," I said.

"You're impossible—you know that? Impossible," she said. She turned, started to walk away but then stopped. "You know what your problem is?"

"No, what's my problem?" It seemed an important question and one I needed an answer to.

"You're selfish—you can only think of yourself."

"I'm just a guy trying to keep two feet on a piece of ground he doesn't want to lose," I said.

"We'll have to see what happens."

I didn't like the tone of her voice—the way she said, 'we'll see what happens' like she already knew what lie ahead—I didn't like any of it.

I seen all of this coming awhile back but tried to duck from it. Sooner or later, though, there's only so much ducking you can do until the facts come out—until the real world is staring you square in the face. There were plenty of times I thought I could change—be more tolerant of Irene, give up the drinking and try going to Mass with Christina and being God-fearing and all that, but I always slipped back into my old self—my old ways. That was me, I reasoned, and didn't feel like leaving that person behind. It's like buying new harness when the old one's wearing out and you know sooner or later the old one's going snap on you, but it slips onto the horse so easily and feels so good and supple in your hands you can't bring yourself to try the new—then the old one breaks. That's the fix I was in.

Christina seemed set on moving to town and she had her reasons, but what bothered me most was not being able to see Irv as much as I did. I loved all my children—even Irene—but I had to confess I loved Irv the most. I wouldn't tell the others that—it was just a secret I kept to myself. The girls had their mother and Irv had me, and that seemed the way it should be but it wasn't shaping up that way. I wanted Irv to stay and work the ranch, but Christina wasn't having it.

"You going to help us move when the time comes or do my brothers have to do it by themselves?" she asked.

"I want Irv to stay with me," I said.

"That's not going to happen—you should know that," she said. "He needs to be in school and needs a family life, and I don't see that happening if he stays with you."

"When the time comes—and that's what you want," I said, "I'll help you move."

"I appreciate that," she said. "It doesn't have to be harder than it already is."

I felt bad about all of this the next few days—worse than I felt in months. It seemed like everything was coming apart in my life—my family was leaving me, the chickens were dying off, and I didn't know how much longer I could keep the ranch. Christina was now talking about buying a house instead of renting one and wanted me to cash-out her share of the ranch. I didn't have that kind of money and she knew it.

The harsh news was coming at me from all sides—so harsh I started drinking early on my route one day and by my last stop—Jess Dye's Tavern and Grocery on the East Side—it was all I could do to stand up. Two ladies from the silk mill were drinking at the other end of the bar and I chatted them up as best I could—the words coming out of me in bursts—until pretty soon I sided up to them and bought them drinks and we just kept talking.

There's nothing two women like to hear more than some poor sap spilling his guts out about everything he done wrong. I don't remember the details exactly, but what I do remember is walking out with one of them and lying down in the back of the wagon with her and staring up at the stars, and everything whirling around inside my head. Pretty soon the wagon starts moving. "Don't worry," I told her, "The horse knows his way home."

"Your horse knows its way home?" she said.

"Sure as Wilson's president," I said.

Well, I don't have to tell you what happened next, do I? Ike rolled into the ranch, right into the hay barn the way he usually does. It was near dark by now and I was still flat on my back with the silk mill lady lying next to me snoring. Next thing I see is Irv looking down at me from over the sideboards. And then I heard Christina's voice—the voice of doom. "Is he in the wagon?" she asked Irv.

"Yeah, he is, Ma," Irv said.

"Well, then rouse him," she said.

"He ain't alone, though, Ma."

"What'd you say?"

"I said, he ain't alone."

By now I saw the outline of Christina hovering over the side-board. I couldn't see her face—I didn't have to—I could *feel* it—white hot with anger, disappointment—take your pick. I'd just driven another nail into my coffin.

"You do this to hurt me?" Christina asked. "You can't wait a couple of weeks until we're out of here before bringing women back?"

What could I say? "I don't know who she is," I finally said.

"And that makes it all right?"

She had me there.

"Worse still bringing some floosie home—"

The woman—I'd forgotten her name—slept through the whole exchange, and when she did wake up, propped herself on her elbows, looked around and asked, "Where am I?"

"South of town," I said. "Lakeville."

"How I'd get here?"

"You rode in the back of a wagon—with my husband," Christina said.

"Your husband?" The woman looked at me and then at Christina. "You didn't tell me you were married."

"I don't remember what I told you," I said.

"So, Arnold Bert Miller—what are you going to do with her?" Christina asked. "Invite her in to stay for the night?"

"Can't we make a bed for her in the house?" I asked. "Then I'll take her back to town in the morning."

"Irv," Christina said, "Go and bring back some blankets—enough for *two* of them. You like each other so much you can sleep together—right here in the barn."

"Christina—"

"You're not sleeping with me tonight!"

Irv returned with the blankets, tossed them over both of us, and then I heard Christina say, "Take the harness off that horse," and next thing I heard was Irv leading Ike away and then it was quiet and dark in the barn. I heard an owl in the distance. The woman—Eva—I remembered her name—looked at me. "I need to be at work in the morning," she said.

"Don't worry," I said. "I'll get you there. Then she turned away from me and fell back asleep.

So there I was, sleeping with a woman in the back of my wagon—and that's all we done—a woman I didn't even know five hours ago, while fifty yards away sat my wife so disappointed and so upset, counting the hours until she could finally leave me.

I don't point fingers. If I did, they'd all be pointing back at me. I shouldn't have gotten so drunk and I sure-as-shit shouldn't have brought the woman back home, but she climbed in with me when all my will-power—my faculties—were gone and I was left with who I was—some poor egg farmer whose chickens were dying, whose soul was a bottle of eighty-six proof bourbon—some guy who always pushed his limits—stretched them out to paper-thin—seeing how far he could take things until they all broke apart in his face—a guy blessed without a lick of common sense.

75

Not All Bad News

· · · · · · · · · · · · · · · · ·

I drove Eva back to the silk mill the following morning. We didn't talk much enroute—what was there to say? I apologized to her for the embarrassing situation with Christina, she stepped down from my wagon, disappeared inside the mill, and that was the last time I saw her. I continued on into town, bought eggs from the wholesaler, Myron Shanksky, and serviced my routes for the day. The hang-over was a bad one—mostly from lack of sleep—so I pulled Ike over to our favorite sycamore and napped for a solid hour. It was a golden sleep—a king's sleep. I woke up feeling better but with a terrible dry mouth and ducked into Grove's Saloon for a quick beer to cut the thirst—just one, I told myself. I sat there nursing the lager, staring at myself in the tavern mirror like I'd done so many times, wondering who that person was staring back at me. It was troubling times—no doubt about it.

I picked up a couple sacks of chicken feed from Golden Eagle for the few chickens I had left and feed for the milk cows—that left me with a dollar twenty five for the day's work—not enough to keep the ranch, not enough to keep much of anything. Some hard decisions were coming up fast.

We drove back—Jigs sitting next to me, his little stub tail moving like a Aero-motor—and I thought how lucky dogs could be—especially when they land with the right owner. "You know that, Jigs?"

When he heard his name, he turned quickly toward me and put a front paw on my arm. "You don't know how good you got it—there's food in front of you twice a day, you're free to roam, plenty of rats around—but it did cost you your nuts, I realize that—but I don't know if that's such a bad thing after all. I mean—I kept mine and they keep finding trouble for me."

Back at the ranch, I noticed Christina's horse and carriage gone, and that was relief—I didn't have it in me to face her—not after last night. I unloaded the feed and stripped the harness off Ike and walked out to the mailbox. I opened the box and there sat a letter addressed to me—it was from Carlotta. I didn't know what it said, of course, since I hadn't opened it yet, but my mind ran off with all sorts of possibilities: she'd had a change of heart toward me and decided to dump the sickly senator, she said she couldn't live without me and begged me to return to her ranch—the kinds of thoughts a desperate man thinks.

I opened the letter and began reading:

Dear Bert:

I hope this letter finds you in good health. I'm writing to share some good news with you regarding the recent incident between my brother and Tino. Granville Harris, the owner of the Union Livery where Tino worked, and a good friend of my brother, has acted as a mediator between the two. In exchange for dropping all charges against him, my brother has agreed to leave town. E.J. Miley, a principal in the Humboldt City Copper Mine and a former business partner of my brother's, has offered my brother a position as courier for his mining operation, and Percy has accepted the offer. This, to me, is good news for both parties.

Fondly, Carlotta.

It was good news—at a time when I needed to hear some. Tino wouldn't have to linger in jail and hopefully with Sheers out of town, the healing could start. I wanted to mend things with Tino, too, because ever since courting Christina, I'd felt guilt about what I'd done. There were folks I needed to settle up with—Tino for one, and Christina for another.

I set about doing the evening chores—slopping the hogs, feeding the chickens and gathering the few eggs they laid. The days were growing shorter, and I was already using the eggs I'd water-glassed back when days were longer and egg production up. It still wasn't enough. All the time I worked—pretty much all through the day and sometimes when I awoke at night—I'd be thinking about how to save this ranch with Christina gone and wanting her share of it paid back. Nothing I thought of penciled out. Not enough cream, not enough eggs, not enough hogs—not enough of anything. I couldn't even borrow the money—I'd have to sell off everything for collateral—and with nothing left—no horses, no cattle, what the hell could I farm with?

76

A Settlement

· · · · · · · · · · · ·

Christina and I hadn't talked, hadn't even seen each other, for several days. The times we crossed paths at the dinner table with our three kids, the tension between us was thick enough to slice with a knife. She'd look around the table—look right past me like I wasn't even there. I hated it and she did, too, until finally she said, "After the kids go to bed tonight, you and I need to talk."

I agreed—we did. So after all three of the children were in bed and asleep, we sat facing each other at the kitchen table. She looked at me and asked, "What are you going to do, Bert?"

I looked around at the kitchen walls, hoping the answer might be written somewhere—maybe behind that picture of a windmill or that one with the red blacksmith shop. It wasn't. "There ain't much I can do," I said. "You're holding all the cards. I want to keep the ranch and don't see how I can if you're gone and want your cut."

"You've made it pretty much impossible for me to stay," she said. "The drinking. The women—"

"I know—I ain't been much of a model husband, have I?"

"No, you haven't."

"And I'm not asking for another chance—"

"That's good because you're not getting one," she said. "You run your string out—just like your dad used to tell you." She looked at me from across the table. Worry had eaten away at her like it'd eaten away at me—the lines around her eyes were deeper, her forehead was lined with furrows—her skin had lost its glow. "We don't have to hate each other—you know that, right?" she said.

"I don't hate you—never have," I said.

"I just see us going different ways, Bert—you're this free-spirit sort of person that hates rules, doesn't like someone lording over

| 542 |

him and I'm different. I like certainty around my life. I believe there's rules to follow and consequences when we don't."

"Certainty?"

"Yes, certainty," she said. "I don't want everything up in the air all the time—all this hand-to-mouth living—this never knowing when you're coming home, whether you'll be sober or not, And like the other night—who you'll be coming home with—"

"There wasn't anything that happened between us—"

"It doesn't matter—just the fact you brought her home," she said. Christina folded and unfolded her hands. "That kind of thing is acceptable when it's just yourself to think about, but when you got a family—and a wife—it changes everything. You just can't be that kind of person anymore, Bert. It's like you've never grown up—never grown into responsibility."

I couldn't mount much of a defense—everything she said was true. I was irresponsible and had a weakness for the drink and was unwilling to do anything about it—even if it meant losing my family. I couldn't tame my thirst—I tried again and again—I told you enough times already, so there's no sense in repeating myself. It had me by the balls. I thought I could work out a bargain with it—drink just enough to keep everything together, drink just to the point where it was tolerable for Christina and no further—but I always pushed my luck, always took that extra shot or two because I liked the way it made me feel, and if I drank more, my reasoning went, then I'd feel even better. I wasn't crazy about the coming-down, though, and I sure didn't like the mornings-after, but I was in the throes of it and didn't think that far ahead. Fact was, I didn't think much further than the next glass and who was buying the round.

"I told you about the house on Keller Street, didn't I?" she asked. I nodded my head.

"Turns out, it's two houses on an L-shaped lot," she said. "The kids and I can live in the larger house and I can rent out the smaller one, and when the kids are gone, I'll move into the one bedroom place."

"Sounds like you got it all planned out," I said.

"Well, someone has to do the planning."

"I'd sure like it if Irv could stay with me," I said. I tossed it out there, but already knew what she'd say, but I asked her anyway.

"You know that's not going to happen, right?" There were those eyes of hers—drilling straight through me. "What are you going to do—drag him into every bar and tavern in town so he can watch his father drink and make a fool of himself? No," she said, "I'd rather die first than see that happen."

"So, we just the sell the place—just like that? What we've worked for—"

"Unless you can find a partner—someone willing to buy my share out," she said. "You thought of that?"

"No, I haven't."

"You seem to be a man with connections around town now. You can't think of anyone who'd go into business with you?" she asked. "You're a hard worker—I'll say that about you—and you got a gentle side to you, Bert, and a good heart—but it's a wandering heart that doesn't know what it wants—and I can't live with that—I tried and it won out. "

"It ain't like I didn't have hard decisions before—"

"We all have them," she said. "You're a smart guy—you'll figure it out. Besides, things are changing around us, Bert, in case you haven't noticed. More cars and trucks on the road, and more machines doing what we used to do by hand—and everything's speeding up as a result." She looked at me. "You can't tell me you haven't noticed—"

"I see it all right—I just wanna keep the hundred acres we have and everything else around us can go as fast as it wants," I said.

Christina laughed. "Bert Miller on his hundred acres, feeding his two hundred chickens and slopping his dozen hogs while the rest of the world just carries on without him—"

"Sure. I mean, why can't I?"

"Because it doesn't work that way, Bert." A silence lingered between us. "Everything's getting bigger and faster—in ten years—no, maybe even five—folks'll be looking at you and your horse and your wagon loaded with eggs and ask, "Who in the hell is that guy? And what century is he from anyway?"

"I don't see that happening," I said. "Besides, I don't give a shit what people think."

"It's happening already—the world you want to live in is leaving you in the dust," she said. "Sometimes I wish it wasn't but it is."

"You don't know everything," I said. "You don't know everything that'll happen."

"Bert, I don't want to sit here and argue over things we got no control over—it's a waste of breath." Her eyes fastened on mine. "Bert, I'm doing what I think best for the children and myself—it's not out of any spite toward you, no ill will—none of that. It's what I think best given our circumstances. You can still see your children. Irv can spend time with you—I won't interfere with that. I'm sorry—but this is how I see it."

Christina and the kids moved out of the Lakeville ranch and into the house in Petaluma a week later. I helped them pack up, loaded the wagon, and with each trip the Lakeville house grew emptier, more hollow-sounding, until my footsteps clattered against its walls. She managed to rent the Petaluma house—the big house faced Prospect Street, the smaller one, Keller—with an option to buy once she received her share of the ranch. I looked for takers—asked John B. if he was interested, but he had all he could handle with the Mark West property. Everyone else I asked couldn't come up with cash to buy out Christina's share, so I sold the sheep and half the hogs at the auction yard, kept what chickens survived—and the ranch went on the market. It broke my heart to see it that way, but I had a heart used to being broken. I think if you could look inside and found my heart, you'd see it all covered with bruises and wrapped in gauze but somehow still beating. I don't want your pity, though—I broke hearts, too—I know I broke Christina's. Hers was just as damaged as mine.

When Christina and I met to figure out what our shares were, it turns out she had everything written down right to the penny.

I don't know why that surprised me—she'd done that since the day I met her—but it did. Every day for all the time we were together—some fifteen years and counting—she filled her ledger books with figures—the amount of eggs, cream, potato salad I left for town with, the time I left, the time I returned, and the amounts in the cash box at the end of each route. If there was a difference, and I hadn't spent it on essentials—chicken feed, potatoes, harness, clothes for the kids—whatever she figured was essential—she assumed I spent it on myself—and 'myself' meant I spent it on liquor.

Christina had put down the larger chunk of down-payment, as well, and she figured that in as part of the settlement. An appraiser came out and looked the place over and figured with implements, the remaining cattle, the ranch was worth about eight thousand dollars. After all her figuring, and adding and subtracting and whatever else she done, she said my share was twenty five hundred dollars. I didn't argue with her—twenty five hundred seemed fair enough if it meant the kids had a roof over their heads.

Frank and I stayed on working what was left of the ranch—milking cows and feeding chickens, gathering eggs and selling the eggs in town. The whole place seemed empty now without Christina and the kids, and I could hardly stand it. Prospective buyers would stop by and ask me all sorts of questions about the place and I'd tell them it was a fine ranch and if I had my druthers, I wouldn't be selling it. But the ranch finally did sell. Allan Erickson, a dairy farmer with a place south of Lakeville, bought it for his oldest son who'd just married and was looking for a place to start out on his own, so I sold him the milk cows and the seed boar and a half dozen hogs—just about everything I couldn't take with me. I kept my three horses and my two wagons.

Gertie told her father, Joe Keebler, about our situation. Joe lived north on Lakeville Road on a big dairy ranch but he also farmed over a thousand acres of oat hay, and he offered me a job driving his teams of horses. Besides milking cows, Joe was partner in a big land company and they built levees around tidal land to open the land up to farming. These fields were hundreds of acres and to work them, Joe and his partners had teams of horses, sometimes numbering fifteen to twenty all pulling one big implement—a ten-bottom plow, sets of discs, and something called a field planer that went along with its big blade, leveling out the field. Joe told me he needed a good teamster to drive them, and he told me that I was that man, so I signed on.

I lived in a little farmhand's house on the ranch—almost shouting distance from the one we use to own. I kept my three horses and wagons—that made me feel good. I hated the idea of ever having to give them up. I brought a couple of colony houses with me, as well, from our ranch, and seeded them with the surviving chickens. I still wanted to raise birds and keep some of my egg customers around town. I told Joe I needed that contact with folks, that I didn't want to spend all my time on a ranch, that I had some town-life in me, too, and he agreed. The time in town was also a chance to visit my kids.

So, another chapter in my life was beginning—one chapter ending and another one starting up—just like all those books in Carlotta's library. I wanted more than anything to keep the ranch Christina and I bought, but I got no one but myself to blame that I couldn't. I felt bad about all of it—the disappointment I caused, the damaged pride, the kids moving to town and being separated from them—but they liked living there—even Irv. He got a paper route and bought a Stanford bicycle and pretty soon was pedaling all around town like he owned the place. And Irene was in her glory, making new friends, and according to Christina, already serious about a certain boy named Ernest. With Nanette still sickly and weak, making new friends was harder, but she was closer to her doctors. And me? I was driving teams for Joe Keebler and when the days stretched out and the chickens started laying again, I'd load up the wagon twice a week and head to town and service my remaining customers. I drank with them, of course, and told stories and unloaded some of my heartbreak—you can't talk about this life without talking about heartbreak—it's all woven in there together. I don't know if that would ever change about me—how disappointment followed in my footsteps, but I figured I wasn't any different from the next man or woman that stuck their neck out and tried something new. It left a bitter taste in the mouth, but you learned to swallow around it, and pretty soon something else grabbed your mind.

And all along I hoped I'd change—be that kind of man that Christina wanted me to be, but I didn't know how that would happen—didn't have the foggiest idea. Maybe I'd come face to face with a burning bush like that guy in the Bible—or be struck by lightning. But I seen myself enough times standing at the edge of a cliff, asking that question—can I change and step back, or do I stay on the same path and leap over the side? But as much as I thought about changing, I fought off every change I could.

This new life wasn't exactly what I wanted, but it was exactly what I got. I still had two feet on the ground and wasn't six feet under it. I was working with horses again and had my chickens and some of my independence back, but it all came at a price. I missed having the kids around—yes, even stubborn, distant Irene, and I missed Christina—not her hard judgments on me so much, but those rare times her eyes softened and that hidden smile of hers came out. I'd gotten used to all my family—used to them the way your hand slips into a worn glove. Christina found a tenant for the small house, was back to making potato salad, and the kids were in city schools. All our lives would go on—nothing really stopped, nothing really ended. We got moved around, re-settled, and life moved in the direction it wanted to take.

77

The Accident
· · · · · · · · · · · ·

Saturday was my usual route delivery day. I'd load up my wagon with eggs early that morning like I'd done for years now, harness up Little Ike and the three of us would head to town. Jigs was graying in the muzzle and couldn't jump up on the wagon like he did when he was young—even the rats could outrun him now— so I'd lift him up onto the wagon seat and lift him back down. I kept just a few customers—they were mostly ones I could sit and drink coffee with early in the morning, and then as the day wore on, I'd hit the saloons and taverns where drinking shifted to the harder stuff and where I could shoot the shit before moving on to the next stop.

There wasn't any big clock saying I had to be here or be there and that was fine with me. If it took me all day, it took me all day. I'd often stop by Christina's to say hello to the kids before I left town. She'd smell my breath and shake her head. Irene continued to avoid me but I hugged Nanette—she was so pale and thin—and, of course, it was always good to see Irv, and we'd plan to hunt or fish but that never seemed to happen—we pretty much had separate lives by now. Like I said, there wasn't any clock I was punching—I was keeping my own time and Irv was keeping his.

With my Saturday route, I'd start at East Washington Street, with the Tivoli and the Yosemite, the Chop Suey house, then move down Main to the Petaluma Cafe, the Egg City Cafe, Baldwin's Bakery before turning onto Western Avenue to Van Morter's, Athan's, the Continental, the New York Oyster and Chop House and finally ending up right where Western took off up the hill at Romelio's Grotto Bar.

There was all kinds of talk in the air during this time—the war was going on over in Europe and folks in the bars would argue over whether we should join it or not. Wilson was trying to keep us out of it, but I figured it was just a matter of time before we joined the fight. I'd sit in Leo Catelli's Saloon and the talk went back and forth—half the saloon saying we had no business over there fighting and the other half saying, "You wanna fight the war over here, instead?" The other talk going around—and this talk affected us right here, right directly— was the movement to ban the sale of alcohol—"Prohibition," they called it. There was temperance groups already marching around town, and talk was with enough signatures, this prohibition horseshit would get on the ballot and maybe even become an amendment to the Constitution. We all prayed it wouldn't happen—those of us who prayed.

One time I staggered out of Klein's Center Club on Main, and there on the sidewalk facing me was an agitated group of mostly women carrying signs and decrying the drinking of alcohol. "Have you no shame?" one of them shouted at me. "You know what alcohol leads to?" another asked.

I looked to see if Christina was part of it—she wasn't. All of them standing there caught me by surprise, and I tried to think of an answer and the best I could come up with was, "Alcohol leads me to want another drink," which seemed a most honest thing to say.

"Think of your family," another one shouted out, and this remark shot right to inside me.

"I think of them all the time," I said.

"And are they—at this very moment—praying you'll stop your sinful habits?" another voice asked. They were all taking turns pumping me with questions.

"I don't know what they're doing 'at this very moment,'" I said, "but, yeah, they could be praying. I'll take all the prayers I can get."

I'd been working at Joe Keebler's now for several months. It was dusty work driving those big teams and I'd wrap a bandana across my mouth and nose, but it still didn't stop the coughing and spitting up big wads of dirt and phlegm all day and into the night. The coughing got so bad I gave up smoking cigars. The dust was everywhere during the summer and fall—a layer of it covered the furniture and worked its way into my ears and every opening in my body until I made stopping at the hot baths in town a thrice-weekly occurrence. Just washing up at the ranch wasn't enough.

I'd finished my route early one Saturday afternoon, took a hot bath and stopped by Christina's to see if Irv could join me for dinner. He said, "Sure, I'm hungry," and the two of us drove to Romelio's at the foot of the hill on Western Avenue. Ike and the wagon were tied up just on the other side of the avenue.

We sat in the barroom, Jigs at the foot of the table, and ordered steaks while Romelio and I talked back and forth. I drank bourbon and Irv drank Coca Colas and talked to Jigs, the dog. "That's a fine boy, you have there, Bert," Romelio said. And I beamed with pride.

We were halfway though our steaks when I heard the noise— the first sound was the sound the automobile and truck horns made—a kind of "Aoooooooogah" followed by tires skidding on the hard pavement and then a terrible crashing sound—like wood and metal all busting up—then one big, short squeal. I can still hear that squeal to this day.

We all ran for the door and looked out and what I first saw didn't make any sense—my eyes saw it but my brain couldn't think. It was a flat-bed truck loaded down with milk cans and it had pushed a car on top of my wagon.

I ran out to the street with Irv following and looked closer— and my heart just sank—I don't know how else to put it—my heart just fell out of me—because the truck had rammed the car right up over my empty wagon and the car landed on top of Ike. My horse was lying on his side—blood from his nose mixing with the spilled milk across the pavement. His rib cage heaved up and down—his nose fluttering, his breathing coming in big gulps—almost like that day nearly thirty years ago when he slid out from inside his mother.

I ran right up to Ike and could see the life draining out of him— there was nothing I could do. He lie there, the car's front tires resting on his rib cage. Then he stopped breathing, not moving a twitch, blood already pooling around his nose and mouth. Irv and me both stared down at the horse—hoping against all odds he'd come back to life. I touched the side of him. "Hey ol' man," I said. "You can't go out like this. We still got routes to do—you just can't."

The truck driver's face was covered with blood. "That car didn't stop," he pointed at the car on top of my wagon.

The car's driver stepped out onto a bed of splintered wood. The car sat there like some big hand had lifted it up and set it on top of Ike and my wagon. The wagon was all busted wood by now—its wheels collapsed, the axles snapped. "I had nowhere to go!" the truck driver said.

I just looked up at him and then down at Ike.

"Was that your horse and wagon?" the driver asked.

I nodded my head.

"The horse's name was Ike," Irv said.

"I'm sorry—I really am," the truck driver repeated.

Romelio had handed the driver his bar towel and the driver wiped the blood from his face. The car's driver and the truck driver argued back and forth about who was to blame.

A policeman arrived shortly afterwards. A small crowd had gathered. Irv stood next to me cradling Jigs in his arms while the truck driver walked over to us and apologized again. The policeman asked both drivers a series of questions and wrote down their answers in a little notebook. He looked around and asked if there were other witnesses—there was none.

"The car didn't stop," the truck driver said. He looked over at the driver of the car. "You didn't stop, man—you know you didn't."

The car driver didn't say anything. The policeman took our names and said he'd call for a tow truck and the tallow company to haul away Ike.

We went back inside Romelio's. I couldn't finish my steak—had no appetite left in me. Irv couldn't eat either. I ordered a double-shot of bourbon though and laid my money on the bar before leaving, but Romelio said, "No, no charge, Bert—not today," and he handed the money back to me.

I thanked him. By now the car had been pulled off Little Ike, and my wagon, its spokes broken, its box splintered into a hundred pieces, squatted on the pavement like a giant insect that lost it legs.

It was hard to look down at Ike and see him that way—I could have cried, and I did. I looked over at my boy and big tears ran down his cheeks.

"Let's walk back to your mother's," I said. He set little Jigs down and took my hand. We walked across town that evening neither of us talking much. Sometimes I'd say something but mostly there were long stretches of silence between us as we crossed from block to block.

"I never seen anything die before," Irv said. "Not like that."

"I seen all kinds of death," I told him. "You never get used to it—regardless of how much you seen."

We kept walking.

"It's like I got punched square in the guts," Irv said.

"It always brings me up short—even the things I killed myself." I looked over at Irv. "To tell you the truth, son, I never liked seeing things die. I never liked killing them, either. I liked tracking them and getting them in my sights, but so many times I hated just pulling that trigger—and many times I didn't. I wanted them to live just as they were."

"So why'd you kill things?" Irv asked.

"Because that's what we done," I said. "That was the whole point of it—you tracked something down and then you killed it."

"And you still didn't like doing it?"

"No, I didn't—I know that must sound crazy to you, but it's how I felt."

"I sure liked Ike," Irv said. "I know Ma didn't, but I did."

"Ike was foaled from your grandad's mare," I said. "On the same day we buried your grandfather. The priest was mumbling prayers and Alfonso, one of the ranch hands, came into Carlotta Stamm's parlor where the service was and motioned me to follow him."

"Was grandpa old when he died?" Irv asked.

"No, he wasn't—maybe fifty years, fifty five—when he was shot."

"Shot?"

"Yeah—he had a temper and it got him killed." I stopped here. "I told you all this before, didn't I?"

"Yeah, but you could tell me again," he said.

So I told Irv about the events of that day. I'd never told him the whole story, though, until this night when I felt I had to— when it carried such a weight I thought I'd collapse right there as we were walking if I didn't unload some of it.

"I'm not a religious person, Irv—your mother's probably told you that enough times—but I always felt my dad's spirit had jumped from his body right into Little Ike's when Ike was born—like my dad's spirit never died. It just found someone—something else to carry it along."

"So who has his spirit now that Ike's gone?" Irv asked.

"Maybe you do, son," I said. "It might be in you right now and you don't even know it."

"Will I feel it?"

"A time'll come when you will," I said. "You can't order it to come, either—it just shows up—you feel it."

On the walk back to Christina's, I kept hearing that truck's horn and its tires skidding on the pavement and the sound of my wagon busting apart, and in the middle of all that, Ike's last squealing sound as though asking me, "Who's going to haul those eggs now? And who knows all the stops along the route like I do? And what are you going to tell Margarite from the Yosemite when she comes out with her handful of carrots and I ain't there? And who are you going to talk to when your whole world's caving in? And who's going to take you home when you drunk too much?"

I hugged Irv good-bye when we reached Christina's. "You coming inside?" he asked.

"No, I'm not—I'll walk from here—I don't feel like talking to your Ma right now. Tell your mother and sisters hello. "

"You'll walk the whole way?"

"Yeah, the whole way," I said. "I think Jigs can make it. I'll carry him if he can't."

I got as far as the Eastside Tavern before stopping, went inside and ordered bourbon with a beer to keep it company—my usual. Jigs sat at my feet. Mario stood behind the bar polishing glasses. "You look like you lost your best friend," he said.

"I think I did, Mario." And I told him what happened earlier that evening.

"Everybody talks about that horse," he said. "He's like a legend around town—how he knows all the stops on your routes, and all the times he's hauled you home. We all have our own story about him."

"Yeah, he was something, wasn't he?"

"I'm sorry to hear about it," Mario said. He poured me another bourbon. "More and more cars and trucks these days—bound to happen sooner or later."

"Yeah, I guess it was."

"I know this just happened, but you thought about what to do?" he asked me.

"No, I ain't thought about it—there won't be another horse like him—I know that," I said. "Foolish to even think about it." I finished my bourbon. "It's like the end of something, isn't it?"

"It is—I hate to admit it, but it is," Mario said. "There's so much going on now—the war, everything speeding up, folks talking about outlawing alcohol—can you fuckin' believe it—outlawing alcohol? So many things happening, it just gets your head spinning."

"You think it'll leave us all behind?" I asked.

"I don't know—"

"It's like a train," I said. "You either hop onboard and it takes you where it takes you—or you don't. You watch it leave the station, watch it disappear down the tracks and you're left standing there, wondering whether you should have gotten on it or not—of course, by then, it's too late."

Mario poured me another and I was tempted to just keep drinking until I couldn't stand up, but then I remembered Little Ike wasn't around to haul me back home, and it was a good three or four miles still to go. I was on my own now.

I banged the last shot down and said goodbye to Mario, and Jigs and I walked the rest of the way down Lakeville Road to Joe Keebler's. All the earlier events came playing again and again in my mind—I couldn't stop thinking about them. By the time I arrived back at my little place, I was cold sober, tired and heart-broken like I hadn't been in years—but I was sober. Christina would have been surprised.

78

Changes
· · · · · · · · ·

I stayed on at Joe Keebler's for another three years. The war finally
ended during this time, Prohibition passed, there was a terrible
flu epidemic and Christina's petition to divorce me, after filing one
year earlier, was finalized in Sonoma County Courthouse. I didn't
show up for the final hearing—I only asked she let me see my kids.
We'd settled on the ranch sale—she took the bigger part and had all
the figures to show why. It left me with a little chunk that I salted
away. Both my big horses had to be put down. Kris Knudsen came
out and done it—I couldn't do it myself—just no heart left in me
for that kind of thing. They'd given me twenty-five years of work
and they were worn out. And Jigs—he finally died from old age—
his hips stiffened and got to the point he was just dragging around
his rear legs. Then he stopped walking altogether. He'd look up at
me with those sad eyes—like it was all his fault—and I told him it
wasn't—that it's what happens to all of us if we live long enough.
I went to rouse him one morning and he was cold and stiff. I dug
a hole under a gum tree and laid him in and cried like a baby the
whole time.

Change was in the air everywhere. Big tractors with iron wheels—
looking almost like those machines of war—those tanks I'd seen in
the newspapers—were replacing teams of horses in the field—replacing them everywhere—and I was feeling like a man watching the
whole world he was used to living in slowly disappear and change
into something else. Most times I didn't know what to do, so I kept
drinking—alcohol sales were prohibited but that didn't stop the flow
of alcohol. You learned quick where the places were that sold it—the
"speakeasies"—they called them, and the locals who were distilling
their own, as well, and selling it out the back door. Vinny Vincera,
at the north end of town, made some fine bourbon—the best in

all these parts. He'd been distilling it for years in a shed behind his restaurant. He let it age in oak barrels—not like some of that white-mule going around. It was the real deal. I'd ride my bicycle up there, buy a few bottles, stash them in my clothes drawer, and pull one out regular-like and sip Vinny's fine work.

Irene married her fellow, Ernest, during this time, as well. He was from a prominent family that lived up on the hill. I was on Casa Grande Road at Len Hartman's the day of the wedding, looking at a new rat terrier when the wedding party drove by—a whole line of cars with the front one pulling a string of tin cans behind it, and all the cars' horns blasting away. I watched them drive by—Irene sitting next to Ernest, the veil from her hat blown to one side of her face. Len looked at me and said, "Bert, I don't mean to stick my nose into other people's business, but ain't that your daughter that just rode by?"

I nodded my head and said, "Yeah, that's my daughter all right." He just looked back at me and didn't say anything else. I decided not to buy the dog.

I liked working at Joe Keebler's. He treated me well and I had a roof over my head and he tolerated my drinking—to a point. But the years of working in all that dust played hell with my lungs. I coughed all the time and had no wind. I didn't need any doctor to tell me I had to get out of working in the fields. Joe saw the shape I was in and he recommended me to his friend Tony Armini, an egg wholesaler in town. I dried up for a couple of days and went to see Tony and he hired me on the spot. "Joe Keebler spoke well of you," Tony said, "and that's good enough for me."

I rented a little shack on Wilson Street on the eastside and worked loading cases of eggs onto Tony's trucks. The horse and wagon days were mostly over, and now it was Autocars and Fords instead of Clydesdales and Percherons—but Tony kept a horse and wagon, and he gave me a little route in town, so I was able to get out and hob knob with folks. It wasn't like the earlier days with Little Ike, but it was better than staying in a warehouse all day. I didn't like working in one place, and I told Tony I wanted to learn to drive truck. He set me behind the steering wheel of an Autocar and I took to it as easy as driving horses. It wasn't the same, of course. I couldn't walk alongside an Autocar and whistle it to stop the way I could with Little Ike. I couldn't talk to it either. And when Margarite saw me at the Yosemite, she'd have a handful of carrots and run out to see Little Ike but see a truck instead, and when I told her Little Ike was gone, her long face got even longer.

Tony Armini drew out routes for me, and I'd start each work morning with a truckload of eggs and a list of stops for the day. He told me no drinking on the job. It wasn't like the old times, though. I was punching a time clock and had to move right along to finish the route in time. I couldn't linger the way I used to, down a draft and shoot the shit, talk about the ballgames, the boxing matches, and who died, and who got married, and who was carrying on with someone else's wife. I mean, we still talked about those things, but there was a clock ticking inside my head all the time, and I had to keep moving from stop to stop.

The trucks improved each year and could travel further and faster than the ones before them. Tony was now taking on customers in San Rafael and points south, and I'd sometimes haul a load of eggs down to the ferry at Sausalito and ride it across to a warehouse in San Francisco owned by one of Tony's partners. On these trips to the city, just before leaving Petaluma, Tony would say to me, "You don't see nothing, right? If someone asks, you don't know nothing either, okay?"

"What'd you mean, Tony?" I asked him.

"I mean, when they're unloading your truck at the warehouse and somebody asks about the load, you say, 'I don't see nothing, okay? I just drive the truck." Tony laughed a lot, even with a cigar stuck in the corner of his mouth. His nose was shaped like a potato and his big, round belly spilled over the top of his belt. He had a lot of sayings—his favorite one was: "I didn't make a lot of money today, but I made a lot of friends." He liked to swear in Italian, too—the only Italian he could remember. It was a mystery to me at first, but it didn't take long until I figured out that in the middle of that load of eggs were cases of bootleg liquor Tony meant for his partners.

"I don't know if I want to do this or not," I said to Tony.

"I'll toss in an extra twenty as a sweetener," he said. "Does that change your mind?"

"Twenty dollars?"

"Yeah, twenty—and if anything happens, you don't know nothing—who loaded the truck, what's inside the truck—nothing!" he said.

For a couple of trips I was okay—nervous, but okay—but the worry about getting caught outweighed the extra cash I made. It seemed like dirty money to me and I didn't like it. All my life I'd been telling myself it wasn't the money I was after—and if it was just for the money, then I'd do something else. If I chased money, then Tino and me would have loaded our skiff up with ducks the way the cash hunters done or dynamite pools where the big trout hid the way Sheers and his guys done—but I couldn't do that. I tried to live clear of just doing things for money—that my heart had to be in it—and if it wasn't, it was on to something else. I know that's what I told Irv, and here I was doing what I said I wouldn't.

Tony offered me even more if I'd deliver to several different warehouses in the city, and at first I told him no, the worry was eating at me. "No worries," he said. "These are my friends, some of them even family—most I've known all my life." Tony stuffed twenty dollars into my coat pocket. "This kind of money," Tony said, "you can buy your own truck."

"I'll do it this one time," I said, "and then, that's it—no more."

So I drove the truck onto the ferry at Sausalito and crossed the bay to the Embarcadero, where I drove onto the city streets, headed for the North Beach area. I found the address and pounded on a warehouse door and a fellow opened a little sliding window in the door and asked, "You the egg man?" and I said, "Yeah, I'm the egg man."

He pulled the warehouse door open and I drove inside. I didn't have to do anything the whole time—they even brought me a cup of coffee and the newspaper. Workers there unloaded the truck while I just stood by and watched. When they were finished unloading, they backloaded my truck with empty egg cases, opened the warehouse door and I was back on the street again and on my way to the Embarcadero.

One day I'd driven about a block, maybe a block and a half from the warehouse, when I saw a woman walking along the sidewalk—long dark hair, graying and braided. I don't know why she caught my eye—there were plenty of women walking along sidewalks in this city—but this one did. It was something about her—I can't explain it—even to this day. I slowed down and drove ahead but then stopped and watched her approach in the truck's mirror. When she finally looked my way I was stunned. It was a face I'd seen before—I knew that—an older face by now but one that had lingered in my memory for twenty years or more. Instinctively I just called out, "Della!" Her eyes caught mine and it was a look of surprise.

She looked over at me. "Do I know you?"

"Are you Della who worked at the woolen mill in Santa Rosa?"

She hesitated. "Yes, I used to work there—several years ago. Who are you?"

"Bert," I said. "Bert Miller."

"Bert Miller,'" she repeated to herself. "What department did you work in at the mill?"

"I never worked at the mill," I said. "I met you in a little place called The Golden Bobbin on the west side of Santa Rosa."

"Now this is weird," she said. "How you know this about me."

"I went home with you—you rented a room on the bottom floor of a house that faced a park. It had a carriage house in the back where my horse stayed."

"Ohhhh—it's starting to come back now—"

"I went to look you up the following week and your landlady said you'd moved back to the city just days before—she first thought I was the one arguing with you and had to convince her I wasn't."

"Bert, did we—"

I nodded my head. "We did," I said, "and it was wonderful."
Her face flushed red.

"I wanted to see you again," I said, "and was so disappointed
to find you gone—I looked for you for days afterwards."

"Really?"

"Just as sure as I'm sitting in the seat of this truck talking to
you," I said. "So much has happened since then I don't have time
to tell you everything."

"Do you live in the city now?" she asked.

"No, I haul eggs down here from Petaluma once a week—I'm
thinking about quitting, though."

"You're an egg man?" and she laughed. "Why do you want to
quit?"

"Mostly, I like it," I said, "but there's things about it I don't."

I didn't know whether I should tell her everything about the
job right then or not. I didn't know exactly what to do or what
to say—it'd all been such a surprise, but I wanted to keep talking
to her—I didn't want her to disappear again. I kept looking at
Della—at the little scattering of freckles across her nose and cheeks
that I hadn't noticed until the morning after. I looked at her dark
brown eyes and her olive skin—still not believing it was her—that
if I closed my eyes and opened them again, she'd vanish from sight.

"What about you, Della?"

"I work at a fish company—Lucia's— down at the wharf,"
she said. "I weigh the catches when they come in and write down
the amounts. Sometimes I work on the line—can't seem to avoid
working in mills or factories. But I like the people I work around.
The worst thing about it is the smell—you can't get out of your
clothes and you have to scrub hard to get it off your skin."

"No bosses like the one you had at the woolen mill?" I asked.

"I told you about him?"

"Yes, you did—"

"He's why I left Santa Rosa," she said. "I learned my lesson
about warming up to bosses—they hold it over you—think you
owe them something."

"Are you married?"

"Once," she said. "Divorced now. I'm not too good for the long haul—I should tell you that right out-front."

"I wasn't too good at it myself," I said.

"I thought it'd work out." Della looked down the street and then back at me. "I mean, we started out pretty good—"

"It usually does—then it changes, doesn't it?" I said. "I know it did for me."

"Something happened," she said. "But I'm not sure what. We both liked a good time—I mean, who doesn't? And then all of that started wearing off for both of us—not just me. He saw someone else that caught his eye, and I said, 'Okay, if you want to play that game, I'm pretty good at it myself. And before I knew it, he wasn't coming home at night and I worried less and less about it."

"I'm sorry to hear that," I said.

"He said all the right things at the beginning and I figured, why not give it a try? I was getting tired of my old ways." She looked at me. "So, Bert, what's your story? Is it a sad one as well?"

"Yeah, they're all sad stories, aren't they?"

"Did you have the wandering eye, too?

"No, I didn't," I said. It wasn't the complete truth but close to it. "Sure, I noticed women—what normal guy doesn't? But I'm not sure what happened. I proposed to her because I was afraid she'd go with someone else."

"She was with someone else?"

"Yeah, my best friend, Tino—he had designs on her."

"And once you butted in Tino was out?"

"Yeah, that's pretty much what happened. Tino and me didn't talk for years because of it."

"So, you're the jealous type?"

"I hate to admit it, but I got some of that in me—it's just a feeling that rises up and I can't do anything about it," I said. "It's like I don't notice the value of someone until that someone is with somebody else. I don't trust my own judgment. Does that make any sense?"

"I think it does."

I hadn't bared so much of myself in such a short time to a woman I hadn't seen in over twenty years—and right there on a street in the city. It caught me by surprise. I was a guy who talked a lot when the situation felt right—in the company of friends, to anyone I thought would listen, a glass of bourbon in my hand—but I was careful about going too deep inside me. There were things I felt folks didn't need to know about me—so I'd just scratch at the surface of what I was feeling. It was all a mystery— all stuff I kept hidden—and I figured folks didn't want to hear about it anyway.

"I need to head back to Petaluma now, Della, and I was wondering if—"

"You could look me up?"

"Yeah. Is that something you'd like?"

"Sure," she said. "I always need a friend, someone I can talk to." She took a piece of paper and pencil out of her coat pocket and wrote her address down. "I live on Chestnut Street—not far from here," and she pointed north.

"I'll look you up—I promise—and you won't run off to Santa Rosa?"

We both laughed.

"Bert, I live my own life, okay?" she said. "I do what I want and I'll always square with you— so don't go trying to build a fence around me. I hope you understand."

"Fair enough," I said. "You live your life and I'll live mine."

She started to walk away.

"What about next Sunday?" I asked her. "Could I see you then?"

She turned around. "Sure—next Sunday's fine."

"Next Sunday—you won't forget?"

She smiled. "No, I won't forget."

I think the truck and I floated above the street just then. I watched her walk away, then turn the corner and she was gone and I wondered if I'd ever seen her again. Hope and excitement both ran through me—like a strong shot of bourbon—like when you think something good is going to happen but you're never entirely sure. You got a whole history to look back on that tells you so. She'd disappeared once; she could disappear again. And her warning about not being good for the long haul—that rang in my ears, too, because already little scenes with her were forming in my mind, little pictures of the two of us together that leaned toward the long haul. Already I was writing our story in my mind minutes after just seeing her again.

I drove back to the ferry terminal and crossed the bay and thought of her the entire way back to Petaluma, remembering as much of that night some twenty years ago as I could—her sitting by herself in The Golden Bobbin, warning me off that her boyfriend might arrive any time but didn't, and the walk back to her place with Little Ike following us and the time in bed—how do you forget something like that? I couldn't.

I remembered especially the disappointment I felt when her landlady told me she was gone—I didn't know what to think. Was I just another guy—another pigeon— she bedded for the night? Just another lonely Joe that wandered into the same bar she'd wandered into and you thought it was all Fate? That it was meant to happen this way? Had she really returned to the city or was it a line she and her landlady worked out ahead of time? And who was this boss that threatened her? What did he have on her? So many questions then, and now—all this time later—so many of them returning. Did I even want to get mixed up with her again? Toss my heart into the fray? I had to think about that one, but I already knew the answer. It was the woman just out of reach that I wanted— the woman surrounded in mystery that kept saying 'no' that drove me wild with desire.

Over the next days, Della stayed on my mind, crowding everything else out. So much so, that at times, I couldn't even bring up a picture of what she looked like I'd thought about her so much. I didn't quit driving for Tony like I said, either, because now the driving job and Della were linked together, and each trip to the city would bring me closer to her—or so I hoped. What was going to happen, I didn't know. How do we know anything about this life?

A week ago, Della was some distant memory, someone I'd almost completely forgot about with only a little brief picture of her popping to my mind's surface before disappearing again. Fine with me. Just diappear. Now she was all I thought about. She filled every space in my mind, every space in my imagination. What a big crapshoot this life was! I'd been saying that for years, and it was still holding true.

And so I'd made a date with a woman I'd already slept with but other than that, didn't know much about. Was she a heart-breaker? Maybe—all women can be heartbreakers—all men, too. Just depends what end of the stick you're on. And what did I wantto happen between us? Another roll in the sack? Thank her and then be on my way? It wasn't so easy anymore to do that—to just walk away like nothing happened—like those earlier years when you'd plunked your money down on some strumpet, got your choad off, put your pants back on, and that was that—hardly a thought about it.

Now I was older—not necessarily wiser—and that kind of thing didn't do much for me anymore. But was I ready for another relationship when I'd washed out of the big one before? How do you get ready for one, I wondered? Was there something you could study? Some model you could copy? Or, was it like I done with everything else—just over-thinking the whole thing? Maybe trying to put square pegs in round holes? Why not just see what unfolded instead? Why not be the person you are—the person you ended up being—without a whole lot of trying to be someone else? And why not let her be the person she is, and then see what the mix is like? That seemed the simplest thing to do—better than all that thinking and planning and hoping—and most of it ending up just wasted breath anyway. Why not let it alone and see what settles out? And then try to live with what you find?

79

Della

．．．．．．．．．．．．．．．．．．．．．．．．．．．．．．．

I rode the ferry across the bay that following Sunday morning,
found her little place on Chestnut Street. She invited me in. It
was a studio flat, a small room with the bed and kitchen table just a
couple of feet from each other. It had bright curtains and jade plants
on the window sills. "It's not the Palace Hotel," she said, "but I like
it—particularly the view."

She was right—it was a great view of the bay below, looking
down on the roofs to the warehouses, and beyond the roofs, the
wharfs where the fishing boats were docked. A good part of the
city had been rebuilt by now after the earthquake and fire. She
brewed a pot of tea and when we'd finished drinking, she put on
her coat and a knit cap and we walked toward Golden Gate Park.
The morning fog had burned off, leaving a sunny but cool day.
We walked all around the park with her arm in mine. I felt like a
king—like I owned the park and every beautiful tree and shrub in
it—like I owned the entire city and was presenting it to this lady
beside me as a gift to her. When we tired of walking, we'd sit on
a bench and watch folks strolling by. We'd make up stories about
some of them. If they were couples, how they met, or what odd
pairings they seemed. We'd poke fun at the hats they wore, the dogs
tugging at their leashes. We were like two little children—laughing
at the world around us with hardly a care to burden us down.

"I brought us a little something," I said, and pulled a flask out
of my coat pocket. "Care to partake?"

"Sure," she said.

I handed her the flask, she took a quick look around, then
brought it to her lips and drank. "That tastes pretty good," she said.

"Can I tell you a little secret? But you got to keep it to yourself,
though."

"I'm pretty good with secrets," she said.

"Each time I haul eggs down here, I haul cases of this liquor down here with me. The liquor's hidden in the middle of the load."

She looked over at me. "Oh, so you're not just the egg man?"

"No, I'm not just the egg man, but the moonshine man, too," I said. "I'm a bit torn about hauling the stuff."

"Why, because it's illegal?"

"Yeah," I said. "And I'd always told myself I wouldn't do anything just for the money and here I am—"

"We're all working for the money, though, aren't we?"

"I guess."

"You're an outlaw, Bert MIller," she laughed. "I don't need to know anything else, okay? Other than I like drinking it."

She'd moved closer to me on the bench.

"Tell me about yourself, Bert—what you've been doing these past years? You got married and divorced—you already told me that. Any children?"

"Three," I said. And I told her about my oldest, Irene, who was married now and how we never got along. And I told her about Nanette and her health problems, but I especially told her about Irv. "I know you're not supposed to play favorites with your kids," I said, "I love them all, but Irv's my favorite."

"And your ex-wife?" she asked. "How do the two of you get along?"

"We're civil to each other," I said. "I told you we bought a ranch together and tried to make it work—"

"And why didn't it?"

"That was mostly on me," I said. "We argued a lot."

"About what? Money?"

"About everything—it seemed. The arguing over money came later."

I didn't know how much to tell her right then but I figured she'd find out sooner or later. "We argued mostly about my not towing the line. And my drinking—she couldn't tolerate it."

"You drank a lot?" she asked.

"Any drinking was a lot to her," I said. "She called me selfish—putting myself and my habits before the rest of the family."

"Well, I drink," she said. "It's something I've learned to live with—"

"The same for me," I told her. "I've learned to live with it and not beat myself up every time I have a taste."

"These times make it difficult, though—like you're some kind of outcast," she said. "I don't like it—this whole prohibition thing was such a mistake." She moved closer to me on the bench.

"I don't like it either," I said.

We sat there and I thought about what part of the last twenty years to share with her. All of it ran together with high points and low points and mostly long days of working in between. It wasn't any special life I lived—pretty ordinary the more I thought about it. What seemed so important at the time—so memorable—got swallowed up by the daily push and pull.

"Let's walk," I said.

We left our bench and walked. Della took my hand.

"I'm curious, Della, what did you think of me back then?"

"It's awhile back, Bert—you're testing my memory."

"I know that—I was just wondering what you remembered about me or about that night."

"There were lots of things going on then—"

"Yeah, I know there were."

"If I say things—things you may not want to hear—it's not to hurt your feelings, okay? I'm saying them as honestly as I can."

"Sure, give it to me straight," I said. Why varnish over it? If it's something I don't want to hear—well, then it's something I don't want to hear—better than blowing smoke up my ass.

"I forgot about you—figured you were just someone who happened along and that was that. Men come into my life and then they go."

"But you're the one who left," I said.

"Because I had to—I thought I explained to you what was going on," she said.

"You did, but I wanted to see you again—went back to Santa Rosa and combed the streets up and down looking for you—"

"I was in a bad way then—nothing would have worked," she said.

"What about now?"

"What about it?"

"Are you in a bad way now?"

"No, not like before—I still got my devils—I think all of us do, but I feel much freer now—more in control of myself. It's a good feeling."

"What did you feel when you saw me last week?" I asked.

"Surprise, of course—and a little confused—"

"About what?"

"Whether I wanted to keep talking with you or just cut it off, and be on my way."

"And not go digging up the past?"

"Yeah—the past."

We walked and I didn't say anything—just let what she said seep in. Like I said, I wanted to hear the straight stuff and not have it twisted around to something I wanted to hear instead. I thought I was strong enough for any of it. But I wanted to hear something different, too—I wanted the "straight stuff" to be that she'd really thought of me, that I made an impression on her and that she wanted to see me again—but I wasn't hearing that.

"I'm cautious about first meetings, Bert—particularly in bars," she said. "Folks can tell you anything with a little alcohol in them. But from what I can remember, you had a certain charm about you—almost a kind of innocence that attracted me. You seemed vulnerable, but honest, too."

"Vulnerable?"

"Yeah, vulnerable—sensitive—like you'd been hurt before."

"Hasn't everyone?"

"Yeah, but a lot of folks I know—men, in particular—try to hide it. Try to pull a thick skin over themselves and act like nothing bothers them. I didn't see you doing that," she said. "I mean, I don't take every man I meet back to my place."

"That's good to know," I said. "It could get a bit crowded."

We both laughed.

"There was someone—someone I was holding out some hope for," I said, "but it didn't happen. Her heart was with someone else."

"Awful when that happens, isn't it?"

Yeah—awful."

"And then another person comes along that makes you forget about what happened earlier—"

"Yeah, another person came along all right," I said, "but I'm not sure she made me forget what happened before—it was all kind of rushed."

"Why was that?"

"I already told you about her. I saw her with my best friend— damn, this is embarrassing to talk about—"

"Oh, yeah, the jealousy thing."

"Yeah, that's what happened," I said. "Until then she was just someone I helped out a little—built a brooder house and a layer house with her brothers and delivered potato salad to her customers when her wagon had broke down. Wasn't really feeling anything romantic toward her, to tell you the truth—just afraid Tino would win her over and I'd be left out."

"Doesn't sound like solid grounds for a marriage," Della said.

"She was a good woman, though—no disputing that," I said. "A hard worker, honest to a fault, reliable—she'd already lost her fiancé and my feeling was I just didn't stack up against him. He was someone she had her heart set on, and then a load of lumber crushed him, and I was second fiddle. She never said that—it was just a feeling I had about her, and I thought with enough time I could learn to love this woman—that it's all right not to be head-over-heels in love because a lot of that wears off in the long run anyway. What was important was to just get along—and we mostly did that—"

"Until you drank—"

"Yeah, until I drank—mind you, I wasn't one of those mean drunks, either—didn't go tearing up the house and beating her—none of that. There was other things going on, too—I worried about giving up too much of my freedom, not having the say over my life that I did before—but it was the drinking that usually set things off. It was a sore spot with her even though on the day I proposed, I said I liked my drink and wasn't about to give it up, but it wouldn't be an excuse to treat her bad, beat on her or anything like that—and I didn't. I kept my word."

"I married a lout—a smooth talker," she said. "Big plans. He told me he was headed for the top," she said. "And I swallowed all of it. He was headed for the top, all right—the top of the shit pile."

"What happened?"

"I told you something about him already—he was a womanizer—something I always suspected but he'd always have an excuse—always some reason why he was late or if he'd been seen with a woman, why he was with her—a business deal, friend or wife of a partner. At first you want to believe all his crap—give him the benefit of the doubt—but pretty soon you start seeing through it. Pretty soon he runs out of excuses and you run out of patience," she said. "I left him—filed for divorce and haven't seen him since."

"Both our stories have sad endings, don't they?" I said. "But it's good talking about them—getting them out in the air where they can breathe—"

"Instead of being locked up inside?"

"Yeah, better to get them out, don't you think?"

She nodded her head.

"I've been carrying around all this stuff for years—thinking about it too much but never really talking about it—I used to with Tino, but he was the guy that I saw with Christina—"

"And that ended that?"

"Yeah, it was never the same between Tino and me."

"Have you ever seen him since then?"

"Yeah, in the county jail in Santa Rosa," I said. "He shot at his father, and his father shot at him. Both had been drinking or they would have killed each other—"

"If they hadn't been drunk?"

"Yeah, being drunk saved them both," I said. "How often does that happen?"

We walked in the park until late afternoon, stopped and ate Chinese food in Chinatown before returning to her flat. At the door, we embraced. I kissed her on the lips, and I wanted to kiss her longer, but she pulled her face away. I wanted her to invite me in, too, but she didn't. We weren't picking up where we left off some twenty-odd years ago—it wouldn't be that easy. Was I disappointed? I was. I hated uncertainty more than anything—not knowing what was going to happen between us—if anything would happen at all. I was flying blind—the way I always flew.

"I enjoyed the day together, Della."

"I enjoyed it, too—you should go so you don't miss the ferry back.

"I'd have to stay here if I did—"

"Go—you've got time."

"I can see you again?"

"Yes."

So I rode the ferry to Sausalito and from there took the train to San Rafael and later, the train to Petaluma. I arrived back home late, stripped out my clothes, fell into bed and went right to sleep.

80

Another Death in the Family

• •

I tried to see my children whenever I could, but we all seemed to live separate lives now that we were no longer together. Christina was good about letting me spend time with them. Irene was married now, and living on top of the hill with Ernest. She'd pretty much erased me from her life. That hurt—but it was her choice, but what could I do but accept it? I'd take Irv out to dinner at least once a week, and we hunted quail and ducks when the seasons rolled around. He grew up fast. I gave him an L.C. Smith double-barreled shotgun for his fifteenth birthday.

He was a fine boy, always asking questions, considerate of others, and I felt damn lucky to have him. He helped his mother, too, caring for his ailing sister, and I give his mother credit for how good he turned out.

Then there was Nanette. She was a sweetheart of a girl who'd battled poor health—a serious blood disorder, a faulty heart—from the day she was born. She'd somehow survived the flu epidemic, but it kept her locked inside mostly—much of that time bedridden. Her condition had taken a turn for the worst lately and she was now in the General Hospital. Irv and I went to visit her, and she didn't look good at all. She'd lost even more weight and her eyes were sunken and dull—her skin so pale it seemed you could look right through to her bones. It was all I could do just to keep from crying. I looked at her and saw Christina's features—but all of them so sharpened now—the nose, the cheekbones.

"How are you doing, sweet Nanny?" I asked her.

"Not too good, Papa" she said. "I have no energy. I asked the nurse if I was going to die, and she said, 'No, you'll fight it," but I'm not so sure—I'm tired from fighting it."

"We all love you very much," I said. "Don't we, Irv?"

"I love you, Sis, and hope you get better," Irv said. "When you get out of here, we can ride bicycles together—all over town."

"Can you take me home now?" she asked.

"Not yet, Nanny," I said.

"I'd like to ride bicycles with you, Irv—more than anything. I want to be like everyone else." Nanette forced a smile.

"We're all praying for you," I said. Praying, I thought—a word I didn't use too much, if at all, but I prayed—even us non-believers—in desperate times, when everything was out of our hands, when all we could do was mutter some words toward the sky, toward heaven, toward a God we hoped would be there—anywhere—and hoped just this once he was listening to us.

Doctors said Nanette had some kind of rare blood disorder—something she'd had since birth— and we knew all along that the chances of a long life for Nanette weren't good—that she was living on borrowed time. She was a fighter—just like her mother—but it wasn't enough. Just days short of her twentieth birthday—worn down and pale as a bedsheet—the fight nearly drained out of her, she died. Irv and I had just left the hospital an hour before.

"She's gonna make it, isn't she, Dad?" Irv asked as we walked up Sixth Street toward the center of town.

"I hate to say it, Irv, but I don't think she will—doctors say there isn't much they can do."

"She was always sick," he said. "Doesn't seem fair, does it? Someone born sick like that—and nothing they can do about it."

"No, it's a bad deal all the way around," I said. "She didn't deserve any of it."

"Did you ever wish she'd never been born?" he asked me.

"No, I never did—I mean—it's a question you bat back and forth in your mind, but once they're born, they're yours—healthy or not," I said, "And you accept it." I looked over at Irv. "Your Ma thinks it was everything going on around us at the time—our fighting and disagreeing—that caused it, but I told her it wasn't so—that it didn't work that way—that sometimes right in the middle of war, and couples fighting and the worst things happening, healthy babies are born."

Christina made the funeral arrangements. A Mass was said for Nanette at Saint Vincent's and after the Mass we were part of the funeral procession to the cemetery on Magnolia Avenue. Christina dabbed at her eyes the entire time with a handkerchief, and we'd embraced and I told her how sorry I was that our daughter had died. "She's in a better place now," Christina said.

I hoped it was true.

First, it was my dad, then Ma, and now my daughter—even the horses and my dog, too. You never get used to death around you regardless of how often it happens. You think you can shore yourself up for it—keep a brave front—but you're only fooling yourself. Each death takes something from you—some little piece that you'd always saved for them and that they brought out in you, and now that piece is gone. So, what's left? Only the memories of them you hold inside you—that's all it seemed to me.

Wouldn't they be in heaven? Someone like Nanette? If there was a heaven, she'd be the first one in. And, for her sake, I hope there was. But like I said all along, I didn't take much shrift in it, myself. I stopped believing years ago. My feet were here on the ground—the only heaven and the only hell I'd ever know. I'd take the real heart beating over the imagined one anytime. And the soul? I didn't know about the soul. Maybe it had a life of its own and was too big for me to understand—too big for me to even doubt. Days and weeks later I'd find myself wanting to ask where Nanette was, why I hadn't seen her when I stopped in to visit with Irv, and all those old feelings—the ones I braced myself for—the ones I thought I could handle—well, they spilled out again and I felt as helpless as I ever felt.

81

An Unwelcome Visit

· · · · · · · · · · · · · · · · · · · ·

Weeks had passed since I'd last seen Della. After Nanette's death, I realized yet again that a long life wasn't a given, and so I spent more time working locally, staying closer to Irv. We fished along the Petaluma Creek and hunted quail and doves in the hills above Stage Gulch. One time we hunted so far south along the creek, we had to hitch a ride back to Petaluma before it got dark. We were packing shotguns and nobody picked us up. Later, it turned out, it was the same day townsfolk strung up a pair of bank robbers in a Santa Rosa cemetery that had shot and killed a deputy sheriff. A Petaluma constable stopped us when he saw our guns, and after explaining to him we had nothing to do with the hanging, gave us a ride back into town.

We rode our bicycles together and sometimes struck out for the countryside. He always wanted to race and show me the different tricks he learned on his bicycle—how he could ride without any hands and even stand up on top of the seat while the bicycle rolled forward. I'd watch him and a cold, sharp feeling would race down the middle of me—right down to my groin—afraid he'd fall and hurt himself. With all this time I spent with Irv, I still thought of Della and what the chances were of us ever getting together as a couple. Those kinds of thoughts never left me. I wanted to see how my feelings settled out toward Della in her absence, as well— how I'd feel with time between us—as if twenty years wasn't long enough.

I couldn't stop thinking about her, though, and one Saturday— on a giant impulse—I rode the train down to Sausalito and crossed over to the city on the ferry, and found myself just a few blocks from Della's place. I'd stopped and bought some flowers along the way and as I climbed the stairs to her flat, my heart felt like it would explode out of my chest. One part of me said 'knock on her door' but another said 'maybe this is a bad idea.' I stopped just outside her door, caught my breath—told myself I've come all this way— and knocked.

At first, no answer. Maybe she was gone—out in the city somewhere. I left the flowers by her door. I turned, started to walk away before hearing her voice on the other side of the door. "Who is it?" she asked.

I turned around. "It's me—Bert."

She opened the door slightly. "This isn't a good time to visit," she whispered.

Then I heard a man's voice from inside. "Who is it, Della?"

"No one—just someone who knocked on the wrong door," she said, looking straight into my eyes. She closed the door and I stood there feeling all sorts of things—but mostly feeling pretty goddamn foolish—like I'd been snookered again and the world was having one more big laugh at my expense. And I'd even felt a betrayal of sorts, too. I'd taken a few steps toward the stairs when Della appeared in the hallway, the door closed behind her.

"You can't just drop in on me like this," she said in a loud whisper. "We don't know each other that well yet."

"I'm sorry—I was thinking of you and wanting to see you—"

"Fine, but let me know ahead of time."

"Who's that guy?" I asked.

"A friend—that's all I have to tell you about him."

"A friend—like I'm a friend?"

"Yes, I have friends—male friends," she said. She looked at me and must have read my disappointment. "I told you right-off, Bert, that I don't hide things—that I'm out front with my life, and you said that you were okay with it, right? And that I don't have to tell you every little detail about my private life? Didn't I tell you that?"

"You did."

"Well, I don't—we're not at that point yet, do you understand?"

"I guess we're not," I said.

"No guessing about it—we're not there—"

"I guess I'm not okay with it then—"

"Well, Bert—I'm sorry you're not—but that's the way it is."

"I'm not too good at sharing—"

"Oh, that's right—you're the jealous type—now I remember," she said. "But that's okay. At least you know that about yourself—you know the people and the situations to avoid—so you're probably better off avoiding me."

"I wish I was different—I wish I could change that about myself."

"Maybe you can—I don't know," she said. "Didn't your ex-wife want you to change, as well?"

"Yeah, she did."

"And how did that go?"

I shook my head.

"Look, Bert—I appreciate your interest in me—you're a good guy and maybe we can be friends—maybe—but I want to be free to live my life. I don't want a man controlling me—men have tried that before and it never worked out.'"

"I can understand the unhappiness part," I said.

"Then good—you know what I'm talking about then."

"I'm sorry for showing up like this—I thought you felt different about me."

"How do you know how I feel about you, when I don't know myself?"

The door to Della's flat opened and a man stepped out into the hallway. "Everything all right out here?" he asked.

"Everything's fine," she said. "I saw an old friend and we're catching up on the news."

He turned around and went inside.

"I won't bother you anymore," I said.

"You're not bothering me, Bert—I do live by some rules and I'd like the people around me to honor them."

"Now I know one of them," I said.

"That's right—now you know one of them."

"Well, good-bye then."

"Good-bye, Bert."

And so I left her place, feeling about as low as I'd felt since Nanette died. It wasn't the same feeling exactly—with Nanette, it was a long grieving, a long witnessing to her suffering and then her death. There was a hope—a slim one—that she'd recover, but as much as I wanted that to happen, I never believed it would. With Della, it had started with hope, too—a hope that this small flame might grow into something larger—and then she vanished for twenty-five years. And seeing her again after all this time, nothing she said or nothing she'd done—outside of being kind and thoughtful to me—encouraged this kind of thinking, this kind of hoping. I'd done it all by myself. The grieving only came later after all the hope and desire went up in flames the second I heard that man's voice from inside her apartment.

On the ferry ride back, I felt for the flask in my coat pocket and walked out to the bow of the ship and took a deep gulp. I looked down at the water, how it sliced away from the ship's hull. The water looked cold and gray, and I imagined how it would feel if I climbed overboard and fell into it. Would I just sink to the bottom? Or would I stay afloat? Would I try to swim and save myself from drowning—realizing I'd made a big mistake—or, just give up, feel the rush of water into my lungs, maybe the last flailing of the arms, and then the blackness? And it was all over—no more heartbreak, no more nothing.

The bourbon gave me the expected numbness. At times, it made me forget what I was feeling earlier, numbed the pain that settled around my imaginary heart. Another woman had disappointed me—certainly not the first time—possibly not the last. I wondered yet again why things turned out this way with me. Did I set it all up knowing in the end it would fail? Was that the plan from the start? Didn't Flo mention something like this to me years ago? And Emma Hansen, too? If it was, I was a lot harder on myself than I ever thought. And what had I done to make me hate myself as much as I did? Sure I wasn't perfect—far from it. I poached, I lied, I cavorted, drank too much, let a perfectly good woman get away—I'm sure if you dug deeper, you'd find even more things wrong in there, as well. I never claimed to be a saint, never pretended to live like one. I was the common man—the regular guy—the poor schmoe who kept a dream or two in his coat pocket and pulled them out when life's disappointments became too ordinary.

Maybe the next morning, I'd feel different—it often happened. I'd go to bed feeling like the whole world had squatted on top of me, crushing me—but sometimes by the following morning, the load had lifted and I didn't feel nearly as bad. Nothing had changed, really—just the way I looked at things. They were only as bad as you let them be—only as bad as you could see them.

"Got another load for the city," Tony said to me one afternoon. I'd been working locally, using Tony's horse and wagon to make deliveries. I'd hauled liquor, too, from Vinny Vincera's at the north end of town back to Tony's warehouse. I hadn't been to the city since that fateful Saturday visit to Della's and was glad for it—I didn't want to ever see her again. My plan was to stay away, forget about her, if I could—never an easy thing to do—but that was the plan.

"Ready to take this load in the morning, Bert?" Tony asked.

"Sure," I said. "I'm ready."

The following morning I was up early and drove the Auto-car with its load of eggs and Vinny's bourbon down to the ferry and crossed the bay. The usual fog hung over the bay waters, and I watched as the ferry bumped up to the dock at the foot of Market Street. I crank-started the Autocar, drove it off the ferrry and onto the city's streets. Twelve blocks later, I knocked on the warehouse door, and a little slat opened on the door and I could see a fellow's eyes through the slat. "It's me," I said. "The egg man."

"Well, good morning, mister egg man," the man said.

He slid the warehouse door open and I drove inside. Just like before, the warehousemen opened the back doors to the van, loosened the cargo bars and unloaded my truck while I drank a cup of coffee and watched. When the off-loading was finished, they back-loaded with mostly empty egg cases—although sometimes the guys in the warehouse often filled the empty cases with dozens of salami and rounds of Italian lunch meats to bring back to Tony. Product was always moving back and forth between the two warehouses.

I felt the pull of Della each time I was in the city—even thought of writing her and planning a visit, but decided against it. I couldn't deal with other men in her life—the jealousy would kill me. And I wasn't any good at competing, either—afraid I'd always lose. No, I settled on what I settled on before—and that was trying to forget about them. It'd take time, I knew that, but I'd be better off for it in the long run. A couple of months—maybe longer—and it'd be like I'd never seen her.

I was about to leave the warehouse when the foreman walked up to the side of my truck and handed me a letter. "I almost forgot," he said. "Some gal came by a couple days back and told me to give this to the "egg man from Petaluma." I'm guessing that's you."

"That's me, all right."

I waited until I was out on the street, away from the warehouse, before pulling over and opening the letter. It was from Della, of course—who else in the city knew I delivered eggs from Petaluma? It read:

> *Bert, you arrived at an awkward time your last visit. It's not that I don't want to see you again. I do, but can you tell me ahead of time—via letter, perhaps—when you'd like to stop by? You can post it to this address: 345 Chestnut Street, Apt. C, San Francisco.*
>
> *Best, Della.*

I was relieved—pissing-my-pants happy. She wanted to see me again! It felt like a weight lifted from me—and, yes, it was only good manners to alert someone that you wanted to visit. But I was still uncertain about any future with her. Two of the times I saw her, there were always other men involved, and that never settled with me.

For the past days and weeks, forgetting her seemed the best solution. She was someone, I reasoned, who would only bring heartache—the other men, her free spirit—these were all things about her that troubled me. Didn't Carlotta tell me the same thing—that she was unconventional? And I tried to ignore it. No, I wanted someone I could control more—I had to admit it—who only did the things I approved of, who thought of me only and not some other guy, but how realistic was that? It wasn't. Christina had those traits, and look how I treated her. No, I seemed attracted to only the long-shots—the dangerous ones—the ones that kept eluding me as I tried tracking them down, hoping to stuff them into my game pouch. I had to keep re-learning this about myself again and again. How was Della, after all, any different from Carlotta?

82

Into the City

· · · · · · · · · · · ·

Della's letter stayed on my nightstand for nearly two weeks. I'd open it every so often and re-read it, trying to sift out some hidden meaning, something I'd missed in all the earlier readings, but it was all pretty clear, pretty straightforward. She said she wanted to see me again, and though that would normally be good news, I went back and forth about what to do. I finally sat down and wrote a short letter to her, and despite all my misgivings, asked if I could see her next Saturday. I posted the letter on a Monday morning.

I worked local deliveries and pick-ups that entire week. I was going out to ranches now and loading up eggs along Bodega Avenue and out Liberty Valley, sometimes as far out as Two Rock and all along Pepper Road, and hauling these eggs—ranch-run they called them—back to Tony's warehouse where they were candled and sorted according to size. I liked being out in the country and often thought of Little Ike as I drove Tony's wagon from ranch to ranch. I missed that horse—all my horses— so much—like a big piece had broken off of me and gone with them.

Della wrote back, and I received her letter on Friday saying she looked forward to my visit. So, once again, I put on a good suit and a starched shirt and an extra serving of hope, and set out for the city. I brought two flasks with me. It rained that morning and I saw how the clouds hung over the hills and how the rain drops trailed past my train window. The train stopped at Novato, then Terra Linda, before arriving at San Rafael. From San Rafael it continued on to Sausalito. Once on the ferry, I wandered all around its decks, trying to walk off my nerves. I leaned out to breathe in the fresh air, take in all the sights of the bay. My lungs felt strong again after those years of working in the dust at Joe Keebler's. I didn't cough anymore like I used to and never went back to smoking cigars.

I walked from the Ferry Building to Della's. It was raining in the city—a kind of drizzle. I brought my umbrella. Once again, I stopped to buy her some flowers. Just before noon, I knocked on her door and she opened it.

"Are you alone this time?" I asked her.

She smiled. "Yes, I am—my previous guest just left."

"Really?"

"No, Bert, I'm just joking with you."

She invited me inside, asked how the train trip was. "Do you want to hang your coat by the heater?" she asked. "Then we'll have some tea."

"Sure," I said. "Maybe later we could go out for lunch?"

"In the rain?" she said.

"You've got an umbrella, right?"

"I do—and I know some good places to eat," she said. "I remembered you liked Chinese food."

She sat opposite me at her little table. Her hair was unbraided now and it fell down her back and the front of her shoulders. In the noon light I saw every little pore in her face, the scant lines around her brown eyes, the full lips, the sprinkling of freckles across her nose and cheeks—some of her many features that captivated me.

"Bert—I want to talk about your last visit and get something clear between us," she said. "I don't feel that I should apologize to you. It was awkward—for both of us—three if you wanted to include Thom—I realize that, but I do have my own life."

"Yeah, I'm figuring that out," I said. "It takes me awhile."

"I don't have a lot of friends, but the ones I do have, I value," she said. "I'm not sleeping with all of them—"

"Just a few?"

"I'll pretend I didn't hear that remark," she said.

"I'm sorry, Della—it was a stupid thing to say."

"We have our own lives," she said. "Everything I've lived up to this point has been without you, just like what you've lived has been mostly without me."

"That's right."

"I don't want it all to get so serious so quickly, Bert, and I have the sense that's what you want—or what you expect."

I couldn't deny it. "I get locked into things wanting to be a certain way," I said. "And that's all I know—the only way I want to see it."

"That isn't going to work with me—maybe with some other women—but not with me," she said. "I want to take things easy— enjoy each other, get to know each other—you may find out, you don't like me. Or I don't like you—that could happen, couldn't it?"

"Yes, it could."

"And then what? Keep seeing each other even though we don't like each other? Does that make any sense?"

"No, it doesn't," I said.

The tea kettle started to whistle, and she got up from the table and turned the gas off, poured hot water over a basket of tea into each of the cups.

"Are you okay with us talking like this?" she asked. "I know some people aren't."

"It's awkward for me, Della, but I'll try," I said.

"Why is it awkward?"

"I guess because I'm not used to talking to women like this."

"How do you talk to them?"

"I mostly avoid talking about feelings—the times I do, what I say gets turned back on me," I said. "And the next time I feel different." I stared down at the cup of tea. "I try to make them laugh, instead, or talk about my work or something they're interested in—a lot of the times it's just to cover my nerves."

"Are you nervous now?"

"I think I'm always nervous."

"And vulnerable?"

"Yeah, vulnerable—there's that word again."

"So, what's the alternative?" she asked. "Not talk about feelings at all?"

"I don't trust my feelings," I said. "They change on me too much. One day I feel a certain way—the next day I feel completely different. I can't bank on them. Sometimes they make me feel like I'm a liar—like I'm blowing out a lot of hot air."

"But we're always feeling something, aren't we? You can't just shut them off because they might change, can you?"

"No, you can't shut them off," I said. "I tried."

Della sipped at her tea then set her cup down. "What do you feel toward me, Bert? I'm curious. When you look at me, what do you see? And have those feelings changed at all?"

"I'm attracted to you—almost from the start after first seeing you at The Golden Bobbin."

"You liked how I looked?"

"Yeah, I liked how you looked—and still do."

"Thank you—I'll take that as a compliment."

"It's hard to say how I feel—because I think you scare me—"

"Really?

"Yeah, you do—your independence—the feeling I get is you can take me or leave me, and it wouldn't matter a lick."

"I don't fall at a man's feet anymore," she said. "I learned that lesson long ago.

I looked over at my coat hanging on the back of her chair. "I brought something to drink—you care to join me?"

"Sure, I'd love to," she said. She stood up, opened a cupboard door and brought out two glasses. She set one in front of me and one in front of her. I poured two inches of bourbon into each glass.

"Cheers," I said, raising my glass.

` `"Cheers!" she responded.

We both drank. "That's first class," she said.

"Yeah, Vinny's been at it awhile—long before Prohibition. It's not like any of that rot-gut going around, either. His is the real stuff—aged in barrels—the whole shooting match. It's what I haul down here—along with the eggs."

"Bert, the egg man and Bert, the hootch runner." She laughed and I laughed, too.

"Never thought I'd be running liquor—"

"What'd you think you'd be doing?" she asked.

"I don't know—I figured I have a tame little egg route around town and do my farming and be like everyone else trying to scratch a living out from this world.—I mean, I've got an egg route now but it doesn't seem enough—"

"Enough money?"

"No, with hauling the liquor, I making more money than I ever did—but that isn't everything, Della. I don't know exactly what it is, either—just something missing from all of it—like it doesn't mean what I thought it would mean. You think you have it and it's supposed to make you feel different, but you still feel the same. I've had that feeling most of my life—that I finally got my hands around it but something's still missing—like there should be more to it—something bigger that grabs at you—but it never comes along. Maybe I'm asking too much from this life."

"Is it your family you're missing?"

"Partly—I mean, I didn't do a very good job there. I run the wife off—a daughter that won't talk to me—another one born sickly—"

"You're feeling sorry for yourself, Bert—you did what you wanted to do, right?"

"Yeah, I did what I wanted to do."

"Not everyone can say that," she said. "You did it and you learn to live with the consequences—like we all do. It isn't any big mystery."

I poured us another drink and we clinked glasses.

"See, it's not so hard talking about feelings," Della said. She set her glass down on the table.

"It seems easier with you than the others," I said.

"Even your wife?"

"Especially my wife—I hid all kinds of feelings from her. I didn't want her to know any of them—just the safe ones, the ones that scratched at the surface that wouldn't upset her so much—but I didn't go much deeper than that."

"But she knew, didn't she? Even if you didn't talk about them—she knew. Women have that sense about them—I don't know about men—"

"Some men know, too," I said. "Maybe not as quickly as women, but they catch on when something's being hidden from them—or it's not being told to them straight." I looked over at Della and stared into her eyes. "We all want to hear just the good stuff—especially at the start—and then as time goes on and the harder things crop up—things that bother you about the other person, things that bother you about yourself that you take out on the other person—you start blaming them and they start blaming you back."

"Sounds like you've thought this out," she said.

"More than thought it out—I've lived it—seen it roll out in front of me every time—and every time hoping it'd be different."

I poured another drink and poured one for her. The alcohol was loosening me up, freeing my tongue as it often does and making me freer with my words—not careless—although that happened often enough, too. It was like confession—this time with Della—talking about the things that bothered me and there were plenty of them—the divorce, the drinking, hauling illegal liquor.

There were other things, too, that ate at me—things I had no control over—like the way the world was changing, the way everything was speeding up and being mechanized, and I didn't want it to change. I wanted Little Ike to be around forever and Jigs and Irv sitting alongside me on the wagon seat and we'd live out all our days, hauling eggs in a Studebaker wagon and stopping at every other tavern and watering hole to swap tales and show my boy off. But that wasn't going to happen anymore—those days were gone. It was that feeling returning again and again that this world was leaving me behind—that the world was that train that had just left the station and I was five minutes late, watching it disappear down the tracks.

"You're a romantic, Bert," she said.

"A romantic?"

"Yeah, you want to live in a certain world, in certain way, and it's not co-operating, is it?"

"No, I guess it's not."

"So, what do you do?" she asked. "Avoid it? Or just live in it the best you can? That's what I decided—to try to live the best I can."

"That sounds like a good way to live your life."

"What are the choices?" she asked.

We finished the first flask together and I felt a common bond growing between Della and me—more than just the liquor—I was feeling that, too, but something else. I don't know what it was exactly—I hardly ever do—but it felt good sitting there opposite her and talking like we did, the rain falling outside and the feeling there was no place either of us had to be except right there, talking to each other.

"Are you hungry?" she asked.

"No, I'm fine. Right now I'm just fine."

"I was hoping we could walk," she said, "but the rain keeps falling."

"Maybe it'll stop and we can go out then," I said. I walked over to where my coat was and brought out the other flask.

"You sure?" she asked.

"We don't have to drink the whole thing," I said. "And I don't wanna leave here with a full flask."

"Well, in that case, pour a little of it in my glass—I might add some ginger ale to mine to stretch it out," she said.

And so I did. I poured some into both glasses and we toasted the rain. We toasted the sun whenever it was going to show itself. "And a toast to you, Della."

"Well, thank you, kind sir."

"Could I ask you something?"

"Depends what you're asking me," she said.

"Who was that fellow with you?"

"His name is Thom—Thom Dyson. He's a fisherman—owns his own boat—very enterprising guy."

"Do you like him?"

"Of course, I like him—we're friends."

"I mean, do you *really* like him?"

"Are we in love? Are we lovers? Is that what you mean? No, we're not," she said. "I weighed his catch one morning and we started talking and we've become friends."

"That's all?"

"That's all I need to tell you, Bert." She placed her hand on top of mine. "You ask too many questions—"

"I just want to know—"

"Know what? And why?"

"I guess where I stand with you," I said.

"It's awfully early to ask about that, isn't it?"

"I told you already I'm guy who hates uncertainty—"

"At this point, Bert, it's all uncertain," she said. "Sorry, but that's the best I can tell you." She looked at me. "You don't need to know everything, okay? There's things we don't know and our lives go on just fine."

Della's words hit yet again at my own insecurity—my fear of women, my fear of all the things I had no control over. For all the times I thought I was on top of the world—in control—there was as many times when I felt it crumbling underneath me. With women, I felt I had to know everything about them—all their past, all their secrets. And why, I asked myself? Why did I need to know all this? So I could hold sway over them? Control them? Not be so intimidated? These were all flimsy reasons when I thought about it—all the reasons of a guy scared out of his shoes—but they were the real reasons.

Alcohol loosened my tongue and often relaxed me—I've told you this enough times already—like I've told you about the numbness—but it sometimes had an opposite effect, too. It could make dark moods darker, turn me deep into myself and see the many things there that unsettled me—the things I didn't like about myself. It could stoke my anger, too—shorten the fuse the way I'd seen it shortened with my own father. So, it was always something I had to be careful with—something I just couldn't give free rein to all the time—although often I wasn't careful enough.

"Bert—you're not talking," Della said. "Is everything okay?"

"Sorry—I was just thinking—"

"You do that a lot, don't you?"

"I do."

"That's okay—it's just that it makes you seem distant at times," she said. "And I'd rather you were closer."

"I'm sorry—"

"I just want you to be aware of it—that's all. It makes me feel a bit funny when you're doing it—like you're not here anymore and you're off somewhere, someplace distant."

"I guess it comes from being alone a lot," I said.

She put her hand on top of mine and I pulled her closer to me. I could feel her breath on my face, smell the trace of bourbon. I looked into her eyes and she looked into mine and then we kissed—a light touching of the lips before she moved her mouth away.

She got up and walked to the window. "It's still raining," she said, "but I have an umbrella. Let's go out and walk and find someplace to eat. How does that sound?"

"Sounds good," I said.

So we put our coats on, and I took the umbrella and we walked downstairs into a light rain. Out on the sidewalk, I opened the umbrella and Della tucked her arm inside mine and we walked toward Chinatown. I told her about the Chinaman, Ho Tzu, and how Tino and I sold ducks and pheasant to him, and how we smoked Ho's opium tar balls. I told her how we were always hiding from Percy Sheers, too, and how he stopped us outside Ho Tzu's once and wanted the money Ho Tzu paid us for the birds Sheers claimed we bagged on his land. "What'd you do then?" she asked.

"I told him he could piss up a rope," I said, "and as we walked away from Sheers, Tino dropped his pants, showed him his bare ass, and said, 'you can kiss this, too'."

Della laughed. "Bert, are you dangerous?"

"No, I'm not dangerous—to tell you the truth, danger scares me."

"But it sounds like you do a lot of dangerous things, though."

"When I was young, I did—not so much anymore."

She leaned closer to me. "But what about what you haul down here—that's dangerous, isn't it?"

"Yeah, I guess—I wouldn't do it if I thought I'd get caught—"

"That's probably what most criminals say."

"You calling me a criminal?"

"Well—at least, you're a likeable one."

We walked along Grant Avenue and we stared into the store windows at all the things I'd never seen before—the trinkets, the dragons, the colorful rolls of silk—everything.

"It's like a different world here," I said.

The smell of incense drifted out to the sidewalk.

"That's because it is," she said.

We found a tiny restaurant on Grant Avenue that Della favored. It was narrow and barely fit a half dozen tables. Our waiter knew Della and she introduced me. He bowed slightly and we shook hands. We ordered noodles and lightly fried fish and chop suey and he brought us all kinds of little dishes I'd never seen or heard of before. I pointed to one. "What's that?" I asked.

"Octopus," Della said.

"Octopus—that thing with all them legs?"

"That's right."

"I'm gonna pass on that one," I said.

I tried using chop sticks—they were awkward at first, but Della showed me her method.

"You know, I feel sorry for the Chinese," I said.

"Why?"

"The way they're treated—they do all the shit work—build fences out of rocks from the hills and lay railroad track—hard labor—and when they're done, and can't be used anymore, nobody wants them around," I said. "In towns around Sonoma County, they're crowded into dingy neighborhoods, kept out of sight like they got some kind of disease—and when folks think there's too many of them, think they're some kind of threat, they want them all sent back to China. It doesn't seem right."

"No, it doesn't," Della said.

We finished our meal and once we were on the sidewalk again, we noticed it had stopped raining. "Let's walk along the Embarcadero,"

Della suggested. "I love to see all the boats, and look across the bay."

And so we walked arm in arm. As we approached the Ferry Building, I looked at Della and said, "I should be thinking about returning home. Doesn't the last ferry leave soon?"

"Why don't you stay the night?" she asked.

I looked at her. "Really? You want me to spend the night?"

"Sure—it wouldn't be the first time, right? You can take the ferry back tomorrow."

I felt light—like I could jump into the air and it'd be seconds—no minutes— before I touched ground again.

We lingered along the Embarcadero and watched the last rays of sunlight burn across the bay before heading back to Della's. There was still the better part of the second flask left, and we mixed ginger ale with the bourbon to make it last longer. We moved from the table to the edge of the bed, where I put my arms around her and pulled her close to me. We kissed. She struck a match and lit a candle.

"This was a wonderful day," I said.

"I'm glad you enjoyed it."

"Did you enjoy it, too?"

"I did—very much."

We fell back onto the bed, our bodies alongside each other. We kissed—longer kisses now—and when the kisses ended, I looked over at Della and then turned and watched the candle-light dance across the ceiling.

"Let's get out of our clothes," she said. "But, Bert, I want you to just hold me—that's all—okay?"

"I'll try."

She stripped out of her clothes and I stripped out of mine, leaving just our underclothes on. We pulled the blankets over us and we embraced, and I felt the smooth skin of her back and shoulders and felt her hands rubbing my back. I got excited—my breath and her breath starting to race—and she'd pull back. "This is gonna take some willpower," I said.

"You can do it—you've got the willpower."

I wasn't sure.

I backed off—felt the load settle down. I wanted her hands to touch me there. "Could you?" I asked her.

And she did—gentle strokes of her hand, and as I was about to shoot, I pulled the covers back. It spurted, big drops of it falling on my stomach and chest.

"My! My!" she said. "You've been storing it up."

We both laughed.

"Saving it for you, Della." We looked at each other and kissed.

"I'll have to do the same for you," she said. "I want you to—I really do—but I want to wait, okay?"

"Sure. We can wait."

We held each other until the apartment grew dark. Soon I heard her breathing deepen and become more regular. "I feel good with you, Della," I whispered.

She murmured something—a little sound. Maybe she heard me, maybe she didn't. I put my arm across her back while my mind thought a thousand different things. I don't know if I slept at all that night—I didn't much care. I was where I wanted to be—in the arms of a woman I could finally talk to—the first one in a long time—maybe ever.

83

Too Many Men
• • • • • • • • • • • • • • •

The following morning there was a loud knock on Della's door. She got out of bed, put her robe on, went to the door and opened it as far as the door-chain would allow. I heard a man's voice, then Della's, saying, "You can't come in now, Thom, so, please—go away."

"But I want to see you," the man said.

"No, we talked about this before—so go, goodbye! Please!" And she closed the door.

I pulled the covers back and slipped on my pants. I walked over to where Della stood. "Was that your Thom friend?" I asked her.

She nodded her head.

"Unfinished business?" I asked.

"I thought I'd made myself clear about our relationship—that I wasn't looking for it to go any further than being friends—"

"But he had different ideas?"

"Yeah, and it's my fault."

"You slept with him?"

"I did—once—and that gave him the wrong idea. I was careless." She knotted her hands together. "I tried to make my position clear, but his mind was set on something different. I'm finding out how stubborn a person he is."

I couldn't help but think how Thom's appearance compared with my earlier one, when he was on the inside and I was outside, and it was Della telling me I had to go—now Thom and me had switched places and it was him on the outside.

"You must think I'm a terrible woman," she said. "But this isn't what I do—it's certainly not something I like—or even plan."

"Two guys like you," I said.

"And I have enough trouble with just one."

"I don't know what to say, Della—I like you—I like you very much but I'm a jealous guy—I told you that already—and with somebody else around—well, that's not going to work for me," I said.

"I thought he and I agreed on just being friends—"

"But he got a taste of you and once that happens it's not so easy just being friends—everything becomes more complicated. You can say whatever you want and agree to all kinds of things, but what's really happening inside? That's what decides."

"Can you and I be friends?" she asked.

"I told you I'd try—but if you're sleeping with someone else, though, I'm out the door—I can't handle that, sorry—I tried it once and it didn't work."

"You men just want to possess."

"I'm just not comfortable with sharing—if you call that 'possessing' then that's what it is," I said. "Seems like you have to make up your mind, doesn't it?"

"It does seem that way."

"Della, if it's Thom you choose, that's your choice and I'll disappear. I won't be knocking on your door with surprise visits—I'll leave you alone—I promise."

She turned around and put her arms around me and we embraced. "I'm sorry this is so confusing."

"You're an attractive woman and two guys like you," I said. "It isn't so hard to figure that one out."

"It's never simple, is it?"

"No, not when it concerns matters of the heart—it always gets complicated."

"It doesn't have to be—"

"With a lot of folks, it isn't," I said. "Take Christina's brother, for example—he's introduced to a woman and a couple of weeks later they're engaged and then they marry and start a family—simple and easy as pie—but you and me? Well, we're not like that."

"Why do you think that is?" she asked.

"I don't know—maybe because we're restless types—never satisfied. And I think we both seen the other side of the street, too."

"Or it just doesn't settle with us—things don't add up to our liking," she said.

"Yeah, there's always a burr under the saddle."

"It's terrible to be that way, isn't it?"

"To be always looking?" I asked. "Yeah, that can take a toll, all right—but it's just as bad settling with something you know inside isn't right."

"Do we even know what we're looking for? Do you?" She looked deep into my eyes.

"I always told myself I'd know when I found it—that my heart would know—but I've learned the heart's a fickle thing—it dances around and fools with you, takes you in, and then just as sudden, it drops you like a rock—leaves you behind wondering what hit you."

"Yeah, you can't always trust it, can you?"

"You can't—you live by the heart and you can die by the heart," I said.

"So what do we do, Bert? Just scramble around all our lives—jumping from one flame to another? What's going to satisfy us? God? Religion?"

"That's what satisfied Christina—but it didn't work with me—all that faith stuff. I didn't have it and that's why I floundered like I done with her. I never thought it was that simple—that it was just a matter of belief and having faith. People believe all sorts of things and they're just as screwed up and lost as I am. "

"Nothing like some light conversation to start your day off, right?" Della said. "How about I make some coffee?"

"We can certainly agree on that," and we both smiled.

I walked over to the window and looked out to where the bay was, but it was covered in a layer of fog. It had stopped raining and I was thinking ahead of what the day might bring. Sometime in mid-afternoon, I'd have to ride the ferry back to Sausalito and from there catch the train to Petaluma.

"I don't think I've ever talked to a woman the way I've talked to you, Della—I'm always dodging around issues—afraid to bring them up—or unable to say what's on my mind."

"I think that's healthy, don't you?" she asked. "To talk about these things?"

"Yeah, even though it makes me uncomfortable—to have to admit stuff about myself—"

"It shows you're growing, Bert."

When the coffee finished perking, Della set two cups on the table, brought out a loaf of sourdough bread and sliced it on a wooden board. She set out a cube of butter, too, and a jar of marmalade. I sipped at the coffee.

"Well, we didn't solve the world's problems, did we?" she asked.

"We're never gonna do that," I said. "I just want to be clear on things—and that's difficult."

"Lots of stuff to sift through—lots of things blocking our view," she said.

"I think if you and I are straight with each other—that's a start. No lies, no bullshit."

She put her hand on top of mine. "No lies, no bullshit," she repeated. Then she leaned across the table and kissed me. We finished our coffee. The morning fog still hung over the bay.

"What do you want to do now?" I asked her.

"Oh, I can think of something," she said, and stood up and led me to her bed. We both lay down and held each other. My hand found its way through her robe—I rubbed her stomach and soon my hand fondled her breasts. I touched them lightly. "Is this okay?" I asked her. "I mean—you're not going to take a poke at me, are you?"

"No, it's fine," she said.

We held each other as if we were in rough seas. I loved how she smelled—a very faint breath of lilacs—and I loved her dark eyes, and the fullness of her mouth—and how she moaned so slightly. I liked how she enjoyed being touched, too—how she invited it—so different from Christina that way who could never relax—who always seemed to hold a tightness in her body.

Della was different from so many of the women before her— freer, outspoken, no God hanging around her that she had to constantly please—not a church-goer or tea-totaler, either. We seemed to share the same tendencies. That's what I thought and felt lying there next to her—that I'd finally met my match and I didn't care much about what I felt in the past, what I felt toward those other women—all that was behind me now.

I didn't know what was going to happen between us, but who does? No one—that's who. There were all kinds of possibilities, weren't there? A thousand different things I could never see or even imagine. Everything was changing, I knew that—and I didn't always want to fight that change—how could you? The horse and wagon were disappearing before my eyes—and nothing I could do about it. The big teams of horses I once drove at Joe Keebler's were now replaced by huge tractors with steel wheels. The old world was disappearing in clouds of automobile exhaust.

Other changes were happening, too— happening inside me. I could feel things shifting. My heart felt like it was opening up again—and that was both scary and exciting. Scary because I never knew where that led—it could be to the top of the heights or down deep into the rabbit's hole. Would Thom re-enter her life? Would there be others? Would my heart take me to the summit, right to the edge of the cliff and then push me over the edge and watch me fall?

But what was happening was exciting, too. My life had turned hum-drum—working all the time—and my heart had grown lonely living by itself. It wanted company—someone it could talk to— someone it could take inside and share what was all stored up. There were risks, of course—I know. I've been telling you this all along—that I don't know where any of it is going—and of all the things I've told you, it was the most honest. We're all in a dark cave, moving ahead step by step, our hands feeling in front of us along the cave's walls, trusting our senses—the sounds we hear, what we feel, what we smell—it's all we have to go on. But what's at the end of the cave? What's there waiting for us? We don't ever really know.

84

The Bear Comes Out

· · · · · · · · · · · · · · · · · · · ·

My life fell into a regular routine by now. I worked the local routes for Tony, but instead of his horse and wagon, I was driving a truck—a 1925 Mack 2, Model AB fitted with a covered van. It had forty-five horsepower and a shift box with four gears. I'd drive the routes, make the pick-ups, and cover an area I never thought possible in the earlier days with just a horse and wagon. I was making the bi-weekly runs to the city, too, often stopping by the wharf area to say hello to Della before returning north. Irv was eighteen now. He'd dropped out of school after the sixth grade—something his mother wasn't pleased about—and went to work on his brother-in-law's ranch on the hills above the old adobe. He fed cattle and did the outside work, and during harvest, worked on the hay press. Ernest kept a horse and wagon there, and Irv would drive it around the ranch, hauling hay, spreading cow manure. We'd hunt or fish when we both could find the time, but time was riding in one of those cars passing me on the roadway.

I continued to see Della on the weekends and sometimes we talked about moving in together, but she was a city girl—bred into her bones—and had no taste for returning to country life. And I wasn't sure about living in a city. I'd only known the country, but I liked her enough to consider moving—to give city life a shot.

We got on pretty well together—Della and me. We liked each other's company and we could talk until the cows came home—talk about anything—God, sex, men, women—whatever popped up between us. We walked in Golden Gate Park and ate in Chinatown and North Beach—did things you couldn't do in the country. I'd never been this close to a woman before—not even Christina, whom I was married to for twenty-two years. With Christina, I was always walking on egg shells around her—she never liked the drinking—and

I never liked the idea of giving it up. And the closeness between us was different, too. With Della, it just seemed more sensual and deeper than it did with Christina—Della enjoyed it more, but with Christina it was like she had to do it to please me. I never cared for that—I always wanted it to be an even trade-off, if that was possible.

We all have our dark sides, too, and Della wasn't any exception. She liked to drink—maybe even more than me, but she'd reach a certain point, and once past it, she could turn on you, unleash some pretty harsh language. I called it "letting the bear out" because that's what it seemed like. She'd be going along with things, we'd be drinking and then something inside her got triggered. After a long bout of drinking one time, she'd accused me of being unfaithful, of wanting to return to Christina—of not loving her anymore. All this caught me by surprise. "Where do these ideas come from?" I'd ask her. "You just brew them up when you got nothing else to think about?"

"Never mind," she'd say. "I know these things about you."

"But they're not true—it's the alcohol that's talking."

"I know—I know all about you men—you can't trust any of you," she'd say. "You're all the same."

I felt powerless when she slipped into these states. Nothing I could say or do would change her mind. There was no reasoning with her. The only thing was to wait her out, let her sober up, and when she did, she'd apologize again and again and tell me she didn't mean those things—at least, those things she could remember saying. Many of them she couldn't unless I reminded her.

Then she'd lead me to bed and in a fit of lovemaking more charged than usual, I'd forget about those hurtful things she'd said earlier. The more hurtful, the more charged the lovemaking. I had no resistance. I gave in—the threats of leaving her vanishing inside me with every kiss. All I could do was watch her alcohol consumption—count the drinks she took and cut her off when she approached her limit. Sometimes it meant pouring perfectly good liquor down the drain so she wouldn't drink anymore. "That's it, Della," I'd say to her. "It's all gone."

"But you can get more, right?"

"No, I can't."

"Just bring more the next time," she'd say. "Put another bottle or two in that truck of yours—you can do that, right?"

"Yeah, I can—"

"But will you?"

"I'll try to remember," I said.

This was the first time I thought seriously about drying up—about not drinking anymore and seeing if Della would go along with me. No surprise there—she wouldn't.

"Then let's not drink as much," I said.

"Okay, we won't drink as much," she said, and mostly she'd hold true until we'd get together with some of her friends and the drinking started. Then there was no holding her back. She'd slip into the kitchen and pour herself a fresh one when I wasn't looking. As the evening went on, she got louder, sometimes laughing uncontrollably, teetering and nearly falling over. If I took a drink away from her or said something about her behavior, she resented it. "You're not my father, okay?" When it was time to leave, she almost always didn't want to go. I'd grab her coat and move her to the door, and she'd turn and push away from me.

"Della, your drinking is a problem," I said to her one night after leaving her friend's house.

"It's my problem, okay?"

"No, when I'm with you, it becomes *our* problem—yours and mine."

"So?"

"So something has to change—"

"Or what?"

"Or I'll leave you—"

She stared back at me. "You won't leave me—you love me too much," she said.

"I do love you—but I don't love that person you become when you drink too much."

"All right—then cut me off when I reach that point—"

"I try to but you just ignore me—push me away."

"I'll try harder the next time—I promise."

Before, it was all those people warning *me* about my drinking—Ma, Dad, Cameron, Carlotta, Christina—a whole list of folks right on down the line. Now, the shoe was on the other foot, and it was me warning someone else. It was a whole different game now, except it wasn't a game. I'd lie awake at night, wondering what to do—hardly sleeping at all, my stomach tied up in knots. I had no appetite for anything. Should I stop drinking all together and see if Della would join me? Or, just keep drinking, weather the barrage, and know that it'd end sometime and there was always that powerful lovemaking as a kind of reward for sticking it out? Or, a last resort—something I hated to think about—should I leave her?

I didn't much care for that last choice. It scared me and was only something I'd do if everything else failed—what folks called 'a last resort.' I hated to even think about it—couldn't imagine life without Della at this point. I loved this woman—even told myself I'd go to hell to be with her—but my better senses told me I needed to draw the line somewhere. The two of us couldn't keep on like this.

On my next visit to Della's, I decided to bring just one flask of liquor as a way of limiting our drinking. I poured two glasses and she added her ginger ale and we sat and talked. This is what I enjoyed most with her—talking, laughing—while our heads were still clear, looking into those beautiful brown eyes of hers. But after we finished the first flask, she looked at me and said, "Time to bring out the other one, Bert."

"That's all I brought," I said.

"That's all you brought—one flask? What were you thinking?"

"I was thinking we don't need to drink so much—"

"Oh—because of me, right? Afraid I'll drink too much and fly off the handle?"

"That's right." I said. "I thought the best way to limit ourselves was to not have as much around."

"Well—I want something more to drink—"

"Then drink your ginger ale," I said.

"My ginger ale? No, I've got something better." And she went over to bottom cupboard and pulled out a bottle of liquor. "It's not as good as Vinny's stuff, but it'll do in a pinch," she said.

"Can't we just drink what I brought?"

"It's gone, Bert!"

"So, let's not drink anymore," I said.

"Just like that, huh? You're going to cut us off just like that?"

"That's right—let's see if we can do it."

"I don't want to, okay? I want another drink—"

"Go ahead, then," I said.

"Okay, I will. Are you going to join me? Or, do I have to drink alone?"

Here was my chance to remain strong, to say no, to take a stand and show her I meant what I said, but I couldn't bring myself to do it. I thought about it—one side of me arguing with the other, back and forth, back and forth, it went—until I gave in—my will-power all shot to hell. "All right, fix me a drink," I said.

She came over and kissed me. "See—it's not that difficult, is it?"

I drank her liquor and it wasn't very good—certainly not as good as Vinny's. I let it run around my mouth—it had a bad bite to it. "This is pretty rough stuff," I told her.

"I never had to drink it before because some fellow I knew north of here always brought me something better—and for some reason, this fellow from the North Bay—he didn't do it this time," she said.

"You know why I didn't."

"Are we going to argue about this again?"

"I don't want to argue," I said. "I just want you to remain that person I've fallen in love with."

"You've fallen in love with me?"

"I have—I thought that was pretty obvious—"

"Well, we say things in the middle of—"

"That we don't mean?

"Yes, that we don't mean," she said.

"Well, I mean it," I told her. "When you're like this, you're easy to love, but when you drink too much, you change—you become like a different person—you turn on me when I don't deserve it, accuse me of all sorts of things. Where does that come from, Della? I'd like to know."

I could see tears forming in her eyes. "I don't know where it comes from, Bert," she said. "I guess it's just stuff stored up inside me—it's always there and the alcohol stirs it up."

"Can't you leave the drink alone—or, at least, be more moderate about it?" I asked.

"I'm like you, Bert—I can't leave it alone—it's like falling in love with each other—we can't live without it."

I knew what she was saying. We both had bad cases of bottle fever—fighting something that always seemed to kick our asses. But I thought here was a person that I loved enough to make me want to quit—and thought she'd love me enough to quit in return, but it wasn't working out that way. She could see no good reason to swear off it.

"Are you aware of how you change when you drink too much? Do you have any idea?" I asked her. "Because I see it and wonder if you do, too."

"Not when I'm in the middle of it," she said. "It isn't until the next day when someone tells me how I acted or what I said—"

"Then how do you feel?"

"Ashamed of myself—"

"And that isn't enough to make you want to quit—or, at least, cut back?"

"For awhile it is—then the thirst, the craving builds up. You know how it is."

Unfortunately, I did.

"And when I'm back to it—not heavy, but back to it—certain times I feel the urge more than other times," she said. "If I'm feeling really sad or feeling really happy—it doesn't matter. The urge comes and I want to drink."

"And if I asked you not to—if it meant my not seeing you again—would you still drink?"

"I don't want to make that choice," she said. "I want both of you in my life."

Then she walked over to where I stood and put her arms around me and kissed me on the mouth. "I think we're talking too much, don't you, when there's something else we could be doing?"

And I followed her to her bed and she pulled me down alongside her. We kissed and embraced and fumbled with each other's clothes until we were both naked. My resistance was gone—shattered, dissolved—wherever resistance went when it was bettered by a stronger force. We made love and she didn't turn on me or accuse me of anything—she just acted like the woman I wanted her to be. But for how long? I knew for how long, but right now it didn't matter. She was in my arms and I was in hers and to be here was worth any price—the heartache she caused, the doubts, the grief, the uncertain future—all of that didn't matter when I was in her arms.

85

Visiting Irv

· · · · · · · · · · · ·

It's funny the turns this life takes, isn't it? All through my teen years, Ma and Dad warning me about drinking, then twenty years and counting with Christina, and those same warnings, and all the time shrugging them off like it didn't bother me. And then what happens? I meet someone and she drinks, and I think, well, at last, a partner in common, but drinking with her is dangerous. You never know when that big, ugly bear inside her is going to show its face, when she slips her beautiful skin and becomes something else—that something you dread and fear—that bear. The one thing you do know, though, is if she keeps drinking, that bear gets restless. It's just a matter of time. So, I tried to live with it—but it was always living afraid—waiting for that bear to come out of its cave.

Despite all this, Della and I continued to see each other. With every serious drinking bout, I vowed that was it—it was over, but I was under her spell, and I kept going back for more—I couldn't get enough. It's like a dog that gets beaten and his master whistles and he's right there by his master's side again, ready for that little treat— until he gets beaten again. I'd dry out during the week— mostly—and do my routes and pick up eggs all through the Liberty Valley area, and every other week, I'd stop at Vinny Vincera's and load up for the trip to the city. When the weekends rolled around, I'd think of some excuse not to hop on a ferry and go to Della's, but the excuses never held much water. I'd hear her voice calling somewhere, feel that hunger in my groin, that need to see her, and how it felt inside her, and before I knew it, I was boarding the train south, hopping on a ferry and staring across the bay as the city sky-line spread out in front of me, wondering what lie ahead.

During this time, I'd gone up to see Irv at his sister's ranch to say hello to him. We didn't spend much time together now, and I didn't want him forgetting about me. We both had our own lives, I knew that, but still, I wanted to stay close to my boy—you just never know when they're snatched from you. I found him out in the field spreading hay to Ernest's dry stock and walked out to meet him. He was driving a pair of horses pulling a flat-bed wagon.

"You look just like me up there with those horses," I said. He was a picture, all right—sitting high in the driver's seat, a ten-foot pile of hay behind him in the wagon and two stout horses, and off in the distance, the Petaluma Valley with the sunlight catching its ribbon of water winding toward the center of town.

"I like driving them," he said. "Sometimes that's all I want to do."

"Me, too—I sort of miss them with driving truck now. It ain't the same." I looked around. Ernest and Irene's house stood above us and beyond their house, the big hay barn and the gray milking barn. "How you like it up here?"

"Okay—kinda lonesome, though," he said. "All's I do is work."

"Then find something else to do if being alone bothers you."

"Been thinking of applying to J.C. Penney's," he said. "I filled out the application but never dropped it off." He looked down at me. "It'd be different than what I'm used to here."

"Sure would," I said. "You'd be a town boy, then—starched shirts and ties—none of this cow shit sticking to your boots."

Irv laughed. "I don't see you much anymore, Dad," he said. How you doing?"

"Working the egg route for Tony, still."

"Ma says you got a girlfriend now—"

"How'd she know that?"

"Didn't you tell me once you can't keep a secret in this town?"

"I probably did," I said. I put my boot up on the wagon wheel. "Her name's Della."

"She live around here?"

"No, she lives in the city—works down at Fishermans' Wharf."

I told Irv how we'd met something like twenty-five years ago in Santa Rosa—before I was even married—and then I saw her one day as I was leaving a warehouse in the city. And after that we'd been together pretty much ever since.

"You guys serious?" he asked.

"I like her a lot—but she's got issues—some things we need working out."

"Don't we all?"

"We do—ain't any of us perfect."

"What kind of issues?" Irv asked.

"I know this might sound funny to you—but she drinks too much."

Irv looked at me as if he didn't hear what I said. "She drinks too much?"

"Yes, she does."

"That does seem a little funny coming from you," Irv said.

"Except it's not so funny." I told Irv all about our pattern of drinking—didn't see any sense in not telling him—and how it went along well until the bottom fell out, and we'd end up clawing at each other's throats. "Every time I think to myself, this is it—this one's taken me over the top—no more."

"Then what happens?"

"The simplest answer? I take the bait again," I told him. "Never had a woman hold such power over me—just never thought it would happen."

"And now it has."

"I'm in deep, son." I told him. "Sometimes I think, too deep."

"You can't just walk away?"

"I try—done it half dozen times—but after a few days I go running after her like a goddamn puppy-dog looking for his mother's teat."

"Sorry to hear this, Dad," he said.

"There's times I don't know which way to go." I ran my hand through the loose hay on the wagon. "Back and forth, back and forth—"

"You can't reason with her?"

"I try, but it's like talking to that wagon wheel there—doesn't do any good," I said. "She'll get her feathers up or worse and when the yelling's done, she starts crying—bawling like a baby until I'm feeling it's all my fault—"

"But it isn't," Irv said. "She's her own person, right? We all are—isn't that what you told me?"

I nodded my head.

"Just don't see her anymore—"

"It's not that easy—you don't know."

"It's not like she's just around the corner, right? She's fifty miles, a train and ferry ride away, for crissakes—"

"It doesn't matter—the further away she is, the more I want her when she's not there—she could be on the other side of the country—and I'd go there," I said. "I don't know what in hell to do."

"What's the longest you've gone without seeing her?"

"Two weeks and I was plain miserable—the first few days were okay, but then it got tougher and tougher until I thought about her all the time—couldn't eat, couldn't sleep. I was a mess."

"Was it her or the drinking you were missing most?"

"It's all mixed in together, son," I said. "I don't know where one ends and the other starts—I'm in pretty deep—I gotta tell you—pretty goddamn deep."

"I'm sorry to hear this, Dad."

"I'm sorry I have to tell you this, but I had to tell someone."

"What can I do?" he asked.

"There ain't much you can do," I told him. "I dug the hole I got myself in and now I gotta figure a way of digging myself out."

"You will—you'll figure something out."

"Thing is, Irv—I lost all faith in myself—don't know where it's gone."

"You'll get it back."

"I don't know—this time it feels different than before. I been through all kinds of shit—but I never thought it was deep enough I couldn't pull myself out. Now, I'm not so sure—don't have that trust in me I used to have."

Irv looked off. "No faith, huh?"

"Gone—just when I need it the most."

"You'll get it back," he said.

"If you don't see me in a long while," I told him, "I want you to look me up—I won't be here in Petaluma, either—likely I'll be in the city—1025 Chestnut Street—that's her address. Can you remember that?"

"1025 Chestnut Street," he said out loud.

"I want you to come down and get me, all right? You go down there and bring me back to the country, okay?"

"Sure, Dad, I can do that."

"You promise?"

"I promise," he said.

"What's that address again?" I asked him.

"1025 Chestnut," he repeated.

"Here I am telling you all my troubles and not asking about you—you doing okay?"

"I already told you about applying to J.C. Penney's—"

"Except you haven't turned in the application yet."

"I did—they got a position open in Healdsburg, but Ma doesn't want me taking it—"

"Why doesn't she?"

"She says there's too many Indians living up there—"

"Too many Indians? Don't go listening to her—my best friend growing up was half Indian—"

"Tino—right?

"Yeah, Tino—so don't let that talk about Indians bother you. There's good people and there's bad people across all the races— being Indian or being a Chinaman doesn't make you bad. Remember that."

Irv nodded his head.

I looked around the field, up to the barns and the house. "What's it like working for your sister and brother-in-law?" I asked him.

"She doesn't have a lot of good words to say about you, Dad."

"She never did—ever since she was a little girl. It's like the die was set early on and nothing I could do about it. I tried—your Ma would say, I didn't—but I tried."

"I don't like to hear it when she talks that way," he said.

"Maybe 'cause some of it's true?"

"Doesn't matter—I still don't like hearing it—and I told her so."

I felt so proud of my boy just then—standing up for me. I don't know how many people would, to tell you the truth. I've stepped on toes all my life and rarely said, 'Excuse me.' Christina was right—I could be out and out selfish, thinking only of myself and not whether I hurt folks or not. But sometimes you have to look after your own skin because you're the only one who will. You get trampled on if you don't, or some son of a bitch'll put his hand in your pocket trying to pry that last five out of you. I tried drumming this into Irv's head because he's so good-natured—too good-natured, if you ask me. He thinks everybody's looking out for him—but I tell him not everyone is.

"I gotta get to feeding cattle," Irv said. "Irene's probably looking out her window right now."

"Sure you do—it was good catching up with you, Irv."

We shook hands. "I may not see you a lot, but I think of you all the time," I told him, and walked back to where I'd parked the truck. Just before I crank-started the Mack, I looked across where Irv was forking out the loose hay, and—I know I keep saying this—but it was like I was looking at myself again years earlier when I had a good, strong back and whiskers just starting to sprout across my face, and a hard-on every time I saw a good looking woman—but, damn, he was a fine boy, if I say so myself.

Irv—I hoped—would turn out better than me. He was honest and hard-working and didn't have any vices following him around like they done with me when I was his age. I give his Ma a big share of credit for his raising—for all three of ours. She'd say I was always off somewhere—chasing a floosie, chasing after the next drink—and she wouldn't be entirely wrong. I done most things she said—I admit it. But I never completely deserted them—I couldn't do that.

86

City, Country, City

• • • • • • • • • • • • • • • • • •

For all my good intentions of trying to deal with Della's drinking, nothing came of it. I pretty much waved the white flag, showed up at her place with two bottles of Vinny's best, and we'd polish off both of them before I boarded the ferry on Sunday afternoon back to Petaluma. Sometimes we never left her apartment—except maybe to grab some Chinese or Italian dish—before heading right back to her place and resume the drinking.

We'd sit opposite each other at her table and I'd drink it straight while she added a ginger ale chaser. We'd talk back and forth—mostly civil—until I'd say something she disagreed with or I'd disagree with her—innocent stuff, mostly—and then she'd reach that point and blow up, and before I knew it, she'd turned on me—and out came that bear again. I grew to expect it by now—and my only defense was to either leave or keep drinking until she passed out—usually deciding on the latter. She'd bark at me, accuse me of cavorting with other women and not loving her, and I'd tell her she had bats in her head, and she'd snap back, and I'd say, "Okay, I'm leaving—that's it. Enough of this crap!"

Those were the magic words, it seemed—all it took for her to apologize and say she didn't mean it, and she'd go to unbuttoning my shirt and slipping her tongue inside my mouth—and you must know by now what followed. One ttime, though, I didn't fall for it and walked out. She screamed at me all the way down to the sidewalk.

Before I knew it, two cops had shown up. "Everything all right here?" one of the cops asked me

"Everything's fine, officer—just a little disagreement between us," I said.

"Well, we got a complaint from one of the neighbors and had to check it out," one of the officers said.

"No, we'll be fine."

The two officers turned and left.

I started each work week at Tony's with a bad headache and my stomach in knots, and he'd usually say something—a vague warning, a suggestion—that I take it easier. "Just don't bring it to work, okay?" he'd say.

"Don't worry," I told him. "I'll just bring the tail-end of it with me."

"Who you spending time with?" he asked me one morning. "Anyone here in town I know?"

"No," I told him. "She's a city gal."

"And you go back and forth every weekend?"

"Like clockwork—I go down there and receive my punishment—can't seem to break out of it."

"Why don't you find someone closer?" he asked.

"I don't know, Tony—I latched onto this one, and she latched onto me, and now we're in the thick of it. We tell each other we were destined to be together."

"Regardless of what happens?"

"Yeah, regardless of what happens," I said. "Through thick or thin, high water, low water—we're in it together. It's not exactly what I wanted but it's exactly what I got."

"It's none of my business what you do on your off-time," Tony said. "But I want you to know that I worry about you, Bert. You drag yourself in on Mondays looking like hammered shit—"

"Well, most of the time, Tony, I *feel* like hammered shit."

"So, do something about it," he said.

"Now you're sounding just like my son," I told him.

"It's your choice how you feel, right?"

I nodded and agreed with him, just like I nodded and agreed with everyone else before Tony. I reached that point where I didn't know what to do but surrender to Della—that seemed the easiest. I told myself I loved her—that life without her was worse than life with her, and for all the pain she caused, she still thrilled me like no other. The reward for enduring her sharp tongue, her attacks on me, was to fall back in bed with her and make love like nothing else happened, like nothing else mattered—only the two of us being together in her little flat by the bay.

But all kinds of things mattered. I could put all our problems aside for awhile but they always came leaking back, bigger and more troublesome than before, and I wondered and worried—what happens if I can no longer be seduced? Would that time ever come? I tried not to think about it but it was always there lurking in the back of my mind.

We kept drinking. The first part of it I always liked—feeling the alcohol flow out to my fingers and toes—and how we always found something to laugh about. Then the numbness followed—like a thick fog through my whole body. We'd keep drinking and our words and thoughts started breaking up—she'd finish a thought I started or I'd finish one of hers, and she'd say, "That's not what I was thinking at all." Sometimes we'd laugh at the combinations we came up with and that was all good fun—but any slip of the tongue, anything she saw as an attack on her—well, out jumped that bear again.

You're probably asking yourself—what's the trade-off here for me? I travel two hours every weekend down to the city. We end up drinking everything I brought—almost always argue and disagree—and I leave there half the time vowing not to see her again. How does that make any sense? If I wanted someone to argue with, I could find someone a lot closer—I could walk down to the nearest speakeasy, shoulder myself in and find some gal to swap sad stories with, and it'd start out grand until it didn't—until a monkey wrench fell into the gears, and I'd look at her and say, "Hey, you're not the person I thought you were," and she'd look back at me, and say, "You're not the person I thought you were, either."

When it was good between Della and me, it was good, but when it was bad, it was downright awful. Funny thing was, we'd almost always make-up. As far as she'd run her string out, she kept just enough on her spool where I could reel her back, where we could salvage a peace and everything was calm for a couple of weeks—but it never lasted.

One weekend, after one of those calm periods, the two of us went on a bender and I just gave in and matched her drink for drink, passed out cold and missed the ferry back north—missed a whole day's work, in fact, and limped into Tony's warehouse on Tuesday morning. He wasn't happy about it—which was something of an understatement. "You got a good record up until now," he said. "Try to keep it that way."

I felt what I always felt in these situations—guilt. I promised Tony it wouldn't happen again, but when I heard myself making that promise, it was like listening to someone hollowed out inside—someone with nothing left in there—just some skin covering a whole raft of bones and a lame-ass voice trying to convince himself he meant what he said.

87

The City

· · · · · · · · ·

During one of our benders—one of the more civil ones—Della almost convinced me we should marry. She'd been sweet to me now for weeks, and I thought we'd weathered the worst of it and it was smooth roads ahead. So, we started out toward the courthouse on a Monday morning when I should have been working instead, but didn't get any further than two blocks before turning around, heading back to her apartment and discussing the issue over two more drinks.

"I don't think it's a good idea," I said. "Not right now it isn't."

"You love me, don't you?" she asked. Her finger circled the rim of her glass.

"Yeah, I love you but—"

"But you don't love me that much—is that it?"

"I don't see any point in it," I said. "You're not aiming for kids, are you? And I already got three of my own."

"No—it's getting too late for that—"

"And besides—we've both been through the marriage ringer already."

"Yeah, but not the two of us together—we'd be different," she said.

"I don't know," I said. "Don't see much point in it."

"To show that you really love me?" she said. "What about that?"

"I can do that without getting married—I've been doing it all along."

"It's not the same—"

"It is to me," I said.

"No—exchanging those vows in front of somebody else—that's different. That means you mean it."

"I don't see it that way."

"You *are* selfish—your ex-wife was right—you think only of yourself!"

"Why? Because I don't say in front of folks what I tell you most of the time?"

And before I knew it, we were at each other's throats again—this whole business about not loving her enough or having another woman—it always lurked just below the surface.

"Where does all this crap inside you come from?" If I asked her this once, I asked her a hundred times.

"I don't know—it just comes up."

"Something happen when you were young?"

"What's that supposed to mean?"

"I don't know—things happen to us when we're young and sometimes it's a lifetime to shake it—sometimes a lifetime to even figure out what happened—most folks never do."

"Nothing happened to me, okay?"

"Look, Della, I'm trying to understand us—"

"Understand us? Why—what's that going to prove?"

"It won't prove anything—just give us some more understanding—"

"So you can tell me how screwed up I am? Is that it?"

I just shook my head. "That's not it at all."

"The past doesn't exist for me, okay?" she said. "At the end of every day, I lay it to rest and just try to forget about it and start the next day all new again."

"I've tried that forgetting, too, but it doesn't work for me—never has," I said.

"You just want to carry it around with you all your life, is that it? You one of those types?"

"No, I don't want to carry around anything—but it isn't something I can just forget about—it won't let me."

"No, *you* won't let it." And she drove a finger into my chest.

That's the way it sometimes went between Della and me—especially when we were drinking. We'd start out civil-like and before I knew it, she was putting words in my mouth or flying off the handle about something, and I was having to back-track on what I said and even apologize when there was nothing to apologize for—I did it just to keep the peace.

"That's not true—if I could forget, I would," I said.

"This is stupid, us talking like this."

"I don't think it's stupid at all."

She looked at me and laughed. "Men."

"Look, when I leave here, I go back home and work all week—every evening I'm back at my place—alone."

"Why do you even have to go home?" she asked. "Why don't you just stay here—"

"Stay here?"

"Yeah, move in with me. You can find work around here. I can ask around," she said. "You're a driver—there's plenty of driving jobs around."

"Move in with you so we can fight all the time—not just the weekends," I said.

"What if we try being nicer to each other?" she said. "And I won't drink as much. How about that?" Her voice softened and she moved close to me and kissed me on the lips. "Would you like that?"

"I need to think about it, okay?"

"Well, you go ahead and think about it—think about it good and hard." And she smiled at me as if she already knew my answer.

I showed up for work on Tuesday morning, and my route truck was gone. I walked back into the office and asked Tony what the deal was. "My son's taking over your route," he said. "I've got to let you go."

"Just like that?" I asked. "I miss a day's work and you've got someone to replace me already?"

"Junior's been wanting to drive—bugging me all the time—and I figured this was his chance," Tony said. "Your mind's somewhere off in the city, Bert, chasing some skirt down there. I just can't rely on you anymore."

"But I missed just two days," I said.

"Sorry, Bert. I paid you through this week—"

"Just like that, I'm down the road, huh?"

"Sorry—you're a good man and you'll find something else to do." He took my hand and shook it.

Well, it wasn't the first time I'd been canned, but like getting your heart broke, it's something you never get used to—it still just flattens you. I had some cash in a savings account left over from the ranch sale, so it wasn't like I was flat broke, but I felt bad just the same—like I'd been a failure all over again—and didn't know what the next move was. When that happened, I did what I've always done when the world comes crashing down—pull the cork out of a bottle and pour myself a stiff one. Irv happened to stop by that evening and we talked it over.

"Never thought Tony would can me," I told him.

"He didn't cut you much slack, did he?"

"Hardly any at all," I said.

"What are you going to do now?" he asked.

"Della wants me to move in with her," I said. "She's even talking marriage."

"You you think that's a good idea—what with the way you fight and all that?"

"She says she'll try to be nicer—not drink as much, either."

"Will she hold to it?"

"I don't know—but I'm not too keen on the marriage idea—"

"Then don't get married," he said.

"I'm holding firm on that one—but I am thinking of moving in with her—seeing how that goes. Maybe give it a trial—for one month, something like that—and I'll know in short time whether it was a good idea or not. My rent's up at the end of the month, anyway," I said.

"Don't you want a calm life like everyone else?" he asked me.

"A calm life? What the hell is that?"

"Yeah, you know—a regular life—like most folks live—not all this fighting and moving around and—"

"Drinking? Was that what you were going to say?"

"Yeah, that's part of it, right?" he said. "You think if you didn't drink, there'd be all this commotion in your life?"

"I don't know, son,' I said. "There's just as much commotion when I don't drink."

My next trip to Della's I told her I warmed again to her idea of me moving in. She was happy about my decision and we went right to bed to celebrate. The week spent apart sharpened both our appetites—I'd been feeling it ever since last leaving her and it was all stored up.

"What made you change your mind?" she asked, as she slipped out of her robe.

"I don't know—I got to thinking things over and it started making more sense—"

"So, you're going to be a city boy now—there's no chickens down here, you know?"

"I know." I undid the buckle on my belt and dropped out of my pants. "The other thing, Della—"

"What's that?"

"I got canned."

"You did?"

"Sure as Carter's-got-pills, I did."

Della stroked my arm.

"Yeah, I shouldn't have stayed over last week," I said. "It was just the opening Tony was waiting for, and he hired his kid—he'd been wanting to do it all along."

"I'm sorry to hear this," she said. "So you decided to leave Petaluma?"

"Yeah, I got to thinking things over and it started making more sense—you know, a new start and all that—a change of scenery."

We both sat on the edge of her bed and as she laid back, she pulled me with her. "I'm glad you thought it over," she whispered in my ear.

"It'll be okay, won't it?" I asked. Her face was just inches from mine. "I worry about us fighting all the time—being around each other more."

"I'll try to be nicer," she said.

"And we won't drink as much?" I knew that was the key to all of it—the big question mark hanging over everything.

"I'll try—but you gotta try, too," she said.

We made love and it was sweet and satisfying, the way making love is after the fighting ends and you make promises neither of you are sure you can keep, but you make them just the same, and both of you feel good about it.

"A new chapter," I said.

"Yeah, a new chapter, Bert." She rolled over on top of me and kissed me on the lips. "Any place else you'd rather be?" she asked.

"I can't think of any," I said. And right then I couldn't.

And so my rent ran out, I packed up my few belongings, Irv borrowed his sister's Ford, and we drove down to the ferry at Sausalito. We stood together on the ferry's deck and watched the waves ripple away from the ship's bow and felt the bay breezes hit our faces. Sausalito disappeared behind us as we sailed past Angel Island and through the wisps of fog, San Francisco's wharf line started to appear—a wharf line I was learning well.

"I hope this works out for you, Dad," Irv said. "I know you must like this woman."

"Yeah, son, I do. For all we put each other through—I do like her." I put my arm around him.

The ferry bumped up against the landing dock and dropped its wide plank so vehicles could drive off. Once on the Embarcadero, we headed toward Della's place on Chestnut Street. We arrived there just before noon.

"So, this is your boy, huh, Irv?" she asked as we entered her apartment.

"Yeah, this is Irv," I said. "Irv, this is Della."

The two of them shook hands.

"He sure looks like you," she said. "The eyes, the nose —everything—"

"He's got everything I got, but with more brains and no bad habits," I said.

Irv looked around the apartment and then walked over to the window. "Nice view," he said. "Never seen the bay like this—and I can see the bridge they're building."

"They're calling it the Golden Gate Bridge," Della said.

Irv and I walked back down to the Ford to carry the remaining valises up to Della's. At Irene's car, I turned to him. "Well, what do you think of her?"

"Too early to tell—she's a looker, though—I'll give her that much," he said.

"Yeah, she's got a spell on me for sure."

"The place is kinda small, isn't it?"

"Yeah, it is—but if it works out we'll move to something bigger."

"You gonna look for work?" he asked.

"Got a couple of leads already."

"Good," he said. "Because you don't want to be around each other all the time—not in that cramped place."

"I know—that's good advice."

Della brewed a pot of coffee and we sat around her table, drinking and making small talk. "What kind of jobs you got lined up?" Irv asked.

"There's a driver's job opening up where I work," Della answered. "Not a very glamorous one," she said, "but it's a job."

"What's he hauling?" Irv directed his question toward Della.

"Fish guts," she said. "Down to South City—they make fertilizer out of it down there."

Irv looked at me. "Fish guts?" he asked.

I nodded my head. "Yeah, fish guts."

We finished our coffee, Irv said goodbye to Della and I walked with him back down to the car. We shook hands. He started up the car. "Good luck to you here, Dad," he said through the open car window.

"Thanks, Irv."

He started to pull away. "Life's an adventure," I said.

"Is that what it is? An adventure?"

"Yeah, that's what it is," I said. "All the way up and all the way down—one big goddamn adventure—oh, and another thing—"

"What's that?"

"Don't forget how to find this place, okay?"

"No, I won't forget," he said, and drove away.

88

Drinking's Claim

· · · · · · · · · · · · · · · ·

Imoved in with Della, and two days later I was driving a flat-bed truck loaded with drums of fish entrails, fish heads, crab shells—whatever a person couldn't eat—to a fertilizer factory in South San Francisco. The route I followed went along the Embarcadero and into China Basin before running south along the bay's western shore and into Brisbane. Here there were still dairy farms, but a growing industrial area was crowding the last of them out.

The fertilizer factory smelled terrible—about as bad as those drums of fish entrails I was hauling. When you popped the lid off those drums, that first wave hit you strong enough that whatever was in your stomach came halfway up your throat. You never thought something could smell this bad, but that was death. "How'd you get this job driving the gut wagon?" the fellow working the dock area asked me my first day driving.

"Lucky, I guess," and he laughed like hell.

The smell bled through your clothes and into your skin—so bad that Della made me wash up and change clothes before I could even touch her. I wasn't sure how long I wanted to keep this job, but there was a depression going on, and jobs, any kinds of jobs were scarce, and at the end of the week there was always a paycheck waiting for me.

So I kept at it, leaving the apartment at daybreak, walking down to where the truck was loaded and waiting, drove off to Brisbane and was back at the wharf by mid-afternoon with all the drums empty and washed out. Sometimes I'd walk over to where Della was working and if her shift was over, we'd walk back home together, stopping off to buy a bottle of bourbon and some ginger ale—by now the government finally came to its senses and ended Prohibition. I'd wash up and she'd have a glass of bourbon waiting for me on the table and we'd drink until the bottle was empty. Most evenings we were too tired to argue. The days spilled into weeks like this and the weeks into months. Then months became a couple of years.

About this same time, Irv sent me a postcard saying he'd been hired by J.C. Penney's and was taking a job in Santa Cruz, selling shoes. The postcard had a picture of a big Ferris Wheel and next to it a giant roller coaster. "Greetings from the Santa Cruz Boardwalk" the card read. *"Saving up to buy a car,"* Irv wrote on the other side of the card. *"I'll stop in and see you sometime. Irv."*

Things had mostly settled down between me and Della. We had our bouts—there was no avoiding them—and I'd threaten to leave and she'd ask me, "Where you going to go, huh? Who's going to take you in?" And I'd fumble around for an answer but never came up with a good one. I didn't know where I'd go—if I'd go anywhere. Seems like I burned a bunch of bridges behind me and had run out of options, so I kept driving the gut wagon and hanging my clothes on a hook outside in the hallway and drinking bourbon every night and thankful for any stretch of peace between us. When things were good, we were as warm and loving as any couple, but when they weren't, we'd avoid each other as much as two people living in a twenty-by- twenty square could.

I guess I'd fallen a long way—it had all been so gradual, one disappointment at a time—you hardly notice—but pretty soon you find yourself looking up from the floor, wondering what happened—what hit you. You start out with big hopes and they get chipped away, and what's left is whatever hasn't deserted you.

I never had any big picture, any big dream of what I wanted to be, what I wanted to do—even when I was a youngster—and I had less a picture now. I never planned for anything. Never thought I could be someone other than who I was at that moment. Things just happened to me and I'd follow where the chips fell until I ran out of chips. Sounds like a helluva way to live your life, doesn't it? But I didn't know anything else.

All the drinking was catching up to me, too—catching up with both of us—and not just a hangover either, but something more serious. I could feel it inside me things weren't right—a constant pain in the guts, losing weight and growing a belly on me round as a basketball. My eyes were always puffed out, and the veins in my nose and cheeks broken. I'd get the shakes, too, especially when I laid off the liquor—and it hurt to piss. When I threw up, I'd see little traces of blood.

It was happening to Della, too, but even worse. Her dark hair and dark eyes always made her seem paler than most, but now she looked unhealthy—big, purple circles under her eyes, her face getting boney, the skin yellowing, and she was growing thin as a rail. She complained of having no energy, either, and hurting all over, and had to cut back on her work hours. We never thought of seeing a doctor—figured we'd rely on our past good health and heal ourselves—but that wasn't happening. We were in a fix.

Her health worsened—to the point she couldn't get out of bed. I finally took her to the hospital. They run some tests and the doctor there said her liver was failing and didn't know how much longer she had.

"Is she gonna die, doc?"

"I don't know—she's pretty sick," he said.

She'd been on the outs with her family as long as we'd been together. She tried not talking about them, but they always seemed to come up in her conversations—she'd make some reference to them before she caught herself and clammed up—and if I asked about them, she'd change the conversation or not want to talk about it. I sensed they were never far from her thoughts—that there was a wound there that had never healed, so I looked her mother up from an old address book Della kept. The mother lived in the Mission District, and I told her Della was in a bad way. Her mother stared at me and asked who I was and I told her I was a friend.

"We don't talk for so long," she said. "My fault—both our fault."

She was sorry to hear the news about her daughter. I met her mother at the hospital along with two of her sisters. They all looked alike—the long black hair, the same brown eyes—that Italian nose. We stood around Della's bed and we held her hands and talked to her. The sisters remembered earlier incidents from their childhood. Della tried to stay awake, but then she'd drift off and her eyes would close and we'd stop talking.

A week later Della died. I went in to visit her after working my shift and the doctor met me out in the hallway and said Della had suffered a massive organ failure and they couldn't save her. He said he was sorry, they'd done all they could do. The news knocked the wind right out of me—like a hard punch to the gut. I looked at the doctor and looked at the walls around me, the floor, my shoes—anything my eyes could find to light on—as if I looked hard enough I'd find an answer somewhere and, miracle of all miracles, Della would be healed.

Like all the deaths before me, I tried to make sense of what I'd just been told, tried to tell myself that this is what happens to folks—that none of us get out of here alive. But no amount of explaining helps—nothing makes any sense of it. I kept hearing that doctor's voice, and what he'd just told me, until I broke down right there in that hospital hallway and cried like there was no tomorrow.

The funeral was a simple one. Her family attended—what was left of her family, at least. Della's father had died years earlier. Some of her fellow workers were there, as well—even Thom Dyson, the fellow she'd been with on my unannounced visit to her apartment. We shook hands and I thanked him for coming. We drove in cars out to Colma, where there was a graveside service. The priest recited some prayers and shook a wand of holy water over her casket. I dropped some red roses on it, as well, and said goodbye to her.

And just like that she was gone—a woman I'd chanced upon years earlier in a west Santa Rosa tavern, who took me home to her place, and then just as suddenly as we met, she disappeared for the next twenty-odd years until chancing upon her on a San Francisco sidewalk. And from that sidewalk meeting and that one night years earlier, we cobbled a relationship together and like most relationships, it was an uneven one, to be sure—full of highs and lows, filled with bouts of drinking, love-making, laughter, arguing, long talks—all those things that settle out between them when two people rub their lives together.

89
Left-Over Pieces
· · · · · · · · · · · · · · ·

I gave them notice at the fishery and stayed on driving for a month after Della died. It was back again to square one with my life after thinking the two of us—Della and me—for all our differences, would live the rest of it out together. I should have known by then about plans—big plans for our lives—and the monkey wrench that's often tossed into the gears whenever you start thinking about them.

I know I couldn't stay in her apartment—everything I looked at and touched and smelled there reminded me of her. Even when I left her place to go to work or just to go out and walk, she was all I ever thought about. I'd see a woman walking toward me and think it was her, see the kind of hat that Della used to wear—that walk of hers—and all my thoughts tumbled toward her. I'd hear laughter and think it was her laughter. See a woman's hair in braids or a dark pair of eyes, and it was Della's hair or Della's eyes that I was seeing. There were times I'd sit on the edge of her bed holding a scarf of hers and cry my eyes out that she wasn't sitting there next to me. There were times, too, when I didn't want to live anymore—that I'd had enough. Drinking wasn't the same, either, without her. I'd turn sad and blubbery after one glass before putting the cork back in the bottle.

In the middle of all this, Irv showed up just days before I was giving up Della's apartment. He'd driven in from Santa Cruz in his Ford roadster, wearing a twenty-five dollar suit if it cost a penny. I'd written to him just after Della died.

"You got your things packed?" he asked me.

"The few I have," I said. "Where we going?"

"I wrote to Tony, your old boss," he said, "And he's got you a job at a chicken ranch west of Healdsburg—out Mill Creek way with a guy named Slim Casper."

"A chicken ranch, huh?"

"That's right—you need to get out of here, Dad—this isn't doinng you any good."

Irv looked around the apartment—the place was a mess— the bed undone, dishes in the sink, dust everywhere and worse— the place smelled like dead fish. I stopped hanging my clothes out in the hallway after Della died—just wore them right into the apartment and dropped them on the floor there.

"I let myself go to hell," didn't I?"

"I've seen you in better shape, that's for sure," he said.

"We can drive across the Golden Gate Bridge now," I said. "I've been watching them build it all along."

"We sure can," Irv said.

He put the top down on his Ford and we cruised along like nobody's business. This same trip that once took me hours in a 1925 Mack truck, we made in half that time. I breathed in the air, and for the first time in a long time, I felt like living again. He wanted to stop in and say hello to his mother, and I told him I'd like to see her myself. She lived on Keller Street now, in the smaller house, and rented out the larger one on Prospect. She still made potato salad for Pedrona's Delicatessen, her only customer. I hadn't seen her in several years.

When Irv and I reached Novato, I saw the highway sign pointing toward Sonoma. I'd been thinking of Tino, and how it'd been ages since we last saw each other—that visit in the county jail— and how I always wanted Irv to meet him. "What about a little detour through Sonoma, Irv? I'd like you to meet someone."

"Sure, we can do that," he said. "Who do you want me to meet?"

"Tino," I said. "I've talked enough about him."

We drove east across tidelands, crossed the Petaluma Creek, and five miles later we were working our way north up the valley toward Sonoma. I knew this side of the valley well—it was Sheers' land with the creek further east winding through the tidelands.

We drove down Broadway and the town had a different look to it now from when I remembered it years ago. It was all cars and trucks—you hardly saw a horse or wagon anywhere. New businesses had sprouted up, and some of the old ones gone now. We pulled up to the Union Livery, but it wasn't a livery anymore but a business called Napa Milling—a feed store.

Irv parked his roadster and we walked inside. I recognized Tino right-off. He was hand-trucking several sacks of grain to a waiting pick-up.

"Tino!" I called out.

He looked at me. "I'll be go-to-hell!"

"Tino, this is my son, Irv." They shook hands.

"The livery's gone, huh?"

"For years now," he said. "Sold to an outfit in Napa. They kept me on and now I'm managing the place. The race track's gone, too."

"Progress," I said.

"I guess."

"You still the egg man?"

"Haven't been for awhile," I said. "I was living in the city and now I'm heading toward Healdsburg to try my luck there—it's back to the eggs."

"We all lost track of you, Bert."

"Well, I lost track of myself, too," I said.

"Your name comes up every now and then. Flo remembers you. 'Any word on that handsome Bert Miller?' she asks, and I tell her 'not a word.'"

"So, it's all good around here?" I asked.

"Calm. Not like before." And Tino laughed and shook his head.

"That's good," I said.

There seemed a million things to talk about just then, a million questions, but we'd planned to see Christina in Petaluma first, and then on to Healdsburg where folks there were waiting to meet me. I told Tino I'd stop by again when we had more time, and that it was good seeing him and I was glad the waters around him had calmed a bit from before. We shook hands again and Tino said Irv was a fine looking boy. Irv and I left Sonoma, and drove over the hill to Petaluma, a route I knew like all the lines in my hands and face

"Well, hello Bert." Christina met us at her front door. "It's been a long time."

"Hello, Christina," I said. "Yeah, it's been awhile, hasn't it?"

She'd aged—I mean, that's what happens to us, right? There aren't any waters from the Fountain of Youth we can drink, nothing that makes the years go backwards. Wasn't any magic lamp you could rub or some genie coming out of a bottle to make you young again. The only thing that came out of a bottle killed Della and nearly took me with her. I looked into Christina's face and saw the years there. She was older than me, to begin with, by some ten years, although it never really mattered. Her eyes still had a cold, hard gleam to them, and I could see Irv and Irene and Nanette in her face.

"I was sorry to hear about your lady friend," she said. "Irv wrote and told me about her."

"We should have seen that one coming," I said. "But we didn't."

"And now you're going to Healdsburg? No more city life?" she asked.

"No, I'm done with it."

"You'll be back to being Bert the egg man," she said.

I laughed. "Yeah, that's me—Bert the egg man."

The three of us ate lunch together at Christina's. She'd fried a chicken earlier in the morning, and of course, there was her potato salad—I'd forgotten how good it tasted. And she baked an apple strudel, too. After lunch, we thanked her, and as we left, Christina and I hugged. "I'm sorry," I whispered in her ear, "for everything I put you through—you didn't deserve it."

She just nodded her head.

We drove north on the Redwood Highway. There were more houses now, but it was still the countryside I remembered—the walnut and prune orchards, the vineyards, the long sweeps of open fields with wild oats, the fog banked up above the western hills. We passed Mark West Springs Road and I thought of the times I rode Little Ike up there after an evening in the big town, and the times I drove my wagon up to John B.'s loaded down with lumber from the Russian River mills.

At Healdsburg we drove west on Westside Road until we came to Mill Creek Road. We followed it as it wound through rolling oak country and vineyards before narrowing into a little valley with redwoods and a clear creek running below the trees. "You sure this is the right road?" I asked Irv. "It doesn't seem like a place you'd find a chicken ranch."

"It's what Tony told me," Irv said. "I wrote it all down so I wouldn't forget."

We continued on, and sure enough, the little valley widened enough, and there, just beyond the creek, was Slim's house, and beyond his house, several rows of chicken barns. The birds were up in metal cages now, with the sides of the barns walled in with redwood slats that let fresh air move through. Irv pulled his roadster into Slim's yard and Slim walked out to meet us. A little terrier dog ran up and pissed on Irv's roadster's tires.

Slim was tall, a little bent at the waist, with white hair that streamed out from under his cowboy hat. A big white moustache covered his upper lip. He greeted us with a wide smile.

"Found the place all right?" Slim asked.

"Wasn't sure at first," Irv said.

"You don't expect to find chickens back here, do you?" Slim looked at me.

"No, sir, you don't," I said.

Slim and I shook hands. "Tony said you're an old egg man from way back." Slim wore cowboy boots and he toed at the ground.

"Yeah, I guess that's true when I think about it," I said. "My brother, John B. and I, we built our first brooder house forty-odd years ago over in Sonoma for a woman named Carlotta Stamm."

It felt good to say her name now after all these years and not feel bad or sad or any of those things I once felt when thinking about her—like, finally, after all these years, she no longer had a hold on me.

"Forty years?" Slim said. "That makes you an old-timer."

"I guess it does," I said. "Is that what happens when you live long enough?"

"So I don't have to tell you much about chickens, then, right?" Slim looked at me and smiled.

"You can tell me anything you want," I said.

"I'll show you around the place," Slim said. "There isn't much to it, really. The wife and I been doing most of the work with a hired hand, and we thought our boy would want to run the place, but he's got different ideas about what he wants to do—go off to college and make moving pictures." Slim looked me over. "We were looking for someone who could manage the place so we could take a few days off at times and get away."

"I'll certainly try my hand at it," I said.

"Never wanted to stay with the chickens, huh?"

"No, I had other ideas," I said.

"What about you, Irv?" Slim asked.

"Yeah, I thought Irv here would be driving horses all his life and what happens?" I said. "He ends up a salesman at a J.C. Penney's store in Santa Cruz. Go figure."

"Sorry, Dad, if I disappointed you."

"No, you haven't disappointed me," I said. "You do what you want to do."

"We got a little house in the back here—it's where the missus and I lived before we built the bigger house," Slim said. "But it's comfortable and served us well."

We walked back to the smaller house. It was a white clapboard cottage with roses all around it and from behind the cottage you could hear the creek running. Tall redwoods grew all along the creek. The air felt cool and clean here.

"We dam the creek up during the summer and draw water from it," Slim said. "And it makes a damn fine swimming hole, too—especially on a hot day."

I liked everything I saw about the place. I liked Slim and his dog, Mitzie, that followed us around, and once away from the chickens, I liked how fresh the place smelled, too. Slim opened the door to the little cottage and we walked in. It was cool and damp inside.

"Ain't no one lived here in a couple of months," Slim said. "Needs airing out, don't it?"

There was a tiny living room with hardwood floors and an over-stuffed chair and a floor lamp next to the chair. Along one wall in the living room was a row of mounted deer antlers. "I can tell you a story about each one of them," Slim said. "You ever hunted wild pigs?"

"No, never have," I said.

From the living room, you walked right into the kitchen. It was painted yellow with a white tile countertop. A little nook with four chairs and a table pushed out from one side of the kitchen. A short hallway from the kitchen led to the one bedroom and the bath.

"This is all furniture from when the missus and I first got married," Slim said. "It's got some wear on it—"

"It's fine, Slim," I said, "Just fine."

From the cottage, we walked over to the chicken sheds. The birds were housed now in steel cages hung waist-high with a concrete floor underneath. A long metal trough ran along the front row of the cages and this is where the chicken feed went. There were water fonts in each cage. Slim had a low-profile tractor he could walk be-hind with a two cylinder gas engine and a blade in front of it that moved the chicken shit down to one end of the shed where it was hauled away in the ranch truck.

"They don't touch the ground anymore?" I asked Slim.

"No, they started going to these battery cages they call them a few years back," he said. "Production. Production," he said. "That's what it's all about now."

Slim's hens were all Rhode Island Reds. They looked healthy enough, but I hated seeing them in cages like this—I hated seeing anything in cages. It didn't seem natural. Chickens like to scratch in the soil—and most folks don't know this—but they like to run around, too. At Carlotta's and the folks' place and over at Joe

Keebler's, the chickens would see me coming from yards off and race to where I tossed them hen-scratch—sometimes going air-born a dozen feet, flapping their little wings—before plunking down to earth again. They'd peck and scratch in the ground with their feet, and cluck, and chase one another off, and they always made me laugh. And after they ate—depending on the time of year—they'd go back to their nests and as a thank-you, leave you a few eggs. I remembered Carlotta saying they were about as perfect an animal as you could find, and she was right.

"What'd you think?" Slim asked me. "Look like a place you could work in?"

"I think so," I said. It looked fine to me, but I was at a point where anything would. It was country—I could breathe the air and not smell fish guts—here I smelled chicken shit, instead. City air for country air with a hint of chicken dust—that was the trade-off.

"Any questions?" Slim asked.

"None right now," I said.

Irv and I walked back to his roadster and we pulled out my two suitcases and walked toward the cottage.

"Is that all you have——just two suitcases?" Slim asked.

"That's it," I said. "It's all I got left."

I'd sold off everything I owned before moving to the city. Joe Keebler bought all my harness and my two wagons—and I gave Irv all my rifles and shotguns to hold onto, so it was pretty much down to just the clothes I wore.

"Well, put 'em in the cottage and come back to the house. The missus has coffee and cake for us."

Slim's wife, Eleanor, invited us into her house. She was a gray-haired woman with a pleasant, welcoming smile. When we were all seated at the table, she looked at me. "So, Bert, you're going to be working with us here?"

"That's right," I said.

"Well, good," she said. "I hope it all works out—and, to tell you the truth—I'd enjoy the company. With our son gone, there's just Slim to talk to."

"Yeah, just me," Slim said, and he laughed.

She set a piece of chocolate cake in front of each of us and filled our coffee cups. Through the opened windows, I could hear the creek running. I liked this place already. We talked back and forth although it was mostly Slim who talked. He'd inherited the ranch from his folks and enjoyed reminiscing about earlier times.

"You like to hunt, Bert?" Slim asked me.

"I used to hunt and fish like crazy when I was young—even made a half-assed living from it one time. I hunted with a buddy— half Indian. We poached, Slim, and we were pretty good at it," I said. "I've told Irv all about him. In fact, we just come from seeing him."

"My friend's a foreman at the Canfield Ranch— got a thousand acres off of Skaggs Springs Road, and every winter a bunch of us hunt wild pigs up there," Slim said. "You're sure welcome to join us when the time rolls around."

"Wild pigs, huh?"

"I asked if you already hunted them, right?" he said.

"No, sir, I haven't."

"We usually take a couple of dogs with us, but you don't get there in time, those boars'll cut up a dog like slicing bread. We lost two dogs in the past three years—those boars'll charge anything," Slim said.

I hadn't hunted in a couple of years—hadn't even held a gun during that time.

"I don't like Slim hunting those pigs," Eleanor said. "It's too dangerous."

"Oh, come on, Eleanor—"

"We talked about this before," she said. "I just don't like it."

After coffee and cake, we thanked Eleanor and walked back to Irv's car.

"Good luck here, Dad," Irv said. "Think you'll be all right?"

"I think so, son." I looked around. "I mean, the creek, the trees—this place is beautiful."

"You need anything, you write, okay?"

"That's what I'm supposed to say to you, isn't it?"

"Hell, I don't know."

We hugged each other and he got in his car and drove off. Slim walked up to me. "You make yourself at home, okay? Work day starts at seven in the morning."

"Okay," I said.

I walked back to the cottage and carried my suitcases into the bedroom and laid them on top of the bed. I snapped the latches open. I'd bought two new pair of pants and a couple of new shirts and several changes of underwear before leaving the city and had stacked all of them neatly into the suitcases. I bought a new pair of boots, too. The clothes I wore while hauling fish guts, I dumped into a garbage can in the alley behind Della's. I put my clothes away in the chest of drawers, and hung my two jackets in the closet before deciding to walk down to the creek.

It was a late July afternoon. I found a big rock near the water and sat down and skipped stones across a little eddy in the creek. Long lines of sunlight streaked through the trees. The light seemed golden and breathing. I sucked in the air, let it fill my body, and thought about this next chapter in my life, wondering what it would bring after the last one that started out so promising, but left me feeling so low and so heartbroken.

And all those chapters before this one? They were building up, leading to something—but I didn't know what, didn't have any idea what would happen next. Some little thing, some little incident, could push it one way or the other—I could walk into a tavern and there at the end of the bar sat a whole new direction my life would take—but I had to keep telling myself that regardless of what happened, I was in control. Right now, though, it was a hard-sell. I didn't feel in control of anything. I was floating with the tides, feeling beat-down, counting on a little bit of luck to keep me from drowning.

I walked back to the cottage and realized I hadn't thought about a drink for nearly three hours. That was something—some kind of record for me. I vowed that with the new job, the new place, I'd cut back on the drinking—not give it up entirely—I didn't think I could do that, but just cut back—not slam it down like the world was going to end tomorrow. Besides, I had a job here to do—it wasn't like I could drink all the day without a worry. That said, I found one of my flasks, and poured myself a house-warming drink.

I sat in that over-stuffed chair and let the bourbon run through me, let my mind run off, let it take me where it wanted—let it fly off like a bird just freed from its cage. What it came up with first, was how my life seemed to follow one big circle, how it kept repeating itself. Every chapter, I thought, a new one, but it really wasn't. It was an earlier scene being played again and again, and I didn't know why. Did it keep replaying until I got it right? Was that it? What did 'right' mean, anyway? Here I was signing on as a ranch hand, living in a ranch hand's quarters, thinking my life was taking a new turn—that I was leaving the past behind when it wasn't a new turn at all—it was just more steps backwards. It was like what I'd done at Carlotta's years earlier—moving in there with my secret desire to have her and all of it building up inside me head. And you could say, I done the same with Emma Hansen—but without the desire—before Carlotta's.

What I wanted then was that shot of bourbon waiting for me on Emma's front porch at the end of a working day. Wasn't anything bad about it—all those chapters—it's just the way life comes at you. And maybe my life was like everyone else's—it kept repeating itself, wanting to slip back into those earlier tracks already laid out in front of it. And, I guess, my aim was to keep it from slipping back into those tracks again—to find a new road and follow that one, but it was damn hard for me.

And with women? It was that same circle repeating itself—those early stages filled with promise, big dreams, building our lives together, until little by little, life whittled away the promise and whittled away the dreams, and you were left with the remaining pieces—a little bit of hope there, a little bit of purpose here, some determination, some resolve and a heaping of good luck—seeing what fit together and what didn't. Maybe that's where the real work took place in this life, I thought—what you could assemble out of the remaining pieces—after most of it had all blown up and scattered to the winds.

I heard a scratching at the front door, opened it, and there stood Slim's terrier, Mitzie, wagging her little stub of a tail. I let her in and she circled the living room, her nose to the floor, before she went into the kitchen and then down the hallway. Her nails clattered on the hardwood floors. I sat back down on the chair and when she returned, she jumped right into my lap. "Well, make yourself at home, little girl," I said. She reminded me of Jigs. You reach this point in your life and something always reminds you of something else, something that came before it and was no longer around.

It'd been two months since Della died. I thought of her all the time, replaying scene after scene with her, wishing things hadn't turned out the way they did—the same way I'd thought of my dad all the time after he was killed, and the way I thought of Nanette and Ma, and how it didn't seem possible they were dead and gone—that they were still alive and it was only when I thought of them, and remembered what had happened, that they were dead. The rest of the time, they were still alive, and there was still time to change up what had happened so they'd never die—but then it sunk in all over again and it was like they'd just died—and I'd only been fooling myself all along.

Screwy thoughts, I know, but that's where my mind took me, always tiptoeing back to the past for some reason, peeking through a half-opened window or a door left ajar—looking for clues about who I was or who'd I become. Did I want to go back there? Did I want to live it all over again? If I could pick the moments, sure— I knew just the ones. But if I couldn't? I wasn't so sure then. Right now, though, I was grateful—grateful to be out of the city and out of that apartment I shared with Della and grateful not to be hogging drums of fish guts around. I was grateful, too, that the liquor hadn't killed me the way it killed Della. Maybe I was luckier than most to make it this far.

I heard Slim whistle and the terrier jumped off my lap and ran out the front door. I took one more drink and saved what was left in the flask for another day. That was saying something, I tell you. Other times I would have drained it—said 'to hell' with tomorrow. I may not be alive tomorrow, but today I am—but I didn't do that this time. I screwed the top back on and set it in the top drawer of the dresser where it wouldn't be staring at me all the time. I set it right next to the other one.

90

Settling-In (Again)

A way from the hen houses, it was quiet out at Slim's save for the sound of the creek, but the creek didn't seem like noise to me—it seemed like a backdrop instead, like a sheet of painted canvas behind players on a stage, and against this painted canvas my thoughts strutted out and said their lines. So many of these thoughts, of course, centered on Della. I missed her terribly these past weeks—missed holding her, talking into the night the way we used to, walking to the concerts in Golden Gate Park on Sundays or along the beach at the Presidio—even our more raucous times when we argued and shouted at each other in those drunken fogs. We were both alive then, full of spirit. Now, I'd wake in the middle of the night and reach for her, but there was nothing there—nothing to reach for—just a dead calm all around and the sound of the creek babbling through an open window .

I don't know how much Tony or Irv told Slim about my past, my struggles with things, but I could tell by the way Slim asked how I was doing, and how he'd take a second look into my eyes as I answered, that he knew more than he let on. He didn't pry though. He went on about his business, and I went on about mine.

Both Slim and Eleanor were kind to me—she'd knock on my door and hand me a plate of food, and say it was left-overs anyway, and would I like it, and of course, I always took it. She often asked if there was something I needed, something their little cottage lacked, and I told her, no, everything was fine. Slim walked me through the jobs he wanted me to do around the ranch. He was patient, and if I didn't do something the way he wanted, he didn't complain, didn't shout at me the way my old man used to, but, instead, would show me all over again how to do the job. It wasn't anything too complicated but as always, my mind still drifted.

"You like it here all right?" Slim asked me a few months into my stay.

"I like it fine," I told him.

"You don't miss the big city?"

"Oh, there's things about it I miss. I liked living near the bay, watching the ships come in, and the fishing boats—seeing all different kinds of people—"

"Yeah, it's different here, isn't it?"

"It's a good change for me, though."

"Tony told me you lost your wife—was sorry to hear that."

"She wasn't my wife," I said. "We lived together but we weren't married. We'd talked about it but never tied the knot."

Slim didn't ask me how she died. I figured he already knew.

"It must be rough," he said, "losing somebody like that."

"It is—we all lose people in our lives," I said. "You just pick up the pieces and move on—ain't that many other choices."

Twice a week I'd take a load of eggs in Slim's truck down to Tony's warehouse in Petaluma. I liked driving down there, driving down the Redwood Highway and remembering all the times I covered this same distance with two horses and a wagon. Those days were gone now—it was a rare time you even saw a horse and wagon—but I still thought about them a lot and wished somehow they'd come back. Slim had a 1936 Chevrolet flatbed, dual wheels in the back, and it cruised along about forty to forty-five miles an hour. With a tail-wind I could get that truck up to fifty.

I liked to drive with the windows open and the wind blowing through my hair. I couldn't look around as much as I could driving Molly and Dolly, and I couldn't let my mind run off like it used to, either. Now I had to stay focused on the road in front of me and watch for other cars and trucks. It was a different world now. I know, I keep saying that, but it was. Everything moved faster and there were more people—more of everything—and I wasn't sure if I fit in it or not.

I liked driving through Petaluma and seeing all the places I used to stop at on the routes with Little Ike—I could recite them all—from

Vinny's at the north end of town all the way south to Moffet's Café on the south. I could tell you who owned the place, who worked there, what they ordered, how often they paid, even who the regular customers were. Some of them were still in business, but many of them were gone now, the little wooden taverns and stores torn down and something new built in its place—some modern thing built out of concrete. That seemed like another century when I looked back—and mostly it was.

As I said before, you didn't see any horses and wagons anymore unless they were in a parade. The old-timers had all died, and the ones who didn't, sat on park benches and hobbled around with their canes and told the same stories to anyone who'd listen, stories about the prime of their youth. And like so many folks that died, I wished they were still around—that I could buy them a drink and talk about old times and how they lived their lives and share some belly laughs. I missed that the most, and wished they could live forever, or at least, outlive me because I wasn't any good at this grieving—wasn't any good at watching folks die, watching everything change around me without feeling sad and lonesome. It just sucked the life out of me.

Tony was always glad to see me and he'd slap my back and ask if I was staying out of trouble, and I told him I mostly was. With Prohibition ended, Tony was all legal now—dealing in eggs and whatever else he could sell on the side.

"You and Slim hittin' it off all right?" he asked me.

"We get along fine," I said.

I was getting to be an old-timer myself—pushing sixty years now and wondering where all those years went. My old man used to say that aging was something that happens when you live long enough. I remembered a lot of things he told me—they made more sense now than they did years ago when I was still wet behind the ears, when I thought I knew everything there was to know, and argued with him just for the sake of arguing.

When I look back, I realize I didn't know shit—I just thought I did—but I was dumber than a fence post and there wasn't anything he could tell me that I didn't think I already knew. I fooled a lot of people, but mostly I fooled myself, and the more I thought about it, the more I thought that's why I struggled with so many things, particularly women the way I done—I always thought I knew all the answers, was always trying to be someone else, someone I wasn't—and women—they have an extra sense about those kinds of things. They could see right through me, and when they showed me who I really was—first thing I did was doubt it—or deny it. And they'd say,' it's all right, there's nothing wrong with being yourself.'

Still, I hated being told that—no other way to describe it. I wished I'd learned this earlier. It would have saved me a lot of grief because there wasn't anybody I knew that walked around longer with his tail between his legs than me. If there were trophies for most broken hearts suffered—those trophies would be lining my mantle—if I had a mantle to line them on. If there was a prize for who could brood the longest—I'd take that one home, too. But I didn't point the finger at anyone else—I can say that much in my defense. I took the blame, said it was me all along—that it was my own doing.

I'd borrow Slim's truck and drive down to see John B. a couple of times a month. He was just down the highway ten miles and up Mark West Springs Road. Weeks earlier, John B. had lost another son, Friedolin, when the boy tossed his shotgun over a fence while hunting quail and the shotgun touched off, and blasted open Friedolin's chest. Gertie heard the shotgun fire from her kitchen window and heard Friedolin cry out, but by the time they got the boy to the hospital he was dead. It was the third child John B. had lost and there were no words that could comfort him. You don't go through this life without losing someone, but with John B. it seemed downright unfair—that he didn't deserve all these deaths within his family.

Folks at the funeral I overheard said it was God's will—and, of course, that's always the priests' message—but I didn't know what to think about this God. If he existed—and I wasn't sure he did—he didn't seem very merciful or just like folks made him out to be—but more like an avenger, going around settling scores with people he didn't even know.

Work became routine at Slim's. Ramon, Slim's ranch-hand, and I gathered eggs every morning in a little cart and put them in flats and we fed the chickens twice a day. Every other week, I'd drive into Healdsburg and haul back sacks of chicken feed and once a month I'd haul the chicken manure away. Slim helped out when he could.

"You work with *Mexicanos* before?" Ramon asked me.

"I have," and I told him about the three brothers at Carlotta's ranch, and how Alfonso, one of the brothers, and I would haul lumber back from Sonoma Landing to build brooder houses.

"He always thought I'd end up marrying Carlotta, the woman who owned the ranch," I told him.

"And you didn't?"

I laughed and shook my head. "No, I didn't—you think if I did I'd be here shoveling chicken shit with you?"

"No—you be shoveling it at your own *rancho*," he said.

I laughed.

"How you end up here?" he asked.

"Ramon, it's a long story," I said.

"Maybe you tell me someday?"

"Sure—someday when we've got lots of time, I'll tell you parts of it—what I can remember, at least," I said.

"It's a good story?"

"A good story? I don't know, but like most stories, it's got its high points and its low ones, too. Times when you're on top of the world and times when you're not," I said. "There's people dying and there's people being born— like one big circle going 'round and 'round, Ramon. Disappointments, broken dreams—stuff like that—the way life usually is."

I shoveled more manure into the wagon and then stopped and leaned on my shovel. "I'm trying to write some of it down while I can still remember what happened. It's not all sad, though. There's other parts that are better—probably just like your story, Ramon—no different."

"You think people are all the same?" he asked.

"Mostly—I think we all want the same things in this life, don't you?"

"I want to have a car," he said. "I don't even know how to drive one but I want to have a car."

"There you go—I do, too. We're all the same," and we both laughed.

It had been several months now since Della died, but I wasn't thinking of her so much like I used to. Sure, some little scene with her would play out before my eyes—sometimes even imagining she hadn't died at all but then remembering that she did and it was like feeling the hurt all over again.

Some mornings I imagined her walking right into Slim's ranch, walking into my little cottage there and pouring herself a bourbon and ginger ale, and things would be like they always were between us—without all the fighting— and both our bodies healthy. But that's all they were—just imaginings—like I spent half my life doing. But that's what I did, making up little scenes the way I'd always done, trying to fool myself into thinking what had happened hadn't really happened at all. I knew she was gone, but you can't tell a stubborn heart something it doesn't want to hear. It grabbed onto that hope and there was no reasoning with it.

I wasn't drinking as much, either, and that was a good thing. My mind seemed clearer as a result. I'd seen what it'd done to Della— what it'd done to a lot of folks— but it didn't scare me enough to give it up entirely. Slim had tried to wean me off the harder stuff, introducing me to some local wines. I was drinking reds and whites now and cutting back on the bourbon—not getting drunk nearly as often—although a couple of times the voices would call out, and I'd wander into Healdsburg, shoulder up to a local bar, and order my old stand-by—a shot with a beer back-up.

If a lady was sitting at the bar by herself, that same little voice started gnawing on my ear, calling out to go over and start talking her up and buy her a drink—sometimes I did—because old habits live a long life. The urge was to keep hammering them down with her, but I knew where that always got me—besides, Slim and Eleanor had been good bosses, and I didn't want to mess it up by dragging some floosie back to their place, or, worse yet, not showing up for work. I'd done that enough already. I was never not going to drink—I told you this before—because the times I stopped, drinking was all I thought about. It got so big in my head I thought I'd have to wear two hats, so I figured I'd keep drinking, but not as much. Maybe I was making excuses here—I didn't know.

On my time off, I liked to walk along Mill Creek, breathe in the air under the redwoods—amazed at their size—and stare up through them to the sky. Slim had read all about the redwoods, how old they were, and how the valleys around here, particularly the Russian River Valley, had been so thick with them there was no other place on earth with this many trees in such a small area. But that didn't last long. Along came man and he logged them—logged these beauties. And after the earthquake, logged them even more to rebuild the city. It was lumber from these same trees I'd hauled to Carlotta's and the Koblentz ranch and down to Lakeville and at the time thought nothing of them ever disappearing. Like a lot of things in this life, I thought they'd last forever.

Irv had driven up a couple times to see me. He still lived in Santa Cruz, still worked for J.C. Penney's, although he was talking about leaving there and returning to Petaluma. He'd grown into a fine looking man—handsome as the devil. He sent me a photograph with him dressed in a fine suit, his foot up on the running board of a Ford roadster. I pinned the photo on the kitchen wall.

"Why you want to leave there?" I asked him. He had a car and an apartment, a couple of tailored suits, liked to go dancing down at the halls along the Boardwalk. He had lady friends knocking at his door— seemed like an ideal life to me, and I couldn't see any reason for wanting to leave.

"Ma's been after me to move back," he said.

"So?" I asked him. "You gotta do everything she says?"

"No, I don't, but I'm missing the country—missing my friends here," he said.

"I guess that's reason enough then," I said. "You do what you want."

"I'm not interested in sales anymore, either," he said. "I want to be outside. I stopped at Western Dairy on the east end of D Street and inquired about work there."

"What'd they say?"

"There might be a job opening with Quality Control," he said.

"Quality Control? What's that mean?"

"It's a fancy term. It means I go around to different dairies in the area and check on the ones that are having problems—lower butterfat, high bacteria counts—stuff like that. Then you write up what you see and make recommendations," he said.

"You know how to do all that?"

"Some of it, I do. The rest I'll learn," he said.

The next time I saw Irv, he'd moved back to Petaluma and told me he'd got that job at Western Dairy. He drove all around the area in a company truck, stopping at dairies and trying to figure out how to solve some problem they were having. He'd write everything down. "I like the writing part," he told me. "Never thought I would, but I took to it right off."

He drove up to see me and said he liked his new job fine. I was glad to hear it. "You don't miss your girlfriends back in Santa Cruz?" I asked him. "You don't miss dancing with them?"

"No, I go to the dances up at the Russian River now, and sometimes Joe Silva and I go over to Boyes Springs and dance with the girls there," he said.

The country was finally coming out of the Depression and more folks were back at work. The newspapers said that Europe was in turmoil and that another war was brewing and could break out any time. Like the earlier war, there were folks against us getting involved and folks who thought just the opposite. It all seemed so far away to me, but I knew we were all connected. I tried not to think about it. I worried that Irv might get called up for military service. I knew it was the patriotic thing to do—and there were posters up urging young folks to enlist, but, still, I didn't want to see him go, didn't want him in harm's way—I wanted him to live out a long, happy life.

91

The Dream

· · · · · · · · · · ·

One result of cutting back on the drinking and working long days on Slim's ranch—I was sleeping better than ever. None of that tossing and turning like before with my stomach in knots, my nerves jangled— getting up several times a night to piss. Now when my head hit the pillow, it seemed like just a few minutes and I was asleep. And along with the sleep, somewhere in the middle of the night came dreams, too, long, detailed ones like none I'd ever dreamt before—dreams that I remembered long after waking up.

One dream, in particular, kept repeating itself. There's a large nest made up of torn flannel and broken wagon parts, long stalks of curly dock and milkweed all woven together, even my old jacket—the one with the torn elbow—and in the middle of this nest, there's a dozen eggs. I'm inside one of these eggs, and I'm feeling inside its shell, looking for some weak point where I can break out of it, punch through and free myself. I find that one little crack, and smack it hard, and the top of the shell breaks away. I look around me at the other eggs, and I can hear their shells breaking and see arms and hands reaching out through the broken shells and sloughing all the pieces off. With every egg that breaks open, someone from my past life appears. The egg closest to me breaks apart and out steps Dad and Ma. They're holding hands, their eyes goggling at each other like I imagined they'd done the day they met. We say hello to each other. My dad's looking at me and smiling! Can you beat that? My old man looking at me and smiling!

Another egg breaks open, and this time it's little Nanette with her rosy cheeks and not a trace of sickness about her. She's ironing one of her little dresses. "Mom says I can go to school now and play with the other kids—that I'm all better," she tells me. She walks up to me and takes my hand.

More eggs break open: Molly and Dolly step out of a jumbo-sized egg, and right beside them, in their own egg, Little Ike pulling the Studebaker wagon and Jigs sitting up high on its driver's seat, barking to clear the way. It's like one big reunion. We're all smiling. Jimmy Murdoch breaks out of another. "Where's Christina?" he asks me. Do I tell him she hasn't died yet?

And finally, the egg I've been waiting for—and, yes, it's Della. She steps out and walks toward me, offers her hand, and I take it. The color has returned to her face. Her eyes are clear now—as clear and bright as I've ever seen them. "Hello, Mister Bert," she says. "I've been waiting for you."

"Well, Della, I've been waiting for you, too," I said.

"How long have you waited?"

"A life-time," I tell her. "Maybe longer."

92

Planning the Hunt
· · · · · · · · · · · · · · · · · · ·

January finally rolled around and all Slim could talk about was the pig hunt. I'd been working at his ranch now for nearly two years, and though I hadn't entirely given up the bottle, I wasn't visiting it nearly as much as when I lived in the city—I couldn't—and still live a normal life. Sometimes I'd drive into Healdsburg to pick up chicken feed and with some time to spare, I'd find myself at the end of a bar, a glass of bourbon and a beer back in front of me, and I'd try to remember all the bars I sat in just like this, looking at my face in the mirror above all the bottles, wondering what direction my life would take, but there were too many bars to count and I just gave up after a dozen, maybe two dozen. There were a couple bars, of course, that stood out—bars I'd never forget for the rest of my life—mostly for the people I met there and what these people I met led to. You probably know the ones I'm talking about.

I had no social life to speak of other than visiting John B. once or twice a month. He had ten acres devoted just to orchards, along with his milk cows, sheep, some Angora goats, a firewood business, a water company—he even built a school for the neighboring kids, and despite losing three children of his own—two at birth and one from a hunting accident—he and Gertie had carried on with the kids they had left, despite the losses. Like he used to tell me, "What are the other choices?"

Irv drove up occasionally from Petaluma, as well. He loved his work, and I was a little envious of him myself because there was nothing I liked better when I was younger than just moving around all the time, watching the ground slide out from under my feet. Irv had plenty of stories to tell, as well. His favorite was when he was visiting the Stucken dairy—they were a family of Swedes—out East Washington Street. The butterfat levels in the milk they shipped had dropped off and Irv was sent out from Western Dairy to find the reason why. It was Christmas time and he'd knocked on their door, but they were inside singing Christmas carols so loud, with the mother banging away on an old upright piano, they couldn't hear Irv knocking. Finally he just walked into their house and they stopped singing, and the old man poured him a hot brandy. Irv sat at the table and said he heard a grunting sound, and goddamn, if a sow pig and her litter of piglets weren't nested behind the piano! "Damnest thing I ever saw," Irv said. "Right there in the living room!"

Slim told me it was usually five to six hunters that joined the hunting party. They'd trailer horses to the Canfield Ranch off Skaggs Springs Road and ride in from there. The terrain was all steep hills, wet this time of year and covered in a stubble of new grass with stands of oak and buckeye spread across the hills. Because of the steepness, Slim said they only brought sure-footed horses in. Slim had invited Irv to join us and I asked Irv to bring my rifle up with him—a 300 Savage lever-action.

Irv showed up Saturday evening and we ate dinner with Slim and his wife. After dinner, Irv and I walked down by the creek, and I told him about this recurring dream of mine with all the eggs in a nest and the eggs hatching into folks from my past life.

'It's just folks that have died already?" he asked.

"Yeah, folks, and my horses—even Jigs the dog," I said. "What do you think it means?"

"I don't know, Dad—dreams don't always have to mean something, do they?"

"I guess not," I said.

Irv went to bed early and I stayed up—a bit anxious about hunting in the morning, but also scribbling down some last details about the day before turning in. I'd been writing now for several months—ever since arriving at Slim's—trying to write everyday about my life or as much of it as I could remember. I enjoyed my time doing this and thought of it as something I could leave behind—something I could pass on, like a keepsake or a piece of jewelry—a way of saying this is what I've done with my life so far. I only wrote down what I thought I knew.

Epilogue:
Going Back Home
· · · · · · · · · · · · · · · · · · ·

I found my dad's writing a week after he died. I already told you this at the very beginning how I went up to Slim's to gather up his belongings, and how I found his writings in a corner desk, and how I read through it one entire night. When I was done reading, I felt I had to finish his story because he ran out of time to finish it himself. I thought just then that finishing his story was my job—maybe the biggest one in my life so far.

On that Sunday morning early—an hour before sunrise—we gathered at the Canfield Ranch off Skaggs Springs Road. It was Will Canfield, Slim Caspers, a fellow named Leonard Betts who'd hunted with Slim for years, another guy, Gene Baldocchi, my dad and me. Will and Baldocchi brought horses for Dad and me. Slim had his own mare. Will had two hunting dogs, as well, and a pack horse to carry out any pigs we shot. While we were saddling up, Will's wife brought out a pot of coffee and cups for us. Dad asked if anyone wanted a sweetener, and we all nodded yes, so he poured a dash of brandy into each of our cups.

"You pretty good around horses?" Baldocchi asked my dad. Baldocchi wore a sweat-stained Stetson and his right cheek bulged out from a wad of chewing tobacco.

"Bert's been around them all his life," Slim said.

"Good," Baldocchi said, "Because this mare a little skiddish," and he slapped the mare on its rump.

"I should be okay," Dad said.

"We ride in this first draw here," Will Canfield pointed to where a little creek ran down alongside his hay barn, "until we're up to a ridge that drops down into Wolf Creek. Once at Wolf Creek we'll split into two groups and work each side of the creek. If there's pigs around, the dogs'll smell them out and start barking. Once they start barking, we gotta get to 'em fast 'cause them dogs got no sense and they'll charge them boars—I already lost two dogs that way."

Dad looked over at me. "How you doing, Irv?" he asked.

"Good—I guess," I said. "A little nervous." Everything Dad and I hunted to this point didn't charge at you and try to rip you into a hundred pieces.

"Yeah, those pigs ain't nothing to mess with," he said.

"There's gonna be places where you'll have to dismount and walk," Will said. "Places where it's a steep son of a bitch."

I rode a big bay gelding named Harry. Dad rode Baldocchi's mare named Brenda. She was the fidgety one—I could tell right off—light on her feet and always moving around while Dad threw a saddle on her and tightened the cinch.

After we saddled the horses in Canfield's yard, we buckled rifle scabbards to the sides of our saddles. Will took the lead with the dogs in front, and the rest of us followed in single file. From the ranch yard, we followed a narrow trail along the creek bed where the terrain stayed mostly level, but in no time it grew steeper and steeper until it seemed I could reach out and touch the ground above us. Once out of the shade of the creek, the sun bore down on us, and I welcomed its warmth. The day started out clear and cool, perfect for climbing these hills. Slim made sure we'd all brought plenty of water with us.

The deeper we got into the hills, Will would point where the pigs had torn up the soil, rooting mostly for mushrooms—white-caps he called them—but they went for worms, tender roots, whatever they could find. The soil looked like a plow ripped through it. Thick clumps of coyote brush and Scotch broom grew out on the open hillsides here, as well.

"How long you been hunting pigs?" I asked Slim.

"I don't know—maybe twenty-five, thirty years now," Slim said.

"Why you hunt them?" I asked.

"Why you hunt anything?" he said. "So you can eat 'em." He pushed his hat back on his head. "You ever eat wild pig sausage?"

"No, I haven't," I said.

"It's the best—nothing like it," he said. "A couple of sausages and some eggs—now you're talking a real breakfast. Ask your dad if you don't believe me."

We rode along, with just the creaking of the saddle leather, the horses snorting, the moosh of the horses' hoofs on the damp trail the only sound. The air smelled of wetness, but in places you'd get a whiff of pepperwood coming up from the creek, and you'd breathe it in deep and it felt good in your lungs. Dad said the smell reminded him of that section of Sonoma Creek that flowed behind Carlotta Stamm's house, that section where his dad had built Carlotta a gazebo and where he could still see Carlotta sitting inside it, reading her novels or painting with her water colors. The dogs ran ahead, but only one, the terrier mix, would turn around and run back to us to make sure we were following them. The hound, a Blue Tick named Luke with saggy jowls and ears that hung down like long flaps, was nowhere in sight. Will said that dog could run forever. The dog that stayed with us was a big, curly-haired mutt—a mix of terrier, shepherd and maybe pointer. "Ain't nothing scares that dog," Will said, "And that's his problem."

Betts and Baldocchi hardly talked at all. They were all business—looking around constantly, twisting one way in their saddles and then the other. I could hear both of them spitting tobacco behind me. They were prune farmers with orchards along Westside Road south of Healdsburg and had gone to school in Healdsburg with Slim and Will.

We reached a place where the creek we'd followed flowed from the bigger Wolf Creek and we all stopped here. The horses had already worked up a lather. I drank from my canteen. The hills were mostly open above us, broken up with stands of oaks that grew out of the hills' creases, but around the creek there were thick bunches of pepperwood and buckeye and thickets of poison oak, and you had to ride around them up the sides of the hills to stay on the trail. Through last year's grass, new green blades were shooting up. Will grazed cattle here during the spring and they'd made trails along each draw the horses could follow.

"We'll split up here into two groups," Will said. "Each group'll take a side of the creek and work its way up. There's some steep places, so watch out." Will looked at my dad. "Watch that mare, Bert, on those steep places, okay? She'll get those happy-feet if you're not careful."

"I'll keep an eye on her," he said.

"Far enough along, the creek'll cut through a couple of ravines," Will said. "And then you're into open ridges again. Bert and Irv can ride with me. The rest of you know the terrain. Once you get to the ridges, turn and work your way back down." Will looked around to the group. "We all clear on this?" he asked.

Everyone nodded their heads.

"There's places where you're better off dismounting and let your horse trail behind you," Will said. "You can set point, too, and wait for something to stir up. By noon, maybe a little after, we start heading back to this spot, okay?" Will pulled a watch out of his pocket. "It's seven o'clock now—noon, twelve thirty, okay?"

Dad and I followed right behind Will's horse. This kind of hunting was new to me. Like I said, everything I'd hunted to this point didn't charge and want to rip you open the way these pigs did. It made me a little jittery. I could sense the nerves in Dad, as well.

We followed Will along the side of Wolf Creek and all along the way, smaller creeks—some of them barely trickles—drained into it from above. It was steep here, so steep I wanted to dismount and lead my horse, but Will stayed on his and I figured I'd do the same. Big clumps of coyote brush stuck out, too, and forced us higher up the slope. The terrier dog was out of sight by now, but as we rode around this one stand of brush, I heard the hound start baying way off in the distance. "He's smelled something," Will pulled his rifle out of its scabbard and chambered a shell.

I was on extra alert by now. I could feel my pulse quicken, and I scanned everything around me for any movement, my ears cocked, too, for any sounds. I kept looking back to Dad. Hearing the dog bark made me even more nervous. The hound kept baying and I wondered what was going to happen. Will didn't say anything. He'd just keep on riding ahead, stopping every couple of minutes to listen before motioning us forward.

Luke's baying, that earlier seemed distant, now got closer like he was working his way back toward us. The baying got louder and louder until I heard a crashing through some under-brush and before I knew it, a boar hog had charged out, his snout just inches from the ground, heading straight for my horse! I froze.

Will touched off a round that nicked the pig's shoulder, turned him in a different direction, and now the pig went right for my dad's horse. The mare saw the hog charging, reared up on its hind legs, its ears pinned back, and Dad nearly slid off the end of the saddle but caught the saddle's pommel with his right hand and stayed on. Then the mare reared up again with the hog right at its legs, and this time I saw the mare's back hooves slip out from under it, and both the horse and my dad fell backwards, the full weight of the horse landing on my dad.

They rolled and tumbled down the side of the slope—two full turns—the bulk of the horse falling full on my dad with every roll. With each tumble, I watched helpless, felt sick inside seeing what was happening.

I heard another shot ring out and heard joints cracking, and my dad letting out yelps and groans. When they stopped rolling, the mare came to rest alongside my dad. Its whole rib cage was heaving in and out like a blacksmith's bellows and it was breathing hard, but it found its legs and managed to stand up.

In the middle of all this, I heard another rifle shot. Will had dropped the pig. It fell over dead not ten yards from us.

By now Will and I were both standing over my dad. "Bert, you all right?" Will asked.

"I don't know," Dad said. "Feels like I'm all busted up inside."

We pulled him away from the horse and when we did, my dad let out a yell, a yell I can still hear to this day.

"I gotta ride out of here and get help," Will said. "You stay with your dad, Irv!"

Dad lay there with the sun beating on him. I found his hat and covered his face to shade him from the sun. The mare was standing up beside us now, breathing heavy and fluttering its nose.

"Goddamn pigs," I heard Will say. Then Will mounted up. "Keep him calm, Irv. I'll be back as soon as I can." Then Will rode off.

I got my canteen and unscrewed its cap. "Drink, Dad," I said. "We'll get help quick!"

"I don't feel too good, son," he said.

"You'll tough it out—I know you will." I soaked a handkerchief and ran it across his forehead.

"I ain't ever hurt like this." he said. "I been kicked before by several horses, punched square in the chops one night by some loud-mouth, but nothing hurts like I'm hurting now."

"You'll be okay, Dad."

He looked up at me and I could see the worry in his eyes.

"You ain't gonna die," I said. "I won't let you."

"Naw, some busted bones—that's all," he said. "They won't kill me—but I'm sure a hurtin' son of a bitch, though. Ain't never stung like this one before."

"That pig come out so sudden wasn't anything we could do," I said. "Will shot it—twice— but by then it was too late. It's lying over there now—not ten feet away."

I looked into Dad's face—there was worry there, and then he seemed to relax, even forced a little smile, and the worry was mostly gone. "I'll be okay," he said. "Soon as I get out of these hills."

"We'll get you out, Dad," I said. "You just stay with us, okay?"

"Where'm I gonna go like this?" he asked.

"I don't see any blood anywhere," I told him—and I didn't. I picked bits of grass and pebbles out of his hair, looking for any sign of blood. None. Then I looked again and saw it—a drip of blood coming from his nose, and then more blood. I covered his nose with the wet handkerchief.

"That's 'cause it's all inside me, sloshin' around," he said.

There was times I looked at Dad, and I'd see his eyes start to roll back inside his head and I'd shake him awake again. "Dad? Dad? Stay with me, Dad! Please!"

"Did we get those ducks, son?" he asked me. "Tell Tino—he knows right where they are. He'll bring the skiff up and we'll scoop 'em right out of the water."

"Okay, I'll tell Tino," I said.

"Do you see the mountains, Irv? The cows are grazing up there."

"I see them, Dad. They're just like you're describing them," I said.

"I always liked the mountains, son," Dad said. "But I couldn't wait to leave them."

I brushed more of the mud from his clothes.

"Will warned me about that horse, didn't he?" Dad tried to sit up.

"He did, but there was nothing you could do—it all happened pretty fast."

"I'm all busted up—I can feel it inside."

"We'll get you help—you just hang on!"

"Where am I gonna go like this, huh? You tell me?"

I brushed the hair back from his face. He tried a deep breath and his face screwed up with pain.

"Son-of-bitch—going out like this—"

"You ain't going out—you just hang in there," I told him.

His eyes rolled back inside his head, and I shook him lightly. "You just keep talking, Dad."

"Did I ever tell you about the dream?"

"The one with nest and all the eggs? Yeah, you told me, Dad."

"Pretty goddamn good dream, don't you think?"

"Yeah, it was a good one, all right—"

He closed his eyes again and didn't move for several minutes. I stared into his face, and thought for a second there, I'd finally lost him. I felt the side of his neck for a pulse and he still had one— weak but he still had one. I didn't know what to do—either to shake him awake or just let him rest there.

"Dad?" I said again. "Stay with me!"

"I slipped away there, son. For awhile I was young again—and none of my bones was broken."

"We'll get you help—hang in there! You got to!" I said. "Will's gone, but he'll be back soon!"

"The heat's growing inside me now," he said. "I ain't young anymore, am I? Or none of this would bother me."

"No, you're not—you're the age you should be."

"You didn't leave the gate open, did you?"

"No, Dad, I closed it."

"You know that horse of your mother's, don't you?"

"I sure do—she'll eat 'til she falls over."

Dad smiled.

"She was hoppin' mad that time—your mother— wasn't she? You remember?"

"When she wanted to go to church? That time? And we had to harness up Little Ike?"

"Yeah, that time," he said.

"And Ike done what he always done."

"He sure did—that was the damnest horse."

Dad's eyes closed again, but a smile creased his lips.

"Dad, you just be still now," I said. He shut his eyes and everything went quiet. I held his hand and brushed more grass and mud from his hair.

On the other side of the creek, I heard horses and riders approaching. I looked up and it was Betts, Baldocchi and Slim. They rode up close to us and dismounted.

"We heard the shots," Betts said. They all three looked down at my dad. "What the hell happened?"

"Will went for help," I said. I told them about the pig charging and Dad's horse going over backwards.

Slim bent over my dad. "Bert, you stay with us, okay?"

My dad moved his head.

"He ain't gonna die, is he?" Baldocchi whispered.

Just as soon as Baldocchi whispered, Dad's eyes opened again. "Tino's mad at me for stealing his girl."

"Who's Tino?" Baldocchi asked.

"His buddy," I said.

"Tino says I stabbed him in the back," Dad said.

"I recognize all the folks he's describing," I said.

"He ain't making much sense," Baldocchi said. "Talking away like that.

"I say, let him talk—that way he's still with us," I said.

"Will left on his horse, but it's miles from his ranch to town in a '36 Ford pickup," Betts said half under his breath, "And then the ride back to the ranch and up to Wolf Creek." Betts shook his head.

"He could be dead by then—is that what you're saying?" I asked Betts.

"I ain't wishing it," Betts said, "I'm just saying."

"This ain't so bad, though," Dad said. "Better than festering away, isn't it? Dyin' in your sleep?"

"Your time isn't up yet," I said.

"That dream's making more sense now, isn't it, Irv?"

"Yeah, it is, Dad."

"Where's he coming up with all of this dream stuff?" Betts asked.

"It's what he's lived," I said. "It's coming back to him in long snatches."

"Damn sure is!" Dad spoke out. "And Ike's stopping all along Washington Street, waiting for his handouts. Here comes Margarite from the Yosemite and Charlie the Chinaman from the Chop Suey House! There ain't a happier horse in town! It's the damnest sight, Irv, you'll ever see! You can see them, can't you, Irv?"

"I see them now, Dad—yeah, I can see all of them—Molly and Dolly and even Jigs the dog. They're all lined up."

Help didn't arrive for Dad until late afternoon, and it was Will and Sheriff Coombs lugging a canvas stretcher between them up to where the accident happened. The sheriff had a first-aid kit with him but when he looked at Dad, he realized there was nothing in his kit that would save him.

We carried Dad back on the stretcher to the farmyard, where an ambulance was waiting. He moaned and groaned whenever our footing slipped, the movement jarring his body. I kept talking to him, all the way to Healdsburg General Hospital, the siren blaring, wishing the ambulance could just up and fly there.

They wheeled him out of the ambulance and into the Emergency Room, and that was the last time I saw my dad alive. He died at eleven that night.

There were no wounds about him, no bleeding, except from his nose right after the fall. You could look at him lying in that hospital bed and think he'd just laid down to rest awhile, a little bit of mud in his hair, the color drained from his face, but the doctor told me all the damage was internal—that's where the bleeding was—and they couldn't do anything to stop it.

I thanked the doctors and rode back to Will Canfield's to get my car, and then I drove to Petaluma and woke up Ma and told her the news. She sat up in bed, stared straight ahead, and I could see the years she spent with my dad all rolling past her eyes.

I knew they weren't all good years—far from it—because my dad was as imperfect a man as you'd find, but he had a true, good heart, and he followed where it led him, and it led him to some hard places—but that made him nearly perfect in my eyes—that he was willing to go there, to these hard places, regardless of the risk.

He left some damage behind him—he was the first to admit it—and it bothered him right up to the moment that pig charged out of the brush, right up to that moment some hours later when Little Ike took him home for good, back home to all the things he loved, back home to all the things he'd left behind. They were all there, every one of them, just waiting for him to return.

January 20th, 1939

Made in the USA
Columbia, SC
12 November 2021